Activists speak out about *Direct Action*

(Organizations for identification purposes only)

Affinity groups, consensus decision-making, and solidarity come alive. These are engaging stories of real people — stories that can be laughed at, cried over, and treasured.

— Karen Pickett, Earth First!

Fascinating, steeped in reality... Brings alive a part of our history and offers its lessons and legacy to the present.

— Starhawk, Reclaiming Pagan Cluster, author of ***Webs of Power: Notes from the Global Uprising***

Draws you into the vital core of the era and relives the sense of utopian possibility. If you want to experience the evolution of today's anti-authoritarian models of organizing, this book is essential reading.

— Brian Tokar, Institute for Social Ecology, author of ***Earth for Sale***

Deftly evokes the complex issues, events, tensions, and victories... Sinks into our bones as only well-told stories can.

— Culebra De Robertis, Bay Area Women Against Rape

Bulk and group discounts

Discounts as low as $12 per book! See page 6 for detail or contact www.directaction.org, (415) 255-7623.

Study and Action Guide

Turn ideas into action right where you live or work with this chapter-by-chapter guide. Perfect for reading circles, grassroots organizations, classes, or affinity groups. Free at www.directaction.org/guide. $3 each in print (order one and make copies). Free guide with bulk orders of five or more books. See contact info above.

Activists speak out about *Direct Action*

(Organizations for identification purposes only)

Captures the spirit of possibility that ignited a generation of activism. The characters are lofty and gritty, idealistic and practical, complex and striving.

— Andrea Prichett, Copwatch and Rebecca Riots

Dramatically brings to life the experience of nonviolent direct action in the tradition of Gandhi and Martin Luther King, Jr.... A new generation of activists will read and learn from it.

— Daniel Ellsberg, author of *Secrets: A Memoir of Vietnam and the Pentagon Papers*

Shows the chaotic beauty of an individual coming to grips with fears of defying societal norms that tell us to "just obey," and crossing the line to challenge a government out of control.

— Dress, East Bay Food Not Bombs and Critical Mass

Direct Action is righteous tree-flesh, capturing lessons of the Livermore actions — that we may live more. Let's hear it for staying alive.

— Wavy Gravy, Camp Winnarainbow

Your heart will alternately ache and soar with the highs and the lows of that tumultuous time... The International Solidarity Movement, which organizes internationals to participate in nonviolent direct action in occupied Palestine, takes its process and structure directly from the anti-nuclear direct action groups of the 1980s.

— Kate Rafael, International Solidarity Movement

DIRECT ACTION

DIRECT ACTION

an historical novel

by Luke Hauser

GroundWork • San Francisco

GroundWork
San Francisco, California

Hauser, Luke
Direct action : an historical novel / Luke Hauser

ISBN 0-9740194-0-2
LCCN 2003105136

Printed in the United States of America
GroundWork
PO Box 14141
San Francisco, CA 94114

PUBLISHER'S NOTICE

This is a work of historical, documentary fiction. While the narrative is based on actual events involving real people, the characters and their behaviors and words are either the product of the author's imagination or are used entirely fictitiously. There is no consistent connection between the actions of any character and any specific individual. Any connection between individuals in photographs and the characters in this book is entirely coincidental.

The author researched many sources in an effort to ensure the accuracy and completeness of the information contained in this book. Any responsibility for errors, inaccuracies, omissions, or inconsistencies herein lies entirely with the author, not the publisher. Any slights of people or organizations are unintentional.

ORDERING INFORMATION

Via the internet — www.directaction.org/order, or info@directaction.org
Via mail, $24.95 per copy (includes postage and CA sales tax) to:
GroundWork, PO Box 14141, San Francisco, CA 94114, (415) 255-7623

BULK DISCOUNTS as low as $12 per book for multiple copies to one address. Great for study groups, classes, spiritual groups, gifts, or premiums. Free Study and Action Guide with orders of five and up.

1 / $24.95 • 3 / $60 ($20 each) • 5 / $90 ($18 each) • 10 and up / $15 each

Price includes sales tax and postage — subtract $3 per book if you pick them up!

STUDY AND ACTION GUIDE — see Appendix or website for more info.

WWW.DIRECTACTION.ORG — more photos and images, additional stories and dialogs, historical documentation, links to grassroots groups, downloadable versions of the study guide, handbook, easy ordering links, and more.

Dedicated to my friends,
who made this book possible

I have a dream that one day . . . we shall be able to transform the jangling discords of our nation into a beautiful symphony of brotherhood. With faith we will be able to work together, to pray together, to struggle together, to go to jail together, to stand up for freedom together, knowing that we will be free one day.

— Martin Luther King, Jr.

A LAG contingent joined this August 1983 San Francisco march to commemorate the twentieth anniversary of Martin Luther King, Jr.'s "I Have a Dream" speech.

Table of Contents

Acknowledgments 11
Foreword by Starhawk 12
The Narrator to the FBI 16
The United States c. 1982 19
Maps 21
Cast of Characters 24
Direct Action: An Historical Novel 29

Appendices

About the Author 698
Handbook 700
Fact and Fiction 736
Graphic Credits 746
Resources 748
Study and Action Guide 749
LAG Discography 750
International Day Call 752
International Day Participating Groups 755
Glossary 758
LAG Structure 766
Last Page of the Book 768

The telephone numbers on virtually all of the posters and flyers reproduced in these pages have changed. Please do not disturb the current users of those numbers. For information on current organizing, contact GroundWork — see page 6 for contacts.

Acknowledgments

Livermore Action Group, Vandenberg Action Coalition, Abalone Alliance, the War Chest Tours, and the many other groups and events mentioned in these pages were collective creations. To write a full list of credits would mean naming every member of every affinity group — and a lot of their friends and family to boot. Not to mention the cops, guards, and other officials who did their part to make these stories possible.

At the sad pain of having to terminate this list arbitrarily, I mention here only those people directly involved in producing the book. For all those who helped via inspiration, interviews, memories, research, laughter, feedback, and encouragement — without you, this book would not exist. I thank you and ask your forbearance that I can't name you all here.

Thanks to my writers' groups: Cynthia Lamb, Mary Klein, Susan Shors, T. Thorn Coyle, Culebra De Robertis, Denise Mewbourne, Kate Rafael, Pamela Harris.

To the GroundWork collective: Tori Woodard, Steve Nadel, Margo Adair, Steve Leeds, George Franklin, Kris Lee, Heidi Lieberman.

To those who helped with design and production: Jennifer Privateer, Elka Eastly, Adrienne Crew, Starhawk, Bob Thawley, Ken Nightingale, Sheila Harrington, Tamara Thompson, Patrick Diehl, Joe Liesner, Lynx Leshinsky, Jonathan Furst, Kat Lilith.

To Keith Holmes for consulting on the visual structure of the book.

To the incredibly generous photographers and artists whose names are listed along with their specific graphic credits in the Appendix.

Special thanks to the Funky Nixons, COMA affinity group, Change of Heart cluster, Reclaiming and the Reclaiming Quarterly production cell, La Peña, Ashkenaz, Dia de los Muertos, Earth First!, Food Not Bombs, and the defenders of People's Park and common spaces everywhere.

Foreword

by Starhawk

In Direct Action, Luke Hauser writes fiction so steeped in reality that he reproduces an era for us, with all of its excitement and frustrations.

Although the 1980s are generally thought of as a kind of dead zone for progressive activism, in the San Francisco Bay Area the early part of the decade was a time of fervent activism around nuclear issues.

Hauser's novel, set in that era, recreates the emotional and political milieu of the anti-nuclear blockades at Livermore Lab, Vandenberg Air Force Base, and the San Francisco Financial District. The nonviolent direct actions of the 70s and early 80s against nuclear power and nuclear weapons were the forerunners of a style of organizing that came to fruition in the blockade of the World Trade Organization in Seattle in 1999. Many of the assumptions about nonhierachical organizations, the power of nonviolent direct action, and many of the tactics and strategies that inform the global justice movement today were pioneered at that time.

Hauser was one of the organizers of Livermore Action Group, which focused attention throughout the early 80s on Livermore Lab, run by the University of California — one of the two places in the U.S. where nuclear weapons were designed and developed. Livermore Action Group was born when organizing against nuclear power expanded to include nuclear weapons.

New Models of Protest

In the 1970s, as nuclear power plants began to be brought online, the dangers of nuclear power were becoming highly evident. The near meltdown at Three Mile Island in the Spring of 1979 increased opposition.

On the East Coast, a group called the Clamshell Alliance pioneered a new mode of organizing in direct actions against the Seabrook Nuclear Plant at Seabrook, New Hampshire. Movement for a New Society, a Quaker-based social action group in Philadelphia, had conducted trainings in nonviolence and helped mold an organizing style. Instead of a central committee making decisions, the actions were organized by affinity groups, small groups of like-minded people that included both activists willing to risk arrest and those who would offer support. The affinity groups made decisions by consensus, and sent representatives to spokescouncils that made decisions for the whole action.

In California, Pacific Gas and Electric had begun building a nuclear plant on the ocean at Diablo Canyon, just west of San Luis Obispo. Huge public opposition was aroused — especially when it came to light that the plant was being built over an earthquake fault. After a long campaign of legal challenges, the plant was finally ready to be licensed in the summer of 1981. As legal modes of opposition were exhausted, a group called the Abalone Alliance formed, modeled after the Clamshell Alliance. They held rallies and small blockades in the late 1970s, but their major organizing efforts went into a call for an emergency response, to blockade the plant and prevent the operators from loading the fuel rods, once the license for testing was granted.

This 1982 Hall of Shame Tour sponsored by Abalone Alliance was a forerunner of later urban actions.

The Diablo blockade took place in September 1981, and lasted about three weeks, during which nearly 2000 arrests were made. For everyone who took part, the blockade became a life-changing event. Three weeks of collective decision making and shared leadership gave us a strong sense of our own personal and collective power. Getting arrested, confronting authority, surviving custody, and often getting out of jail and returning to the blockade gave us ample opportunities to test our power, courage, and commitment — and come out stronger. While in jail, we used our time to hold workshops, talent shows, and meetings, and to discuss strategy. Reagan was pushing to build up our nuclear arsenal, characterizing the Soviet Union as the "Evil Empire," and talking about how to make nuclear war winnable. Nuclear war seemed a real possibility in the immediate future. Our new mode of organizing, combining direct democracy and nonviolent direct action, was so empowering and powerful that some of us decided we should expand and organize in a similar way against nuclear weapons.

The Birth of LAG

AND SO Livermore Action Group was born. LAG, as it was familiarly called, organized its first blockade in February of 1982. It was followed by a larger blockade that June, on the Summer Solstice. In these days of computers and the internet, when international organizing is easy and expected, it seems quaintly archaic to remember that we organized across borders by using regular mail and occasional long-distance phone calls. We had allies in the German anti-nuclear movement, and later developed allies even further afield, in Kazhakstan and Palau, wherever weapons had been tested and toxic residues left behind.

LAG soon acquired an office in Berkeley and a small paid staff — underpaid, but paid. There was always a tension in the organization between the paid staff and those who identified with the affinity groups: between a pull toward some centralization and core leadership, and an outward push into more direct democracy. The tension was mirrored by the emergence of a new group, Vandenberg Action Coalition, which formed to oppose missile testing at Vandenberg Air Force Base in Southern California.

Vandenberg Action Coalition was more "pure" in its devotion to nonhierarchical organizing, with no paid staff, no coordinating council, only representatives from affinity groups and working groups. LAG and VAC planned two actions in 1983 — a fixed-date action in January, noteworthy because almost all of us contracted dysentery from the camp food, and a floating date action that was planned to interfere with the actual testing of the MX.

Arrest at a military base meant federal, rather than state, charges. After the January action, everybody was "banned and barred" from coming back to the base, but most were not charged. Repeat trespassers, however, faced greater risks in the Spring action. We planned a jail solidarity strategy — that we all would stay in jail to keep pressure on the authorities to drop or reduce charges, or at least to insure that second-timers were not treated more harshly. Part of that strategy was to withhold names, to keep them from simply releasing some protesters and singling out others for prosecution.

Hauser's novel traces the tensions and conflicts as well as the creative interactions between the different approaches to organizing. He recreates the feelings, the issues, the controversies, with great fidelity. The central part of the narrative takes place during the extended jail stay after the June 1983 blockade. LAG planned a jail solidarity strategy which proved vitally important when the courts attempted to give us all (in addition to ten days in jail) a long period of probation, which would have prevented us from civil disobedience for months or years.

We ended up staying in jail for nearly two weeks. Hauser does an excellent job of recreating the experience: the frustration, the waiting, the high points of mutual support and solidarity and the low points of depression in our unexpectedly long sojourn in custody. He brought back the experience so vividly that I could smell the unwashed bodies, feel the cold and the rough wool of the blankets, and taste once again that inimitable combination of spam and fruit cocktail the guards called, "The Empire Strikes Back!"

A die-in protested a lethal toxic spill by Union Carbide, outside corporate offices in San Francisco.

THE BOOK continues through the following Summer, culminating in a series of corporate-focused direct actions around the 1984 Democratic National Convention in San Francisco that were precursors of today's vibrant direct action movement.

Anyone interested in the history of social movements or the antecedents of the global justice movement kicked off by Seattle will find this book fascinating. Hauser tells a good story, and creates characters that live and breathe. But he does more — he brings alive a part of our history that might otherwise be forgotten, and offers its lessons and legacy to the present.

Starhawk is the author of many books on Goddess religion and grassroots activism, from The Spiral Dance to the recent Webs of Power: Notes from the Global Uprising. Her writings and teaching schedule can be found at www.starhawk.org

The Narrator to the FBI...

HAVE YOU EVER been part of a news event, picked up a newspaper the next day, and found yourself thinking, "Wait a minute, I was there — that's not how it happened."

Well, that's exactly how I felt when I read our government files, obtained by members of the legal collective under the Freedom of Information Act. To hear the Naval Intelligence Service tell it, all those of us from Livermore Action Group who were arrested at Vandenberg in January 1983 skipped the action. To see police reports on the War Chest Tour period, you'd think we were a bunch of ultra-Bolsheviks conspiring to destroy the American Way of Life, not a loose-knit community of anarchists who had trouble agreeing to show up at the same place on the same day.

Even if I am just a fictional narrator, I'm disturbed. If a government doesn't do a good job spying on its own citizens, how are we supposed to trust it with spying on the rest of the world?

But I also feel a bit guilty. Do we in the direct action movement have a clear idea who we are, what we are doing, or what our structures are? No wonder the FBI is mystified.

Therefore, as part of my good citizenship merit badge, I undertake to document (both for the government's sake and for that of posterity) exactly what happened in those troubled times – lest you have nothing more reliable to turn to than police reports and the mainstream media.

BEFORE I BEGIN my somewhat lengthy narrative, here's a few things I want you to know. First, everything in this book actually happened. The author was present, or interviewed people who were present, at every incident described in this book. Some events and details have been moved to different dates for the sake of the narrative. These changes are documented in the "Fact and Fiction" appendix.

Names of affinity groups and clusters are all real. However, actions, dates, and details that are attributed to a specific AG or cluster are often fictional.

Narrator is seventh from the left in the thirteenth row.

Why a novel? The decision was reached after frustrated attempts to write a history book, a set of dialogues, and an anthology of articles from Direct Action newspaper. As each of those methods came up short, it became clear that only a living re-creation of the events and actions could do justice to the many-colored tapestry that was LAG.

Unfortunately, no one was available to create a living tapestry on such short notice. So we decided to do a novel instead. One with lots of pictures.

Narrator Jeff Harrison blends in with his surroundings at the October 1983 financial district action in San Francisco.

All of the photos and graphics except scenic shots and murals are from the early 1980s. Many are from the LAG/Direct Action archives. Others were loaned specially for this book, and are printed here for the first time. A detailed list of photo credits appears in the Appendix.

As closely as possible, photos are matched with the correct action. It is likely that some are misplaced.

The photos document the actions, not the individuals who happen to be pictured. Any connection between anyone pictured in a photograph and any fictional character in this book is coincidental. No photo should be taken as indicating that a specific individual was even present at the action to which the photo is (perhaps erroneously) linked, or is in any way connected to any fictional character.

While this book describes real events involving still-living people, it is not biography. The characters are fictional composites of the actions and words of innumerable individuals. The dialogues have been put in the mouths of fictional characters based on dramatic needs, not biography. No actions or words should be attributed to any specific individual based on the text.

To be totally clear — *all* of the characters are fictional. Even me — Jeff Harrison, the narrator of this tale. I'm a composite, and have been placed into situations according to dramatic needs, not the biography of the author.

Overall, it's worked out well. I saw a lot of amazing things, including actions the author only heard tell of. And I had the pleasure of working with as fine a bunch of characters as have ever gathered between covers.

Still it must be admitted that the strain of appearing in every scene, dealing with obsessive rewrites, memorizing last-minute dialog, and humoring an, shall we say, "eccentric" author, only to watch my favorite parts of a chapter end up on the cutting-room floor — all this has taken its toll. While I never wavered in my commitment to this project, I have nonetheless resolved to take a long break from this sort of work.

AT THIS point, the perceptive reader might venture the question: Why, if he claims to hew so closely to history, has the author chosen to merge his actions and most private thoughts into a fictional narrator? Is it a misplaced sense of residual Midwestern modesty? A quasi-religious veneration of the anonymity of the Medieval artist? Or perhaps simply a concern for personal privacy?

The answer, of course, is "D" — all of the above. Most of all, the awareness that this book is the result of many people's work, thinking, and creativity. It would be impossible to name everyone whose actions, words, misadventures, and love lives fill these pages. So the author opted to name none, including himself. If ever there existed a collaborative creation, it was LAG.

And so we reach the end. Or perhaps the beginning. While you glance at a background-history sketch, I will retire to the makeup room to prepare for my entrance in the sixth paragraph of the Prologue.

Bon voyage, dear reader.

— *Jeff Harrison, Narrator Emeritus*

P.S. — the direct action handbook, which is edited from the Diablo Canyon, Livermore, Vandenberg, and International Day handbooks, immediately follows the text. Skim this fairly early. There will be a pop-quiz.

The LAG office was located in the present site of the Northern California Land Trust, 3126 Shattuck Avenue in South Berkeley. The adjacent Long Haul is a key organizing hub for Food Not Bombs, People's Park, and other grassroots projects in Berkeley and Oakland. La Peña and the Starry Plough are across the street.

The United States c. 1982

A Brief Overview

Ronald Reagan was sworn in as president on January 20, 1981, with George Bush the Elder as vice president. The ensuing years saw skyrocketing military budgets, massive social service cuts, and a catastrophic surge of homelessness that still persists.

The 1980s were the New Cold War era, with hundreds of billions of dollars spent on developing new conventional and nuclear weapons. The USSR tried to keep pace, but contrary to Reagan's rhetoric always trailed far behind the U.S. in weapons technology. The strain of the arms race helped bring about the collapse of the Soviet Union in 1989, while permanently weakening the U.S. economy.

California, after the liberal 1970s of Governor Jerry Brown, went sharply Republican in 1982. The prison industry and law enforcement boomed. The urban tax base was destroyed via "Proposition 13," which slashed the corporate property taxes that had underwritten social services and education.

Reagan straddles the nukecycle for a ride through downtown San Francisco — July 16, 1984.

The onset of "Reaganism" was a harsh and abrupt cultural shift. Traditional political forms such as rallies, pickets, and chanted slogans appeared ineffective in mobilizing opposition. This created an opening for groups like LAG that combined feminist process with direct action, the personal with the political.

The development of Abalone Alliance, LAG, VAC, and the California direct action movement was a synthesis of the nonviolent activist legacy of the Civil Rights and Vietnam eras with a West Coast emphasis on personal awareness and growth.

The 1970s had seen the development of the Women's Liberation movement, Gay Rights organizing, New Age consciousness movements, and an explosion of alternative healing and psychology trends. Cumulatively, these movements helped create "feminist process," a loose term for consensus, nonviolence, and small-group, non-hierarchical structures.

The anti-nuclear direct action movement blossomed first on the upper East Coast, leading to late-1970s mass actions at Seabrook nuclear power plant in New Hampshire. California saw actions at Diablo Canyon nuclear power plant from 1976 to 1981. The 1981 protest resulted in 2000 arrests and helped delay licensing of the plant for years. Following that action, Livermore Action Group began meeting in Fall 1981, with its first action at Livermore Nuclear Weapons Lab on February 1, 1982. Chapter One of this novel picks up the story at that point.

Culturally, flash and polish were the order of the day — Madonna, Prince, Michael Jackson, Bruce Springsteen, and Van Halen ruled the music charts. The avant-garde included Talking Heads, Gang of Four, Herbie Hancock, and The Clash. Rap evolved around 1980, but didn't break into the mainstream until 1984 with Run-DMC's first album. Punk arose in the malaise of the late 1970s and took solid root in the 1980s, but was still mainly underground music. Reggae had been popular in the U.S. since the mid-1970s. South and Central African music made their first significant inroads into the U.S. market around 1980, a harbinger of the growing interest in "world music."

Direct Action newspaper (1982-1986) was produced with electric typewriters, photocopy machines, and gluesticks. Personal computers were so rare that no one working on the newspaper had one. Email, the internet, faxes, and cell phones were years away.

Some people had answering machines, but they weren't ubiquitous. Communication mainly meant seeing people in offices, at meetings, or at actions. A majority of LAG organizers lived in Berkeley or North Oakland, many within walking or biking distance of one another.

Bay Area rents already rivaled Manhattan, but were not yet extortionate. Many activists and artists worked part-time and still managed to live in Berkeley or San Francisco. Berkeley had a much higher percentage of tenants and (not coincidentally) working-class people than it does today.

Southside Berkeley, around Telegraph Avenue, was a bohemian neighborhood of cheap apartments and post-college noncareer types. Today, after nearly two decades of soaring rents, it consists mainly of UC-Berkeley students and home-owners.

It is doubtful that anyone will ever be nostalgic for the 1980s.

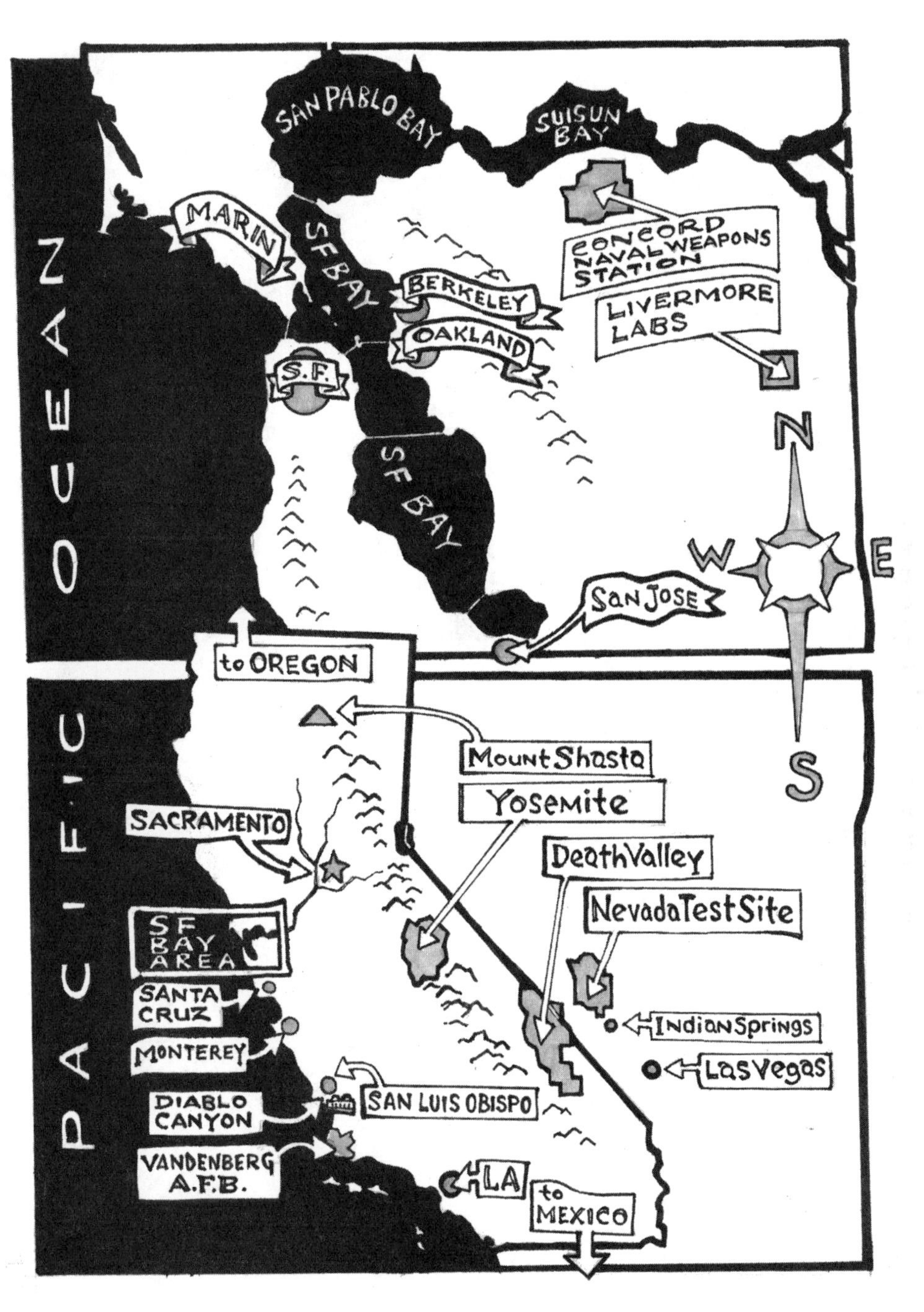

Bay Area maps on next page. Map of Livermore Lab in Handbook.
San Francisco Financial District, see beginning of Chapter Five.
Maps on these pages by America Narcoleptic.

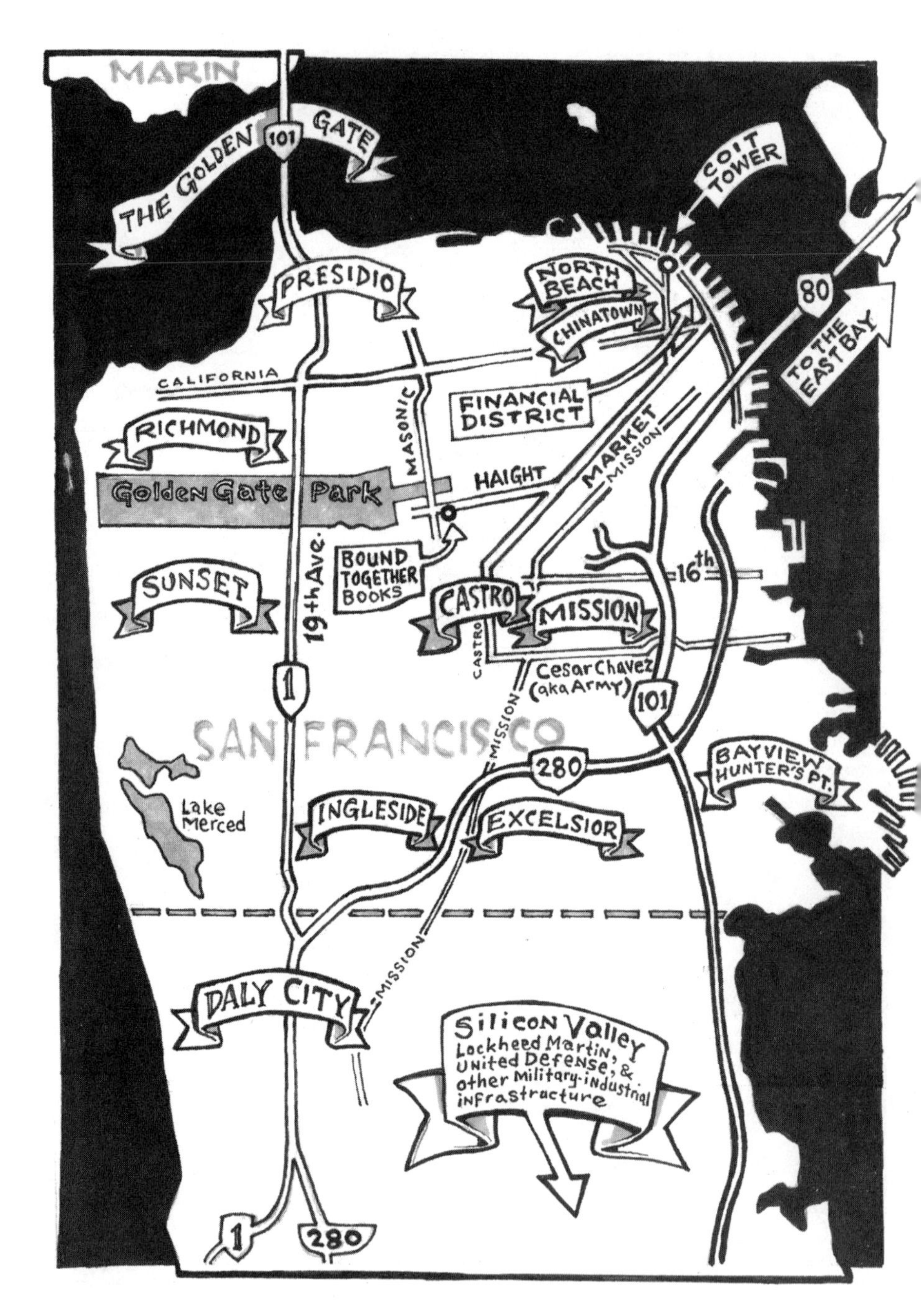

California was home to numerous Native American tribes for thousands of years, and was then a Spanish and Mexican province, before being seized by the United States in the mid-1800s. Discovery of gold in 1849 built San Francisco into a booming port city where alternative and radical ideas found a home. Maps by America Narcoleptic.

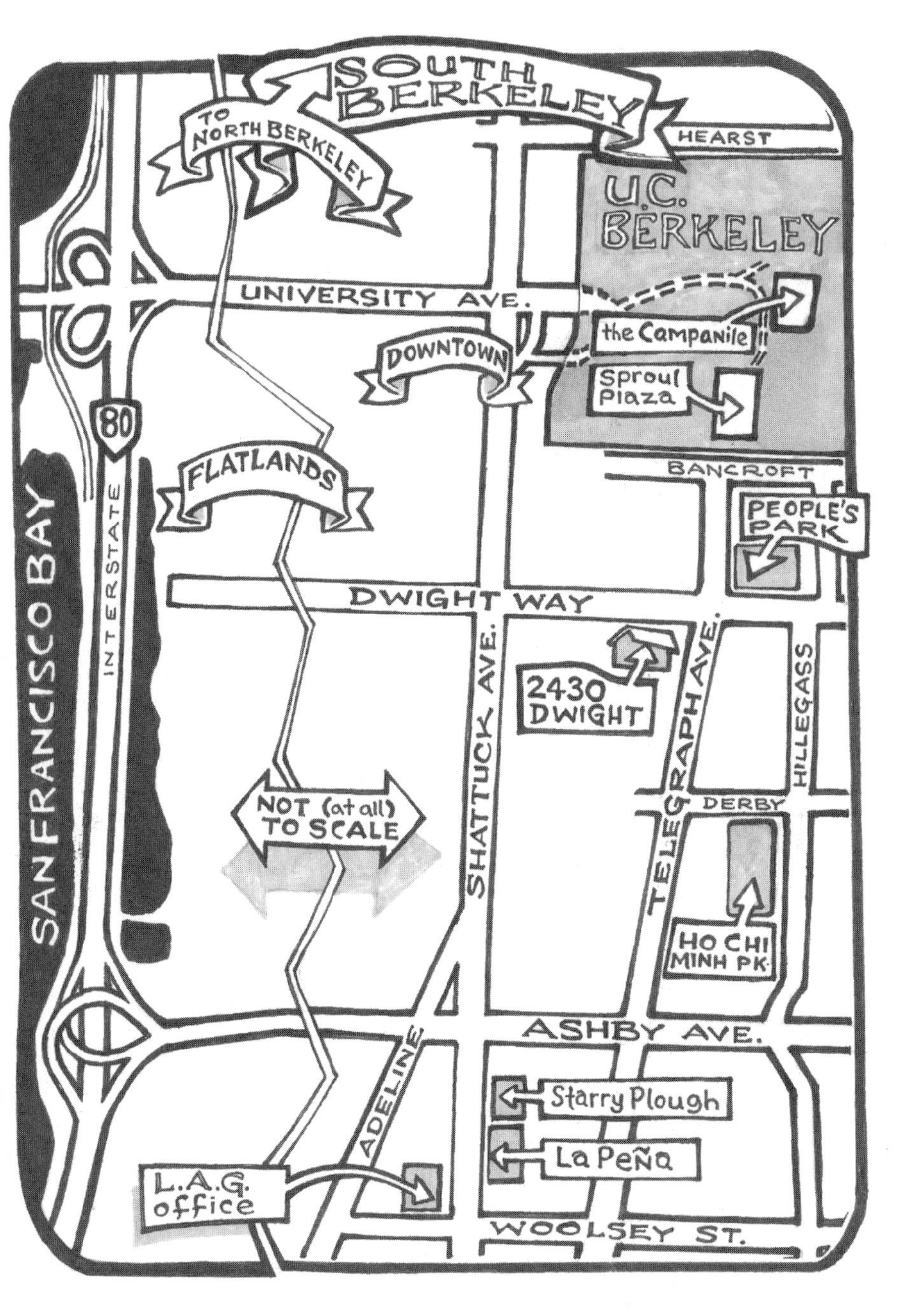

A quiet college town from the late 1800s through the 1950s, Berkeley got on the map in the 1960s with a series of protests including the Free Speech Movement, huge anti-Vietnam marches, and the fight for People's Park. More recently, Berkeley has been a pioneer in community recycling and in building an audience for world music in the United States. Most of the city is residential, a mix of houses and small apartments.

Dramatis Personae

Ages are circa mid-1983

Alby (24) In Red Menace AG and Change of Heart Cluster. Anarchist but active in LAG.

Angie (24) Works as part-time secretary, volunteers in LAG office. Works on Direct Action. Pagan, member of Change of Heart Cluster. Lovers with Jeff later in book.

Antonio (50) Professor of creative writing at Laney Community College, Pagan, in Lifers AG and Change of Heart cluster. Works on International Day.

The LAG-a-Tron tested for radiation at the 1984 Democratic Convention in San Francisco

Artemis (45) Pagan, in Matrix AG. Works as a cook, and on Peace Camp kitchen.

Belinda (40) In Spyderwomyn AG and Feminist Cluster. Co-parent with Doc.

Caroline (28) LAG staffer 1982-1983, then involved in Central America support work, goes to Nicaragua. Holly's best friend.

Claude (42) Artist/muralist, leftist. Active since 1960s.

Claudia (32) LAG cofounder and staffer 1982-1983. Active in women's movement.

Craig (29) LAG cofounders, office staffer 1982-1983, active in Overthrow Cluster.

Daniel (35) Ex-professor at Cal, LAG staffer from mid-1983. Works on International Day.

Doc (40) Hippie, Pagan, Enola Gay AG, Change of Heart. Co-parent with Belinda.

Flint (32) Anarchist, no interest in LAG, considers even War Chest Tours to be too tame.

Hank (30) Electrician, restores pinball machines. In Spectrum AG with Jeff, later joins Overthrow Cluster. Builds nukecycle.

Holly (30) LAG staffer 1982-1983, later cooks for a cancer patient. Works on International Day, peace camp, Direct Action. Lovers with Jeff.

Jacey (28) Anarchist, works on War Chest Tours. Not active in LAG.

Jeff (29) Narrator. Apartment repairman, works on Direct Action, in Change of Heart Cluster. Studies history. Has read Marx and Lenin, but sympathetic to anarchist views.

Jenny (24) Roommate of Angie, partner with Raoul. Office staffer from mid-1983, works on Direct Action. Anarchist, works on War Chest Tours.

Karina (23) Lover/housemate of Sara, lover of Alby and Walt. Pagan, in Noah's Ark AG and Change of Heart Cluster. Office staffer from mid-1983, works on War Chest Tours.

Lyle (30) In Overthrow Cluster, goes to Santa Rita jail with Jeff.

Maria (34) In Spirit AG. Uses a manual wheelchair. LAG staffer from mid-1983.

Melissa (39) Christian, in Spirit AG, pacifist. Active since 1960s. Focused on Livermore.

Moonstone (31) Hippie, Pagan. In Deadheads for Peace and Change of Heart Cluster.

Mort (30) Solar physicist, Marxist. In Overthrow Cluster, works on Direct Action.

Nathaniel (52) Staffer for American Friends Service Committee. Jeff's nonviolence prepper, pacifist, active since Civil Rights movement in early 1960s.

Norm (39) Joins LAG for 1983 Livermore, volunteers in office, works on peace camp.

Pilgrim (65) Active since 1950s anti-nuclear movement. Starts book with about 30 arrests and adds a dozen more. Cofounder of LAG, focused on Livermore.

Raoul (25) Printer, partner with Jenny. Anarchist, works on War Chest Tours.

Sara (26) Lovers with Karina. Jewish and Pagan, in Change of Heart Cluster. Anarchist, but stays active in LAG. Works on Direct Action.

Sid (19) Lives at Urban Stonehenge. Arrested at Livermore, but main focus is San Francisco actions. Anarchist critic of LAG, works on War Chest Tours.

Tai (23) Graffiti and poster artist, active in Overthrow Cluster.

Walt (31) Lawyer, does pro-bono work for protesters. In Change of Heart Cluster.

Abbreviations and Acronyms

for detailed glossary, see Appendix

AG Affinity group, "A-G"

BARF Berkeley Anti-Reagan Festival, "barf"

Bay Area Short for "San Francisco Bay Area"

BCA Berkeley Citizens Action, "B-C-A"

Cal See UC

CD Civil disobedience, "C-D"

CISPES Committee in Solidarity with the People of El Salvador, "sis-pes"

East Bay East side of San Francisco Bay, includes Oakland and Berkeley

ERN Emergency Response Network, "E-R-N"

LAG Livermore Action Group, "lag"

RPF, RWP Revolutionary People's Front, Revolutionary Workers Party

Telegraph Telegraph Avenue, main drag of Southside in Berkeley, also called "The Ave"

UC University of California at Berkeley, also called "Berkeley" or "Cal"

VAC Vandenberg Action Coalition, "vac"

U.S.-funded death squads execute Salvadoran dissidents. Street theater sponsored by CISPES, San Francisco, July 17, 1984.

Oh, you may be sure this drama is no work of fiction, no mere novel. It's all true, so true that each of us may recognize its elements within ourselves.

Balzac, Père Goriot

Prologue / 1984

Monday, January 23, 1984

HALF A DOZEN soldiers, tugging at their uniforms and whispering among themselves, approached the band of peasants huddled against an alley wall. One soldier gestured sharply. "Let's get going."

The peasants conferred hurriedly, then gathered their small bags of supplies and followed the soldiers toward the street. As they reached the corner, two soldiers began arguing over whether to proceed or not. "We're too early," one insisted. "We'll ruin it for the others."

A peasant woman stepped toward them. "My watch says it's only ten till eleven. I think we should wait."

WE WERE IN an alley off of Fifth Street in downtown San Francisco, twenty of us from Change of Heart Cluster masquerading as soldiers and peasants. It was a brisk but sunny Winter day, actually warm if you could keep out of the shadows of the old South-of-Market office buildings.

People were pacing around, reiterating plans in clipped voices. We stayed back in the alley, trying to be inconspicuous. We weren't sure if the police had learned of our action, but we didn't want to get nailed before we even got started. Hopefully we were close enough to the cable car turnaround that the cops would assume we were going to do street theater for the tourists.

I was trying to talk Jenny into switching helmets with me. Jenny was a year out of college, five years younger and a head shorter than I was. She pulled her frizzy brown hair back in a knot that emphasized her pale cheeks, making her look more like a member of an Ivy League equestrian team than a Salvadoran death squad. "Try this helmet with a visor," I urged her. "It'll make you look more cold-blooded."

"My helmet's too small for you," she answered in a concerned voice.

"That's okay, my whole uniform's too small." The theatrical aspects of the action were lost on me. Chalk it up to my Indiana roots — I just wanted to get the job done. How I dressed wasn't a major concern.

But theatrics were the order of the day. Doc, a forty-year-old hippie with a tanned, weathered face and dark blue eyes, approached us dressed in peasant garb: old blue jeans, a weather-beaten jacket, a red bandanna around his long graying hair, and a couple of dirt smudges on his face to show he'd been out in the coffee fields. "Hey Jeff, Jenny," he greeted us. "Has anyone talked to the other clusters today?"

We shook our heads. Sixty people from Livermore Action Group and a couple of Central America solidarity groups had joined in calling the action. Somewhere nearby, Overthrow Cluster and the solidarity activists were preparing for a second target, while a faith-based cluster was heading for a third site. At exactly eleven o'clock, all three clusters would converge on their targets, located on different floors of the Flood Building at Powell and Market.

Out on the Fifth Street sidewalk, shoppers and office workers hurried past, intent on their missions. "They're so dedicated to their shopping," I said, thankful for living in slower-paced Berkeley. "It looks like a religion."

"My sister is like that," Jenny said. "A cup of coffee and a charge card."

Doc laughed. "Get out of her way!"

Someone called out: "It's five till." Conversation ceased. Without another word we surged out of the alley and up Fifth Street toward Market, nervously laughing at our own spectacle and downtown's complete indifference to us.

"10:58" read the clock in the store window on the corner. We stayed on the south side of Market, steering clear of the police over by the cable cars. Jenny pointed. "That's it, the Flood Building." The twenty of us furtively slipped across the four lanes of Market Street, dodging taxis, buses, and bicycle messengers. We ducked under the portico of the old ten-story office building that rose above a Woolworth's. There was no sign of the other clusters.

I looked at Jenny. "Should we go ahead?"

"It's better than waiting here!" We headed through the doors into the marbled lobby.

There was no sign of building security. Two elevators arrived simultaneously. Ten people crammed into the first one, but the rest of us had to wait while several business-types disembarked from the second and gave us the once-over. We slipped past them. "Fifth floor, push it quick!"

The doors slid shut, and silence fell over us. The elevator reminded me of going to the orthodontist with my younger brother to get our braces tightened. Afterward we'd go downstairs to the lobby and play pinball. Probably there'd be no pinball today. I thought about my brother, still living back in Indiana, and wondered what he'd say about this elevator ride. Probably the same thing he said when I moved to California: "Have you stripped *all* your gears?"

The doors slid open. Whispers from our comrades greeted us as we stepped out. "Shhh! This way!" We tiptoed down the shiny waxed floor. The block-long hallway was punctuated by translucent glass doors bearing names of law firms, corporate branches, and government bureaus. Jenny pointed apprehensively at the silhouettes moving like ghosts behind the glass, but none of the doors opened.

Ahead, some of the peasants were gesturing excitedly at room number 508: Consulado General de El Salvador. Our destination. Doc tried the handle. It turned with a loud squeak and we burst through the doorway.

We hadn't fine-tuned the details of our entry. I grabbed Doc's arm and pushed him against the desk of the bewildered receptionist. Other peasants followed. We butted them with our cardboard rifles, herding them into the center of the little front office. The receptionist, a middle-aged woman with reddish skin and gold-frame glasses, backed away. From the next room, two secretaries gaped at us.

"This is what you get for rebelling against the government of El Salvador," yelled one of the soldiers. We pulled out squeeze bottles filled with red paint and began drenching the peasants, who collapsed in a groaning heap. Some lay writhing in the middle of the floor. Others dragged themselves into the second office and sprawled across the desks of the secretaries, who retreated to the far end of the room.

From a side office, a business-suited man stuck his bald head out of the door. "Don't worry, sir," I called to him. "These peasants won't trouble your puppet government anymore!"

Several of the peasants began clawing their way across the floor toward the official, who glared at them, then retreated into his office and slammed the door.

The moaning and groaning tapered off as Sara and Karina stood up. Karina, at twenty-three the youngest in our cluster, stood resolutely in front of the receptionist's desk. Her small shoulders were thrown back, and her wavy black hair cascaded over them.

The San Francisco Consulates of El Salvador, Guatemala, and Honduras were occupied in protest of their governments' complicity with Reagan's wars in Central America.

Sara, straight brown hair framing her serious face, produced a white plastic bottle filled with a quart of Karina's own blood. The color seemed to drain from Sara's cheeks, and her eyes grew wide as she held the bottle in front of her.

I felt queasy. Paint was one thing. But blood? I leaned against a door frame. The peasants propped themselves up on their elbows to watch. Sara snapped the lid off the bottle. She took a long, hesitant look at Karina, her mouth hanging slightly open. Then she flung the blood. Most of it splattered on the wall, but some hit Karina, who slumped onto the desk, smearing the dark liquid over files and telephones.

Finally Karina slumped to the floor. The rest of us took a breath, and an awkward silence ensued. Jenny leaned over to me and Alby. "Did anyone tell the secretaries that this is a nonviolent action?"

"Yeah," Alby announced, "This is a nonviolent action. *Es una acción no violenta...*"

One of the secretaries, a young woman with shiny brown hair, buried her face in her hands and started crying. Jenny went over and gingerly tried to reassure her. People attempted to explain the action to the other two office workers — our opposition to the collusion of Central American governments with Reagan's bloody war on the people of El Salvador and Nicaragua. But the secretaries seemed more concerned with rescuing files from the paint and blood.

Not a big surprise, I thought. It's their job. Had the planners thought about what it meant for a bunch of mainly White activists to barge in on three Latino office workers? The Salvadoran government certainly deserved protest. But I wondered if we'd picked the best venue for expressing our views.

The door to the side office opened again. This time it wasn't the bald-headed official who emerged, but a huge, grim-looking bodyguard. He was at least six-foot-six, with harshly-cut hair framing a leathery face. All eyes focused on Goliath. He took a couple of steps toward Sara and Karina. Whether on

Protesters staged mock executions, splattering paint and blood around the consulate offices.

higher orders or his own initiative, however, he stopped, folded his arms across his massive chest, and gave them a death stare. Under his icy surveillance, conversations slowly rekindled.

We expected the police to show up right away and bust us, but the consulate officials were reluctant to call them, apparently hoping we would leave without a further scene. As a few people talked with the secretaries, the rest of us made ourselves at home. I found a chair by a window facing a barren courtyard. Somewhere in the building the other protesters were occupying the consulates of Guatemala and Honduras. I didn't see any sign of them out the windows. A few pigeons winged their way around the prison-like courtyard, then soared toward the sky, which was turning as gray as the stone of the building.

My eyelids felt heavy, and a wave of exhaustion passed over me. I had spent the previous night with Angie, only our second time together, and we didn't quite have the sleeping part down yet. Not that I had minded at the time. But now it was catching up with me. A yawn stretched my lungs, the first deep breath I'd taken in the past hour.

It wasn't just lack of sleep that was so taxing. It was my first foray into non-monogamy, the first time I'd slept with anyone else since Holly and I got together a year and a half earlier. Holly and I had an open relationship, so it was all legal. But with the three of us in the same affinity group and working on the newspaper together, it was a strain on everyone.

Angie had decided to do the action with the Quaker AG in the faith-based cluster. Holly sat on the floor with her back to me, talking to Jenny and Sara. Was it coincidence, or commentary on my relationship with Angie? Sweat formed on my forehead. I pushed the window open and inhaled the cold air. What was I doing getting arrested? I should leave before the cops arrive. I wasn't in any mood to spend the night in jail. Just the thought made me feel claustrophobic, desperate to be outside, free.

No, I had to stay for the arrest. Skipping out would feel like breaking solidarity. I looked over at Doc, who was sitting on the floor with several other guys from his affinity group, Enola Gay. Doc and I had met at the first big blockade at Livermore, and we'd been through a lot together. I couldn't just walk out on him.

But would it really matter if one person left? There were probably plenty staying. I felt desperate for time alone. I hadn't had an evening to step back and reflect for weeks. Every waking thought was absorbed in immediate problems.

Of course, what else mattered? Who could guarantee a future? The U.S. government was starting to deploy the new Cruise and Pershing II missiles in Europe. The Soviet Union had responded by putting their nuclear forces on alert. One false move and we could all be annihilated. The future, whether it was the ultimate destiny of the human race or something as mundane as the upcoming baseball season, seemed hypothetical, almost illusory.

My attention was called back to the present by a few supporters who brought us news from the other two consulates. The cluster in the Guatemalan consulate had taken over the phone and called in a live report to KPFA, and Melissa talked directly with the Guatemalan ambassador in Washington.

Down at the Honduran Consulate, the religious cluster site, the police were called right away. A couple of people tried to slow down the arrests by chaining themselves to the radiator. The police threatened them with extra charges while they waited for bolt cutters, and then roughed them up while cutting them loose.

I glanced over at Karina and Sara. Would they get extra charges for the blood? In a way, it was their action. The two of them had initiated the protests after it became clear that LAG as a whole was never going to come together on a Winter action. At first, I was upset that they were planning the consulate occupations autonomously, instead of working to get LAG to sponsor it as part of a larger action. After a thousand arrests at Livermore each of the past two Summers, it was hard to get excited over a protest this size. But the way people were tearing LAG apart over what to do next, you had to wonder whether we'd ever consense on anything again. So when they invited me to join the action and loaned me a soldier's outfit, I jumped on the bandwagon.

But now I wanted out. Escape. It wasn't too late. Tell people I wasn't feeling well and split.

I might have done it, but at that moment a commotion erupted out in the hall. A shock ran through the room. The guys from Enola Gay swung into an arc to meet the police. The rest of us took up positions behind them.

Instead of cops, a small squadron of reporters came barging through the doorway. Flashbulbs popped. Karina sprawled photogenically across the desk, her blood now congealed into a dark brown paste on the folders and telephone.

It was great to get press coverage. But figuring we'd be arrested right away, no one had prepared a statement. Confused, we thrust Antonio, a professor of creative writing, in front of the outstretched microphones. He paused dramatically, ran his fingers through his thick silver hair, then launched into a passionate discourse on nonviolent resistance. His concluding words stuck in my mind.

"We have developed technology to dazzling heights, and with it our economic and military might. Yet we are less secure than ever before. Why? Because we have no vision of a world truly at peace. If we fail to save this planet, it will not be a failure of technology. It will be a failure of vision."

The police arrived a little later, separated the protesters from the reporters, and busted us one by one. Most people stood up, got handcuffed, and were led out the door. But Doc, just ahead of me, refused to stand. Two cops bent over, wrenched his arms behind his back, cuffed him, then looped a baton through the cuffs and lifted until they forced him to his feet. Doc's face contorted in pain, but he refused to make a sound. With his arms twisted upward he was half-dragged out the door.

I winced. I hadn't even considered non-cooperating. My jaw tightened as an officer loudly informed me that I was under arrest and ordered me to stand. I stood and folded my hands behind my back.

A San Francisco police officer contemplated posters on the walls outside the Guatemalan consulate.

He handcuffed me and marched me out of the offices. The hallway was lined with spectators peering out of the other offices. On the marbled wall outside the consulate door someone had slapped a bloody handprint.

The cops hauled us downstairs, stuffed us into paddywagons, and drove us across town to the Hall of Justice. We were dumped out in the underground garage and herded into a windowless concrete tunnel flanked by a long counter on the left and a row of holding cells on the right.

The women were being directed into the first cell, and I caught a glimpse of Holly sitting on a bench talking with Sara and Karina. I started to call out to her, but hesitated to interrupt, as if sleeping with Angie forfeited my claims to Holly's attention. An impatient cop prodded me along, and it was too late.

Our group of men was steered into the next holding cell, where we found the guys from the other consulates awaiting us. Hank, who was in Overthrow Cluster, a loose network of more traditional lefty types, greeted me at the cell door. He was about thirty, a little older than me, with a stubbly beard and a long black ponytail. He had been in my first affinity group, and was my oldest LAG friend. "Welcome to the luxury suite," he said, gesturing around the cell. The eight-by-fifteen-foot space, three sides concrete and one side steel bars, was made even smaller by the backed-up aluminum toilet at one end.

I found a seat on the floor away from the toilet, and spent the next half-hour talking or reading random sheets of the morning newspaper. Once everyone was in, someone suggested that we do a check-in. We formed a rough circle and went around, each of the two dozen men saying how he was feeling and whether he planned to remain in jail overnight. Most were staying till arraignment, which would probably be the next day. If we spent the night, we might get sentenced to time-served and be released right then.

But I kept thinking of home, of going back to Berkeley and having the apartment to myself. Taking the phone off the hook, making a bowl of popcorn, playing some guitar. Over the next three hours I went back and forth a few times, but when it came my turn for booking and fingerprinting, I knew I was citing out. I said a quick goodbye, signed a citation to appear in court in a month, and was led into a little cage to wait for the elevator. It took forever to arrive and even longer to reach the main floor, but finally the door opened and I stepped out into the lobby. Out! I longed for that burst of energy. Out! That charge of freedom. Out...

But it wasn't quite there. I couldn't shake the feeling that I was deserting people. Plus, I'd have to come back later to deal with the court and a possible return to jail. Not that I wanted back in. There was just no sense of triumph. Only relief.

The stale air was suffocating. I hurried across the lobby and out the steel doors into the cold night. It was sprinkling, and the streetlights glared off the pavement. "Bail Bonds — 24 Hours," flashed the neon. "Coffee to go."

A cold mist drifted past the streetlights as I headed around the monstrous gray jailblock onto Seventh Street, past the empty parking lot, under the freeway. Five blocks to the BART train. Seventh Street was deserted. Or was it? Vague forms lurked in the doorway of an auto repair shop. Was I going to get mugged outside the jail?

I clenched as a man stepped out of a shadowy alley. Should I run back? Or on toward the Greyhound terminal a block ahead? But the man scurried by and jumped into a car. I didn't unclench, grinding my teeth as I hustled past the Greyhound station, past porn shops and Burger Kings, on through the shabby fringe of downtown. Enshrouded in the misty rain and dismal shadows of Market Street, I clutched my jacket tighter and hastened on toward the benign sterility of the BART station.

Sunday, February 26, 1984

"Has anyone seen the rest of the AIDS vigil story? I had it here a minute ago." Sara poked around the litter-strewn worktable.

"Oh, no," I said. "If it's lost in this room, forget it. We might as well re-xerox it." Hundreds of scraps of paper, everything from hand-scrawled notes to finished copy, cluttered three tables and most of the funky living room where we were pasting up our monthly newspaper, Direct Action.

"No, it has to be here someplace. I was just getting ready to paste it down." Around the tables a half-dozen people were bent over layout boards in various stages of progress, while on the floor in front of the window several more people spread out their pages in the last patch of afternoon sunlight. Nigerian pop rolled out of a cassette player on the mantel of the old South Berkeley house.

It was Sunday afternoon, and we had a long way to go if we were going to finish by Tuesday night. Hopefully the toughest decisions were behind us. We'd reached an uneasy peace over which actions would get top billing, and with luck we could avoid further arguments until after the paper was at the printer.

People were pasting up various two-page boards. My task was keeping an overview of what stories were going on each page. I had a pretty good handle on it, but I was glad Holly was coming by later. Sure, there was a simmering tension over my relationship with Angie, and our communication hadn't been the best lately. But as far as Direct Action, Holly was the person I most counted on. I trusted my own thinking more when we thought together.

Mort looked over my shoulder at the story list. "What happened to the plan to cut down to twenty pages?" he asked. Mort was one of my closest friends of the past two years, a thirty-year-old transplanted Brooklynite with dark freckles on his reddish skin, set off by a brown Lenin-esque goatee. The tail of his button shirt hung out of his jeans, which were brand new and a couple of sizes too large. He flipped through the story list. "Don't we ever say 'no' to anyone?"

"What else can we do?" I humored him. "It's hard enough getting people to write for free without cutting their articles. Besides, we have more room for the international section." I pulled a sweater over my head, rolled the sleeves above my elbows, and picked up a folder from the table. "Holly wants to design the Eastern Bloc pages. Why don't you start on the Middle East board?"

Mort mumbled an okay. I went back to making a list of who was working on which pages. Around the room, which was ringed with several old couches and a broken TV, low conversations and jokes mingled with the Nigerian music.

Over by the mantel, Melissa was surveying the page on the Democratic Convention with a perturbed expression. We'd learned the previous Fall that the Democrats had chosen San Francisco for their 1984 convention, and Direct Action was covering the several coalitions that were forming as everyone in the Bay Area scrambled to influence or protest the Democrats.

Melissa scowled as she read. She was a tall woman in her late thirties, with short hair that showed streaks of gray against her olive forehead. Melissa had been involved in protests since the late 1960s and was one of the founders of LAG in early 1982. Even after two years of working with her, I was still slightly in awe. She looked up as I approached. "I don't see why we're giving the Convention so much attention," she said. "We're just legitimizing the Democrats by protesting them."

Should I answer? We'd discussed it before, with little to show for the effort. Let her have her say-so and move on.

Mort wasn't so diplomatic. "We can't ignore the Convention, or we'd be totally marginalized," he said as he situated his layout board.

"We'd be doing our own work, instead of getting distracted by the Democrats," Melissa answered.

"If we're not part of this organizing, we're irrelevant," Mort said.

"Besides," I said, trying to head off Melissa, "a lot of LAG people are already planning to do things in San Francisco this Summer. We need to work with that, not ignore it."

"The police aren't going to let you do anything during the Convention. Plus, a protest like that could get out of hand. We shouldn't risk our credibility as a nonviolent group." She put her hands on her hips. "I don't understand why people want to drop the June blockade when it's been our most successful action the past two years."

I sighed. Livermore Action Group had formed two years earlier to do civil disobedience at Livermore Nuclear Weapons Lab near San Francisco, the most tangible local symbol of Reagan's escalation of the arms race. Several thousand people had been arrested there in the past two years. But was Livermore Lab the only thing we should be protesting?

Native American Struggles

The Nuclear Fuel Cycle Begins and Ends on Indigenous People's Land

Leonard Peltier Fasts for Religious Freedom

April 10, 1984 Leonard Peltier, Standing Deer and Albert Garza began a spiritual fast in Marion Prison, Illinois to protest the denial of their freedom to practice their religion. They are not allowed to pray with the sacred pipe. They are denied the drum, feathers, rattles, gourds, medicine bag, sage, sweetgrass. They are denied the purification of the sweat lodge and can only speak to their spiritual advisors through plexiglass and over the phone. This is a violation of the Constitution, of Human Rights and of specific laws guaranteeing Native Americans the right to practice their religion. It is part of the U.S. Government's continuing drive to either assimilate or destabilize and disorganize Traditional Indian people whenever and wherever possible. The imprisonment and harassment of Leonard Peltier -- a well-known A.I.M. activist and respected leader in the resistance to corporate exploitation and its ally, government Indian policy -- constitutes a specific and selective attempt to suppress his religion as a method to weaken his resolve.

Leonard Peltier has been granted an evidentiary hearing based on material gained through the freedom of information act proving the fabrication of the case against him by the F.B.I. The miscarriage of justice surrounding his case has provoked an international scandal. 50 members of Congress (Ron Dellums, Barbara Boxer, Sala Burton, Vic Fazio, George Miller among them) have signed an Amicus brief in his support. Two major books have been written exposing the case.

Friday, June 1st, a march and rally were held in San Francisco for Leonard, Standing Deer and Albert Garza. At that point Albert had still taken no food, only liquids. Leonard and Standing Deer, under the threat of force-feeding another violation of their civil rights, had taken enough food from their trays to prevent the force feeding. All three men consider themselves to be still spiritually fasting: refusing to eat voluntarily until their religious freedom is restored to them. Despite the life-threatening extremes of this fast and the issue that has brought it on -- the denial of religious freedom for political purposes -- there has been an almost total media black-out. Ten days of intensive work on the part of Leonard Peltier supporters did not succeed in bringing the media out to the march or rally. Yet there has been daily coverage of Sakharov's fast in Russia. Bobby Sands' fast in Ireland was also covered extensively by local media.

The government is trying to suppress this case and the media black-out is assisting them. It is obvious that only the support of many people can change this situation. The religious community has called for a national day of fasting for the prisoners June 16th. Contact the Ecumenical Peace Institute 391-5215 to see how you can help to publicize this. Remember that the three men in prison have been fasting for all of us. It has been in Leonard's words "in solidarity with all the peace movement and nuclear resisters in the world so that we can stop those madmen who rule the world from destroying Mother Earth and our beloved children's future."

Ask your local news station and newspapers, why do they broadcast no information on this situation. Demand they interview the prisoners. Demand they address the issues.

PHONE: Inquire about the safety and welfare of Leonard, Albert Garza and Standing Deer to: Warden, U.S. Medical Center, Springfield, Missouri (417) 862-7071.

TELEGRAPH!: Demand human and religious rights be restored to these prisoners!:

Norman Carlson, Director
U.S. Bureau of Prisons
320 First NorthWest
Washington, D.C. 20537

Jerry Williford, Warden
U.S. Penitentiary
Box #2000
Marion, Illinois 62959

WRITE!: Demand a full congressional investigation into abuse, violence and suppression of religion from your own congressman and:

Representatives
Den Edward / John Conyers
House Office Bldg.
Washington, D.C. 20515

Rep. Bob Kastemeier
2136 Rayburn Bldg.
Washington, D.C. 20515

For more information, contact International Indian Treaty Council: 441-7841

--by Denise Ferry

Athletic Events Pay Tribute to Jim Thorpe

Jim Thorpe wrote Olympic History in 1912 when he won the Pentathalon and the Decathalon in Stockholm, Sweden. In 1913, it was learned that he had received pay ($60 a month) four years earlier, unknowingly breaking his pledge of amateur athletics. The Olympic Committee voted to strip him of his medals. From 1913-1919 Thorpe played professional baseball for the New York Giants, Cincinnati Reds, Boston Braves and Milwaukee Brewers. When he wasn't playing baseball he played pro-football. In 1920, the American Professional Football Association (today's NFL) elected him their first president. In 1950 the A.P. poll named him "The Athlete of the Half Century". He died in 1953.

Born May 28, 1887 in Oklahoma, Jim Thorpe was Sac & Fox, Pottawatomi, Irish and French. He said: "I am no more proud of my career as an athlete than I am of the fact that I am a direct descendant of that noble warrior, Chief Blackhawk." After 70 years of diligent work by Native American Tribes and other organizations led by family and friends, Jim Thorpe's 1912 Olympic medals were restored by the International Olympic Committee on January 18, 1983 at a special ceremony in Los Angeles, CA.

Now a cross country run, pow wow and games are being held in his honor. Runners have left, and will continue to leave, from various starting points from May through July throughout the U.S. They will converge in L.A. July 20th for a pow wow and memorial games on July 21-28. May 28th runners left Onandaga Reservation in New York for a 3,600 mile run which will take 54 days and cover 14 states. Another group will leave July 1st from Vancouver, B.C. These two groups will converge July 13 in Sacramento. In the words of Dennis Banks who is National Co-ordinator of the Run:

"This is a spiritual run. We carry with us the medicine of our people and greetings to our relations in the west, that we are still carrying out our duties given to us by the creator. We will offer tobacco in our sunrise ceremonies. We will remember our old ways and ask our young to grasp the meaning of these duties and carry on after us. We will ask our younger generations to live a good life, to respect the elders, to observe the beaver, the eagle, the fish, and to learn from them some responsibility. We will ask our young to follow this path which we follow, to eat natural foods and abandon the foods which are unnatural to our bodies, and to build a strong, healthy body. This is our purpose. And in our purpose we will remember JIM THORPE."

Everyone is urged to join in the following activities to celebrate the arrival of the runners and to honor Jim Thorpe's memory:

July 13: runners arrive at Sacramento. Rally on east steps of Capital. Welcome dinner at D.Q. University.

July 14: Spiritual Ceremony on Alcatraz. Boat leaves Pier 49 in San Francisco at 6:00 a.m. ($3.50 or sliding scale.) Call Dennis Banks Support Committee for more information at (415) 641-9010.

1:00 pow wow at D.Q.U.
3:00-5:00 community dinner

July 15: runners leave for L.A.

Help is needed to provide the supplies and food for the meals and pow wow at D.Q. Runners need sponsors. If either Affinity Groups or individuals can provide assistance, phone Darrel Standing Elk (916) 756-6082/758-0470 or Andy Reynap (916) 441-1683/371-5256.

Corruption Fuels Big Mountain Relocation Tragedy

Public Law 93-531, passed in 1974, requires partition of 3,000 square miles of lands and the removal of more than 10,000 Navajo people by 1986. The lands to be cleared are in the heart of the Navajo and Hopi Reservations, in the center of the Black Mesa of the Colorado Plateau.

The cleared lands are not only some of the most energy and mineral-rich lands in the world, but they are also crucial to the global climatological balance. Several scientific studies have shown that these lands are essential in maintaining the world's electrical and magnetic balance, these energy fields being the main regulators of global weather patterns.

Big Mountain is located in the center of the lands which are to be cleared, the area known under U.S. law as the Joint Use Area (JUA). The people of Big Mountain trace their occupancy of the area back for centuries.

P.L. 93-531 was passed as the result of a 24-year campaign by special interest Mormon attorneys, some of whom were also on contract to Peabody Coal, the largest leaseholder on the reservations. The excuse was to separate Navajo and Hopi people who were supposedly in dispute with each other.

The traditional religious and spiritual leaders of the Hopi and Navajo confirm that they have shared a good and mutual relationship for centuries. They are unified in their opposition to the forced removal under P.L. 93-531. Both people say that the law violates their treaty rights and human rights under international law, as well as their inherent rights as sovereign and independent people. They are appealing directly to the people of the U.S. to remove the U.S. intervention in the form of P.L. 93-531.

The first "Tribal Council" in the U.S. was Navajo, and was invented in 1923 by the Department of Interior, as a "Business Council" to sign leases with U.S. corporations. The office of the Tribal Chairman is an invention of U.S. law and the chairman is an employee of the U.S., his primary role being to substitute for the "chiefs" whom the U.S. designated in the 1700's and 1800's to sign imposed treaties.

There is a dispute, between these incorporated Tribal entities, chairmen and councils, whose income is totally dependent upon mineral leases and U.S. aid.

Main instruments of removal are (1) the Navajo-Hopi Indian Relocation Commission, which has spent $50,000,000 to coerce, bribe and engage in psychological operations against the people, while planning economic conversion of the JUA to a mineral and cash economy, and (2) the Bureau of Indian Affairs, which carries out livestock raids under the auspices of "range management" regulations. The people on the land understand range management as a polite term for the same burn and destroy starve-out tactics used by Kit Carson in his 1863-1864 military campaign.

The Relocation Commission needs approval from Congress every year for continued funding, and in March of this year requested another $70,700,000 for the year starting in October, 1984.

Since January of 1984 there have been several exposes and investigative results released which indicate that not only have unscrupulous realtors made a fortune off the removal, but that the Relocation Commission itself may have been party to the corruption.

Since March of this year there has been a nationwide initiative to freeze the Commission's funding and to obtain a full Congressional investigation of the Commission. Initial hearings on the appropriations were held on March 20 and 22, 1984, and for the first time in the history of the Commission, the committees carried over deliberation of the appropriation. Congressional sources indicate that this was solely because of the growing scandal around the Commission.

Goal of the initiative is to (1) freeze the funding of the Commission in order to halt its practices which appear to be corrupt from a variety of perspectives, (2) investigate the Commission in a public manner in order to better determine and expose its practises, and finally (3) call for a reconsideration of the issue of full repeal of P.L. 93-531.

PLEASE CONTACT YOUR CONGRESSPERSON: Representative ________, Washington D.C. 20515
Senator ________, Washington D.C. 20510

Ask them to contact Representative Sydney Yates, or Senators DeConcini or Melcher.

--Big Mt. Support Group,
1412 Cypress, Berkeley CA 94703
(415) 841-6500 or 525-9218

14

Native American News was a regular feature of the paper.

Melissa looked at me imploringly. "I don't see how we can claim to be a nonviolent group and then call a City action where a riot is a real possibility. We have to create situations where everyone is committed to nonviolence. That's what it means to be a pacifist."

I laughed, hoping to lighten the mood. "Melissa, we're not all Gandhians here! Some people do nonviolent actions without converting to pacifism."

Sara, seated on the floor by the window, looked up from her layout board with a pained expression. She tilted her head, and her long brown hair fell over one shoulder. "I'm a pacifist," she said. "But when the Democrats are here,

I'm going to be in San Francisco protesting. What's the point in pacifism if we only protest when we think we're safe?"

Melissa tried to answer, but Mort talked over her. "We should be talking about the real issue — how to protest the Democrats without helping to re-elect Reagan."

Sara twisted a strand of hair around her finger. "I think we should forget the Democrats and focus on corporations and how they corrupt elections."

"Great," Mort said, "as long as we're not criticizing voting altogether."

"Why not?" Karina interjected as she came back from the kitchen. She tossed back her dark hair. "Most people don't even bother to vote."

"That's not the point," Mort sputtered. "Everyone knows that national elections are a joke. But people still equate voting with democracy."

"Liberals do," Karina said.

Mort threw his hands in the air. "If we want to have *any* effect in the real world, we might have to learn to work with people outside our privileged little radical ghetto. We're not going to change anything alone. We need to be part of coalitions if we're going to accomplish anything."

Karina turned away. Melissa was still looking at the Convention pages and shaking her head. I hesitated, then asked, "You don't want LAG to do *anything* around the Convention?"

"Not if it means people running around in the streets. Besides," she said in a lower voice, leaning toward me, "Without the support of the whole group, a protest at the Convention would be divisive for LAG."

She'd hit my weak spot. Why do an action if it was going to rip the group apart? But the Democrats were coming to town. If we didn't respond, LAG was superfluous, a quaint anti-nuke group with no relevance to the wider struggle.

The front door opened, and a gust of cold air stirred the papers on the worktable. A cat stepped inside, took one look at the chaos, and scurried back out the door.

A moment later Holly appeared. She hesitated in the doorway, unwrapping her scarf. Thick red-blonde hair fell over her wool sweater. Her skin was pale from the cold. I set down my gluestick and walked over to her. Holly was thirty years old, tall, and self-possessed. As she pulled off her knit gloves, she looked at me and smiled slightly, setting off a memory of meeting her two years before — her warmth, her poise, her radiance.

I welcomed her as she stepped into the living room. She hugged me, but I sensed a reserve. Was it about our relationship, or was she just bracing for the onslaught of questions and information?

"Hey, look who's here," Mort said. "Just in time to figure everything out."

Holly loosened up as people welcomed her. I gave her a quick overview of our progress. She nodded and picked up the Eastern Bloc folder. I sensed that she didn't want to go over the whole story list, so I spared her that detail. Maybe we'd talk about it later.

Mort put on a tape of South African music. As the guitars picked out the opening rhythms, people settled back into their work. Holly took her layout board and sat on the floor next to Sara and Karina. The three of them talked in low voices about the upcoming court appearance for our consulate actions. Most people had stayed in jail overnight, then cited out the following morning. We all got the same court date, and there were no extra charges against people for throwing blood or chaining themselves to the radiator. Sounded routine, but if we got any additional jail time, I'd have an extra day to serve for leaving early.

A while later, as I was putting the finishing touches on my layout, Sara suggested that we make a list of what remained undone on each page. Before we got far, though, I was interrupted by the telephone.

It was Moonstone, just returned from the protest at Diablo Canyon, where a nuclear power plant was being built. He tried to tell me about hanging a banner and then getting inside the fence at the construction area. But I persuaded him to save his thoughts and write a story. "Keep it short," I said, "and we'll squeeze it in somewhere."

"Cool," Moonstone said. "One other thing. I saw Angie down there."

"Angie?" I pressed the phone closer to my ear. "How was she?"

"She was doing great. She said to give you a kiss." He smooched into the phone. "I'll get the Diablo story to you by tomorrow night."

I hung up and stood there for a minute. I hadn't seen Angie in a week, the longest we'd gone since we started sleeping together. Usually she was right in the thick of newspaper layout. I remembered working late with her one night before we became lovers, keeping each other awake until three a.m. with rambling conversation and repressed desire. If only we could return to those days...

Back in the main room, production was wrapping up. Sara showed me the "to do" list, then she and Karina headed out. As Holly packed up proofreading to take home, Mort and I walked out onto the porch. "Do you and Holly need a ride?" he asked. "It's past eleven."

"No," I said, looking up at the stars shimmering through the hazy fog. "We're going to walk."

"Okay," he said as he parted. "See you tomorrow at Coordinating Council."

Holly and I crossed Ashby and turned up Russell, a shadowy street lined with trees. She slid her arm around my waist and I looped mine around her shoulders. Holly was nearly as tall as me. I leaned my head toward her and felt her thick hair brush my cheek.

Other than bed, it was our first time together in several days, and it felt good to settle into our accustomed gait and stroll the familiar South Berkeley streets.

Low branches arched over our heads in a leafy canopy. We walked a block in silence. Then Holly sighed. "I hope we get the paper done by Wednesday morning," she said quietly. "I want to go back out to the peace camp. We need more people. Can you come out this weekend?"

"Maybe," I hedged, thinking of how much work I needed to get done. I rubbed her shoulder. It was a sore point with Holly that I'd spent so little time at the Livermore peace camp, which opened a couple of weeks earlier on farmland about a mile from the Lab.

Holly stayed outside while I went into a corner store for a candy bar. As I waited in line, I chided myself for not supporting her more on the peace camp. It was the first thing she'd really been excited about since quitting the LAG staff the previous Summer. Was I really so busy that I couldn't spend a night or two out there? Lucky that Holly and I still shared the newspaper. We weren't connecting on much else.

Even though Holly and I hadn't discussed it much, I sensed that my relationship with Angie was pushing us apart. What I saw as a passing fling seemed to be weighing more heavily on Holly, which made me feel guilty and also a little scared that she might leave.

Ironically, our sex life had improved since I started sleeping with Angie, in quality if not in quantity. It seemed to me that Holly was less interested in sex than when we first met, but maybe she was responding to my ambivalence. We didn't talk about it much, and I tried not to see it as a problem. But sometimes

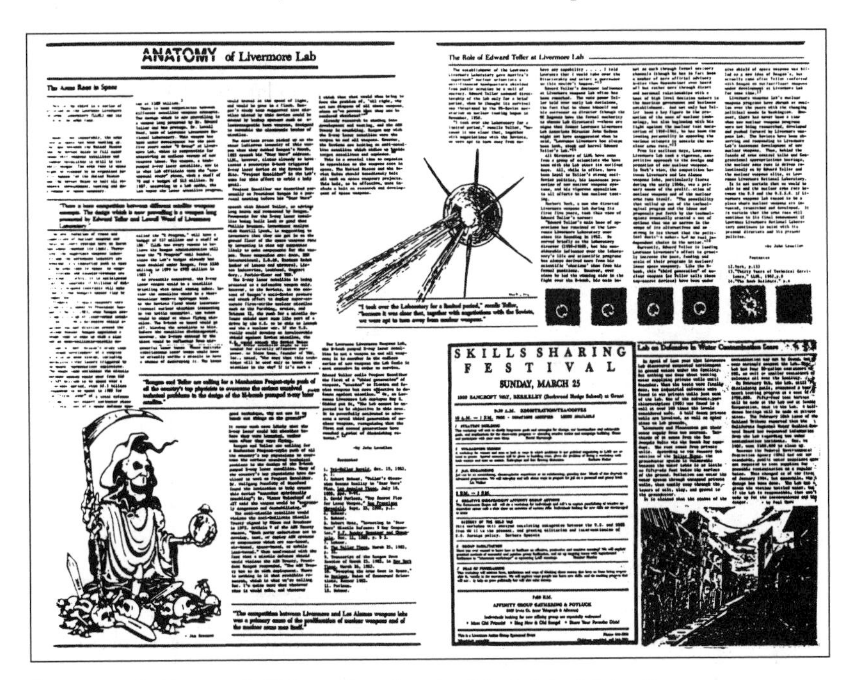
ANATOMY of Livermore Lab

The Arms Race in Space

The Role of Edward Teller at Livermore Lab

SKILLS SHARING FESTIVAL

SUNDAY, MARCH 25

Lab on Defensive In Water Contamination Issue

"Anatomy of Livermore Lab" focused on the role of the Lab in driving the arms race.

after we made love, I'd roll over on my back, relieved — we're still here, together.

When I met her outside the store, I must have given her a searching look, because she tilted her head and looked back at me quizzically. Realizing she wasn't having similar thoughts, I tried to let it go. She took my hand, and we headed back down Russell Street. We stopped to admire a spot-lit cactus garden lined with glittering white stones, and talked about urban gardening, one of her favorite topics, the rest of the way home.

We were living in the building where I had my part-time maintenance job, a big three-story apartment complex on Dwight right off of the main strip of Telegraph Avenue. Being near the Avenue and People's Park, the neighborhood was a little downbeat, but it was close to the campus library, various book and record stores, and most importantly for political activists, cut-rate xeroxing.

Our apartment was on the third floor, a two-bedroom box with white walls, tattered gold carpet, and a motley collection of reclaimed furniture. Scattered around the living room were a dozen well-tended houseplants, with an eight-foot-tall philodendron tumbling out of one corner. The walls were covered with collages of Medieval and Renaissance art prints. The pièce de résistance was the west wall, where a sliding-glass door opened onto a little balcony with an incredible view across the Bay toward San Francisco and the Golden Gate.

We pitched our coats on the old recliner next to the door. I got out a bag of peanuts and filled up my pipe while Holly heated water for tea. I put on a tape of folksongs by Ferron, then sat down at the table and flipped open a book on Roman sculpture.

She poured herself a cup of tea and sat down at the table next to me. "Guess what?" she said. "Caroline sent me a letter from Nicaragua. She was part of a construction brigade that built a schoolhouse in two weeks. She talked about how much people give of themselves, because they believe they're building a new society."

I closed my book. "Sure sounds different from here. Do you think we should print her letter in Direct Action?"

She weighed the idea, massaging a knot in her shoulder. "No, we can't add another story now, even a short one. We have to stick with the list. That makes me so tense, the way we're always adding stories, it gets so frantic — "

She caught herself and cleared her throat sharply. "I was getting into it again! Let's talk about something besides LAG." She yawned, then smiled at me with red eyes. "What I should really be doing is sleeping."

I was going to stay up and play guitar, but I followed her around as she got ready for bed, then slipped off my jeans and T-shirt and got under the covers with her.

We cuddled together and lay silently, gently caressing each other. Holly sighed as I massaged her temples. After a while, she leaned her head back and looked at me with soft eyes, her hair fluffed out across the pillow. "We need some non-political time, Jeff," she sighed, reaching out to touch my cheek. "We need to get away. Let's go down to Santa Cruz or Monterey soon, okay?"

"Yeah, I'd like that," I said. "Santa Cruz especially." I reached up and clicked off the light. "Do you want me to put on some music?"

"No, I think I'd like it quiet tonight. Goodnite, sweetie."

"Goodnite, Holly." I curled up around her and kissed her hair. She pressed against me as she drifted off. I closed my eyes and felt her warmth radiating into my chest. Still together. My mind wandered ahead to my guitar, but Holly suddenly rolled over. She looked at me searchingly. "One more thing I almost forgot," she said. "Did you call Hank about getting his peace camp photos?"

"Yeah," I assured her. "They'll be in by Tuesday."

She pulled the covers up around her neck. "Okay. Goodnite." She was asleep in a moment. I stretched out on my back next to her, took a deep breath, and yawned. An image flashed through my mind of the days before Holly, the hyper moods I used to get in, obsessing over productivity: numbers of pages read or written, numbers of hours practicing music... How I'd cast off my history studies and musical ambitions to charge into the direct action movement full tilt, ready to take on the world... And how fortunate I'd been to meet Holly. What a difference to have a partner. Someone to share the ups and downs, to hear my ideas and give me sympathetic criticism. Someone to help me keep my head together when things got crazy.

Holly stirred, and I curled around her, feeling her warmth, feeling how lucky I was to be with her. She'd been the center of my life for the past two years, the core of my connection to LAG. How could I be risking our relationship by getting involved with someone else?

Friday, March 2, 1984

WE LEFT THE LAG office about eight, Angie and I, headed for the bank at Ashby and Adeline. The sun was an hour down, the sky sprinkled with more stars than usual. A cool breeze swept into our faces as we ambled down the dusky back street. At the corner a teenager was shooting baskets, and some kids ran past playing cops and robbers.

Angie was ten inches shorter than I, but moved so fluidly that she easily matched my strides. We sauntered down the sidewalk talking nonstop, kidding around, bouncing off each other. With just one night a week together, it didn't matter if we were joking, arguing, or making love — we did it all in high gear.

We'd seen each other on Friday nights the past two weeks. After Angie got back from Diablo Canyon, she and Holly had a talk, and they agreed that a predictable schedule was better for both of them. I felt like I was dancing on thin ice anyway, and whatever would put things on more stable ground was fine with me.

Angie had been in good spirits since coming back from Diablo. Angie and the rest of Change of Heart Cluster got the usual four-day sentence. "It's great to know your sentence in advance," she said. "You can plan your life around it."

I put my arm around her shoulders. Angie rubbed her hands together. "The only bad part was, we were so cold in jail," she said. She twisted her neck to extricate her walnut-brown braid from under my arm. "And by the last day, I was getting really bored."

I nodded sympathetically, although I hadn't done any time lately. I'd managed to evade jail for the consulate action, though not without some courtroom drama. In our preliminary hearing a week earlier, we got an ill-tempered judge named Azman who harangued us about damaging private property with our paint-throwing. He brushed aside any attempt to explain our moral or political motives. "That's irrelevant," he said. "You are charged with defacing property. How do you plead?"

Doc, Sid, and I were standing off to one side watching this bastion of judicial impartiality. Sid, a wiry nineteen-year-old who never stood still, had appeared before Azman the previous Fall for LAG's financial district action, and all of his boyish charm failed to move the judge's stone heart. On the contrary, Azman conceived a strong dislike for Sid's courtroom demeanor, a dislike he generously extended to all of us. "I am concerned only with your destruction of property," he droned.

Sid stepped forward and spoke in a high, clear voice. "The action wasn't about property. We were protesting U.S.-sponsored terrorism in Central America."

Azman waved his robed arm. "Your motives are of no importance to me." He scowled down at Sid. "I have no respect for what you do."

Doc and I looked at each other in disbelief, but Sid never missed a beat. "Your honor," he proclaimed, "the feeling is mutual." The rest of us erupted in laughter and further commentary as Azman banged his gavel for order.

Needless to say, we used our one challenge to get rid of Azman. We wound up before a more sympathetic judge who let the prosecutor know that we would be sentenced to "time served" no matter what the charges, since the county jail was overflowing. The consulates wanted to avoid the publicity of a trial, and after making everyone waste another day in court, the prosecutor dropped the charges and we went free.

Angie and I rounded the corner onto Adeline Street across from the Ashby BART station. Headlights and streetlights glared at us as we approached the biggest intersection in South Berkeley. A tired-looking man leaned against the wall of the corner store. "Spare fifty cents for a bite to eat?" Angie stopped and fished a few coins out of her pocket. We waited for the green light, then hiked across the four lanes to Bank of America.

B of A didn't squander its investors' money on architects. The one-story branch office squatted alone and brooding on the hectic corner, isolated from the neighboring buildings as much by its stark facade as by its wraparound parking lot.

We stopped in front of the ATM machines. Angie reached into her bag and pulled out two stencils. I glanced quickly up and down Ashby. "Do you want to be lookout first?" I asked in a low voice.

"We don't need a lookout," she answered in a raspy whisper. "We can see a block in every direction. If we see cops, just act like we're stopping to tie our shoes. It'll go faster if we both do it."

We looked around again, then pulled out the spraypaint. I shook up a can of fire-engine red and began stenciling a neat row of eight-inch replicas of the B of A corporate logo, one per sidewalk square. Angie followed close behind, spraying the words "Blood of Africa" below the logo in glossy black Krylon. I'd done four logos and she had finished three when headlights flashed in the parking lot — a car was coming around the back of the building. I snapped to my feet and stashed the paint in my bag as the front of the car emerged. I gestured anxiously to Angie, who stayed still, kneeling next to her stencil.

BLOOD
OF
AFRICA

A big old Buick cruised out of the parking lot and onto Ashby, paying us no mind. Angie scooted over and finished the last one. "That's enough for here, don't you think?"

"Yeah, let's go."

She tucked her can away and wrapped the stencils in newspaper, then stepped back to admire our job. "There's no hurry now. Nobody can tell it was us who did it."

I still wanted to split. We ducked around the building and headed up Adeline Street toward downtown. Angie took my elbow and slowed me down. I laughed to myself and matched her step. We were hardly graffiti veterans. We had each done a few, but not the weekly forays of some people we knew.

Earlier, while we were at the LAG office cutting stencils, who had stopped by but Sara, one of the spraypaint hardcore. We showed her how we had enlarged the bank logo from a brochure to make the stencil.

Sara's endorsement was important. She carried a can of spraypaint in her daypack at all times, "just in case." And her affinity group had scored the graffiti coup of the season by spraying "Who's Illegal?" in big letters on the Oakland jail, where illegal immigrants were being detained.

Our stencils passed Sara's inspection. "That's a nice idea," she said. "I don't usually go to the trouble of making a stencil."

As Angie and I rounded the corner onto Ward Street, she laughed about it again. "How perfect that Sara would show up right when we're doing our first action together. She probably thinks this is what we do every Friday night."

We passed into a quieter stretch, walking past small houses and shadowy gardens. I was engulfed by a yawn. "God, I haven't sat still all week," I said, yawning again. If it wasn't the strain of trying to be in two relationships at once, it was a People's Convention meeting the same day as a Livermore spokescouncil. How long could I keep it up? Something had to give. But what?

Angie stopped in her tracks and pointed to the ground. On the sidewalk in front of a quaint little cottage someone had painted, in neat red letters, "Be Tasteless."

"Now there's a slogan I can get behind," I said. "People should write on sidewalks more. Send messages to each other. 'Be Tasteless.' That's so perfect."

"Why do you want to be tasteless?" she asked. "Or *more* tasteless?"

"Hey, good taste is a liability," I said. "Why is it an advantage to enjoy only expensive food, or new clothes? Or to appreciate music only if it's played over a thousand-dollar stereo? Why not cultivate a taste for cheap things? Then you can enjoy everything."

Angie eyed my tattered jeans and sweater. "I admire your dedication to your principles," she said, followed by a mischievous giggle that made me laugh, too.

We filtered into downtown Berkeley and made our way to the B of A on Shattuck. Restaurant patrons and moviegoers passed five feet away, but no one paid us any notice as we knelt outside the main entrance and stenciled three logos. When we added one at the corner, though, a well-groomed preppie on his way to the Versatel stopped to survey our design. "How infantile," he muttered, and went on to transact his business.

"Your deposits support apartheid," I answered.

He ignored me, and Angie took my arm and steered me clear. "I don't think you're going to convince him," she said. "Let's get out of here."

I nodded, smiling at my zealousness. We headed up toward Cal. Our plan was to cut through campus, stop on Telegraph Avenue and buy a Patti Smith album, then head on up to College Avenue and do the North Oakland B of A. From there we could catch a bus to Angie's place in central Oakland, where we were spending the night.

"Let's stay away from California Hall," she said. "I see enough of that." Angie worked mornings as a secretary at UC. "And I spend my afternoons volunteering at LAG," she mused. "To think that after college, I swore I'd never work in an office again!"

We crossed Sproul Plaza, site of the Free Speech Movement in the mid-1960s. A campus cop eyed us lazily. Although Cal was no longer a hotbed of radicalism, I still felt pride in Berkeley's history when I walked across the plaza.

I usually saw Telegraph Avenue in the daylight. At night it seemed dingier, the day's litter congealed in the gutters. Café windows were open to the street. The crowd at Blondie's Pizza spilled out onto the sidewalk, forcing a skateboarder to dismount to get around them.

At the corner, against the backdrop of a neon-lit clothes store, a bunch of teenagers were clustered around several young guys breakdancing to rap music.

We stopped to watch. Angie stuck her hands into the pockets of her button sweater. "I want to dance every day for the rest of my life. That would be magic."

"I thought you were telling me last week that language was magic," I teased her.

"They both are," she answered thoughtfully. "Language, dance, ritual, those are the specific forms. Magic is the broad category. Opening up, breaking loose. That's magic." She mulled it over some more. "Anyway, I'm going dancing with Jenny and Raoul tomorrow night. There's two world-beat bands playing at Ashkenaz. It's been a long time since Jenny and I have gone out dancing together."

As she finished speaking, she pointed at a Bastille-like building on the opposite corner. "Look! We forgot all about the Telegraph branch."

"Oh, yeah..." I was less than enthused, with people everywhere and cops patrolling on foot, not just in cars. "Maybe we should do it later at night."

But Angie was already crossing the street toward the bank. I followed her to the side entrance on Durant. Angie took a quick look up and down the street, then pulled out the stencils. "Come on, here inside the grating." I shook the can of red. She grabbed it from me and started laying down a B of A logo.

I was shaking the second can, still scanning for cops, when a street person wandered over and stood practically on my toes. He looked down at the stencil. "What are you doing? Graffiti?" he asked, wobbling unsteadily.

I got so distracted that I forgot to keep a lookout. Just as Angie took the can of black from me, a patrol car spun around the corner. Headlights raked the wall. My stomach jumped, and I couldn't even get the words out to warn Angie. The lights flashed over us. I grasped for an alibi. But in the general turmoil of the Avenue we must have blended right in, because the cops rounded the corner and cruised on up Telegraph.

Meanwhile, the street person had bent over to read the "Blood of Africa" bit. As Angie sprayed a circle-A signature next to the stencils, the guy stood up, right in my face. "Oh, it's politics, huh?" He stuck out his hand at me. "That's good, politics." We shook on it, and he sauntered away.

Angie and I strolled away as casually as we could, silent till we were two blocks down Telegraph. Finally we stopped in front of Moe's Bookstore and burst into laughter. I leaned into her, and she clutched me until the tremors subsided. Finally with a yawn she released me. I looked at her expectantly. She lay her head against my shoulder. "Carry me home," she ordered.

"We still have North Oakland to do."

She slumped. "I don't think I have the energy to walk all the way up there. It's already going on ten. Let's head home." She was rocking back and forth, still leaning on me.

"Okay," I said. "But wait — we forgot to get the Patti Smith album. We should go back for that, shouldn't we?"

"Sure," she said, rocking herself upright. "And we can check out our graffiti. Come on, we'll return to the scene of the crime."

Friday, April 6, 1984

THE NEXT several weeks passed in a blur of meetings, mailings, and answering machines. Somewhere I gave up hoping the April actions would pull LAG back together and started hoping simply that the April actions would be over. The Livermore demo was going nowhere. We'd be lucky if there were a hundred arrests. And the San Francisco action, despite a core of committed affinity groups, might be even smaller. I had to admit I didn't want to get busted myself. If it weren't for feeling responsible for the Livermore action, I might not even go to it.

I stuck around the office that afternoon especially to talk with Jenny about Convention actions she was part of. But there was plenty more going on. Angie and Norm were making phone calls for Direct Action. Sara and I put together a mailing about the April actions, while awaiting a flyer that Holly was dropping off.

Angie must have figured I'd be nervous that Holly was coming by, and had been teasing me all afternoon. She'd unfasten a couple of her shirt-buttons and lean over the table, or drop her pen into my lap and artfully pick it up.

I kept thinking of Holly. It wasn't a good moment to rock the boat. Earlier that afternoon, when she left for work, Holly left me a note saying she wanted to talk that evening. She'd been pretty quiet the past few days, as if she were making up her mind about something. An ultimatum? A decision to move out of our apartment? That's what I was afraid of. What would I do? Live with Angie? Too scandalous. Besides, we'd probably chew each other up. Live with another friend? But who could move on such short notice? Sublet to a stranger? Just the thought made me feel like I was growing old alone.

I wondered where she was. Holly — a former LAG staffer — didn't stop by the office much anymore. I knew that the commotion and clutter depressed her. And today, at the end of the week, the place was in peak form. The clutter started ten feet high, cascaded down the wall in a torrent of posters, flyers, and newspaper clippings, sprawled across the worktables that filled our fifteen-by-forty-foot space, and climbed back up the opposite wall.

Above this sea of paper, reaching up to the ceiling and spanning most of the north wall, was a mural left from the days when the storefront office had been Congressman Ron Dellums' community center. On the left side of the mural were arrayed The People: workers, farmers, artists, and children in deep Earth tones. On the right, surrounded by snarling metal dogs and fiery nuclear explosions, huddled a menagerie of generals, government officials, corporate executives, and their ilk. In the center, a ferocious conflict lit the wall in jagged patches of color. And judging from the shocked expressions on the faces to the Right, the struggle was going well for The People.

Meanwhile, back on ground level, business was getting done. Sara polished off a stack of envelopes and took them down to the mailbox. Norm finished his last phone call and handed the list to Angie. "I'm going to the Plough for a beer," he announced.

Angie and I had been hoping to go across the street to the Starry Plough, too, to eat home fries and hang out in one of the side-booths. But both of us were running behind, so we had to content ourselves with a furtive session behind the file cabinets under the loft. It made me nervous, knowing that Holly might show up. But I craved time with Angie.

One of only two known photographs of the inside of the LAG office on Shattuck Avenue.

She didn't seem quite so urgent. When I tried to kiss her, she pulled up my T-shirt and gave me a raspberry on the stomach. I laughed, but it faded quickly. It was Friday, our usual night together. But this weekend Angie had decided to go on a solitary retreat, at a hostel in an old lighthouse down the coast. "I need time alone to think," she told me. "It's nothing ominous. I'm not going to leap into the sea. I just need some time to myself."

So much for our night together. So much for commitment. I laughed dryly. Commitment? Maybe I better not give that speech.

She tried to tickle me, and I used it as an excuse to wrap my arms around her from behind and hold her tightly. I leaned down and kissed her cheek. She turned her head to kiss me in return, biting my lip, and sending a pulse through my body. I eased my grip. She slid around to face me, kissing me again. But as I tried to press her to me, she slipped away, gave me a squeeze on the butt, and headed back to the front of the office.

I tucked in my shirt, feeling a flush of embarrassment and frustration as I emerged from behind the file cabinets. Angie was pulling on her sweater. There she goes. I wanted to walk her out, but her breezy tone convinced me not to. Oh well, I thought, at least she'll be gone when Holly arrives.

But politics is never that simple. As she was saying goodbye to people, Angie mentioned that she might not be in the office Monday because of jury duty. Karina, previously absorbed in her work, turned around and spoke lightly. "How could you be on a jury? It just legitimizes the system."

Flyer for the War Chest Tours at the Democratic Convention in San Francisco, July 1984. Organizing went on all Spring.

Angie responded with exaggerated patience. "That's like saying that voting props up the system."

"Well, it's true. What do we really accomplish? If the corporations want an election badly enough, they'll buy it. All we do by working on elections is drive up the price. For us, it's our lives, our time, and our energy. For them, it's just more money."

"Right, and they pass the cost along to us, anyway," I said, hoping to ease Angie out of the discussion and on her way.

Angie picked up on the escape, but not without a final word. "As long as there's an election, it's stupid not to vote against Reagan."

Karina tried to answer, but Angie blew a kiss to me and was gone.

Karina shrugged and turned back to her work. I envied her nonchalance. With Angie gone, I breathed easier, but I felt flat as I cleared off the table. Without seeing her on Friday night, the weekend seemed pointless.

The office door swung open. I looked up, expecting Holly, but in bustled Jenny, back from a xerox run. With a brusque nod to me and Karina, she went straight to her desk. I could tell by the way she was shoving things around on her desk that she wanted to finish her work and get out. But I needed to talk with her.

Jenny, the cornerstone of the current LAG staff, was involved in planning a Democratic Convention protest called the War Chest Tours, aimed at showing that the same corporations funded both the Democrats and the Republicans, that it was all one corrupt system. Although the organizers included a lot of anarchists who weren't part of LAG, I figured they'd want the Tours to be LAG-sponsored, to take advantage of our name-recognition.

Which was exactly what I wanted. They'd organize the War Chest Tours, while others of us would work on People's Convention or the Central America march. We were all in the struggle together, and LAG was the thread that bound us.

After all, wasn't that the point? I thought of my college and post-grad years, frittering away time on little projects, waiting for something like LAG to come along — something that united us in our struggle to change the world.

Jenny looked up at me nervously, strands of curly hair escaping from their tight bun. I broached the subject carefully. "It's a great idea, the War Chest Tours," I said. "I really like the focus on corporations."

"On the whole financial district," she said. She scooped up a stack of papers from her desk, crammed them into a drawer, and forced it shut. "We'll do die-ins and disrupt offices and traffic, that sort of thing. It'll be affinity group autonomy, so it'll be harder for the police to control."

"Unless they bust everyone," I said. It felt a little paternal, but it wasn't the first time that I worried over what Jenny was getting into. Partly because she and Angie were such good friends when we met, and partly because Jenny reminded me of my younger sister, with keen brown eyes and an anxious smile. "They might just sweep up everyone who looks suspicious. Or bust the organizers and charge you with felonies."

"Well, we can't hold back because they might arrest us," she replied. "But getting arrested isn't the point. The goal is to disrupt the financial district for as long as possible."

"Sounds good to me, but I can picture how people like Melissa are going to react. Even if you say it's nonviolent, it's hard to see LAG consensing on roving street demonstrations."

Jenny stopped shuffling papers and looked at me. "Well, then that's LAG's problem!"

It wasn't the kind of thing I expected to hear from a LAG staffperson. She must have read the surprise on my face. "It's not an attack on LAG. But we can't let the Democrats walk in here and not do anything. If LAG doesn't want to call an action, other people will. And I know where I'll be."

The phone rang. Jenny turned to answer it. Frustrated, I stepped aside. Hopefully I'd get more of a chance to talk with her when she got off the phone.

I tried to refocus on the mailing. I wondered where Holly was with the flyer. I hoped she hadn't gotten depressed and forgotten about it. Should I try to call her?

Before I could decide, the office door burst open and Raoul and Sid barged in. "Ho! It's Friday night!" Raoul hollered. "Come on, the revolution is on vacation. No more work on Friday night." Raoul, Jenny's lover of the past nine months, was twenty-five, a bearish guy with drilling eyes behind black-rimmed glasses. He ambled over toward where I was standing.

"Opening Day," he intoned. "Oakland A's versus Detroit Tigers." He went into a slow-motion windup and fired an imaginary curveball. "Home opener, a week from Tuesday. Jenny and I are going, plus a couple of guys I work with at the print shop. Wanna go?"

It was here — the baseball season I'd thought would never arrive. Through the interminable Winter, ever since the U.S. and the Soviets put their nuclear forces on alert, I couldn't see more than a week or so into the future. One false move... I didn't see how the world could survive another day, let alone make it until baseball season. But now Spring training filled the sports pages, and opening day was just around the corner.

Still, when I thought of my calendar, I had to be realistic. "I should wait and see if I have time. Think the game will sell out?"

Raoul dished up another curveball. "Sure, on opening day. 45,000 people."

"45,000?" I shook my head. "That's more people in one afternoon than we get in a year of demonstrations."

"Well, it's a better spectacle," he said.

Sid loped over, vaulted off Raoul's shoulders, and bounced up in front of me. He looked like a beanpole next to Raoul, just as tall but half as wide. A jagged white stripe ran down the center of his black hair. He picked up a LAG button and started doing coin tricks with it. "How's the Pupil's Convention going?" he bantered.

"The Pupil's Convention?" I answered bleakly. "Give me a break."

"You should work on the War Chest Tours," he said. "That's where the action's going to be."

"Yeah," I said. "Jenny was telling me about it."

"It's time to push things in the streets," Raoul said. "We don't need another peace march. We need to shut the City down."

I knew that kind of talk would never fly with people like Melissa. My hopes of getting LAG to co-sponsor the War Chest Tours were fading. "What makes you think you'll even get started? The cops might just arrest everyone in sight."

"They might," Raoul answered. "It's a risk we take."

Sid looked at Raoul, then at me. "We can try stuff out at the Kissinger demo and see how the cops respond. Have you heard that Kissinger is coming to town on April 16th? It's perfect timing."

I wasn't so sure, with LAG's Tax Day actions already set for that afternoon. "I just hope it doesn't take energy away from our action," I said.

"It'll probably bring more people, if anything," Raoul said.

Jenny hung up the phone and started toward us. Maybe she'd see some middle ground. But suddenly she froze in her tracks. "Oh my God, I forgot to call about our float in the Gay Pride parade!" She made a beeline for her desk.

"It's super-organizer!" Sid called after her. "Never misses a phone call! Always a clean desk!"

"Oh, shut up," Jenny muttered, scattering papers as she searched for the number.

Raoul reached in his daypack and pulled out a hand-drawn flyer. "Have you heard about the punk shows at Vats, over in the City? They're happening on Sunday afternoons, outside this old brewery in the warehouse district. It's more than the music, it's a total scene. The cops have cruised by, but they've left it alone, since it's not really bothering anyone."

"That's not going to stop the cops from harassing people," Sid said.

"Aw, the police don't want to mix it up with a bunch of punks," Raoul retorted. "They like easier fights."

Jenny came back from the phone looking relieved. "I need to get going. You want a ride to the BART station?" she asked Sid, who nodded.

Outdoor punk concerts at an abandoned San Francisco brewery were a meeting ground for street activists, squatters, and punk rockers.

Raoul stretched, yawning loudly. "Let me know if you want a ticket for the A's opener," he reminded me. "Leave a message on my machine down at the print shop."

"Sure," I called after him half-heartedly. Watching them walk away, I knew the War Chest Tours were gone. The whole street-action wing of LAG was splintering off. And where did it leave me? Sitting at a desk working on People's Convention. Was this what I'd abandoned my history studies and my music for?

In the sudden quiet, I could hear a radio playing in the back of the office.

It was KPFA, the community radio station, with some story about how Vice President Bush and the CIA were implicated in a cocaine-smuggling plot to finance illegal weapons sales to mercenaries in Central America.

It sounded intriguing, but it was too much to follow. I paced around the deserted office, my head spinning. Livermore versus People's Convention versus the War Chest Tours versus the Kissinger Demo versus the Next Big Thing. Everything was coming unglued. Something had to be done. But what?

And what was I going to do about Holly and Angie? Maybe it was out of my hands. What did Holly want to talk about this evening? What if she insisted that I make up my mind? "Sure, just give me another month or two..."

Of course, by that time, Angie might find someone else, and Holly might move out. Keep stalling, and you'll lose them both.

Ironically, when she got home later that evening, Holly postponed our talk. She seemed in good spirits, but said she was too tired for a serious conversation.

I assented, relieved. Apparently there was no immediate crisis. But I knew it was only a respite. I had to make a decision soon, and I didn't like the options. All I could do was press ahead and hope my vision cleared in time.

Monday, April 16, 1984

Henry Kissinger, architect of Richard Nixon's genocidal five-year extension of the Vietnam War, will speak in San Francisco on Monday, April 16th. Dr. Kissinger has just returned from Central America and is touring the United States drumming up support for U.S. intervention in Nicaragua and El Salvador.

—*from a flyer for the demo*

You could tell right away it was going to be different. A block from the hotel, helmeted riot police were redirecting traffic and giving hard stares to anyone who didn't take the hint and turn back. Angie and I hurried past the cops and joined the crowd gathering in front of the San Francisco Hilton, where Henry Kissinger was addressing the Commonwealth Club at their monthly luncheon.

The San Francisco Hilton was a sheet-glass monolith that covered an entire city block, dwarfing the small stores and apartments on the surrounding streets. Fifteen stories on Mason Street, the building towered to twenty-five on the opposite side, its shiny facade sealing the rich in and the rest of the world out.

Over the entrance to the hotel, three flags flapped in the gusty breeze: the United States', California's, and the Hilton's own banner. Underneath the flags a row of riot cops clenched their nightsticks and eyed the growing crowd. At the right-hand end of the block, a half-dozen mounted police paced their anxious horses around. Beyond them, another squad of cops came marching down toward the hotel.

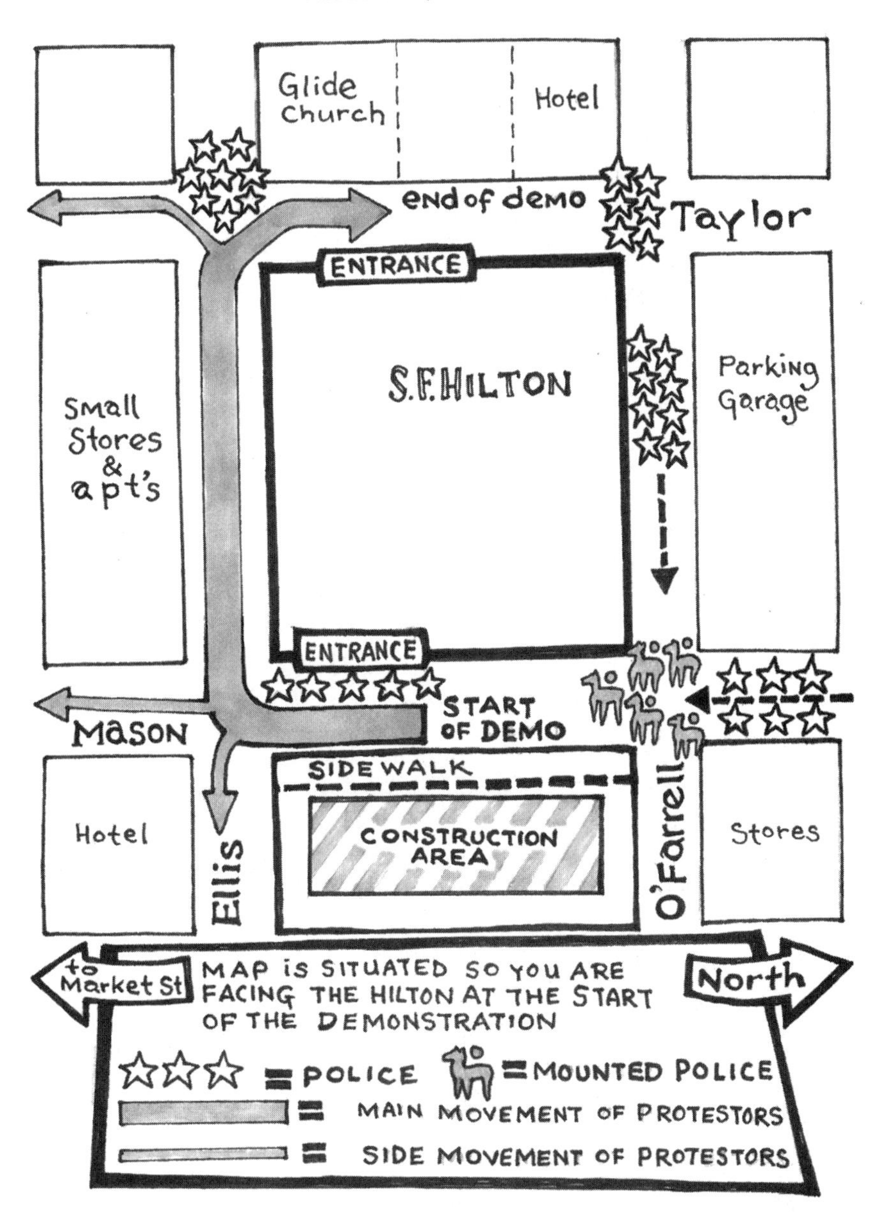

The layout of the demonstration against notorious war criminal Henry Kissinger on April 16, 1984 was typical of many in San Francisco during this time, with a thousand protesters squaring off against a couple of hundred riot cops. What was different about this protest was its occurring two months before the Democratic National Convention came to town. The day served as a testing ground for activists and police alike. Map by A. Narcoleptic.

A thousand people turned out to protest the visit of Henry Kissinger on April 16, 1984.

Despite it being noon on a workday, nearly a thousand people gathered across the street from the hotel to protest Kissinger's visit. When Angie and I arrived, the crowd already filled the ten-foot sidewalk that butted up against a construction area. The monitors, volunteers from some of the traditional leftist groups, had gotten part of the demonstrators to march in a picket loop and chant.

One especially vocal contingent seemed to consist largely of Central American people. Many were carrying pots, pans, and metal utensils, which they beat in time to the chants. How different from the LAG folks, who milled around or talked in small groups off to the side.

If there were arrests, the difference would be even more accented. I doubted that many immigrants, documented or otherwise, would want to risk arrest. That privilege was best left to those of us born north of the border.

The restless feeling on the street heightened the friction between Angie and me. Walking up to the Hilton from BART, we got into a disagreement about the foggy weather. She loved the fog and wanted to live in San Francisco, but I preferred the East Bay, where the sun shone more. We finally let it drop, but once we got past the cops we went our separate ways.

Riot police and mounted officers patrolled the street, forcing protesters back onto the sidewalks.

The whole situation felt impossible. How long could I juggle two relationships? Nothing had been resolved between Holly and me, and a crisis loomed. Meanwhile, my relationship with Angie, once a source of such pleasure, seemed tenser each time we got together.

What was I supposed to do? Sometimes I wished a higher authority would make the decision for me. Sure, I'd probably rebel against it. But reacting to someone else's decision seemed a lot easier than making my own.

The scraping of boots on concrete called my attention back to the present. A fresh squad of cops marched in and replaced the ones who were monitoring the Hilton entrance. "The changing of the royal guard," someone said.

The squad leaving the hotel marched past the crowd, who greeted them with loud boos and catcalls. A leftist group, the Revolutionary People's Front, shook their signs and accused the officers of collaborating with the enemies of the working class. The sticks holding the RPF's signs were pretty stout, as were the poles holding their banner.

At the right-hand end of the block, up near the horse cops, Jenny and Raoul's affinity group huddled together. I felt a twinge of envy, wishing I were part of their schemes. Why hadn't I planned anything?

Closer to the picket loop I saw Antonio, who had canceled his creative writing classes so he could be in our Tax Day action at Bank of America later that day. He was standing off the curb talking with Claudia and Sara, and had to jump back as a squad of cops came sweeping up the street.

The cops were forcing people back onto the sidewalk, but mostly they were doing their own little drill. It was this funny exercise where they would come shuffling up the street in two lines, eyes rigidly forward, batons gripped against their chests. At the end of the block, they would do a sharp about-face and come back past us, their heavy boots scraping an insistent rhythm on the cement. They weren't trying to hit anybody, but most people gave them a wide clearance anyway.

I started up toward Antonio and Sara, but Hank intercepted me. Hank was tall with broad shoulders, and seemed to bear down on me. He was wearing a baseball hat, and looked like he hadn't shaved for a day or two. "Hey, buddy," he said, giving me a quick, energetic handshake. "How's it going?"

I was glad to see him, and even happier that he had flagged me down. The demo felt like being stuck at a party where I hardly knew anyone. "Are you thinking of getting busted?" I asked.

As the protest stretched on, mounted police became more aggressive in their crowd-control maneuvers.

"Not today," he said. "I've got a wiring job that's supposed to be done by today. Gotta keep the boss happy."

Hank had driven a truckload of signs and props over to the actions. One of them was Change of Heart's Tax Day prop, a ten-foot nuclear missile made of paper-machéd tax forms. "It's still on the truck," he reported. "I'm not too worried about anybody stealing it. I'll take it over to Bank of America later."

We surveyed the scene. The police had closed the block to all traffic except limousines bringing the local elite to hear Kissinger. As two limos snaked their way through the police cordon and disgorged their passengers, the crowd raised a righteous chorus of jeers. The monitors, who were trying to keep the picket circle going, cranked their bullhorns up another notch. The cluster of Central American protesters started banging on their pots and pans, and everyone yelled even louder at the arriving aristocrats.

As the tumult peaked and subsided, Doc and Melissa walked up to me. I was surprised to see Melissa at a street demo, but it turned out she was actually in the City to go to her job at a senior hospice, and was just swinging by the protest on her way there. "What a hostile scene," she said, her arms folded across her chest. "I don't even see the point. It's just us and the cops. Who are we going to reach with this kind of energy?"

I shrugged. It was an old argument between us, and I didn't feel like taking it up again.

Doc tugged on his graying beard as the bullhorns pounded out a chant. "It's bad enough dealing with riot cops," he said, raising his voice. "But we're putting out the same aggressive tone."

Melissa pointed up the street. "Look at the horses. They can't stand still. They know something's wrong." She crossed her arms again, her olive skin standing out against her blue shirt. A sad look clouded her eyes. "On the way up here I heard some people talking about throwing marbles under the horses' hooves to trip them up. Who would do something so cruel to a horse? What ever happened to nonviolence?"

I didn't have an answer. Doc spotted some other men from Enola Gay and went over to greet them. Melissa reminded me of a few logistical details for the next day at Livermore, then headed off to work.

Although the picket loop was still chanting and the cops persisted in their shuffle drill, the general energy had ebbed. Jenny and Raoul's AG was still plotting. I walked over to Sara, who had come straight from her downtown office-temp job. She was dressed in a fluffy sweater and a billowy skirt, and her hair was pulled back in a long braid.

"I guess you have to look the part when you work down here," I said.

"I hate dressing like this," she said. "The dumbest part is, I have to shave my legs. Can you believe it?"

Sara eyed the cops patrolling the entrance. "I wish I had figured out a way to get into the hotel. Out here, we can yell forever and they probably can't even hear us. I'll bet if we got dressed up and waited for some hotel guests to arrive, we could follow them right in. There's hundreds of guests at the Hilton. How do they know who's who?"

It sounded plausible to me. Sara started to expand on the idea when Karina walked past, waving to us. I'd heard rumors that their relationship had hit stormy weather. I was amazed that they'd managed to navigate two years of non-monogamy. Holly and I had barely lasted three months and were coming apart at the seams. As Karina walked on past, Sara's smile vanished. Her mouth hung open, and with a quick goodbye she headed after Karina.

I stepped back and looked around. Up toward the horse cops, Angie was talking with Norm. I edged over to where I could see her better. They were laughing about something. I thought about joining them, but it felt like I'd be chasing after her. Maybe in a while.

Jenny and Raoul's affinity group had finally broken out of their huddle. They were dressed like somber peasants, in tattered black and white. Jenny was talking with a guy from her AG named Jacey whom I'd run into at a couple of Berkeley demonstrations. He was about twenty-eight, with short hair and a broad, open face. He was critical of LAG and nonviolence, preferring to "mix it up in the streets," as he said. He had a chipped front tooth that gave him

credibility, and I had to admit he had a lot of guts when it came to confronting the police. But I got the feeling that Jacey wouldn't be real torn up if the cops responded by attacking the entire crowd. "It'd radicalize people, getting attacked by the cops," I imagined him saying.

Jacey turned away as I approached. Jenny greeted me with a sharp squeeze of my arm. "How are you doing?" she said. "Have you heard anything from Holly?"

"No," I fumbled, caught off-guard. "No, I haven't." I hadn't thought about Holly all day, and it felt weird to be reminded.

"She's probably okay," Jenny assured me. "I wonder if they've gotten caught?" Holly was part of a small action at Site 300, Livermore Lab's local test area for non-nuclear devices. They had gone over the fence before dawn that morning. It embarrassed me that I wasn't sure whether she planned to elude the cops or just hike in and be arrested.

Jenny didn't seem to notice. She stepped off the curb, her sharp eyes searching beyond the horse cops and on up the Mason Street hill. "We hoped Sid's AG would get here before we started," she said. "But maybe they got busted." Two peace-punk affinity groups, Domestic Terrorists and Gruesome Rebels, were doing a roving tour of the financial district on their way to the Kissinger protest.

"What's your plan?" I asked.

Jenny straightened the white scarf around her head. "We're supposed to be ghosts of the Vietnamese peasants Kissinger killed," she told me, "returned to haunt him for his Central America policy. Did you hear that we actually saw him earlier? You should have seen it. We were walking by the garage around the corner on Ellis. Kissinger got out of his limo wearing this big trenchcoat, and Raoul and Jacey started howling like wild animals and screaming at him, 'Murderer! We want you, Henry!'" She laughed nervously as Raoul stalked over our direction.

"It was the dogs in our souls," he hissed menacingly, his big frame hulking toward us. "The first scent of fresh game."

Jenny looked at him uncertainly, then let out a sharp laugh. Her hands flitted around as she spoke. "We're going to creep into the street like ghosts, groaning 'Henry! Henry!' Then we'll throw red paint on each other and maybe do a die-in. Hopefully other people will come out in the street, too." She looked a little dubious.

I scanned the street without replying. The squad of shuffling police had finally come to a halt in front of the entrance. Up behind the horse cops were still more officers, ready for action. "There's a lot of cops," I observed with an air of foreboding. I looked at Jenny.

But it was Raoul who responded. "They've brought all their goons out," he said. "It's a test run for the Democratic Convention, getting the troops ready for battle."

The crowd was still on the sidewalk, but taunts and an occasional crumpled-up flyer were being hurled across the street at the cops who lined the hotel entrance. The chanting fizzled out, and an eerie stillness hung over the nearly deserted street.

Jacey and some others from their AG approached Raoul and Jenny. "We should do it now. We can't wait any longer for the punks. Now's the time." Their circle braced. I squeezed Jenny's shoulder. The group inched off the curb, hesitated, then started crouch-creeping into the street. My eyes went for the police, who gawked around for orders. The AG reached the middle of the street. "Hen-ry! Hen-ry!" they moaned. "We want you, Henry!"

The picket line stopped as everyone focused on the spectacle. Raoul pulled out a bottle of red paint and doused the other peasants with it. "Hen-ry! Hen-ry!" they cried. The cops got orders to advance, and a dozen officers moved stiffly out from the hotel entrance, batons ready to strike. The AG melted back into the crowd, then re-emerged farther to the left. "Hen-ry! Hen-ry!" Jacey was gesturing broadly to the crowd. A few other people stepped cautiously into the street, then retreated hastily when the cops advanced in their direction.

Angie, Sara, and Doc had moved a few feet off the curb as the cops swung the other way. "Come on!" Angie called to me. My chest tightened, but I was spared a decision as the cops about-faced and moved our way, sending everyone jumping back to the sidewalk. Angie stepped over and looped her arm through mine like we were going to the theater. "We can take the street down here," she pointed, tugging on my arm. Twenty or so people in our little group edged out into the street again. I followed Angie reluctantly, craning my

Protesters used die-in tactics to shut the street as mounted police looked on.

neck for undercover police. "Don't be so nervous!" Angie rasped. "You're making me uptight."

"I don't even see the point of being out here," I answered under my breath. "The cops are just going to chase us back." My prophecy was fulfilled as the police turned back our direction, batons shoving the slower people out of their way.

Angie watched the street intently as Jenny and Raoul's AG dodged the increasingly hostile cops. "We have the right to be in the street," she insisted. "They can't tell us where we can protest!"

Her spirit was drawing me in, but I had to be realistic. With obligations at Livermore tomorrow I couldn't risk getting busted here.

A few more bands of protesters were edging into the street. The mobile squad of cops was outnumbered. The reserves up the block weren't moving.

Police backed their nervous horses into the crowd.

"What do they really care?" Angie asked with a sweep of her arm. "They've re-routed all the traffic anyway. Are they really going to fight us over the principle of keeping the street clear? Is it really just a power-trip for them?"

I wasn't as optimistic as she was, but it was hard to resist when she tugged on my arm. The squad of cops stopped to regroup, and we joined a dozen more protesters venturing off the sidewalk. The monitors made no attempt to impede anyone, and some people carried their banners out into the street. It felt like we were claiming the territory, conquering the street for peace.

The squad of cops soon moved on us, jabbing with their batons. We gave ground but stayed in the street. The cops circled around and we eluded them a second time. We were congratulating ourselves on our brilliant maneuvering when several mounted cops came riding down our way. Alarm gripped me. People started to retreat. Raoul called out, "Hold your ground! Horses won't step on people."

Whether they willingly would, we never learned. When the cops reached our group, they wheeled their mounts around and backed the nervous, high-stepping horses toward us. Angie seemed as scared as I was, and made it back to the sidewalk ahead of me.

We leaned against each other, studying the street. My eyes were wide open, my muscles taut. As the horse cops rode back up to deal with Jenny and Raoul's group, someone yelled, "Down here!" and we were out in the street again.

I hadn't lost sight of the other cops off to the right. As the first squad regrouped, the second geared up to join the sweep. Damn, I thought. Out of a thousand people at the demo, only about fifty of us were in the street. Counting the second squad and the horse brigade, there were almost that many police. I tried to scope out our retreat route to make sure no more cops were coming up that way to surround us, but I couldn't tell.

The police lined up facing us. They clenched their riot clubs and pawed at the pavement, awaiting the order to launch their sweep. With no chanting and no traffic, it was eerily quiet. I studied the cops, then gauged the distance back to the sidewalk, bracing myself for the onslaught. But just as they were about to strike, a commotion erupted in the intersection behind them. The cops looked around, confused. I craned my neck to see — the punks had arrived!

As the cops floundered about, their battle plan in disarray, seventy or eighty young punks came parading around the corner to join us in the street. A spike-haired woman carried a sign proclaiming, "Kissinger is a Tax-Paid Terrorist." I spotted Sid near the front of the march with a black Circle-A flag. A broad smile crossed his face as he greeted Jenny and Raoul. The punks merged into our crowd, more than doubling the number in the street. Their festive spirit infected the entire demonstration, and spontaneous chants and cheers echoed off the plate glass of the Hilton as we celebrated victory.

It took the cops ten minutes to work out a new plan, and when they finally moved to clear the middle of the street, the punks were ready. Migrating down toward Ellis, they started a countdown that could be heard up and down the block. "10! 9! 8!" They occupied the intersection. "7! 6! 5!" The rest of us took up the count as we moved down toward them. "4! 3! 2! 1! Aaaaagggghhhh!" A hundred people dropped in the street, screaming in the agony of a die-in.

Two squads of foot cops double-timed down our way, ready for action. But it wasn't clear what they could do with us lying on our backs. They halted ten feet away. We still had the street, and might have held it longer. But out of nowhere the Revolutionary People's Front materialized, taunting the police and brandishing their banner poles like pikes and spears. It was the crudest sort of confrontation, and the authorities seized the opportunity. The foot cops fanned toward the outside of the crowd, chopping with their clubs. The horse squad came galloping down the middle of the street toward us.

The cop-baiters scattered. The rest of us scrambled to our feet. Angie and I broke for the sidewalk, but I collided with Hank, and both of us staggered. He grabbed my arm and we jumped back as the cops rode past, batons swinging at

The mounted police finally got the order to charge.

anyone they could reach.

We made it to the sidewalk. Several people were hurt. One man was bleeding from his head. As friends tended to him, I felt a rush of anger. That could have been me! Out in the street, the police were re-forming their lines. "Jerks!" I yelled at them. "Stupid jerks!"

Next to me, Jacey hollered something similar and shook his fist.

But Hank eyed me suspiciously. "This is insane," he spouted. "Why provoke them? We're going to lose every time at this game."

I edged away from him. I didn't have an answer, but I wasn't giving in.

Angie joined me, and we looked around. The crowd in the street had been split in half. Sara and Sid were trying to get over to where we were, but the foot cops deterred them. Doc, on our side, had been separated from his affinity group. Enola Gay was in a crowd being forced away down Mason Street by the horse cops, and when Doc tried to get over to them, he was clubbed back toward Angie and me.

Doc glared at the cops. Next to him another protester grabbed an orange sawhorse from the construction area behind us and dragged it in front of the cops. Doc grabbed another one and pulled it into the intersection at Ellis, which was still open to traffic. Angie stepped out in front of an oncoming car and flagged it to a stop as Doc and I hauled another barricade into the street. Angry motorists honked and cursed, but had little choice except to stop as protesters dragged more sawhorses, newspaper stands, and other debris into the intersection.

As flimsy as the barricade looked, it felt like we'd done something, impeded business as usual. The clutter slowed down the cops as they stopped to sling the objects out of the street. But their mood got uglier. Billyclubs swung freely whenever a protester retreated too slowly. Twenty feet behind us a cop whacked a guy in the side and sent him sprawling to the pavement clutching his ribs.

"Around the block!" Jacey shouted. "Stay near the hotel or they'll disperse us! Around the block!" The cops had split off a large part of the crowd and forced it back onto Mason, but the rest of us turned the corner and started around the hotel on Ellis. Angie and I were still together. Doc was up ahead, with Jenny and Raoul just behind. Sara and a friend of hers slipped past a line of cops and hurried after us.

We pushed up the long block toward Taylor, where there was rumored to be a second hotel entrance. I was breathing easier when behind us Jenny let out a cry. I whirled around and saw her duck away from a cop who brought his club down right across her back. She lurched forward, arms flung out as she hit the ground. The cop raised his nightstick again.

Before he could strike, Raoul sprang in front of him. The cop was in full riot gear, but Raoul presented an imposing obstacle as he squared his shoulders to confront the officer. The cop froze, arm still in the air, then abruptly turned and hurried away to join a squad roughing up some people back by the barricades.

Raoul stood staring at the cop. Jenny scurried to her feet, grabbed his arm, and pulled him toward us. Angie put her arm around Jenny, who had a scraped arm and a sore back but otherwise seemed okay. "I never even saw him till he started to hit me," she said.

Angie tapped Raoul on the stomach. "Good job," she said.

Raoul's breathing was still fast. "Aw, you could see the fear in his eyes right through his riot mask. If you stand up to cops, they're such cowards."

Angie looked Raoul up and down. "Well, it probably helps to be six-foot-five."

The horse cops were moving our way, but some people had stretched their banner across the street to slow them down. Good rearguard defense, I thought.

We figured to take a right turn onto Taylor and shut down that entrance to the Hilton. But when we reached the corner we were met by a phalanx of cops who had cordoned off the whole block of Taylor in front of the hotel. You could still get over there, but it was obvious that you were walking into an arrest. The alternative was to go left on Taylor, where you would be blocked away from the action.

"Divide and conquer," Raoul groaned, his big shoulders slumping. He and Jenny conferred, then announced that they were going to the right.

"We *have* to stay, even if arrest us," Jenny said. "If we leave, it's like admitting they had the right to disperse us."

"Yeah," Raoul muttered. "We have to contest their definition of public space."

Angie gestured to me. "Are you coming?"

"I can't," I said awkwardly, hiding my relief at not getting arrested. "I have to be at Livermore tomorrow. People are counting on it."

A hint of vexation rumbled in her sigh, but as the horse patrol advanced, she relented. "I forgot about Livermore," she said. "I guess you can't get busted here. But I have to." She stepped over and gave me a hug. Standing there in the intersection I squeezed her to me, imprinting her soft form onto my body-memory.

Finally the looming horses forced us to break away. Angie headed after Jenny and Raoul, and I ducked away from the cops.

Once I got under a store awning on the other side of Ellis, I caught my breath and let out a big "Phew!" It startled the curious business-types who were gawking at the row of cops in the intersection. They were the first outsiders I'd seen in over an hour, and I gave them a rude stare.

A television crew was pressing toward the cops, trying to film the protesters in the street behind them. I edged up behind the TV crew, wary of the burly undercovers who I suspected would be sneaking through the crowd. My eyes searched the boisterous protesters clustered in front of the Hilton. I spied plenty of familiar faces, but Angie's eluded me.

Frustrated, I turned back toward the gawkers across Ellis. What did they think this was, some kind of circus? The turbulence of the past hour welled up inside me. "Welcome to Ronald Reagan's America!" I yelled at no one and everyone. "Welcome to 1984!"

I turned and strode away, agitated, disconnected, discouraged. The action was over. What was there to do? Just get out.

But Sara and Doc intercepted me. "You doing okay?" they asked solicitously.

"Yeah, yeah, just blowing off some steam," I assured them.

We eyed the scene over in front of the

Protesters marched around to the back side of the hotel...

Hilton, where people were shouting and waving their banners defiantly at the encircling police. "Have you seen Karina?" Sara asked us. "I don't know if she's getting arrested or not." Doc and I said we hadn't seen her. Sara continued to survey the two hundred or so people facing arrest.

...where they were greeted by more mounted cops.

"Tell me if you see Angie," I said to her, then turned to Doc. "Are you getting busted?"

"Yeah, I guess." Doc scuffed his shoe on the sidewalk. "But I feel frustrated with myself. I was criticizing the monitors for their aggressive tone, and then I go hauling barricades into the street. There was confrontation in the air, and the worst part of me bought into it."

"What's wrong with barricades?" I answered. "The cops were attacking people. You've got to do something."

"It's not what I want to be doing," he said. "It's militaristic, fighting over the street, over 'territory.'"

A caravan of paddywagons rolled up Ellis Street. The cordon of cops opened to let them pass, then closed ranks. Behind their lines, other officers began arresting the people trapped in front of the hotel.

"I don't want to get arrested," Sara said, more to herself than to us. "But I know if I don't, I'll feel like I didn't do anything." She sighed and tugged on her baggy sweater. "I guess if I'm not sure, I should just do it. I can always decide later it wasn't such a great idea."

As I reflected on her logic, Sara turned to Norm, who was approaching us. "Seen Karina?"

"Not since earlier," he answered. His face was red, and he seemed out of breath. "Half of LAG is getting arrested, though. I just saw Pilgrim and Craig getting handcuffed."

"Craig?" I said. "I didn't even know he was here today. What about Hank? Is he in there? He has the keys to the rental truck."

"Hank? I'm not sure," said Norm. "He probably is."

"What about Sid?" Sara asked. "I never saw him after the barricades."

"You didn't hear?" Norm burst out. "Sid got beat up by undercover cops. They had to take him to the hospital."

"Damn!" I shivered. "What pigs!"

"Yeah, they caught him trying to let the air out of a cop-car tire."

I laughed involuntarily. "I sure hope he's okay."

Antonio came over. "I'm going over to Bank of America, in case people start showing up there for our action," he said. "I'll drive back by the jail later to see if people from here are citing out."

"I won't be citing out," Sara replied austerely.

"I won't, either," Norm said. He turned to me. "I'm going to get busted here and do jail solidarity, so I won't be at Livermore tomorrow. Sorry."

It was the first time I'd considered the effect of the arrests on the Livermore action. Even more, I thought about what today would mean as far as LAG consensing on anything around the Democratic Convention. The anti-Convention people would be flipped out over what happened, while the street-action people would be more determined than ever to push things in San Francisco. Of course, the whole thing might rally LAG together, people refusing to be intimidated. But I wasn't optimistic.

We studied the cordon across the street. The line of cops served not only to hold the arrestees in, but also to fence the rest of us out. Down toward the end, a guy who tried to get a message to someone inside got clubbed away. "What priorities," Norm said. "Beating the hell out of people because they blocked traffic."

Doc nodded. "They're afraid that if one person is allowed to disobey, the whole system will crumble."

Suddenly Sara sparked to life, waving and hollering to Karina, whom she had spotted in the arrest crowd. Karina didn't hear her, but Sara said a quick goodbye to us and headed across the street toward the Hilton.

I looked after her with wonder. Did she see a magical opening in the police line?

No one else seemed surprised. Norm went to make a phone call before getting arrested. Doc turned and gave me a hug. "See you," he said. He started across the street after Sara. I shook my head. There's determination for you.

The line of police stood with helmets fastened and clubs at an angle across their chest. As Sara paused in the intersection, another cop came over and poked her in the side with his nightstick, pointing toward the opposite sidewalk. Sara ignored him, and he poked her harder, ordering her out of the street.

With a flash of irritation, Sara turned on him. "What's your badge number?" she snapped. The cop seemed taken aback. Sara squinted at his badge and read the number aloud, then deliberately re-focused her attention on the cordon of cops. She turned toward the edge of the line, searching for an opening. But as she started away, the cop lurched forward and lashed out with his club, striking her across the back of the head. Sara staggered a step or two, turned around, then crumbled to the ground.

The cop strode away. Doc grabbed Sara and pulled her to her feet. Antonio and I ran to meet them as Doc steered Sara toward the sidewalk. Sara made it to us, then slumped to the ground. Doc bent over her frantically. "Stay awake, Sara! Stay awake! Don't pass out!" He looked up at me. "Get some water! She could go into shock if she passes out."

"We need to get her to a hospital," Antonio said, and went to get his car. I headed across the street to a deli, where I got a cup of water and hurried back. Several other people clustered around, trying to keep Sara alert. She was still conscious, but only vaguely aware of what was happening. "Why does my head hurt so much?" her glazed eyes seemed to ask as I dabbed water on her cheeks. "Why won't you let me go to sleep?"

Antonio pulled up in his car, and we eased Sara into the back seat. Several people got in to ride to the hospital with her. "I'm taking her over to Oakland if she can stay awake," Antonio told us. "If she checks into a San Francisco hospital they'll come arrest her."

They pulled away. Doc and I looked at each other. I wondered if he felt as bleak as I did. Without a word, we hugged. Then he turned and headed across the street. The cordon had eased a bit, and Doc slipped past a cop who had his head turned and joined the arrest crowd.

I sighed, feeling lost. What do you do after something like this? Go to Bank of America with our missile and leaflet the customers about war taxes? Maybe I should just get on BART and go home.

I was mulling it over, half-watching a TV crew maneuver, when Norm came running up the street toward me. I tensed, ready to spring. "Jeff! Down here!" he hollered from twenty feet away. "Angie's getting arrested. The cop is choking the hell out of her!"

My stomach tightened. I ran with him to a vantage point and climbed on top of a mailbox, but we couldn't see Angie anymore. "She was non-cooperating," Norm told me. "This big cop got hold of her by the neck, he was dragging

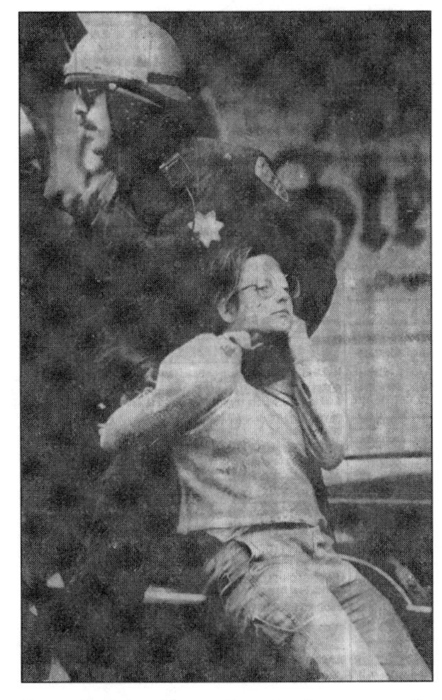

One of the nearly two hundred arrests at the Kissinger protest.

her away, she couldn't get her feet on the ground, I don't see how she could breathe!" He pointed across the street. "Look! There she is!"

My eyes cut through the crowd just in time to see a cop lift Angie off the ground by her neck and drop her in the back of a paddywagon. She sat there, stunned. Then the cop gave her a shove and she disappeared.

I gaped for a moment, then climbed down off the mailbox and slumped against a lightpost. A dull gray fog blanketed the City, and the chill stiffened my muscles. Ellis Street was practically deserted except for photographers. The whole spectacle receded, as if I were watching it on TV.

My mind drifted off to Holly. I pictured her at the Site 300 protest, dealing with cops away from any media or support people. Was she faring any better? Would she be in jail overnight? I wondered when I'd see her again.

And when would I see Angie? I chastised myself for my indecision, as if my failure to commit to one or the other was the cause of their being held in jail. And suppose one of them was released, and spent the night with me. I'd feel like I was betraying the other...

My reverie was broken by a commotion behind the police lines. The cordon of cops twitched their batons, but maintained a taut line. TV crews jockeyed for position. Although I couldn't make out what was happening, I figured I should split before I wound up getting busted myself. That was the last thing I needed.

But before I could move, a heavy hand clasped my shoulder. My body snapped, then froze. Unable to speak, let alone cry out, I felt myself dragged away, slapped into handcuffs, thrown into the back of an unmarked car...

...Slowly my eyes came into focus. Someone was speaking to me. "Hey, sorry! Didn't mean to scare you." It was Hank. "I thought you saw me coming!"

I sucked in a breath through clenched teeth. Hank gave my shoulder a shake. "Really, I'm sorry!"

Suddenly I burst out laughing. "God! I thought I was gone!" Then I turned serious. "I thought *you* got busted."

"Naw, I couldn't," Hank answered. "I've got to get the truck back to the rental place by five. But we should get out of here. Come on, let's take the tax-missile over to Bank of America and see what's happening there."

Blockade Livermore Lab!

June 21, 1982

Over 1300 protesters were arrested in a nonviolent blockade of Livermore Nuclear Weapons Lab on Summer Solstice.

Top: Janet Delaney
Center: Keith Holmes
Bottom: Bette Lee

Over 100 affinity groups (AGs) blockaded all four entrances to the Lab.

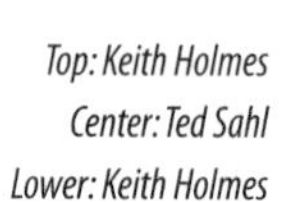

Top: Keith Holmes
Center: Ted Sahl
Lower: Keith Holmes

Youth AGs were a dramatic part of the action. Blockaders under 18 were arrested, booked, and released into their parents' custody.

Blockade Livermore Lab!

June 21, 1982

All photos: Bette Lee

Any connections between the people pictured in the photographs and the characters in this book are purely coincidental. The characters are fictional. No photo should be taken as implying that an individual is in any way connected to a fictional character.

A few of the 1300 arrests at Livermore Nuclear Weapons Lab, June 21, 1982.

Another 80 people were arrested in a follow-up action the next day.

Top: Keith Holmes
Center: Ted Sahl
Bottom: Ted Sahl

One / 1982

In politics, obedience and support are the same.

— *Hannah Arendt, Eichmann in Jerusalem*

Tuesday, May 25, 1982

"Stop the Bomb Where It Starts — Blockade Livermore Lab!" The poster stood out from a clutter of paper and tape on the Berkeley phonepole. Demonstrations happened all the time in the Bay Area, but in 1982, anti-nuclear protests were special. For the first time in my adult life, large numbers of people were doing civil disobedience.

I'd heard about CD since I was young — Henry David Thoreau, Susan B. Anthony, Martin Luther King, Jr., the Berrigans. Inspiring, sure. But something that other people did. Heroes and martyrs.

In the late 1970s, in the wake of the Three Mile Island nuclear accident, activists on both coasts turned to civil disobedience in their protests against nuclear power. But the actions weren't in the Bay Area, and I didn't hear much about them. It wasn't until February 1982 that the spirit reached me. The newly-formed Livermore Action Group sponsored its first action at Livermore Nuclear Weapons Lab, forty miles east of San Francisco. One hundred seventy people were arrested, and the local papers gave it front-page coverage.

One hundred seventy people? That changed the equation. The part that worried me most was being alone in jail. If there were one hundred seventy others with me, well, that felt different.

I'd been out of the political loop for a few years after being involved in campus-type organizing at Indiana State in the mid-1970s, mainly cultural work like coffeehouses or literary journals. I got my degree in political science, but that didn't seem to mean much in the real world.

Music seemed more promising. Since college I'd been writing blues and folk songs satirizing Republicans, landlords, generals, and other obvious targets. In 1980, I got serious about it. I dropped out of grad school in Berkeley and took a maintenance job in a Southside apartment building. Two or three nights a week I performed at open mikes or played with a couple of friends at a pizza joint down by the Bay. I liked seeing people laugh and nod as I sang, but something was still missing.

Soon after the February 1982 Livermore blockade, I saw a flyer for a LAG meeting in Berkeley. Why not go by and sing them a couple of anti-nuke songs? When I arrived, there were fifty people crowded into the community room of the Savo Island co-op, overflowing couches, leaning through doorways, filling the floor. Most were White, and they ranged in age from students to seniors.

I asked for five minutes on the agenda, and someone said, "Why don't you sing now while we're waiting to start." I didn't even have time to get nervous. I wasn't sure if it was nuclear power or weapons they were protesting, so I covered both.

The cheers rang in my head for days afterward. Singing to a roomful of protesters, I felt involved. If my singing inspired them, and they went and shut down a nuclear plant, I'd had an effect. Sure, it was indirect. But you have to start somewhere. The memory stuck with me all Spring, and when I saw a poster for a protest co-sponsored by LAG in May, I decided to take the afternoon off my maintenance job and go.

LAG joined the Committee in Solidarity with the People of El Salvador (CISPES) for this non-CD protest of a Livermore Lab weapons conference.

Livermore Lab was hosting a weapons-research conference entitled, unbelievably, "Tougher Targets: Upgrading Lethality," a title which eloquently captured the mission of the federally-funded Lab — the creation of ever more deadly weapons for the U.S. government.

LAG joined with several Central America solidarity groups in calling a protest of the weapons conference, which wasn't at the Lab itself but at a nearby country club. I'd been hoping to witness my first arrests, but apparently no one in the crowd of a hundred was planning to blockade.

We lined the roadside, chanting and singing for

ourselves and a couple of dozen police. Off to one side, a group called Overthrow Cluster set up the "Hard Times Soup Line and Crumb Kitchen" to dramatize the sudden increase in homelessness as the Reagan administration slashed social spending to fund the arms race.

Seven o'clock came and went, and I was wondering whether the conferees had snuck out a secret exit. Suddenly two police cars came cruising down the road with their lights flashing, followed closely by several chartered buses. From both sides of the road, people surged forward, chanting and yelling and finger-pointing. The police fell back a step before bracing and bringing their clubs to attention. Through the narrow corridor crept three shiny tour-buses. As they came parallel with our lines, our shouting coalesced into a chant: "U.S. bombmakers, you can't hide! We charge you with genocide!"

The Hard Times Soup Line and Crumb Kitchen, organized by Overthrow Cluster for the May 25 protest.

From behind their sealed windows the delegates gawked and nervously laughed. A few even waved or flashed the peace sign as the buses inched past.

"U.S. bombmakers, you can't hide!" For a minute, I felt a jubilant sense of release. Then they were gone. My eyes turned back toward the direction from which they'd come. There had to be someone else to yell at. But the cops were packing up. Clearly they thought the action was over. Now what?

"The delegates are going to Howard Johnsons!" The rumor swept the crowd. People scrambled for the cars. No one seemed to mind who rode with whom, and quickly an entire caravan was speeding down the highway with the state police hot on our trail.

We found Howard Johnsons, and were out of our cars before the last bus emptied. Several dozen of us descended like locusts on the delegates. Most of them scurried for the cover of the cocktail lounge, but a few of the thicker-skinned ones stopped to explain themselves.

"What about the Russians?" a condescending delegate in a gray jacket argued. "We're supposed to stop our research while they move ahead?"

"We could stop for a while," a protester countered, "and see if the Soviets do the same. Someone has to take the first step for peace."

I was still pumped up from the earlier scene, and cut loose in a loud voice.

"Why bother with him? He's a sellout. He gets paid big bucks to talk the government line."

The man inspected me through a veneer of imperturbability. Other protesters elbowed me away. "Come on, let the man talk. Let's hear what he has to say."

I waved my hand. "It's a waste of time. He's paid not to think."

A picket line formed in front of the lounge. Although a row of police barred the doorway, we could see the delegates through the windows. I joined the ranks, and we chanted and sang as the cool Spring evening set in. Maybe we couldn't get directly at the bombmakers, but at least they couldn't ignore our presence.

Gradually the protest wound down, and I caught a ride in a van heading back to Berkeley. As we got settled in the back, a tall woman whose brown hair showed streaks of gray looked over at me. "I heard you hassling that delegate," she said pointedly. "You weren't facilitating communication."

Other eyes were on me. "No, I guess not," I admitted. "I was just sick of him acting so calm and casual about designing weapons."

"But do you think it's nonviolent to yell at him?"

Another woman spoke up. "Come on, Melissa, anger isn't violence. Anger shows respect. It can open communication."

"There was no communication going on out there," Melissa said. "Shouting at someone just creates an us-them dynamic."

"But we *are* against them," I said. "I'm totally against what that guy does."

She looked at me as if she'd had to explain herself one too many times. "That can be expressed in an open and caring way. If we truly want peace, we have to show it in our own lives, in the way we treat our adversaries."

"Oh, come on," an older guy in the front seat said. "We have to have some release or we'll all get ulcers."

"Then we have to find a better way," Melissa responded. "That's why I get arrested. Yelling and chanting doesn't accomplish anything. But civil disobedience shakes their whole system. If they prosecute us, we clog their jails and courts. If they drop the charges, we go back and do it again. Getting arrested is the only time I've ever felt like I was being heard by the government."

That got my attention. "You've been arrested?" I said. "What's it like?" No one else in the van had done civil disobedience, and we peppered Melissa with questions. She had been busted in LAG's February blockade at the Lab. She'd gotten a seven-day sentence, which she served with dozens of other protesters. She had a misdemeanor on her record, which wouldn't keep her from getting a job anywhere. The police had been rough, the jail guards were liars, but the other inmates at the county jail had mostly been supportive.

She told us about the next action, a blockade on the Summer Solstice. By the time we got back to Berkeley, I was ready to go. Maybe not to get arrested right off, but at least to be part of the protest.

"You should call the LAG office and sign up for a nonviolence prep," Melissa told me. "Everyone involved has to have one. It gets you ready for the police and jail."

What a concept. When I thought about civil disobedience before, the idea of a prep session hadn't crossed my mind. Had I thought people just showed up at the Lab and sat in the road? And the possibility of being a supporter hadn't occurred to me before today. No wonder I was hesitant! But here they were, offering a do-it-yourself CD workshop. How could I turn that down?

It was about a month till the June 21st blockade at Livermore. I thought I'd probably get arrested, but I didn't tell anyone right away, in case I changed my mind. It worried me in some ways. I'd never had a run-in with the law, not even a speeding ticket. They didn't have my fingerprints or anything. So why should I turn myself in? Wouldn't it be more effective to stay anonymous, underground?

But I had a nagging feeling that I wouldn't take myself seriously if I didn't do it. I knew that the world had to change, and that I had to do something about it. But what? Music? I wanted to *do* something, not just sing about it.

The LAG office in 1982.

After a week of thinking it over, I decided to visit the LAG office. It amazed me that LAG had an office. Unions have offices, and political parties. But a group whose major purpose was breaking the law?

There it was, though, a small storefront on Shattuck Avenue, right at the Oakland/Berkeley border. The front windows were pasted over with posters for the upcoming blockade, and for the big June 12th anti-nuclear march sponsored by the Freeze and other mainstream peace groups. I pushed on the front door, which stuck. I gave it a harder shove and made it into the office.

The space was about forty feet long and fifteen feet wide, with an exceptionally high ceiling. Desks and file cabinets lined the walls. Worktables filled most of the rest of the area. The space was shared with Berkeley Citizens

Action, "BCA," a left-leaning electoral coalition. In their half of the office, several older Black women worked on a mailing while a high-powered young White guy talked on the phone.

I made my way to the LAG area in the back, where half a dozen young White folks were working amidst posters, mailings, tangled phone lines, and a hundred important scraps of paper.

"Who's in charge?" I asked. A couple of people laughed.

"Hi, I'm Caroline," said a tall, round-shouldered woman. "I'm *not* in charge. What can we help you with?" She had an open, welcoming demeanor, and I felt like I'd come to the right place.

"I want to sign up for a training for the June blockade," I said.

"You mean a nonviolence prep?" She turned to another woman behind her. "Claudia, where's the sign-up sheet for preps?" Claudia rooted around on her desk and produced a handwritten list of twenty names. "Can you make it June 19th?" Caroline asked.

A flicker of disappointment passed over me. I was counting on the prep to make up my mind about getting arrested or not. "That's only two days before the blockade. Isn't there one sooner?"

"No, they're all full. That's the next open one in Berkeley."

"Okay, I'll be there."

LIVERMORE WEAPONS LAB
BLOCKADE/DEMONSTRATION
HANDBOOK

NONVIOLENT PROTEST & CIVIL DISOBEDIENCE

JUNE 21, 1982

The Livermore handbook was based on the Diablo and Seabrook handbooks that came before it.

"It's from ten till six," she said. "Make sure you're there on time and can stay for the whole prep. It's really important." As I finished signing the list, she gave me a newsprint booklet. "You should read this, too. It covers the action and consensus and stuff. It's one dollar."

I paid the dollar and thanked her. She turned back to the mailing she was working on. As I headed out, I looked around at the posters tacked over every inch of LAG's wall-space — from Germany, Japan, Italy, New York, Wyoming, everywhere the same message: No Nukes, Not Here, Not Anywhere.

When I got back to my apartment, I watered the

plants, made some popcorn, and opened the handbook. I leaned forward on the table and flipped through the pages, catching glimpses of the titles: Consensus, Nonviolence, Feminism, Nonhierarchy, Jail Solidarity.

I'd been wanting this for a long time. I came into political awareness at the tail end of the Vietnam era. The protests were over, but the world was still a mess. What should I do? Campaign for the Democrats? I tried it during college, and I felt like a cog in a rusty machine. Work on a referendum? If it could really change anything, it would never be allowed to pass. That much I understood. Electoral politics was hopelessly corrupt, chained to the pocketbooks of the rich.

Through my music and writing, through studying history and economics, I groped for a handle: How to shape my talents and interests into a tool to change the world. The quest had its own rewards, like my recent awakening to Medieval art. But sometimes I wondered how much I clung to "searching for a niche" to avoid having to *do* anything.

Since Reagan's election in 1980, I had been experiencing flashes of anxiety. One day it was the spectre of nuclear war or toxic disaster. Other times it was more personal, a devastating car accident or a brutal mugging. Always the images were haunted with a sense of the entire world falling apart.

I knew I had to do something. But what? I wasn't a pacifist, but neither was I going to pick up a gun and head for the hills. Acting alone or with a few friends, the only options I saw were to be an artist exposing the injustices of society, or a social worker struggling to alleviate the suffering.

Leafing through the handbook, I caught a fresh vision. A vision of a better future — and of a new way of living and working right now.

I read about the Seabrook and Diablo Canyon actions, where thousands of people raised their voices against nuclear madness. I read again about the February blockade at Livermore. 170 arrests. My wake-up call. And I read about the plans for the June blockade. What would that be like? Two hundred people? Five hundred? Maybe these LAG folks were on to something. Maybe it wasn't hopeless after all.

Saturday, June 19, 1982

THE DAY-LONG nonviolence prep, held at the North Berkeley Quaker meeting hall, brought it all together for me. There were twenty of us, aged seventeen to fifty-five. Two were Asian American, and one woman identified herself as

Latino. The rest seemed White. Most looked middle-class, which somehow didn't surprise me.

As far as our daily lives, we were pretty diverse: a couple of teachers, a couple of students, a mother and daughter, gays, straights, and bisexuals, a wealthy couple from Marin County, the secretary of a plumbers' union, several underemployed marginals, and even one man who confessed to voting for Reagan. One thing united us — no one had ever been arrested at a protest.

Nonviolent direct action preps were held all over Northern California before 1980s actions such as Livermore and Diablo Canyon.

The preppers were two veteran activists. Maria was about my age, twenty-eight. She had helped start LAG, and been arrested at the Lab in a small action on Mothers' Day after chaining her wheelchair to the front gate. Nathaniel was around fifty, a staff member at American Friends Service Committee with an arrest record dating back to the Civil Rights and Vietnam eras.

The prep included some theory and discussion of nonviolence, but mainly we role-played protests — dealing with the cops, talking with Lab workers, making consensus decisions under pressure, getting arrested, and jail solidarity actions. We formed an affinity group, calling ourselves Spectrum. I was so inspired that I even volunteered to be one of our AG spokes at the final spokescouncil the next day.

For all we covered, I still had a hundred unanswered questions at the end of the prep — not the least of which was, am I going to get arrested? Several times during the day, I was sure I'd blockade. But I could see the wisdom of going to my first action as a supporter. Check out the real thing before jumping in headlong. It wasn't like nukes were going to disappear overnight. And neither was I. With the prep, the handbook, and all the great people I was meeting, something more was awakening. Some long-buried desire not simply to take action, but to be part of a movement dedicated to changing the world. I was especially struck by the emphasis on consensus and feminist process, which seemed like a blueprint for building a new, cooperative society. We weren't just protesting — we were forging an alternative.

Knowing that this movement existed — or was coming into existence — how could I be anywhere else? Sure, no one had asked me to sign anything or pay any dues. I could walk away at any time. But we had a chance to make a difference. Wasn't that the whole point of my studies and writing and music? I'd found my calling.

Sunday, June 20, 1982

AROUND TWO HUNDRED people gathered for the spokescouncil in Berkeley's Martin Luther King, Jr. Park. It was lunch break, and I was sitting around in the warm grass with people from other affinity groups in our new cluster, "Change of Heart." The name came from a documentary film being made about Noah's Ark, one of the AGs in the cluster.

Karina was in Noah's Ark. She was in her early twenties, with bright eyes and thick brown hair that fell over her shoulders. Her laughter summoned a growing circle as she recounted episodes from the filming. "Can you imagine fifteen people trying to name an affinity group with video cameras capturing every word?"

"That's great," I said. "Sounds like a pressure test for consensus process."

"It was terrible," Karina said. "Everyone knew that we needed the cameras to be off for a while, but no one wanted to be the one to say that on camera!"

Final pre-blockade spokescouncil in Berkeley, where spokes (reps) from dozens of clusters and over a hundred affinity groups worked out action and jail solidarity agreements. Spokescouncils met periodically for several months before major actions.

We got to talking about the number of people blockading the next day. Earlier in the afternoon the spokescouncil had taken an informal poll of AGs. Everyone hoped the number would significantly exceed the one hundred seventy arrested February 1st. But no one was prepared for the estimated total — nine hundred fifty!

As the crowd erupted in applause, I inclined toward getting arrested. I could help push the total past a thousand. That would be pretty amazing, a thousand people. I smiled to myself — here I was, keeping a scorecard on the protest. Probably not the best motivation for my decision. But still....

The only bad moment came at our cluster meeting. I was so inspired by

June 19 pre-blockade rally, Mosswood Park, Oakland.

the gathering that I led a song and offered to facilitate the meeting. I called on other people to speak, but interjected my own opinions after most speakers. Finally a tall woman with long red-blonde hair interrupted me from across the circle.

"I don't think the facilitator should talk so much," she said plainly. "If you want to argue, you should let someone else facilitate."

I flushed. She was right. I awkwardly proposed that someone else facilitate, and didn't speak much for the rest of the meeting. I could see I had a lot to learn.

The main topic at the meeting was whether to non-cooperate during the arrests. Most people planned to get up and walk, but a few were talking about going limp when the cops came for them.

"Do you think they'll carry non-cooperators, or use choke holds?" someone asked.

Karina tossed her head back. "Choke holds? If we're lucky. They'll probably use wrist locks and other pain holds. They're not going to carry a thousand people."

I shivered. Even if I did get arrested, I didn't see the point in non-cooperating. Why bring on pain when they're going to make you move in the end?

A man next to me raised his hand tentatively. "Maybe we should consense that we won't non-cooperate?"

Hank, one of the other spokes from my AG, jutted his chin out. "No way," he said. Hank was about my age, a tall, muscular guy with a dark stubble. He worked as a electrician in a Berkeley auto shop, and looked like he'd had a few run-ins with the police in his day. "I'm not cooperating with a cop busting me for blockading a death lab."

"Amen," Karina said. "If they're going to arrest us, at least make them work for it."

The meeting broke up. For the first time all day I felt alone, lost in the milling crowd. I wandered over to where a couple of AGs had prepared dinner for us. As I waited in line, I saw the blonde-haired woman who'd challenged me at the cluster meeting. She moved with casual grace as she surveyed the salads and breads, taking only a couple of small servings from the table. "You're not getting much food for your money," I kidded her, trying to show I didn't hold a grudge.

"No," she said, turning toward me. Her blue-green eyes were friendly, but I couldn't read any further. "I'm not supposed to eat wheat or dairy." She got a bowl of broccoli soup and some rice, then walked toward the last sunlit spot in the park.

Ordinarily, I would have taken it as a hint if someone walked away from me. But I couldn't drop it quite so easily this time. I'd been single for a year, wishing and waiting for the right person to come along. Maybe she just had. The graceful stride, the calm smile, even the gentle yet direct way she'd criticized me at the meeting — I better not let her slip away.

I went over and sat down on the ground next to her. "My name is Jeff," I said, reaching out to shake her hand.

She took my hand, which looked red next to the pale yellow of her skin. "I'm Holly." She seemed amused at our handshake. She was about my age, and had a calm, collected air about her. "I wasn't trying to give you a hard time at the meeting," she said. "I just thought you shouldn't try to facilitate and debate at the same time."

"That's okay," I said. "I needed someone to slow me down." There was a moment of silence. I bit off a chunk of bread and searched for something to say. "Is this your first arrest?"

She looked up from her soup with a thoughtful expression. "Yeah. I went to the Mothers' Day action at Livermore last month, but as a supporter. This time I'm blockading. How about you?"

"I'm not sure," I said quietly. I creased my brow. If she had been a supporter

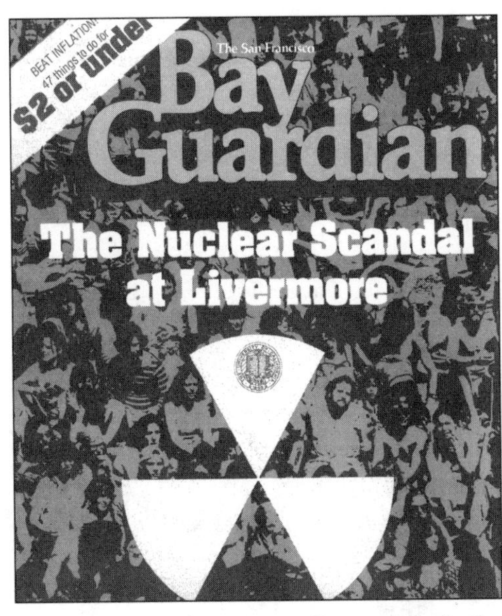

Bay Area alternative media, especially the Bay Guardian, helped alert the public to Reagan's abrupt escalation of nuclear weapons programs.

the first time, why couldn't I? I changed the subject, asking her what drew her to LAG.

She looked at me thoughtfully. "Partly I was seeking community," she said. "I wanted to be in an affinity group. But it's political, too. I wanted to make a statement. I don't know if we can shut the Lab, even for a day. But I want people around the world to realize that not everyone in America is passively accepting the arms race."

I nodded. "That's the same for me, making a statement. Plus, if the world blows up, I want to die knowing I tried to stop it."

She smiled, and I relaxed a notch. I asked about her affinity group.

Holly's eyes sparkled. "We named it for a civil defense song from the 1950s," she said. "In case of nuclear attack, Duck and Cover! We've been meeting every week since our prep in April."

"Wow, my AG just met for the first time at our prep yesterday," I said.

We talked a while longer, till we finished eating. Then she excused herself to go meet with her AG. "We're leaving for Livermore at three tomorrow morning."

"Yeah, us too," I said. I wanted to ask for her phone number, but it seemed like pushing things. She hugged me lightly. As she turned to go, I called after her. "I'll see you out there in the morning."

She looked back and smiled. "Good. I'll see you then."

Monday, June 21, 1982

As we pulled off the freeway and passed through the sleeping town of Livermore, a cloud of foreboding crept over me. Was it a premonition, a warning to stay on the sidelines today? Or a projection of fears that I needed to face?

It was still dark as we stopped along a country road outside Livermore. I groped my way out of the car, and could make out a ditch and a field beyond it.

"The Lab is down this road," Hank said as he squeezed his big frame out of the car. "It's an easy walk from here."

Change of Heart was part of the first wave at the East Gate, and I wanted to get up there and see what the place looked like. The sooner I got to the site, the better

Supporters at the June blockade.

picture I'd have of my options.

"Don't worry, we're way early," Cindy said. "It's only four a.m. There won't be anyone to blockade yet." Cindy was a special-ed teacher in her mid-thirties, and she herded us together like we were kids on a field trip. She pointed down the road, away from the Lab. "We should go that way and block the road leading in. The police are expecting everybody at the gate. We could blockade a lot longer out here."

"But there's media and support people at the gate," someone argued. "The police can't be as rough."

I silently nodded. Going off on some unknown adventure made me nervous. Of course, if I weren't getting arrested, it wasn't my decision to make. But I still hadn't quite ruled it out.

"We agreed on the gate at our prep," someone else said. "It takes a new consensus to change our plans."

"If we're serious about shutting down the Lab, we should go down the road," Cindy persisted. But only Hank backed her, and they gave up.

We walked quietly up the road toward the gate. My angst had subsided. For most of us it was our first time at the Lab, a two-square-mile complex of office and research buildings surrounded by an eight-foot barbed wire fence. Even though I knew what went on at the Lab, it was hard not to be awed by this bastion of "scientific research."

We arrived at the gate, a simple two-lane asphalt entrance road with a chain-link fence on either side. A couple of hundred protesters were already bunched along the sides of the road. The police had set up barricades inside the gate, and were standing nervously at ease, waiting for the blockade to start. People were hurrying around making final arrangements and saying goodbye to friends. The AGs from our cluster, Change of Heart, congregated in the gravel area to the left side of the Lab entrance.

Two other clusters formed the balance of the first wave at the East Gate. Before our AG arrived, there had been a coin toss to see which cluster would go first. Sonomore Atomics, a cluster from Sonoma County, won the toss. Change of Heart came in second, which meant that there were fifty or so blockaders ahead of us. Good, I thought. Gives me time to see how it all works.

The affinity groups within our cluster needed to meet to determine the

A youth AG joined the June 21 Livermore blockade.

blockade order. Tony, the plumber from our AG, volunteered to be the spoke. The rest of us pressed up to the road. A row of police were stationed right at the gate, and some protesters harangued them about the arms race. Although it was barely dawn, a few cars were arriving, and everyone wanted the action to begin. Chants kept breaking out, then dissolving into shouts and applause.

Finally, the first AG from Sonomore Atomics strode into the street. A cheer went up from the crowd. Several dozen California state troopers buckled down riot helmets and pulled on leather gloves. The blockaders situated themselves across the Lab entrance and sat down in the road. The rest of their cluster chanted, "Shut it down! Shut it down!" A couple of cars pulled to a stop. The drivers leaned out of their windows, chagrined.

A squad of troopers marched in and surrounded the affinity group. "You are obstructing a public roadway," blared their bullhorn. "If you do not move immediately you will be subject to arrest."

"Shut it down! Shut it down!" the crowd yelled back. One by one the protesters were led away to an open area just inside the fence, where they were frisked and handcuffed. The lone non-cooperator was dragged by the arms.

As soon as the first AG from the Sonoma cluster was cleared away, a second took its place, followed soon by a third and a fourth. Lines of cars were backing up in both directions. As the drivers stopped their engines and settled in for the wait, protesters handed out leaflets. Some workers accepted them, some angrily threw them away.

Hank and Cindy and I stood at the edge of the road taking in the panorama. "We'll be up in no time," Hank said.

"Yeah," Cindy answered. "It's going too fast."

Too fast. My chest tensed. Should I do it? Why not? Well, for one, I hadn't actually asked for any time off work beyond today. I'd have to cite out after a day or two, and break solidarity. Let it go, I told myself. Don't be impatient. You don't have to get arrested at your first blockade. Use today to watch and learn.

I craned my neck for a better view as a man in a wheelchair was hauled away by several police. The arrestees were being handcuffed with flexible plastic strips, disposable cuffs that looped together behind the back. The police must have figured they didn't need to handcuff the guy in the wheelchair. But as soon as they turned away, he steamed back into the intersection to the cheers of the crowd.

The second time, the police cuffed his chair to the fence. Fifty or so people were now in custody, and Change of Heart's turn was rapidly approaching. The last affinity group from the Sonoma cluster took to the street: animated high-schoolers with painted faces, balloons, and bright, hand-lettered signs pleading for the future of the planet. The police seemed reluctant to begin the arrests. When they began busting the teens, booing and cries of "Shame!" filled the air.

Tony, our spoke to the cluster meeting, rounded us up for the final briefing. "We drew straws, and we're the fifth AG," he said. "We're after Fish Without Bicycles, and before Duck and Cover. Look, there go the first people from our cluster."

A dozen people from Short Meetings AG stepped into the road, holding hands. The rest of Change of Heart applauded them, then joined in the old Pete Seeger song, "If I Had a Hammer."

We sang through several verses as the police arrested them one by one. I tried to picture myself seated on the concrete. Should I do it? If you're not sure, it's better to wait. Focus on supporting those who are arrested.

Next to me, Hank fidgeted and shifted around. "It's only been a half hour, and they've busted eighty people," he said. "It's barely dawn. We're walking right into their arms."

"It's kind of late to change our plans now," said someone else from Spectrum.

"No, come on," Cindy said. "Let's go back up the road. We could be way more effective if we got away from the cops."

As other members of our AG joined the debate, though, it was clear that most preferred to stay at the gate. People talked about their blockade plans. I drifted out of

People using wheelchairs were arrested and jailed with the rest of the protesters.

the discussion, having spotted Holly fifty feet away, circled up with Duck and Cover. They had their arms around each other, and looked very close-knit. I felt happy for her, but wished their meeting would break up so I could go talk to her before she got busted.

A woman from Fish Without Bicycles came over to us. "We're going now. You're next." A current ran through our group, blockaders and supporters alike. We huddled together. People grabbed drinks of filtered water, took vitamins, and got a final round of hugs. "One of our support people should go tell Duck and Cover that we're going," Cindy said as the moment approached.

"I will," I volunteered, seizing the opportunity. I hastened over to Holly's circle. "Spectrum is going next — then it's you," I told them, looking right at her.

Holly looked back at me and smiled. "We're still discussing what we're going to do." She pointed past me. "There goes your AG. You better hurry!"

Sure enough, Spectrum had just walked out into the road. I looked back at Holly, still smiling at me. I held her gaze, and suddenly it was completely clear. I turned and headed toward the blockade.

"Come on," Hank hollered as he saw me hustling after them. I caught up and grabbed his hand as we circled in the intersection. In a glance I took in the faces of the others — excitement, fear, pride, concern. I shared all their feelings, simultaneously.

We barely got seated before the troopers surrounded us. Photographers darted in and out. We started singing a song we'd learned at our prep:

"Circle round for freedom, Circle round for peace...."

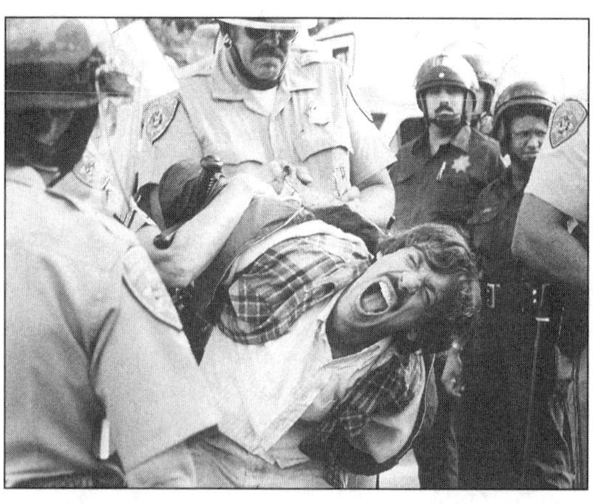

Some non-cooperators were dragged (opposite), others had pain-compliance holds used, depending on the police force making the arrest. Police were called in from all over the Bay Area, plus the California Highway Patrol.

My heart pounded, but I brimmed with confidence in what I was doing and in the people I was with. How could I have doubted that I belonged here? We gripped each others' hands, letting go only as the police pulled someone up.

The first few stood and were led away, but when they came for Hank, he remained seated. "Come on," came a cop's gruff voice. "You're under arrest!"

Hank stared straight ahead. The rest of us kept singing nervously. A helmeted cop bent over and wrenched Hank's arm behind his back. Hank leaned forward to ease the pressure. The cop yanked the twisted arm up and forced Hank to his feet. I sang in a thin voice, embarrassed that I planned to cooperate.

Our song faded. Heavy boots scraped the concrete behind me. "You're under arrest." Leather gloves gripped my arm. I staggered to my feet, scared and excited. On either side an officer held my lower arm, ready to twist. I walked with them to the waiting schoolbus, where other Change of Heart people yelled support through the windows. My wrists were pulled back and cuffed. A wave of elation swept over me. I was doing it.

The police did a cursory pat down, then pushed me up the stairs into the bus. There was a guard at the front, but otherwise it was all blockaders. I made my way past rows of laughing, shouting people to the back seats where the rest of Spectrum had gathered.

A woman from Short Meetings came toward us brandishing a pair of nail clippers. "Who wants out?"

Hank stood up. With a few quick snips, the clippers cut through his plastic handcuffs. He yanked free and massaged his shoulder. "Damn, I think they sprained it."

I leaned up in my seat, taking in the scene, joining in the songs and chants that kept bursting out. Karina from Noah's Ark was kneeling on the seat in front of me. Her hands were free, and she stuck a piece of granola bar in my mouth. "You want out?"

"No," I said, wriggling my bound wrists behind my back. "If I'm going to get busted, I want the total experience." I settled into my seat as best as I could, and a feeling of satisfaction wafted over me. We'd closed the weapons lab. They had to arrest us. It was official now.

The bus pulled out and headed across the Lab grounds. "They're taking us out the back way. I'll bet they have roads that aren't on the map." We cruised on for a few minutes, then came to a stop for no apparent reason. We were still yelling and singing, and it took a while to realize we weren't going anywhere.

"What's the delay?" griped Karina. "I want to get to jail."

"Yeah, come on," called out Hank. "I need to use a toilet!"

But we sat. The cop at the front of the schoolbus refused to answer questions. Karina opened a window. She leaned out, then ducked back in and hollered, "It's blockaders! They're blockading our bus at the edge of the Lab!" A cheer went up and we pulled open more windows to shout encouragement.

It took ten minutes to clear the road, and we resumed our journey to the county jail. When we got there, we were led off the bus and into a small gymnasium to be booked. "Women this way, men over there!" yelled a guard. People quickly hugged whoever they were standing closest to, and we said goodbye to half of our cluster.

The guards clipped the plastic cuffs off the few of us who still had them on, and formed us into a long line facing a row of makeshift booking tables.

"Where can we go to the bathroom?" someone asked.

"Out there," a guard pointed.

"Against that wall?"

"Well, there's nowhere else," he shrugged.

A few of us started that way, but someone called us back. "Don't! It's a trick, they're gonna bust you!"

I hesitated, but Hank waved the guy off. "Come on, we've already been busted."

Apparently the guard wasn't tricking us. "There's our first lesson in arbitrary authority and the prison system," someone half-joked.

Booking went just like the role-play in our nonviolence prep. We gave our names and addresses, got weighed, measured, and photographed, and then were led to a long table where a row of deputies were waiting with ink pads and fingerprint cards.

"Right hand first. Just relax your hand and let me roll the finger over. Now the thumb." This was the creepiest part. I recalled how as a Boy Scout I had started working on the fingerprinting merit badge, but never got around to the final challenge: submitting my prints to the FBI. How lucky, I later thought. If I were ever involved in any illicit radical activity, my prints wouldn't give me away. So now here I was, donating a complete set to the government.

"Left hand, all four fingers together. Okay, wash up over there." The deed was done. As I wiped off my hands, I felt an unexpected wave of pride. No more hiding, no more dreaming of some hypothetical act of resistance. I was officially a protester.

After booking, the men were led back to the bus and driven across the Santa Rita jail grounds. We peered out the windows at the decrepit facility. To my right, behind a tall barbed wire fence, I saw a row of barracks.

Our bus drove past the barracks for a quarter mile or so and stopped in front of a big warehouse. "The inmates are kept in the barracks," someone said. "But they don't have room for us. We're probably being kept in this warehouse, and the women in that gym we saw."

The bright morning was rising over the valley as we filed off the bus to a round of applause from the fifty men who preceded us. The guards handed each of us a sheet, a blanket, and a paper bag. I opened the bag in search of breakfast, but instead found a toothbrush, soap, paper, a pencil stub, and a shiny New Testament. "That's going to honk some people off," Hank said, holding his book at arm's length as if avoiding contamination.

The warehouse, which had a thirty-foot ceiling, was lined with row after row of olive-green army cots. We made our way down the narrow aisles and staked out a corner for our AG. Other Change of Heart AGs settled nearby, and we did a quick check-in to see if everyone in the cluster was accounted for.

"Wait," someone said. "There's only eight AGs here. We started with ten."

"Fish Without Bicycles was all women."

"But where's Duck and Cover?" I looked around. Sure enough, the men from Holly's AG were missing.

"We were supposed to blockade after them, but they were still discussing what to do, so we went ahead," someone from another AG said. "They're probably on the next bus. There it comes now."

We yelled and applauded as another thirty men disembarked and checked in. But there was no sign of Duck and Cover.

Several more buses arrived, and we hollered ourselves hoarse greeting them. The warehouse was filling up fast, but still no Duck and Cover. We asked the later arrivals if they knew anything.

"They were at the East Gate?" someone said. "Isn't that where the Oakland motorcycle cops were?"

"Oh, great," Hank said. "They can be real pigs."

It was hard to picture someone as tranquil as Holly tangling with motorcycle cops, but I was starting to worry. Once trouble started, everyone in the area would be in danger.

Another bus arrived, and I went out to ask if anybody had been at the East Gate and seen what was happening. No one knew specifically about Duck and Cover, but people talked about the cops getting rougher as the blockade went on.

The next bus pulled in, and I was hearing the same story, when suddenly the men from Duck and Cover emerged.

"Where were you?" I asked a young guy from the AG. "The rest of us got here an hour ago."

"We saw how fast the cops were scooping up people at the gate," one guy said. "So we hiked down to an access road and blockaded there. We shut down traffic for a long time before the police got it together to come arrest us."

Later in the morning the guards opened the doors of the warehouse and let us out into the yard, an old asphalt parking lot broken apart by sun-bleached weeds. Bales of hay served as the only seats. A token coil of barbed wire demarcated the yard. Obviously no escape attempts were expected.

"We're overflowing the warehouse," Hank reported. "There's more of us than they have beds for."

"They're putting the rest of the men in holding cells in the main jail," someone told us. "There must be over a thousand arrests." We felt great about the numbers, but it wasn't yet noon. A thousand arrests, and it would be over by lunchtime.

I thought about Cindy wanting to go up the road to blockade. "It would have been more powerful if we kept them out for the whole day," I said.

"That wasn't the point," said a man from our cluster named Antonio. He was in his forties, with sharp eyes and a precise, impassioned voice. "We reached their hearts. They may get into the Lab, but I don't believe they'll get any work done today. They'll be too busy talking about the blockade."

The shriek of a diesel horn almost drowned out his last words. Highway 580 was only twenty feet beyond a double fence at the edge of the yard. One protester was out by the fence pumping his arm at the trucks rolling by, and every few minutes a driver would blast his support.

I sat down on a bale of hay. I was finally winding down, and for the first time, the expanse of dead time hit me. An entire day with no guitar, no books, no baseball game on the radio, no beer or candy bars. I thought about what I'd eat when I got out. A burrito. No, a hamburger. And a big bowl of popcorn.

Some guys were talking to a guard behind me. "You wouldn't want to be in the general population," the guard was saying. "Those guys would hate you."

"Aw," someone argued back, "We passed a truckload of inmates going out on work detail and they were all cheering us. Well, except one guy who flipped us off."

"No, you'd see," the guard insisted. "The Blacks and Whites and Latinos, they all hate each other. It's a jungle. You're lucky to be out here."

Around eleven a.m., Change of Heart gathered for a cluster meeting. We reviewed the legal situation, which was simple. We were charged with a misdemeanor, obstructing a roadway. People who non-cooperated had an additional charge, but no one seemed to think it would stick.

Then we did a go-round to see who from our cluster needed to cite out. "They're expecting me on a job tomorrow," said Tony, the plumber from Spectrum. "But I could call the union hall and get someone to cover it. I'm good for at least one more day."

As my turn approached, I wished I'd told my boss that I might get arrested. She was pretty conservative, though. Probably best not to bring it up if I didn't have to. "I could take one more day off my repair job without having to explain where I am," I said. "After that, I might need to cite out."

Moonstone, who had been leaning back on a cot, sat up slowly. His tie-dyed shirt stood out against the muted canvas cot. Moonstone looked to be in his early thirties, with a long ponytail and a scraggly beard. "Time-wise, I could stay. But unless they serve vegetarian food, I may need to get out after a couple of days."

"Maybe we should make it a demand," someone suggested.

"No, we shouldn't ask for special treatment," answered Doc, an intense man with flowing hair and a long, graying beard. He was in Enola Gay, a self-described "faggot" affinity group. "We shouldn't ask for anything different from what the regular inmates are getting," Doc said. "But you could trade meat for bread or cheese."

Moonstone's AG, Deadheads for Peace, included a few CD veterans. They suggested that our cluster consense on some basic solidarity points to be considered at the first jail spokescouncil. "At Diablo last Summer," one guy said, "everyone agreed on 'no fines, no probation, and equal treatment.' No fines because it's economic discrimination. No probation because it keeps us from getting busted again. And equal treatment for everyone, including non-cooperators."

There was a bit of discussion, but we consensed to the solidarity proposals pretty quickly, and chose a couple of guys to be spokes at the meeting.

A little later, lunch was served — balogna and American cheese on white bread, plus an apple and Kool-Aid. I bartered for a triple-balogna sandwich, trading my apple to Moonstone for his cheese and balogna, then swapping both cheeses to another vegetarian for his balogna and Kool-Aid.

"Can we have your cup?" someone asked. "We're making a peace sign." A few guys were collecting all the styrofoam cups and wedging them in the chain-link fence to create a giant peace sign facing the highway. "If we get enough we can spell out a message."

After lunch, four of us from the cluster sat down together on a couple of cots: me, Hank, Antonio, and a guy named Daniel. Daniel looked and spoke like a college professor. "As impressive as this blockade is, it could be the seed of something greater still," he said. "What if each of us were to bring in five new people next June?"

Next June. It was in the air already, almost taken for granted. "Yeah, we should blockade again," said Hank. He was leaning forward, lacing up his hiking boots. "We oughta do it earlier in the Spring, though. Doing it on the Solstice is too new-age for a lot of people."

Antonio sat up on his cot. "No, no, we have to stay with the Solstice," he said. "It's a truly global day, beyond any one movement or nationality. It's in tune with the natural rhythms of the planet."

Hank started to reply, but Daniel preempted him. "We should call on other people to join us next June — locally and across the country — to band together on the Solstice to protest nuclear weapons. It's an idea whose time has come."

"Why focus just on nukes?" I said. "It would reach more people if it covered more issues, like the environment or unemployment."

"Nuclear weapons are the fundamental issue of our era," he said.

"I absolutely agree," Antonio chimed in. He ran a hand through his silver hair. "Other issues divide us. Nuclear weapons are the one issue that touches everyone. We're all at risk. People who would otherwise never be in the same room can make common cause in opposing nuclear weapons. We have to set aside our differences and join together. If we can't stop the nuclear madness, no other issue will mean anything."

Hank tried to say something, but just then a cry went up from the yard. "Out to the fence! The guards are trying to tear down the peace sign!"

We jumped up and hurried out into the yard. Several hundred guys were packed against the tall chain-link fence, squared off opposite a dozen guards. Everyone was arguing about what to do, but we finally managed to choose two guys as spokes. They went over and conferred with the guards while the rest of us determined to go limp and non-cooperate if the guards tried to clear us away.

The spokes came back. "The guards say they have orders to remove the peace sign. They don't want to force us to move, but they have to obey their orders."

I was amazed that the guards would admit their reluctance. It was like confessing they were human. People started arguing again as the guards eyed us nervously.

"Let's not polarize the situation," someone said. "It's not their choice. This order came from higher up. There's no point in turning this into a confrontation."

"Let's just sit down in front of the sign," another guy suggested. "What can they do?"

Hank laughed rudely. "Step on us!"

Ideas were flying every which way, and the guards were getting itchy. It looked like we would never reach consensus, but Doc raised his voice to get people's attention. "Maybe *we* should take the sign down. That way we defuse the conflict, but keep the power of action ourselves. We don't turn it over to them."

Not everyone agreed, but no one had a better idea. The guards seemed mollified, and backed off. Slowly, one cup at a time, the peace sign was removed. As the last cups were taken down and turned over to the guards for proper disposal, someone started an "om," and it caught on. Several hundred men linked arms and formed concentric circles. The "ommmmm" filled the air, swelling and fading, swelling and fading. Here and there men let their arms float upward, reaching for the sky. As the tones finally faded, some people knelt and spread their palms on the ground. "Returning the energy to the Earth," one man explained.

I nodded to myself. That was an interesting way of seeing it.

Eventually people drifted away, but a few men stayed behind and built a small monument of stones at what had been the center of our circle.

A legal spokescouncil convened in mid-afternoon. I wanted to be right in the center of the action, and was hoping to be one of the spokes for Change of

Heart Cluster. But I didn't want to nominate myself, and two other guys were chosen. I wandered outside to watch. There wasn't much definite to discuss at the meeting, although we had heard some rumors from guards and late arrivals. One account had us getting a week in jail or a $500 fine. Another had our charges being dropped to an infraction — a jaywalking ticket — and all of us released with sentences of "time served."

"Rumor control, rumor control," called out Claude, a tall guy with graying hair and a long, sharp nose. Hank had pointed him out as one of the artists who had painted the great La Peña and People's Park murals in Berkeley, so I was especially inclined to trust his opinion. "This is all speculation. Let's stick to what we're sure of," Claude said.

The main order of business was determining what sentences we would consider acceptable. As the forty or so cluster spokes weighed in, I looked up at the stark sun. Compared to coastal Berkeley, the parched Livermore valley, with little shade and no cold water, felt like a desert.

As the meeting stretched on, I heard someone behind me mutter, "junior lawyers." I turned to see an older guy I'd met at lunch. He had been part of "peace navy" actions during the 1950s, sailing into restricted areas in the Pacific to delay atomic tests.

His remark about junior lawyers stung me, since I had wanted to be a cluster spoke. "What's the option?" I asked him. "We have to make decisions somehow."

"No, we don't," he tossed back. "Why not just sit in jail until the government throws us out? This legal dickering is just playing their game, playing by their rules. No matter whether we plead innocent or guilty, they win. We acknowledge their right to arrest and prosecute us. But suppose we said, 'You don't have that right, and we're not going to cooperate with you in any way. We're going to sit in jail until you get sick of us and throw us out.' What could they do? They'd eventually be forced to let us go, and that would be like admitting they were wrong to arrest us in the first place."

"They can force us to go to arraignment," I answered uncertainly.

"You think so?" he laughed. "If we refuse to cooperate every step of the way, do you think they can come in and force a thousand people to go to court? We've got them over a barrel. All this legal nonsense is just weakening us."

"Why don't you say that to the spokescouncil?"

"They don't want to hear it. They're too wrapped up in their own importance."

He turned away. It was a lot to take in. With a little less ardor, I refocused on the meeting, which was trying to discuss specific demands to make to the judge. A lot of spokes thought we should plea-bargain to get the charges dropped from misdemeanors to infractions, with a sentence of time-served. "We'd probably get out in less than a week," someone said.

But there was a sizable group of people who were demanding a mass arraignment, all thousand of us at once, prior to any plea-bargain. The most vehement proponent of this tactic was a man with a weathered face and white hair named Pilgrim. I heard he had been arrested over thirty times, and he certainly had the attention of the meeting. "Holding out for a mass arraignment might cost us an extra day or two in jail," Pilgrim said. "But it would get as much media coverage as the action did. If they refuse a mass arraignment, we'll all plead not-guilty and demand a thousand separate trials."

The proposal caused a buzz, but most people favored a plea bargain if it would get us out sooner. Someone pointed out that we didn't all have to do the same thing, but the overall sentiment favored unified action. "We have to stick together," Doc said. "Their whole strategy is to divide us."

The meeting continued until dinner, which was a warm plate of pasty spaghetti. I saw Doc talking with Claude, and went over to join them. I worked across the street from one of Claude's murals on Telegraph Avenue, and I couldn't help putting him on a pedestal, "the great Berkeley political artist."

Claude and Doc each looked to be twelve or fifteen years older than me, and I imagined them to be veterans of the Civil Rights and Vietnam eras. Both had worked on LAG all Spring, and they were talking about what would happen after the blockade. "Do you think LAG will organize more actions?" I asked, hoping it was the right question.

"That's assumed," Claude said in a nasal voice. "I didn't spend the last six months of my life working on a one-shot coalition."

I nodded, trying to catch his eye. "A lot of people will want LAG to keep going."

Doc furrowed his brows. "The question is, what will it be? Will LAG be an affinity group network, or will it turn into one more 'progressive' organization with an office and a permanent staff?"

"It has to go beyond affinity groups," Claude answered. "It's time to think in terms of building a movement, not just doing actions. LAG is the first step, a group that lasts beyond one action."

I was going to second that point, but a commotion at one side of the yard interrupted the discussion. A hundred men were already clustered around, and more were hurrying over.

"It's the lawyers! They let the lawyers in!" We finished our scant meal and headed over to where two members of LAG's volunteer legal collective were being mobbed. Walt, a recent law school graduate who was in one of the Change of Heart AGs, stepped up onto a bale of hay. "We really don't have anything solid to report. We just wanted to check-in with people."

Someone called out, "We heard that the two local judges have disqualified themselves and that there would be a new judge appointed."

"We heard that rumor too!" Walt laughed. "But that's all it is."

"Has there been an offer to negotiate?"

"Nothing definite yet," Walt said.

"What was the total number arrested?"

Kathleen, a short woman with wavy brown hair and a sharp jaw, waved some papers. "We show a little over thirteen hundred —" A cheer punctuated her remarks. "— And I've heard there might be fifty more tomorrow. There's a meeting tonight for people who want to get arrested."

There were more cheers from the hundreds of guys clustered around the lawyers. I wondered what the largest-ever anti-nuke protest was. I'd heard people talking about Seabrook on the east coast, and Diablo Canyon in southern California, but I didn't know much about them. Maybe we'd broken the all-time record.

I surveyed the five hundred men crowded around the lawyers, and suddenly felt the need for some privacy. Some room to think. I drifted away from the gathering, laid down on my cot, and mulled over the situation. How long would we be here? Could I really cite out? It would be hard to leave before the action was over. Maybe I should call in sick for the extra days. Or just tell my boss where I was and hope she'd be cool.

I looked around the warehouse. I had expected the average age of the blockaders to be mid-20s, but it seemed more like mid-thirties. Hair styles ran the gamut from blow-dried professionals to home-cut dropouts. Regardless of age and appearance, a pervasive politeness and tidiness made me think of my own middle-class upbringing.

Most of the men were White, with a smattering of Asian Americans and Latinos. I'd noticed two Black men earlier, both middle-aged. I wondered how they felt about being in such a minority. Had they expected it all along?

I thought about the "real" county jail, where most of the inmates were Black. In the February action, the one hundred seventy arrestees were mixed in with the general population. What a different experience that must have been.

A loud voice cut short my daydreaming: "You too can be sssssssssssucked up in the Tornado of Talent!" Earlier in the day, Wavy Gravy, a longtime activist who was a Merry Prankster in the 1960s and an emcee at Woodstock, had posted a sign-up sheet for an evening talent show. I had taken a slot, figuring to share a song, but I hadn't given it much thought through the day.

Now, as Wavy assembled us for the show, I hurriedly hummed a few scales, trying to get loose. The names were drawn out of a hat, and I wound up with slot number one, which seemed like a tough assignment. Luckily, Wavy warmed up the crowd. We packed onto the cots in the center of the warehouse. Knowing that we had all chosen to be there together, it felt like a big state-sponsored Summer camp. Wavy was the jovial head counselor, and the guards, who were standing off to the sides, seemed like the maintenance staff relaxing at the end of a long day.

Wavy told a few jokes, then launched into a story from the Sixties, when he was in Washington, DC, for a Vietnam protest. "I went inside a government building and found an empty room," he told us. "I took off all my clothes and hid behind the door." Wavy pantomimed the scene. "Then one of my friends called in a bomb scare. They emptied the building, and the cops went room to room searching for the bomb. When they came to my room, I jumped out and screamed — scared the daylights out of them!"

I was on. I planned to sing one of my own songs, "After the Nuclear War." But as I stepped onstage and faced five hundred expectant faces, a different inspiration seized me. I grabbed a breath and launched into Elvis's "Jailhouse Rock." With no guitar, no harmonica, and no microphone, I had no idea what to do with my hands. I nervously snapped my fingers. Instantly dozens of people picked it up, and the raucous cheering as I finished told me I'd hit the mark.

Skits, poetry, mime, comedy, songs, magic, and dance filled the next two hours. "And this is only the first night," Wavy said late in the show. "Wait till we get warmed up!" We ended the evening in a huge circle around the perimeter of the warehouse, holding hands and singing the old Civil Rights-era standard, "We Shall Overcome."

Finally we reached the end of the longest day of my life. The blockade that morning was distant, and the previous night — before I'd been arrested — seemed like a prior lifetime.

We talked in lower voices as we settled in for the night. No one wanted to let go, but finally the guards insisted that we be quiet. They turned off a few of the overhead lights, but it was still pretty bright. I tried to get comfortable. The canvas cot was barely as wide as my shoulders. The building wasn't insulated, and the chill night air seeped through my army blanket. I pulled the blanket tighter, then decided to use the portajohn one more time. I got my shoes on and trekked to the far end of the warehouse.

A dozen other guys had the same idea, and were lined up at the door. "They're only letting us go one at a time," someone told me.

"Why? There's eight portajohns."

"Right. But they don't want us to forget who's in charge."

Tuesday, June 22, 1982

It seemed like I was awake all night, vibrating with the rhythms of the action. But somewhere I dozed off, and Hank had to rouse me the next morning. "Come on, there's something happening out at the fence!"

I staggered up, pulled on my jeans and followed him out into the gray dawn, where we joined a crowd of men along the fence facing the highway. Out in the median strip a van had pulled over and a half-dozen Asian men with shaved heads and white robes were chanting solemnly to a simple drumbeat.

"It's a group of Buddhist peace monks from Japan," someone said.

"Japanese monks?" exclaimed Tony. He pushed his way up to the fence. "I was on a peace march last year with some monks from Japan." He squinted through the fence at them, then started waving and yelling. "It's him, it's Matsahiro!" Tony jumped up and down, waving and hollering.

At first the monks stoically continued their drumming. But then one of them took a few steps toward us. He peered across the highway, then started waving back. He ran over to his comrades and pointed at us excitedly.

People tried to pick up the chant. Most of us never quite got the words, but our toning voices filled the air as the State Police arrived and chased the serenaders away.

Soon after, the guards dispensed a breakfast of gummy oatmeal and white bread. While we were eating, a guy came around announcing the resumption of the spokescouncil. "Every cluster should send a spoke empowered to decide on our basic legal demands."

It made sense to me, but several people gave the guy a hard time. "Who are you, calling the meeting?"

"I was a spoke yesterday," the guy answered. "Don't get paranoid."

Sometime mid-morning, the guys who had been put in holding cells the night before were brought over to join us. Enough men were citing out to make room for them, but we still filled the warehouse. If as many women were staying, we still numbered a thousand.

We traded stories with the newcomers. Toward the end of the previous day's blockade, a Pagan AG, The Web, had spun a ritual web of yarn and string across the road where the Oakland motorcycle cops were harassing people. The cops thought that a web of yarn was no big deal, and one tried to ride through it. The web held, and the cop fell off his bike. Although a number of people got knocked around as the cops retaliated, it sounded like everyone was inspired by the action. "I think there's a metaphor somewhere in that yarn," said Antonio.

The guards brought in a few *Chronicles* and *Tribunes* so we could read about ourselves. We got banner headlines in both papers, with plenty of pictures. We were celebrities! It was the first time I'd ever been involved in a front-page story. The papers circulated around the warehouse, read aloud over and over.

Along with the papers, the guards brought two rumors: they told us eighty more blockaders had been arrested that morning, and the two local judges had in fact disqualified themselves from the case. The former information was soon verified by the arrival of about forty more men to new rounds of cheers. But no one could corroborate the story about the judges.

Several workshops got underway in the afternoon. The one that appealed to me was veterans of earlier movements sharing their experiences in a big circle out in the yard. I leaned back against a bale of hay as Nathaniel, my nonviolence prepper, told a story about a Civil Rights sit-in.

"In the Spring of 1960," he said, "I was working in Washington, DC, with a group of students from Howard University, a Negro College, as it was called then. By 1960, the lunch counters and cafeterias in Washington had been integrated, but those in Maryland and Virginia, just across the border, had not. Even diplomats to the United Nations, if they were Black, couldn't sit at the counters and be served.

"There had been some sit-ins in Maryland that Spring. We'd go down there for the weekend, get arrested, sit in jail singing freedom songs and sharing stories, and then on Sunday night they'd let us out and we'd go back to school for the week.

"But in Virginia, they passed a law saying that anyone arrested at a sit-in would get a $1000 fine and a year in prison. Also, the American Nazi party was active in Virginia, and had threatened to lynch people who came there. They seemed serious, so at first, no one tried.

"But some of us talked it over, and felt we had to stand up to them. We decided to do a sit-in after school ended that year. We did intensive nonviolence trainings, and asked anyone who didn't think they could maintain nonviolence not to take part. We actually punched people in the stomach during the preps, to test our responses. Finally, eleven Black students from Howard University and I decided to do it.

"In early June, we went across to Arlington, Virginia, to a place called, ironically, People's Drug Store. We went inside and sat down at a Whites-only counter. Within five minutes, the police arrived with paddywagons. But the owner said he didn't want arrests — it would be bad publicity — so he closed the counter.

"We decided to stay and wait. We wound up being there for two days, which were the two most challenging days in my life. Word got out fast, and people came from all around, Nazis and others. They harassed us, shoved and punched us, sometimes so hard you'd fall off the stool. Then they'd start kicking you. The worst part was when people put lit cigarettes down our backs. The police had left, of course. They had no interest in preventing the violence.

"The whole time we tried to respond as nonviolently as we could, looking people in the eyes, trying to treat them as human beings.

"For me, the peak came toward the end of the second day. A White guy came up behind me and called me a 'nigger lover.' I turned around and saw the most terrible look of hatred I have ever seen. He was holding a switchblade about an inch from me. And he said, 'If you don't get out of this store in two seconds, I'm going to stab this knife through your heart.'

"Luckily, I had a lot of experience by that time. So I looked him in the eye and said, 'Friend, do what you believe is right, but I'm still going to try to love you.'

"This guy was just shaking with hatred. When I spoke, his jaw dropped, and his hand shook even more. He didn't say a word. He just turned on his heels and walked straight out of the store."

I released my breath, wondering if I could have thought so fast. And what if one of the Black students had said the same thing?

"Later that evening," Nathaniel continued, "we finally decided to leave. We were dead tired, after two days of this. We prepared a written statement, saying, 'We appeal to local religious and community leaders to get these eating establishments open and integrated. If nothing has happened in a week, we will be back.'

"There was a crowd of about five hundred people outside, yelling and throwing things at us. But there were also some friendly media people, and they helped cover us as we left. Otherwise, I don't know whether we would have gotten out of there alive.

"We went back to Washington, DC, and tried to resume our lives. Five days passed, and we wondered whether we had the courage to return. On the last day, we got a phone call from Arlington. People's Drug Store had decided to open its counters to everyone. The religious and community leaders had used their authority to bring it about. After hundreds of years of segregation, twelve students had touched their hearts."

The group of listeners was sitting in spellbound silence. Nathaniel paused and collected his thoughts, then concluded his story.

"As I reflected on my experience, especially on the man with the knife, I realized that what I did was the most effective thing I could have done to protect myself. If I had tried to fight back, I probably would have gotten stabbed. Even if I'd won the fight, his hatred would have grown stronger. But by reacting in this way, it made him realize he couldn't go through with it. He had to change.

"I've been involved in civil disobedience actions for over two decades now, but I have never seen such a striking example of the power of nonviolence. There's a crucial lesson here — if we treat our opponents as humans, there is a good chance that they will respond that way. It also shows the strength of a small, committed group of people — an affinity group, you could say. Together we were able to maintain our nonviolence and be there for each other with emotional and physical support.

"We weren't alone. Thousands of people went through similar experiences in those years, and helped bring about the transformation of society. I've seen it happen."

LATER ON, Daniel Ellsberg gave a talk about the arms race to a large gathering of men in one corner of the warehouse. Ellsberg was a former government employee whose revelation of the secret "Pentagon Papers" in 1971 had blown the lid off the lies and cover-ups surrounding U.S. policy in Vietnam, and helped turn the tide against the war. Since that time he had been a key spokesperson against U.S. nuclear and military policy, taking part in civil disobedience actions on both coasts.

By the end of his talk, I was losing steam, and retreated to my cot to lie down. Two guys near me were playing chess with little pieces of paper. Antonio and Doc were rounding up Pagans to plan a new moon ritual, and some other guys in our cluster knotted a few T-shirts and headed out to the yard to play football. I lay on my back, exhausted but too wired to sleep. I wished I had something to read. I flipped through the New Testament they'd given us, but it didn't hold my attention. Too sketchy. I wished I had a Russian novel. Something by Tolstoy or Dostoyevsky to pass the hours. Or the days.

How long would we be in? People at the February action had gotten a week. Since the state had gone to the trouble of setting up the warehouse, they might just let us sit here for a while. By tomorrow, I was going to have to cite out or call my boss and tell her where I was. Not something I looked forward to.

Moonstone and some other guys were talking and laughing on a cot near me. I rolled over the other way. I thought about how long I'd craved my own apartment, which I finally got a few months earlier — and here I was spending my vacation in a five-hundred-man dormitory.

Try as I might, there was no way to tune it out. One guy talked about being arrested at the 1977 occupation of Seabrook nuclear plant on the east coast and enjoying the action more than the Livermore blockade. Moonstone, who was pacing around wearing his bedsheet as a toga, said he liked the 1981 Diablo action more, too. "There's something about a backcountry occupation that a street blockade just can't match."

Someone else said they had heard that our thirteen hundred arrests were the biggest one-day total ever for a California anti-nuke protest.

"Yeah," answered a younger guy. "But we didn't really disrupt anything. It was all so orchestrated. Put this kind of energy in downtown San Francisco and we could shut down the whole business district."

There was an idea, I thought. Shutting down the financial district. How about the stock exchange? If we disrupted trading, it could be statistically verified. We could make headlines in the business section.

A little later, word filtered around that the legal spokescouncil was reconvening. Sleep seemed hopeless, so I decided to go watch the meeting. As I headed outside, I heard Wavy Gravy decline an invitation. "I've been going to jail for fifteen years, and I haven't been to a meeting yet." He lay back down on his cot.

The spokes circled up. Many clusters had rotated their spokes, and it took an hour just to do check-ins and catch everyone up on the previous day's discussions. The main issue was still whether to bargain for lower charges and agree to plead no contest, or to accept the misdemeanor charges and demand a trial.

"We could use the courts to put Livermore Lab on trial," someone argued. "We could present evidence on why we blockaded, and use it to indict the Lab and the government."

Claude was standing with his arms folded across his chest. "That kind of testimony would probably be suppressed by the courts," he said. "They don't typically allow political defenses."

The spokescouncil discussed the trial question for a while, but there was no consensus on what to do. Luckily a couple of our lawyers arrived. They had some definite information: local judges Lewis and Hyde had voluntarily disqualified themselves, and Judge William Chotiner had been appointed to hear our cases.

"Chotiner's the judge from Diablo Canyon last Summer," Moonstone said, bouncing excitedly on his toes. "He's the guy who gave us four-day sentences."

Shouts and joking rang through the space, even though some people reminded us that we might be in jail for several more days.

"Lewis and Hyde had to step down, they couldn't take the heat," Hank said to Doc and me. "The county can't afford to keep us here, but the local judges can't afford to let us out or it would ruin their political careers. So they had to step aside."

Doc squinted. "Lucky for us they disqualified themselves," he said. "We could have challenged them, but that takes time. They could have kept us sitting here for a week or more."

The legal spokes reached consensus that we would all stay in solidarity until it was certain that everyone was getting equal sentences. The lawyers said they would convey our decision to the women's jail.

Dinner came and went, along with a great rumor that we were getting out that night with sentences of time served. The spokescouncil reconvened, but I stayed behind this time. The lawyers had brought in some books, and I was reading a copy of Kurt Vonnegut's *Slaughterhouse Five* that had been torn apart and was being passed around serially.

Around sunset the lawyers unexpectedly returned. From around the warehouse people converged, and the air was electric. Walt was urged up onto a chair to fill us in. "Your charges have all been dropped to infractions," he announced, "and all resisting arrest charges for non-cooperators have been dropped." Shouts and applause burst out, then subsided just as quickly so Walt could continue. "Judge Chotiner has indicated that he will give a sentence of time served to anyone who pleads no contest, and the arraignments can begin this evening if you accept the offer."

I could hardly believe what I was hearing. And it was icing on the cake when Walt added, "The judge has agreed to arraign you by affinity groups, in the order you were arrested."

I spontaneously hugged the guy next to me, a huge smile on my face. The warehouse echoed with cheers. Everyone was talking at once. There was no question that most people were ready to accept the offer. A few people called for process, saying that spokes should check-in with their clusters and then reconvene to see if we consensed to the offer. But the warehouse was in chaos, with people laughing and yelling and hugging as if they were about to part forever.

The spokescouncil had barely gathered before a deputy with a bullhorn began reading the names of the first twenty men to leave for arraignment. The guys looked around for guidance. Some people still argued that we should coordinate with the women's spokescouncil and formally consense before anyone left for arraignment. Others argued that immediate arraignment was a major victory, and we should go for it. Clearly most people wanted to get the legal proceedings underway. With a final round of hugs, the first group of men left for court. The spokescouncil heard a few complaints about process and how we hadn't ever reached consensus, but gradually the debate wound down.

Blockaders in night-court for the June 1982 Livermore blockade signaled agreement ("consensus") with someone's courtroom statement by twinkling their fingers in the air.

Wavy got another talent show going, which most people gathered around for. My AG, though, stayed on our cots talking. We heard from the guards that about one hundred fifty men would be arraigned that night, and we had easily been among the first one hundred fifty brought to the warehouse the day before.

We talked in low, hurried tones about the action, mostly in the past tense, looking ahead to the next time. Everyone was pretty sure they'd get busted again, especially if there were a blockade next June at Livermore. I had no doubt, and even hoped there'd be another action before then. If all we were getting was two days, I could do it more than once a year. I wasn't feeling tired anymore.

It must have been about midnight when our names were called and we boarded a bus that drove us across the jail grounds to a makeshift courtroom. Fifty or so supporters and press people who had gotten jail passes greeted us with applause as we were led in and reunited with the women from our AG. We sat with our arms around each other as the judge read the charges. Then he called our names one by one, took our no-contest pleas, and asked if we had a statement to make before sentencing.

A few people gave short speeches on why they had blockaded — for their children, for the planet, for the future. The rest of us waved our hands in the air to signal support. But most of us skipped statements to speed things up for the people after us.

"Jeffrey Harrison," Judge Chotiner said as I stood before him, "If you have no statement, I sentence you in the name of the People of California to two days in the county jail. That time has already been served, and you are free to go."

I stepped away, hardly believing it was over. I thought back over my time in jail, the blockade, the Sunday meeting in the park, the nonviolence prep — what a long four days! I'd been swept into an alternate reality where every minute was packed with meaning, where every day was half a lifetime. My innocent bystander days were over. I barely remembered what it was like not to be involved.

We were led back out to the buses, men and women together. Everyone seemed to have extra bounce in their step. Even the guard driving the bus got caught up in the spirit, telling us "off the record" that he and some of his colleagues supported our action.

"Why did you jail us then?"

He laughed. "That's what you wanted, wasn't it? We didn't want to disappoint you."

"Join us next year! We'll be back — join us!"

"No comment," he said. "No comment."

The bus dropped us off at the edge of the jail grounds at about two a.m. The driver pointed up the road. "I think some of your people are over there." We started off hesitantly, then we heard shouts and calls. At least a hundred people were waiting for us. They welcomed us to freedom with hugs, extra jackets, and four types of trail mix.

We waited a couple more hours for later people, trading stories with the women from our cluster. Karina entertained me and Hank with a long story about some women who burned one of the New Testaments and were dragged away by the guards, setting off a big commotion. I didn't get the story quite straight, but I figured I'd hear it again at our AG meeting a week later.

I was hoping Duck and Cover would get arraigned so I could see Holly, but they were too far down the arrest list to get out that night. Finally, the last bus of the night unloaded, and we all headed home.

Karina offered me a ride back with a woman named Sara, whom I took to be her lover. Sara was in her mid-twenties, with dark, serious eyes. She was involved with Central America support, and made sure I got a handful of flyers when she dropped me off at my apartment.

It was past five a.m. when I finally made it to bed. I had scarcely slept for two entire days, but even after drinking a beer I lay awake for a long time reverberating from the impact of the past 48 hours. I scribbled frantically in my journal, trying to capture every detail.

When I awoke that afternoon, I lay in bed for a while replaying my mental tapes of the blockade. A hundred scenes reeled past, and dozens of faces swirled through my mind. But one person in particular kept popping up: Holly. I couldn't wait to see her. I had no idea whether she was single or not, and I didn't even know how to get hold of her except that she volunteered at the LAG office. It seemed like a good time to do some volunteering myself.

Friday, July 16, 1982

THE FIRST FEW times I stopped by the office, Holly wasn't around, so I looked at the literature rack a while and then split. Finally one time she was there, working on a mailing about the LAG Congress that was being called for the first weekend of August. I offered to help, and afterward caught her alone for a minute and asked if we could get together later in the week.

She thought for a moment, a slight smile on her lips. Then she looked at me and said, "I've been wanting to go for more walks. How about Thursday afternoon?"

On our first couple of dates, we went for walks around South Berkeley and the UC campus. Conversation flowed freely, everything from theories of social organization to the nuts and bolts of the latest LAG mailing. Back in my day-to-day life, the blockade sometimes seemed like a dreamworld. But when I talked with Holly, it seemed as if it were only yesterday, and I was filled again with the passion, the power, and the hope.

The third time we got together, I met Holly at a house in South Berkeley where she was doing some gardening. We were going to a show at the Freight and Salvage coffeehouse that evening, but it was only about five o'clock. "Want to walk to my house?" she asked. She pulled on a gray sweater and zipped up her daypack.

We wended our way down to Grant, a quiet street that ran most of the length of town. An anarchistic array of flowers, shrubs, and little lawns crowded up against the sidewalk, enlivening the small wood and stucco houses. Kids were playing up and down the street, and music filtered out of an occasional window.

We hadn't talked much about the past, and I was surprised to learn how recently Holly had moved to Berkeley. Until the previous December, she had been working as office manager for an alternative energy company down in Monterey, and living with a guy named Frank. Their relationship mostly ended in late 1981. "I say 'mostly' because I'm still really close to Frank," she told me.

I felt a twinge of jealousy and steered away from the subject. "So you moved to Berkeley?"

"Yeah," she said. "I got laid off and was getting unemployment, so I had a lot of free time. I always wanted to live in Berkeley. It seemed like a place where so much was happening."

I nodded. "Did you know about LAG then?"

"Not initially. I went to a forum sponsored by a group called Urban Ecology, and I decided to join them. In fact, I wound up moving into the house where Urban Ecology has its office. Then some of us went out to Livermore to support the Mothers' Day action. Seeing the arrests was powerful, but what especially struck me was how the women doing the action were so intimate and caring toward each other." She slowed almost to a halt and looked at me. "That really touched me. I was searching for community. Being new in Berkeley, I felt like I was meeting people superficially, even in my house. I was looking for a deeper connection."

I could help with that, I wanted to say. But it didn't seem like the moment for a joke, even a serious one. "I know what you mean," I said, looking at her.

As I spoke, we reached University Avenue, the dividing line between south and North Berkeley. Four lanes of traffic interrupted our reverie. "A rude reminder of the state of civilization," I commented. "This city is getting overrun with cars."

"It sure is," she said. "Urban Ecology wants to get most cars out of Berkeley. We have a plan to route all traffic onto a few major streets. The rest would be plowed up and made into playgrounds or parks or community gardens."

"I like it," I said. "I had this idea for getting rid of cars entirely. Everyone who had to drive would park in underground garages at the edge of the city. Then, to get into town, there'd be these giant roller coasters running into the different neighborhoods. It'd be energy efficient, since gravity would do the work. And it would be really fast!"

She laughed and put her arm around my waist. I put my arm around her shoulders and breathed deeply. Along the sidewalk, flowers swayed in the evening breeze, drinking in the last sunlight.

We turned off of Grant onto Cedar and headed up a slight hill, approaching a two-story wood house set back about fifteen feet from the sidewalk. Behind a little picket fence was a yard full of wildflowers and an apple tree. "This is it, the Urban Ecology house," she said.

"I recognize this house," I said. "Didn't it used to have an old convertible parked out front that was filled with dirt and had a garden growing in it?"

"Yeah, the Veggie Car. We had to move it. It's in a park down in West Berkeley now." She unlocked the front door and ushered me into the living room. "I need to call Claudia at the LAG office."

"It's after six. Do you think she'll pick up?"

"I'll call on the night line. I'll be back in a minute."

She walked toward the back of the house. The night line. I hadn't heard of that before. Was it a secret phone number for the initiates, or could anyone ask for it?

I stepped into the living room, which had high ceilings and lots of wood trim. The room was furnished with old couches and chairs draped with patterned cloths. More fabric hung on the walls. The aroma of baking bread wafted out from the kitchen, but it was overpowered by the scent of fish emulsion plant food, which had the house smelling like Ocean Beach at low tide. I looked around at the dozens of potted plants filling the living and dining rooms. "Why don't you use instant fertilizer?" I innocently asked Holly's housemate Randall.

"Are you kidding?" he asked, pulling his head back for effect. "You're feeding right into the petrochemical industry when you use commercial fertilizer. Fish emulsion is a sustainable resource and requires practically no processing."

I nodded noncommittally, wondering how you emulsed a fish. "Too bad the room doesn't get more light. The plants would do better."

"Funny you should say that," he said enthusiastically. "We're getting ready to knock out the whole front wall and build a greenhouse. It's a perfect southern exposure." He beckoned me out onto the front porch. "The apple tree will give it enough shade so the plants won't scorch."

I tried to visualize how a greenhouse would attach to the front of the narrow two-story house with its tiny yard. "It'll be two stories, all glass," he explained, "shaped like the front three sides of an octagon. It'll be a model for indoor gardening."

Holly came to the door. "Do you want to eat while we're here?" We followed her back into the kitchen. "There's miso soup heating up, and we have some tabouli..."

I tried to decline, having no idea what I was being offered. "I'll just have some tea," I said.

But Randall wouldn't hear of it. "No, no, try the miso soup, it tastes just like tamari, only more intense — you'll love it." He set a big bowlful in front of me. Holly helped out by offering me some crackers and cheese.

I wished we'd have some time to hang out, maybe up in her room. Our strolling conversations were great, a chance not only to relive the blockade, but to envision the next steps and brainstorm how to make them real.

Until the past month, sweeping social change had seemed like a remote fantasy. Talking with Holly, though, the radical reworking of our entire culture along the lines of peace and social justice was transformed into a challenging organizing problem to be solved by thorough discussion, careful planning, and direct action. I was grateful for our talks wherever they took place, but the idea of making love and then lying in bed plotting nonviolent revolution seemed wonderful.

When we finished dinner, though, Holly told me that she had to deliver a phone list to the LAG office before we went to the show. "They need it for phone-banking about the LAG Congress. I should warn you, Belinda and Monique are there — we're probably walking into the middle of a fight over the Bible-burning."

The Bible incident was still being debated, especially since the Feminist Cluster announced that they weren't sending spokes to the LAG Congress. I had never formed a clear picture of the incident, and I asked Holly about it as we took a bus across town. I opened a sliding window, then turned in my seat to face her. Her eyes met mine, then drifted away.

"We were held in a big gymnasium. Two-thirds of the floor was filled with six hundred cots, and the other third was open space, for meetings, rituals, sharing circles, or whatever. Over in the back corner you had the Feminist Cluster. Their AGs had names like Revolting Hags and Sisters of Lesbos, and they were a lot more vocal than most of the women, chanting and yelling at the guards all the time. A lot of them already knew each other from the Women's movement. They stayed separate in jail, and there was definitely prejudice against them. They were seen by a lot of people as 'big, loud dykes' who were stirring up trouble."

"So they burned a Bible?"

"We were never totally clear on what happened. After lunch on the second day, most people were napping or talking in small groups, waiting for some word from the legal team. Suddenly there was a terrible scream. Two women from the Feminist Cluster came bursting back into the gym from the restroom, chased by several female guards. Before anyone could react, the guards grabbed the two women and dragged them out of the gym."

Holly's voice was rising, and she seemed to check herself. "I still get wrapped up in it, three weeks later! More guards squared off, guarding the door. Women from the Feminist Cluster ran up and demanded to know what was going on. Most of the other women gathered around. The guards said that the two women had started a fire in the restroom, endangering everyone in the gymnasium."

"Did you believe them?"

"I didn't know what to think," Holly said. "The Feminist Cluster challenged it, and kept demanding

Since the 1300 arrestees would overflow the county jail, women were held in a gymnasium and men in a warehouse on the jail grounds. This drawing was done in the gym.

the return of their sisters. But some other women wanted to know what had been set on fire, which the guards told us — one of the New Testaments that everyone had been given."

"That's the part I heard," I said.

Holly nodded as the bus lurched to a stop. We shifted in our seats. "A spokescouncil was called to discuss what to do," she resumed. "Their cluster wanted solidarity actions, but others didn't want to hold solidarity with people they felt had violated the nonviolence guidelines by destroying property.

"Finally the Feminist Cluster got fed up. Twenty women walked out of the spokescouncil, marched to the front of the gym, and started pounding on the doors and chanting. The doors were locked, and the guards didn't respond. So the women kept pounding and yelling. Belinda and a few others went to support them, but most people stayed at the meeting. Some of us were just confused over what to do, but a lot of people were offended by the Feminist Cluster."

"So what happened to the two women who got grabbed?"

Holly laughed slightly. "Nothing. Toward the end of the day, with no explanation, they were returned. That was the end of it."

I shook my head. "Just like the whole incident never happened," I said.

We'd reached our stop, just up the block from the LAG office. As Holly had predicted, tensions were simmering as we entered and made our way to the back. Claudia, whom I'd met before, nodded in our direction. Holly introduced me to Belinda, who barely looked up, and Monique, who said hi and asked how we were doing.

Holly joined them around the worktable. I felt a little extraneous, and busied myself straightening the flyers on the literature rack, where I could hear the talk without interloping.

Monique was about my age. Unlike practically anyone else in LAG, she wore makeup and styled her auburn hair. Monique was a member of the Walnettos affinity group, which had its base in Walnut Creek, an affluent suburb east of Berkeley. I'd met her once before, and although I liked her, a geographic and cultural gulf separated us.

With Belinda there wasn't a gulf. We were from totally different planets, and I gathered there wasn't much room for me on hers. She wore a bright red T-shirt that proclaimed, "I Like Big Women." Belinda was a big woman herself, with wire-rim glasses and crewcut blonde hair. Her face flushed with anger as she turned back to Monique. "Who can blame the Feminist Cluster for boycotting the Congress," she said. "They got no support at all in jail."

"There was some support," Holly said. She spoke slowly, as if reluctant to enter the argument. "The spokescouncil consensed that we wouldn't leave jail until the two women were returned."

Belinda shook her head sharply. "It wasn't enough. Solidarity failed. When your sisters are singled out like that, you do everything you can to get them back. The Feminist Cluster knew what solidarity meant. While everyone else sat around debating, they acted."

I nodded to myself. Abrasive as Belinda was, I liked what she said.

Monique looked distressed. "All their yelling just turned people off. And in the end the guards brought the two women back, anyway."

"Maybe that was because of what the Feminist Cluster did," Claudia put in. Claudia was a wiry woman with spikey brown hair. She was one of the two LAG staffers, with a sharp mind and sharper tongue. She eyed Monique. "The guards knew that if they didn't bring the women back, the Feminist Cluster would raise hell all night."

"I think that's probably true," Holly said, looking apologetically at Monique.

Monique turned to Holly with a pleading expression. "It split the group," she said. "They escalated the tactics, and then expected solidarity. That's coercive. We could have gotten the women back by less confrontational means, like refusing to go to arraignment until they were returned. The Feminist Cluster just alienated people."

"Well, the lack of solidarity alienated other people!" Belinda gesticulated. "Lesbians are subjected to this all the time. As soon as we stand out in a crowd, the authorities clamp down, and the straights stand by and say, 'Oh, they shouldn't have made such a scene.' Well, we're through being quiet. And if straights don't like it, who needs them? We'll go do our own work!"

Damn, I thought. What could anyone say to that? Monique seemed cowed by Belinda's tone, and didn't respond.

I caught Holly's eye, and nodded toward the clock. She looked torn between mediating the clash and trying to get as far away from it as possible. My hint about the time seemed to settle the matter. She gave the phone list to Claudia, and we said our goodbyes and took off.

We headed for the Freight and Salvage, which was down in West Berkeley. Originally Holly had suggested going to Ashkenaz to dance to a Cajun band. I didn't want to admit that I was incompetent on the dance floor, so I talked about how much I wanted to see the band that was playing at the Freight that night. To my relief, she went for it. Sure, sooner or later she'd figure out I couldn't dance — but not on our first musical outing.

Our route took us directly into the remnants of a patchy red sunset, and we walked along quietly. But my mind kept drifting back to the argument at the office. "That's intense," I said. "There was nothing like that in the men's camp. People argued, but nothing so divisive."

"Yeah," Holly said. "It definitely polarized people. When the guards brought the two women back that evening, Karina and I went over and welcomed them. But we were about the only ones from our cluster who did." Holly nodded to herself. "In a way, I felt intimidated by the Feminist Cluster. But not by their behavior — it was their experience and analysis. These women had spent years discussing feminism and solidarity. They were way ahead of most people, and that caused problems."

"Kind of ironic that it was the women who had the conflicts, and the men who ran smoothly."

Holly yawned. "It wasn't all conflicts. That was the only divisive incident. Most of my time in jail was amazing. It felt so easy to connect with people. My cot was right next to a Buddhist AG from the Zen Center in San Francisco. I meditated with them on the second and third days. And there was a Pagan ritual led by people in Matrix AG who call themselves Witches."

I had met a couple of male "Witches" in jail, and although they seemed like nice guys, I was skeptical about the whole Pagan thing. But just then, Holly pointed to a poster on a phonepole. "Look, the San Francisco Mime Troupe is doing their new show in Berkeley next weekend. Want to go?"

"Sure," I said, glad to pin down a future date with her.

"How about Sunday? Because on Saturday, I'm going to the Future Actions work group. We're going to decide what actions to propose to the LAG Congress next month."

"Is that the coordinating meeting you were telling me about?"

"Coordinating Council? No, that's different. Coordinating Council is a meeting of spokes from all the work groups. It's an overview group that meets every Monday. I might go next week. We'll probably hash out the final plans for the Congress."

That was news to me. I had gone with Holly to a planning meeting for the LAG Congress the previous week. I went mostly to have something to work on with her, but I was starting to feel invested in the two-day Congress, which was charged with calling future actions as well as designing an organizational structure for LAG. It bothered me that some other group was setting itself up as the overseer, making the real decisions. I felt cut out of the loop. "Who's on this Coordinating Council?"

"Mainly spokes from work groups. But anyone can go," Holly said. "It's not a closed meeting."

"Do you think you'll go?" I figured that her presence would make me feel more at home if I decided to check it out. I had been going back and forth on how much to get involved in LAG, since it was taking up time that I wanted to be reading history or playing music. Still, if Coordinating Council was where the real decisions were being made...

The Good Old Persons were playing at the Freight and Salvage that night, singing bluegrass and country swing. My thoughts drifted off to my family in Indiana, who might like this music. A rare point of agreement. What would they make of LAG? I'd talked with my mother just before the blockade, and hadn't mentioned it. As far as she knew, I was still saving up money to go back to grad school. If I mentioned civil disobedience, she'd start talking about careers and how an arrest record would jeopardize my brilliant prospects. Maybe I could tell my younger sister or brother about it, but what would it mean to them? They'd think it was one more weird thing that Californians did — sit in hot tubs, follow gurus, and get arrested at protests.

My family were your basic "good Americans," silently assenting to whatever the government did. Did they ever secretly imagine that things could be different? That their efforts could matter? What would it take to reach folks like them?

The one ray of hope was my newfound faith in LAG, that we were the cutting edge of a fresh wave of resistance. Despite Reagan's momentary ascendancy, people were waking up. Seabrook, Diablo, Livermore — we were lighting the torches of a new rebellion.

We stayed through two sets, then took off. Walking home, our conversation died more than once, which was rare for us. I wondered what she was thinking. Was she enjoying the silence, or was it making her uncomfortable?

Tentatively, I put my arm around her shoulders. She slipped her arm around my waist. Her hand lay lightly on my hip. I closed my eyes, letting my steps match hers. What was she thinking? Did she want me to kiss her? Or was she just enjoying my company? What would happen when we reached her place?

As we approached her house, she slid her arm from around my waist and reached into her pocket for her keys. "Do you want to come in?" she asked casually.

"Sure," I said nonchalantly. Holly stepped in and removed her shoes. I followed suit. "Let's make tea and go up to my room," she suggested. Despite feeling some jitters, I smiled to myself. This was more like it. A kettle of hot water was already on the stove. Holly made a cup of raspberry hibiscus tea for each of us, and then led the way up the stairs.

Her room was at the front end of the hall, overlooking the street. The old hardwood floor squeaked as we stepped through the doorway. She closed the door behind us. There were no chairs, so I sat down on the end of the big bed, which took up most of the room. A thick white comforter crumpled under me. Holly picked up a stack of papers from the bed and moved them to the orderly shelves lining one entire wall. A potted ficus tree arched out of one corner, and deep green vines circled the top of the walls.

"Looks like you're really into plants," I said.

"They do really well in here." As she reached out to light a candle, her hair tumbled over her shoulder, looking reddish against the light skin of her arm. "We have a garden in the backyard, too. It's all organic. I love it, it keeps me at peace with the Earth."

"Sounds spiritual to me," I joked, reminding her of a recent conversation.

"It is, it's a spiritual connection," she said, sitting down next to me on the foot of the bed. "We sang this song in jail, 'The Earth is our mother, we must take care of her.' I believe in that."

From our previous discussions, I knew we didn't see eye to eye on spirituality, and I regretted bringing it up. "Let's put on some music," I suggested, spying a cassette player on the shelves.

"There's some tapes over there," she pointed. "Pick whatever you want to hear." As I got up, she sat down on the side of the bed.

Most of her tapes looked like sound tracks for meditation. I picked North Indian flute music and put it in the player. "Do you meditate?" I asked as I sat next to her on the bed. The flute sketched a haunting melody, joined by tablas and an organ-like drone. I wished it were a little louder, but I didn't want to get up again.

She lay back on the bed, her hair fanning out and framing her face. She folded her hands across her stomach and gazed up at the candlelight flickering on the ceiling. "Yeah. I wish I did it more. I guess I'm a one-passion person. And right now, that passion is politics."

She lay on her back, breathing gently. A curl brushed across her forehead. Her eyes shimmered blue-green. I hesitated, then leaned down and kissed her lips. She slid her arms around my shoulders and looked up with an enigmatic smile, as if to say, "Yeah? Now what?" I eased down and pressed my body against hers. We kissed again. She rolled toward me, and the softness of her breasts against my chest sent a shiver through me. I threaded my fingers deep into her thick hair, then burrowed down to kiss her neck.

She laughed slightly, which caught me off-guard. "Are you ticklish?" I whispered.

"No," she answered. "It just made me laugh. Here we are on the bed together, we're probably going to make love, and neither one of us has spoken a word about it."

I looked at her intently. "Does it bother you?"

"No, it's just interesting." She leaned up on one elbow so our heads were at the same level. Her eyes were full of warmth, but I couldn't make out what she was thinking.

"Is there something you want to talk about?" I asked.

"Well, I guess there's one thing — condoms. I have some if you don't."

"I have one in my jacket." I went to get it, turning up the flute tape at the same time. Holly slipped out of her jeans and pulled back the sheets. She stretched luxuriantly on her back, arms behind her head, her breasts outlined through her T-shirt. An angel, I thought. Truly an angel.

As I slipped into bed, I flashed back to meeting Holly, in the park the day before the blockade — how lucky I felt to have met her, and how much I wanted to see her again. Here we were, in bed. Was this for real? She leaned over and kissed me sweetly on the lips. What a dream.

Wednesday, August 18, 1982

THE CROWD pressed in on both sides, singing and shouting. From the left they danced after flutes and drums, from the right a trumpet and sax. Attired in brilliant colors, they converged on the small double doors. A huge guitar played by two thick hands soared overhead. And from the flames above the doors rose a fiery phoenix.

IT SWUNG like a rainbow over La Peña's facade, a mural commemorating the struggles of the Chilean people against their CIA-sponsored military government. The doors, the focal point of the mural, were carved with intricate Andean reliefs.

While Mort locked his car, Craig and I looked over the familiar painting. Craig pointed up at the weathered hands holding the big guitar. "Claude says he's going to renovate the mural next Summer. BCA swung a city grant."

We made our way into the crowded restaurant area of La Peña, the local Chilean cultural center and a favored watering hole for Berkeley activists. Craig went to the bar for a pitcher of beer while Mort and I found a table under a row of multicolored shawls hanging along the back wall. A photo collage showed the Guatemalan village where they were made.

We pulled up another chair for Hank, who was expected momentarily. Hank had engineered our gathering to share his blueprint for a giant Grim Reaper for the October Livermore protest, one of three actions we consensed on at the LAG Congress.

Three actions. If I had any lingering doubts, that hooked me — a radical organization with a full year of actions. Even before the Congress I was going to a couple of meetings a week plus stopping by the office every few days. Now we had three actions in the next ten months, each building off the previous,

The original mural on the front of La Peña, the Chilean cultural center that serves as a community gathering spot for South Berkeley. The new mural closely follows the original.

culminating in another June blockade of Livermore. With good organizing, who knew how many thousands might join us this time?

Not everyone was so sanguine. I knew that Mort and Craig thought we were spreading ourselves too thin. But how could there be too many actions? You can't hold back people's desire to protest.

Craig set the pitcher and mugs on the table and pulled up a chair. We were all practically the same age: Craig and I were twenty-eight, Mort twenty-nine, and Hank thirty. We shared a cultural history, growing up at the end of the Vietnam era, and I had gravitated toward them over the past month or so.

The other three had met earlier in the Spring, and I envied their easy rapport. I wanted to be part of their circle, and I was glad to have an hour or so to spend with them before joining Holly, who was at a meeting across the street at the LAG office.

Craig poured the beer into our glasses. "Cheers," he said. As we clinked our glasses and drank, I studied Craig. He was stocky, with neatly-trimmed brown hair, and wire-framed glasses. His green short-sleeved button shirt contrasted with the light skin of his arms. Craig had helped initiate LAG the previous Winter, and had been a staff member since the Spring. I'd met him at the office and a few Coordinating Council meetings. He was usually so brusque that it took some adjusting to see him leaning back in his chair drinking a beer.

By comparison, Mort seemed like an old friend. We worked together on the LAG Congress, and he'd given Holly and me a ride home from several meetings. Mort maintained a consistently unkempt appearance: long brown hair tucked behind his ears, a wispy Lenin-esque goatee, shirt tail falling out. Only a pocket-protector crammed with pens suggested that by day he worked as a solar engineer.

I asked Mort and Craig about their cluster, Overthrow. The idea of a socialist-oriented direct action group intrigued me. It had a lot more bite than the amorphous nature of Change of Heart Cluster.

"It started as a refuge for people who didn't like the new-age tone of most of the affinity groups," Craig said.

Mort nodded and set his glass on the table. "Our goal is to get discussions going about the wider context of LAG's work. No one ever talks about economic relations, or political power and social classes. The affinity groups just want to know when the next blockade is."

He was cut short by Hank, who loped up and said, "Let's see who's radioactive." He started scanning Craig with a small Geiger counter. Immediately it began clicking. "Jeff? Sure enough." The box clicked again as he checked Mort. "Good, I see you've all been getting your daily dose of radiation."

"How are you doing that?" Mort said, leaning over to see the dial of the instrument.

"I was turning the counter up to peak sensitivity," Hank explained. "It was picking up background radiation. Reassuring, huh?" He pulled up a chair. "Hey, I just got tickets for the Dead shows next month. They'll probably sell out by tomorrow."

We poured Hank a beer and got to talking about all the great 1960s bands from the Bay Area — the Grateful Dead, Jefferson Airplane, Creedence Clearwater Revival, Santana, Country Joe and the Fish... How as teenagers living in different parts of the country, we'd listen to them and dream of moving to San Francisco and joining a hippie commune.

Growing up in Indiana, I nurtured an image of San Francisco and Berkeley: everyone was political, everyone was an artist, and the whole culture was steeped in radical creativity. Which wasn't far off the mark. But despite playing political music around Berkeley for several years, I had been doing it by myself or with others who were in it for the music, not the message. LAG was my first time being around a whole community of creative political people.

"I feel really lucky to be here in Berkeley," I said as I refilled our glasses. "Politics seemed so hopeless in Indiana. It probably does everywhere outside of a few liberal cities. What can you do?"

Craig sat up, and his eyes met mine. "People can take action anywhere," he said. "That's the message we have to spread. No matter where you are, you can find a few others and act."

"Five people can't go organizing a blockade," I said.

"Not at first. But you can do something. The key is to act, not just sit around talking. Do an event that unleashes people's creativity and gets them working together. Paint a banner and hang it off a rooftop. Perform a skit outside the student union. It doesn't take a thousand people to make your point."

Mort nodded. "In a place where nothing's happening, you might actually get some media coverage. You could reach a lot more people than you think."

I thought back to my years at Indiana State. Not exactly prime organizing territory. Some friends and I had set up a coffeehouse and a couple of folk festivals, trying to rekindle the spirit of the '60s. Without a lot of luck. Oh well, I figured, I had to start somewhere. Look at it as a warm-up for LAG.

Craig doled out the rest of the beer and asked Hank, "What about this Grim Reaper idea of yours?"

"I'm glad you asked that question," Hank said. He pulled a sheaf of crumpled papers from the pocket of his leather jacket and showed us a sketch. "I'm picturing a ten-foot Reaper, with a long black robe and a death head. We mount it on a flatbed truck and drive it through Livermore in October — think they'd get the message?"

We all laughed. "I'll work on that," Mort said.

Craig emptied his glass. "I like it. But I'm worried about the October 9th demonstration, overall." October 9th was the thirtieth anniversary of

Livermore Lab, and Lab brass were planning a big celebration. People at the LAG Congress felt that October was too soon for another big CD action, so we consensed to a legal demonstration at the anniversary bash. "It's a fine idea," Craig said, "but hardly anyone signed up for the work group."

"There's still time," I said.

Ignoring my remark, Mort looked at Craig. "No one wants to work on a legal demo. It's not glamorous enough for the AGs." He pulled out a couple of dollars. "Who wants more beer?" Several more bills were tossed onto the table, and Mort made his way to the bar.

While Craig and Hank talked about the Reaper idea, I leaned back in my chair. Mort's disdainful attitude toward affinity groups bugged me. Even though Spectrum hadn't met since right after the blockade, Hank and Cindy and I had been spokes at the Congress, and I figured our AG would come back together for the upcoming actions.

Even more, I noticed that when the talk got serious, Mort and Craig talked right past me. Sure, they knew each other better and were in Overthrow together. But I'd had enough of politics as a spectator sport.

Mort returned with a pitcher. "I just ran into Pilgrim at the bar," he said. "His AG spraypainted another draft billboard last night. We should drive by and see it later."

I saw an opening. "Did anyone see the anti-nuke billboard that the Freeze bought downtown? The top says 'Stop the Arms Race.' We could alter the lower part so it says 'Blockade Livermore' instead of 'Vote Yes on the Freeze.'"

"No, we've got to support the Freeze, whatever we think of it," Craig answered. The Nuclear Weapons Freeze referendum was on the California statewide ballot for November, and Livermore Lab had joined a multitude of defense corporations in lobbying heavily against it. "If it loses in California, Reagan will claim that people are behind his insane escalation of the arms race."

"Sure, I'll vote for the Freeze," I said. "It's still a powder-puff."

"It's not that simple," Mort said. He shifted in his chair, slinging his arm over the back, but didn't look any more comfortable. "It's about building alliances. Civil disobedience is a fringe tactic. It's easy for the government and media to dismiss us. But if LAG is working with the Freeze, it situates us on the political spectrum. It keeps us from being totally marginalized."

Clearly they'd done more thinking about it than I had. At least they had responded to my idea. I shifted to a lighter vein. "I had an idea for a ballot initiative. How about a Northern California secession referendum?" They laughed, but I pursued it. "It would probably pass. We could secede from the

United States and start our own country. If it worked, other places would do it, and we could completely dismantle the U.S. government."

"Why couldn't they just blockade us?" Mort said. "The secession idea has been floated before. The problem is, if it's just the Bay Area, they could isolate us and starve us out. We have to build a national movement, not just focus on a few key centers."

"The government wouldn't need to blockade us," Hank put in. "They'd just cancel our military contracts, and our economy would collapse."

"We have all the farms in the Central Valley," I said as I filled my mug. "We could start our own economy."

"Think so?" Craig answered. "Take a look at Nicaragua. They had a socialist revolution in 1979. So what happens under Reagan? The CIA is spending millions of dollars funding right-wing guerrillas and terrorist attacks

Berkeley activists targeted draft billboards in 1982, eventually driving them from town.

to destabilize the Nicaraguan economy. We have to restructure our entire society, not just secede."

"Besides," Hank said, "if the Bay Area secedes, the U.S. would become even more reactionary."

"An excellent point," I said, glad to have a graceful retreat from my proposal. "As long as there's Berkeley, there's still hope." Just then I noticed Holly and Daniel walking toward our table. Holly had a bounce in her step, and was talking over her shoulder to Daniel, leaning back to tell him something over the noise of the crowd.

I smiled to myself as they approached. Holly greeted us warmly, her eyes sparkling as they lighted on me. Her buoyancy re-animated our table, and a ripple of pride ran through me as she came over and gave me a hug.

She pulled up a chair next to me, and I noticed how the others immediately included her in their conversation. Holly's opinions mattered. I slid my arm around her, feeling myself drawn into the inner circle by her presence.

Holly and Daniel were coming from a meeting to start planning the International Day of Nuclear Disarmament, the most ambitious of the proposals we'd consensed to at the Congress.

"How did it go?" Craig asked.

"Great," Holly said. "There were over twenty people. We did a long visioning process led by Antonio, sharing our greatest dreams for International Day. Then we formed work groups and started to draft a Call to send out to peace groups all over the world."

"Inviting them all to come to Livermore?" Hank joked.

"No, groups will do local actions, wherever they are. Some will blockade, some will do vigils or teach-ins." Holly's eyes were open wide, her cheeks full of color. "Schoolkids will paint murals and have festivals, churches will have special services — in a few years, it could become an international holiday."

"Precisely." Daniel's professorial voice came from behind me. "We're issuing a Call for groups to do local, decentralized actions on or around June 20th next year. We'll do another blockade at Livermore, but we envision actions all over the world."

"Isn't it premature to start organizing internationally before we even have a local coalition that we can work with?" Mort asked with a scowl.

Some of the color drained from Holly's face. "I think we can do both."

"I agree," Daniel said dryly. "And I suspect that we'll find more kindred spirits in other cities and countries than among existing leftist groups in the Bay Area."

"Depends on your definition of kindred," Mort retorted.

Craig gestured toward Mort, as if signaling him to ease up. "The time may be right for national and international organizing," he said. "The key is to reach out to local groups, too. We can't expect to shut Livermore Lab single-handedly."

"We're planning to do a lot of local organizing," Holly said. "Melissa and I are going to join the Outreach collective."

"Well, I hope so," Mort said.

"You could work on International Day if you have so many ideas," Holly said with no enthusiasm.

"I'm thinking about it," Mort said. He fidgeted with his napkin. "Is anyone seriously asking how we're going to organize an international coordinated action plus three actions of our own in the next ten months? People were consensing to everything at the LAG Congress. It'll amaze me if we can sustain this level of involvement for a year."

Craig nodded slowly. No one else responded. I wasn't sure what to think. Mort was pretty sharp, but he struck me as pessimistic. Why couldn't we sustain our momentum — even grow — over the next year?

We finished up our beers. Mort pulled on his jacket. "Well, I've got to work in the morning. Anyone want a ride?"

Craig and Hank got up to join him. Craig put his hand on Holly's shoulder. "We'll talk some more about International Day next time you're at the office. I have some ideas about publicity."

"Great," she said, regaining some of her élan. "I'll be in tomorrow afternoon."

As the others took off, Holly and I stood together on the sidewalk outside La Peña. She yawned, and I put my arm around her shoulders. "Are you meeting'd out?" I asked her.

"Just about," she said. "Three nights in a row is pushing it. But the meeting tonight was so good, it was worth it."

It had been a few nights since I'd seen Holly, and I was looking forward to walking home alone with her. But it turned out that she had invited Caroline, who was still over at the office, to walk with us.

Not that I didn't like Caroline. I remembered her signing me up for the nonviolence prep the first time I went into the office. Anyway, maybe she was only going a few blocks.

We jaywalked over to the LAG office, where Caroline was just emerging. Her shoulder-length brown hair was tangled on one side, and her glasses were slightly askew. Her forehead creased as she turned her key in the office door lock. "I finally got the books balanced," she told Holly. "It doesn't look very good."

"We need to get a mailing out right away," Holly said. "If we announce the actions, people will be excited about donating."

Caroline nodded, but her forehead didn't unfurrow.

"Don't think about it now," Holly said. "Leave your worries at the office."

We were all silent as we passed under a shadowy canopy of branches and leaves. As we emerged into the streetlight, Caroline looked at us beseechingly, as if to say, help me not obsess about LAG's finances!

Holly picked up the cue. "Let's talk about the actions," she said. "Are you going to do Vandenberg?"

Caroline twisted a strand of hair around her finger. "I think so," she said. "We could possibly stop the missile test, or at least delay it, if there are enough of us. So for me, well, I'm pretty sure I'll do it."

"Me, too," Holly said. "I want to do a backcountry occupation, to reclaim the land."

"The land" was Vandenberg Air Force Base, located on the central California coast near San Luis Obispo. A test launch of the new MX missile from Vandenberg was slated for late January 1983. Activists around the state were gearing up for it, and though it wasn't yet clear how LAG was going to relate to the Vandenberg Action Coalition that was taking shape, we had adopted the action as our Winter focus.

"Between that and International Day and Livermore, we're going to have our hands full," Caroline said. "Plus we consensed to start a regular newsletter."

The newsletter. I caught my breath. At the Congress, there was a proposal to expand LAG's periodic mailings into a newsletter that carried announcements and articles about our actions. There was even talk of doing a four-page tabloid newspaper.

Publishing a radical newspaper was a dream of mine since childhood, ever since I read about Ben Franklin and Tom Paine during the American Revolution. What better way to forge a new radical organization out of disparate elements? Give people a common publication, a meeting ground for all views, and let the truth emerge.

In college, some friends and I quit the stodgy student daily and started an "independent" tabloid. Alternative, yes. But radical, it was not. It mainly carried concert reviews, humor, poetry, and campus news, with only the occasional environmental or anti-nuke article.

This would be different. LAG had a vision not just of ecology and global peace, but of restructuring the world from the bottom up. Who better to launch a paper dedicated to nonviolent revolution?

After the Congress, Claudia had encouraged me to draw up a subscription proposal for LAG's September mailing. If enough subscriptions came in, we'd have the money to do a tabloid. I wrote a Dickens-esque spoof on the "ghosts of actions past, present, and future," helped stuff it into hundreds of envelopes, and crossed my fingers for a good enough response to pay for a real newspaper.

Caroline parted from us on Derby Street, where she was house-sitting, and finally I had Holly to myself. We stopped under a willowy tree and hugged. Holly gently kissed my face, then my lips. I sighed and held her close for a moment. Hand in hand we strolled the last couple of blocks to my apartment.

As we came into the lobby, the clutter of old newspapers and junk mail and litter distracted me. I had been neglecting my job. I resolved to devote more time to cleaning the place up.

Inside my apartment, I turned on some music and flopped onto the cushions in the living room. I tried to coax Holly down with me, but she seemed preoccupied. I looked up at her. "Is something wrong?"

She reached down and took my hand. "My mind is still racing from the meeting," she said. "Let me get some tea, and then we can go lie down." She let go of my hand and went into the kitchen.

I tried to be a good sport. She's here, I reminded myself. She's staying the night. Still, wouldn't you think that after three days apart she'd find me more irresistible?

She got her tea and we headed for the bedroom. Holly had an Urban Ecology project the next morning, so she set my rarely-used alarm. I put on a tape of troubadour songs and lowered the volume. At last we lay down together. I rolled onto my back and drew her to me. She nestled her face into my neck, and her fingers laced through my hair. I took a deep breath and slowly released it. The breath was followed by a deep yawn, which Holly echoed. I smiled to myself. At last, we were in synch.

Even though I'd pictured us making love, I wasn't disappointed that what evolved was cuddling and quiet talking. We spun a quilt-like conversation, meandering from the LAG newsletter and International Day to organic gardening and troubadour tunes, weaving together patches of our lives. In her thoughts and words, in her caresses and light kisses, I could tell that Holly was totally present. What more could I want?

At last she couldn't keep her eyes open any longer. She lay on her side, her hair flowing across the pillow. "I'm sorry, sweetie," she murmured. "I'm falling asleep. I love being here with you."

I kissed her goodnight, stroking her hair as she settled in. "I love you, Holly," I whispered. "Goodnight."

She was asleep in a minute. I lay beside her for a while, the threads of our conversation still slipping through my mind. Finally, I slid out of bed and went back out to the living room.

As I filled my pipe, I thought back over the evening with Holly. Now that she was asleep in my bed, my earlier worries seemed out of joint. I sat down in the big olive-green reclining chair I'd salvaged from a vacant apartment a couple of weeks earlier. The vinyl felt cool against my arms. My eyes played over a collage of Renaissance art prints that covered the longest wall in the living room, coming to rest on Botticelli's "Birth of Venus." The flowing blonde hair and graceful pose of the Goddess on the half-shell made me smile at her resemblance to Holly.

I took a hit off my pipe and reached for my journal. I leaned back in the recliner and gazed at Botticelli, then turned to a fresh page.

Saturday, October 9, 1982

ON OCTOBER 9th, Livermore Lab celebrated "Thirty Years of Excellence."

The Lab was founded in 1952 by Edward Teller and other nuclear scientists as a competitor to Los Alamos National Lab in New Mexico. Los Alamos was the home of the original hydrogen bomb and other early nuclear weapons, but conflicts within that lab led Teller to persuade the government, then deep into the Cold War, to open a second weapons design facility.

I'd asked Claudia recently why the government ran research labs, when the actual production of nuclear weapons was farmed out to the defense industry. "Why not have defense contractors do their own research?"

"What would be the profit in that?" she answered. "Corporations can make a guaranteed profit on weapons production, but they don't make a penny off research. That's why the government set up the weapons labs, and why they put so much military research money into places like Stanford or MIT."

"The government controls the budget," I said. "Why don't they tell the defense industry that if they want the big contracts, they have to pay for their own research?"

"Who do you think the government is?" Claudia responded. "Practically every top-level official has come out of the corporate world, and is headed back when they leave office. Why would they want to cut corporate profits, when they can pass it on to taxpayers?"

To celebrate thirty years of creating nuclear weapons, Livermore Lab's brass invited the seven thousand employees and their families to a picnic at the Lab. There was a feeling in LAG that we had to respond, if only with a legal demo. A small planning group reserved a park in Livermore, organized a rally, and got a permit to march four miles through town and out to the Lab.

The work group chose a funereal theme for our march. People were asked to wear gray, black, or white, and to bring muted signs and props for a solemn procession through Livermore and out to the "Death Lab."

I had plenty of black clothes, so that part was easy. But even with the right colors, I was feeling weird.

What triggered it was Holly going on a two-day excursion to Monterey with her old lover, Frank. They were still occasionally sleeping together, which made me jealous. The night before she left to see Frank, Holly stayed with me.

The next morning, I woke with her, hoping we would make love. But she got right out of bed and pulled on her T-shirt and jeans. I propped myself up on my elbow and asked when she was getting back.

"Sometime Friday evening," she said. She flexed her shoulders and released them. "I need this vacation. I'm already getting obsessed with International Day, and it's only October. I've got to pace myself. Plus, Frank is going through a hard time, and he needs my support."

Good for Frank, I thought. "What about Friday night when you come back?" I asked. "Do you want to get together?"

"I'll probably get back late and feel like heading home," she said as she laced her shoes. "Maybe we can talk on the phone. We'll have all day Saturday together at Livermore."

I rolled onto my back. Holly had told me once that when she and Frank lived together, they couldn't keep their hands off each other. What a difference from us.

Holly folded her sweater and put it in her daypack. After a minute she looked at me. "I feel like you're trying to manipulate me," she said. "You're trying to make me feel bad about seeing Frank."

"I'm not manipulating you," I said. "It just gets me down that you're still sleeping with him, that's all."

She sighed impatiently. "Frank and I love each other a lot. I really like spending time with him, and if that includes making love, I'm not going to set artificial limits on it."

I couldn't argue with the logic, but I also knew that I wanted Holly to myself. Sure, she could go visit Frank. But did they have to sleep together?

"You know where I am with Frank," she said. "If you have questions, fine. But don't manipulate me."

Her words stung. I forced a smile. "I'm not trying to be this way. Can we let go of it?"

"We have to," she said. "I need to get going." She knelt down and gave me a quick kiss. I tried to pull her onto the bed and hug her, but she resisted. "I have to go," she said. "I'll see you in a few days."

"Yeah," I said. "See you sometime." Right away I was sorry for the sarcasm. There was no time to move beyond it as she picked up her daypack and headed for the door.

"I'll try to phone you Friday night," I called after her.

She turned and looked back for a second. "Okay. I'll be there later in the evening. We can talk then."

It made for a dismal few days. We did talk a little on Friday, mainly to make plans to carpool out to Livermore the next day with Caroline. On the ride out, we sat together in the back, holding hands and leaning together. She didn't seem anxious or upset. Still, I wished we'd had a chance to talk.

As soon as we got to the protest, Holly was swept into setting up the

International Day table. I didn't have a specific task, and I wandered off, feeling at loose ends. I walked to the edge of the rally area and looked over the panorama. After some early fog, it was turning out to be a beautiful Fall afternoon, a great day to hang out in a park and listen to music. Unfortunately, the "park" we had reserved — the only one the Livermore city government would let us use — was simply a huge parking lot outside of town, solid gravel as far as the eye could see. In the middle of the barren plain, two dozen assorted peace and anti-nuke groups set up literature tables. Opposite me, a woman played guitar from a makeshift stage on the back of a flatbed truck. A few hundred people milled around.

My shoulders slumped. I had expected the day to be like a blockade reunion. But everyone seemed standoffish, huddling in furtive cliques. I saw a couple of people from my affinity group whom I hadn't seen since right after the blockade. We talked about doing the Vandenberg action in January, but there was no spark, and they moved on.

If only I could disappear for a while, go do something else, and come back fresh once the event picked up some steam. But in the expanse of the parking lot, there was nowhere to disappear. What a perfect image for the protest — nowhere to hide.

I looked around for a familiar face. Over by the flatbed stage I spotted Hank. He was standing in front of the Grim Reaper that he and Mort and some other Overthrow guys had finished the night before: a ten-foot insectoid demon with white face, black cape, and a long silver scythe. The Reaper loomed ominously over the crowd, its beady red eyeballs flashing on and off like a sci-fi spectre.

As I started over toward Hank and the Reaper, Monique headed me off. I appreciated having someone actually walk up to me, and gave her a hug, feeling the springiness of her styled hair against my head. Her affinity group, the Walnettos, had organized a small blockade at the Lab earlier in the week, and she was still wired from the experience. "We were arraigned the same day, pled no contest, and our sentence was community service," she told me. "I'm doing mine at a senior center. Can you believe it? Next time we might trespass, so they have to give us misdemeanors and we can take them to trial."

Personally I wasn't real optimistic about our prospects of justice in the suburban Livermore area. Monique and the Walnettos were from the suburbs, though. "I don't know if we would win an acquittal," she conceded. "But we could bring a lot of issues like toxics and groundwater contamination before the local people."

As Monique walked off, Claudia and her partner Rebecca wandered by. "Is this supposed to be the rally?" Claudia asked.

I looked around. There were about five hundred people by now, but not much was happening. "Maybe it'll pick up," I said.

She wasn't buying it, I could tell, but it didn't bother me. I was still glad to be talking with her. As one of the LAG staffers, Claudia was the center of our amorphous universe. I'd gotten used to her steering projects my way — press mailings, workshop flyers, typing up the mailing list. And now with the newspaper, I had a project of my own. It was happening. The subscription appeal had raised almost a thousand dollars. A work group with Craig, Holly, Caroline, Mort, Monique, and me had met a week earlier and consensed to produce a monthly four-page tabloid, starting in November. I volunteered to keep track of articles and paste up a subscription ad. "The first issue or two will be called the 'LAG Rag,'" I told Claudia. "We'll have a contest to pick a permanent name."

Claudia nodded and cracked a wry smile. "That's great. What amazes me is that no one has complained about it." She shared a knowing glance with Rebecca. "After a while, you start expecting criticism for whatever initiative you take."

As she spoke, Doc and Belinda walked up. I hadn't seen them since the Congress, and welcomed them warmly. But Claudia stepped back, acknowledging them with a sharp nod.

I wanted to ask Doc about the Vandenberg meeting he'd been to. Before I could speak, Claudia preempted me with a non-political query. "Where's Jeremy?" she asked.

Jeremy was Doc and Belinda's six-year-old son, raised according to the strict nonhierarchical values the two of them espoused. Doc and Belinda were a couple, a gay man and a lesbian who had joined to raise a family. I liked Doc a lot, and being around Belinda at the Congress, I'd gotten past my stereotype that she'd automatically hate me for being a hetero male. She wasn't looking to win any charm points, and she wasn't going to budge an inch when we disagreed. Still, I didn't feel any personal animosity from her.

"We left Jeremy at a friend's house," she said. "He decided he didn't want to come to the march. I think they're going to the zoo."

"Sounds like a tough choice for a kid," I said, looking around the little circle. Maybe this was what today was about, I thought. Bury the conflicts and spend the afternoon together. Comrades in the struggle.

Then Doc knit his eyebrows and leveled his gaze at Claudia. "Listen, I

The Grim Reaper rode through Livermore on the way to the rally. The signs came off to make the truck a stage.

need to talk to you. I heard Rudolph got treated pretty lousy when he took the Vandenberg Action Coalition proposal to Coordinating Council last week."

I was caught off-guard by his vehemence, but Claudia didn't seem fazed. "Well, no wonder," she said. "He parachuted into the middle of our meeting asking for $1500 for posters and a handbook. He didn't have any written budget, just a vague request for money that everyone knows we don't have. What do you think we are, a fund-raising committee? No one from VAC even comes to Coordinating Council unless it's to ask for money."

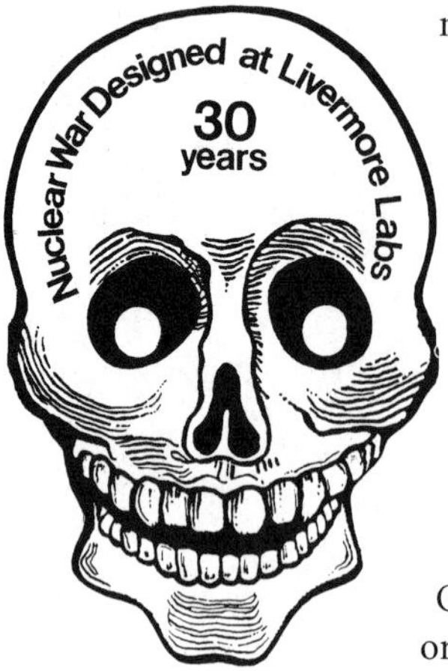

"What do you expect?" Belinda retorted. "When someone from VAC does go, look how rudely they get treated."

"Hey, everyone gets treated rudely at Coordinating Council," wishing they'd lighten up.

Belinda ignored me and glared at Claudia. "That's why no one wants to go."

"Well, someone needs to represent VAC," Claudia answered.

"I don't see why," Doc said. "Coordinating Council isn't in charge of the protest. VAC is the organizing group, and LAG is just one member of the coalition."

Claudia laughed without humor. "LAG has been paying all of the phone and postage bills. And we've gone into debt to hire Craig as a staffperson for —"

"That's exactly it!" Belinda cut in. "Hiring a staffer for Vandenberg is one more example of how Coordinating Council is trying to dominate the organizing. LAG doesn't own the action — it belongs to the people doing it. And that's who VAC represents."

She was cut short by a group of skeleton dancers. They wove through the crowd passing out laminated skull masks. I was relieved at the interruption. Did everything have to turn into a fight? I tried on a mask. Claudia walked away, and our circle broke up.

The argument stayed with me, though, and left me rattled. I looked around for Holly, and spotted her checking out the literature tables. I started over to join her, but Mort waved to me. He stood beside the flatbed truck holding a clipboard, coordinating the performers on the stage. The Reaper towered over him, its red eyes blinking relentlessly. "Looks like he's enjoying the show," I said as I walked up. "That's quite a creation."

Mort lifted a corner of the black robe to reveal the metal structure. "Check it out. Hank welded the frame at his shop, and I wired in the eyes. Tai and Lyle just finished painting the face this morning."

The welded frame under the robe caught the sunlight and reminded me of jail bars. Not that I'd actually been behind any. Not yet, anyway.

I turned back to Mort. He was working with Holly on both the International Day and Outreach collectives. I wasn't on either, but I had a bit of news. "Holly told me that she and Daniel and Antonio have a new version of the International Day Call," I told him. "She said it was a lot less 'new-age' than the first one."

"I don't see how it could be any *more* that way," Mort said, suddenly agitated. "The first version was just one long poem to Mother Nature, and how all conflicts are really only in our heads. There's no way we could do outreach to local groups with that Call."

His response caught me off-guard, and I was sorry I'd brought it up. He flipped through the papers on his clipboard. I looked around the parking lot. More people were arriving. A folk trio sang on stage, and a crowd had gathered to listen.

Melissa came by and handed Mort and me a flyer. "Are you going to the Vandenberg protest in January?" she asked us.

"No," Mort said, "I couldn't take that much time off work. But there's an action the same week out at Concord Naval Weapons Station. Some Central America groups are planning a demo against arms shipments to El Salvador. I'm going to the coalition meeting next week."

"Do you think it will pull energy away from Vandenberg?" I wondered aloud.

Melissa shook her head. Her olive forehead glistened in the sun. "No, it's different crowds. I've been talking to all kinds of people who are doing Vandenberg. It could be as big as Livermore."

I was weighing her assessment when Walt came hurrying up. He looked at us breathlessly. "Daniel and I just drove up to the Lab," he said. "The police have totally cordoned off the South Gate. They're not going to let us get anywhere close to the Lab's picnic."

Nowhere close? Why were we even here? The others started analyzing the situation,

Was it the proximity of Halloween that brought out so many costumes?

but I sagged. All afternoon I'd been holding my feelings at bay, but the latest development was too much. I kicked at the gravel. "Why'd we come to the middle of nowhere," I said. "We should have held our rally in Berkeley."

Melissa's eyes grew wide. "We don't have to obey the police," she said. "I don't think they're prepared to arrest a thousand people if we nonviolently walk around their barricade. The police depend on us obeying them. They only have as much power as we grant them."

"They don't have to arrest everyone," Mort scoffed. "They could bust a few people, press heavier charges, and use it to teach everyone a lesson."

Melissa started to respond, but she was drowned out by the thumping of drums. Just behind us, a Danse Macabre troupe led by a corps of drumming skeletons began a contorted, expressionistic Dance of Death. The crowd of a thousand gathered around to form an amphitheater. Some of the dancers drummed and chanted, while others mimed a nuclear explosion and its agonizing aftermath. Their silent moans swelled into an anguished cry, ending in a *tableau vivant* of death and desolation.

There was a smattering of applause when the piece ended. Clapping didn't seem appropriate, so I nodded my head. Beautiful, if not very heartening.

The troupe gathered themselves and began a spiraling procession, winding outward from the center. Through the crowd, people hoisted their banners and props, fell in behind the drummers and dancers, and headed down the road into town.

It was a somber procession, draped in mourning, trudging to the dirge-like beat of the Danse Macabre. Gray banners bearing skulls and mushroom clouds floated through the funereal crowd. At the rear, hovering menacingly over us from the flatbed truck, followed the red-eyed Grim Reaper.

Our route led through a residential part of town, but the streets were completely evacuated. From behind their tidy lawns, from behind the curtains of their suburban homes, the townspeople of Livermore peered out at the slowly-passing procession. A few adventurous souls came out and stood on their porches, pointing at us and talking in hushed tones. Some leaflets had been made up, but hardly anyone would come close enough to take one.

I was feeling adrift in the crowd, and I looked around for Holly. Finally I spotted her toward the back of the march talking with people from Change of Heart. She looked more like a gardener than an undertaker in her gray denim shirt and straw hat. She gave me a hug, but there was none of her usual vibrancy. "I'm really tired," she said. "I might have to go home early."

We walked along together, but it seemed like we were in different worlds. "The march feels weird to me," she said. "I wish we weren't using such negative images. That's what the Lab is all about, death. We ought to be about life."

I felt a twinge of irritation. "It's not like the Lab ever admits to what they're doing," I countered. "They paint this rosy picture of science serving humanity. Sometimes you need to use art as a mirror to say, here's reality —

The thousand protesters on October 9th marched several miles through the town of Livermore out to the weapons lab, which lay on the outskirts.

here's the true meaning of what you are doing."

"That's not the sort of art that reaches me," she said. "I need to see an alternative, a vision of a better future. What if we did a festival showing what we believed in, something really colorful, and invited the townspeople to come see who we are? I'd like to have some dialog with the people of Livermore, not just scare or guilt-trip them."

I didn't see much future in dialoguing with Livermore people, many of whom were families and friends of Lab employees. But I didn't want to argue with Holly, either.

We walked along with Karina and Sara for the last stretch of the march. I wondered what their relationship was like. Next to Karina's exuberance, Sara seemed downright contemplative. She was tall, with a long nose and straight brown hair that hung nearly to her waist. "I can't believe they're building condos here," she said, pointing to a billboard announcing a future development in the abandoned farm field just up the road from Livermore Lab.

"Comes complete with a lifetime supply of radiation," I joked.

"Imagine raising a family across the street from a nuclear lab," Sara said. "Who would live here?"

"Lab workers," bantered Karina. "They're already in total denial." Sara laughed. Karina beamed and took her hand as we strolled along the roadside.

"It's not exactly denial," I

Affinity groups created funereal costumes and props for the march.

said, thinking back to my own education. "It's faith. People are taught this unquestioning trust of science. Science solves problems, it doesn't create them. Even when they distrust the government, people believe in science."

"Sounds like a new religion," Karina said. "Better living through radioactivity."

I laughed, but Sara looked pensive. "Americans can be so oblivious," she said. "We think that the planet exists for us to exploit and manipulate, and there will never be any consequences. The Earth might have ideas of Her own." She made it sound like such an ordinary observation that I found myself nodding.

Melissa fell in step with us. "We should ignore the police barricades and try to walk to the Lab gates. Just refuse to acknowledge them."

Musicians and dancers led the October 9th funeral march.

I tried to assimilate the idea. To me, the police seemed like an impersonal authority with boundless power to enforce their edicts. Even when we did CD, it was with the understanding that we would inevitably be arrested, that there was no escape. Defying police orders and getting away was another leap.

Karina seconded the proposal with such buoyant enthusiasm that Melissa took a step back. "The only problem is," Karina told us, "I can't risk arrest today. As soon as the march is over, Sara and I need to catch a ride back to the City for a pro-choice vigil."

We arrived at the southwest corner of the Lab, where we were handed a red, black, or white carnation. Daniel and a couple of other organizers pointed to a billboard-sized frame up near the intersection. The flowers were to be fitted into designated spots in order to spell out a simple message to the Lab workers and guests: "Convert the Labs."

"Is this your idea of positive imagery?" I kidded Holly, trying to lighten our mood.

"It is," she answered. "Flowers reach people who shut out negative images. The world is so harsh already. It's up to us to offer an alternative."

"The system already has an alternative," I said. "Disneyland. Nothing negative is ever allowed to happen." As the words came out I winced, wishing I hadn't been so flippant.

Fortunately Holly seemed to take it in stride. "Yeah," she conceded with a smile. "But we need to offer real-life alternatives, examples of beauty and peace."

As we finished our bit of the flower-sign, we followed others down East Avenue toward the barricades between us and the picnic site. Police were routing most of the exiting Lab traffic away from our demonstration. Only people leaving from a small parking lot up Vasco Road would have to pass us.

"What the hell!" said Hank as he climbed out of the Reaper-truck. "We march all the way out here and no one will even see us."

"Doesn't look too promising," I said.

"We should have stayed in town," he said. "Then people would at least have to see us as they come home."

Some people took their signs to the small exit on Vasco, while others talked about how long it might take to hike around to the other side of the Lab.

Holly looked uninspired by the options, and went back to help Daniel with the flower-sign. I went up toward the barricade, where a hundred people had gathered. The barricade itself was simple enough, a bunch of metal sawhorses bedecked with yellow "Police Line — Do Not Cross" ribbon. Behind that stood a double row of riot cops armed with three-foot batons.

Among the protesters, there was no concerted plan of action. One AG was trying to get a song going. But those up front seemed more interested in venting their frustration at the line of cops, and their shrill voices carried the day.

All around, signs and banners drooped at odd angles. I followed Melissa and a few other people out toward the end of the police cordon, but both sides of the road had chain-link fences, and the barricade reached almost to them.

I was trying to rally my spirits when Caroline walked by wearing a forlorn expression. "We lost money on the rally," she said. "I was counting on today to raise money, not lose more."

I reached out and rubbed her shoulders, which were hunched. But I couldn't think of anything uplifting to say, and Caroline drifted off.

Needing an energy boost, I worked my way right up to the barricade, where the tirades continued. Across from us, the column of cops rocked on their heels and fidgeted with their batons while protesters took turns haranguing them.

Melissa wasn't one to abuse the police, but she was in a sour mood. She sought out the squad captain at the edge of the barricade and loudly expounded her views on freedom of speech. She demanded to know why a nonviolent group was not allowed to peaceably assemble up at the gates. The captain listened for a moment, then turned away. Melissa took a step around the end of the barricade, still lecturing him. He turned abruptly and barked at the line of cops. Two officers closed in on Melissa, and she stepped back across the line, still jawing at the retreating captain.

Finally she turned away, and stalked over to where I was standing with Pilgrim and Walt. "It's like talking to a brick wall," she said with exasperation as she joined us.

"Of course," said Pilgrim. "They don't have to pay any attention to us if we're not risking arrest. I don't know why we bother with non-arrest actions."

I could see his point. But Walt's brow creased. "The Lab is working around the clock to destroy the planet. We can't just disappear till the next blockade."

I could see his point, too. Face it, that was about all we were going to accomplish today, anyway. Might as well appreciate it.

Melissa left us and wandered back toward the barricade. She walked out to the far end of the line and started admonishing a couple of cops. She tried to give them a leaflet, and shook the paper at them when they declined.

Pilgrim and Walt were still talking, but my mind drifted away. The baseball playoffs were on that evening. I hadn't had time to listen to any of the games so far, but if I headed home soon, I could catch the St. Louis-Atlanta game. Get my mind off politics for a while.

A scuffle at the far end of the barricade jerked my attention back to the protest. People hurried down that way. The cops bunched up to hold their line. Melissa, clutching a handful of leaflets, had actually slipped beyond the barricade. The cops on the line didn't go after her, but a roving officer came over and used his club to shove her back toward the crowd. "You can't come through here, this road is closed."

"I need to get up to the gate to leaflet," she stated, regaining her balance and stepping forward. People pushed against the barricades, but the cops held firm. Melissa was alone on the other side of the police line. "I have the right to leaflet in a public place."

Other cops headed for her. People yelled to warn her, but she was focused on the officer who had shoved her. He stepped back, and as Melissa took another step forward, two other cops grabbed her by either arm. Her leaflets went flying. Everyone was yelling, and a few people tried to follow, but the poised nightsticks of the barricade cops dissuaded them. Melissa went limp. The cops dragged her to a nearby van and shoved her in the back. They slammed the doors, and in a minute the van was gone.

Some people kept yelling and jostling the barricades, but a lot of us just stared in disbelief. Claudia walked past and said something about Melissa knowing what she was doing and being alright, but it didn't do much for my mood. I felt deflated, knowing I didn't have the nerve to follow. Sure, I'd join a blockade and even get arrested. But defying the cops on my own and getting hauled away? I wasn't ready for that.

A moment later, Caroline came by to tell me that Holly had taken off. "She was feeling tired, and someone offered her a ride back to Berkeley if she went right away. She said to tell you goodbye, and asked if you would call her tonight."

"Sure," I answered, as if I expected Caroline to convey the message to Holly. Caroline walked away, and I stood alone, scanning the scene as if watching it on a movie screen.

The blue sky receded before the incoming fog. The sun was an orange dot over the distant hills. My mind drifted back over the Summer, over my months in LAG. Coming out of the blockade, I had seen LAG as almost a magical movement. From one hundred seventy arrests in February to thirteen hundred in June. Why couldn't we keep growing like that — growing till the government could no longer resist our numbers? Nonviolent direct action would accomplish what no armed insurrection had a chance of doing in this country.

This demo shook my confidence. Where had everyone gone? I felt sad, gray. LAG was fallible.

I thought about Holly again. How different it would be if we lived together, and she was waiting for me when I got home. I sighed. It wasn't the first time I'd thought about living with her.

Cars were coming out of the little lot on Vasco Road, so there was finally someone to wave signs at. But I felt an inclination to slip away, hike back to Livermore, and catch a bus home. It would feel good to be alone with my thoughts. And I could probably get home in time to catch the end of the baseball game.

I surveyed the bedraggled scene one last time, then turned to head back to town. But before I'd cleared the intersection, Hank and Mort flagged me down. "Hey, Jeff," called Hank, "We're heading back to Berkeley with the truck — you want a ride?"

I felt an impulse to make an excuse about running an errand in town. But who was going to believe I had an errand in downtown Livermore? "Does the truck have a radio? I think the playoffs are on."

"Yeah. Come on, the game's already started."

I GOT HOME around seven. Should I call Holly right away? Or hold off? Wait a bit, I thought. Listen to the end of the ballgame. St. Louis was up by a run when Hank dropped me off, but Atlanta was coming to bat. I flipped on the radio and tried to follow the action, but the announcer got on my nerves with his non-stop talking. I was relieved when the inning ended and I could switch it off. I didn't even catch the score. I put on a South African jazz tape. It was still on the hectic side, with a saxophone blaring over multilayered rhythms, but at least there were no words.

I paced around the living room. What was Holly doing? Was she expecting my call?

One hour and one large bowl of popcorn later, I was still debating with myself. Finally I punched out the number and listened to the jangling ring. Maybe she wasn't home. It rang for the fifth time. But then she answered. "Hey, Jeff." She sounded happy to hear from me, like she was expecting my call. "Feel like coming over?"

"Sure," I said. So it was as simple as that? I hung up the phone. Something felt unreal. Was it just me? I finished the popcorn and headed out. Maybe everything was fine between us, I thought as I walked across town. Maybe my fears that she'd get back together with Frank were unfounded.

And maybe they weren't. Was she asking me over to tell me that her feelings had changed? Surely not.

How well did I know Holly? Suppose she did want to break up? I had no idea how she'd go about it.

She greeted me with a hug. I leaned forward and kissed her lightly on the lips. Her eyes were welcoming, although, as usual, I couldn't make out what was going on under the surface. She leaned up and kissed me gently. I felt at a loss, and hugged her again.

"We could take a hot tub," she said.

I nodded, glad to have a plan. She led me through the house and onto the back deck. We lifted the lid, and a wisp of steam rose into the cool night. Holly lit a couple of candles, and we slipped out of our clothes and into the water. She leaned back onto the rim of the tub. "When I left Colorado, this is what I was looking for," she said.

I looked at her, wondering if she meant the hot tub, me, or both. I still felt uneasy. Should I bring up our relationship? Or just try to relax and enjoy the evening? I groped in the water for a seat. "This is harder than I thought," I said, not quite sure what I meant.

"What is?" She looked at me carefully. "Is there something you're wanting to ask me?"

"Well," I said, not sure how to answer, "I guess I'm wondering how it went with Frank."

She looked into the night. "Really nice. In some ways, we're growing apart. But in others, I feel so close to him."

I nodded quietly and didn't reply.

Holly looked at me. "If what you're asking is whether Frank and I might get back together —"

I tensed.

"— that's not going to happen, Jeff. I love him, but there were reasons we broke up, and they're still there."

I took a slow breath. Did I want to know the details? Yeah, in a way. But the night was short. This was a time for me and Holly. Enough about Frank.

We sat silently, submerged to our chests in the warm water. I bent over and kissed her cheek. She leaned her head against my shoulder and rubbed my leg gently. A warm breeze rustled the tall trees along the back fence. Overhead, a sprinkling of stars glimmered through the haze. Had Berkeley ever been more beautiful?

Thursday, October 28, 1982

It was just before Halloween when Change of Heart Cluster gathered for the first time since the June blockade. Holly's AG, Duck and Cover, had called the cluster meeting to start planning for the Vandenberg action, which was just three months away.

I remembered the Livermore blockade back in June — meeting my affinity group two days before the action. What a distance I'd traveled.

The cluster meeting was at Doc and Belinda's house in the Castro district of San Francisco. Holly and Karina and I rode over with Sara, who wasn't in the cluster but was going to a poetry reading at Modern Times bookstore after dropping us off.

The three of them talked about the Spiral Dance, a Wiccan ritual they were going to on Saturday night. Karina, up front next to Sara, turned in her seat to face Holly and me. "Our circle is building the south altar. We're invoking fire and passion."

"Actually," Sara said, glancing at us in the rearview mirror, "if you know anyone who has a red bodysuit, we need to borrow a few. We're going to dance around the altar with red veils before the ritual."

"We should paint our bodies red and do it nude," Karina said. I studied her profile. Her jaw jutted out, and she had a bright, expectant look on her face.

Sara shook her head. "You can do it, but I'm wearing a bodysuit."

We got to the City early, and decided to walk through the neighborhood. Sara and Karina made last-minute plans, then kissed a long goodbye. Holly put her arm around me, and we kissed, too. "It's a double date," Holly whispered in my ear.

As Sara drove off, we headed down Castro Street, the heart of Gay culture in the City. It was dusk after a warm day. The big neon sign of the Castro Theater shed a soft glow over the Scarecrows, Dorothys, and Wicked Witches waiting in line for the "Sing-Along Wizard of Oz."

Across the street, Halloween looked to be getting an early start as men in elaborate and risqué outfits sauntered up the sidewalk to the cheers and catcalls of bystanders.

"This is nothing compared to Halloween night itself," Karina told us. "Last year, Castro Street was closed for three blocks, and all the side streets, too. It drives the cops crazy."

We turned off Castro onto Nineteenth. After a few small storefronts, the

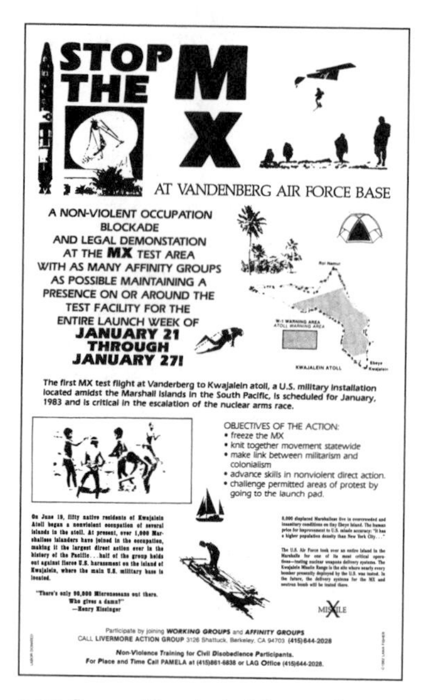

LAG flyers seldom lacked for words, as this Vandenberg leaflet shows.

block turned residential, lined with old Victorians. Doc greeted us as we climbed the stairs to his flat. He flashed his bright orange fingernails for our inspection. Despite his flowing hair and long gray beard, Doc presented a fairly low-key demeanor, and the orange nails jumped out. "Halloween is my favorite holiday," he said as he welcomed us. "I can let out a part of myself that I spent years hiding."

"Yeah, let it out," Karina said, throwing her arms around him.

Twenty people from seven AGs gathered in Doc's front room. It wasn't a huge room to begin with, and overflowing bookshelves and record bins made it seem even smaller. Luckily, a wide doorway let a few people stand in the hallway. The rest of us filled two old couches, and a few sat on cushions in front of a bay window overlooking the street.

I knew about half of the people present, mainly men: Hank, Walt, Doc, Antonio, and Daniel. Among the ten women, I recognized only Holly, Karina, and Cindy.

We spent a little while checking in, then pitched into the Vandenberg action. Spokescouncils for the action had started up, every other Saturday. A number of us from Change of Heart had been at the first one. It had been unfocused, spending five hours and accomplishing little beyond agreeing on an agenda and facilitators for the next meeting.

But the spokescouncil was memorable on other grounds. One of my few political heroes had stopped by the meeting: Daniel Berrigan, the dissident priest. I'd heard of his protests since I was a teenager first coming into political awareness. He and other religious activists did "Plowshares" actions where they went into military offices and poured blood on files, or broke into assembly plants and hammered on nuclear missiles.

His anti-war actions reached me in Indiana and helped rouse me from my patriotic upbringing. If someone believed enough in peace to go to jail for months or years, maybe I should be listening.

Berrigan's visit t0 the spokescouncil was a surprise. There were fifty of us at the meeting, and we had a spirited talk with him about tactics and organizing. He was about to go on trial with several other activists for hammering on missile nosecones at the Electric Boat plant in Connecticut.

"We couldn't do that," someone said. "LAG's nonviolence guidelines say, 'No Property Destruction.'"

"A missile is not property," Berrigan answered. "What's 'proper' about a nuclear weapon?" We laughed, but he pursued the point. "Property means something that is proper to human beings. So I don't think that it's 'property damage' to hammer on a missile whose purpose is to destroy human life, or to break a window to gain access to it."

We started discussing it again at the cluster meeting, till Cindy called our attention back to the agenda. She was working on the handbook for the Vandenberg action, and gave us a background report on the MX. The new missile would have multiple nuclear warheads capable of striking Soviet targets with extreme accuracy, dramatically destabilizing the balance of terror.

The MX still required a series of test firings, though. The Democrat-controlled Congress, despite caving in to every military funding request that the Reagan administration put forward, had approved only limited initial funds for the MX. If we could successfully delay the tests, Congress might yet find the stomach to say no to the Pentagon and the military corporations.

Ideas for the January action started to fly, but Cindy had one last item in her report. "We need to remember that the MX test schedule is just tentative," she said. "We should be prepared in case the test is delayed."

"Prepared for what?" Hank asked. "We're not going to delay our action, are we? There's still plenty there to protest."

Everyone agreed with him, although one woman said she'd probably wait to get arrested until they

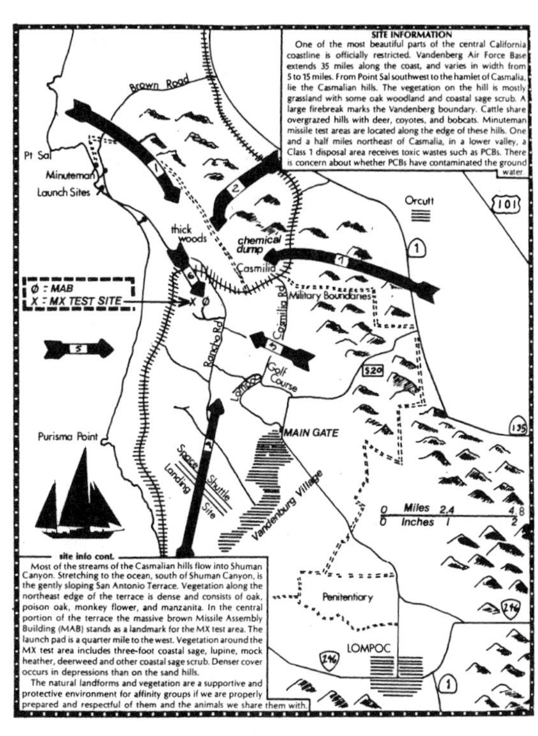

Vandenberg Action Coalition activists studied Vandenberg AFB and produced this site map, which guided protesters at the January, March, and June actions.

actually tried to test the MX. "I only get two weeks vacation all year," she explained.

"Well, so far *Aviation Week* says that the preparations are running right on time," Cindy assured us.

"Great," Karina piped up, "World War III is right on schedule."

We moved on into reports on the rally and campsite. VAC was trying to get farmland near the base to set up an encampment modeled after the 1981 Diablo action, a place where AGs could meet and network before going onto the base, and where support people could stay during the legal proceedings. "It's been hard finding land," Doc reported. "The FBI is talking to local farmers and scaring them out of letting us use their property. But the folks in Action for Peace and Disarmament down in San Luis Obispo are working on it."

Karina was next with the scenario report. She was kneeling on the floor in front of an old green couch. "This action is ideal for a backcountry occupation," she reported as she passed out a xeroxed map. She pointed to the upper portion of the map. "Most of the north area is wilderness. It's not even fenced in. We could go on the base at night, take cover during the day when they're searching for us, and move again at night. Even if they spot people by helicopter, it may be hard to get to us, since there are hardly any roads through the backcountry."

"I have a question," I said. "How bad is the poison oak?"

"Face it," Hank spoke up, "You can't go backcountry down there without running into poison oak."

That squelched some of my enthusiasm. I was willing to risk a lot for world peace. But poison oak?

Several other people looked just as queasy. Doc pointed out that even a blockade at the main entrance would disrupt the base and call attention to the arms race. But most of the cluster still favored a backcountry plan.

Walt was working on the legal collective for the action. "The key legal issue will probably be whether or not you are arrested on Air Force property. For people who blockade the road outside the base, it's the same as at Livermore — state charges. People who are arrested inside the gate will probably get federal trespass charges. If you go backcountry, trespass is also likely, but you may be risking additional charges like obstruction of federal property."

"What about a trespassing charge? What would we get for that?" Cindy asked.

"It's hard to say. There aren't a lot of precedents for mass arrests on military bases. But for a first offense, about two weeks seems likely."

"Two weeks?" Everyone started talking. It was a long stint, but for most people, two weeks seemed tolerable, especially if we were kept together.

"There's one other possibility," Walt added. "It's this thing called ban-and-bar, where they give you a written warning and throw you off the base. You go free at the moment, but they can hold it over you if you get busted there again. It's a way for them to avoid the immediate legal hassles."

"Not for long," Antonio said emphatically. "We'd return and occupy it again. We are not going away." A ripple of approval ran through the room.

Doc gave the Vandenberg work group report, and took a dig at Coordinating Council for trying to control the organizing. I started to respond, but most people seemed ready for the meeting to end, so I let it pass.

International Day was the final topic of the meeting. Holly gathered her papers. "A dozen groups from across the country and in England have already pledged to do local actions next June, and a lot more are discussing it. Members of the work group will be traveling around the U.S. and Canada over the next few months to meet with groups that responded to our first mailing. And Les and Aurora are planning a trip to Europe to network with peace groups there."

Few stop-signs in Berkeley lack a political footnote.

Holly passed around copies of the latest draft of the International Day Call. "The Call is still being hashed out," she said. "We need to get it mailed out soon, but if you have feedback, we're still open."

People gathered in a closing circle, arms around each other. "Should we sing a song?" someone asked.

"Wait," Karina jumped in, "I have something I forgot to announce. My affinity group is organizing an action next Saturday night. We have these bright red bumper stickers that say 'The Arms Race' that we're going to stick across the bottom of every stop sign in Berkeley. Here's a photo of one we did as a test. We need a lot of people, so tell your AGs."

The meeting broke up, but most people hung around talking for another fifteen minutes. Finally the last of us stepped out onto the sidewalk. The night had cooled, and I pulled on my sweatshirt. Up ahead of us, Hank called: "Is everyone going to go out next Tuesday and vote?"

"Yes, teacher!" Karina called back.

I wondered if they actually would. I planned to vote, but it was funny how little anyone I knew talked about the election. If you can *do* politics, why bother talking about Republicans and Democrats?

Daniel gave Holly and me and a woman named Megan a ride, steering his old Buick station wagon through the Mission district toward the freeway entrance. Daniel and I rode in the front, Holly and Megan in the back of the big family car.

Daniel was in his mid-thirties, married, and the father of a two-year-old boy. Holly liked Daniel, but I hadn't warmed to him. When we talked, I felt put down. Partly it came from Daniel having a Ph.D. in Medieval literature, whereas I had dropped out of grad school and was studying history on my own. But it also related to the imperious way he dismissed Marxism, as if it were some simplistic prejudice that mature minds had cast aside. I was no hardcore Bolshevik or anything, but I had read Lenin and Trotsky and Gramsci, and it rankled me to hear them dismissed out of hand. I wasn't sorry to have him and Holly do the talking.

Holly sat in the back seat sorting index cards on her lap. "We're pasting up the first LAG Rag this Sunday," she said. "We need to have an International Day article."

Daniel gave a wry laugh. "Maybe we should reprint all the arguments over the International Day Call. Of course, that would fill the whole paper, and I don't see where it's gotten us. I have a hard time grasping the objections."

His tone goaded me out of my silence. Claudia and Mort had voiced major objections to the Call, and I shared them. "I don't think it's a big mystery," I put in. "The new-age tone annoys people."

"Yes," he replied, "I suspect what they'd prefer is a bland, voiceless piece of traditional leftist rhetoric."

"It's not about rhetoric," I said. "It's the content. There's no mention of any sort of oppression or injustice, no sense of conflict."

"That's because we're speaking about fundamental levels of being, not about humans' narrow perceptions," Daniel said flatly.

"Conflict seems pretty fundamental to me," I came back. "Workers and owners, tenants and landlords — these aren't superficial distinctions. It's reality."

Daniel tilted his head back slightly, keeping his eyes on the road. "Of course such conflicts exist," he said. "But I don't subscribe to the viewpoint that contradictions and oppositions between humans are inherent."

"Okay, maybe conflict isn't some inherent, unchangeable part of human nature," I said, warming to the debate. "But we're born into a world that is divided. We live in a world of polarities that we didn't create and can rarely escape."

He nodded knowingly. "Yet look closely at any so-called polarity, and it dissolves into a complex array of individual actions and motivations. Reality is overwhelmingly complicated. Any approach that starts from the idea that there is an 'enemy' to fight against is wrong. That's why nonviolence is so important. Moving beyond dichotomies and polarities is the underlying assumption of nonviolence."

"Maybe for nonviolence as a morality. As a tactic — "

"I was never interested in nonviolence as a mere tactic," he interrupted. "As a tactic, it's just another transitory device. It doesn't operate for basic change. As an ethos, it has the possibility of fundamentally altering the world."

I felt like we'd gotten away from the original issue: conflict. I tried a different approach. "Isn't a group that does direct action implicitly acknowledging conflict? It's hard to blockade someone without entering into conflict."

"I'm not arguing that the world is or can be free of conflict," he said. "The question is, how fundamental is this opposition? Most dichotomies are a function of limited perception."

"Limited perception? That's easy for us to say. What about the civil war in El Salvador? The army has killed fifty thousand people in the past decade. That has nothing to do with limited perception. You get to the hills and pick up a gun, or you'll be murdered in your home."

"Now you're positing that there's only one alternative," he said imperturbably. "Submission or violence. There are other ways."

Although I tried to clarify my point, he out-talked me. "For instance," he said, "Nonviolent organizing groups are working to protect the rainforests in Brazil. Of course, you may end up dead that way, too."

It still seemed that he was avoiding the core issue. I thought about reading Trotsky the previous year. "Aren't there moments of crisis," I said, "when the blurred lines and ambiguities become very clear, and you're either striking a deal with the ruling class, or you're rebelling and you're in great danger? Aren't there times in history when the polarities are objective? That's the question."

"But what are these polarities?"

"To submit or to fight."

"To stay and fight involves a wide range of choices."

"Sure — but the choices are no longer to 'appreciate the complexity of the situation.'"

For the first time, Daniel was ruffled. "I object to that," he said with evident restraint. "This is not a patrician position. I think you would find plenty of so-called proletarians who realize that things are a lot more complicated than the simplistic rhetoric of American leftists. If you look at a situation like the civil war in El Salvador, if you look at the actual individuals, you'll see that the ties of friendship and family cut across the supposedly clear lines of the conflict. Human reality exceeds all our boxes. And it's not just philosophizing to say that. It's a description of how people actually experience the world."

I didn't have an answer. Daniel settled back into his usual professorial mode as he turned off the freeway into Berkeley. "This is the problem that the traditional left has in communicating with the public," he said. "Marxist analysis is so remote from how life feels. It doesn't speak to the reality of people's daily lives. We have to learn to speak in a language that touches people's hearts."

Holly, whom I didn't even realize was listening, leaned up between the seats. "The vision of International Day is aimed at people outside traditional left circles, people of ecological consciousness, people who have a holistic view of the world. People like that are rising up all over the planet. That's who our Call will reach."

I shook my head. "But how is a new-age Call going to work as far as building a local coalition? Mort said he'd be embarrassed to take it to the Central America support groups."

Daniel sighed. "I don't especially want to work with those traditional White leftist groups," he answered. "The forms in which they operate are an obstacle. I'm not looking for a coalition. I want people to get involved directly in our actions."

It seemed like a hopeless disagreement. I knew how Mort and Claudia felt, and Daniel was intransigent. I didn't envy Holly's having to try to resolve it at the next International Day meeting.

As Daniel pulled up in front of my apartment building, he changed the subject. "Holly tells me that you're interested in Medieval and Renaissance music. I have a fairly extensive record collection from my academic days that you might want to look through. You're welcome to borrow and tape them."

"Thanks," I said, struck by his generosity. "I have a few that you might not have, too."

As Daniel drove off, Holly turned to me and smiled. She put her hand gently on my arm. "I guess I just assumed it was okay for me to spend the night with you," she said.

"Sure," I said. We stopped outside the front door and hugged. My chest tingled with the warmth of her embrace, and I took a deep breath. "Sure," I whispered. "You can stay here anytime."

Tuesday, November 9, 1982

ELECTION DAY brought a big victory for the local progressive slate, Berkeley Citizens Action. Despite being heavily outspent by the landlord's party, BCA held the mayor's office and captured most of the seats on the city council, rent board, and school board.

Holly and I got up in the middle of the night to go "door-knobbing," hanging slate-cards on every doorknob in our precinct, and I felt like I was part of the victory. Part of the vanguard. Let the media make fun of "far out" Berkeley — we were forging the path of resistance to Reaganism. How long till the rest of the country followed?

The question clearly alarmed the rest of Alameda County, and the suburban majority on the Board of Supervisors took up the struggle. Sorely vexed that some demonstrators in Berkeley had burned an American flag and gone unchastised, the County Supes ordered the Berkeley city council to humiliate itself by reciting the Pledge of Allegiance at the beginning of its meetings. The city council naturally refused, and the Berkeley school board entered the fray by voting that the purchase of state-mandated American flags for the classrooms would be given the "lowest priority" in the new budget.

Into the heated controversy stepped the newly-formed Commie Dupes affinity group, who decided to honor the supervisors with a special musical visit. Cindy from my old AG was in the Dupes, and invited me to join the chorus. Given how little singing I'd had time for lately, it sounded like fun, even if the dress code was a stretch: "We want to make a good impression on the suburban supervisors," Cindy said.

Now there was a challenge. Luckily, Holly's housemate Randall loaned me a dinner jacket that was only a little too small. I scored a pair of slacks and a button shirt for two dollars at a thrift shop on Telegraph, and I was styling.

Catching BART during the crush of the morning commute was a wake-up call. I arrived in downtown Oakland jostled and craving sugar. I found a donut shop and got a couple to go, then made my way to the Board of Supervisors' chambers.

Our crowd, seated together on the left side of the room, numbered two dozen. And a nattily-attired group it was. Most of the men were wearing ties and jackets. Daniel sported a monogrammed handkerchief in his pocket. Women wore gowns and make-up, and a few were in high heels.

Cindy handed me a songsheet of patriotic classics. I scanned the lyrics, confident I knew most of them by heart. It would feel good to be singing, no matter what the content. It felt like weeks since I'd really opened up my voice.

At nine o'clock on the dot, the supervisors emerged from backstage and stepped to their places on the podium. The audience rose to recite the Pledge of Allegiance.

I kept my eye on Cindy, figuring she knew the timing. Along with the rest of the crowd, she recited the Pledge. I followed along, saying by rote the words I'd mouthed every day in grade school.

As everyone else sat down, we remained standing. Cued by Daniel's rich baritone, we launched into "My Country 'tis of Thee." Others in the crowd, no doubt impressed by our fashion finery, joined in. Up on the podium, the supervisors reacted with surprise and pleasure. A couple sang along.

We worked our way through "You're a Grand Old Flag" and several verses of "America the Beautiful." The supervisors looked irritated, and a couple besmirched their reputations by conferring with anxious aides during our performance. But when we struck up the "Star-Spangled Banner," everyone in the room dutifully rose and faced the flag with hand over heart through all four stanzas.

We could have held the supervisors captive all day by repeating verses, but we were holding up the meeting for everyone else as well. As the strains of the national anthem faded, Cindy stepped forward and faced the dais. "We'll stop imposing our patriotic gestures on you — and we call on you to do the same. Patriotism should be a voluntary act, not a display mandated by the government."

We applauded her words as we filed out of the room. And I heard more than a few people in the audience applauding, too.

Monday, November 15, 1982

THE HIGHLIGHT of the next couple of weeks was an action at Livermore by Pilgrim and Imagine affinity group. Their AG had been doing monthly leafletting at the Lab since Spring, keeping the protests visible.

Apparently too visible. In September, Lab security warned Imagine to stay clear of the entrance gates or face arrest.

That was the wrong threat to make to Pilgrim, who counted the June blockade as his thirty-first career bust, and had notched number thirty-two with the Walnettos in October. Once he heard about the ban on leafletting, he and his AG announced the date for their return visit, and asked other LAGers to come out and support them.

Mort, Hank, and I took the afternoon off and rode out to the Lab together. A light drizzle coated us as we stood along the roadside holding signs, waiting for Pilgrim and Imagine to finish their last-minute planning. In the crowd of twenty supporters I spied Monique and Melissa, but no one else I knew.

Traffic was sparse, and I walked over to where Melissa was holding one end of a banner. It was the first time I had seen her since her arrest at the October demo. She had been away visiting her family, and although I knew she'd gotten out of jail okay, I hadn't heard anything else about it.

"Hey Jeff, I saw the LAG Rag," she said as I approached. "It looks great."

I welcomed her praise, proud that she knew I'd been involved. Holly, Caroline, and I had coordinated the all-day production marathon, and I also wrote a short critique of the Freeze campaign. The paper turned out to be eight pages, since on production day we wound up with twice as much material as would fit into the four pages we had planned. Not bad, eight pages. That was no newsletter — that was practically a newspaper.

I buttoned my jacket against the misty rain, and asked Melissa what had happened after her arrest at the October demo.

"Wow, that seems like a long time ago," she said. She gazed into the distance. "I was just fed up with their trying to tell us where we could and couldn't protest. You know what was funny, though — when they took me in for booking, there were all these tables set up with fingerprinting pads and stuff. They were obviously ready to arrest us all if they had to!"

"Sounds like we've got them worried," I said. "Do you still have to go to court?"

"No," Melissa said scornfully. "I didn't commit any crime, so they never filed any charges. It was just harassment."

"Typical," said Mort, who had put down his sign and joined us. "The point is to grind us down."

Melissa got me to hold her banner-pole while she tied on a scarf to keep her head dry. "So how are other things going with LAG since I left?" she asked. "Daniel told me that the International Day Call got mailed out."

LAG RAG

LIVERMORE ACTION GROUP NEWSPAPER

50¢

INSIDE:

Non-Violence Code on Property

THANKSGIVING ACTION

BAY AREA CALENDAR

VANDENBERG MEETING

OCTOBER 9TH

INTERNATIONAL DAY

Spokes Meeting

CISPES RALLY

SING-ALONG

Introducing Our Newspaper . . .

LAG Rag #1, November 1982

"The Call!" Mort said. "Four pages of new-age drivel."

Melissa recoiled. "I thought the Call was beautiful when I read it," she said.

"Sure, as poetry," Mort said. "It just happens to completely disregard reality. Every problem in the world is reduced to individual motivations. There's no awareness of class conflict or the control of wealth and resources. New-age 'no conflict' ideology is totally irrelevant to most political groups. There's no way we can build a local coalition around it."

I didn't disagree, but I wished Mort would tone it down a notch. I could imagine how this played out at International Day meetings: Mort going off about power and class, Daniel dismissing it all as superannuated leftism, Mort sputtering back about privilege and analysis, Daniel rolling his eyes.... And Holly wedged between the two of them, trying to get some work done.

"Maybe the Call isn't perfect," Melissa said, taking the banner-pole back. "But we have to put forward a vision. After the June blockade, people around the country are looking to us. If we put out a proposal, it might catch on."

"And then what," Mort said impatiently. "There's this fantasy that we'll do International Day year after year, and the blockades will get bigger and bigger until the arms race ends and the government collapses and we all live happily ever after. What a strategy! Growth means a lot more than bigger numbers.

There's this naive idea that if enough people do civil disobedience, the government will be paralyzed. As if the government needs our consent to operate! Even if they did, they wouldn't ask for it — they'd manufacture it."

Melissa started to say something about keeping faith, when someone from her AG interrupted her. Mort seemed satisfied with himself. I thought again of Holly trying to mediate the disputes, and asked Mort if he had raised these issues with Daniel outside of meetings.

"Oh, I've tried," he said with a wave of his hand. "It's pointless. Any criticism is taken as an attack. It would just turn into a fight."

I looked away in silence. With that attitude, it probably would, I thought. I had a hard time listening to his attacks on International Day and Holly's work.

Just then Monique caught my attention. I started to say hi, but she cut me off. "People in my affinity group were really upset over your Freeze article in the LAG Rag," she said sharply. "A lot of them worked on the Freeze."

I groped for a response. What could I say? Knowing that the referendum had passed, I felt free to vent my true feelings. I called the Freeze a distraction from real organizing, and accused it of sucking energy into a non-binding advisory measure that the government would completely ignore. Not that I didn't believe those words. But my face reddened as I recalled being mad at Mort for attacking other people's work.

"I was criticizing the electoral system," I said apologetically. "It wasn't meant as an attack on individuals."

"Well, that's how they took it," Monique answered. "The Freeze got a lot of new people involved in the peace movement, and they felt like the LAG Rag was minimizing their contributions. Nuclear weapons are the single biggest problem facing the world today. We don't need divisiveness. We've got to work with anyone who will join us."

I shuffled uncomfortably. I wanted the paper to reach out to all blockaders, to pull people together, not cleave to a purist line. "Maybe you could write up the other side of the argument," I offered.

"I'll think about it," she tossed back as she walked away. I took a deep breath. Next time, think before you pop off, I told myself. I didn't want to jeopardize the paper's support by having it — or myself — seen as representing one viewpoint or clique.

Imagine AG finally broke from their huddle. The rest of us shored up our picket line and held our signs high as six men and two women came up the roadside toward us. Pilgrim, full of bustling vitality, was out in front in his usual jeans and flannel shirt. His sparse white hair jutted out of a bright red

Imagine affinity group organized many small actions at Livermore Lab, particularly involving leafletting rights. April Fool's Day was another Imagine favorite.

headband. As he reached our lines he turned, and his AG joined hands in a circle for a moment. Then, armed with leaflets and xeroxes of anti-nuke articles, they strode up to the Lab gate.

One of the cops at the guardhouse ambled over, wearing a tired smile. "You're not planning to get arrested again today, are you, Pilgrim?"

"No, officer, just came to exercise our right to pass out a few leaflets."

"Do you have a permit to do that?"

"Sure have," Pilgrim said politely.

"Let's see it."

"It's called the United States Constitution, first amendment."

The cop shook his head. "Not good enough. If you attempt to distribute any materials we'll have to arrest you."

Pilgrim reached into his sidebag. "Would you like a leaflet, officer?"

The police quickly took Pilgrim and the others into custody. The arrests didn't come as a shock to anyone, least of all the AG, who planned to plead not-guilty and try to get a trial.

"There's a good chance of them winning, or of getting the charges dropped," Melissa said as we gathered up the signs and banners afterward. "They can't stop you from leafletting in a public space. It's still a free country."

"Appreciate it while you can," Mort tossed out.

"Yeah," Hank said. "1984 is coming up fast."

We hit the highway back to Berkeley. Hank and Mort planned to get a burrito, pick up a six-pack, and play some pinball at Hank's shop. "I just got El Dorado working," Hank told us. "Fastest flippers in the house."

I had reserved the evening for reading and guitar, but I figured I could hang out with them for a while. I pictured Hank's shop as a mytho-poetic lair of flashing pinball lights and 1960s paraphernalia. When we arrived, what I saw was a dilapidated twenty-foot-square building with cinder block walls, whitewashed wooden rafters, and a corrugated roof. In the middle was a big steel workbench, surrounded by the tools of the trade. Beyond a row of acetylene torches and metal scraps, a bunch of banged-up old arcade games lined two walls. Several had their playing fields tilted open to expose the under-wiring. In front of one machine was a big cardboard box overflowing with tools and wire.

Hank walked past the workbench, reached behind a toolbox, and flipped a switch. Miraculously, the place sprang to life. A dozen classic pinball machines filled the room with twinkling colored light. A Wurlitzer in the corner started playing "Jumpin' Jack Flash" by the Rolling Stones. Neon signs glowed on the walls, along with an animated display of a waterfall filling a Schlitz beer mug.

Hank opened a small refrigerator under one of the machines and handed each of us a Pilsner.

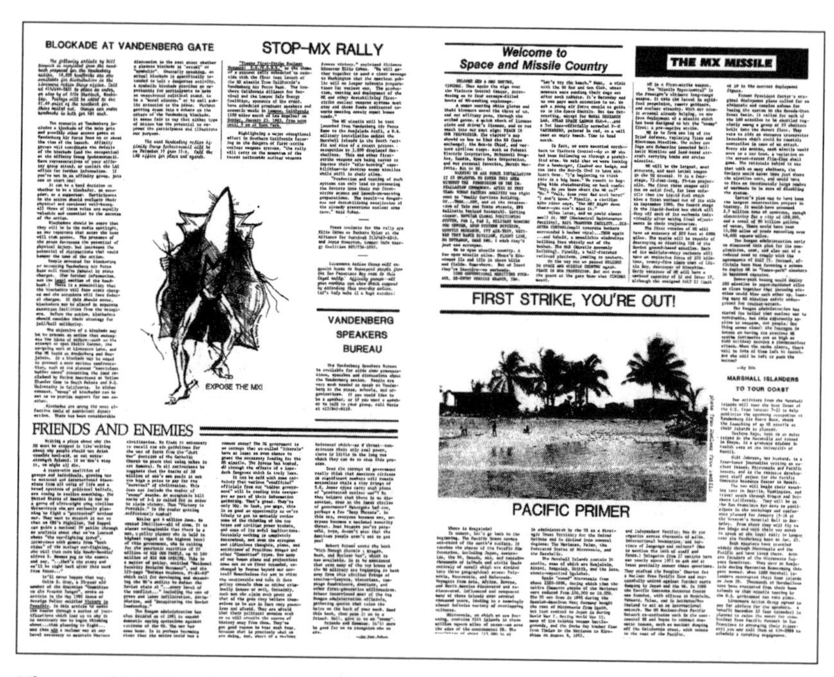
BLOCKADE AT VANDENBERG GATE

STOP-MX RALLY

EXPOSE THE MX!

VANDENBERG SPEAKERS BUREAU

FRIENDS AND ENEMIES

Welcome to Space and Missile Country

THE MX MISSILE

FIRST STRIKE, YOU'RE OUT!

MARSHALL ISLANDERS TO TOUR COAST

PACIFIC PRIMER

The second LAG Rag featured two pages of articles on different aspects of the Vandenberg action — a forerunner of later "theme sections."

"The games are all wired to play for free," Mort told me. "Just push the reset button."

"That's great," I said. "These things used to bust my budget."

Hank tinkered with the wiring on one of the open machines. "The idea is to restore them, then convert them from bloodsucking capitalist mercenaries into socialist workers at the service of true revolutionaries everywhere."

I laughed. "What a noble mission!"

We played a few rounds on different machines, my favorite being Queen of Diamonds, which I remembered from my teenage years. Between games, Mort pulled out one of the largest joints I'd ever seen, lit it up, and passed it to me.

"Hey, we forgot the train," Hank said as he passed the joint back to Mort. He went over by the jukebox and flipped a few switches. Above the machines a model railroad engine chugged into gear, hauling several cars in its wake. Between a couple of boxcars was a silver missile launcher with an American flag on the side.

"Every model train should have one," I said.

"Check out the last car," Hank said. "A friend of mine from Earth First! just gave it to me." I took a closer look. Neatly stacked on the yellow flatcar was a load of clear-cut timber, heading for the market.

"What's next," Mort said, "a nuclear waste car?"

We shot pinball for another hour. Hank and Mort talked about going to a movie, but I decided to head home.

"Where's Holly?" Mort asked.

"Holly? I'm not sure," I said. "She has a friend visiting from England. I didn't talk to her today."

"Oh, that's right. I was thinking that you two lived together."

His comment was innocent, but it hit home. I'd been thinking of asking Holly to live with me lately. I imagined how it would be if she were at home, and I were heading back to spend the rest of the evening with her, talking, listening to music, making love.

If I knew she'd say yes, I'd have asked her already. But Mort's remark triggered the other side, the reality that she had other friends, other commitments, and a house she considered her home. Did I expect her to give it up and move into my box-like apartment? It wasn't impossible. Just steep odds. Was I ready to risk asking?

Thanksgiving Day, 1982

HOLLY AND I were seeing each other two or three nights a week, sleeping over at her place or mine. But it was rare that we spent a whole day together. She mentioned going to the Native American Un-Thanksgiving at La Peña, but I wanted to set aside the day for just the two of us.

Holly sometimes spent holidays with her family in Colorado, but stayed in Berkeley for this one. Myself, I hadn't gone home for a holiday since my freshman year in college. Drinking whiskey and watching football on TV wasn't my idea of a Great American Tradition I wanted to perpetuate.

Still, as a young kid worshipping God and Country, Thanksgiving had been my favorite holiday. I devoured tales of the American Revolution — Ben Franklin, Samuel Adams, Betsy Ross, Paul Revere, John and Abigail Adams — never doubting that their legacy lived on in our times, that my country really was the land of justice and freedom, and that our disproportionate wealth was a divinely-ordained reward for the truth and light we brought into the world.

Coming of age toward the end of the Vietnam era, I'd let go of most of that baggage. But Thanksgiving was still a romantic season for me.

Lately I was dreaming a lot about living with Holly — how great it would be to spend every night with her, to see her every day without making special plans. A week or so earlier, while we were out on a nighttime walk, I asked her in a roundabout way if she'd thought about it.

Ocean Beach shorebirds enjoy dinner at low tide.

She took my hand and turned to face me. Her hand felt warm in mine. "I really like being with you, Jeff," she said. "I'm committed to our relationship. But I'm not sure I'm ready to live with a lover again. I think I need the challenge and support of a collective house." She paused and looked directly into my eyes. "But I want you to know that I love you."

Under a corner streetlight we hugged. I pressed Holly to me, feeling the warmth of the best relationship I'd been in since college.

But afterward I wished I'd been more direct. She hadn't exactly said "no" to my question. Maybe if she knew how much I wanted her. How much I wanted to know that at the end of the day, whatever else had happened, we'd be lying in bed together...

For Thanksgiving, we planned a trip to the ocean, followed by dinner at my place. We met at noon, and by one o'clock we were rolling through San Francisco's Sunset district on a sparsely-populated Muni train. Retail shops mixed with houses lined our route. The buildings got progressively smaller as we approached the ocean.

The train let us out at the four-lane road that cut the beach off from the rest of the City. We made it across the road, crested the iceplant-covered dunes, and looked out over the ocean. From the boundless west, low waves washed onto the beach. The sun sparkled against the cool blue sky, scattering patches of emerald green amid the white of the surf.

To the north, where a craggy promontory rose, breakers dashed against rock-islands jutting out of the sea. On the tip of the promontory was perched the Cliff House, a nondescript commercial building that added a quirky touch to the picture. Beyond the Cliff House, a patch of low-lying fog was gathering. Beautiful as the blue sky was, I almost wanted the fog to roll in and give the day more of a gray Thanksgiving feel.

Holly and I stood at the edge of the dunes, gazing over the vast beach. I felt an impulse to go running down the sandy incline to the water, but Holly took my hand and steered us along a more leisurely route.

She was telling me about a guy named Jerald who had been arrested earlier in the week down at Vandenberg. "He was scouting out routes through the backcountry and the military police spotted him. He pled no contest and got ten days."

"Ten days," I repeated. "That's less than we were expecting. Not like it would be a picnic, but I think I could handle ten days, if it's with other protesters."

We strolled along the tide's edge. Holly looked out at the ocean. "The hardest part would be being away from the office for ten days. Every day there's something new to think about for International Day."

I nodded. Thinking about International Day was Holly's job. She had been hired along with Caroline as a LAG staffer. People at Coordinating Council were worried that we were already behind on pay to Craig and Claudia, but everyone agreed that we needed an International Day staffperson, and Holly was the obvious choice. After that, we had little option but to entrust Caroline with trying to raise the thousands of dollars we planned to spend in the next eight months.

Holly pitched into International Day with all her heart. She was out of bed at dawn every morning, brimming with purpose. It was a dream job for her, using her administrative skills to help organize an international peace protest.

Just before Thanksgiving she had visited DQ University, the Native American school near Sacramento, for an encampment and pow-wow. "We did some good networking for International Day," she said. "But mostly it was an honor to be included in the ceremonies. You would have loved the drummers and dancers. It was so beautiful, you could feel their kinship to the Earth, to the air, to growing things."

Holly stopped to tie a scarf around her head, and I put my arm around her shoulders. Even if I didn't share her enthusiasm for spirituality, I loved the softer, reflective facet that it brought out.

"You should write it up for the LAG Rag," I said.

"I was thinking about that," she said. "We should run it by other people."

"It's true, we already have a lot of stories." We'd held an editorial meeting for the upcoming issue and made a story list — a great leap forward from the spontaneous first edition. I took responsibility for a feature section on Vandenberg, with stories on the MX missile, the military and political background, and the action scenario.

"There's just one thing bugging me," I said, picking up a piece of driftwood and sidearming it out into the surf. "The name, 'LAG Rag.' It feels like a joke. I want the paper to have a serious name, something that says what we're about."

She smiled. "People like 'LAG Rag.' It's humble. You know what I want to bring up? Production process. The last issue was so frazzling, everyone racing in at the last minute and dropping their articles off." She gritted her teeth.

The "Dutch" Windmill in the northwest corner of Golden Gate Park, San Francisco, designed by Alpheus Bull, Jr. and completed in 1903.

"I kind of liked that frantic feeling," I confessed. "It felt like things were jumping."

"I know you liked it," she said in a bemused tone. "But it's not how most people like to work, especially when they're volunteering. Our lives are frantic enough." She stopped and took my hand. "Want to turn around and head back?"

We had walked a good distance down the beach, which stretched far to the south before ending at some low hills. We turned toward one another. I gazed into Holly's eyes, which radiated warmth. I soaked it in. She loved me, I couldn't doubt it.

And yet, however much affection her eyes conveyed, there was never urgency or need. Was something missing? Yet she seemed happy enough. She even told me recently that she and Frank had stopped sleeping together. Wasn't that what I wanted? Why couldn't I let go of the doubts?

We meandered along the wet sand at the tide line. Little shorebirds darted in and out of our squishy footprints, scouring the freshly-washed beach for their Thanksgiving dinner. Holly danced her fingers in imitation of the frenetic birds. "What hard work!"

To the north, beyond the promontory, fog was rolling in toward the Bay. But our part of the beach was still sunny. We were coming up on the southern corner of Golden Gate Park, a wild stretch that ran along the ocean for about half a mile. Near the edge of the park stood an old windmill with its arms removed. I was curious about the missing arms, and we hiked across the highway to inspect it.

The Cliff House, at the northern end of Ocean Beach. To its lower left, looking like a tiny temple, is the camera oscura room.

We entered the park and circled the thirty-foot wooden tower, which had been brought over from Holland years earlier. The arms, made of huge beveled beams connected by lighter latticework, were piled up on the ground. "What a work of art." I said, inspecting them closely.

"And totally ecological," Holly said. "We haven't advanced over this."

"I wish it were working." I looked up at the dome-shaped top where the arms would have been mounted. The sky was still bright blue, but fog clouds were condensing and blowing past, forming a picturesque vista behind the wooden tower.

Camera oscura chamber, descended from a design by Leonardo da Vinci.

"I think the one at the other end of the park is working," Holly said.

"I never noticed that there were two," I said. "Let's go see it." We hiked north on a narrow trail that skirted the edge of the park, winding through scraggly underbrush and low, wind-gnarled trees. We talked about the windmills, thinking how they might have been made by our own European ancestors. In either of our genealogies might be a great windmill engineer.

"It's funny," I said, "I study history, but I never think about my own family line beyond my grandparents. I wonder what my ancestors were doing ten generations ago? I'd be curious to know."

"Rituals are good for that," Holly said matter-of-factly. "At the Spiral Dance last month, we did a trance-journey to the Isle of the Dead, and each of us called upon an ancestor."

I tried not to sound skeptical. "Did you hear anything?"

"I felt like I did," she said, seeming to gaze back to that moment. "I spoke with a peasant woman who raised ten children and became a village healer in her old age. I told her I didn't want to have children, but that I wanted to do healing work for the planet. I could tell she believed in me."

I noted Holly's calm, focused expression, and nodded silently. Talking to the ancestors? Well, who was I to doubt her? Holly wasn't prone to making wild claims.

We arrived at the second windmill, its arms attached and turning gracefully in the steady ocean wind. Against the backdrop of weathered trees, it looked like a huge creature guarding the entrance to the park. "No wonder Don Quixote thought they were alive," I said, tracing the circuit of the majestic arms.

"A windmill on the ocean probably never stops turning," Holly said. "Why doesn't every house in San Francisco have one? It would be free energy."

"That's just it," I said. "There's no profit in free energy."

The fog was taking hold, and the grayness of sky and ocean imparted an autumnal spirit. As we ascended the hill to the Cliff House, a wave of good feeling washed through me, and my earlier doubts ebbed. What a beautiful day.

We got juices at a café and went back outside. "Want to see if the camera oscura room is open?" Holly asked. She led me to a little round building below the Cliff House. The door was open, and we stepped through a curtain into a dark room. In the center, several people were gazing down into a shallow dish eight feet across, where a projection of the ocean was displayed so clearly that you could spot seagulls flying from rock to rock. "The light comes in through a tiny opening in the roof," a guide explained, his voice filling the dark chamber. "The image is projected by mirrors onto this dish. The camera oscura was developed by Leonardo da Vinci, the famous painter."

Back outside, I said to Holly, "Leonardo da Vinci, now there's a guy I could imagine as my ancestor."

"Maybe you could go to a ritual and talk to him," she suggested. I wasn't sure whether she was joking or not, but it made me smile. Go to a ritual and talk to Leonardo. There's an idea I had never considered.

We stayed a little longer, gazing out at the choppy gray waves. Finally we headed back toward Berkeley. The plan was to go to my apartment and have dinner, then over to her house to take a hot tub and spend the night.

Traveling through the transbay tunnel on BART, the train was too loud to talk, and we sat silently. I found myself thinking again about living with Holly, how nice it would be if we were heading "home" now.

It wasn't like she was holding me at a distance. Lately we had talked about forming an affinity group with Caroline, Walt, and a few other people that we actually had an affinity with, not just for the Vandenberg action, but as an ongoing support group. And working on the newspaper gave us our first shared project. Our activism was right in synch.

But I wanted more. I wanted to feel like we weren't just co-organizers, but that our lives were twining together. I loved being with Holly, loved how relaxed I felt whether we were alone or in a crowd. If we lived together, I thought, I'd feel her presence even when she wasn't around.

Dinner was simple. I had baked a turkey drumstick and some potatoes the day before, so all I had to do was heat some frozen corn and stovetop stuffing, open a can of cranberry sauce, and voila, Thanksgiving. Holly had brought some lentil soup and a salad. "I got us a vegan pumpkin pie, too," she said. "I'll heat it while we're eating."

We sat on the floor with the food in a circle around us. I put on a classical guitar tape, and Holly lit a couple of candles. I knelt and slipped my arms around her from behind, burrowing into her thick blonde hair to kiss her neck. She leaned back and squeezed my arms to her.

Right now, I thought. Here's the moment. Ask her to live with me.

I almost did. But with all the food ready, it didn't seem like the moment.

We ate our fill, and opened a bottle of wine. It was unusual for her to drink, but she sipped at a glass. Pushing the dishes aside, we stretched out on the carpet, quietly listening to the music. My eyes roved over the art prints on the wall, but my mind was still sifting through thoughts about Holly. A Bob Marley album played in the background. "I'm jammin'," he sang plaintively. "Hope you like jammin' with me."

Holly and I lay on our backs, our heads sharing a pillow. What if we were together like this every night? I looked over at Holly. Her eyes were closed. "Holly, I want to live with you, it's really important," I imagined saying.

No, I chided myself, be patient. Let her enjoy tonight just as it is, then ask her next time you see her.

I propped myself up on my elbow and gazed down at her. She opened her eyes and smiled. "Holly, it would be so wonderful to have you live here," I whispered. "Have you thought any more about it?"

She paused for just a moment. Her eyes moistened. "Yes," she said in a soft voice. "I'd like to."

A tear rolled down my cheek, and I held her to me. My heart swelled, not with giddiness, but with deep satisfaction.

We lay together on the carpet for a long while, holding each other. When the tape player clicked off, neither of us moved, and for once, I felt like I could live without music. I looked into Holly's eyes, drinking in their deep greenness, their steadiness and subtle twinkling. "I want you so much," I whispered.

She stroked my hair. "I knew the moment you spoke that I'd say yes," she said. "I love living at Urban Ecology, but I don't have time for that now that I'm working full-time for LAG. Still, I wasn't sure what I'd say until you asked again."

Asked again. I'd done it. Without knowing the answer. And look what happened.

We lay together a while longer. Finally she stretched and said, "If we're going back to my house, we better do it now, or I'll never make it."

She lay languidly on her back. I leaned over and kissed her. "We can take a hot tub this weekend," I said. "How about staying here tonight?"

Holly assented. We went out on the patio to get some fresh air. I gazed out across the Bay toward San Francisco, but Holly looked up at the moon. "Waxing," she said. "That's a good sign."

Monday, December 20, 1982

Stand on the moon and look at the Earth. In sunlight and solar wind it hangs, a pearl infinitely precious, whole and entire.

Stand on a mountaintop, stand by the sea. Land, air, water — they move round the great arch of Earth to meet themselves again.

About the globe the mantle of life clings, no less seamless than what it clothes. There are no breaks or barriers, only a million kinds of continuity.

Yet life threatens life with death. Human beings have distorted the variety of life into oppositions and polarities. Many have forgotten that life cannot be divided, only destroyed. In the pursuit of limited and local gains, we risk the loss of everything.

We are killing each other, and killing our planet. Everything we do affects all of us. We need to work together, consciously, for our common good.

— *from the International Day Call*

ANTONIO HANDED ME a crisply-printed copy of the final version of the International Day Call as I reached the top of the stairs.

"Thanks," I said. "Holly showed me a copy, it looks great." I remembered how excited Holly had been the day it came back from the printer, staying up late working on a mailing to dozens of activist groups.

The last Coordinating Council meeting of the year gathered at Melissa's house in the hazy zone between the Mission and Castro districts, where bookstores and burrito shops alternated with leather bars and artsy cafés. Melissa lived with five other high-powered activists in the upper flat of an old Victorian. She and her roommates were involved in so many projects that they were practically a coalition among themselves.

As we assembled for the meeting, one topic was on everyone's mind. We'd learned a couple of days earlier that the government had thrown the long-

A CALL FOR

INTERNATIONAL DAY OF NUCLEAR DISARMAMENT

JUNE 20, 1983

PROPOSAL:

A day of coordinated local actions around the world to resist nuclear arms and power, militarism, intervention, and their social and ecological consequences. People will use whatever nonviolent means they think appropriate—civil disobedience, strikes, marches, vigils, demonstrations, individual initiatives, etc.

OBJECTIVES:

To further the causes of 1) global nuclear disarmament, 2) demilitarization and non-intervention, 3) equitable distribution of wealth and resources within and among nations, and 4) a sustainable relationship between the human race and the planet.

To protest, halt, and disrupt the design, production, transport, and deployment of nuclear weapons worldwide for at least one working day.

INTRODUCTION

Stand on the moon and look at the earth. In sunlight and solar wind it hangs, a pearl infinitely precious, whole and entire.

Stand on a mountaintop; stand by the sea. Land, air, water—they move round the great arch of earth to meet themselves again. About the globe the mantle of life clings, no less seamless than what it clothes. There are no breaks or barriers, only a million kinds of continuity.

Yet life threatens life with death. Human beings have distorted the variety of life into oppositions and polarities. Many have forgotten that life cannot be divided, only destroyed. In the pursuit of limited and local gains, we risk the loss of everything.

We are killing each other, and killing our planet. Everything we do affects all of us. We need to work together, consciously, for our common good.

The roots of war are deep, and the A-bomb, the H-bomb and the neutron bomb are its most poisonous flowers. They must be eliminated, for they threaten the very existence of life on earth.

At the same time, if we hope to achieve a lasting peace, nuclear disarmament can only be the beginning, the necessary pre-condition, of a profound process of transformation and rebuilding.

The June 1982 U.N. Special Session on Disarmament demonstrated the unwillingness of the world's nuclear powers to disarm. It is clear that we cannot rely on governments to promote peace without serious pressure from their citizens. We as individuals, working with one another all over the earth, must take upon ourselves the responsiblity of stopping nuclear destruction.

On the days leading up to the Solstice in June 1983, we call for people all over the world to say NO to nuclear weapons and to the increasing world militarism which squanders precious resources needed for basic human necessities.

We call for, in fact, the celebration of an annual world holiday for peace and justice.

THE ISSUES

The threat of nuclear war increases each second. An emergency situation confronts us as the world's nuclear powers move closer to deploying first strike weapons, designed not to deter an attack but to launch one. Two of these weapons, the cruise missiles and the Pershing IIs, are slated for deployment in Europe this year, 1983. Plans to test the MX missile in the Pacific also continue for 1983. These dangerous plans must be resisted with all our will.

Funds for human needs are increasingly siphoned off for war preparation while world unemployment, malnutrition, infant mortality, lack of adequate housing, and other societal ills abound. We must work diligently to change the existing social, political, and economic order, nationally and internationally, wherever it fosters suffering and favors war.

Accelerating militarism increases the likelihood of war, and new "conventional" weapons make war much more violent. Military conscription forces young men, especially poor men, to coerce other people, to kill, and to die. The current military build-up pushes us toward destruction and away from a civilized, peaceable world.

Intervention in the domestic affairs of other countries is bringing death to hundreds of thousands of people each year, and untold misery to others. Wherever intervention exists, it must be opposed, and the right of people to self-determination affirmed.

Discrimination by race, class, sex, age, and religion, is reinforced by a militaristic world. To change that world, we must begin now to live as we would in a more equitable society, and to eliminate these inequities in our daily lives and institutions.

The opening page of the International Day Call, which was drafted by a LAG work group and sent out to grassroots groups around the world in Winter 1982-83.

Hundreds of groups responded, and over three hundred groups in North America, Europe, Japan, and Australia did events around Summer Solstice 1983. Over twenty groups did civil disobedience, some for the first time. See participants' list in Appendix.

Visit www.directaction.org for more information on the 1983 International Day of Nuclear Disarmament. Full text of the International Day Call in the Appendix.

feared monkey wrench into our Vandenberg organizing: the MX test was delayed. "You can't count on the government for anything," Claudia said in genuine aggravation as I sat down next to her on the couch.

We were meeting in the living room, already crowded with couches and cushions and now heaped with coats and scarves. Claudia, Daniel, and I sat on an old couch along the back wall. Holly, Hank, and Lois were on cushions on the floor, with Mort, Caroline, and Craig on the next couch. Walt and Antonio set up folding chairs by the door.

A minute later, Doc and Belinda stepped in, and the temperature in the room rose a couple of degrees. They represented VAC, which had been sending rotating spokes to our meetings for the last couple of months. Belinda eyed the room suspiciously before greeting Melissa. Doc took a seat next to me on the couch, and I welcomed him to the meeting. Being in Change of Heart, Doc and I had a special bond, even if we were on opposite sides in the Vandenberg disputes.

I was less excited about Belinda's presence. She sat with her feet planted firmly on the floor, one hand squarely on each knee, as if impatient for the meeting to begin. I knew she and Doc would go over the organizing with a fine-toothed anarchist comb. But in a way it was good to see both of them. What better evidence that despite all our differences, we were working together as the action approached?

Regardless of who attended, Coordinating Council always had its share of tense moments, as we hashed out every last detail of every conceivable topic. For me, it was a weekly seminar in grassroots organizing — how to get the next action together, how to pull a coalition together, how to keep LAG itself together.

And with the newspaper I'd found a niche. Several of us at the meeting were involved with the LAG Rag, but I was the one who kept track of the details and had the scoop on our production timeline. When people wanted to get something in the paper, they'd look to me to make a note.

Melissa brought in a tray with tea and coffee. People pulled their feet in, and she set the tray in the center. "Has everyone heard about the religious protests at the Lab this month?" she said as we got situated. "Today there was an AG that got arrested praying in the road outside the gate."

"Was that the Catholic Worker group?" Craig asked.

"No, they were last week. Today was Mustard Seed affinity group. Every day there's a different group organizing something. There have been Jews, Buddhists, Christians, and tomorrow, for the Solstice, there's a Pagan ritual."

I looked over at Holly, who smiled at the mention of Pagans.

Walt offered to facilitate, and the meeting got underway. The tensions around the MX test delay simmered through a few other topics, until finally we moved on to a report from Saturday's Vandenberg spokescouncil.

People shifted and leaned forward as Craig laid out the cold facts. "The

Washington Post reported that due to a technical failure, the test launch has been delayed at least a month. January is out. I've heard that because of satellite positions, the next possible launch date would actually be late March. And that presumes no further delays."

Different people tossed out comments about what it meant for us, but Claudia cut through. "We've called an action for January 24th. There's no question, we're going ahead with it."

It made sense to me. Several people raised their hands. Daniel addressed the importance of keeping our focus regardless of what the government did. A couple of others spoke to the same effect.

All the while, Belinda was steaming. When her turn came, her face was red, and she bit off her words. "I've been part of the Vandenberg planning, and I would say this changes a lot. If the test is delayed, our major action should be delayed."

Although Claudia tried to respond, Craig had his hand up first. He spoke quickly and firmly. "LAG called an action for January 24th. We've been organizing all Fall. Even if there isn't a test launch, a January demonstration would draw attention to the MX and the arms race." He looked around the circle, his gaze stopping on Belinda. "Besides, LAG has other commitments later in the Spring."

Protesters and security don rain gear for a wintry blockade of Livermore Lab.

Exactly, I thought. Wasn't that the point of LAG's three-action annual plan, to leave us the entire Spring to work on Livermore?

Doc was next. His brow furrowed, and he spoke deliberately. "I don't think this is a matter for Coordinating Council to decide."

Melissa looked astonished. "What is there to decide? It would be completely irresponsible to postpone an action that we have led people to plan for. We have to carry through on our word."

Others echoed her sentiments. By the time it came back to Belinda, her face was even redder, and her voice barely controlled. "If LAG wants to do an action, fine! But VAC called an action for the MX test date. If it's postponed, we need to start planning for that."

"I don't think many people will scrap January for a vague floating test date action," Craig rejoined. "People have to plan ahead for an action of this magnitude. It's clear where we should be putting our priorities."

"It's clear to *me* where our priority should be," Belinda shot back. "On stopping the test."

I wished I saw some way to defuse the tension, and I was glad when Melissa asserted herself. "Process, process," she called out. "This is turning into a personal debate. Obviously LAG is still committed to a January action. It was called for that date at the LAG Congress, and Coordinating Council can't call it off. People are also free to work on a floating test date action if they want. Is there anything else we need to discuss here? Can't we please move on?"

The combatants reluctantly agreed, but the mood remained edgy. I leaned over to catch a glimpse of Daniel's watch: nine o'clock. And that was before Walt delivered a legal collective update, and Mort gave a long report on the Central America protest at Concord Naval Weapons Station in late January.

Next came the finance report. Caroline fumbled with her papers. I winced for her. I'd been helping her with fund-raising, and knew how anxious she felt. She didn't seem quite ready to speak, despite having waited for the past two hours. Her eyes flickered with doubt, and her shoulder-length brown hair was knotted in the back from twisting it around her fingers.

"As I reported last week, or was it two weeks ago, yeah, anyway, LAG is close to $5000 in debt." The debt wasn't news, but hearing exact figures was sobering. We stared back at her. "And we, that is, by my calculations, LAG will be $7000 in debt by the time of the action." More stares and a few sighs answered her.

She picked up a sheaf of notes. "But the mailing, the fund appeal, is finally getting out to people, although we do need more volunteers to stuff the rest of the envelopes, but I'll bring that up later. And the Grand Raffle — "

She bent over and rooted around under her chair, producing a stack of raffle tickets. "We're hoping we can raise $5000 by selling raffle tickets. Grand prize is a trip for two to the hot springs in Baja, Mexico. Plus there's lots of other prizes."

Hank cupped his hands over his mouth. "Get your red hot raffle tickets here!"

"Exactly," said Caroline. "We're phoning AG contacts to get them involved."

"Get AGs to help with fund-raising? Good luck," Claudia tossed in.

Walt tried to move the meeting along, but Caroline raised one more item. "I wanted to say that the LAG Rag is still bringing in money." She pointed at me. "So far we've received over $2000 from the subscription appeal that Jeff wrote."

DECEMBER, 1982

LAG RAG

50¢

PUBLISHED BY THE LIVERMORE ACTION GROUP

This Is Not A Test! It Is An Outrage!

—by Ken Nightingale

ISLANDERS RELUCTANTLY LEAVE HOMES

The Occupation of Vandenberg AFB

DEADLINE FOR NEXT ISSUE

LAG Rag #2, December 1982

The commendation caught me by surprise. "That's great," a few people said, and I felt a flush of pride that lasted through the next couple of reports.

We got through the rally and outreach okay, but then Doc got a look at the publicity flyers. "These Vandenberg flyers don't have VAC's contact number on them."

I winced as Craig snapped back, "That's because they're meant for LAG organizing."

"They make it look like Vandenberg is totally a LAG action," Doc countered.

To my relief, there was no support for pursuing the argument. Even Claudia seemed unexcited. "Let's get International Day done and get out of here," she said.

With that ringing introduction, Holly cleared her throat. She sat upright on her cushion and surveyed the notes on her clipboard.

She and Daniel and Antonio had just returned from the Mobilization for Survival conference, a gathering of grassroots groups held in Austin. "The Mobe officially adopted our proposal for International Day," Holly reported, her voice gaining brightness. "We talked with dozens of groups, and a lot of them are going to do something in June."

Mort scrunched his face, although I couldn't tell if it was about the Mobe specifically, or the mere mention of International Day. He twisted in his chair and tugged at his goatee, but refrained from commenting.

Doc's brow furrowed, and he raised his hand. "I heard that in order to get this proposal on the agenda, we had to join the Mobilization for Survival."

"We affiliated," Holly answered carefully. "Coordinating Council agreed last month to affiliate with the Mobe. It's a coalition of grassroots groups like us."

Doc shook his head slowly, almost sadly. "Joining a coalition is not a decision for Coordinating Council. It should have gone to the spokescouncil."

Claudia let out a sigh. Doc turned sharply on her. "It's clear that Coordinating Council doesn't trust the AGs or the spokescouncil," he said.

"Is it any wonder?" Claudia answered impatiently. It was hard to tell if she was more irked at Doc's point or at the delay in the meeting. "If it weren't for Coordinating Council, half of the Vandenberg organizing wouldn't even get done."

Belinda smacked her knee in disgust. "It's exactly that kind of attitude — "

"Process, come on, process," Walt pleaded. "This is not the issue we're discussing."

"I don't see the point in discussing any of it," Belinda retorted. "The damage is already done."

"Then let's move on," Claudia said bluntly.

Belinda glared at her but didn't respond. Walt looked at Holly. "Did you have anything more to add?"

Holly's face was pallid. I felt sorry for her, having International Day dragged into the Vandenberg fighting. She added a few more details and wrapped up her report.

With that, the last item was struck from the agenda. We straggled into a closing circle. As we draped our arms around each other, a palpable relief filtered through the room. The conflicts still rumbled under the surface, but people seemed willing to let them rest. Here we are, I thought. Working together. Even if Claudia and Belinda won't make eye contact, we're all in the same circle. As I looked around at the familiar faces, I was struck by the personal rapport I had with each person. Holly, Mort, Doc, Claudia, Hank — the whole bunch. More than any time since I moved to California, I felt like I had found my people. We were building something together.

It was past 11:30 when the closing circle broke up, but the discussions kept on going as we put on our coats. I went over to talk with Doc, to let him know that I appreciated his viewpoint even when we disagreed.

He peered at me from under his bushy eyebrows. "I don't have a problem with disagreements," he said. "Clearly LAG has its priorities. What bothers me is when people try to control the movement, making decisions without consulting the affinity groups."

"I don't think it's control," I answered, standing my ground. "We called an action for January, all of us, at the Congress. No one is saying that VAC can't call a floating test date action later on. But most people have to make definite plans. They can't put their lives on hold for months waiting for the missile test."

Doc shook his head. "That may be true, but it isn't a Coordinating Council decision. It's for the AGs to decide at a spokescouncil." His eyes locked in on mine. "Most people on the VAC work group want nothing to do with LAG, and this is precisely why."

I started to say something conciliatory, but Belinda was gesturing to him to go. "Well, happy Solstice," he said, giving me a hug. "See you next year." I hugged him back. If we couldn't settle all the politics, at least our parting was warm. I even stepped over and gave Belinda a hug, although that felt like a formality on both sides.

We finally made it down the stairs and out the door. "Don't forget, no meeting next week!" Hank called to everyone. "And there's a New Year's Eve party at my house in Oakland, everyone's invited. Costumes optional, dancing compulsory."

Sunday, January 2, 1983

It was production day for the newspaper, so I didn't want to stay too long at the Vandenberg spokescouncil. But I figured I'd stop by and check it out.

The meeting was in the main hall of La Peña. Coming in from the street, it took my eyes a moment to adjust. The thirty-foot-square room was filled with disheveled rows of folding chairs. To the left was a large stage cluttered with microphone stands and cables. Framed photos of villages in the Andes were highlighted by small spotlights on the far wall.

Fifty people were milling around, swapping leaflets and listening to a mandolin player. I was surprised how few people I knew. Craig was talking with Lyle from Overthrow cluster. Claudia and Lois came in a little later. Walt and Alby from Change of Heart were there, and a woman named Ariel from Urban Stonehenge, an anarchist household over in San Francisco. There were a few more people I recognized from the Livermore blockade, but otherwise it was unfamiliar faces until Karina came bopping in.

When she entered La Peña, it was as if the lights came up. She was wearing a tight sky-blue sweater and her customary smile, and her spirit radiated into every corner of the room. I hadn't seen her much in the past few weeks, since she stopped coming to Coordinating Council. She shared Doc and Belinda's frustration around hierarchy and control. Compound that with the subtle condescension she had to take for being young and outspoken, and it probably wasn't the most inviting milieu.

I crossed the room to greet her, and we hugged for a long moment. "It's great to see you," I said, and couldn't help adding, "You've got to come back to Coordinating Council. We need you."

She squeezed my arm. "I will, I've just been too busy lately." We talked another minute, then someone else called to her. "Let's ride down to Vandenberg together," she said as we parted.

"Sure," I answered. "I think Hank is driving a van down."

I walked up front and looked over the handwritten agenda. It focused mostly on the upcoming Vandenberg action, with topics like the camp, action logistics, and an MX update. Partway down the magic-markered list was "Future Vandenberg Actions," which figured to set off some sparks. The test was delayed at least till March, and probably longer. But with nothing concrete to go on, I didn't see what arguing over a nebulous future action could accomplish.

As usual, the meeting was a half-hour late in starting. By that time, I'd made up my mind to split and work on the paper. I checked with Craig to make sure he was going to write a report after the meeting and bring it over. Then I headed for Caroline's new place down in the Berkeley flatlands, where we were doing layout.

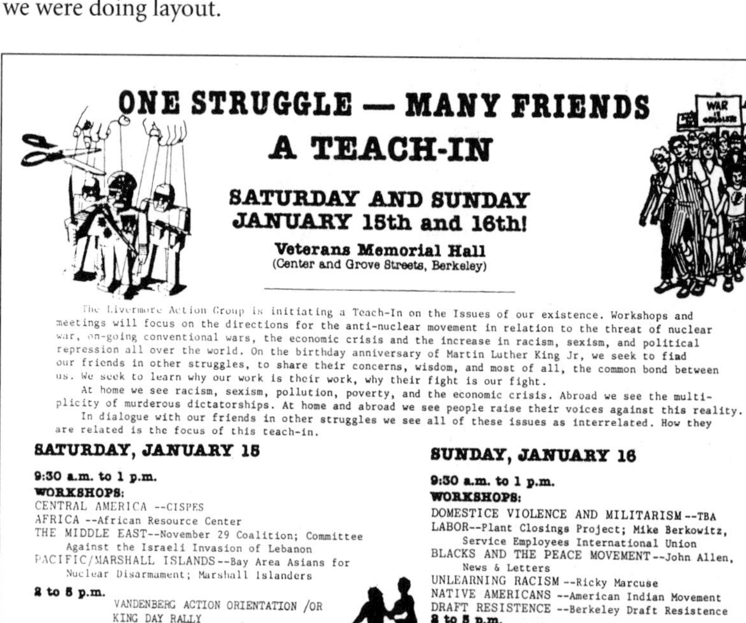

ONE STRUGGLE — MANY FRIENDS

A TEACH-IN

SATURDAY AND SUNDAY
JANUARY 15th and 16th!

Veterans Memorial Hall
(Center and Grove Streets, Berkeley)

The Livermore Action Group is initiating a Teach-In on the Issues of our existence. Workshops and meetings will focus on the directions for the anti-nuclear movement in relation to the threat of nuclear war, on-going conventional wars, the economic crisis and the increase in racism, sexism, and political repression all over the world. On the birthday anniversary of Martin Luther King Jr, we seek to find our friends in other struggles, to share their concerns, wisdom, and most of all, the common bond between us. We seek to learn why our work is their work, why their fight is our fight.

At home we see racism, sexism, pollution, poverty, and the economic crisis. Abroad we see the multiplicity of murderous dictatorships. At home and abroad we see people raise their voices against this reality.

In dialogue with our friends in other struggles we see all of these issues as interrelated. How they are related is the focus of this teach-in.

SATURDAY, JANUARY 15

9:30 a.m. to 1 p.m.
WORKSHOPS:
CENTRAL AMERICA --CISPES
AFRICA --African Resource Center
THE MIDDLE EAST--November 29 Coalition; Committee Against the Israeli Invasion of Lebanon
PACIFIC/MARSHALL ISLANDS--Bay Area Asians for Nuclear Disarmament; Marshall Islanders

2 to 5 p.m.
VANDENBERG ACTION ORIENTATION /OR KING DAY RALLY
Bart to 12th Street & March to Rally

9 p.m.
BENEFIT DANCE AND GRAND RAFFLE

SUNDAY, JANUARY 16

9:30 a.m. to 1 p.m.
WORKSHOPS:
DOMESTICE VIOLENCE AND MILITARISM --TBA
LABOR--Plant Closings Project; Mike Berkowitz, Service Employees International Union
BLACKS AND THE PEACE MOVEMENT --John Allen, News & Letters
UNLEARNING RACISM --Ricky Marcuse
NATIVE AMERICANS --American Indian Movement
DRAFT RESISTENCE --Berkeley Draft Resistence

2 to 5 p.m.
TRENDS AND DIRECTIONS IN THE GLOBAL ANTI-NUCLEAR MOVEMENT: ALLIANCE BUILDING, CLASS VIOLENCE, PROPOSALS FOR ACTION --Marcy Darnovsky, Adam Hochschild

Childcare available. Wheelchair accessible.

Livermore Action Group, 3126 Shattuck Avenue, Berkeley, CA 644-3031

Members of LAG's Outreach Collective organized this multi-issue teach-in to develop a broader context for the anti-nuclear protests planned in Spring and Summer 1983.

We had finally renamed the LAG Rag. I kept bringing it up until someone suggested calling it "Action," which people liked okay. Then Mort added the prefix "Direct," and we knew we had it — Direct Action. We decided that two of our eight pages should cover other direct actions besides LAG, one page for the Bay Area and the other for national and global resistance.

A folk music show was playing on KPFA when I arrived at Caroline's, a small adobe house which she shared with three roommates. She, Holly, and several others were seated around a couple of small tables, working away.

I gave Holly a hug. Then Caroline took me on a tour of her new house. Caroline looked less stressed than when I'd last seen her, partly due no doubt to LAG's finances improving as we approached the action. But also, she had been subletting and house-sitting for as long as I'd known her. "Having a stable place to live makes such a difference," she said as we came back into the living room. "I didn't realize how much that had been distracting me till I moved in here."

We went over to the production table, where Holly was reviewing the story list. I put my arm around her. "How is it looking?"

"We're making progress," Holly said, showing me the page line-up. "We have to go up to twelve pages, though. There's way too much stuff for eight."

I was glad to see the paper growing, but I glanced at Caroline, knowing the extra expense would worry her. She pouted her lower lip, but nodded her agreement with Holly.

"Well, twelve pages sounds good to me," I said nonchalantly. "Anything that I can paste up?"

Holly pointed to a folder on the table. "How about typing up the Native American news and the letter about your article?"

Monique had written up the Walnettos' response to my diatribe on the Freeze. "Is that my punishment, that I have to type up my own criticism?" I said as I sat down at the typewriter.

As I got going, Mort came in the door carrying bread, chips, and a six-pack of Sierra Nevada ale. "Here's some supplies," he greeted us. "And I brought the ad for the Teach-In."

"How's the Teach-In shaping up?" I asked, looking over the ad.

"I think it's coming together," Mort said. "We have workshops or panelists from almost twenty groups. We'll get great cross-fertilization among the issues. Now we just have to get LAG people to show up."

"That's what the paper is for," I said. "We need to print more copies. We distributed all seven thousand of the second issue. I was lucky to grab a few for the LAG archives."

"Did we send Reagan a copy?" Mort asked.

"No way," I said. "He's got to subscribe like everyone else."

We toiled on through the afternoon. We figured that if we worked late that night, and then a few of us came back the next morning, we could get it to the printer by that afternoon.

I did a quick survey of production. Several pages were almost done, and the front page lacked only Craig's spokescouncil story. We were cruising along, listening to Joan Armatrading's "Show Some Emotion," when the front door swung open.

Craig stood in the doorway, his face impassive, his mouth slightly open. He fumbled for words, then burst out, "They called another action!"

No one moved. "What?" Mort said in a creaky voice.

"The spokescouncil just called an action for the end of March!"

Mort got Craig to come in and sit down. But in a moment he was up, pacing the floor. "I knew VAC was thinking of a future action, but I never suspected they'd call theirs before the January action was over. This totally undermines our action. And a March action will interrupt our organizing for Livermore this Spring."

"This is crazy," Mort scoffed. "This is the VAC work group?"

"Well, part of it," Craig muttered. He named a few people I vaguely recognized. "You wouldn't know them from LAG meetings," he said. "They don't think LAG as an organization should even exist."

"Doc and Belinda?" I asked tentatively.

"No, they weren't even there. They'd never have done it this way." Craig stopped pacing. His eyes swept our circle. "It's totally parasitic. We spend all Fall organizing and mobilizing people to do an action at Vandenberg — and then VAC not only pulls out of January, but they go and call a March action deliberately designed to draw people away from ours. They could have at least waited till ours was over!"

Craig paused, then flared again. "It's just backstabbing. These people — they said decisions I made — there was all this talk of hierarchy — they said I was leading a conspiracy in Coordinating Council, that I was betraying the movement..." He looked away.

Caroline walked over to Craig. "Didn't you or Claudia or anyone argue back?" she asked.

"Claudia had left by then. Lois argued some, but there was no real dialog. I certainly wasn't in a position to challenge them, after being declared the king of a headless organization." He chuckled for the first time, although in a jaded tone. "I could have made a legalistic appeal to the Congress decision, but VAC could claim that was just LAG's decision, and they aren't bound by it."

"I can't believe it," I said. "What about process? Aren't AGs supposed to have time to discuss new proposals?"

"Only LAG goes by that process, I guess. Anyone else can call any action they want," Craig said quietly.

Caroline put her hand on Craig's shoulder. "How are you feeling?"

Craig met her gaze, and his eyes reddened. "Well, to be trashed openly, to be humiliated and declared worthless, what can I say? It's just too much. A March action —"

His voice cracked, and he coughed sharply. "It's a deliberate attempt to undermine us."

I tried to think practically. "What should we say in the paper?"

Craig pointed at page one and spoke rapidly. "We'll have to tear up the front page. We need a big headline saying that the January action is still on. We have to show that LAG doesn't call off actions just because the government can't meet its deadline. The MX missile and first strike are still part of the government's plans. There's no reason to call off the protest."

January, 1983

DIRECT ACTION

50¢

PUBLISHED BY THE LIVERMORE ACTION GROUP

THE RIGHT ACTION AT THE RIGHT TIME

VANDENBERG ACTION STILL ON

FIRST MX TEST FLIGHT??

Direct Action #3, January 1983

No one disagreed. Craig took off to write his story. I turned back to my layout work, but Caroline sighed. "The split over the dates doesn't surprise me," she said. "You always get power struggles. I don't entirely blame VAC for calling another action. I mean, Coordinating Council *is* kind of controlling."

"But what's the alternative?" I said. "Somebody has to make sure that the work is getting done. If VAC wants to do it differently, fine. But Craig's right — this is a competing action. It's bound to pull people away from January. Makes me wonder who's paying them."

"No," Mort said sarcastically. "They've got plenty of reasons to attack LAG. We're an affront to their adrenaline-rush mentality. For us to plan a year's worth of actions like we did at the Congress is a challenge to absolute affinity group autonomy to do whatever is hot at the moment."

Holly slowly looked up from her layout, as if measuring her words carefully. "We don't have to see it as an attack on LAG," she said. "Some people find LAG's organizing too hierarchical and centralized, and they want to do it differently. We don't have to take it personally."

"But a March action undermines our organizing," I put in.

"Some people will probably wait and do the March action," Holly conceded. "Some might do both."

"Well, I'm still doing January," I said. I looked across the table at Holly, who had looked back down at her pages. I hesitated, then asked, "How about you?"

"Probably not," she answered, looking up. "If it's not the actual test date, it doesn't make sense to take that much time off when we're so busy with International Day."

I searched for words and came up empty. All along I'd pictured us doing the action together. Our action — where did that go? I stared blankly at her.

She set down her work and came around the table. "I'm sorry, Jeff," she said as she put her arm around me. "I should have told you that I was thinking of not doing it."

"Yeah," I said sadly. "I hope everyone won't decide to wait."

"I'm still going to do it," Caroline told me. "It'll be a good action. A lot of people are psyched for it, they won't want to wait."

"You're probably right," I said. But I still felt deflated, as if what I was pouring my life into wasn't quite as important, quite as central, as I had thought it was. Why would people undermine us? LAG seemed like the best thing that had happened in the Bay Area in my five years here. I couldn't understand why everyone didn't see it that way.

Watching the pages of Direct Action coming together allayed some of my dejection. I finished typing the letters page and hunted for a good graphic. Caroline pasted up a page that covered Greenham Common Peace Camp in England and Native American news. Holly and Mort designed a new layout for the front page emphasizing the January action, so all we needed to do was plug in Craig's story the next morning.

I surveyed the pages as I finished my beer. "If we get it done tomorrow morning, we'll have it back from the printer by Thursday."

Ad from the January 1983 Direct Action.

"We could work on the mailing at the office that night," Holly said. "It could be in the mail by Friday."

"And people would get it by the first of next week," Caroline picked up. "Once people know the action is still on, they'll plug in."

I appreciated her buoyancy, but the split over the date weighed on me. I tried to dismiss it as a conflict of personalities or organizing styles, but I knew there was no evading the core issue: control.

And I knew where I stood. I didn't have a problem with VAC or the spokescouncil. I liked the vision of a leaderless, collective action where everyone involved took a fair share of the responsibility. But if I were heading off to federal prison, who would I trust to keep track of the big picture — the LAG office, or a bunch of rotating AG spokes who met every other Saturday?

Sunday, January 16, 1983

HOLLY HELD the crystal up to the sunlight, rotating it to catch the rays from different angles. We were lying in bed on a Sunday afternoon, feeling lazy after making love. Bessie Smith's blues floated out of the tape player, and I had just opened a bottle of beer.

"The cluster meeting yesterday was really encouraging," I told her. "There are fourteen people from Change of Heart doing the action, plus Walt doing legal. Hank and Cindy from my old AG are going, Antonio from Lifers, Karina, and you know who else? Doc. He wasn't at the cluster meeting, but Rick was there from Enola Gay, and he said Doc is doing it."

Holly was still rotating the crystal, which she had hung in our window first thing after moving in. "I keep going back and forth," she said, "But I shouldn't get arrested."

"You're still riding down there with us, aren't you?"

"Yeah," she said, turning on her side to face me. "I'm looking forward to camping together on Sunday night before the action." She caught my eye. "Do you want to go backpacking sometime this Spring?"

"Well, maybe if we go to the ocean or the desert, so I don't have to worry about poison oak," I said. I thought about poison oak at Vandenberg. "Luckily for me, Change of Heart is doing our action at the front gate. Only a couple of people were in favor of going backcountry since the MX isn't there."

"Craig told me that Overthrow decided the same thing," Holly said. "But they aren't going to announce it, to keep the government wondering."

"How's Craig doing?" I asked.

"Craig? He's been totally absorbed in his work. He's on the phone all day, rocked back in that old tilting office chair he found." Holly seemed to be gazing at Craig, and got a concerned look on her face. "He acts like he's doing fine, but I think he's burying himself in the organizing to avoid his feelings. It must really have hurt him to be attacked at the spokescouncil when he's put so much of himself into the movement. But his attitude is more like, 'So what, who needs them? We're doing all the real work.'"

"Well, we are," I said half-jokingly.

"No, we aren't," she answered. "The spirit at the office has been good, though," she said. "The day we got Direct Action back from the printer, everyone was in a great mood. And the Vandenberg fund appeal we sent out last month has brought in over $3000."

"That's great," I said. "I'll bet that's helped the mood."

She lit a stick of incense. I lay back on the pillow and watched the first gauzy stream of smoke rise. A slight breeze rustled the curtains, sending shimmers of light across the wall.

Holly lay down next to me. Her thick hair brushed against my face. "Someone called last week from San Luis Obispo," she said, "and told us that a woman from the Chumash tribe, the original people of the area, will be at the action to lead a ceremony honoring the land at Vandenberg."

"That's great," I said.

She gazed up at the crystal again and drew a deep breath. "There's something perfect about it," she said. "We're not just blockading. We're reclaiming sacred land."

Reclaiming Vandenberg

January–June 1983

In January, March, and June, Vandenberg Action Coalition and/or Livermore Action Group organized actions at Vandenberg Air Force Base near Santa Barbara, protesting test launches of the MX missile.

Most of the nearly 1000 people arrested served one to ten days in jail, but some received sentences up to 60 days for second arrests.

Top: The Reaper at the pre-action rally, by Alice Rogoff

Bottom: Action camp, by Ted Sahl

Reclaiming Vandenberg

January–June 1983

The sprawling Air Force base lent itself to "backcountry" occupations. Here, January protesters occupy a meadow near the main gate. Other affinity groups did more clandestine backcountry actions, particularly in March and June.

Top left: Ted Sahl
All others: Bette Lee

Any connections between the people pictured in the photographs and the characters in this book are purely coincidental. The characters are fictional. No photo should be taken as implying that an individual is in any way connected to a fictional character.

January arrestees were led out of the meadow to waiting buses, which took them to detention facilities on the base.

Photos by Ted Sahl

Reclaiming Vandenberg

January–June 1983

Two / 1983

"(A government) is preserved so long as the ruling class succeeds in putting over its economic and political forms upon the whole of society as the only forms possible."

— *Leon Trotsky, "Dual Power," The Russian Revolution*

Sunday, January 23, 1983

"SHOOT! DAMN wiper's stuck again!" Hank hit the windshield with his fist.

I pointed to the dash. "Try turning it off and on. That worked last time."

He yanked the knob back and forth and the wiper started up. Hank settled back behind the steering wheel of his old van. He'd been talking about a wiring job he'd taken, on top of his regular forty-hour week. "I've got to make some money. I'm buying four classic pinball machines from a place in Omaha that closed last year. The shipment comes in next week."

"Your shop is already overflowing," I said. "Where are you going to put them?"

"I can fit a couple more near the door, I think." He stuck a Bob Dylan tape into the player and fiddled with the tone control. "Anyway, I hate to miss too much work. I'd vote for a state blockade, with a shorter sentence. But if people decide to do a federal action, I'll do it."

"You could do it and cite out," I said.

"Naw," he said. "Once we're in jail I'll hang to the end. How can you leave when everyone else is staying in solidarity?"

I nodded and looked out the window. A row of trees bordering a farm field swayed as the wind carried banks of gray clouds inland. "I'm staying till the end," I said. "I have two weeks off work, and I'll take more if we have to. But maybe there'll be so many of us that they'll have to dump us out like they did at Livermore last year."

"I don't know, it'd be sort of a letdown after all our — damn, stuck again!"

This time the on-off trick didn't work, and Hank steered to the side of the road. In the back of the van, voices grumbled. "Are we there? What time is it?" I fished a roll of toilet paper from under the seat and climbed out into the light mist. "Watch out for poison oak," Hank called after me. "That's all you need, two weeks in jail with poison oak."

Poison oak. I winced. Two weeks. I ducked behind a row of trees back from the road. Federal prison, maybe. And that might mean the Federal Marshals. Federal thugs. Anxiety cut through me. What were we walking into? What if they stuck us in prison for a year? What if they broke my wrist or fingers and I could never play guitar again? What if we never even got there? That was the immediate concern. An old van on a slick highway...

As I waited behind the tree for results, the mist gathered into beads on my skin. I wiped it from my brow like sweat and shivered. Damn, think about something else or I'll be here all day with my pants down. Think about the trip. Two more hours of riding left. A slight nausea fluttered through me. The Marshals. Were we ready for this? Maybe they won't be there. Maybe they'll leave it to the soldiers to deal with us. That would be weird, getting arrested by enlisted guys younger than me. That's not how I picture authority.

Flyer for the legal rally the day before the action. Legal rallies preceded or accompanied nearly every LAG action.

When I returned, Hank had gotten the wipers running. People shuffled around and tried to get comfortable in the back of the van. I took another shift in the rider's seat. Caroline sat on some packs behind us and leaned up between the seats.

As we pulled back onto the road, Bob Dylan launched into "Highway 61" — an auspicious sign, I thought. I turned in my seat to face Caroline. "This is your first arrest?" I asked.

"Yeah," she said slowly, pouting her lower lip. "Seeing everyone else arrested last Summer, well, I knew I had to do it the next time. And I'm going to non-cooperate when they arrest me. I can't stand up and walk with them."

"Right on," Hank pitched in.

"What if it's the Marshals who arrest us?" I asked her.

"Oh, it won't be. I heard in the office last week that it'll probably be soldiers who arrest us, and then the Marshals will take over as guards."

"Why would they do that?" I asked.

Hank laughed coldly. "Easy. They don't want the Marshals beating on people in front of the media."

A few of the hundreds of people who marched to the gates of Vandenberg AFB following the rally.

Caroline nodded slowly. "I'll still non-cooperate, even if it's the Marshals."

Hank fiddled with the heater levers. "What's your sense of how many people will get busted?"

Caroline mulled it over. "From what I've heard at the office, I'd guess maybe two hundred," she said. "It's too bad about the split over the date. I think there could have been a whole lot more."

I nodded. I hadn't been thinking about it much lately, but when solid numbers were spelled out, my jaw tightened. Two hundred arrests. It might have been a thousand. My resentment rose at the people who had split from LAG and called the March action. Get in line, I felt like saying, then felt irked at myself. Get in line?

We made it to Lompoc by late afternoon. But between dropping off a couple of people in town, getting something to eat, and making a few wrong turns, we didn't get to the rally till it was over. We pulled up at the deserted site and hailed a few stragglers. "Where is everybody?"

"They left about twenty minutes ago," a guy with a short, curly beard told us. "They're marching to the main gate."

Hank wheeled the van around and headed up the road. Wild fields stretched out on either side, merging on the horizon with the low gray clouds. "The edge of the base," Hank pointed. "Most of it is just open land. Look, there's everybody." As we caught the tail end of the march, little clusters of people waved, pulling their banners taut and shaking their signs. Hank honked and hollered, "Bunch of hippie freaks!"

He spun the van into a gravel turnout across from the gate. As I stepped down onto the gravel, the earlier nausea welled up again, and I clutched the door to steady myself.

Holly, who had ridden down earlier with Antonio and Daniel, walked up at that moment, and looked alarmed. "Are you okay?" she asked, putting her hand on my shoulder.

"I think I'm fine," I said in a thin voice. I wobbled a step forward. "Just motion sickness." She took my arm and steadied me as I walked off the nausea. Welcome to Vandenberg.

The brisk evening air soon cleared my head. Holly went to talk to Caroline, and I crossed the street to check out the protest at the gate. The entrance to the base was a simple two-lane road flanked by trees and open fields. A steel arch spanned the road, bearing a large sign: "Vandenberg Air Force Base — Peace Is Our Profession." Underneath stood a row of young soldiers, struggling to avoid eye contact.

Several hundred people filled the entrance road and spilled out into the intersection. Some pressed forward to lecture and plead with the tight-lipped soldiers. Others dropped back to talk with friends. Off to one side, a cluster sang peace songs.

Through the crowd I spotted people I hadn't seen since Livermore. A guy with long, scraggly hair and a tie-dyed sweatshirt breezed by, dancing after a conga player. "Moonstone," I called. He turned and enveloped me in a hug. "Hey," I said, "How are you doing? Have you been down here at the camp?"

"Yeah, three days, been going onto the base, at night, scouting out the routes. Whoa!" He bent over to catch his breath, dangling his arms, still laughing. "I want to try a backcountry action, but other people in my AG want to do a state blockade, then come back when the MX is actually being tested and do backcountry. We'll decide tonight, I guess."

A Vandenberg Action Coalition work group edited and produced this 56-page action handbook.

Hank and Doc walked up. "Can you believe how young those soldiers are?" Hank said. "I was trying to talk with them, but they won't even tell you where they're from."

"They're ordered not to speak, I'm sure," Doc said. "I did a stint in the military when I was their age. Privates don't make their own decisions."

Hank looked back and forth from me to Doc. "They've never seen anything like this before. They're all worried about the gate — we should just walk down the road and sneak onto the base right now. We could come up behind and surprise them."

Moonstone and I laughed, but Doc furrowed his brow. "Surprise them? You want to keep on living?"

"Yeah, you're right," Hank said. "But wouldn't it be funny? They think they know our plans, they're all set to deal with us in the morning, and we show up at their headquarters tonight."

Doc looked past us toward the gate, which was spot-lit as dusk settled in. "The entrance is so small. I was picturing more maneuvering room. If we do a trespass here, they'll just sweep us right up. It would be totally symbolic. We wouldn't disrupt anything."

I kicked at the road with my toe. Change of Heart was leaning toward a front-gate action, and given my fear of poison oak, I wanted it to stay that way. "It's going to be symbolic anyway, if the MX isn't here," I said. "We might as well do the action at the gate and see what media coverage we can get."

"Then why do a federal action?" Doc answered. "If we don't want to get on the base, our best tactic would be to do a state action and blockade the entrance road. I want to feel like we're doing something, not just walking into their arms."

"I'm not arguing," I said.

Holly came over and took my hand. "There's a Chumash ceremony to reclaim the land starting over there. Want to go?"

I felt like I should be spending time with Holly since we were parting the next day. We only had a few waking hours left. But a ritual? I squeezed her hand. "Not right now," I said, grasping for an excuse. "I want to find Craig."

Holly, Doc, and Moonstone headed off to join the circle forming across the road. I wandered through the crowd still milling around the gate. Looking for Craig was as good a mission as any. Although the rain was holding off, everyone had hoods and hats pulled tight. In the fading light it was hard to recognize anyone without staring right into their face. I ran across a few more people I knew, but no Craig.

After the ritual, Hank rounded up the van-riders. Amid a flurry of people hastening to their vehicles, I spied Holly talking quietly with Doc. I signaled to them that we were leaving, then got into the van. Holly followed soon after, and we sat together just behind Hank's seat. I put my arm around her, but had trouble getting comfortable. The milling at the gate had left me agitated and impatient. Maybe I should have gone to the ritual after all.

Hank tried to follow a couple of cars back to the encampment, but we lost them right away, and wound up creeping down a muddy country road between two tall rows of trees. There were no lights anywhere. All I could think about was how old the van was and the weird noises it kept making. But Hank said he was sure it was the right road. He'd been here in December when they were looking for a site for the camp and was sure he remembered the turnoff. We kept driving.

A light flashed up ahead, then disappeared. Hank slowed the van. "I think I can see a car up ahead. It might be off the road." He rolled down his window and leaned out. "Yeah, it is."

The light reappeared and moved toward us. "Better hold it right there," a voice called out.

Hank leaned his head out the window and called back. "What's the problem?"

"It's solid mud from here to the camp," came the answer. "Unless you have four-wheel drive, you'd better park."

The camp. We'd made it. My chest relaxed a notch. I eased out of the van into a light drizzle. Holly and I gathered our tent and other gear and made our way up the road. Walt tromped by in heavy galoshes. "Why be so careful? You're gonna get wet anyway. The sooner you get to the camp, the sooner you can dry out by the fire."

Holly pointed through some trees. "Look, there's a light over there."

Walt peered through the trees. "That's it, that's the camp. I'm going backcountry." He plunged into the brush directly toward the lights. His route looked no worse than ours, but my respect for poison oak kept me to the road.

We set our bags under a canopy and made our way to the welcoming campfire. The flames were roaring, but all around was sloshy mud. A few pieces of plywood provided the only solid footing. Holly and I pressed up to the fire, toasting our chilled hands.

"There's food in that tent over there," someone said. "You'd better hurry, they're getting ready to close the kitchen."

We headed toward an off-white canvas tent, where Turning Tide AG had set up a camp cafeteria. As we ducked inside, the aroma of vegetable soup greeted us.

Holly stopped to talk to someone she knew. As I approached the table, I recognized Artemis working at the big butane stove. She was a broad-shouldered woman in her forties, active in Matrix AG. She and I had co-facilitated a tough Coordinating Council meeting a couple of weeks earlier, so I felt a special bond with her.

"This is amazing," I said as she turned to greet me. "I'll eat better here than at home." I filled my plate with potatoes, green beans, and corn chips.

Artemis handed me a bowl of soup. "I can't say I always cook like this at home. Interesting how when we gather as a community, we eat better."

I admired a knife rack fastened to one of the tent-posts. "What a great set-up. And I'll bet there's not a dryer spot in camp."

"I know, I've been sleeping in here the past few nights."

"You've been here all weekend?"

"Yeah, it's been great except for the rain." Without setting her mixing spoon down, she wiped her brow with the back of her hand. "People have been going onto the base at night to scout entry routes. My AG is still thinking of doing a backcountry action, but they're leaning toward state charges. How about you?"

"Change of Heart is thinking about federal trespass at the gate," I said. "No point in going backcountry if there's no missile to stop."

"Sure there is," she said. "Backcountry actions get you in touch with the land, with the Earth we say we're fighting for. It feels less symbolic. I'll probably do backcountry at the March action, whether or not the missile is there."

"So you're planning to do the VAC action?" I asked.

She shrugged. "I don't think of it as VAC or LAG. It's about shutting Vandenberg. We ought to be glad there are more protests."

"Well, it feels like having a second date weakened this action," I said, giving a forced shrug.

Before Artemis could respond, one of the other cooks called her back to the stove. I drifted back outside with my plate of food, feeling unsettled. Craig walked by, looking surprisingly relaxed. I followed him over to the fire. "How did the rally go?"

"Really good," he said. "Especially considering we had three weeks to organize it after VAC pulled out."

"Yeah, the whole scene came together well."

"Shows who was doing the real work all along." He held a shoe on a stick over the edge of the fire. "We've done all we can do. Tomorrow we'll see who steps up."

I looked off toward the camping area, where flashlights darted around like fireflies. The mist congealed into a light rain.

Antonio walked up and put an arm around each of us. "Gentlemen!" He greeted us in his warm, resonant voice. "This beautiful weather reminds me of why we chose to hold International Day on Summer Solstice."

"Yeah," tossed out another guy. "We're out of synch with the natural rhythms of the planet."

I laughed, assuming he was joking. Craig pulled his steaming shoe back from the flames. "Unfortunately," he said, "the government doesn't follow the natural cycles."

"Which is one more reason not to respond to the government," Antonio said. "We have to take the initiative, declare our own calendar."

We were interrupted by Claudia. "Are you guys going to the spokescouncil?"

I polished off the last of my dinner, tossed my plate into the fire, and followed the others up to the meeting tent. I wasn't a spoke for Change of Heart, but I figured I might pick up some information on the next day's action. And apparently most people felt the same way. There wasn't a spare seat in the tent. The dark green canvas absorbed most of the light from the four bare bulbs dangling overhead, and my eyes couldn't quite get used to the dimness. The ground was cold and damp even through a layer of straw. A hundred people crammed onto plastic dropcloths, sitting back-to-back to keep our muddy shoes off the sheets.

At the front of the tent, next to the medics table, the facilitators huddled. I recognized one of them, a back-to-the-land type from Humboldt County whom I'd seen at a couple of meetings in the Fall. He turned and addressed us. "Okay, everybody, my name is Abelard, and this is Janet, we're the co-facilitators tonight. We want to try to get through the agenda as quick as possible so everyone can get some sleep." He was bouncing up and down and slapping his hands together, and he seemed relieved when Doc raised his hand.

"Why is the solidarity discussion at the end of the agenda?"

"Well, we figured that people would want to talk first about what actions they're doing, and get the legal review out of the way, and we have to do camp support, we can't put that at the end or we'll never get to it — yeah, Melissa?" He stopped bouncing and pointed to her.

"We put off the solidarity discussion at the last spokescouncil and said we'd do it here, when everyone was together."

Janet stepped in front of Abelard. "We'll try to get through the early parts fast so we have plenty of time for solidarity."

Melissa muttered to herself. Someone called out: "Who chose these facilitators, LAG?" Several hands shot up. "Process point, process point," someone yelled. Everyone was shuffling around and the plastic dropcloths were making a racket. Abelard was bouncing up and down and pointing, "Process point, let's hear the process point!"

"Never mind, I withdraw it."

Janet waved for quiet. "Me and Abelard were chosen at the end of the last spokescouncil. You don't have to treat it like a conspiracy."

"Process," someone yelled. "Can't we just get on with the discussion so we can get to bed?"

"That's what we're trying to do!"

Everyone was arguing over what to do next. The facilitators conferred hurriedly. Finally Janet pointed to Moonstone, who was waving his hand.

He stood up and looked around the tent. "I just want people to know that one affinity group is already on the base, and another one is going backcountry in about an hour."

The tent erupted again. Moonstone was besieged with questions.

"Do you think you should be announcing that here?"

"Why not?" he said. "The Feds know we're coming. They've been looking for us all week and haven't caught us yet." Scattered applause and laughter rippled through the tent.

"So you're definitely doing federal?"

"Yeah, we can probably make it to some test areas. And if not, we'll at least get a better idea of the base for next time."

The final spokescouncil the night before the action was more like a general meeting, with half the camp crowded into the tent.

Melissa raised her hand. "It's obvious what we need to decide — whether to do a federal action in solidarity with the backcountry people, or do a state action and leave them to deal with the federal government alone." Her prejudicial remarks seemed to rankle the facilitators, but Melissa talked over them. "I propose we do a straw poll and see how many people are willing to do federal charges, either backcountry or at the main gate."

Someone objected. "I need to check back with my affinity group before we do that. Let's take a break and report back to our clusters and AGs." The facilitators wearily consented, and we scattered around the camp hunting people up.

I was pretty sure what Change of Heart would decide. I stopped at the fire to talk to Antonio and a couple of other people while Doc went on down to the tents to look there. Hank trudged up from the distant row of portajohns. A silent mist coated us as I filled people in on the latest developments.

Doc returned from the tents with Karina. We warmed our hands one last time and headed back to the meeting. The place was even more packed than before, and we had to search for a corner of plastic to sit on. The wind sliced through the flaps of the tent, snapping them at their anchor ropes. We huddled together to cut the draft.

During the break, the facilitators had stepped aside. When we reconvened, Abelard proposed that Artemis facilitate. No one objected, and the straw poll began. In no particular order, a spoke for each AG or cluster stood and called out their name and decision while Janet tallied them.

"Spiderwomyn AG, seven federal, main gate."

"Truth and Dare Cluster from Santa Cruz, twelve federal backcountry."

"Soviet Agents affinity group, eight state. We need to get out of jail sooner, but we support the federal action."

"Overthrow Cluster, twelve federal, main gate."

Doc got to his feet to report for our cluster. Our decision had been easy. Once we knew that some people were doing federal, there was no question. The only issue was backcountry versus front gate, and with a majority favoring the gate, the rest agreed. "Change of Heart, fourteen federal, main gate," Doc announced.

Yeah, I thought as the final clusters checked in. Solidarity. Count me in.

People intending to risk arrest at Vandenberg wore these armbands.

Artemis added up the figures. "I get one hundred seventy-two federal, thirty-four state." There was some applause and even a cheer or two. People started standing up. Artemis waved her arms and pointed to the rest of the agenda, but half the people in the tent were saying their goodnights and heading for bed.

"I knew this would happen," Melissa groaned. "We agree to do federal, but there's not going to be anyone here to discuss solidarity tactics." Even as she spoke, more people were trickling out.

"We'll never have a serious discussion now," Antonio said. "People can talk before the arrests, or in jail. We might as well get some sleep."

People consensed with their feet, and after a few more announcements, the meeting fizzled out. We headed toward the camping area. "See you tomorrow around ten," Doc said as we parted. "That should be early enough."

"Good. Ten's a civil hour."

Holly rolled over as I crawled into our tent, making room for me next to her. "Here's your sleeping bag. The floor is dry except right near the door."

I zipped the bag and scooted it up against hers, shivering as we curled together. I was glad we'd made love the night before, because I couldn't imagine getting out of my sleeping bag. "It's colder in here than outside," I said.

She put her arms out and hugged me as I tried to get warm. We lay there a while, listening to the rain on the tent. I wished she were getting arrested with us. I imagined sitting in the road holding her hand. How poetic...

But even if she wasn't doing the action, her presence was calming. I remembered the days before the Livermore blockade, feeling agitated and alone with my decision on whether to get arrested. How different it was this time, being here with Holly.

"What got decided at the meeting?" she finally asked. "Is it federal charges?"

"Yeah, for most people," I told her. "Change of Heart is trespassing at the front gate."

"That's good for you," she said. "You can keep your new shoes dry."

I smiled at my own foresight. Figuring it might never stop raining, I brought along a brand new pair of sneakers to put on just before our arrest. The front-gate action meant I would start my jail time with dry feet.

Holly rolled over so I was behind her and our bodies spooned. "This is our last night together for a while," she said. "Our apartment is going to seem empty. That will be hard after spending every night with you for the past two months." She pulled my arms tight around her. "It feels hollow knowing you and all my friends are getting arrested, and I'm just watching."

"Yeah," I said, feeling thankful that if we had to part, I was the one going to jail. I kissed her hair, then leaned up and kissed her face. She turned so our lips gently met. "I'm so glad to be here with you, Jeff," she whispered. "I love you."

Monday, January 24, 1983

CAROLINE'S AG WAS the first to cross "the line." Vandenberg officials apparently figured that if they discouraged us from trespassing at the gate, we'd just be more likely to go backcountry. So they painted a white line across the entrance road and ordered the soldiers to remain well back of it, giving us plenty of room to commit federal trespass.

The rain had let up, but the pavement was still wet as Caroline's AG strode past the gate and sat down in the road, blocking a couple of incoming cars. A squad of soldiers moved up behind them.

I was standing with Holly, several rows back in the crowd of protesters bunched around the front gate. Holly was slightly in front of me, and I gazed at her as she watched Caroline. We were about to be separated for who knew how long. Ten days? Two weeks? I reached out and took her hand. She squeezed mine in return but kept her eyes on the protest.

Caroline was seated in the middle of her AG, wearing an army-green poncho. It was keeping her pants dry, but even more, it was making life difficult for the two soldiers who were trying to pry her arms out and make her stand up. Caroline's brow was taut, and she refused to acknowledge the presence of her tormentors. Finally, after a few clumsy attempts, one of the soldiers succeeded in getting a wristlock on her. Caroline grimaced and lurched to her feet. The crowd yelled encouragement to her, but Caroline stared stoically at the ground, ignoring the soldiers as they half-dragged her to a bus.

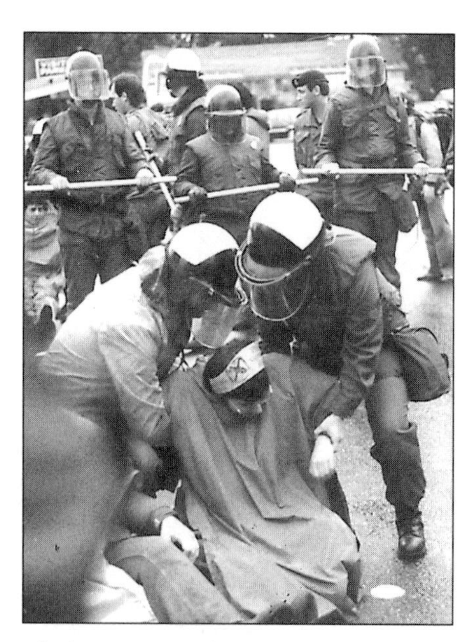

The first protesters of the day were arrested blockading the base entrance.

More arrests followed. Forty or fifty people had crossed the lines by the time Change of Heart circled up for a meeting in the gravel turnout across the road. We started talking about when we wanted to go, but Doc changed the topic.

"We can't just walk into their arms," he said. "They've got the buses right there, waiting to haul us away."

Karina jumped in as soon as he finished. "I just walked down the road and found this huge meadow, right past those trees. If we walk down there real casually,

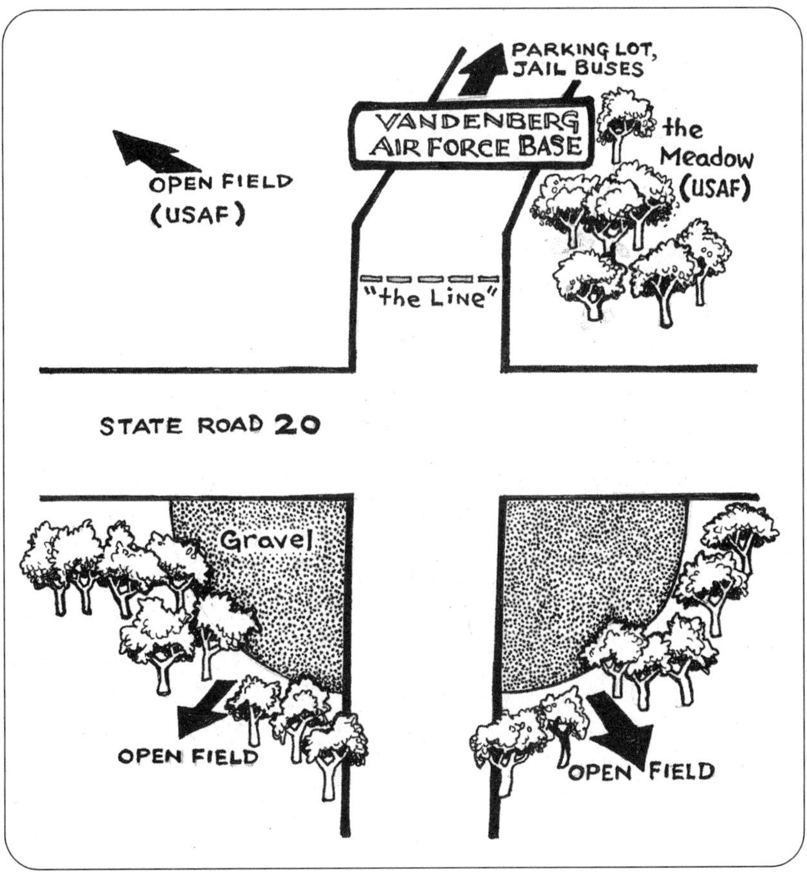

Main gate at Vandenberg AFB in 1983 — not to scale. The area has been built up since then, with low buildings in the meadow and subdivisions in nearby fields.

then all of the sudden head out into the meadow, it'll catch them completely off-guard."

Karina's remarks set off a passionate debate. "Surprising the soldiers is too dangerous, even in daylight." — "But if we go into the meadow, we're actually occupying the base." — "We should stick with what we already agreed on." — "The whole point of affinity groups is to be flexible." — "The gate is under their control. Occupying the meadow takes back the initiative."

My concern was mostly for keeping my feet dry. Even though it wasn't raining, I was carrying my new tennis shoes around in a plastic bag, aiming to put them on right before we got arrested. Naturally, I favored the gate over the wet meadow. But I wasn't going to admit to that motivation.

Back and forth it went, around the circle. No one gave in, and no comment quite clinched the debate. "Let's do a straw poll," someone finally said. "How many want to do the gate? Seven. And the meadow? Seven." Laughter and applause vented some of our jitters.

Karina reached in her pocket. "Let's toss a coin." More applause. "Here, Walt, you toss it, you're neutral."

Walt, who was working on the legal collective for the action, placed the nickel carefully on his thumbnail and held his arm out. "Heads for the gate, tails for the meadow." He let it fly. The coin bounced off the gravel and landed in some tall grass. "Tails! The meadow!"

"Wait, he has to catch it," someone said.

"No way," Karina shot back. "Come on, let's go!"

We strolled away from the gate with a casualness that attracted thirty or forty supporters and several photographers while evading detection by the military. I felt uneasy about our change of plans, but I was relieved to be getting on with the action.

Holly slid her arm around my waist as we fell behind the others. "I'm planning to stay in camp for three more days," she told me. "Then unless it looks like you'll be released in the next day or so, I'll probably go home, and come back down when you get out."

Up ahead, people were bunching in front of a large "No Trespassing" sign, as if that were our destination. I put my arm around Holly's shoulders and pulled her close. Amid the tumult of feelings, I couldn't think of anything to say that didn't sound trite. "I'm really going to miss you," I finally whispered.

She slowly released me. "I wish I were going in, too," she said sadly. "I knew I'd feel this way."

I knelt to lace up my new shoes. "Even if we got busted together, we'd get separated right away," I said.

"If we were both in jail, I'd feel like we were still together," she said. "It's different if I'm on the outside."

I weighed her comment as I tied the second shoe. Then I stood up and hugged her one last time. "I love you, Holly. I'll write if they let us."

We kissed, then parted. Change of Heart clustered. Only a token strand of wire separated us from a huge green field, lush from the rain. Way off across the field was a row of trees. With the skies trying to clear, my worries over dry

Several AGs moved down the road and entered a meadow, symbolically occupying the Air Force Base. Trespassing on the base raised the charges from state to federal, risking longer sentences.

feet subsided, and I felt an impulse to take off running and see if I could reach the trees.

Karina looked around our circle. "Here? Now?" No one objected. She ducked under the wire. Cindy and Doc were close behind. I glanced back at Holly. "I love you, Jeff," she called as I slipped under the wire.

I grabbed Hank's hand as we formed a ribbon and streamed out into the field. My feet sunk deep into the sod carpet, as if the Earth were welcoming our celebratory incursion. Shouts and laughter reverberated in the crisp air. The field expanded to immense proportions, and I sensed our spirit permeating the entire base.

In the distance I spied three soldiers flying down to intercept us. As they zoered in, we swung the line around to form a circle. We thrust our clenched hands into the air in a victory salute. We were occupying Vandenberg!

The three soldiers hastily conferred, then fanned out and "surrounded" us. Someone started singing "We Shall Not Be Moved." We took it up at the top of our voices, drowning out the

Soldiers surrounded and arrested clusters in the meadow.

The military seemed ill-prepared for the mobile, decentralized affinity group action that developed.

attempts of the soldiers to communicate with each other.

Overhead, patches of crystal blue shone through the clouds. Two other groups followed us into the field. Overthrow Cluster got within fifty feet of us before several more soldiers raced down and headed them off. Most of their cluster circled up, but Tai got up on Lyle's shoulders and the two of them came galloping toward us yelling, "Overthrow! Overthrow!" When two of our soldiers ran over to corral them, Change of Heart took off again. Arms linked, we chorus-lined another fifty feet onto the base before the final soldier grabbed Karina's arm. We stopped and circled up.

Reinforcements rushed down, mostly young battle-helmeted privates ordered around by a few officers in black berets. The arrests began almost immediately. We sang "This Land Is Your Land" as two soldiers gingerly took Doc's elbows and led him back across the field toward the gate area. Daniel and Cindy soon followed. Nearby, the first couple of people from Overthrow Cluster received a similar escort.

Pain-compliance holds and pressure were used on some non-cooperators...

But when two soldiers came for Lyle, who was seated near us, he didn't budge. The soldiers took hold of his arms and tried to twist them behind his back. Lyle stared intently ahead. One of the soldiers removed his gloves, reached in his pocket, and pulled out a short wooden dowel. He took a long breath, then bent over and jammed the dowel into the soft spots behind Lyle's ears.

Lyle stared straight ahead, his jaw firmly set. As one soldier twisted his arm and the other jabbed with the dowel, I wavered unsteadily. I gripped Karina's hand for support. A private fastened onto my elbow. I didn't resist, and he led me away from our circle. As we passed Lyle, who had risen to his feet but refused to walk, the private started twisting my arm. My elbow twinged in pain, and I looked around at him. "Hey, I'm not going anywhere," I said. He eased up, but wouldn't look at me.

... while others were carried out of the meadow by military police.

Emboldened, I leaned forward, trying to catch his eye. "How does it feel to arrest American citizens? Is this why you enlisted?" He yanked my arm forward, but it seemed to get under his skin. And sure enough, a moment later, when I proposed veering out of our way to avoid a marshy area, he silently acquiesced, as if to show that he had a heart.

He led me up an embankment to the gate area where the buses were parked. After a quick pat-down he handcuffed me with white plastic bands. Then another soldier carefully wrote the number "R-56" on my hand.

Most of Change of Heart and Overthrow wound up on the same bus. People were yelling to each other, leaning out the windows to razz the soldiers, and laughing up a storm. We had survived a confrontation with the U.S. military, even out-maneuvered them for a few minutes! The nail clippers came out, the plastic bands were cut off.

I held my wrists out as Cindy snipped my cuffs. I stuck them in my back pocket — maybe I'd get to keep them as a souvenir.

Once free, people bounced around the seats. Secret stashes of fruit and nuts and even a few candy bars were passed around as the last protesters came aboard.

The driver closed the doors. The two guards at the front ordered everyone to sit down, and the bus pulled out and headed into Vandenberg. "They're keeping us on the base," I said, settling into a seat next to Hank.

He shook his head. "Naw, they're probably just taking a back road."

"Remember what you see for the occupation next time," Karina announced. "This is our chance to scout it out."

We rolled down a two-lane road, passing an occasional nondescript building. Without discussing it, a number of people began industriously rubbing the numbers off their hands. Hank went a step further. After smearing out his number, he borrowed a pen from me and inked a fresh one over it. I leaned toward him, trying to make it out. He held it up and read it aloud. "4Q-U812."

He started laughing, read it again, and laughed even more. "4Q-U812 — I always wanted to use that!"

I laughed, even though I wasn't sure it was such a great idea to mess with the system that way. But I didn't want to be the only one still numbered. I rubbed out most of my R-56.

The bus pulled up in front of what looked like a junior college classroom complex. I turned to Hank. "We're still on the base, I told you!"

An officer with an unnecessary bullhorn leaned into the bus and barked: "Everyone out! Single file!" Out the windows we could see a pack of guard dogs straining at their leashes, snarling at the first people stepping off the bus.

They herded thirty of us, men and women together, into the first building and through a doorway so low you had to stoop. We found ourselves in a twenty-foot square room with a high ceiling, painted entirely white except for a couple of horizontal black lines running around the walls.

"What's this," I said to Hank, "The brainwashing chamber?"

"No, it's a squashball court. See, up there's the cage for spectators."

"Or to spy on us!" I said.

"It's pretty convenient for them," Doc said as he joined us. "They can watch us without having to be in the room. They don't want the soldiers around us. They're afraid we'll corrupt them."

A woman I didn't recognize suggested that we make basic solidarity agreements not to move unless we all moved together. "There's thirty of us in this room — we have to stick together," she said as people gathered around.

"They'll want to separate men and women," said a woman named Aurora from Spirit affinity group. "That's usual."

Doc raised his hand even though no one was facilitating. "Just because it's 'usual' doesn't mean we have to agree to it."

"I can't support invoking solidarity over that issue," said Aurora. Most people seemed to side with her, and Doc let it go.

After fifteen or twenty minutes, we consensed to "no fines, no probation, and equal sentences," chose a couple of spokes for when the soldiers returned, and the meeting dissolved. People milled around, as if unsure whether to bother getting comfortable. We could be here for five minutes or five hours. I figured the Feds were in no hurry to deal with us, and sat down to unlace my new shoes. The moment of truth: the canvas was wet, but inside, my socks were dry. Success.

Some people took seats against the white walls, sitting quietly or talking in twos and threes. Others paced the floor. Karina, not content to pace, danced around the room, using people's bodies as props and balance beams.

I took a seat in the corner by Doc, who rubbed at the back of his hand. He held it up to the light, rotating it to see if the number showed from different angles. I looked down at my faded R-56, still hesitant to efface it completely.

I wished there were a clock in the room. When's recess? Was this chamber my home for an hour or a month? Didn't they have to let us go outside? Or at least tell us what was going on?

I wasn't feeling especially social, but it was my first chance to talk with Doc in a while, and I was curious about his motives for getting busted. "I'm glad you're here," I said. "But this turned into such a LAG action. I thought you would be more interested in March."

He looked at me thoughtfully. "I am. I'd prefer an action organized by affinity groups. But this first action is critical. It'll set the tone for March and beyond."

Arrestees were numbered and re-numbered.

I pursed my lips and leaned my head back against the wall. "Do you really think VAC can get the March action together without LAG?"

He stopped working on his hand and looked at me. "It's not a question of VAC getting it together. It's going to be organized by AGs. And a lot of this action was, too — look at the kitchen, the medical team, the whole encampment. Those are done by affinity groups."

I crossed my arms and nodded. "But LAG wound up coordinating all the publicity, getting the rally together, and paying for posters and mailings. Plus, the media collective is all LAG people."

"That doesn't mean AGs can't do it," he said. "The problem is, as long as the LAG office is involved, people will assume things are getting taken care of. If there isn't a central organization, it would be clear that AGs have to take it on."

A chafing crept into my voice. "That's too idealistic. If the organizing gets decentralized, who's going to see the big picture? Who is going to make sure that pieces don't fall through the cracks?"

"That's what the spokescouncil is for."

"But every meeting it's different people. The spokescouncil is as transient as a lot of affinity groups. Someone has to provide continuity and maintain an overview."

Doc knit his brow. "What you're describing is a traditional, centralized power model. Maybe it's efficient in the short-term, but it reproduces the social dynamics we're trying to change."

A large paperwad being used as a soccer ball bounced off his leg, chased by two guys kicking at it. As they brushed past, I pulled my legs in, then put them out to reclaim my space.

"People on the office staff or Coordinating Council aren't trying to control the action," I said. "They see their jobs as facilitating the organizing. They're committed to not being leaders."

"It's not that simple. It takes more than good intentions to avoid hierarchy. It's inevitable that an organizational staff will be seen as leaders, and start to act the part."

I thought about Holly. My discomfort must have shown, because Doc quickly added, "This isn't an attack on the staffers as people. It's a critique of the centralized structure."

"So we should disband LAG?"

Doc's brow relaxed, but he continued to look intently at me. "If LAG exists as a network to do actions at Livermore, it has a function. But building an organization shouldn't be our goal. Suppose we succeed, and LAG becomes the acknowledged hub of radical organizing. The government would just know what to sabotage." He paused for a breath. "There's an alternative. A decentralized affinity group network can forge a community of resistance they'll never destroy."

How do you argue with a poetic vision? For me, it all came back to the question of overview. If you're asking people to take risks, you need to know that the support work is being done.

Before I could say anything, though, the door opened and a soldier stepped in. All talk stopped as he counted us, pointing to each person in turn. The two spokes approached him, but he ignored them. Without a word, he backed out of the room and locked the door.

"Maybe they're going to bring us lunch," someone said.

"Or jail clothes," said Karina. "I wonder if we'll get a New Testament like at Livermore?"

Suspecting that something was about to happen put a damper on conversation. Doc went over to talk with Rick from his AG. I sat by myself, feeling restless for some change, any change, just to be on with it.

The little door opened again. Two soldiers ducked in, followed by an officer. "Line up by your numbers," the officer ordered. "You're going next door to be booked."

I looked around to see what others would do. There was some shuffling around, but no one lined up.

"We're not moving unless we all move together," Karina called out.

"We want to see a lawyer," someone demanded.

"Yeah," Hank seconded. "And when's lunch?"

The officer gruffly assured us that we would all end up back together. "You won't be separated. We just need to process you. Now line up by your numbers."

This time his command set off a ripple of half-suppressed laughter, which seemed to perplex the officer until someone explained the situation to him. He cocked his head and growled at one of his aides, who ducked out of the room. "Alright then," he ordered. "Everyone line up along this wall." As he spoke, the aide ducked back in with six more soldiers and a magic marker.

The officer glared at us. "Line up!"

We slowly made our way to the wall. One of the soldiers came down the row and renumbered us. When he got to me, he labeled me A-17. Then he scratched out the rest of my old number, as if reprimanding me for my caution.

Someone called out a proposal that we go ahead with the booking, with everyone making sure that they could see the person ahead and behind at all times. If anything went wrong, we would all sit down and refuse to move. We agreed, and the line was ushered out of the squash court.

The booking was held across the hall in a gymnasium barely bigger than a basketball court. Moveable partitions divided it into a maze of cubicles. As we wended our way through the booking process, protesters bantered with the military police checking our IDs and taking our fingerprints. The guy ahead of me made a hard-boiled-gangster face for his mug shot. I tried to follow suit, but wound up laughing instead.

The only downer was that they took away everything in my pockets, including my pen and paper. So much for keeping a prison journal. I should have put it inside my shoes, the one place they didn't check.

As each person finished the booking, they were steered to the other side of the room and put into a small cage — to save sideline space in the small gym, the team benches were right at courtside, enclosed behind wire mesh.

I joined Cindy, Hank, and about fifteen other people in the cage, followed soon after by Doc and Karina. Karina seemed unusually subdued. She gave me a faint smile as I caught her eye. I wished she'd sit down next to me, but she went and sat with a couple of people from her AG. I looked around the cage, not feeling like talking to anyone. I wished I had a book. I should have smuggled in some pages of a novel in my shoes. Or maybe Trotsky's autobiography. That would make good prison fare.

Daniel was put into our cage. But before the next person could be brought over, the calm of the gym was broken by the sound of stomping boots. A squad of men in khaki fatigues came marching across the floor, and the racket echoed off the concrete walls. We stared through the wire mesh as the squad came to a halt in front of our cage. "Hright, Hace!" The column snapped around to face us — the U.S. Marshals.

Someone called out in a shaky voice: "I don't think we should move unless we all move together." People nodded, but no one took their eyes off the Marshals.

The commander pulled open our cage door. I pressed my back against the wall.

"Cindy Davenport!" he bellowed.

Cindy didn't answer. We stared back at the commander, motionless.

"Move it! Davenport!" No one budged. Cindy was hunched behind two people in the center of the cell. Her head was down, her hair hanging across her face.

The commander glared at us, then stepped out to confer with two of his men. The three of them came back into the cage studying a small piece of paper — Cindy's polaroid photograph.

"That's her, over there!" The three Marshals charged at her, knocking other people aside. They grabbed Cindy by the arms and dragged her out the cell door. Then, as she staggered to her feet, they flung her headlong into a partition. She hit it with a thud and dropped to the floor.

I froze in my seat as the cage door slammed. But Karina leapt up against the wire mesh. "Shame! Shame!" she screamed. Her rage sparked the whole cell. In an instant, everyone was up and shouting, "Shame! Shame!"

The Marshals gawked at us. The commander hollered at his men. "Get her out of here!" Still shaking, Cindy was hauled away. "Shame! Shame!" The shouts rocked the gym. An Air Force officer ran up and talked heatedly with the commander of the Marshals, who kept making sweeping gestures with his arms. "Shame! Shame! Shame!"

Suddenly the Marshals snapped to attention. "Hright, Hace!" The column bristled as the commander strode to the front of the line. And with a step so quick it made us jump, they marched straight out of the gym.

We gaped after them. Were they really gone? Had we shamed them into leaving? Before we could get our bearings, a short man in an impeccable suit stepped up to the cage. "Legal Counsel," people started yelling. "We want to see a lawyer!"

He waved for quiet, a tight gesture that belied his cool exterior. "I'm the assistant federal prosecutor for this district. You'll see your lawyers."

"Where did you take Cindy?" people demanded. "We're not moving till we see our lawyers!"

The prosecutor set down his briefcase and pleaded in a terse, polished manner. Gradually, by various arguments and reassurances about us all ending up together, and getting to see our lawyers, and not having to deal with the Marshals, he persuaded us that it was in our best interest to move back to the squashball court.

A gauntlet of soldiers with riot clubs and helmets lined our path as we were led out the back of the gym. I tried to make eye contact, but they stared blankly away. Behind me, Hank jived at them: "Protecting national security, huh? Feel good about working in a prison camp?"

En route we were given our first chance to use a toilet, a relief I hadn't been anticipating. It surprised me that I hadn't noticed how much I needed to go.

We were steered to a small wood-floored exercise room. It wasn't the squash court we'd been promised, but no one seemed inclined to fight over it. We ducked through the low doorway.

"What's with all these four-foot doors?" I asked Karina.

"Teaches you to stoop," she said.

People sat down in a rough circle and started to discuss what to do about Cindy's being taken away. We hadn't even gotten as far as choosing a facilitator when several soldiers ducked through the doorway. They stopped just behind Hank. Their heads jerked as they sized us up. Suddenly they grabbed Hank by the arms and dragged him out of the room.

I groped to my feet along with a few others, but the door had already slammed. I sagged. How did we fall for that? Of all the amateur...

Hank. What was happening to him? Why had they grabbed him? Was it coincidence, or retaliation for his taunting the guards?

We reformed our circle as a horseshoe so no one had their back to the door. I took a seat on the far side of the room. If the soldiers returned, I wanted a chance to see what other people did before they grabbed me.

Karina, seated near the front, was the first to speak. "Don't let them drag us away. Next time the door opens, let's all get in the corner and link arms. At least make them work for it!"

Next to her, a big guy named Kurt shook his head slowly. "Why fight when we know we can't win? They can move us if they want to."

Aurora from Spirit affinity group nodded. "I don't feel good about fighting them, either. They're not my enemies. Non-cooperating only escalates the confrontation." When she finished, she looked around. "We need a facilitator."

"No," someone said, "A facilitator will get singled out as a leader. Each person call on the next one. It's safer."

Aurora called on Doc. His voice cracked as he spoke. "We've got to make some basic solidarity agreements," he said hurriedly. "There's no guarantee that we'll end up back together if we leave here separately. This is the federal government. They can ship us all over the place if they want to." Several hands went up as he paused, but he waved them off. "Wherever we are, we should all keep demanding a mass arraignment, so we can meet before we go to court. If you get isolated, don't go to arraignment till you've seen one of our lawyers."

A woman across the circle kept her hand up insistently, and Doc finally called on her. "The question is," she said urgently, "What are we going to do when they come back? Are we — "

"Process, process," I called out anxiously. I knew it sounded formalistic, but the scattered energy was hard for me to handle, and I really wanted us to stay focused and make some agreements. "Doc made a solidarity proposal. We should stick to that."

Karina groaned. "We're never going to reach consensus on this."

The woman across the circle spoke again. "We shouldn't be wasting time trying to reach consensus. We should break into small groups based on what we want to do, so people who want to resist can plan it."

But the idea of splitting the group got a cold reception. Daniel spoke next, in his deep, measured tones. "We have to stay together. But that doesn't mean we all have to do the same thing. Solidarity means respect and support for each person, not identical responses."

More hands flew up, but at that moment, the door swung open. "Kurt McCormick," a soldier called out. "Come with us."

Kurt looked sheepishly around, then stood up. The soldiers latched onto his arms, led him out, and relocked the door.

Karina threw her arms up in exasperation. "This is so disempowering!"

"Process," someone yelled over the rest of us. "Let's do a go-round and see what people plan to do when their name is called. It'll give us an idea where we are."

It sounded good to me. I leaned against the wall opposite the door, next to Daniel and Doc. Probably they would both non-cooperate. I pictured twisted wrists and sprained elbows. Was it worth fighting, just on principle? But if the rest of my cluster resisted, how could I *not* do it? Hopefully they wouldn't call my name right away, so I could see what the others did.

The go-round hadn't even started when the door opened. "Aurora Elkhart?"

Aurora rose from the floor, but as the soldiers approached her she knelt down. "I would like a moment to pray." The soldiers stopped and put their hands on their hips, waiting like patient executioners. At last they beckoned to her. She nodded, crossed herself, and slowly got to her feet. Taking her lightly by the elbows, the soldiers ushered her from the room.

Her response lowered the tension, but it quickly rose as people spoke. Daniel's plan made the most sense to me. "I'm going to tell them, 'I can't cooperate with you because of the way you have treated people before me.' Even if they drag me away, it's important that the soldiers understand the consequences of what they do to us."

When the guards returned, it was Doc they called for, and he adopted Daniel's tactic. "Because of the way you yanked Cindy and Hank from the room, I cannot cooperate with you." The soldiers looked at each other, then bent over, took hold of his upper arms, and dragged him out.

I can do that, I thought. I have to. Daniel was right. Somewhere we have to draw the line.

Besides, they're dragging people, not using pain holds. Of course, who knows what happens once they get you out of the room? They might have more persuasive techniques at their disposal.

A few minutes later, Daniel was dragged out. I could be next. I was ready. It felt powerful to declare solidarity with those before me, to join in a common response.

But it was discouraging that there was nothing we could consense on as a group that was more effective than each of us acting individually. It didn't bode well for the coming days.

The door opened. Was it my turn? Two soldiers stepped in and flanked the door. Instead of calling a name, though, they stood at awkward attention, staring at the back wall and pretending not to notice that we were in the room. A minute passed. An unhelmeted head ducked in — Walt!

He surveyed our grim circle and burst out laughing. "Haven't they told you what's happening?" We shook our heads. "They've charged thirty people who trespassed at the gate with misdemeanors," he told us, "and given them three-day sentences. They've already pled 'no contest,' and they aren't asking for further solidarity. All of you here are getting tossed off the base with ban-and-bar notices. You'll be back at camp in an hour."

My initial response was stunned silence. I wanted to believe it was true, but I couldn't quite summon the faith. After all of our preparation, after all we had just been through, we were getting out? I looked around at the others. Everyone seemed dazed. Was it a trick? Or was it really a victory?

Finally Karina clambered to her feet and let loose a whoop. "Yeah! I knew they couldn't handle us! We're free!"

A few others joined her celebration, but the rest of us were still recovering from the shock. Karina caught my eye. I wanted to jump up and hug her, but my body didn't respond. I smiled and shook my head, as if to say, "Unreal, isn't it?"

Walt stuck around to answer a few more questions. Someone asked about Cindy and Hank. "They're both already free," Walt told us. "They dragged them right out to the bus. That's where you're heading, too."

To the bus. Back to camp. And then home. We could be on the road in a few hours. I could hardly believe it. After all our build-up, we got off with a slap on the wrist? Well, why not? Maybe we'd earned it by our willingness to travel halfway across California in the middle of Winter to protest a missile that the Pentagon couldn't even get it together to test.

But it was hard to feel too glib. Our half-baked jail solidarity hadn't exactly forced their hand. It felt more like we'd escaped than that we'd actually won anything.

Still, we had occupied Vandenberg Air Force Base. And for whatever reason, the government had backed away from a confrontation. Score round one for us.

Friday, January 28, 1983

"MAYBE I'LL frame my ban-and-bar notice," I said to Holly as I watered the vines that wound along the walls of our apartment.

"It's still hard to believe that's all you got," she said from the kitchen. She brought her soup and tea out into the dining area. "Have you decided about the Concord action tomorrow?"

"I think I'm going to do it," I said. Mort had been lobbying people to do the action out at Concord Naval Weapons Station since we got back, and I was pretty well committed. "Maybe I'll get busted and cite out. That's what CISPES and the other Central America groups want to do. It's LAG people who want to stay in jail. What are you planning?"

"I'm staying in till arraignment, I'm pretty sure," she said. She sat down at the table, then turned to me. "Will you start the record over? I want to hear that flute song again." Holly and I had walked up Telegraph Avenue earlier and bought an album by Sukay, an Andean group we'd heard recently at La Peña. "Caroline and I are thinking about taking flute lessons," she said. "I need to be doing something non-political."

I turned the volume up a notch, then walked over behind Holly. She set down her spoon and leaned her head back against me. I stroked her long hair as the flutes piped like two kids running up and down green hills on the first day of Spring.

ACTION BULLETIN

INTERNATIONAL DAY OF NUCLEAR DISARMAMENT

50¢

Published by Livermore Action Group — Issue No. 1

INTRODUCTION

Dear Friends,

This is your Action Bulletin. The purpose is to provide a forum for people wishing to take part in actions for disarmament and social justice on or around June 20, the International Day of Nuclear Disarmament. The nature of the material, the length of this publication, and of course, the success of International Day itself, depend on your efforts.

Please send us letters or articles about your plans for International Day and the week leading up to it. We also welcome articles and letters of a philosophical and political nature exploring different approaches within the peace movement. We encourage information-sharing about the arms race and related social evils, and discussions of programs, tactics, long-range plans and organizing strategies to bring about social change. We'd like to include a broad spectrum of views and styles and to provide people with an opportunity to form new alliances within this politically and culturally diverse movement.

As this first issue of the Action Bulletin goes to press, hundreds of thousands of people in Western Europe are participating in Easter week deomonstrations to protest the manufacture of nuclear weapons and their present and proposed deployment on European soil. These weapons and weapon systems are designed in the United States at Lawrence Livermore and Los Alamos Laboratories. Many communities in the U.S. have factories that manufacture or assemble these weapons or weapon systems or have plants that process fuel for nuclear weapons.

Last week Reagan plugged the continuing "space wars" research of Livermore Labs as the answer to the peril of nuclear holocaust. Earlier in March, he again denounced the Freeze movement and warned us about the "evil empire" of the Soviet Union. Meanwhile United States unemployment continues to rise, vital social services are cut, and we expand our military intervention and our support of repressive regimes in the Third World. If there is to be an effective international movement for disarmament and social justice, millions of people in the United States must make a powerful commitment, must be willing to become engaged.

We hope that between now and June 20th you will make time in your lives to discuss these issues with your friends and neighbors and to help plan an action or educational event for June 20th. And we hope that all of our actions on International Day will generate many new organizing skills, new alliances, and a sense of personal empowerment and solidarity with others that will find continued expression in local, national, and international movements for peace and justice.

continued on page 8

CHICAGO

In February, the Chicago Disarm Now Action Group (DNA) sent out a "Midwest Call for Action to Stop the Euromissiles and First Strike", proposing that there should be coordinated actions at as many Euromissile and other first-strike weapons production sites as possible on June 20 -- the International Day of Nuclear Disarmament.

DNA is planning a blockade at the Northrop Defense Systems plant in Chicago. The goal is to protest and disrupt weapons production there for one working day. The Northrop Chicago division produces radar and electronic defense equipment for the B-1 and B-52 bombers, and other aircraft. DNA will be leafletting workers at the plant prior to June 20th in an effort to gain their support and participation in the blockade.

In addition, DNA is encouraging actions at several other major weapons production sites in the Midwest: Williams International, Walled Lake, Michigan (assembles the engines for all 3 cruise missiles); McDonnell Douglas, St. Louis (TERCOM guidance and navigation systems for all 3 cruise missiles); Honeywell, Inc., Minneapolis (guidance system for the ALCM, radar equipment for the SLCM, memory system for Trident); Boeing, Witchita (prime contractor for the ALCM); and Sundstrand Co., Rockford, IL (fuel boost pump for the ALCM). Planning for coordinated actions at Midwest production sites took place on March 19 at the "Great Lakes Euromissile Workshop: Organizing Opposition" in Chicago.

The first deployment of cruise and Pershing II missiles is now scheduled for December, 1983. American resistance at production sites, coordinated with European resistance at deployment sites, will be necessary to stop the missiles, and time is short. The potential for media impact of an international day is immense, and American support for the European resistance would be demonstrated. Resistance means doing more than symbolically protesting or petitioning for change. Direct action is required. This means that while marches and rallies play a role, concrete interference with "business as usual" brings concrete results.

In addition, we must make clear that we value and need the participation of military workers. In the current economic crisis, the military is an island of jobs in a rising sea of unemployment. And war, both conventional and nuclear, becomes more likely as the crisis oeepens. "Defense" workers, even more than anyone else, are lead to believe that the "other side" is the only aggressor. Extensive dialogue should take place long before an action, encouraging participation or independent actions, as well as talking about the issues.

For more information, contact Disarm Now Action Group, 497 S. Dearborn, Rm. 370, Chicago, IL 60605. Telephone: 312/427-2533.

The International Day Action Bulletin began as a separate newsletter, mailed to participating groups. Later editions became the basis of the International Pages of Direct Action newspaper.

"Caroline called this afternoon," she said when the song was over. "She's back." Caroline was one of the people who had gotten a three-day sentence at Vandenberg.

"It must have felt a little like a vacation to her after spending the Fall working on fund-raising," I said.

"Caroline thinks that the reason most people got ban-and-bar notices is so they can come down heavy on the second-timers at the March action."

"Sounds logical to me," I said. "They wanted to show us that they could be tough, play the divide-and-conquer game, then get rid of us and see if we come back." I plucked some dead leaves off the vine that wandered around the Michelangelo collage. "Maybe that was the point with the Marshals, too. They wanted us to see what we were dealing with."

"That makes me want to do the March action," Holly said.

I was a little bugged that she had skipped the LAG action, and now was thinking of doing the VAC one. "Tomorrow at Concord is enough for me to worry about," I said.

"Yeah. I have the whole weekend free if I can get these International Day letters done tonight. I could stay in jail for a couple of days at least. Maybe I'll cite out Monday so I can go to Coordinating Council." She paused. "Then again, maybe I won't. I could use the break."

I opened a beer and a bag of corn chips and sat down beside her. "What are you mailing, the International Day Call?"

"Yeah, the Call. But mainly it's a mailing to raise money for the European networking trip Les and Aurora are starting in February."

"It's really going to happen?"

"They already bought the tickets. But we still need money for their expenses. They'll be gone over two months, all over Western Europe. Les speaks German, and Aurora knows Spanish and Italian, so they can cover a lot of the continent."

"France gets left out?"

"The main response to our first international mailing has been from England, Germany, and Italy. So it makes sense to focus there."

"Do you think there's still time for groups to plan an action for June?"

"Well, even if they can't do much this year, we can get them involved for next year," she said.

I picked up some of the letters and started folding them. "So Mort and Claudia finally approved sending the Call out?"

"Oh, they still can't stand the poetic part at the beginning," she said impatiently. "But we had to quit arguing and get something to the printer. International Day is only five months away."

I glanced at her. She was intent on the envelope she was addressing. I scooted my chair back and stood up from the table. Stepping over behind her, I started massaging her shoulders.

She stopped writing, although her pen remained poised. Her eyes were closed. I worked my thumbs under the uppermost muscle and felt her wince. "Too much?" I asked.

"No," she said. "Would you do my neck?"

I kneaded my fingers up and down her neck, then worked on the lower part with my thumbs. "I could do this better if you were lying down," I said.

She smiled. "If the offer extends till later, that would be great. But I have to get this mailing finished tonight, and make a list of tasks for next week. I don't want to come back from jail and try to remember all these details."

I sat down and finished folding the letters. Holly hand-addressed each envelope in her plain, open script. When we finished, she went into the kitchen and made a cup of tea, got out her day planner, and settled in on the living room cushions. I put on a reggae tape and sat down next to her. I took a hit off my pipe, opened a book on Renaissance architecture, and let my eyes range over the classical forms while my mind wandered forward to the Concord action.

Saturday, January 29, 1983

Jenny and Angie buzzed our door at ten the next morning. I was still groggy as Jenny gave me a quick hug. "Hey — how's it going?" she said. She exuded a charge that extended to the tips of her curly brown hair. Jenny was twenty-three, short and wiry, with freckled skin and bright, expectant eyes. I'd met her a few times at the office, where she was helping Caroline with bookkeeping and Claudia with the mailing list.

She jangled her keys. "Ready to go?"

"Just about," said Holly. "I want to fill a jug of water."

Angie stepped from behind Jenny. In height and age the two were matched, but that was the extent of the resemblance. Angie was quiet, pensive. Her auburn hair, which had been in a loose ponytail the other time we'd met, was woven in several braids. Our hug was casual, but she held on for a moment longer than I expected.

Holly handed me the water and picked up a bag of International Day flyers. "We should take some copies of Direct Action out there too, don't you think?"

I pointed to the stack near the door. "I got a bundle."

Jenny's live-in boyfriend had come along as chauffeur, but he didn't seem very excited about the protest, and drove in silence. Jenny sat next to him, but she turned around in her seat to face Angie, Holly, and me in the back.

"I noticed you have Massachusetts plates," I said to her. "Did you just move here?"

"Well, in September," she said with a guilty look. "We just haven't gotten new plates yet."

"That's only four months," Holly said.

Jenny seemed to review a mental calendar. "It seems like a long time ago. When we came out here, we weren't even sure we were going to stay. But the first week I was here, I heard about LAG, and then visited the Berkeley Women's Health Collective. I knew this was where I wanted to live."

"I know that feeling," I said. "For me it was the first time I saw Telegraph Avenue."

"That's what did it for me, too," Angie said. She worked a braid loose and plaited it again as she spoke. "That and the murals. After I got out of college last Summer, I decided to hitchhike from Boston to the west coast. I wanted to see San Francisco, then go on up to Portland and Seattle and maybe Vancouver. But I never made it past Berkeley."

"There's worse places to get stuck," I said. "So you two met here? I thought maybe you went to school together."

"No," Jenny said. "Angie and I met in the LAG office, then took our nonviolence prep together. Most of us at the prep formed Red Menace AG, and Alby wanted us to join Change of Heart because he's friends with Karina. So here we are."

"Are you staying in jail?" Holly asked.

"Oh, definitely," Jenny said, although she was shaking her head. "That's the main point, to go to jail for what you believe in. If you cite out, it's like you don't really mean it, it's just a gesture."

Holly looked over at me. "Some people have to cite out, to get back to things like work or kids. Even if they cite out, the media still reports it as arrests — it builds our actions."

"Right, right," Jenny said hurriedly. "I was just speaking for myself."

LAG joined the Committee in Solidarity with the People of El Salvador (CISPES) in calling an action at Concord Naval Weapons Station, which shipped arms to right-wing forces in Central America.

Angie looked down at her hands. "I'll stay at least one night," she said. "But after that I don't know. I'll have to see if I can handle jail." I nodded, but she didn't look up.

We cruised over the Berkeley Hills and out into the valley toward Concord, a suburb forty-five minutes northeast. The demonstration was at Concord Naval Weapons Station, located in a semi-rural area outside the town. Concord was the major weapons depot in the Bay Area, and had been a shipping point for munitions to Vietnam and more recently to Central America.

The main organization behind the day's protest was CISPES, the Committee in Solidarity with the People of El Salvador. Central American politics were pretty convoluted, and I was groping to make sense. In El Salvador, the CIA was supporting a right-wing government and its military death squads against a large, popularly-based guerrilla movement. CISPES's role was to build opposition to U.S. policy.

CISPES also did a lot of organizing around neighboring Nicaragua, where a 1979 revolution by the Sandinistas had toppled a longtime dictator. Then-President Carter cautiously supported the revolution. But since Reagan took office in 1981, the CIA had not-so-covertly funneled millions of dollars to right-wing "Contra" rebels trying to destabilize the Sandinistas and reinstall a pro-corporate regime.

It was hard to keep it straight. But weapons from Concord were going to both countries, which simplified the matter for us.

We left the car up the road and walked to Clyde Park, which wasn't a park at all, but a muddy lot the size of a football field. Clumps of straw stuck up out of the lumpy ground on either side of a gravel road. It was hardly an uplifting sight, but its location right next to the main gate made it the logical staging area for the demonstration.

And it was truly a demonstration, not a LAG-style action. CISPES's leadership consisted of more traditional leftist-socialist types. The bullhorns were out in force, the planning committee was conducting scenario briefings, and those of us who planned to get arrested were being assembled into "waves" which would blockade the gate in orderly succession.

In some ways I liked it. Short as my Vandenberg jail time had been, it was sufficiently draining that I didn't mind someone else orchestrating this one.

As I came out from under the briefing canopy, I heard Karina accost Mort, who with a few other Overthrow people had worked on the demo as unofficial LAG reps.

Karina was wearing a dark green poncho with a visor on the hood. "What about affinity group autonomy?" she demanded.

"This action isn't organized by affinity groups," Mort answered.

"Isn't that up to us to decide?" Karina countered. "A bunch of self-proclaimed leaders have worked out all the details ahead of time, and we're supposed to be good soldiers and carry out their orders? That's the whole mentality we're protesting, isn't it?"

Mort threw his hands up in exasperation. "We've been working for months to get CISPES to organize an action with us. They don't want any 'autonomous affinity groups' running wild and upsetting things."

Before Karina could answer, Hank loped up in leather paratrooper boots. "Hey, I thought maybe I was the only one here from Change of Heart."

"No," I said, "Holly's here, and Angie and Jenny from Red Menace, and a couple of other people."

"Maybe you should join Overthrow and do the same wave as us," Mort proposed. "We have about eighteen people here."

"Wow," I said, "That's a lot."

"This is our focus," he said, "building a local coalition."

We rounded up the rest of our cluster and joined the circle of Overthrow people huddling on the gravel road. I recognized a half-dozen, including Lyle, Craig, and Tai. Lyle proposed that we sign up for the last wave. "Since we're planning to stay in jail till arraignment, we should let other people who are citing out get arrested first, so they can get processed sooner. Does everyone here plan to stay in till Monday?"

Everyone nodded. I still hadn't made up my mind, but if all the other LAGers were staying in, it would feel weird to leave.

We consensed to being in the final wave. Lyle shrugged. "Since the steering committee is planning the action, there's really nothing else for us to decide. The march down to the gate should begin pretty soon."

We started to break up, but Craig called us back. "People are lining up over there right now. Let's march over there as a cluster."

"Stop corporate war from Livermore to El Salvador," read Overthrow Cluster's banner for the action.

The crowd looked to be around a thousand people, including a large contingent of church people led by local clergy, a lot of Central and South Americans, various leftist groups, and a healthy sprinkling of LAGers. I saw Nathaniel talking with Pilgrim, and near them Monique and the Walnettos from nearby Walnut Creek. Off to the side, Melissa and several other people from Spirit AG were part of a prayer circle.

Facing this crowd, Overthrow unfurled its brand new fifteen-foot banner, white letters on black silk: "Stop Corporate War, From Livermore to El Salvador." Twenty of us fell in behind the banner and started down the gravel road to join the main group, loudly chanting "Over-throw! Over-throw!"

Our little procession was greeted with enthusiastic applause from the rest of the crowd. The initial effect was indeed a fine blend of stridency and high spirits. Unfortunately, none of the Overthrow lefties stepped forward to lead our march toward the main gathering. Still chanting "Over-throw," we paraded past the crowd and on down the gravel lane, finally coming to a halt facing the portajohns. "Turn around," Craig yelled, "We can march back up!"

"Let's just walk," Karina answered. Her proposal won general approval, and we merged into the main crowd.

In traditional demonstration form, the masses assembled in a column five to ten people wide. Most groups had their own banners, and the more militant had also brought bullhorns to enforce their chants. LAGers drifted toward the back of the line, marching behind a big International Day banner reading, "Thinking Globally — Acting Locally," and talking in small groups as the procession wound out of the park.

We strung like a ribbon along the right shoulder of the country road. The morning rain had passed on to the east, but clouds of clashing gray and white still towered from the horizon. The short march ended across the road from the weapons depot gate. The entrance was a two-lane drive flanked on the left by a single railroad line and on the right by a neat little suburban lawn with a few spindly trees. Beyond the lawn, a chain-link fence and guardhouse ordinarily controlled access. But for the protest, a hundred young Marines in combat fatigues were arrayed behind the fence. In front of the fence stood several dozen California Highway Patrol officers, who I assumed would make the arrests.

Although the base was open on Saturdays, no vehicles were entering the gate. This elicited some murmuring about the point of a blockade when there was nothing to block, but the organizers were undaunted. We did a few chants, and then the first wave of fifty protesters strode across the road and sat down in the entrance.

"Think globally, act locally" — a favorite slogan of the 1980s.

Despite the absence of traffic, the police quickly moved in and busted the blockaders. The second wave of fifty was swept away just as quickly. At that pace, it might not have been necessary to repeat any chants before the arrests ended. But for reasons no one could fathom, the third wave was left sitting as the police abruptly marched off and the Marines moved out onto the lawn.

Speculation had a field day as the third wave squirmed on the damp pavement. Maybe the authorities were nervous about how many more people planned to get busted. Maybe the jail only had room for the first hundred.

Dancing at the gates of the weapons depot.

Maybe the police were taking a coffee break.

Melissa brought up the possibility of going down the road and climbing over a fence. "Then they'd have to deal with us," she said. The idea got some support. But just then, the state police re-emerged. The Marines stepped back, and the cops marched out into the road and arrested the third wave. It was our turn.

Without a chant, or even much organization, Overthrow, Spirit, and other miscellaneous LAGers filtered across the two-lane road and formed a long blockade line. Some people in the crowd started chanting the Overthrow banner slogan: "Stop Corporate War, From Livermore to El Salvador!" But it faded as the police once again marched off and the Marines moved up. Did they hope we'd get bored and go home? Were they getting paid overtime and stretching it all they could? We muttered among ourselves. Someone started a Holly Near song, but no one quite knew the words. Confused, we linked arms. Nervous laughter rippled up and down the line, and when someone kicked their legs in a can-can, the whole wave erupted in a chorus line, to the applause of our audience across the road.

No telling what theatrical heights we might have scaled had the police not returned as suddenly as they had left. We sat down. The cops scraped their boots on the concrete behind us as they waited for orders. Finally a bullhorn made the official pronouncement that we were blocking U.S. government property, and would be liable to arrest if we did not immediately disperse.

No one budged, and the arrests began. Non-cooperators got dragged. The rest of us stood and walked away with our arresting officer. Twenty feet behind the lines, we were patted down for weapons, plastic handcuffs were pulled tight, and we were herded onto a bus — a real prison bus this time, with the windows barred and rings under each seat for shackles. I took a seat across from the door, just behind Holly and Karina. A few more people were loaded on. Then the door slammed shut, and we headed toward the highway for the county jail in Martinez.

Inside a minute, Karina had snipped her cuffs off and was turned around in her seat. "They just built this jail a couple of years ago. We're practically the first protesters to try it out!"

"Yeah, it's one of the new high-tech jails," Hank said from across the aisle.

"I heard it's all done by remote control, with video cameras everywhere. It's like Big Brother."

Karina's clippers cut through the plastic bands around my wrists. "This'll be my first time in a real jail," I said.

"We're starting with the best," she said. "I hope so, anyway. What a drag if they put us in a gym again."

Pilgrim, who was getting arrested for the thirty-fifth time in his illustrious career, hollered for attention. "We need to talk about solidarity before we get off the bus. I propose that we demand mass arraignment, refuse fines and probation, and insist on knowing the sentence before we'll plead."

Melissa, who was one of six people stuck in a little "high-security" chamber at the front of the bus, separated from the rest of us by a mesh grill, interrupted him. "You shouldn't make proposals if you're facilitating."

"It's okay with me if someone else facilitates," Pilgrim answered. "Let's just get on with it! Why don't you do it?"

"I can't from in here. Karina, you do it."

Karina squatted in her seat so she was a head taller than the rest of us. "Okay! Pilgrim has made a proposal. Any clarifying questions?" We turned in our seats to form a rough oval and pulled together a by-the-book meeting. We were on the verge of reaching consensus on "no fines, no probation, mass arraignment, equal sentences" when the bus pulled into the jail garage. The door was wrenched open, and a voice with no need of a bullhorn cried: "Out of the bus, single file!"

"We're having a meeting," Karina shot back.

A husky deputy barreled up the stairs and came to a halt right in front of me. I recoiled, but he grabbed my arm and yelled, "I don't give a damn about your meetings!"

He yanked me down the stairs and shoved me toward a line of deputies. Before I could get my footing, the deputies sent me careening down their gauntlet, shoving me from one to the next. At the far end of the garage two deputies caught me and jerked me upright. I struggled to gain my balance, expecting to be sent sprawling at any second. But the two deputies held me firmly in place. I looked back toward the bus just in time to see Karina dragged out and sent reeling toward me.

After her there was a pause. I caught my breath. Karina's eyes, ablaze with determination and delight, met mine, then turned toward the bus door. A minute passed. The deputy emerged — empty-handed! He flipped his hands in the air and walked over to a telephone. Another minute passed, and another. Then, slowly, one by one, the rest of the people got off the bus.

As Karina and I rejoined them, everyone seemed to be talking at once. Mort wound up behind me as we were led into a hallway for a preliminary booking. "You doing okay?" he asked.

"Yeah, what happened in the bus?"

"After they pulled you and Karina out, the rest of us piled up in the back of the bus. They could tell it would be impossible to get us out of there without a major mess, so they gave us five minutes to finish the meeting."

"Did you reach consensus?"

"I think so."

The authorities photographed us, searched our pockets, and fastened a white plastic ID bracelet on each person's left wrist. Then we were herded, men and women together, into a large holding tank.

A small window and recessed fluorescent fixtures cast a diffused light on the glossy white cinder block walls. The door was cast metal, polished to a dull sheen. Varnished wood benches ringed the cell like a locker room. Even the aluminum toilet glistened.

The cell door opened again, and Karina and Holly were put in with us. Karina said something over her shoulder to the guard, then turned and gave me a hug. She was practically vibrating, and held onto me as if I were an anchor. "Breathe," she said as if reciting a mantra. "Remember to breathe." I held her close, and felt her chest quiver as she laughed to herself.

After Karina, Holly seemed solid as an oak. I leaned into her and swayed a little. Our cheeks pressed together. Hers felt cool next to mine. I whispered, "I love you" and she kissed me gently.

We found a couple of bench-seats and sat holding hands and sharing impressions of the action. Being in jail with Holly gave me a new perspective. Compared to my previous two arrests, I found myself less concerned with "what's next?" or "when are we getting out of here?" Maybe I was getting the hang of jail. But mainly it was due to being with Holly. I thought of the title of a book I'd seen on her shelf: *Be Here Now.* That was easier with her around.

The evening passed in conversation and speculation. The most popular rumor had it that we would be arraigned the next day — Sunday — just to get us out of their hair. Gradually the mood quieted, and I found myself yawning constantly from the stale air.

"Would there be any dinner," someone asked.

"Sorry, you missed it," came the reply. All the granola had been confiscated during the search. Around the room, people moaned about involuntary fasting. We leaned against each other on the benches. Conversations were hushed.

Around 11 p.m., deputies came in dragging thin mattresses and a bunch of army blankets. The booking of earlier protesters was going slowly, they said. We might have to spend the night in the holding tank. We spread the mattresses on the floor. The deputies turned the lights down, and we laid down and tried to get comfortable.

"Isn't it weird how prison is designed to remove you from the people you love?" Holly whispered as we curled together under a flannel blanket. "People who probably need the most affection of anybody, and the state denies it to them."

"Yeah, this is pretty amazing. Here we are, sleeping together in jail. It'd be a whole different thing if you could be in jail with your lover."

Near us, Karina was curled up with Sara. Lucky for them, I thought. They'll get to stay together after Holly and I are separated.

Though Holly managed to fall asleep, I lay awake, my eyes playing with the renegade light beams slipping through the mesh window. Was I staying in jail? Should I cite out if I got the chance? Maybe when we got booked. But why? We'll probably get a two or three day sentence. I might as well stay in and serve it now with everyone else. But wouldn't it be great to get out tonight? Even if it took all night to get home, it would feel so great to sleep in my own bed.

I had just about drifted off when the door opened, bumping my mattress. The lights came on with a jolt. "Everyone up. Pile the mattresses over here. You're going to be booked."

Midnight booking? Were they just messing with us? People staggered up. The guards herded us out of the cell and led us through a maze of brightly-lit concrete hallways and remote-controlled steel doors. From above every door a gray video camera stared down like an unblinking cyclops.

As we traversed the shiny corridors, I thought again about citing out. But now I was so tired that all I wanted was to get back to sleep. Just stay the night. Get some sleep and then see what happens in the morning. Maybe we'll all get out then.

After enough twists and turns to thoroughly disorient us, we suddenly emerged into a large reception area with contoured chairs, drinking fountains, and dark gray carpeting. Hank cupped his hands over his mouth. "Flight 666 for Livermore Lab now boarding rows one through ten."

Melissa sat in a chair and shifted around, seeming unable to get comfortable. "Well, at least it's clean," she said sourly.

"Yeah," Craig said. "You should see the booking area at Santa Rita. It's cement and metal. The windows are all barred up — can you imagine working there?"

"You'd rather work here?" Hank said. "How could anyone be a jail guard? You spend most of your waking hours in prison."

Melissa scowled. "It fills a need some people have to be an authority figure, to be respected, or at least feared," she said in a voice that seemed intended to be overheard.

I looked around at the guards, who were clumped around the booking counter acting bored and disinterested. "They must believe at some level that what they're doing is a service, that they're protecting society," I said.

"How could anyone believe that?" Hank scoffed. "They can see what's going on. Ninety percent of the people in this jail are Black or Latino. Most of them are here for drugs, theft, or prostitution. How many of them are a threat to society?"

A deputy approached and ordered several of us to come over to the counter to be booked. I went first — get it done and get to bed. Melissa and Hank grumbled and followed slowly.

I stepped up the counter, walked through fingerprints, photo, and health survey, and then obediently went to the far side of the lobby to await further instructions. I leaned against the wall and looked back to the booking area, where Melissa gave her name loudly and lectured the woman taking the information about why we had done the protest. She grudgingly consented to being fingerprinted. But when she was led to the camera, she balked. "You already took our pictures earlier."

"We need to do it again."

"No, you don't."

My teeth grated at Melissa's audacity. Did she really think she could flout authority like that? Here, where they hold all the cards?

"Just stand there and hold your head up," the guard directed Melissa. Another deputy steered her against the wall, but her chin drooped onto her chest.

Melissa's non-cooperation was attracting attention. The deputies nervously tried to pry her head up, but Melissa responded by sitting down. Finally the commandant flipped his hand. "Just put her in that cell over there till she wants to cooperate."

As the two deputies grabbed Melissa by the arms, other protesters started moving that way. In a flash a dozen guards formed a cordon as Melissa was dragged to a row of tiny isolation cells tucked into a corner of the lounge.

Some people yelled at the guards, who backed up a step. But Melissa didn't call for any help, and even the other women from her AG settled for calling out encouragement. "We'll stay in solidarity! We won't leave without you!"

The cell door slammed. "That's Melissa all the way," one of her friends sighed. "No one's going to tell her what to do."

Slowly the booking process resumed. The next few went through fine and joined me against the wall. Then Hank stepped up to the counter. His shoulders were hunched, and he wore a clenched-teeth grin. The deputy looked up at him. "Last name?"

Hank stared at the deputy. "Feddup."

"Spell that."

"F-e-d-d-u-p."

"First name?"

"Irma."

"Is that your real name?" Hank was silent, as if he were struggling to keep from laughing. He offered no resistance as two other deputies led him to an isolation cell.

I gazed after him. You think you know someone, but then... Who would voluntarily provoke the guards to isolate them? Well, Hank and Melissa, apparently. I wondered if he thought up the name right on the spot.

People yelled encouragement and promised to stay in solidarity. The rest of the processing went without incident. No one was paying attention to those of us by the far wall, so I went back over to say goodbye to Holly. "How long are you planning to stay in?" I asked.

"At least a couple of days. There's an International Day meeting Wednesday night that I don't want to miss, but they have to arraign us before then, anyway." A look of alarm flashed across her face. "There goes your group! I love you!" She squeezed my hand and gave me a little push toward the departing men. I caught the door just before it closed.

All of the men from my holding cell, except Hank, were present. Mort, Lyle, and Craig were up ahead. Just behind me was Claude, the muralist I'd met at Livermore. To me, he was an elder statesman, and I was glad to be in with him.

Again we were led through the twisting halls, this time on a guided tour by a couple of young deputies who relished showing off their high-tech jail. They explained how the video cameras monitored each door, which opened only after the proper security codes had been relayed back to command central.

At last — at four o'clock in the morning according to the clock high on the wall — we arrived at our new lodgings. In the dim light we could make out the cell-block: an irregularly-shaped central area about half the size of a basketball court, with two-person cells along two of the walls. A wide stairway in the center led up to a balcony and a half-dozen second-story cells.

About thirty-five men had decided not to cite out. The earliest arrivals had been placed in the cells, but by the time my group got there, the rooms were full, and we had to crash in the main area.

As soon as I hit the thin plastic mattress I started to doze off. But I was awake long enough to overhear Lyle go to the door and call for the guards. "It's freezing in here. Can't we get some more blankets?"

"What's your name?"

"Lyle Eisner."

"Okay, go lay down and we'll see what we can do."

A while later we were awakened by guards with a few extra army blankets. "Where's Eisner?"

When Lyle raised his hand, the two guards grabbed him, led him brusquely to a cell, locked him in, and marched out.

I shook myself awake, along with the dozen others sleeping in the main area. We clustered together at the back of the cell-block, trying to figure out what to do. Mort went over to Lyle's cell and knelt down to talk under the door.

"There's nothing we can do now," someone said. "We know where Lyle is. We should just get some sleep."

Claude cut in sharply. "We have to figure out how we're going to resist if they try to grab anyone else."

Nathaniel, my nonviolence prepper, raised his hand. "We shouldn't resist them. Part of civil disobedience is a willingness to accept whatever punishment the state imposes, however unjust. It's our steadfast refusal to fight back that ultimately reaches people."

"I'm familiar with your views," Claude said. "Those of us who feel differently would like to discuss how to deal with the guards."

Nathaniel shrugged. "I've stated my opinion. If anyone is interested in discussing this later, I'd be glad to." He and another man left the circle and went back to bed.

Nathaniel's pacifism was intriguing, but it didn't speak to my heart. Even though I was scared by the guards, I wanted to resist, especially if someone had an idea how to do it. Claude proposed that if the guards reappeared, we all huddle behind the stairs and link arms and legs. We decided not to cooperate until the people confined in cells were let out and we could meet as a whole group. A couple of guys were chosen as liaisons to the guards if they reappeared. We all laid down.

It took a while, but finally I fell back asleep. It seemed only minutes later when I jerked awake. The guards were back! I groped toward the stairs. People called out, "What's happening? Who are they after?" We peered at the guards, who were opening up a coffee machine and filling it with instant crystals. "Sorry, it's decaf," one of them said. "It's all you're allowed to have."

Huddling together and linking arms seemed a bit theatrical, but we stayed together as our spokes approached the guards and demanded to have the cells opened before we'd cooperate.

"Oh, they'll be opened about nine," a deputy said. "Usually they're left open till about ten at night. You're on an open cell-block here. Of course, there aren't ordinarily people sleeping on the floor, but I guess they want to keep you all together, away from the other prisoners."

It was hard to stay militant in the face of such matter-of-factness, and we gradually drifted into smaller groups, talking among ourselves. I lay down again, fantasizing about more sleep. Behind me, Craig and Mort weighed our immediate prospects.

"They'll probably arraign us tomorrow morning," Mort said.

"You never know," said Craig. "I'm sure they want us out of here. The guards were telling people we could cite out anytime. I think they'd like to be rid of us."

"I still wouldn't count on anything happening today."

I looked around the shiny concrete cell-block. The odd angles of the walls gave the place a Kafka-esque feel, but even more striking were the video cameras mounted high on the walls, capable no doubt of surveying every inch of the room. 1984 had arrived early.

Shortly after nine, the cells were unlocked, including Lyle's. But Hank was still separated.

Breakfast followed — a bowl of Special K, a carton of milk, and a banana. Afterward, Pilgrim called for attention. "We should have a quick meeting and see who is staying in and who needs to cite out. Then we could do some workshops."

We gathered in a circle in the open area in front of the stairs and did a go-round. I wasn't feeling an especial desire to escape, mainly because as soon as the meeting was over, I was going to take a nap. Six men did need to leave by the end of the day, leaving twenty-nine to spend a second night. "What else do we need to discuss?" someone asked.

Claude thrust out his chest. "Melissa and Hank are in solitary confinement! The least we can do is find out what's happening to them."

Craig spoke in a calmer voice. "A couple of people should go talk to the guards and try to find out. The rest of us should talk about what we're going to do if they keep Hank and Melissa separated."

"That's fine," Pilgrim said. "But some people already said they didn't want to talk about resistance tactics."

Claude threw up his hands. "Then they don't have to stay at the meeting!"

Nathaniel was standing against the wall with his arms folded across his chest. "I'd like a chance to say something. Then I'll leave you alone to meet." He stepped forward to join our circle, but remained standing. "We have to keep sight of what civil disobedience means. We deliberately break the law, and we publicly submit to arrest, knowing we'll be punished. It contradicts the spirit of nonviolent resistance to try to avoid punishment." His assertions were met with some grumbling, but Nathaniel pressed on. "These two people carried their protest into jail, and refused to cooperate with their booking. They knew what they were doing, and knew they could be isolated for it. Willingness to accept the consequences of our actions is the strongest statement that we can make."

No one ventured an answer to his speech, and Nathaniel quietly left the meeting. Someone put out a tactical suggestion. "Maybe we should wait till we have word from them before we start making plans."

"If they're in solitary confinement, who's going to talk to them?"

"The lawyers will be able to see them. They can let us know what's going on. Until then, we should just agree not to leave jail without them."

Mort and Lyle returned from talking to the guards, who claimed to know nothing except that Hank and Melissa were still in solitary. Claude pushed for some sort of action to try to get them out, but got only lukewarm support, and with a loud sigh withdrew his proposal.

As the meeting broke up, most of the men stayed in the circle for a "life stories" session that Pilgrim pulled together. Each person got five minutes to share who they were and how they got involved in the protest.

I wanted to sleep. I went over and lay down on my mattress. The shiny cinder block walls created an echo chamber, though, bombarding me with stray bits of people's stories.

Nearer to me, Craig and Mort were talking about working with CISPES on the demo. I would have preferred silence, but eavesdropping on them was some consolation.

"This was a big step," Mort said. It was unusual to hear Mort optimistic about anything, and I inclined an ear in his direction. "Of course, only Overthrow people went to any meetings," he continued. "We've got to get people in LAG to connect the issues, get out of our anti-nuke ghetto."

"Reagan's doing his best to help out," Craig said with a wry chuckle. "Between trying to put the Cruise and Pershing missiles in Europe, giving the CIA money for the war in Central America, and cutting social services at home, I'd say he's doing his best to build a united front."

"It does open some doors," Mort said. "Right now, LAG is still pretty isolated. But I can see us a year or two from now as the direct action wing of a coalition that would include everyone from the Nuclear Freeze to the Central America support groups — like the Greens in Germany."

I finally succeeded in drifting halfway to sleep, transfixed by the big clock on the wall. It had no second hand. Each minute was marked by a click of the big hand, driving home its sheer duration. I lay there for nearly an hour trying to anticipate exactly when it would move.

Finally lunch interrupted my endeavors. I welcomed the white bread, bologna and cheese, a little bag of potato chips, and a waxed red apple.

"This isn't real jail food," Craig said. "This must mean they don't have enough people to make meals for us."

Once lunch was done, though, the expanse of time began to weigh on me. A book. Why didn't I bring a book? Just like at Vandenberg, they didn't search our shoes. I could bring in a novel. No, something dense, where each page would last a long time. How about Hegel? I could read that forever and never understand it, so it would always be fresh.

Would we get to go outside? Maybe we could play basketball for a while.

Maybe we could improvise a hoop and ball here. But the idea of organizing anything, even a game, seemed overwhelming.

Midway through the afternoon, a percussion jam developed on the second floor, with a dozen guys hammering on the hollow aluminum railings. I didn't feel inspired to join, but sat on my mattress dreamily listening to the rhythms and shouts echoing off the cinder block walls. I found myself humming a bass line as a tall guy wearing a blanket-cape twirled and pirouetted among us.

Amidst this circus, it took Claude a while to convince us that his shouts and waving arms were not part of the spectacle. "Hey, everybody should come down, the lawyers are here."

Instantly our mood changed from the communal celebration of free time in an exotic setting to the urgent personal need to know exactly when we were getting out of jail. There's the power of the law for you, I thought. We gathered in a horseshoe around Kathleen and another attorney I didn't recognize. They were laughing and talking with Craig. Kathleen turned to the group. "We were just over in the women's section. We came here to tell you the district attorney has agreed to recommend a sentence of time served for everyone, provided you accept arraignment now and come back in a month for the actual sentencing. They're willing to hold the hearing here at the jail tonight, if you accept the offer."

Kathleen had spoken so plainly that it took a moment to sink in. "Sunday night arraignments?" I said to Lyle. "Can you believe it? There's sixty of us in jail, and we're forcing them to hold court on Sunday night."

He nodded. "They can't deal with us. They want us out of here right now!"

Claude called for silence so he could ask a question. "What about the people who got put in solitary?"

"We're going down there next. They'll get the same deal. We'll make sure they get arraigned first, just to be sure. In the meantime, you should decide whether to accept the offer, and we'll try to get back down here in an hour or so."

There seemed no doubt that we'd accept the deal. Unless they agreed to pay us for our troubles, we weren't going to do much better.

It was several more hours before it all came together, so we spent the evening doing a talent show. I was feeling upbeat, and sang a John Prine song called "Flag Decal" that set forth an incisive analysis of patriotism and militarism:

> Your flag decal won't get you into heaven anymore
> They're already overcrowded from your dirty little war...

Around midnight, the twenty-nine men were led into a courtroom within the jail complex, where we were joined by Hank, looking none the worse for his solitary ordeal. The judge quickly arraigned us and ordered us to return en masse a month later for the formal declaration of our time-served sentences.

Out in the jail lobby we were reunited with the women. I saw Jenny and Angie first, and they welcomed me with an exuberant double hug. As they released me, Karina grabbed me in a tight embrace before spinning off to hug someone else.

I greeted a couple of other women, then spied Holly across the lobby talking to Craig. I wove my way through the crowd toward her. As I approached, a smile lit her face. She turned toward me, and I wrapped my arms around her. She seemed surprised at my intensity, but when I let go of her, her eyes were sparkling.

Hank interrupted our twosome to give Holly a hug. "Have you guys seen the control booth?" He gestured toward a glass-enclosed room filled with TV screens. "That's where they monitor all those cameras we were seeing. Look at the bossman, he's in paradise." A jowly deputy was tilted back in his comfy chair, supervising several female operators.

Holly frowned. "Reminds me of too many offices I worked in," she said.

Jenny's boyfriend drove out to pick us up. Six of us piled into the small sedan: Jenny and Angie sat in the front, with Sara, Karina, Holly, and me in the back.

Sara was still mainly a stranger to me, although I'd heard a little about her from Holly. She was involved in Central America support work and helped organize the Concord action. She was sitting upright next to the right-hand door. Her long brown hair flowed over her shoulders and onto Karina's. "Tell people about Johann," Karina said to her.

Sara's brow creased. "While we were waiting for our ride I called home," she said in a pained voice. "After we were arrested on Saturday, my roommate Johann was walking back to his car, and three guys jumped him and beat him up and broke his ankle. He had to go to the hospital. And the guys turned out to be off-duty Marines."

"Marines?" several of us said in unison. Sara nodded.

Angie turned around from the front seat to face Sara. "Did they catch them?"

"Two of them, anyway. The third got away."

"What are they charging them with?"

"Nothing," Sara said. "Johann didn't want to press charges, so they let the Marines go."

"What?" I said. "They broke his ankle, and he didn't want to charge them?"

Sara's brow creased further. "I can understand why he didn't," she said. "It's contradictory for us to protest the state, and then turn around and use the courts to prosecute someone."

Angie gave a skeptical laugh. "But if they attacked you?"

"That's part of nonviolence. Nothing says we won't have violence used on us."

Angie shook her head. "I'm not that much of a pacifist. Sometimes you have to fight back. And if it means using the courts, so what? The state works against us all the time — why not get it to work *for* us once in a while?"

"I don't think that's a consistent anarchist position," Karina intervened.

"I'm not trying to be a consistent anarchist," Angie said. "I'm a realist. The government exists. So does violence. And using the first to fight the second seems practical."

"Well," Karina retorted, "I don't think we should ever do anything that legitimizes the government."

With a growling sigh, Angie paused, then spoke in a level voice. "I agree, we basically should not appeal to the government. But here's a chance to play one part of the state against another, to use the courts to go after the military. We can turn the government against itself."

"But where does it end up?" Sara said in a low voice. "They prosecute a couple of eighteen-year-old Marine privates whom the military couldn't care less about sacrificing. And then they say, look, it's a fair system, we punished the offenders. What does it matter to the government? We're victims, the privates are victims, and the state comes out looking good."

Angie spoke slowly, as if thinking out loud. "But you can't just let it go. You have to give a message to people that we won't be intimidated. Maybe you could threaten to press charges, and offer to drop them if the Marines would meet with you."

As she spoke, the car pulled up in front of our apartment. People got out of the car for hugs under the Dwight Way streetlights, then bid us farewell. As they drove away, Holly put her arm around my shoulder. I turned toward her. We looked into each other's eyes, then kissed.

"I'm so happy to be back home with you," she said.

"You have to admit," I said after another kiss, "we're charmed. Counting last night when we were together in the holding cell, we've never missed a night. Two actions and not a night apart."

Wednesday, February 9, 1983

SINCE MOST OF us from Direct Action had spent the end of January in jail, we decided to hold off for a week or two and do a mid-February edition of the paper that would cover all the actions of the past month.

Production was going on all afternoon and evening, but I had to work at least a few hours, with the pay period coming to a close. Revolutionary journalism didn't pay the rent. Not yet, anyway.

It was a crisp day, overcast with fog. As I raked the leaves in front of the building, I went over what needed to happen on Direct Action, stopping now and then to jot a note. I didn't have a good handle on the issue overall, but I had the feeling that we were running behind. It was going to be a late night.

Around six I got cleaned up and headed over to the big house at Telegraph and Ashby. I wasn't sure if I even knew any of the people living there, but they seemed okay with us taking over their living room for a couple of weeks for newspaper production.

I stepped through the front door. Once-proud couches ringed the ample living room. Bob Marley and the Wailers filtered out of a boom box perched on the cluttered mantle. Spraypainted on the dirty walls were stencils of Ché Guevara. In the corner stood a television set with a smashed screen. Was it art, accident, or spontaneous social criticism?

Half a ping-pong table surrounded by folding chairs formed the central work space. Caroline and Holly were working on a layout together at the table, with Daniel across from them. Angie and Jenny were pasting up pages over in the corner by the TV. Claudia was sitting on a tattered couch proofreading.

I said hi to folks and walked over toward Holly, who looked relieved to see me. "I need to show you where we are," she said. "Then I want to go get some dinner before my meeting."

"Okay." I put my arm around her shoulders. "How are you doing?" I asked.

"Pretty good, considering."

I didn't have a chance to follow it up before Caroline tugged on my arm. "Jeff, glad you're here."

MID-FEBRUARY 1983

DIRECT ACTION

50¢

PUBLISHED BY THE LIVERMORE ACTION GROUP

A WAVE OF PROTESTS RESULTING IN OVER 500 ARRESTS SWEPT CALIFORNIA IN LATE JANUARY, FOCUSING ATTENTION IN QUICK SUCCESSION ON UC WEAPONS LABS MANAGEMENT, VANDENBERG AIR FORCE BASE, AND THE PORT CHICAGO WEAPONS SHIPPING FACILITY. THE CO-ORDINATED ACTIONS UNDERLINED THE CONNECTIONS BETWEEN UNIVERSITY-SPONSORED FIRST STRIKE WEAPONS DEVELOPMENT, MILITARY TESTING, AND SHIPMENT OF ARMS TO REPRESSIVE DICTATORSHIPS.

ON TO LIVERMORE!

DIRECT ACTION
LIVERMORE ACTION GROUP
3126 SHATTUCK AVENUE
BERKELEY CA 94705

BULK RATE
US POSTAGE PAID
PERMIT NO. 20
BERKELEY, CA.

Direct Action #4, February 1983

I gave her a hug. "Hey, I saw your finance report," I said. "LAG is two thousand dollars ahead?"

"At least," she said. A cautious smile crossed her face. "All along, I wanted to believe it would work out."

Holly stepped over to me. "Let me show you where we are. Here's a list of pages that have been started, with a note on who's working on what. Artemis left her pages under the couch. She said she'd try to come back tomorrow to work on them. Melissa came by and picked up pages two and three to work on at home tonight. Here's her number if you need to call her about anything. And Monique is doing the xeroxing."

I was taking notes as fast as I could. "Here's a list of stories that aren't in yet," she continued. "These people need to be called right away. Tell Mort we need his spokescouncil story tomorrow."

Holly tucked her notebook in her pack and said goodbye, but just then Craig came in. "Here's my Vandenberg analysis," he announced, waving densely-typed pages at us. "I hope we have a separate story describing the action."

"No, not really," I said, looking at Holly. "But we're doing a photo page."

"That's a great idea," Craig said. "Showing a successful action is the best way to build momentum for June at Livermore."

"And for the March action at Vandenberg," Holly said offhandedly. She pulled on her coat and turned to speak to Caroline.

"What's happening with the VAC action?" Craig asked. "In the paper, I mean."

"We have a story," I said. "We're going to run it at the bottom of page one, under your story."

Craig didn't miss a beat. "No, we should put the June Livermore story there. That should be on the front page."

I didn't want to contradict Craig, who seemed coiled for a confrontation. "We should ask some other people," I said noncommittally.

Claudia, over on the couch, had been listening to the exchange. Now she put down her proofreading and joined us, pulling Holly in along with her.

Craig reiterated his position that the VAC action be relegated to an inside page. Holly listened for a minute, then spoke plainly. "The purpose of the paper is to promote civil disobedience. There's a major action at Vandenberg next month. That belongs on page one."

"But Direct Action is a LAG paper," Claudia said. "It should focus on our actions. VAC has been very clear that this is *not* a LAG action."

Holly leveled her gaze at Claudia. "A lot of the people involved are LAGers. They'll expect us to cover it."

"I'm not saying we shouldn't cover it," Craig said. "But the June Livermore action belongs on the front page. We agreed at the Congress last Summer that as soon as Vandenberg was over, we would start organizing for Livermore. No one expected a bunch of people to go changing the dates of actions."

That's the essence of the situation, I thought. I hated not supporting Holly, but my sense was, go with Livermore.

As Craig finished speaking, Claudia nodded vigorously. "The whole idea of the LAG Congress was to lay out a coherent plan for the year, so we're not always racing from action to action, burning ourselves out, with no better idea of where we're going than the government has."

Holly shook her head as she wrapped her scarf over her shoulder. "I've got to go — you know what I think."

I followed her out onto the porch and silently hugged her goodbye.

"We don't even have a Livermore story, do we?" she asked.

"We must have gotten someone to write one," I said.

"I didn't. Maybe Craig did." She squeezed me and started away. "I'll see you at home tonight. How late are you going to be here?"

"Oh, eleven or so. Why don't you come back and we'll walk home together?"

"Then we'll both wind up staying till midnight."

Notwithstanding that likelihood, we agreed on the plan. As I stepped back inside, Claudia and Craig pounced. "I'll write the Livermore article by Friday," Claudia informed me. "It should go on the front page, ahead of the VAC story." She turned back to the page she was working on. "We can talk about it Monday night at Coordinating Council if Holly really objects. We can see what other people think."

The door swung open, and Cindy stepped in. "Hey, I've got the prints from our BART action last Friday," she said. I was glad to have a break from arguing. Cindy pulled out photostats of the poster that her AG, the Commie Dupes, had designed. People crowded around the table, eyeing the authentic-looking poster outlining emergency procedures for a nuclear attack.

"We put three hundred of them up in the ad-slots of BART trains," she told us. "It got in the *Chronicle,* and it was on KPFA news, too."

"Did anyone get busted?" Caroline asked.

"We got hassled by the police," Cindy said, "But no one was arrested. They just made us get off the train. So we'd wait a few minutes and get on the next train."

After Cindy took off, I tried to get back to work. I thought about starting

IN CASE OF **NUCLEAR ATTACK**

1. REMAIN CALM

2. AVERT EYES FROM FLASH

3. BRACE FOR BLAST

4. DUCK AND COVER/ PLACE NEWSPAPER OVER HEAD

5. RESERVE MEDICAL ATTENTION FOR HIGH PRIORITY EVACUEES

6. HAVE FOOD AND WATER FOR SEVERAL WEEKS OF ISOLATION

7. COMFORT THE DYING

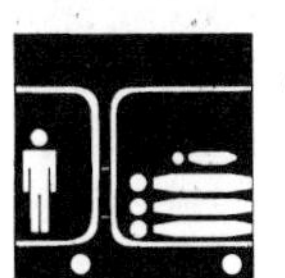

8. ISOLATE CORPSES TO PREVENT SPREAD OF DISEASE

This official-looking poster was inserted in advertising panels on 300 commuter train cars.

the photo spread, but felt like I didn't have a good enough sense of the paper as a whole. The past couple of issues, I'd been the person who kept track of the progress of each two-page spread — what stories went where, who was designing it, what was missing, what was finished. It came naturally, since I liked having the overview, watching the paper take shape. And having a coordinating role, even an informal one, solidified my sense of belonging to LAG.

I drifted around the room taking stock of what was needed on each page. We were in better shape than I had thought. All of the pages were started except the photo spread and the front page.

As I put the finishing touches on the local actions page, Angie brought her pages over and laid them on the table in front of me. "I just need a graphic for the top, and it's done," she said. She tugged on the sleeve of an oversized sweater.

"The layout looks really good," I said. The sweater hung loosely around her small body as she leaned toward me to tape down a loose headline.

I offered to help her look through the graphics file, which was a cardboard box stuffed with anti-nuke graphics from around the world, a bunch of anti-Reagan editorial cartoons, and all sorts of loose pictures torn out of other magazines.

"Copyright isn't a big issue, I take it," Angie said.

"I think of it as 'liberating' the graphics," I said.

She turned the idea over in her mind. "For me, it's a question of giving credit. It's not like we're making money off it. But if we use someone's art, we have to give credit."

I nodded. "Good point. Mostly we do, but that's something we should check during final proofing."

We sifted through another folder with no success. Angie yawned and leaned her elbow on the table. "I think my drugs are wearing off. I'd drink more caffeine, but then I'd need another beer to balance it. I think it's time to call it a day."

As she stood up, her eyes fell on her page and saddened. She straightened a column of type. "I was hoping to find the perfect graphic and have the page done."

I looked over her design. "Maybe Tai could draw something. He's doing the graphic for the subscription ad. Maybe he has time for this one, too."

"Good idea," she said. "I'll call him tomorrow. Anyway, I'm going home now."

I gave her a hug. "See you here tomorrow night?"

"No, I've got something else going. That's why I wanted to finish tonight. I'll run into you at the office sometime soon. Say goodnight to Holly for me."

Right at that moment, Holly walked in. She stopped to say goodbye to

Angie, who informed her of the missing graphic. "What I need is something serious but funny," she told Holly. "And it has to be about nuclear war."

"We have cartoons like that," Holly said. "Daniel brought in a bunch he clipped from British papers." Angie took off her coat and joined Holly back at the graphics box. They thumbed through several folders, all the while discussing how better to catalogue our ever-expanding graphic arts collection. At last their efforts were rewarded with the perfect cartoon. Angie got a gluestick and pasted it onto her page. "Now I can sleep with a clear conscience," she said.

It was almost midnight by the time we packed it in. We locked the door behind us. I put my arm around Holly as we said goodnight to Angie and watched her pedal away. Holly slipped her arm around my waist. "Want to walk on Hillegass?" she asked. "I need to be around more trees."

ACTION BULLETIN

ISSUE 2

INTERNATIONAL DAY OF NUCLEAR DISARMAMENT —JUNE 20—

INTRODUCTION

In the autumn of 1982 Livermore Action Group began circulating a call for an International Day of Nuclear Disarmament on June 20, 1983. In response to the call, groups all around the United States and in several other countries are planning activities on or around that day. This action bulletin is a forum for participating groups to publicize their planned activities, ideas, graphics, and information about the nuclear facilities, military installations, power plants, or other sites at which they will organize protests.

This is the second action bulletin published by Livermore Action Group for the International Day. It includes a summary of Issue No. 1. We intend to publish action bulletins every two weeks if there is sufficient copy from participating groups to print. LAG's May, June, and July Direct Action newspaper will carry the action bulletin so that our readership can learn about activities planned around the world on June 20. For $5.00 you may subscribe to the action bulletin and receive every copy, including the mid-May and mid-June issues which will not be a part of Direct Action.

Please send us your press releases so that we may in turn inform other International Day participants of your activities. By serving as a clearinghouse for June 20 actions, we hope to provide local groups with the information they need to publicize the coordinated aspect of all the activities planned that day.

NEW MEXICO

The June Disarmament Coalition of Albuquerque, New Mexico is planning a week of disarmament activities from June 11–20. Events include a peace camp, forums, workshops, a film festival, a poster exhibit, a spiritual service, a picnic for peace, and non-violent civil disobedience on the 20th.

The focus will be Kirtland Air Force Base on the southeastern edge of Albuquerque, one of the nerve centers of America's nuclear weapons industry.

The Coalition sent the following list of tenants at the Kirtland base, all of whom are heavily involved in nuclear weapons research, development, and management:

A) Air Force Weapons Lab: the lab is a leader in research on "Star Wars" technology that represents the next escalation in the nuclear arms race. Research is being done on particle beams and laser weapons that will eventually replace bombs and bullets.

B) Air Force Test and Evaluation Center: the Center is responsible for providing operational assessments of evolving major systems of various types. AFTEC is presently evaluating more than 90 major weapons systems, including the cruise missile.

C) Defense Nuclear Agency: the Agency plans, coordinates, and supervises the conduct of Dept. of Defense nuclear weapons effects testing as well as provides for the construction and management of nuclear weapon effects simulation facilities and field experiments which simulate nuclear weapon effects. Other responsibilities include working with the Dept. of Energy and the armed services on programs to insure the safety, security, and survivability of nuclear weapons in transit or storage. It also maintains the national nuclear weapons stockpile data base and provides current information on the stockpile to government agencies.

D) Manzano Arsenal: in the Four Hills area of SE Albuquerque exists one of the largest stockpiles of nuclear weapons systems in the western world.

E) Interservice Nuclear Weapons School: the school is responsible for presenting the complete national nuclear weapons program from conception of weapons, design manufacturing and test programs, to employment of weapons and weapon effects.

F) Department of Energy: the Albuquerque Operations Office's primary mission is research, development, production, testing, stockpile surveillance, and transportation of nuclear weapons. The DOE complex includes nine major laboratory, plant and test site facilities in eight states extending from California to Florida. The office manages the entire nuclear weapons production complex.

G) Sandia National Labs: a prime contractor to the Dept. of Energy, Sandia works on nuclear fusing armament and firing systems. Sandia works closely with DOE's other two nuclear weapons labs: Los Alamos and Lawrence Livermore.

MOUNTAIN PEOPLE

Mountain People for a Nuclear Free Future, as an International Day activity, plans on declaring their area a Nuclear Free Zone. They also want to initiate local action toward a Nuclear Free California campaign, which would prohibit nuclear power, as well as bomb technology, in California.

The group reports that some of its members are also interested in participating in the Livermore Action Group's June 20 blockade of Lawrence Livermore National Laboratory in Livermore, California.

For information, write: Lawrence Kay, Mt. People, P.O. Box 19, Friant, CA 93626.

IDAHO

Dear Friends,

The Idaho National Engineering Laboratory (INEL) is a Department of Energy facility that occupies 893 square miles of sagebrush-covered high desert in Eastern Idaho. Fifty-two nuclear reactors have been built at INEL; 15 are operating currently. Some of the most advanced nuclear research in the world is carried on here; much of this research is military in nature.

Sailors are trained here for nuclear submarine reactor operation. Fuels and materials for nuclear submarine reactors are tested here. At the Idaho Chemical Processing Plant, spent nuclear submarine fuel is reprocessed, and the recovered uranium is used to make new fuel for the Savannah River materials production reactors. Over 25% of the nation's military nuclear wastes are stored at INEL including over 93% of the transuranic wastes generated at Rocky Flats.

The INEL is located above the Snake River Plain Aquifer, one of the largest underground bodies of water in the world. Liquid low-level radioactive wastes, containing trace amounts of plutonium, are injected directly into the aquifer from the Chem Plant.

Idaho Peace Groups are organizing events to mark the International Day of Disarmament. Their planning is partially dependent on a decision expected by the Department of Energy (DOE) in April concerning the placement of a new tritium production reactor. INEL is one of three sites under consideration. If the DOE chooses INEL there is talk of a blockade or occupation at INEL, the first such action ever taken at the facility.

Carry on,
Liz Paul
Groundwater Alliance
Box 4090
Ketchum, ID 83340

GREENPEACE/SEATTLE

On June 20th, in coordination with the International Day of Nuclear Disarmament, there will be a peaceful action at the cruise missile factory in Kent, Washington. The intention of the action is to halt production of the cruise missile, focus people's attention on its local production, and demonstrate to the people of the world that people in Washington State think that nuclear weapons production is a matter of life and death for all.

With leadership provided by such groups as Greenpeace, Northwest, it is hoped that as many people as possible will participate from all over the northwestern U.S. A coalition of peace groups is currently mobilizing to organize the action.

The targeting of the cruise missile for protest came about for a number of reasons. The cruise is designed to carry a nuclear warhead. It poses special problems to world peace because it can be easily hidden and is therefore difficult to monitor under arms control agreements. The planned placement of cruise missiles by the United States in Europe would have gravely destabilizing effects. The continuing manufacture of the cruise missile contradicts the strongly pro-freeze sentiment of the American people.

Civil disobedience has been chosen as a form of protest because it is the strongest possible peaceful statement we can make. It is clear that nuclear weapons should be illegal, yet they are part of the vast system of power that effectively disenfranchises citizens of both the United States and the world. Since legal protests and referendums have not cause fundamental changes and since all life on earth is in great peril, direct actions and strong protests by people are now morally necessary.

We are encouraging all to respond to this call for peace. Those not interested in being a part of the civil disobedience are encouraged to come and be supportive. The numbers of people who respond will be the message that carries weight.

All participants in the civil disobedience must first receive nonviolence training and will be organized into affinity groups. While maintaining a non-violent mode of action, the protestors will not, however, cooperate with the manufacturers, military, or the police. The objective is to slow production for as long as possible, rather than trying to demonstrate moral superiority.

In addition to the June 20 action, planning is underway for a women's peace camp at the Kent, Washington weapons facility, which is run by Boeing.

For more information, contact Sherry Klink of Greenpeace, Seattle, Good Shepherd Center, 4649 Sunnyside Ave. North, Seattle, WA 98103. Telephone: 206/632-4326.

JAPAN

Dear Friends,

Thank you very much for sending us the call for International Disarmament Day. I made copies of this call and gave them to my friends.

I would like to put this call in a small magazine, "New World," which I am in charge of publishing so that more people can receive the message. I was very much moved by this appeal; my friends also were moved by this call. We have not yet planned any action for the day, but probably we can eventually have some good ideas for actions.

I pray for your actions to convert Lawrence Livermore Lab for peaceful uses. We want to celebrate June 20th for Survival of all human beings and all lives on the earth. We have to have international solidarity in order to realize total abolition of military expansion. Let us walk together for the future.

Sincerely yours,
Ganzo Kato
Society for World Federation
No. 302, 4-2-4 Hongo
Bunkyo-ku, Tokyo 113
Japan

BERLIN

Activist Michael Lucas reports from Berlin, Germany that he has distributed the International Day of Nuclear Disarmament call-to-action brochure to Berlin peace groups and movement publications. Photocopies of the leaflet were distributed at the monthly meeting of 180 groups, at which actions are planned and information exchanged. There is now a commission within this coalition of groups to coordinate the decentralized actions which are planned for June in response to the International Day appeal.

Some editions of the International Day Action Bulletin were published as pages of Direct Action newspaper.

"Sure," I said. We headed up the slight hill. "Did you know that in Jack Kerouac's book, *Dharma Bums*, the first scene is on Hillegass? It doesn't give the address, but I imagine it being right across from the park where we saw the Mime Troupe."

We crossed Telegraph and passed into a darker stretch. I looked up at the sky. It was a clear, moonless night, and a sprinkling of stars were visible. Holly looked up, too. "We should borrow a car sometime," she said, "and drive out to Mount Diablo. I'll bet you can see the Milky Way from there."

"Yeah. It would be nice to actually see some constellations." I pulled the tip off an evergreen branch hanging over the shadowy sidewalk. The production session was still on my mind. But I didn't want to impose my agenda on Holly. "Do you want to talk about the paper," I said, "or something lighter?"

"How about you?"

"I could go either way."

"Let's just talk about it till we get home," she said. "I want to know what was decided about the front page."

The front page. I'd forgotten that issue. "Well, basically what you heard before you left," I said. "Livermore goes on the front page. Claudia is writing a piece on the Livermore blockade. The March Vandenberg action goes on the back page."

Holly put her hands in her pockets. "It isn't right. Vandenberg is a major action regardless of who is organizing it. Sara and Karina told me that thirty people from Change of Heart plan to get arrested — that's double the January action. How can we call the paper 'Direct Action' and not have Vandenberg on the front page?"

"You should talk to Craig if you want to change it. But you know how he feels."

"I know," she said with a hint of exasperation. "He takes the VAC action as a personal insult."

"Some people meant it that way."

"But that's hardly anyone." Her voice broke, and she cleared her throat sharply. "Only the organizers are fighting. Everyone else is focused on the action. The newspaper shouldn't take sides. We should be getting the word out about any protests that are happening."

We had reached the Dwight Way entrance. I rattled my keys to avoid answering. I hated to be arguing when I had hardly seen Holly for days. "You should talk to Craig and Claudia about it," I said. "They're the ones pushing for Livermore."

"I'll think about it," she said. "I have plenty else to worry about."

I opened the front door. "Well, we're home now," I said as we started up the stairs. "Do you want to talk about something else?"

"Yeah," she said over her shoulder. "But wait — one more thing..."

Of course, her one more thing led me to think of one more thing, which reminded her of one more thing, and soon it was two in the morning.

Finally Holly headed to bed. She sighed as she pulled back the covers and stretched out. "We really need some time away, Jeff. We get so caught in the moment. All we think about is LAG. We need some time for us."

She pulled the blankets up and lay her head on her big feather pillow. "Jenny and Angie are going dancing at Ashkenaz this Friday," she said. "Want to go with them?"

"Sure," I said, "sounds like fun." Actually it sounded terrifying, as did anything involving dancing. At least if we went with other people, I wouldn't be so conspicuous.

I sat down beside Holly and stroked her hair. "How about going down to Santa Cruz sometime soon," I said. "We could rent a car and do a day-trip."

Her eyes lit up, and she rolled toward me. "Maybe the last weekend of this month?"

I nodded. "I can do that."

But then Holly clouded. "No, there's an International Day meeting that weekend," she said. "But maybe the weekend after that..."

Saturday, March 5, 1983

When local resident Arthur Looff (son of the famous carousel builder, Charles Looff) built the Giant Dipper in 1924, he envisioned a giant wooden coaster which would be a "combination earthquake, balloon ascension, and aeroplane drop." With speeds up to fifty-five miles per hour, it's all that and more.

— from a brochure for the Santa Cruz Boardwalk

I tested the safety bar one last time as the train lurched into gear and began the steep ascent. Next to me, Holly sat bolt upright, both hands clutching the black bar that was supposed to keep us from flying out. The people in the car ahead of us laughed and whooped as we crept upward through a narrow tunnel.

Why did they enclose the tracks in a tunnel? Probably so we couldn't see the white-washed wooden scaffolding that held the roller coaster aloft. Given a close look at the rickety structure, half the riders might bail out before we reached the top.

The first car crested the peak, tugging us in its wake. Holly looked at me, eyes wide with terror and delight as we cleared the top and dropped. My stomach flew upward. I gripped the bar and let out a low howl. Holly shrieked and threw her arms in the air. I burst out laughing. No turning back now — we're in this to the end!

Sunday, March 13, 1983

The streets were still damp, but the sun shone through patchy clouds. It was warmer than I'd anticipated. I peeled off my sweatshirt as I crossed Telegraph Avenue, making my way to the Change of Heart meeting in People's Park.

On the way, I stopped at the copy shop to pick up some Livermore flyers. Sure, the cluster meeting was about Vandenberg. But we had to keep Livermore on the table, too.

Coming out of the store, I recoiled as a truck spewed exhaust at me. Was it my imagination, or were there more cars than when I moved to Southside two years before? Seemed like every time I went to cross a street, I had to be watching out for them.

Why was I going to this meeting? I was out of the Vandenberg loop. I had no plans to do the March action, or even to go down to the encampment. But from being around Karina and Angie and Jenny at the office I knew how fired up people were. Even if my official excuse for going was to plug Livermore, I wanted to share the Vandenberg excitement, to be around a crowd of people getting ready for an adventure.

I thought I was fashionably late, but when I got to the Park the only others there were the two facilitators, Sara and Alby. Sara gave me a quick hug. I'd been getting to know her a bit at the office when she'd come by with Karina. She still mainly worked on Central America organizing, but was doing the Vandenberg action with Change of Heart.

"So you're facilitating?" I said by way of making conversation.

"Yes, we're facilitating," Sara said as if I had challenged her competence. I winced. It wasn't the first time I had inadvertently irritated her.

I started to explain myself, but luckily Alby spoke up. "Hi," he said, extending a hand to shake. Alby was about twenty-five, with bushy red hair. He was six inches shorter than me, but his crunching handshake more than compensated.

I extricated my hand and excused myself. "I guess you two need to plan for the meeting," I said, then immediately regretted it.

But Sara didn't seem bothered this time. "No, I think we're ready," she said. "We better be, here come more people."

A dozen people arrived in the next ten minutes, although Walt and Antonio were the only ones I really knew. But then Angie and Jenny arrived. Angie came over and gave me a hug, and I felt more like I belonged.

I was standing on the edge of the circle when Karina made her entrance. Being closest to her, I got the first hug. I held her for an extra moment, then released her to Sara. They kissed, and Karina ran her hand through Sara's hair. Sara leaned up and kissed Karina again before they separated.

Karina hugged Walt, then turned to Alby. I knew Alby was one of Karina and Sara's spraypainting cohorts. Was he one of Karina's lovers as well? The way their hips swayed as they hugged suggested it.

Moonstone interrupted my pondering by hugging me from behind. The contact felt good, and I let myself drop back into his arms. He held me for a minute, then lowered me to the ground, where a circle was forming in the grassy middle section of the park.

I settled in on the low, scruffy grass. Twenty yards away, a guitarist strummed a Grateful Dead song for a small gathering. Further back toward Telegraph, a few people worked in the garden, a former parking lot slowly being reclaimed from the asphalt. Off to one side, a couple of men sifted through clothes in the "free box." Scattered around the rest of the block-long park were little clumps of people, many of them looking like they spent a lot of time on the streets. One woman stopped by our circle and asked for spare change, but after that we were left in peace.

We went around the circle and said our names and AGs. Lots of new people, mostly young, just out of college, it seemed. Jenny, Angie, Alby and a dozen others. A new wave. In the eight weeks since the January action, Change of Heart had almost doubled in size. Several new AGs had joined, and others, like Lifers and Deadheads for Peace, had taken on new members. The cluster was humming, with thirty people planning to get busted and a dozen more making the trip down to the encampment.

Great — for them. My AG had fizzled out. Since January, when four of us were busted, we hadn't met again. The only other active members were moving on. Cindy was in Commie Dupes. And Hank was joining Overthrow Cluster, referring to Change of Heart as "amateur anarchists."

It was a harsh assessment, but not devoid of truth. With the changing of the guard, Change of Heart was becoming a cluster of young anarchists: long on ideals, creativity, and spontaneity, but short on patience for working in coalitions or building an organization.

I considered following Hank to Overthrow, which would be more politically congenial. But a couple of things held me back. One was gender. Overthrow, true to the leftist tradition, was mostly men. In Change of Heart, on the other hand, a lot of the most active people were women or gay men: Karina, Jenny, Doc, Rick, and, increasingly, Sara and Angie. I liked the tone it gave to our actions.

Plus, Holly had proposed that the two of us form an AG. We'd talked it over with a few other people, and it looked like Caroline, Daniel, and Walt were up for it, with Jenny and Angie possibly joining after Vandenberg. Belonging to an active AG would give me more solid footing in the cluster. I'd have a support raft of like-minded LAGers amidst the sea of anarchists.

The meeting got underway with Karina reporting on the previous day's spokescouncil meeting. As she spoke, I looked from her to Alby and back again. I thought of something I'd heard her saying to Jenny recently: "If I care about someone, and we're attracted, why shouldn't we make love? Why put an artificial restraint on it? If I feel love, I want to express it."

Hard to disagree, in theory. But in real life? I remembered Holly continuing her sexual relationship with Frank after she and I became lovers. That was difficult enough. But Karina's interpretation went well beyond that, covering several of her friends at any given time. I wondered how it was for Sara. Did she have other lovers, too?

I looked at Karina, whose head was bobbing up and down as she concluded her report with a glowing estimation of the prospects for bringing Vandenberg Air Force Base to its khaki'd knees. I couldn't help being intrigued by her. Holly and I were doing great, and I didn't want to throw a curve ball into our relationship for the sake of a fling with anyone. But it certainly spiced up the meeting to sit across from her.

Once we finished the reports, the main issue was whether to do a backcountry action, given that the MX still wasn't ready to test.

"We need to scout out the base," Alby said. "When they do try to test the MX, we need to know the terrain."

Angie was lying in the grass sketching on a notepad. She'd draw for a minute or so, then tilt her head and gaze pensively at the pad. Now she looked up and shielded her eyes from the sun. "The whole point is to occupy Vandenberg, isn't it? I want to get on the base and reclaim it."

A couple of people spoke in favor of a front-gate action, but most of the cluster wanted to go backcountry, and consensus was quickly reached. The decision let loose a cascade of brainstorming for the action, but Sara reined the discussion back to the agenda.

"Solidarity is the next discussion. I forget, who put this on the agenda?"

Doc raised his hand. "I did." His tone of voice sobered the meeting. Doc looked around the circle, his heavy brows accenting the intensity of his gaze. "We have to get serious. Solidarity was a failure at the January action. They pushed us around, yanked people out, jailed some, and released others — and we didn't have any idea what to do. There was almost no discussion of solidarity tactics before we got there, and we paid the price."

I nodded, although I still didn't see a lot we could have done if the authorities really were determined to move us.

Walt raised his hand. "It's hard to plan solidarity when we won't even meet most of the other protesters till the night before the action," he said. "The spokescouncils can make some decisions, but it really comes down to the people who wind up in jail together. I don't see that much we can do ahead of time."

Doc's eyes fixed on Walt. "We can make our own decisions, and propose them to other clusters at the action. In a crisis, we'll have a response ready. If one cluster has a plan, others may join."

"Right," Karina put in, "There's no time to have a meeting once they start jerking us around. It's going to be especially risky this time, because so many of us have ban-and-bars hanging over us."

Antonio ran his hand through his thick silver hair. "We need to go into jail resolved to non-cooperate every step of the way, until they guarantee that everyone will be arraigned together and get equal sentences."

Sara spoke up. "Love and Rage AG from Santa Cruz is proposing that we refuse to give our names. Make them identify second-timers by trying to match the January photos."

"Yeah," Karina said. "If they try to separate someone out, we should non-cooperate in any way we can. We have to stay together and refuse to be processed out of jail until we're certain of the legal deal. Don't give names, and leave your ID with the legal collective. If we make it tough enough, they'll have to give all of us the same sentence and let us go."

"Right on," Alby said, "Take it to them, and let 'em deal with it if they can."

Consensus was reached on not giving names, along with a general resolve to physically resist separation. Doc wanted more definite tactics, but time was running out, and it was put over to be discussed down at Vandenberg.

One lingering item remained on the agenda: LAG's role in the action. Jenny delivered the news on LAG's official line — that the office would not be giving logistical support to the March Vandenberg action.

I thought back to last Monday's Coordinating Council meeting, where we had made the decision to focus exclusively on June at Livermore.

Not surprisingly, Holly had been the one person at Coordinating Council to speak strongly in favor of supporting the VAC action. "I've been thinking of going down to the encampment," she announced. "Instead, I'm going to stay here and be the office liaison."

Craig and Claudia, sponsors of the "no help" proposal, were caught off-guard. Holly looked calmly from one to the other and continued. "People are bound to call the LAG office when they hear there's been a big action. I'll deal with it. You won't have to do anything."

Claudia looked away, as if she had no further interest. Craig sat back and shrugged. "Alright," he said, "as long as I don't have to answer any calls."

It seemed reasonable at the time. But sitting here in People's Park amidst thirty people preparing to occupy Vandenberg, I felt embarrassed for LAG. Our decision not to give support seemed lame, out of touch. Jenny reported that Holly would support Vandenberg in the office, and I spontaneously said I would help, too. But compared to LAG's all-out effort in January, it seemed like small change.

Doc brushed back his long gray hair. "We're doing fine without any help from LAG," he said with no rancor in his voice. "There's nothing we're asking from Coordinating Council."

"Yeah," Alby chimed in. "Who needs them?"

Their words stung, and the murmur of approval that followed rubbed it in. I wanted to respond, but that would be to admit my own culpability.

We'd reached the end of the agenda, but Karina had one more item. "We need to make plans for rides home," she said. "We might need them faster than we think. This action is going to be way bigger than January. People are coming from all over California. If we stick together, there's no way they can handle us. We might get out the same day."

As we gathered in a closing circle in the middle of People's Park, I wound up next to Karina. She squeezed my hand as Doc spoke up. "It's great that we're meeting here," he said. "Fourteen years ago, People's Park was reclaimed from the government. Now it's time to take back Vandenberg."

I put my arm around Karina's shoulders, and her exuberance vibrated through me. My heart felt warm and full, and for an instant I was ready to drop everything and join the pilgrimage down to Vandenberg.

We took a breath and released it together. No, I probably wouldn't go down to the action. But Change of Heart was in the thick of it. And that included me. Up till now I had been toeing the LAG line about the March action. I hadn't let myself experience the excitement that was percolating among the hundreds of people heading to Vandenberg. But now it boiled like a cauldron in the center of our circle, fed by our breaths and our resolve. Yes, part of me will be there, too.

After the meeting broke up, Angie and Jenny headed toward Telegraph to get coffee at Café Med, and I walked with them. As we approached the corner we passed the People's History mural — itself a piece of history, as one of the oldest of Berkeley's many murals. I slowed my gait and took in the familiar local history: the Free Speech Movement, the Vietnam protests, the fight for People's Park. Our forerunners. Maybe someday the artists would paint a new panel showing our triumphant occupation of the meadow at Vandenberg, fists thrust in the air. That was us — the next link in the chain.

Thursday, March 31, 1983

WHAT HAD IT been — two weeks? — since people left for Vandenberg? And I hadn't seen or spoken with most of them since.

At least they were getting out. Supposedly. That would be the worst, to drive all the way down there and find out that the judge changed his mind.

I hadn't intended to make the ten-hour round trip down to Santa Barbara. Someone had to pick people up, though, and when Lyle volunteered to drive a van down, I let myself be drafted to keep him company. I felt like I hadn't done much to support the action, and I owed it to people in my cluster to help.

It was hard not to compare the action to LAG's January protest. Incessant rain provided a common element — mud. But there the similarity ended. Maybe it was thanks to our pioneering efforts in January, but this time seven hundred seventy protesters were busted. A lot of them did backcountry occupations even though the MX still wasn't ready to test. The message was clear: March was a dress rehearsal for stopping the missile test.

Backcountry or front gate, the sheer scale was hard to ignore. 770 arrests, hundreds held in jail for a week or more, a two-week encampment under terrible conditions — VAC and the affinity group network proved their mettle.

VAC was being tested in a way that LAG hadn't been. Jail support — challenging even with an office and staff — was a nightmare for the scattered support team working out of the rain-soaked Vandenberg camp or from collective houses like Urban Stonehenge back in San Francisco. Simply keeping

Detail from the People's History mural at Telegraph and Haste, Berkeley. Left, gardening at People's Park. Right, showdown with the police, c. 1970.

track of people was a Herculean task, with protesters held in almost a dozen jails and prisons all over Southern California and even in Arizona.

Arizona. Last we had heard, there were still thirty men there, with no word on when they might be back. "No one is sure why they picked those thirty men," Lyle told me as we drove down early Thursday morning. "It's probably just because they ran out of California jail cells. But they might be planning to prosecute those guys heavier. The misdemeanors carry up to six months in jail."

Lyle had been arrested as well. But since he had a federal ban-and-bar from January, he opted for a state-charge blockade outside the base. "There were about fifty of us. They put us all on a bus and drove us to Santa Barbara County Jail. When we get there, a deputy comes on board and tells us we're going to be issued citations and released until a later court date."

"So they were going to cite you out?"

"Yeah, but then we'd have to return next month for court. Some people said they couldn't do that. Pilgrim especially argued that we should demand an immediate arraignment, and not get off the bus until it was set up. So most people stayed." He nodded his head at the memory. "We were on the bus for about six hours. They gave us at least ten 'last chances' to cite out or get put into general population. Finally, they booked us into the jail. Some people cited out, but twenty-five of us stayed.

"The next day, they took us to court. At first, the judge refused to credit us for time-served for the day we spent on the bus! But we threatened to plead not-guilty, and he had to give in."

"And he let you go on time-served?"

"No, they just dropped the charges against us and told us to get lost. We stayed in solidarity for one day, and they totally caved in."

"Too bad that didn't work for the federal charges," I said. "It's been ten days since the first arrests, and a couple of hundred people are still in jail."

"Yeah, that's what I've heard," he said. "Different judges and magistrates are giving different sentences. It feels like you spin the wheel and you don't know what will come up — a day, a week, a month...."

A light but steady rain was falling as we cruised off the freeway into Santa Barbara. I suddenly felt out of place. Lyle belonged — he had done the action. But me? I felt like a poseur, a hanger-on. I tried to shoo the feelings, but they persisted. How could I not have seen that this was going to be a major action? Why hadn't I at least gone down for the rally?

We were approaching the jail. Maybe people would be waiting outside and we wouldn't even have to get out of the van. Just pick them up and head north.

Sure enough, there they were, huddled under an overhang outside the jail. As we pulled up, a wave of animation swept through the little knot of people. I spotted Karina, Jenny, Moonstone... Forgetting my out-of-place feelings, I hopped out of the van and jogged through the rain to the overhang.

Jenny and Angie were the first people I reached. Jenny greeted me like a favorite brother, wrapping her arms around me. Angie had tears in her eyes. "I can't believe we're out! It's so great to see you!"

It was one continuous welcome. Alby treated me like a long-lost friend. Karina threw her arms around my shoulders. Moonstone squeezed me and held me in a long embrace, as if I were his means of regrounding with the outside world.

Walt took my place up front with Hank. I gladly climbed in the back of the van, finding a spot between Karina and Jenny. My left arm was touching Jenny's shoulder, but our bodies were carefully distinct, like we were sitting in bus-seats.

Karina, on the other side, leaned back against me and draped her legs over Alby's. As she nestled into me, I let my body curve into hers.

The whole crew was bedraggled and exhausted, but they seemed delighted to have someone new to tell their stories to. Karina inclined her head back onto my shoulder, as if to suggest that her words were intended for me. "The first few days they held us at Vandenberg, on the base," she said. "But then they said they were taking us to San Diego, and one of the lawyers drove all the way down there, but they really sent us to Los Angeles, only we wound up spending the whole night on the bus. If you had to pee, tough luck until they decided to let you, and there was no food except balogna sandwiches and not enough of those, but it didn't matter because I was fasting anyway, only later I decided it was better to eat because we were in for so long, and we finally got our one phone call, but what could we say, we had no idea where they were going to take us next."

I nodded, letting my cheek brush against her hair. Jenny rustled on my other side. "Thank God for the lawyers," she said. "They somehow found us. It was so great to see Walt when we were taken before the judge this morning."

I wanted to hear about the backcountry action. I leaned up so I could see Angie, who was on the other side of Jenny. "Did you get onto the base like you were hoping?"

"Yeah," Angie said in a wistful tone. "About twenty feet in. We tried to get over the fence during daylight, but a helicopter spotted us right away."

"Most people went on at night," Jenny explained. "Some of the Pagan groups got way onto the base and did rituals. We blew it."

It's About Times

Abalone Alliance Newspaper

February-March 1983

MX foes get a Vandenberg welcome

It's About Times, published by Abalone Alliance in the early-to-mid-1980s, covered LAG and VAC actions as well as Diablo Canyon protests.

"Too bad," I said. "Did they hold you on the base?"

"The first day," Karina said. "But it was tougher than January. I was in handcuffs for seventeen hours. Megan and I were dressed as pirates. We had these terrific coats, burgundy and navy, and boots and baggy trousers and eye-patches. We had made a parchment map of Vandenberg, with an X marked, 'Here thar be missiles!'"

Jenny yawned. "That was tough, being in handcuffs so long. Someone had a bottle of soap bubbles. It took three people to do it — one to hold bottle, one to hold wand, and one to blow — but they did it."

"There was a lot of that kind of improvising," Karina said thoughtfully. "Later in the week, we did a Passover Seder. We didn't have matzo, so we took the leavened bread they gave us for dinner and mashed it flat to de-leaven it. Someone had managed to smuggle in a little vial of goldenseal, which we used for bitter herbs."

I nodded. "I guess you have to get creative if you're in for ten days."

"Ten days," Angie said. "Mostly it was okay, except for one scene with the Marshals. They were trying to separate out a few women who they'd figured out had ban-and-bars from January. When they came to get them, we all took off our clothes and circled around the people they were looking for. We figured the Marshals would be too freaked out to do anything. Wrong."

"Yeah, that was pretty disgusting," Jenny said. "They came in and threw people all over the place."

"It was a horrible feeling, being naked in front of those gross men," Angie said. She shivered. "A lot of women were crying afterwards. I wouldn't do it again."

"Why didn't they give you court dates and throw you out like they did other people?"

"Because we wouldn't give our names and weren't carrying ID," she said. "They didn't know who we were, so they couldn't force-cite us. That was the only way to keep solidarity with second-timers."

"And it worked," said Jenny. "Everybody in our cluster got the same sentence in the end, regardless of whether they had a ban-and-bar."

"Exactly," Karina said. "They held us for almost two weeks, but in a lot of ways, we won. We kept ourselves emotionally and psychically intact. And even when they succeeded in pulling someone out, people knew that we had done everything possible, and that we would do everything possible for their return."

No one spoke for a moment, as if the deciding word had just been spoken.

Angie leaned up so she could see me around Jenny. "Was the action covered much in the newspapers?"

"Not in San Francisco," I said apologetically. "Not after the first couple of days. They covered the arrests. But it was hard to get ongoing news. All we had
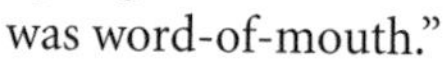
was word-of-mouth."

We stopped at the Vandenberg camp to pick up people's tents and gear. The rain mercifully took a break, and I disembarked to check out the camp. It wasn't quite the quagmire that January had been, but the canvas tents were damp and musty.

I took in the big field bounded by

Encampments modeled on the 1981 Diablo Canyon action — and inspired in part by the 1969 Woodtock festival — provided a gathering place for people preparing to do the Vandenberg actions as well as a home base for support workers. Here, campers gather during a rare dry moment at the March 1983 action.

clumps of trees. The camp had a mellow feel, even though I knew support people must be getting frazzled with driving to Santa Barbara or Los Angeles for court hearings.

We arrived at dinner time. People were gathered around the central fire pit talking and eating. A guitar player was strumming off to one side, and I wished I'd brought a harmonica so I could join him.

I stopped by the kitchen tent and said hi to Artemis, who was back in the kitchen after spending the previous week in jail. I spotted her over by the compost bin. Her shoulders slumped a bit, and her black and gray hair was matted and cowlicked like the latest punk fashion. I wondered how she was holding up, but when she turned toward me, her eyes answered the question. "I could do this full-time," she said as she came out to hug me. "It's been so wonderful. I'm going to stay a few more days, till I have to be back in Berkeley for a meditation workshop I'm leading. That's going to seem so strange after this."

Artemis got together a care package for our journey home, stocked with bagels, fresh fruit, and a brick of chocolate. We said our goodbyes and headed back to the van. Sara, who had been at the camp, joined us for the ride home. I was a little sorry, since I'd been hoping to sit with Karina again. I volunteered to ride up front with Lyle, figuring the others probably wanted to sleep. Before we reboarded, I put my arm around Jenny, and said to her and Angie, "You know there's no vacation after this. We have newspaper production this weekend."

"I have it on my calendar," Jenny assured me. "It'll be nice to get back to normal life."

"Depends on your definition of normal," Angie said. I laughed and hugged her before she got in the van.

Back on the highway, Lyle and I tuned in a country station from Bakersfield. As a Freddy Fender song drifted through the van, I cracked the window to catch the cool evening air and thought back over all I'd heard in the past two hours.

Up till now, the ten-day sentences — and the uncertainty surrounding those still in jail — seemed simply unfortunate, a remote occurrence that didn't affect me. Today's trip made it concrete, something that had happened to a bunch of my friends. And what about the thirty guys in Arizona? How long would they be held?

I'd never done more than one night in jail. Was it just coincidence? What if the guards tried to separate out second-timers at Livermore in June? How far would they go? Could we hold solidarity?

The image of the Marshals throwing around Karina and Jenny and Angie pressed into my mind. Ten days in jail they'd served, and some folks got even longer. What happened to our string of victories? Was this a fluke, or did it signal a crackdown on protests? Either way, we weren't quite as invulnerable as I'd thought.

Friday, April 12, 1983

HOLLY WASN'T at the office when I got there. I was meeting her at the end of the day, but she and Craig had gone to see about permits for LAG's pre-blockade rally in June.

Holly and I hadn't been finding much time together since our trip to Santa Cruz. We talked about another excursion, maybe over to the Sierra foothills, but with the Livermore spokescouncils starting up, plus a couple of weekends every month for Direct Action production, it didn't look promising.

The office was fairly quiet for a change. Sara and Claudia were on the phones, and Jenny and Caroline were working together at a small desk near the door. LAG had recently moved to the front of the long office. Plate-glass shop windows made the front a lot brighter, although posters and flyers always threatened to obscure the sunlight. Up front, a couple of old couches formed a "reception area," while a half-dozen desks and several worktables filled the rest of the space.

I went over to where Jenny was updating donor cards. Coordinating Council had just hired Jenny as a bookkeeper, to keep track of the money we were steadily losing. She was hired only half-time, but the other half she volunteered with Caroline on fund-raising, so it was a bargain for LAG.

At twenty-three, Jenny brought a younger spirit to the office, doubly so when Angie was around. A couple of days earlier I had worked with them sending thank-you notes to Direct Action subscribers. They sang along to a Madonna song, reminisced about salsa dancing over in the Mission, and drew me into a graffiti plot that involved four stencils and six colors of spraypaint.

APRIL 1983

50¢

DIRECT ACTION

PUBLISHED BY LIVERMORE ACTION GROUP

VANDENBERG

continued on back page

June 20

BLOCKADE

LIVERMORE!

AT WHAT COST A BLOCKADE?

DIRECT ACTION

LIVERMORE ACTION GROUP
3126 SHATTUCK AVENUE
BERKELEY CA 94705

BULK RATE
US POSTAGE PAID
PERMIT NO. 20
BERKELEY, CA.

Direct Action #5, April 1983

I wished Angie were around now. Jenny and I were meeting to organize a "Blockade-a-thon," where Livermore protesters would get sponsors to pledge so much per day in jail. Who knew if it would work, but people laughed when we announced the idea at a spokescouncil, so it seemed worth a try.

I pulled up a chair next to her. "How's it looking on the AG outreach?" I asked her.

"I'll call the rest of my list tomorrow," she said quickly.

"I haven't finished, either," I said. "But most people I've talked to say they'll pass out Blockade-a-thon forms at their next AG meeting."

"Yeah, mine too," she said. "And I'll take stuff to the spokescouncil next weekend."

"That's all we can do," I said. "You put out an idea and see if it flies. If not — on to the next idea."

Jenny studied my eyes for an instant, as if I might have said something profound. Then she apparently decided I hadn't, and laughed loudly, which made me laugh, too.

Claudia called me over. "Do you have time to help me with this mailing?" she asked. She gestured to a press release for our June Livermore action as if it were a stack of widgets to be shipped to Acme Hardware. You'd never guess from her demeanor that it concerned the most important event on our calendar, the action that practically defined LAG.

Usually I liked working with Claudia, even if she was in a sardonic mood. But lately she'd seemed increasingly jaded, and I found myself avoiding her. Probably best to counteract that, I thought. I pulled up a chair at the worktable.

BLOCKADE LIVERMORE!

BLOCKADE-ATHON

SPONSORS Name (optional)	Phone (for pledges followup)	check if name is to be added to letter to judge.	Contri-bution	Pledge ($$ per hour, day.)

SPONSORSHIP FORMS AND CONTRIBUTIONS CAN BE BROUGHT TO THE PLANNING MEETING ON JUNE 18, OR TO THE LAG OFFICE, 3126 SHATTUCK, BERKELEY, 644-3031. IF SPONSORS WANT THEIR NAMES ON THE LETTER TO THE JUDGE, BE SURE TO GET THE NAMES TO THE OFFICE NO LATER THAN MONDAY, JUNE 20. (Call 644-3031 for office hours around the action.)

The Blockade-a-thon, in which friends and family members pledged support of blockaders, raised $3000 for LAG while giving donors a personal connection to the action.

"This is going out early," I said as she handed me a stack of envelopes. "It's two months till the blockade."

She folded a half-dozen releases at once, peeled off one at a time and guided it into the awaiting envelope. "You have to start early," she said. "This may not get any immediate results. But you have to keep your name in front of the press, keep coming at them from different angles. Otherwise, you get one story the day of your event, and then you're gone. Look at VAC — hundreds of people in jail and almost no coverage in Bay Area papers."

"The action was halfway across the state," I said, irritated that I had to defend VAC.

"Doesn't matter. A lot of Bay Area people spent a week or more in jail down there. Do your homework, and the media will be hungry for the story. But you can't send out a half-baked press release at the last minute and expect them to drop everything and come running."

"Well, maybe LAG could help out with those kinds of details," I said pointedly. "VAC organized the camp, the legal team, the handbook. And they sure showed they can get a lot of LAG people to come to their actions."

I expected her to snap back, but she kept stuffing envelopes. "The March action happened because of the work that LAG did in January," she said. "So what if it was bigger? As if all we need is bigger blockades. We'll run from action to action till we all burn out. Protests alone can't change anything. We have to build a broader movement. But who has time for movement-building or coalitions? They're too busy getting arrested."

Claudia clearly wasn't in the mood to be dissuaded by facts. Just recently LAG had joined a coalition with local chapters of the Freeze, War Resisters League, and a dozen other peace groups. The focus was a demonstration in

October against the new generation of "Euromissiles," which the U.S. was pressuring its NATO allies to accept — another component of Reagan's First Strike nuclear strategy. I reminded Claudia of the Euromissiles coalition.

She tossed her head back and laughed sharply. "That proves my point," she said. "Sure we joined. But how many people in LAG give a damn about the coalition? It's just another chance to protest."

For once I could trump her. I laid out my cards. "I'm planning to be part of the coalition," I said. "And Mort and Melissa definitely are. They're the ones who proposed it in the first place."

"Well, that's great," she said, loosening up a little. "I'm glad not everyone has tunnel vision."

I took it as a compliment. We finished up the mailing, and I was glad to see her leave for the post office on a positive note. For now, anyway.

Claudia had just departed when the door burst open and Raoul tromped in. Raoul was the burliest man I knew, a linebacker in street clothes. In baggy shorts, a T-shirt, and a backwards baseball cap, he seemed even younger than his twenty-five years. "Hey, the Livermore posters are almost ready," he told no one in particular. "We just finished printing them." He sized up the bunch of us in a glance, then plopped his hefty frame onto one of the couches in the front of the office.

I didn't know Raoul well, but I knew he was one of the thirty men who spent two weeks in an Arizona prison for the Vandenberg action. With their return, everyone was out and accounted for. We'd come through intact.

"Good to see you," I said. I sat on the arm of the adjacent couch. "Thought we'd lost you guys for a while there."

He scrutinized me before speaking. "Felt that way to us, too," he said. "We had no idea what was happening. We were arrested just like everyone else, but then they shackled us and stuffed us into an airplane. We kept trying to figure out why they picked us, but we never found out. We didn't do anything different from anyone else."

Sara and Jenny came over to where Raoul was sprawled. Jenny looked at Raoul intently. "They were making examples of you guys," she said, "to scare everyone else."

"Maybe," Raoul said. "They wanted the second-timers, the people with ban-and-bars. They tried to get us to talk, and offered to let first-timers go. But we never gave in, never even gave them our names. Finally after two weeks, they shackled us again, put us on a bus, shipped us back to Santa Barbara, and dumped us on the street. Totally bizarre."

"But solidarity worked," Sara said. "They finally had to let you go."

"Definitely," Raoul said. "We got shoved around, but everyone got out within two weeks, which isn't too bad. They couldn't isolate a few people and hammer them. But before the next action, we have to think about how we can we keep them from splitting us up. How can we bring more pressure on them?"

"We have to have everyone involved from the start," Sara said. "There were almost eight hundred people arrested at Vandenberg, but only half did solidarity. The pressure we have on them is when we overflow their jails. If everyone stays in jail and refuses to cooperate until we get equal sentences, they couldn't stop us."

"I wouldn't be so optimistic," I said. "Look at the Good Friday action at Livermore last week. They force-cited people, kicked them out of jail, and gave them separate court dates. Sure, that was only sixty people. But why couldn't they do that to a thousand? They can throw us out if they want to."

Sara crossed her arms. "On Good Friday, people gave their names. If you refuse to identify yourself, they can't throw you out, or they're setting you free."

"Maybe," I said, weighing her point. "Seems like they're yanking people around a lot lately."

"That's because they know we'll stay within predictable bounds," Raoul said sharply. He shifted so he was sitting upright on the couch. "We're essentially passive vis-à-vis the police. Civil disobedience is a ritual of submission, with a safe and acceptable outcome for all parties. We have to push the limits. Refuse to submit. Show up where they aren't expecting us. Raise the ante."

Jenny looked at Raoul with fascination. Sara nodded, but her brow creased. For myself, I had to wonder whether Raoul had specific proposals or just a general critique. Anyone could talk a radical line.

But at that moment the office door opened. Holly and Craig were back. A smile came to my face as I stood to greet Holly. Enough of Claudia's cynicism or Raoul and his anarchist rhetoric.

Holly gave me a quick hug, but I could see she was still engaged with Craig. "I'll be five more minutes," she told me.

I turned back to the office. The conversation had broken up, and people worked alone or in pairs. I followed Jenny to her desk and reminded her about the Direct Action meeting the following Tuesday. "We're going to plan the new issue," I told her. "Tell Angie, too, will you? I haven't seen her in a while."

Jenny scribbled a note to herself, then looked up. "Did you hear about Angie's souvenir from Vandenberg? When we were in jail, there was no place to wash our underwear, so the Marshals went out and bought this old 1950s-style underwear at J.C. Penney's. Angie smuggled five pair out of jail. She modeled them for me last night."

"What a prize — McCarthy-era underwear," I said. I pictured Angie striking Marilyn Monroe poses. "I hope you both can make the meeting."

"Yeah, I'll tell her about it. How many pages do you think this issue will be?"

I wasn't sure if she was kidding me about how the paper kept growing, or expressing concern for the financial impact. "Well," I said, "there's all the

International Day reports, plus covering our June Livermore action. And Holly is doing a report on peace camps here and in Europe. I'd say twenty pages."

"At this rate, by next Fall we'll be up to a hundred."

"Or publishing weekly," I said, "Then we'll go daily in 1984."

The place was clearing out. Craig took off, and Jenny shortly after. Sara was on the phone for a few more minutes, and then it was me and Holly.

We wended our way to her nook at the back of LAG's section. "The further I am from the door," she said, "the more work I get done."

She picked up some file folders to take home. I came up behind her, put my arms lightly around her waist, and kissed her on the cheek. A smile crossed her lips, but she held onto the folders. "Sorry, I haven't quite slowed down yet. I've been going non-stop all day, and I have more to do tonight."

"Don't let me distract you," I said. I leaned over her and kissed her ear. She stopped sorting and leaned back into my chest. Brushing her hair from her face, she tilted her head toward me. I leaned forward to kiss her. Just as our lips met, though, the phone rang. She glanced down. "It's the night line," she said apologetically. "I told Daniel he could call me here after six. I promised I'd answer." I kept my arms around her as she picked it up, but it was clear that she needed to concentrate. I let go and stepped back. Curses. Foiled by the night line.

It wasn't that big a deal, I told myself. It was part of the total package. After

ACTION BULLETIN — INTERNATIONAL DAY OF NUCLEAR DISARMAMENT — ACTION BULLETIN

WESTERN NORTH AMERICA

Pt. Mugu Action

IDAHO

NEW MEXICO

OREGON

CANADA

LOS ANGELES

FATHERS DAY

PEACE WEDDING

EUROPE

BELGIUM

FRANCE

MIDWEST U.S.

CHICAGO

WISCONSIN

THE OZARKS

MINNESOTA

INDIANA

EAST COAST U.S.

Protests at G.E.

CONNECTICUT

FLORIDA

Worcester County

ORLANDO

NEW YORK

Each issue of Direct Action grew more ambitious in its coverage of global activism.

all, it was Holly's passion for peace that had drawn me to her in the first place.

Still, I felt a twinge of jealousy as she laughed on the phone. Not concern that she would leave me for Daniel, but that she was using up her laughter and enthusiasm talking about International Day with him.

I shook my head. Take it as a political lesson: Sometimes you're going to get preempted by the night line.

Friday, April 30, 1983

I HEADED DOWN to Hank's about ten o'clock, after stopping by my new night job. I'd stumbled onto a custodial gig at a little office building a few blocks from my apartment. For dumping the trash and sweeping up two evenings a week, I got $150 a month, increasing my income to the unheard-of total of $600 per month. My after-rent income practically doubled.

Friday night's chores took a little longer than usual. But I amused myself thinking of all the records I was going to buy when I got paid the following week. I had my eyes on a four-disk set of Bessie Smith, and maybe a Renaissance lute compilation.

Hank's shop was about six blocks from my new job, in a little industrial zone just off of Shattuck. The area had once fit neatly in the shadow of Berkeley's auto row, but car dealers were being displaced by video stores and restaurants, and the enclave seemed like a relic of another era.

As I came through the door, the Rolling Stones' "Satisfaction" blared out of the trebly juke box. Hank put down the purple lava lamp he was rewiring and gave me a firm handshake. "Hey, welcome to Friday Night Pins," he said. "You're the first to arrive. Want a beer?"

"Sure," I said. Hank produced a bottle of Pilsner. He picked up a massive set of keys from the workbench, flipped expertly through them, and produced a bottle opener. He popped the lid and handed me the beer.

I looked at the lava lamp. "My favorite uncle had one of those when I was a kid," I said. "Only his was green."

"Hey," he said. "Look what I got at the Ashby Flea Market last weekend." He pointed up into rafters, where a rubber mask of Richard Nixon — ski-slope nose, jowly cheeks, and a perpetual five-o'clock shadow — grinned down at us.

"Well, that'll keep us on our toes," I said, shifting a step or two so the mask wasn't looking right at me.

"You never know when it might come in handy," Hank said. "I've had a grudge against Nixon ever since he sent my brother to Vietnam. He and I have a score to settle."

Mort, Lyle, and Craig arrived. Mort set a six-pack of Beck's on the workbench and started a game on Old Chicago, a house favorite. Craig leaned on the next machine to watch. Lyle opened a beer and wandered around, looking more at Hank's work area than the pinball games.

I rang up a game on El Dorado, a western-motif game with the fastest flippers in the house. My first ball shot to the top of the illuminated playing field and careened downward, setting off an array of bells and buzzers before heading straight for the drain. I saved it with a deft double-flipper maneuver, but watched helplessly as it rolled down a side chute and disappeared. My luck wasn't much better on the next ball, and I reset the game prematurely to wipe out my low score.

Before I could shoot again, Hank called out: "Check what I did to the shooting gallery game. I just got it working. It used to be these cute little squirrels and deer that you were trying to kill. When you hit one, the next one would pop up. Check it out now."

I looked into the window of the old game. There in the target range was a miniature photo of Vice President George Bush, his expression frozen halfway between a grin and a grimace.

"Take a shot," Hank invited.

I gripped the mechanical pistol and aimed carefully. Pow! Pow! Got him! Curtains for Bush. Up popped Jesse Helms. Pow! Down he went, and up popped Richard Nixon. Pow! Pow! Pow! A goner. Up popped the big prize — Ronald Reagan.

Craig was looking over my shoulder. "Let me have a shot," he said boisterously. He stepped up and squeezed the trigger. Pow! Missed. Pow! Pow! Pow! No luck.

"He's an elusive character," Hank said. "Try aiming a little higher, right between the eyes." Craig leaned over the gun, eyeing down the sight line. Pow! Pow! Clunk.

"That didn't sound good," Mort said.

Hank went around back and checked the connections. "Shoot, I think we fried the coil. It's not hard to do on these old machines." He looked frustrated, then seemed to slough it off. "Ah, well, it can always be rewired one more time."

"Figures it would get stuck on Reagan," Craig said.

"What a metaphor," I said. "Did you hear what he said the other day? He called the Soviet Union the 'Evil Empire.' It's all a *Star Wars* movie to him. What a joke."

Mort cleared his throat. "I hope it's a joke. But he's got Congress eating out of his hand, funding every weapons system the Pentagon can come up with. Sooner or later, Reagan's going to want to play with his new toys. How long till we send troops into Central America or the Middle East?"

"That's what I've been thinking," Craig said. "Especially with the economy in recession. A war could knock the economy off the front page for a while."

I leaned back on a pinball machine. "I don't see it," I said. "Not direct intervention. People may tolerate CIA mercenaries and weapons sales. But not an open war. After Vietnam, people won't swallow the patriotic propaganda you need to justify sending people to die."

I preempted Mort's reply by pulling out a joint, firing it up, and passing it his direction. "Direct from Mendocino County to Berkeley."

"Ah, nature's bounty," Hank said as he exhaled his first toke. "The sun shines on California."

Lyle punched some Beatles songs on the jukebox. Hank turned back to rewiring the lava lamp. Mort started up a game on Queen of Hearts. Craig and I leaned against the workbench watching him play.

"Hey, how did the meeting with CISPES go?" Mort asked Craig.

"Okay," Craig said after a moment's reflection. "I think CISPES and the Freeze will help organize a legal march this June."

"Do you think they can get their members to come out to the Lab?" I asked.

Craig contemplated his beer bottle. "Even if they don't, it helps our credibility with the media. We need to do a march, anyway. There'll be plenty of people out there who don't want to get arrested. We have to provide ways for them to participate. You can't have people just stand around doing nothing, or they won't come back."

"Well," I said, "if people support the blockade one time, maybe they'll come back and get arrested the next."

Craig nodded. "Exactly. It's about making links to the mainstream, finding different ways for people to get involved." He took a drink, then turned to Hank, who was still at his workbench. "Hey, we need banners and props for the march, too. The Grim Reaper for sure. And what ever happened with that big nuclear missile that Spirit AG made? We should have it in June."

"I think the police confiscated it out at the Lab on Good Friday," Mort said over his shoulder as he worked the flippers on Queen of Hearts.

"Yeah," Hank said. "We saw Melissa and Nathaniel carry the missile into the intersection and chain themselves to it. But then the crosses came out and the prayers started. That was our cue to go back to my van and get high."

"Couldn't take a little praying for peace?" I said.

"Well, we were worshipping in our own way," Hank answered. "Worshipping nature. By the time we got back, everyone had been arrested and the missile was gone."

"Maybe the cops will return it," I said. "Don't they have to give back your property?"

Hank set down the lava lamp and came over toward us. "I want to take the missile idea a step further," he said. His eyes grew large. "I want to build the world's first Nukecycle. It'll be a twenty-foot-long tube with a nosecone and fins. The top will be cut away so four people can get inside it. Then the whole thing will be mounted on bicycle frames, with four seats and four sets of pedals."

We laughed, but Hank pressed on. "I can weld the bike frames together, with double wheels at the front and rear. Turning corners will be a problem, but I'll figure it out. I already got an estimate on a reinforced tube, twenty feet long. It would be about $250. Do you think Coordinating Council would pay half?"

"Then LAG would have its own nuclear missile," Craig said. "It's about time."

"Right," Hank said. "We could paint LAG slogans all over it, then pedal it out to Livermore and do a first strike on the Lab."

"Then we could drive it out to Concord in July," Mort tossed in between shots on his game. "The Central America groups are calling another action out there a couple of weeks after ours. They want LAG to endorse it."

"Great," Hank said. "Get busted at Livermore, rest up a few days, and head out to Concord."

The International Day work group produced this 104-page handbook, consisting almost entirely of new material, in Spring 1983.

"You'll have to think up another pseudonym if we go back to Concord," I said to him. "I think they caught on that Irma Feddup wasn't your real name."

"I've got one ready for Livermore," he said. "Sikov Bullschmidt."

I laughed. "I'd like to see them write that on their booking forms."

"You could use that at Concord, too," Craig said. "It's a different jurisdiction."

Mort stopped playing and turned to us. "We've got to get behind the Concord action. We can raise anti-intervention issues in LAG and build a coalition with CISPES."

"Sure," I said. "That's the way to get people interested in a coalition. CD excites people. Why not use it?"

"The problem is," Mort said, "it becomes an end in itself. The point becomes getting arrested, not building a strategy for political and social change. It warps the organization, so that any other type of organizing gets ignored. Some people didn't want LAG to endorse the October Euromissile coalition, because the Freeze doesn't want to do CD! Between the CD junkies and the new-agers in the International Day work group, it's a wonder we aren't totally isolated."

I felt defensive for Holly. "International Day includes other local groups," I said. "There's a local coalition."

"Sure, other peace groups. But do you see any unions or Central America solidarity groups getting on board? You can't ask people who are engaged in a daily struggle for jobs or lives to line up behind new-age rhetoric." He set his beer down and resumed his pinball game.

Craig leaned against the machine next to Mort. "It's a start. International Day gives us something to build on. It will help with the Euromissiles coalition in October."

"Even the Euromissiles coalition is mostly peace groups," Mort said over his shoulder. "There's got to be more diversity. White, middle-class activists aren't going to change the world by themselves."

"Well," I said, "If the Democrats come to town next Summer, we'll get our chance to form coalitions. Everybody will want in on the action." We had been hearing rumors that the 1984 Democratic National Convention was headed for San Francisco. "That would be wild if the Democrats come here. There'll be protests every day. It'll be a free-for-all."

Mort turned from his game as if he'd been stung. "It's not that simple," he said. "Protesting the Democrats could actually help re-elect Reagan. It's not like nuclear weapons, where the target and message are clear-cut."

His ardor surprised me. "Yeah, I guess not," I said.

Craig seemed unfazed, though. "You've got to admit," he said, "if it comes to pressuring the Democrats, we should be able to form a hell of a coalition."

"Yeah, it could be interesting," Mort said. "Of course, we'll have to deprioritize International Day. Some people talk like it's already carved in stone, and they get all bent out of shape if you question it."

I figured he meant Daniel, not Holly, so I let it slide. Hank screwed the base back on the lava lamp, wrapped tape around the loose wires, then plugged it in. After a moment it began to glow a deep, iridescent purple. "Now we just have to wait and see if it heats the lava," he said. He looked around the circle. "Hey, let's get back to work here. Enough goofing around. These machines need their exercise."

"I'll get us in the mood," Mort offered, pulling out a joint. "Someone ring up Old Chicago for four players and let's go."

Saturday, May 22, 1983

It was coming up fast. The Livermore blockade was barely a month away. By the time we got Direct Action out, it would be down to a couple of weeks.

I was going to meetings practically every night. It was hard to believe that

may 83

DIRECT ACTION

Livermore Action Group
3126 Shattuck Avenue
Berkeley, California 94705

BULK RATE
US POSTAGE
PAID
PERMIT NO. 20
BERKELEY, CA.

DATED MATERIAL

FEMINISM 14–15
INTERNATIONAL DAY
ACTION BULLETIN
9–12

PUBLISHED BY THE LIVERMORE ACTION GROUP

50¢

JUNE 20 LIVERMORE BLOCKADE SCENARIO

LAG Rally
—June 11

DISARMAMENT RALLY—JUNE 11
Mosswood Park
MacArthur & Broadway
Oakland
—NOON—

Entertainment • Speakers • Theatre
• Music • Food • Booths •

Direct Action #6, May 1983

only a year before, I had all of my time to myself, to read, write, or play music. Now my history books seemed like artifacts from that distant time before LAG. And it had been a week since I had touched my guitar. If not for a benefit that I was playing in early June, I might drop it altogether.

At least till after the blockade. Once in a while, especially late at night, I would think how nice it would be to do the action, spend a day or two in jail, and then take a break. Not that I wanted out of LAG. But I wanted a balance. This every-night business was too much.

And on top of that, here I was at a Saturday afternoon spokescouncil. I arrived early with Craig to set up a literature table and talk over the meeting, which Jenny and I were facilitating. We were meeting in the rec room of the student ministries center on Bancroft. A ping-pong table and volleyball net held center stage in the big hall. Windows along one side looked onto a garden, and banners proclaiming "peace," "love," and "justice" hung from the high ceiling.

Craig and I carried the ping-pong table to the side of the room and wheeled out a rack of folding chairs. "We should have another rack handy," he said. "There were over seventy people at the last meeting."

"Yeah," I said. "Solidarity is on the agenda, so that should bring people out."

Craig started setting up chairs. "We've got a lot to cover in five hours."

Jenny arrived with a box of stuff to sell. We covered half of the ping-pong table with flyers, bumper stickers, buttons, and stacks of recent issues of Direct Action. The other half would fill up fast enough with other people's flyers.

Besides being facilitators, Jenny and I were spokes for our new AG, Rabbit Deployment. We'd had our first meeting the previous Sunday — Daniel, Caroline, Walt, Angie, Jenny, Holly, and I. We decided to meet for dinner once a week till the action, then all get arrested together at Livermore.

Rabbit Deployment was named for the proposed Rapid Deployment Force, a special strike team which could intervene militarily anywhere on the globe on short notice. Probably the RDF was just a public relations ploy, a way to get more money for the military machine. But if it existed, Reagan might be tempted to use it. And once the Rapid Deployment Force was committed, more troops would follow. Maybe intervention wasn't as impossible as I thought.

"Did you hear Walt's idea?" I asked Jenny as I made a donations sign for the lit table. "He wants to announce that we're going to deploy hundreds of pregnant rabbits at Livermore in June."

She laughed sharply. "That's terrible! We'll have the animal rights people all over us!"

Craig came over, and the three of us conferred about the agenda, which focused mainly on blockade tactics and jail solidarity. People kept filtering in, and people had to scoot their chairs back to widen the circle. "This is great," Craig said. "We must be doing something right."

I nodded as I copied Jenny's agenda notes. Livermore was right on target. After that, though, who knew what we'd agree on. Beyond June we had nothing except the sketchy October Euromissiles coalition and vague rumors of the Democratic Convention. Still, for the moment, we could play our ace — Blockade Livermore!

Of course, there was a wild card — Vandenberg. About once a week we'd hear that the MX test was imminent. So far, it had been false alarms, and there was no solid evidence that the government was any closer than before. With billions of dollars in defense contracts at stake, the first test had to be perfect. So we could be waiting a while.

The meeting got underway with a quick check-in. Spokes had come from as far as Santa Barbara to the south and Eugene to the north. Reports on media work, the legal collective, and other logistics took too long, but finally we moved into solidarity.

It wasn't an easy topic, since it could mean anything from organizing a hunger strike to pressuring the courthonts to give everyone equal sentences after we'd been cited out. Jenny, who was facilitating, suggested starting with tactics during booking.

Two northern California clusters, the Acorns from Mendocino County and

LIVERMORE ACTION GROUP

Blockade Livermore Lab on INTERNATIONAL DAY OF NUCLEAR DISARMAMENT

Kids Affinity Group, Livermore Blockade June, 1982.

LIVERMORE ACTION GROUP
3126 Shattuck Avenue
Berkeley, CA 94705

Locally, LAG focused its International Day energy on a second June blockade at Livermore.

Sonomore Atomics from Sonoma County, put out similar proposals that no one give their name or provide ID until we had been promised equal sentences, no probation, and no fines. "That way they can't single out second-timers and nail them," said one of the spokes.

"But what about people who need to cite out?" someone asked. "Shouldn't they take ID?"

Several people raised their hands. Doc was first. "Each person will have to make their own choice. But you have to know that if you take an ID, they may find it and force-cite you. Once you're out, you're a lot more vulnerable. Our strength is to be together in jail. We're visible, and we're costing the government money. That's our best leverage. If a thousand people hold firm, they'll have to give in."

"We should refuse to even talk to them," said Cindy. "Maintain complete silence through the booking. They'll just have to call us all Jane or John Doe."

The discussion went on for quite a while. Jenny kept trying to move forward, but someone always had one more reservation or concern. Finally, the spokes consensed to the proposal about not giving names, but decided that carrying IDs and maintaining silence would be optional.

It was already past four, and we only had the room till six. Jenny proposed a ten-minute break, but most people wanted to press on with the meeting. I took over facilitating the last segment, a task I didn't relish.

We moved on from solidarity, agreeing to take it up at the next spokescouncil. Then we took up blockade tactics. Like the previous year, hundreds of first-timers were expected, many of whom would want a predictable scenario. But there was also a sizable contingent of people, not the least from Change of Heart, who wanted to step things up.

I was wary of spending the entire time hearing complaints and concerns that would just divide people. I searched for some way to channel the pent-up energy. Already, a half-dozen hands were up. We had to let the steam off, even if we never got to a concrete proposal. Maybe if we aired the differences, we'd see that we weren't that far apart.

I called on four people, who spoke about keeping our chants nonviolent; the importance of a good flyer to give stalled drivers; mobile blockade tactics; and the possibility of renting a bus so people from L.A. could come to the protest.

Another half-dozen people raised their hands. My jaw tightened. At this rate, we'd use our whole hour talking past each other. The next speaker talked about the symbolic value of shutting down the Lab for the entire day, but didn't say a word about specific tactics.

We had to try something different. Something that would get people talking directly to each other. I thought of a technique I'd seen Artemis use at a Vandenberg meeting earlier in the Spring.

"Let's do a fishbowl on how to make the blockade more effective," I said.

"Specific proposals. Six or eight people with strong opinions come into the center. It's okay to dialog, but when you've spoken a couple of times, step out so someone else can come in."

I must have sounded like I knew what I was doing, because people assented. Hopefully it would focus the discussion without triggering an all-out fight. At the minimum, it would buy me a little time to think of something else. I pulled my chair into the center. Most of those who joined me were people I knew: Karina, Raoul, Hank, Melissa, Monique from the Walnettos, and a few others.

Before we even got the chairs arranged, Karina was waving her hand. "Last year, the blockade was over by noon because we sat down right in front of the cops and waited to be arrested. We should make them catch us. Get up and move every time the cops show up. We need to shut the Lab all day, whatever it takes."

Melissa folded her arms across her chest. "What it might take is renewing our commitment to nonviolence. I propose that we all go limp when they arrest us. It would take them all day."

"Aw, they can handle a bunch of pacifist blockaders," Raoul said. He shifted in his folding chair, which looked fragile underneath him. "If we all do the same thing, that's playing their game. Our strength is spontaneity. We need some people going over the fences, others chaining themselves to the gates, others doing roving blockades. Keep the cops guessing."

Monique bristled. "I hope you don't do that near my AG. We'll be bringing in a lot of new people, and we're planning traditional civil disobedience."

"You can be at different gates," said a man across the circle. "That worked last year: Different zones for different tones."

Good idea, I thought. But I wondered whether anyone had tried going over the fence the previous year. That could complicate matters.

Alby jumped into the circle as Karina stepped out. "We should drive old cars out there and disable them right at the gates," he said before he even sat down. "They'll have to get a tow truck through the blockade to get rid of them."

A ripple of laughter ran around the room, but Melissa didn't look amused. "I assume you plan to stay and take responsibility for what you've done," she said.

"No way." The speaker was Sid, a gangly nineteen-year-old with a paint-spattered T-shirt and spikey black hair that leapt away from his pale skin. He perched on the edge of his folding chair. "That's the whole point. Keep moving. No sitting and waiting to be arrested. Move down the road and blockade again. Make them come to us."

"Wait," Melissa said as if struggling to comprehend. "You're going to disable cars and then run away?"

Raoul jutted his jaw. "Don't we have affinity group autonomy? AGs can do anything, as long as it's nonviolent."

Melissa spread her hands in front of her. "Well, *is* it nonviolent? I don't want to see anybody stirring things up and then running away while others pay for it."

Raoul muttered something, but Claude, who had just joined the circle, spoke over him. "I have another concern about escalating tactics. People could wind up with different charges. Some could have felonies, others misdemeanors. It makes jail solidarity a lot trickier."

"Why can't people with similar charges be in solidarity among themselves?" someone asked.

"No," Claude shot back. "We have to demand equal charges for everyone. We can't let the authorities divide us into different groups."

"Hey," said Hank, who had sat silently through the whole fishbowl. "Don't worry. It'll give us something to argue about at the jail meetings."

Most people laughed. At least we can still make jokes, I thought. We'd just about run the range of tactics and no one had gone ballistic. Still, my secret hope that the fishbowl would magically produce the perfect proposal and make me look like a genius was fading.

Time was running short, and we had reports about outreach, a wheelchair blockade, a seniors' march, and a youth action on the agenda. I had to call an end to the discussion. People grumbled as they moved their chairs out of the center. The woman who was taking notes said she would mail them out to AG contacts the next day, so the next meeting could try to come to some decisions.

I had brought my guitar, hoping to end the afternoon with a song, but the meeting ran on until we had to vacate the space. With minutes to spare we chose facilitators for the next meeting, folded up the chairs, and cleared out.

Craig and Mort talked about getting dinner. I wished I could go with them and debrief from the meeting. Even without any dramatic decisions, I felt like it had gone well. Most of the tactical differences could be contained within the "tones for zones" policy. Still, I'd have liked to get Craig's sense of it.

But that would have to wait. I had plans with Holly. It was our only night together all week, and I was looking forward to going to a movie or a play.

I hoisted my guitar over my shoulder as I angled across People's Park. A group of drummers sat on the edge of the stage, not quite getting a rhythm going. "Hey, play us a song," someone called to me.

"Can't right now," I said apologetically. It nagged at me as I kept walking.

Was I in such a big hurry that I couldn't stop and play a song? But it was too late now. The moment had passed.

I skirted the edge of the garden and headed toward Telegraph. As I waited for the light to change, a headline about the Giants caught my eye. Baseball. I dropped a dime into the newsbox and opened to the sports page. Sure enough, the Giants were playing baseball. I scanned the standings — fifth place. Not a great start. I should go to a game. Maybe Mort and Hank would go. Good idea. Well, after the blockade. No way it was going to happen before then. But once we got the protest behind us, a sunny afternoon in the bleachers would be the perfect kickoff to a belated Summer.

Holly stood to greet me when I got home. I was still pretty keyed up from the meeting. "How about going to a movie?" I asked, picking up a *Bay Guardian* and flipping to the film section.

"Okay," she said with hesitation. "Actually, I'm not sure more stimulation is what I need. I was hoping to spend the evening hanging out and talking. Maybe we could get something to eat."

"Okay," I said, pacing around the living room. "How about some music?"

"Sure," she said. She poured a cup of tea and settled back in on the cushions on the floor. "Something not too loud."

I put on a Flatt and Scruggs tape and sat down next to her. The banjo was too jangly, though. I reached over and turned it down, but then it seemed too low. Just relax, I told myself. I stretched out on the floor, using the cushion she was sitting on as a pillow. I reached over and rubbed her lower back. "How did it go with Caroline today?" I asked.

"Well, good," she said dubiously. "I mean, it was great to spend the day with her. But she is so stressed about money. LAG is deep in debt again. The only hope is that with the blockade coming up, our mailing might bring in a lot of money."

"It worked with Vandenberg," I said.

Holly took a sip of tea. "Jenny was there for a while, too. She and Caroline are organizing a raffle. The grand prize is a trip to the island of Grenada."

"Why Grenada?" I said.

"It's a Caribbean island, for one," she said. "People will buy tickets to go to the Caribbean. But also, Grenada's new government is socialist. And it's the only country in our hemisphere with a Black president."

Grenada seemed far away to me, but Holly had traveled through Central America a few years earlier and spent time on the Caribbean coast. "I think it would be a great prize to win," she said.

She set down her tea and stretched out next to me. "Caroline told me about a friend of hers who went to Nicaragua on a coffee harvest brigade. It sounded wonderful. Since the revolution, people believe they're building a new society. Caroline and I were fantasizing about going on a harvest brigade."

Her words raised a nervous tremor in me. "Going to Nicaragua?"

"It's all a dream right now," she said. "But after the blockade, I'm going to need some sort of vacation. And Caroline definitely does. She's thinking of resigning from the staff after June."

I rolled onto my side so I was facing her. "Really? But she's done such a great job. How could anyone resign such a central position?"

Holly sighed. "I can understand it. It's so stressful. Especially being in the office. When I need to get work done, I have to get out of there."

I reached over and stroked her shoulder. "Is this what you want to be thinking about?" I asked.

She looked at me sadly. "No, you're right. We should talk about something besides LAG. But did I tell you about getting confirmation from the Plowshares people up in Connecticut? They're the people who have been arrested for hammering on missiles. They're going to do a CD at Electric Boat on June 20th."

"Cool," I said, sitting up on the futon. "What about Chicago? Did they ever sign up?"

"Yeah," she said. "Disarm Now Action Group is doing an action at Northrop Corporation. And a coalition of religious groups are doing a vigil in Cedar Rapids, Iowa." She sat up, and her eyes shone. "And you know what the best one is? The traditional Navajo down at Big Mountain, the Dineh Nation, are going to do a vigil in solidarity with us."

"That's great," I said. "That's not the 'usual peace group' that Mort complains about."

"Yeah. Every day there's something new. Antonio is working on a joint press statement that all the groups can use. And Daniel is planning a trip to Europe in the Fall, to help build for next year."

Next year? Wait a minute. What about the Democratic Convention? My jaw tightened. What to say? I didn't want to dampen her exuberance, but I remembered Mort's words about changing priorities, and it didn't seem right to remain silent. "If the Democratic Convention comes to San Francisco next Summer, a repeat of International Day might not make sense."

Holly stretched out on her back. "Why does the Convention make a difference? I don't care about yelling at a bunch of politicians? I'd rather be blockading Livermore as part of International Day."

"But we can't ignore the Democrats," I said. "They've given Reagan everything he wants. They're just as guilty as the Republicans. And just as crooked."

Holly yawned. "We have our focus, with International Day and the Livermore blockade. We shouldn't abandon our plans because of the Democrats."

I was sorry I'd brought it up. Before I could think of what to say, the tape player snapped off. Holly yawned again, and her features softened. "Weren't we going to get something to eat?"

"Yeah," I said, glad for the shift. I sat up next to her. "Do you want to go out?"

"Let's get something on Telegraph. Sara told me that the new Ethiopian place across the street is really good."

We grabbed our sweaters. I wished we were going to a movie, but at least we were getting out for a while. "How's Sara doing?" I asked as we started down the stairs. "I haven't seen her much lately."

"She's okay. Sometimes she has a hard time with Karina and her other relationships. She won't say so, but I think she wishes she had Karina all to herself."

"I can relate."

"What, you wish you had Karina all to yourself?"

We were just going out the lobby door. She passed through ahead of me. I reached out and tugged on her sweater to slow her down. "No," I said. "I'm happy right where I am."

Wednesday, June 8, 1983

"You don't really think they timed the MX test to mess with Livermore, do you?" I looked at Doc expectantly.

"Sure I do," he said. "They know the strength of our movement. And it scares them. Anything they don't understand scares them."

I nodded. Doc and Antonio and I were standing behind a circle of couches and folding chairs in the Savo Island Co-op community room. The seats were filled to capacity. Inside the ring, a couple of dozen people were crowded onto the floor.

I had just walked over from the LAG office, where I'd spent the afternoon helping Holly with her duties as unofficial Vandenberg liaison. As she predicted, dozens of people called LAG after learning that the MX missile test was about to happen.

The MX test. LAG answered the phones, but VAC called the meeting. Dormant since the exhausting March action, the Vandenberg Action Coalition sprang back to life in a day. Here at last was its moment of truth.

I skipped a Livermore publicity meeting to attend the emergency gathering. Even if it was exasperating to see LAG's blockade undermined by Vandenberg, I knew this was the place to be.

The meeting hadn't started yet. I looked around the room. Change of Heart was well-represented: Moonstone, Karina, Alby, Sara, Doc, Antonio, and a couple of others were already present. Karina got up from the floor and came over to Doc and Antonio and me.

"Are you going?" she asked us.

Antonio and I shook our heads, and I felt sheepish.

Doc nodded to Karina. "I'm leaving tomorrow night. And you?"

Karina glowed. "Tonight. This is the point of everything we do, isn't it? If we're on the base, they can't test the missile. It's as simple as that. Even a hundred people could ruin their plans. It's our biggest chance ever to affect the arms race."

The implicit contrast with stodgy old Livermore annoyed me. But Karina's enthusiasm was irresistible, and I leaned closer as she continued.

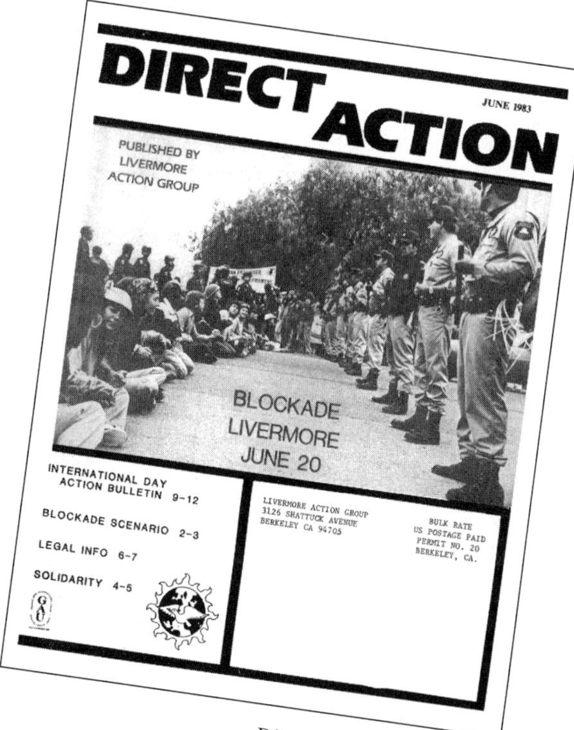
DIRECT ACTION

JUNE 1983

PUBLISHED BY
LIVERMORE
ACTION GROUP

BLOCKADE
LIVERMORE
JUNE 20

INTERNATIONAL DAY
ACTION BULLETIN 9-12

BLOCKADE SCENARIO 2-3

LEGAL INFO 6-7

SOLIDARITY 4-5

LIVERMORE ACTION GROUP
3126 SHATTUCK AVENUE
BERKELEY CA 94705

BULK RATE
US POSTAGE PAID
PERMIT NO. 20
BERKELEY, CA.

Direct Action #7, June 1983

"We know the terrain from last time," she said. "We can approach the MX site from at least three directions. Most people will get caught, but as long as some get through, we can stop the test."

The meeting got underway, and she returned to her seat. I turned to Antonio. "I wonder how many people will skip Livermore and go down to Vandenberg?"

He looked around the packed room. "If Change of Heart is any indication, this is going to hurt the Livermore blockade."

"That's putting it mildly. Change of Heart is losing half its members." I lowered my voice. "Between you and me, it's a problem. LAG needs a strong action. We've got nothing definite planned after the blockade. We need the boost. And this cuts right into our action."

Antonio crossed his arms and tilted his head philosophically. "It's all one movement," he said. "It's not a competition. All of us working together will stop the arms race."

"I don't know," I said. "We're diluting our impact. We can subtract the Vandenberg arrests directly from the Livermore total. We expected the June blockade to be bigger than last year. Now who can say?"

Sunday, June 19, 1983

"SIXTY DAYS?" I could hardly speak the words. "Karina got sixty days in federal prison?"

Moonstone clenched his teeth. "She'll be in jail for the rest of the Summer," he said as we talked at the office the day before the Livermore blockade. "Alby, too. They both had prior arrests. And several others got thirty days for a first offense."

Backcountry actions at Vandenberg began June 10. AGs went on and off the base, some getting busted, some hiding in the backcountry. No one was sure who had been arrested, who was still somewhere on the base, and who had gone back home. There wasn't even a phone at the camp, so messages had to be relayed from a house in Lompoc. All we knew for sure was that about a hundred people made it to the camp in the first few days. For an emergency action, it wasn't a bad start.

But unexpectedly, it tapered off. Maybe because of the heavier sentences at the March action, maybe because of the logistical strain of a long-distance action, and maybe because Livermore had its own emotional pull, Vandenberg didn't build momentum. Only about thirty-five people got arrested in the week before the missile test.

Worse yet, the MX test shot landed close enough to its Pacific island target that the Defense Department could call it a success. At the LAG office, everyone seemed to sag. And for VAC, the launch knocked the wind out of the weary network. Meetings evaporated, and information was even harder to get than for the March action.

Moonstone tried to put a good face on it, talking about the need to organize solidarity actions in support of Karina and the others in prison. But there wasn't really much that could be done.

Jenny called Moonstone over to her desk, and I turned back to Claudia, with whom I was working on a media kit for the next morning's press conference. Claudia had remained silent while Moonstone talked about Vandenberg. Once he was out of earshot, though, she wasn't slow to offer her opinion. "VAC set themselves up for failure, claiming they would stop the missile test," Claudia said matter-of-factly. "And now they've got people with sixty-day jail sentences. Big surprise. You can't pull off actions of this magnitude without a solid organization behind you."

"Makes me wonder about doing small actions," I said. "With thirty-five people, you're left to the mercy of the court. They couldn't get away with this at Livermore."

Claudia shrugged. "Maybe. All we know is that they haven't tried so far."

Walt came in the door. I stood and greeted him with a warm hug. His eyes seemed tired and harried. Walt had represented Karina and Alby at their Vandenberg hearing, and he looked like he felt culpable.

"Come on," I said, "You couldn't know what was going to happen."

"No," he said in a low voice. "But I was more cocky than I should have been. Most people who got arrested pled not-guilty and risked their luck on a later trial, figuring maybe with the missile test over, the courts would go lighter.

"But the five Change of Heart people wound up before a federal magistrate who had given people a ten-day jail term for the March action. I was the only lawyer there at the time. We assumed they would get a similar deal. So they pled no-contest."

Claudia peered at Walt. "And the magistrate hit them with sixty days?"

"Well, he asked why we were before his bench on these charges, and I told him that we were there to stop the government from building first strike nuclear weapons. He didn't like that at all." Walt shook his head slowly. "Next thing we knew, it was sixty-day sentences for second-timers."

"He was probably going to do it anyway," I told him. "How did Karina and Alby take it?"

"They were more angry than anything. But the first-timers who got thirty days were stunned, and this woman named Madrigan was really shaken up. She started sobbing right there in court." He looked at the ground. "It was pretty hard to take."

I felt for Walt, but I couldn't think of anything to say. I pictured Karina. Sixty days in prison. She could be tough when she needed to be. But that sort of sentence would wear anyone down.

Walt and Claudia started talking about the Livermore press conference. I went over to Moonstone, who was up by the couches in the front of the office. "How come you're free?" I asked Moonstone. "Didn't you get arrested?" I asked.

"Oh, I did," he said. "Twice. We were at camp within two days after the alert, and went on the base that night. We got dropped off on a perimeter road at dusk, seven of us from Change of Heart. We hiked the whole first night, took cover and slept all day, and hiked another night."

I could picture Moonstone hiking through the backcountry, burrs clinging to his tattered jeans and scraggly beard, looking like Old Man Mountain himself.

"Some people were getting exhausted," he said. "Not everyone was ready for a week in the backcountry. So we made it to an access road and dropped them off. They got spotted by a helicopter and busted right away.

"That left me and Alina. We hid in some bushes till the cops left. We hiked on for another night, using a compass to steer in the general direction of the MX site, until we ran into a swamp. We're wondering which way to go, sitting there alongside this swamp with our packs. But we were too near an access road, and a military policeman in a jeep comes along. Talk about lousy luck!" He laughed to himself. "The poor cop, he was so desperate, calling for help on his radio and yelling at us not to move. Finally some more cops showed up and busted us."

"Why did you wait?" I said.

"Exactly. We should have run away. At best, he could only have captured one of us."

He scratched the back of his neck. "So we went to jail, spent the night, and cited out. I went back to camp, and immediately get recruited to be a guide. Suddenly I'm the expert! I'd been on the base one time, and made it about halfway to the MX site, and now I'm the guide.

"So I wind up taking Karina and Alby and three others from Change of Heart. We hiked two nights, hiding out during the day while the helicopters were patrolling, and made it back to the swamp just before dawn of the second night. We wanted to keep moving, since it was getting close to the launch date and we wanted to get to the MX site. I told people to stay hidden, and went crawling along the access road, looking for some safe way around the swamp. Well, wouldn't you know it, a police jeep comes along right then! I dive back into the bushes where people are hiding. But the jeep stops and points its headlights at the bush.

"They tell us to stay still, that they have dogs. But I can see there are only

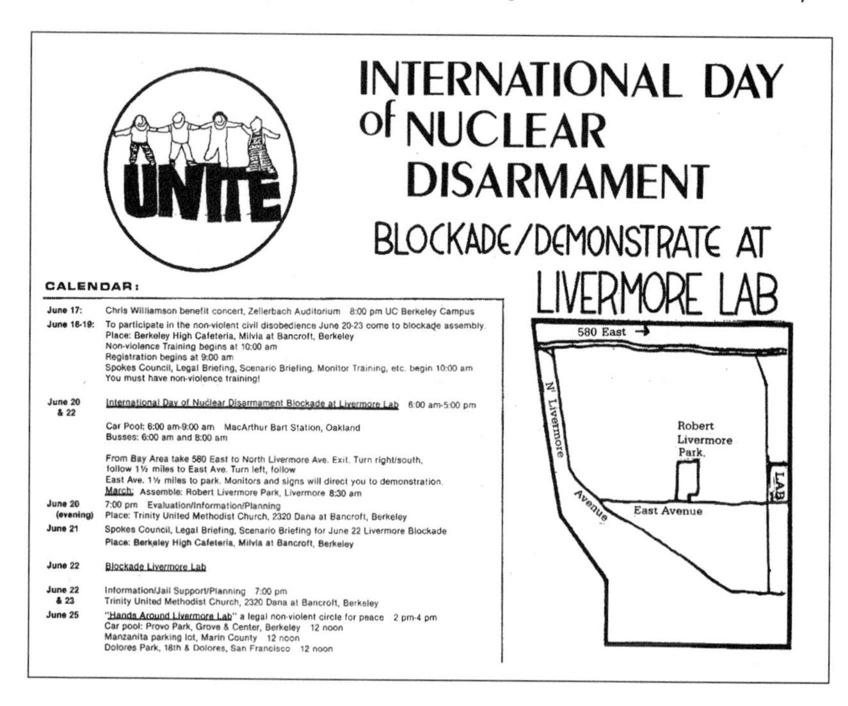

LAG's International Day plans included a rally, a benefit concert, the Livermore blockade, and Hands Around the Lab.

two cops, and there's seven of us. So this time I say to people, 'I'm going to walk, see you later.' And I take off, back up the hill. I get up a hundred feet, find a nice spot, and lie down and listen to them rustling up the other people."

"The others didn't try to run?"

"No, running would mean splitting up, and I was the only one who really had any clue where we were. No one else wanted to risk it."

It surprised me to hear that Karina hadn't taken off. If there was anyone I thought would have been up for an adventure, it was her. But maybe not alone.

Moonstone bent over and scratched his leg. "After they busted the others," he continued, "They come looking for me. They get close, so I do a little ritual. I cast a circle around myself and ask the Goddess for invisibility and protection. The cops are cussing and talking real loud about snakes and wild boars that are going to get me.

"Finally they bring up a dog. It immediately trots right over by me, sniffing, followed by a cop, not five feet away. I'm not breathing. I try to melt into the bushes. Luckily, the Goddess protected me. Also, the dog didn't actually have a scent to go by, and it went right on past, sniffing at the ground.

"They finally gave up and left. I waited there most of the day, and that night tried to figure out how to get to the MX site. But it was hopeless. I could never find a safe route. I wound up going through a big bed of poison oak, and then through a patch of thistles."

A swell of nausea rose in my stomach. His face was a little splotchy, and I'd noticed he was scratching a lot, but I hadn't put it together. I knew poison oak wasn't contagious, but I couldn't help edging away from him. "So how did you get busted?" I asked in a thin voice.

"I ended up near the officers' quarters," he said, not seeming to notice my revulsion. "I walked past the buildings, looking in the windows, till someone saw me and had me arrested. I was so exhausted that I non-cooperated all the way."

"If you got arrested twice in one week," I said, "how did you avoid the sentence Karina and Alby got?"

"They took me to a judge for arraignment, with Daniel and a few others. This was after Karina and Alby got sixty days, so we figured we better plead not-guilty and take our chances later. It was my second arrest, but I got a different judge, and he said he would let me go without bail if I agreed not to come back within two months. Between my exhaustion and the poison oak, I wasn't in any hurry to return, so I said okay."

"And Daniel, too?"

"Yeah, we both wanted to get back up here and do Livermore."

I laughed in spite of myself. "You're going to get busted with a case of poison oak?"

"I might as well itch in jail as out," he said. "I've been fasting, so I'm not feeling it much. And we'll probably only be in for a couple of days, anyway."

I reached out and rubbed his shoulder. He stepped forward and gave me a long hug, which usually I would have appreciated. But I was still feeling a little queasy about the poison oak, and it was hard to return his fervor.

Moonstone released me from his embrace. "I've got to get going. See you in jail." He started away.

"Yeah," I called after him. "I'll see you there."

Monday, June 20, 1983

I HAD A nagging feeling on the pre-dawn ride out to the Lab, a vague sense of going into "enemy territory." I wanted to turn back. But we were already on the highway, heading over the Berkeley Hills toward the Livermore Valley.

Maybe it was the music. Jimi Hendrix was great accompaniment to pinball and weed-fueled political discussions. But on a pre-dawn ride to a nuclear weapons lab?

I was riding shotgun with Hank, who was hauling a van-load of signs and banners out to the action. "Hopefully we can drive in pretty close, so we don't have to shlep them too far," he said. He sneezed hard. "Damn, I'm getting a cold. Too much work and too many meetings. I'm running on fumes."

I looked at Hank and nodded. "I'm glad we're not getting busted today."

Hank and I were among twenty organizers who had decided to delay our arrest till Wednesday so we could help with logistics, media, and jail support during the main blockade. It was important organizing, sure. But more than that, it meant two more nights in my own bed. I figured that the first couple of days in jail would be the toughest. If I got arrested Wednesday, with the legal settlement already in place, I might be released the same day.

Holly was planning the same, as far as I knew. She and Sara had driven out to the Lab even earlier to be legal observers for a women's cluster opening the blockade at the East Gate. Legal observers, being right in the middle of the action, were always at risk of arrest.

What if she did get busted? I'd have the apartment to myself for a couple of days. Get some space to myself before going to jail.

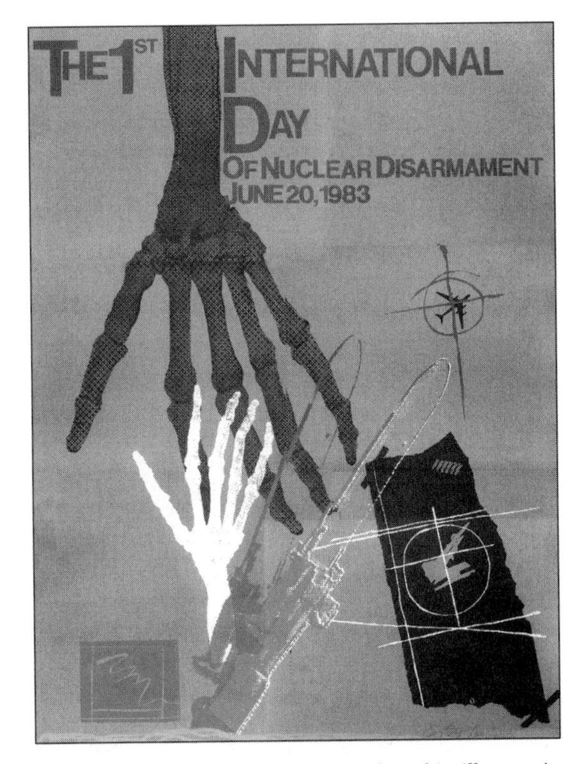

Local artists offered posters such as this silkscreen in support of International Day.

It was still dark as Hank eased his van off the exit ramp and rolled through the deserted little downtown of Livermore. "I'm surprised there aren't cops everywhere," he said. "Wish I had a can of spraypaint."

I twisted in my seat, picturing us trying to drive a van loaded with protest signs up to the Lab. Cops everywhere, ready to bust everyone in sight. And we'd be the most conspicuous target. Why hadn't I volunteered to work in the office with Claudia and Caroline?

As we approached the Lab, the first rays of dawn were visible on the horizon. I could make out clumps of protesters along the roadside. There were hardly any other cars on the road, and Hank was able to drive up to the gravel lot at the corner of East and Vasco, about a half-mile from the South Gate. He pulled up alongside a row of portajohns.

Although the police at the intersection weren't trying to stop us, driving farther seemed risky. I definitely did not want to get busted. And not just for selfish reasons. Jenny and I were doing a last-minute nonviolence prep the next day for any new people who wanted to join the Wednesday action. I had obligations.

Scenes from the June 20, 1983 blockade at Livermore Lab. Over 1100 people were arrested in this, the largest of two dozen civil disobedience actions across North America and Europe as part of the International Day of Nuclear Disarmament.

STOP CORPORATE-WAR
-FROM-LIVERMORE
-TO-EL-SALVADOR
BLOCKADE LIVERMORE
U.S. OUT
NO
TO MX!
OUT OF EL
SALVADOR

Hank decided to go for the gate, though. "Otherwise, we have to carry the signs all that way."

I sucked in my breath and stayed quiet. Hank's headlights illuminated a row of helmeted cops against the backdrop of the Lab's tall chain-link fence. They studied us coldly but let us pass. Pockets of protesters huddled together making final plans. Others hiked toward the gate.

One AG blocked traffic while other protesters gathered along a road near Livermore Lab.

We made it to the South Gate with no hassle. Hank pulled over, and we started unloading the signs and banners that Overthrow had painted. Hank did a quick inventory of the signs, which covered disarmament, nuclear testing, Central America, and social justice. "If we're blockading people," he said, "we might as well give them something to think about."

"Maybe they should be like the old Burma Shave highway signs," I said, "where you read them in succession and they make a poem."

"Yeah, yeah. I had an idea like that. I should've done it. Four signs, and they'd say: It Ain't/No Joke/George Bush/Deals Coke."

I laughed. Some of the tension drained from my shoulders. "Don't forget the fifth sign," I said. "It has to say 'Burma Shave' at the end."

Blockaders came and grabbed signs and banners, and the scene seemed more like a theater production than a protest. We had just about cleared out our stock when a cop came over and poked at the van with his baton. "Gotta move. No parking."

"Thank you, officer," Hank said with exaggerated politeness. "Good to see our tax dollars at work."

The cop cocked his head. "Let's see the registration on this vehicle," he said, pulling out a flashlight as big as a riot baton.

"You've got to be kidding," Hank said.

"Let's see it. And your license, too."

Hank muttered to himself and went to get the papers. Several other cops, having nothing better to do, came over to help hassle us. I instinctively patted my back pocket to be sure I had my wallet in case we got busted.

Suddenly I realized I hadn't emptied my pockets the night before. My pipe. I didn't dare check my pocket or it was a giveaway. I tried to visualize my last toke the night before, with a sinking feeling that I'd put the pipe in my pocket.

Hank returned with the van's registration. His jaw was set, and I thought he was going to fling the papers in the cop's face. Don't antagonize them! I tried to signal him. The cops were on their radios, running a warrant check. Should I try to get away? But I couldn't desert Hank. Besides, trying to leave would make the cops suspicious. And there wasn't anywhere to run.

I started over toward Hank to try to quiet him down. But one of the cops immediately held his arm out. "Back over there, don't move."

I was stuck. And now the cops were watching me. Hank was jawing at them, going on about illegal searches. His voice kept rising, like he didn't care whether he got arrested or not. Maybe he figured if the van was getting busted, he might as well, too. I stayed silent and tried to look insignificant. Maybe they'd arrest him and leave me. It was my only hope.

Minutes dragged by. The cops seemed determined to find a reason to impound the van. Hank was defiant. I felt sick. I'd probably be separated from the other blockaders and left out of solidarity for having brought weed to the blockade. Damn!

One of the cops got on his radio, probably to call a tow truck. An officer over at the side was fiddling with handcuffs. The search would be next. I groped for a way out. Make a run for the cover of the crowd? Plead that I was an innocent bystander?

Just when it seemed like we were goners for sure, the first affinity group stepped out into the road. The chanting and the applause of the crowd drew the cops' attention away. Their commander ordered them to line up and strap on their riot helmets. Hank and I seized the opening, jumped back in the van, and made our getaway.

As it turned out, I didn't even have my pipe on me. False alarm! I felt grateful just the same — saved by the blockade.

A Wednesday action drew newcomers inspired by the Monday blockade.

Wednesday, June 22, 1983

THE DAY DAWNED as we cruised east through the hills. I squinted out the window at the pinkish sky, feeling slightly nauseous.

My eyes traced the silhouettes of the rolling hills that separated Berkeley and Oakland from the Livermore Valley suburbs. Across the great divide. Again. Why didn't we ever protest in Berkeley?

Holly, next to me in the back seat, took my hand, and I felt thankful for the reassurance. Here we were, blockading together on our anniversary. I squeezed her hand.

We'd been living in different worlds the past couple of days, me with my head to the ground, hers in the clouds. My attention was stuck on Monday's Livermore action. Specifically, on the fact that there were two hundred fewer people than last year.

Two hundred fewer. What happened? Vandenberg's thirty-five arrests weren't the difference. Where was the groundswell of activism that the previous year had promised? How could there be fewer people? I tried to tell myself that eleven hundred arrests was a fine showing. And over nine hundred people remained in jail. Not bad at all. But I couldn't help feeling that we'd lost our momentum.

June 1983 Livermore blockaders, who would have overflowed the already-crowded Alameda County jail, were kept in circus tents on the jail grounds. Photos were taken by two protesters who smuggled cameras past the police and guards. Another person smuggled in a small tape recorder and sent live reports to a commnity radio station.

Holly, on the other hand, was basking in the glow of International Day. For the past two days, news had been pouring in about the three hundred International Day protests and events. A dozen groups did CD, most for the first time, and sent jubilant accounts of their actions.

Even now, at six a.m., Holly was telling Caroline, Jenny, and Angie, our traveling partners, about a blockade at Kirkland Air Force Base near Albuquerque where thirty people were arrested. I'd heard about it the day before, and had a hard time getting excited. We'd lost two hundred blockaders at Livermore. Even if Albuquerque gained thirty, I didn't like the math.

Still, if I couldn't share Holly's triumph, I tried not to begrudge it. Hearing her talk to reporters the day before, listening to how gracefully she showcased the actions of other groups while subtly underscoring LAG's initiating role, I felt proud of her and all she had done. But the glow seemed distant, and paled next to our reduced numbers at Livermore. How were we going to change the world if we got stuck at a thousand arrests? It was going to take a lot more than that to turn the arms race around.

I hadn't been tracking the scenery, and I was surprised when we pulled off the freeway onto Vasco Road. Although there were squads of police along the road, we were able to drive up to East and Vasco, at the southwest corner of the Lab. I stepped out of the car and caught a deep breath, remembering my last visit to the site. I patted my pockets just to be sure there were no surprises.

My travel-nausea receded, and I surveyed the spectacle. Two hundred people, maybe. A group of nuns. A few kids. A guy dressed as a skeleton with big floppy bone-hands. Up near the street, Mort and Tai unfurled Overthrow's red-on-black "Stop Corporate War" banner next to a white and blue banner reading "Let Peace Flow Like a River."

Traffic into the Lab was picking up, and the crowd seemed restless for the blockade to start. Rabbit Deployment circled up: Jenny, Angie, Caroline, Daniel, Holly, and I were getting arrested, and Walt was doing legal. Blockading with a bunch of friends — what a difference from the previous year.

We moved up to the intersection. There were about forty people doing the action. A women's AG linked arms and filed into the street. The cops casually buckled down their helmets and moved in to make the arrests. It was shaping up as a routine day on the old blockade line.

At that moment a boisterous figure made his way forward. People stepped aside to let the man through, and I caught a glimpse — Richard M. Nixon was joining the blockade. A confused buzz ran through the crowd. Then it dawned on me — Hank and his flea-market Nixon mask. As he came by I heard him rasp, "It's about time Tricky Dick paid for his crimes!"

Attired in coat and tie, Nixon did a spindly two-step into the street and joined the second group of blockaders. As the others knelt in the intersection, Nixon hunched his neck and thrust both arms in the air in his classic "V-for-Victory" salute. The media ate it up, and I smiled at the idea of tomorrow's paper showing a jowly, grinning Nixon getting hauled away by two burly cops.

It was our turn. Holly and I kissed quickly. Even though there was no legal settlement yet, I figured I'd see her in a day or two, so it wasn't a real dramatic parting. We didn't even sit together in the blockade line. When we went out into the road, I wound up between Jenny and Angie. We sat down in front of a short line of cars, linked arms, and squeezed together. I could feel Jenny and Angie vibrating on either side, as if they were channeling electricity to each other and I were part of the circuit.

Our arrests were a simple affair. The only twist came when the first bus filled up just before my turn, and I was separated from my AG. Oh well, I thought, we'll probably be back together for booking.

Being a small group, we got special treatment: a real jail bus. It looked like a school bus gone bad. The outside was dirty white, with "Alameda County Sheriff's Department" stenciled in big black letters. Thick bars covered the windows. I wondered if you could see anything from inside.

I climbed the stairs and took a seat away from the door. The interior could almost pass for an antique. Everything was made of tubular steel like old playground equipment, once-painted but now worn bare in many places. Wherever the dark gray paint remained, it was etched with graffiti.

The bus pulled out, and I sat back and listened to the others talking. Mostly it was speculation about when a legal deal would be reached, but one rumor put me on edge: that we were going to be housed in general population, not with the other protesters.

We pulled off the freeway and onto the Santa Rita jail grounds. I pressed up to the window and peered through the slats. I made out the main jail entrance, with a tall barbed-wire fence around it. Were we getting dropped there? Or did they have a back gate? General population. The concentration-camp barracks. I wondered if we'd all be kept together in the same unit. Probably not. It'll be a few here, a few there. I wondered if I'd be in with anyone I knew.

The bus trundled past the main compound, though. I watched the barracks recede from view. After that, all I could see was low-cut fields. Finally, the bus turned sharply to the left and jerked to a stop. A sheriff ordered us out. There seemed no point in resisting. Single file, we trouped out into the daylight.

I squinted at the makeshift booking area the deputies had erected in the middle of a scraggly field. A canvas backdrop stretched for thirty feet, as if masking some environmental eyesore. Two long tables formed the processing department. Down at the opposite end I spotted Hank, one of the last of the earlier bus. The cops confiscated his Nixon mask, and he pointedly reminded them that it was his personal property and must be kept and accounted for.

I was released from my handcuffs and directed up to the tables. Off in the distance I heard a chorus of cheers. Had some supporters gotten visitors' passes? It sounded like a lot of people. I worked my way down the booking line. At the end, a cop snapped my photo, then directed me around the curtain.

Emerging on the other side, I saw where the cheers came from. Two hundred feet away loomed a huge red-and-white-striped circus tent. Lined up in front of it were hundreds of men, waving and cheering. Guards lined the periphery. But they seemed like part of another reality. All that counted were the sea of hugs and friendly faces welcoming me to the "Santa Rita Peace Camp."

Hank and I found cots together toward the back of the tent. Coming in late, I didn't wind up near Change of Heart, but that was okay. I didn't want to get sucked into all the meetings. Better to have some distance.

Hank dropped onto his cot and lay there motionless. "How are you feeling?" I asked.

"Not so good," he said hoarsely. "I thought I was better last night. I even got high. But now it feels like it's turning into the flu." He coughed and winced.

I sat down on the edge of my cot and looked around the cavernous tent. It was about eighty feet wide and two hundred feet long. Seven stout wooden poles, twenty-five feet tall, held up the center spine. Thick hemp ropes traced the slope of the red and white roof. The side flaps were rolled up, but the air still felt musty. Probably the smell of the tent.

Row upon row of army cots filled most of the space, with two aisles about six feet wide. The front quarter was open, to use for meetings, talent shows, or whatever. In the center of the tent was a bottled water dispenser, an anomalous luxury. On the tentpole next to it, a makeshift bulletin board was covered with announcements of workshops and spokescouncils as well as poetry, drawings, and inspirational quotations.

I leaned back on the cot. I felt restless, wishing I had something to eat, preferably not bologna and white bread. Don't think about food, I told myself. Do something constructive. Like read.

Yeah, read. I bent over and unlaced my shoes, took a quick look around for guards, and pulled out my stash of fine-print Shakespeare plays: *Hamlet, Richard II, Julius Caesar,* and *A MidSummer Night's Dream.*

The guy on the cot next to me looked intrigued. I lent him *Julius Caesar,* and started in on *Hamlet* myself. It was slow going. The Melancholy Dane. Maybe I should start with something cheerier.

My ruminations were interrupted by a swell of applause from the front of the tent. Around me, men's faces lit up, and they jumped up and headed toward the commotion.

I put down *Hamlet* and followed. Was it the lawyers? Was there some news? Maybe this was the breakthrough. Maybe I'd gotten here just in time to celebrate our release.

It wasn't the lawyers, though. It was the County Sheriff, Reginald Krieg. Sheriff Krieg had been a regular visitor, I gathered, and his arrival triggered an ecstatic response. "We've been doing this twice a day since Monday," Antonio told me. "Every time we have a more elaborate greeting."

Doc joined us. "It was different the first time the sheriff showed up and ordered us to arraignment," he told me. "There were a bunch of deputies surrounding us, ready for action. We thought they were going try to force people onto the buses. All five hundred of us retreated to the center of the tent and linked arms. The sheriff got the message that we weren't going to cooperate, and he was smart enough not to push it."

The cheers rose again, and the sheriff approached, a tall man with wire-rim glasses and a Smokey-the-Bear hat. As he pulled out his bullhorn, the crescendo of shouts and applause brought a smile to his face. He looked embarrassed as the assembled inmates launched into a rousing rendition of an old Summer camp favorite:

We love you Reginald, oh yes we do
No one can say those words, the way you do.
When you're not with us, we're blue
Oh Reginald, we love you.

Raucous cheering followed the serenade. Only after it subsided could the sheriff make his speech, which some of the men seem to have memorized. "Gentlemen, I would like to advise you that Judge Lewis is sitting in Livermore Muncipal Court. You are hereby ordered to appear for arraignment. (Loud boos and hisses.) However, I have been informed that you will not cooperate at this time. (Cheers.) If any of you wishes to be arraigned, please step forward."

Several men who had to leave moved toward the back of the tent. Odd, I thought. Do they exit that way? Then I saw that the rest of the men were forming two long lines down the left aisle, leaving a narrow pathway in the center. I took my place, linking hands with the person on either side. As the departing men passed slowly between the ranks, those remaining sang, "I will never forget you, I will never forsake you." As if our tent were the true reality, and those leaving were journeying forth into the unknown. I picked up the tune, touched by the loving assurance the song offered.

After they left, more cheers resounded, and the old union song "Solidarity Forever" rose from hundreds of throats. I joined in, feeling like I was being initiated into a rite. And it must have worked, because as the song wound down, I felt stronger and more resolute than before.

I thought back to the Vandenberg action, when they were dragging us around, and I'd felt like nothing we could do collectively was more powerful than each acting alone. What a difference here. We might be stuck in jail, but no one was pushing us around.

The day passed as quickly as I could have hoped. When the lawyers showed up late that evening, my hopes rose. But they had nothing new to report. As they departed and I got ready for bed, an unaccustomed sadness mingled with irritation crept over me. The exhilaration of the earlier showdown with the sheriff had melted away. What did it matter? Sure, it felt good to stand up to authority. But at the end of the day, we were still here, and the Lab was still building nukes.

The shuffling, coughing, groaning, and sniffling of four hundred men pressed in on me. If only I could close the door. I longed for an art book, for my Renaissance tapes, for my guitar and a pipe of weed. For home. I pictured Holly sitting on the cushions sifting through her International Day notecards, the scent of her tea filling the air. How beautiful home seemed, and how bleak my present abode.

Friday, June 24, 1983

"DAMN," SAID Hank as the guards rousted us from sleep on Friday morning. "It's hard to wake up without caffeine." He hauled himself to a sitting position.

"Tell me about it," I said, rolling over onto my back. "I don't even drink coffee, and I still miss it." Waking up was even harder than the previous day. Between the cold and the snoring, I hadn't gotten more than a few hours sleep either night.

There was no point lying in bed, though. I wasn't likely to get back to sleep with all the commotion around me. I sat up and rubbed my eyes. "What do you think's for breakfast?"

Hank scratched his stubble. "I'm guessing filet mignon and roast duck, with a side dish of stuffed peppers."

"Wow, sounds great," I said. "I was expecting oatmeal." I looked around the tent at the wrinkled clothes and unshaved faces. People's hair was matted and cowlicked. Some wore their blankets like ponchos. Friday was my third day. But it was the fifth for most of the men. With no end in sight. Unlike the wrist slap of the previous year, the prosecutor was demanding jail sentences of eleven days plus two years' probation. Local judges Lewis and Hyde were backing him up. These were the same judges who the previous year had stepped aside because of "conflict of interest." Something was fishy.

Eleven days in jail was bad enough, but probation was the real sticking point. With probation would come a suspended sentence, probably six months. If you violated probation — in other words, got arrested again within the two years — the judge could throw you in jail for up to six months with no further hearing. It was the state's most effective weapon against protesters.

We saw two choices. We could cite out, demand individual jury trials, and threaten to snarl up the legal system in hopes of forcing them to negotiate. But since we all had the same charges, the court could probably get away with consolidating everyone into one big trial and railroading us. Once we were convicted, the judge could stick us with whatever probation or jail time he wanted.

Our other option was to refuse arraignment and stay in jail. It was a lot of stress since, based on the previous year, few people had made long-term plans to be away from families, jobs, and other responsibilities. But it was our strongest card: to be together and publicly visible. So far, we were holding tight. Out of eleven hundred people arrested, over eight hundred were still in jail on Friday, half of them men. We weren't budging.

But neither was the court. So here we were. Wherever this was. I still didn't quite have my bearings. Someone had told me which way was north, but I couldn't remember. With the sun hidden behind the low gray fog, I had not a clue.

As I neared the front of the chow line, I looked out over the yard area in front of our tent — a thirty-foot strip of crumbling asphalt bounded by a coil of barbed wire. A quarter-mile past the barbed wire, the stripes of the women's tent were visible. Beyond them were the barracks of the main Santa Rita compound, which kept things in perspective. We weren't so bad off.

The California National Guard, called in for the "emergency," had set up several wobbly folding tables in the center of our yard and were dishing up culinary delights. I got my toast and oatmeal and looked around at the scattered clumps of men eating and talking quietly. I was surprised by how few I recognized. Someone had done an informal poll the day before and concluded that about half were there on their first-ever arrest. Only about a

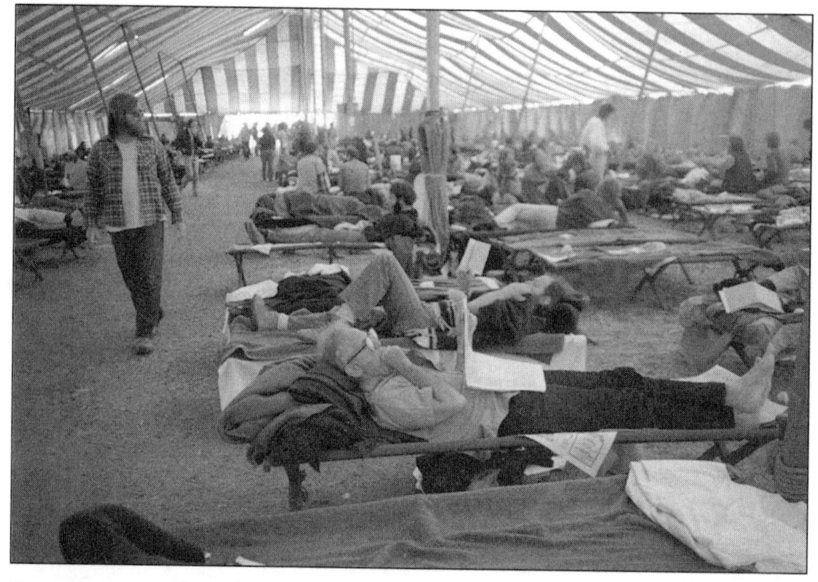

Rows of army cots lined the inside of the dirt-floored tents.

quarter had been at Livermore the year before, with the other quarter being veterans mainly of Diablo Canyon or Vandenberg. I heard that the women's camp was about the same.

The percentage of returnees disappointed me. Everyone had been so fired up when we got out last year. "We'll be back," everyone was saying. I was sure half or more would. Where had they gone? Was this the best recidivism rate we could hope for? No wonder our numbers were down.

Even though it was too early for the lawyers to have stopped by, there was already a fresh rumor circulating as we ate — we were all getting out today with sentences of time-served. Not impossible, I thought. They've gotten five days out of most people. I wondered if I'd have to stay two more days because I came in late. That would mean getting released Sunday. I could handle that, if I knew the end was in sight.

After breakfast, I followed Craig out to the side yard, which was about forty feet wide by the two-hundred-foot length of the tent. The far side was bounded by a low barbed wire fence separating us from a wild field that stretched for what looked like miles. Way off in the distance loomed the blue-ish hulk of Mt. Diablo, the tallest peak in the area. "Not a bad view for a jail," I said.

"No, I guess not." Craig had been in since Monday, and looked weary. I'd expected him to be organizing workshops or strategy sessions, but he was laying low. I asked if he'd done anything the first couple of days.

"No, I'm staying out of the spotlight," he said. "I've caught enough flak for one year."

"That's too bad," I said. "Seems like a loss not to have you doing workshops."

"Yeah, well, Nathaniel did a strategy game the second day. I think about five people showed up." He spoke as if making an irrefutable point, then looked down.

"Maybe people just needed some time to get oriented," I said. "Could be different now. I'd be there."

He glanced up at me awkwardly. "Maybe I'll set up something over the weekend if we're still here."

Around eleven that morning, the legal team came by. I'd done a good job the previous day of not getting all worked up, but today being Friday, I felt anxious to get our situation resolved. When I heard the lawyers were up front, I headed that way, along with half of the men in the tent.

One look at Walt dispelled my hopes. He looked tired and beleaguered as he brought us up to date. "The government is entrenched," he said. "They've already rented the tents and called out the National Guard to feed you. There's no pressure to resolve it before next week." He looked down at his notes. "The courts are closed Saturday and Sunday. Anyone needing out before Monday afternoon should go today. You may not get another chance over the weekend."

The weekend. Another three days in jail. I've got to quit getting excited every time a lawyer shows up. I moved slowly toward the lunch-line. No more. I refuse to get my hopes up.

After lunch I retreated to my cot and tried to read Shakespeare, but the tiny print was irksome, and I didn't make much progress. Mainly I brooded about wasted Summer days. A guy came around announcing a sing-along happening out in the side yard, but I wasn't in the mood for music.

A while later, I got up to use the portajohn. I was just coming out when several panel-vans pulled up in front of the tent and started unloading stacks of plastic bags. "Line up," the guards said. "You're getting your belongings back."

Getting our stuff back? For real? Sure enough, going by our John Doe numbers, the guards returned most of the personal effects confiscated in the arrest. For me it wasn't much of a haul — my apartment key and a few dollars in change. Other people got watches, hats, and belts.

Funniest of all, Hank regained possession of his Nixon mask. He pulled it on and stalked around congratulating everyone on their fine work. People were laughing and talking excitedly: why would they return our stuff unless they planned to cut us loose that day?

A few people warned that it could be a coincidence or a cruel trick, but the mood was ebullient, especially when we learned that the women's camp had gotten their belongings back, too. I thought of Holly. Even though we'd only been apart three days, she seemed far away. What if I got to see her tonight? We could make love, then go for a walk around Berkeley. How beautiful it would be after this.

Plus, I would get to eat the next day. Daniel, Moonstone, and six other men had started a hunger strike, protesting our incarceration by refusing to eat jail food. Everyone joked about how the strikers weren't missing much, but to me, the meals were more than food. They were the prime events of the day, the only punctuation in the monotonous flow.

No, I wasn't a hunger striker. But I'd gotten roped into doing a one-day solidarity fast on Saturday. Supposedly it was a big deal, with a press release and all. But if we got out of jail and I never had to do the fast, I wasn't going to be overly disappointed.

I spied Moonstone standing near the tent entrance wearing his bedsheet as a toga. He looked slightly dazed, and I wondered if hunger-striking was taking its toll. Moonstone had continued his fast since Vandenberg the week before. "I always fast in jail," he said. "I don't trust the food they give us. And it was better to keep fasting than stop for a couple of days and start over. Besides, I figure we'll be out of here any day now."

He adjusted his toga, which along with his scraggly beard made him look like an ancient Greek sage. Moonstone had gotten arrested in a lacy white wedding dress, doing a skit about being the "forgotten bride" of Lab founder

Edward Teller. But since the wedding gown was a bit formal for everyday attire, he fashioned a toga from a spare bedsheet.

"I could go on for at least another week if we have to," he said. "I'm not craving food." Moonstone's voice was ethereal, and he gazed past me. "I'm just tired."

He looked exhausted. And beyond that, his poison oak from Vandenberg looked worse. It made my skin crawl to see the splotchy rash on his face and arms, but he was so spacey from not eating that he seemed not to mind. "I'm meditating a lot," he said slowly. "That helps."

Monday June 27, 1983

Refusal to Eat Statement

Under the banner of "Fast for Freedom," seven blockaders so far are refusing to eat until the final demands consensed upon by spokes council are guaranteed. Some have refused food since our imprisonment began, one week ago; two dozen other prisoners are also fasting in solidarity with food refusers.

By refusing to eat, we are reclaiming the initiative. In the spirit of last week's blockade we are taking direct action. We are empowering ourselves to challenge the attempts by the authorities to crush our movement. The judiciary, as represented by Judge Lewis, who has intimate ties with Livermore Labs and the military industrial establishment, is trying to smash our organized opposition to nuclear proliferation by imposing restrictive probations, heavy fines, and long jail sentences. We are refusing to

A small band of hunger-striking protesters drafted this handwritten press release.

I shook my head. Moonstone smiled to himself. I put my arm around his shoulder, and he drooped against me. "I need to lie down," he said.

I might have skipped the hunger strike altogether, except that Daniel was one of the core organizers. I respected his icy determination and unrelenting resistance. I wanted to show some affinity group solidarity with him, so I went over to his cot and offered to help make copies of the strikers' press release.

He handed me a blank sheet of paper and a pencil. He set the corrected draft down between us, and we commenced our monkish task.

"How's it going?" I asked. I meant it as a personal question, but Daniel took it politically.

"Realistically," Daniel said as he continued writing, "I doubt that ten or twenty people on a hunger strike is going to turn the tide. We need two hundred."

"Well, maybe you'll have it with the solidarity fast tomorrow," I said.

"For one day, we will," he said. "Most of Change of Heart signed on for the whole day, and about half the men have pledged to skip at least one meal."

After we finished copying the press statement, I wandered back to my cot.

I wished someone would come around wanting to sing now. But I didn't feel up to organizing it myself. I checked in on Hank. His eyes were sunk, his nose red. I sat down across from him, and he pulled himself upright on his cot.

"Hanging in?" I asked.

"I haven't croaked yet," he said. "What have you been up to?"

"Helping Daniel with the publicity for the hunger strike."

"Oh, Martyrs Incorporated?"

"I take it you're not going to join the solidarity fast," I said.

"No, I need the nutrition," he said. "Besides, I'm not into that whole self-flagellation trip."

I didn't feel like arguing about it, so I didn't say anything. I knew Hank didn't care for Daniel. But I felt like he was dumping on me, too, for being part of it. We're all in this together. Can't people be more tolerant? Live and let live. Protest and let protest. How are we going to survive if we tear each other apart?

Friday afternoon ground on. The air inside the tent was hot and stuffy. Outside, the only shade was behind the portajohns. I opted for my cot. I took a drink of lukewarm water and lay back, studying the rhythm of red and white stripes overhead. Maybe there'll be showers today, I thought. The previous day, the National Guard had hauled in a tank of water and erected a shower-tent. But there was little soap, no shampoo, and only enough water for about a hundred men to shower. I didn't make it through the line.

At least I had a clean shirt. I'd learned the trick of wearing two shirts and two pairs of socks and underwear to jail. One to wear, one to wash. And I wasn't alone. The guy-ropes of the big tent were strung with hand-laundered clothes.

Around four o'clock the guards ordered everyone out of the tent so they could conduct one of their periodic searches. "Looking for drugs and weapons," Hank scoffed. "Wouldn't surprise me if they planted something."

As we waited in the yard, a slight breeze wafted the aroma of the portajohns our direction. "This is pretty bad," I said. "We'd be better off in the real jail."

"Don't kid yourself," said a guy named Les from Mustard Seed AG. "I was in Santa Rita for the Good Friday action. You've got fifty men crammed into each of those broken-down old barracks. There's one shower hall for the entire compound. Really, what complaints do we have here? Bad food and being cold at night? If you were in the real jail, you'd have a lot more to worry about."

I hadn't expected such a serious response. "Yeah," I said. "You're probably right."

He looked at me as if to say, Probably?

Damn, I thought, gotta watch what I say around here.

Nearby, Raoul was trying to organize a sit-down strike in protest of the guards' raids. He'd gathered a small audience of mostly younger guys. "Next time they order us out of the tent," he said as Craig and I walked up, "we shouldn't budge. What can they do if we don't acquiesce?"

Craig chuckled. "Nothing except crack a few ribs. They've got a few tools at their disposal. It's one thing to defy a distant judge, and another to defy the guards face-to-face."

Protesters used empty water-jugs to improvise a drum circle. Soon after, guards confiscated the musical instruments.

Raoul's eyes narrowed. "We have to let them know that when they jerk us around, we're going to resist. We have to fight them every step of the way for collective control of our environment."

"If the guards want to move us, they have their ways," Craig said. "You're setting yourself up for failure. Don't pick fights you have no chance of winning."

Raoul drew himself up to his full, imposing size. "Maybe we won't lose. And even if we do, it'll make them think twice the next time."

"Yeah, we can't let them push us around," Sid chimed in. He jutted out his chin. "If they mess with us, we mess with them."

Craig walked away. I thought about speaking up, but Raoul turned away, and the circle broke up.

Still, I thought they were wrong. We should pick our fights carefully. We had to conserve our resources, not burn people out by resisting every petty power-trip the guards pulled. Besides, when you non-cooperate, and they inflict pain to force you to move, doesn't it just reinforce their tendency to use violence?

As we milled around the yard waiting for the search to end, some guys took empty plastic water jugs and started a drum circle. Others danced or clapped counter-rhythms. I liked hearing it in the background, but I felt too fatigued to join in, too tired to do anything except hope we'd get out. I didn't even feel like reading. I'd finished three of the Shakespeare plays, and I wasn't up to starting the last one yet. My midSummer night's dream was to sleep in my own bed, not study Shakespeare in jail.

The guards' search turned up nothing. Back inside, a workshop got going on the arms race, facilitated by Daniel Ellsberg. I was debating whether to go to it or try to take a nap when Raoul came by and told me that there was a baseball game on the radio. I thought he was joking, but it turned out that

Pilgrim had smuggled a transistor radio by stashing it in his underwear. Tired as I was, there was something irresistibly poetic about that. I followed Raoul across the tent. Baseball! The real world, at last.

Around Pilgrim's cot sat a little throng of spectators, hardly any of whom I recognized. Most of the men in the tent probably scorned professional sports, so there were plenty of good seats for the fifteen or so who grasped the peculiar charm of professional athletic competition. A couple of guys acted as sentinels, watching for guards who might confiscate the radio.

I settled into my seat as the San Francisco Giants came to bat the bottom of the eighth, trailing 4-2. The team hadn't been very good this season, and when they made the second out in the eighth, nothing suggested that today would be any different.

"They'd be a lot better if they still had Joe Morgan," Pilgrim said. "They never should have traded him."

"Yeah," said Raoul, "Stupidest thing the Giants ever did. He almost won MVP last year."

MVP, I thought. Most Valuable Player. I looked around our little conclave, then at the rest of the tent. MVP. Most Valuable Protester. You'd win a bronze statuette of a blockader getting his arm twisted, with your booking number engraved on the plaque.

People were still discussing the Morgan trade when Pilgrim waved for silence. "Two on, two out," he told us. "Clark at bat."

"Clark? Oh no, he always — "

"Shhhhhhhh!"

We crowded in together. If the Giants were going to turn it around this year, they had to win close games like this. The ballgame, and maybe the season, were on the line. Clean-up hitter Jack Clark stepped to the plate. A double could tie it, and a home run would put the Giants ahead going into the ninth inning.

After falling behind, Clark worked the count full. It was down to one pitch. We leaned toward the radio. There's the pitch — Clark rips it! It's a long drive down the line — hooking — foul ball!...

Nervous laughter ran around the circle. I leaned in toward the radio. Come on, Jack! The pitcher checks the runners, then studies the signs from the catcher. He shakes off one sign, then nods. There's the stretch, and the pitch — Clark coils — he cuts loose with a mighty swing — and it's strike three. He's outa there!

The crowd groaned, and our circle sagged. Sure, there was still the ninth inning, but the steam had gone out of the game. It was a lost cause.

I got up and wandered back toward my cot. Whatever hope I'd felt earlier in the day had dissipated. Sure, we could still be released at any time. But I didn't feel it coming.

Craig, Claude, and Lyle were talking nearby. "I think they're just stalling," Craig said as I joined them. He chopped with his hand to emphasize his points. "Today is a make-or-break day. They can't keep us here forever. They're hoping that when they call for arraignment tonight, a bunch of people will leave, not wanting to face the weekend in jail. That would be a victory for them, to see our numbers drop. They'd think they had us on the run. If we hang tight, they may cave in."

I was swept right along, seeing Craig so upbeat. "The court has its breaking point, too," I said. "Maybe they've just about played out their hand."

Claude scowled. "I wouldn't count on it. It's not the Livermore judges calling the shots. They're pawns. The pressure is coming from Washington, and you better believe there are back room deals being made. They want to make an example of us. We're going to be here a while."

Craig adjusted his glasses. "I hope you're wrong," he said. "But I still think arraignment tonight is the key. If a lot of men leave, we'll be in bad shape. If we hang tough, it puts pressure on the court to accept a compromise."

I folded my arms. I could do it. Sure, I wanted out as soon as possible. The idea of citing out had crossed my mind. But it wasn't like I was on the brink of collapse. In fact, compared to a lot of people, I was doing pretty well. Some men were barely hanging on, calling their jobs or family each morning to ask for one more day of grace. And now it was for the whole weekend. Refusing arraignment today meant not being at work Monday morning. Some people would have to leave.

"Let's just hope Hank's typical," Claude said. I looked over toward Hank's cot, where he was stretched out on his back, oblivious to the world. Sick as he was, Hank refused to cite out.

"That's dedication," Lyle said with a shake of his head. "Let's hope he's not our first martyr."

A rustle swept through the tent. We were about to find out exactly where we stood. The tent-flaps were rolled up, and we spied Sheriff Krieg's convoy pulling up on the road adjacent to our camp. Clusters drew together spontaneously, and all eyes turned toward the front entrance.

There were the usual shouts of "Reginald! Speech!" as the sheriff made his entrance, but it died away. Everyone seemed to sense that the stakes were higher this time.

I did some quick math. Four hundred men still here. If over a hundred leave, we're going to be hurting. Under fifty, we can claim victory. Fifty. That seemed like the magic number. Anything under fifty, and we're okay.

Paper and pencils were scarce. Razors and other amenities were non-existent.

"Gentlemen," the sheriff began, "I would like to advise you that Judge Lewis is sitting in Livermore Muncipal Court..." As he droned through his incantation, I looked around the tent. Gaunt, determined faces stared back at the speaker. Next to me, a guy pulled his blanket tighter around his shoulders. I folded my arms across my chest.

Sheriff Krieg wrapped up his routine. "If any of you wishes to be arraigned at this time," he announced, "Please step forward."

There was an awkward pause before anyone moved. I looked around the tent. Anything less than fifty... Behind me a man hugged his friends goodbye. To my left another guy slowly made his way forward. He looked pretty upset, and I felt sorry for him having to walk away from the fight. A couple more stepped up. Then a pause, and it sank in — only a dozen men were leaving! We had held! Shouts and cheers burst out around the tent, swelling into our mantra, "Solidarity Forever."

As the sheriff marched out with his little detachment, the rest of us gravitated to the open front of the tent, singing and clapping. The energy peaked with a melange of sweaty people pogo-ing in the center. Some waved their arms over their heads. A few rows back from the dancing, I clapped and sang a high harmony as the voices settled into a long, rich "ommmmmm." Sure, we'd all just agreed to spend the weekend in jail. But I probably wasn't the only one who remembered the Sunday night arraignment at the Concord action. We had held firm. Anything could happen.

As I turned back toward my cot, hopes running high, I ran into Antonio. We shared a hug, but he looked sober. "I'm proud of the stand we've taken," he said. "But we've reached a point of no return. Till now, we could have compromised, bargained for shorter probation. By refusing to leave today, we've thrown down the gauntlet. Any compromise from this moment forward will seem like surrender."

I nodded slowly. We had staked out our position. There was no graceful retreat. "We have to hope the court caves in first," I said. "It's happened before."

Before the crowd had quite broken up, the legal team suddenly materialized. I didn't recognize either attorney, one of whom actually carried a briefcase. I hung back at first, but when the briefcase guy said something that made people laugh, I moved in closer.

"The only news, unfortunately, is that there's no news to report," he said. "We don't have any meetings with the judge or DA scheduled till Monday. I don't expect anything to change over the weekend."

Nothing new. Nothing scheduled. Nothing. I turned away. Why did I even waste my time and brain cells? Quit getting worked up. Nothing ever changes.

I wasn't alone in my annoyance. There was a lot of grumbling as we queued up for dinner. I was toward the end of the line, which stretched down the left-hand tent-aisle. Hank and Craig joined me.

"Hey, good to see you up," I said to Hank. "How are you feeling?"

He coughed hard. "I don't know how much longer I can take this," he said. "Besides, I've got to be back at work Monday, or my boss is going to have a cow." He looked around for guards, then whispered to Craig and me. "I've been watching. I can escape from here when they're not looking. We're outside the main security fences."

Craig smiled, but I was afraid that Hank might be serious. His eyes had a wild tinge, and there was no telling what he might try.

"They'd notice that you were missing," I said. "They'd put out a warrant for you."

"They'd know *someone* was missing," he answered. "But they'd never know who it was. I'm just another John Doe to them."

"No, you're not," I said. "You told them your name was Sikov Bullschmidt."

"Well, I am Sikov Bullschmidt," Hank said as we moved up the chow line. "But the deputy wrote down John Doe on my form." He laughed, then coughed again.

People seemed subdued as we ate our meager dinner. Doc talked in a low voice about having to miss San Francisco's Gay Freedom Parade on Sunday. "I've been to it every year since I moved here," he said.

"Me, too," said Rick. "In fact, that's what got me to move to San Francisco. I was visiting one June and went to the parade. It blew my mind, thousands of queers taking over the City. I knew I had to be here."

They were sharing memories of parades past when Doc suddenly brightened. His eyes swept our little circle. "We should do a Gay Pride march here!"

People laughed and applauded spontaneously. The idea spread through the dinner crowd. For the gay and bisexual men in the tent, it offered a chance to stand up to the homophobic prison system. For me, my motives were a little less pure. Solidarity, for sure. But I also wanted to see the guards' reaction to four hundred prisoners marching for gay rights.

Costumes and props would be a challenge. People saved their paper cups, and when a lawyer stopped by, he was persuaded to smuggle in essential items like glue, glitter, and make-up.

Clustosterone, a gay and bisexual men's cluster that had formed for the blockade, met with Enola Gay after dinner and drew up a statement to be sent to the San Francisco Freedom Day rally expressing our solidarity and calling for their support. When the phone lines opened later, someone talked to the women's camp and found out they had come up with the same idea.

"Synchronicity," Moonstone said.

Antonio nodded. "You know you're on the right path when that happens."

The evening passed slowly. I lay on my cot reading *Richard the Second,* my final Shakespeare play, but gradually tuned in to a group of Jewish blockaders holding a Shabbat observance nearby. The quiet voices lent a peaceful tone to our corner of the tent, and when someone read a familiar passage from Isaiah, I felt like I was hearing the lines for the first time:

> They shall beat their swords into plowshares,
> And their spears into pruning hooks;
> Nation shall not lift up sword against nation,
> Neither shall they learn war anymore.

As they sang their closing song, I wondered if any Christian groups were doing services. It was hard to imagine going. But maybe if they sang songs I knew...

Later, during the talent show, I went out and called Holly on the phone lines that people had figured out the first day. By making a single ten-cent call and then passing the phone from person to person, we could keep a line open between the camps for hours.

Holly's voice sounded far away, like an international call. But after a day of nothing but male sounds, I was happy to hear her voice.

WASHING UP

We talked about the decision to stay in for the weekend. It had never occurred to me that Holly would cite out. Without talking to her, I had taken that for granted. Maybe that was part of solidarity — knowing what the other person would do without having to ask.

But despite our shared commitment, Holly seemed remote, as if we were living in separate worlds. She was almost chipper, telling me about a workshop on war tax resistance and a meditation circle she'd been part of. I felt embarrassed to say I'd just been sitting around reading Shakespeare all day, so I told her about Hank and his Nixon mask, which made me laugh again.

One odd thing Holly told me was that Caroline had joined a different AG. "She did it yesterday. She said she felt more comfortable with them. I tried not to take it personally, but I thought that Caroline and I were going to spend a lot of time together here."

I started to ask why, but Holly didn't want to dwell on it. "I've been hanging out with Sara," she told me, "She's really upset over Karina getting sixty days at Vandenberg."

She mentioned Jenny and Angie. I asked how they were doing. "Why don't you ask them yourself? They haven't talked with anyone in the men's camp, it'd be fun for them." I held for a minute, and they all returned together.

"How's it going over there?" Jenny asked. "Are you getting any sleep? Have you been singing in the talent shows?"

"Once," I told her. "How are you doing?"

Jenny talked so fast that I couldn't get all the details, but I sensed she was holding up well. Jenny and her apolitical boyfriend had split up just before the action, partly over her immersion in LAG. I wondered how much her staying in jail was to prove to herself that she'd made the right decision. Hey, if that's what keeps someone in solidarity, we'll take it.

Then Angie got on the phone. What a change of pace after Holly and Jenny. Angie's voice had a whispery, confiding quality that drew me in. "Staying in jail all weekend is hard to face," she confessed. "I'm going through caffeine withdrawal. I've had a headache for three days. I don't know if I'm cut out for this."

"I know what you mean," I found myself admitting. "I miss smoking weed, just kicking back at the end of the day. All I want to do in here is drown my sorrows in books." I told her about my smuggled Shakespeare.

"That's brilliant," she said. "I've had to settle for some cheap novels the lawyers dropped off."

We said goodbye, and I wrapped it up with Holly. "I miss you," I told her. "It feels really strange not seeing you for so long."

"I miss you, too," she said, "But I can feel your presence. It gives me strength to know we're in this together."

As I returned to my cot, I mulled over her words. I wished I could feel Holly's presence and draw strength from her. But it seemed like we existed in alternate dimensions.

Still, how great to get to talk to women. What a different spirit. Could I imagine talking with a man the way I had with Angie? Not likely. No matter how supportive men tried to be, for me there was something missing.

I knew it didn't have to be that way. I saw how the guys in Enola Gay interacted, how caring they were toward each other. But for me and most of the straight men, the most we could say was that we were peacefully co-existing. Which wasn't bad, considering the pressure. Outbursts of pent-up anger must be a routine occurrence in general population.

The talent show was still going, but something more exciting caught my eye. The lawyers had dropped off a couple of boxes of books. I dug in. Mainly it was pulp fiction, with a few self-help volumes tossed in for good measure. But amidst the debris I came across a tattered copy of *The Fall* by Albert Camus. What a find! Now I could afford to polish off Shakespeare.

I retreated to my cot, tucked Camus carefully under my blanket, and lay down to finish *Richard the Second.* As I sifted through the pages searching for my place, Daniel wandered by and asked what I was reading. When I told him, a knowing smile crossed his lips. "Ah, not a propitious choice. You realize how it ends, don't you?"

"No," I said, "Don't tell me."

But it was too late. Daniel seemed to gaze beyond me. "He winds up languishing in prison," he said, "and finally provokes his own execution." He nodded to himself, not seeming to notice my chagrin.

I set the pages aside and tried to get comfortable on my cot, which was barely wide enough for my shoulders and sagged in the middle. I scanned back through the day. Facing down the sheriff. The false hopes when we got our stuff back. The baseball game. The Shabbat service. Talking with Holly and Jenny and Angie. It didn't sound bad. But like the previous two nights, I found myself depressed as the day wound to a close. Missing weed was part of it. But the worst was having no idea how long I'd be here. Give me a certain number of days to count, something to look forward to. I felt like the future had been stolen.

Hands Around Livermore Lab drew 5000 people to the Lab in support of the jailed blockaders.

If only I had an art book and a joint. Would it be that hard to smuggle in? Well, the art book would. Damn. If I could just get high and look at pictures, eat some peanuts...

I shook myself. Don't think about that. You'll go crazy. Stay in the present. Someone laughed a few cots over. Pipe down! Enough of the chatter, the incessant scraping and shuffling. And when the lights went down, it would be even worse — another night of freezing under my single army blanket, trying to fall asleep with four hundred snoring roommates. Earplugs. Why hadn't I smuggled in a pair of earplugs?

There was no escape. At least not tonight. But what about tomorrow? Maybe the sheriff would come back and offer us another chance to cite out.

Saturday, June 25, 1983

HANDS AROUND Livermore Lab. Not one of the more inspiring proposals I ever heard — a legal demo at the Lab the weekend after the big blockade. The idea was to get blockaders to return, joined by thousands of people who wouldn't come to a CD protest, but would attend a legal event with no risk of arrest. Apparently the idea had worked at Greenham Common peace camp in England. Maybe it would work here.

But I wasn't going to be there. I and eight hundred others were cooling our heels in the circus tents. Hands Around Livermore would have to happen without us.

Had I been free to attend, I might have found another way to spend my first free Saturday in two months.

Denied the right to go, however, I felt compelled to attend the alternative — Hands Around the Tent. Unfortunately, the back side of the tent was off-limits, and the guards claimed they were powerless to make an exception. So at the same time as Hands Around Livermore we gathered in the side yard and formed a circle. When it grew to the limits of the yard, we turned it into a peace sign.

"Maybe the media will hear about it and fly over to film it," Moonstone said. Someone phoned the LAG office and asked them to notify the press.

We got a link with a pay phone in Livermore to update us on Hands Around the Lab. Over five thousand people were gathered, we heard — the biggest crowd ever at Livermore Lab. We cheered for those at the Lab and cheered for ourselves. "We'll be on the front page again tomorrow," Antonio said.

We stayed circled in the mid-afternoon sun for an hour, awaiting the mythical press helicopter, until the heat wore down enough people to make an end of it. As the circle dissolved, men turned to one another, exchanged a few parting words, here and there a hug. I hugged a couple of people and talked for a minute with Antonio, but it seemed like something was missing. I stood there for a minute, but I couldn't put my finger on it, and finally wandered back inside and lay down on my cot. Too much sun, too little inspiration.

A legal protest. That's it. We did our protest where the guards permitted. They drew the line, and we acquiesced. Never very empowering.

But there was something else, right at the end. A feeling like I had dropped something, or forgotten some final detail. I tried to focus on the feeling, but it took too much effort. I felt like I'd drained my reservoir for the day.

I rolled onto my side and stared at the wooden tentpole near my cot. Its surface was uneven but smooth. The light wood, stained here and there with dirt or tar, clashed with the bright red and white of the tent.

My stomach rumbled. No relief was coming. It was my day of fasting in solidarity with the hunger strike. I tried to remember what the point was. Making a stand of some sort. Backing up Daniel and the strikers. Proving I could go without food, no matter how boring it made the day. It wasn't an especially uplifting experience. Another legal protest, I noted. Maybe I'd feel different about fasting if it were illegal.

To make matters worse, our National Guard chefs prepared spaghetti for lunch, the best meal they had served all week. Ouch.

I lay on my back, wondering what time it was. Three o'clock? My eyes traced the arcs of the red and white tent-stripes. Doc and Rick came by and asked if I wanted to help with Change of Heart's Gay Pride props, but I couldn't summon the enthusiasm. "I'll be in the contingent tomorrow, but I want to rest right now."

Rick went on ahead, but Doc stopped and looked intently at me. "Feeling run down?"

"Yeah," I said. It felt good to actually say so. "I guess I'm not seeing much I can contribute. I feel like I'm just an extra body, keeping the numbers up. And I wonder how long I can do that."

He sat down on the next cot. "I know the feeling," he said, "like nothing we can do will make any difference. But that's exactly the feeling the authorities want us to have. It makes their job easier if we feel powerless. If they could create that feeling, they would, wouldn't they?"

I laughed awkwardly. "Well, I guess so."

"It's something to think about," he said.

As Doc stood up, shouts and a flurry of activity at the front of the tent alerted us to a surprise visit by Sheriff Krieg, offering a fresh opportunity to cite out.

Cite out? I dimly remembered the previous night. Hadn't I been thinking about leaving? No way. Sure, I wanted out like nobody's business. And I couldn't swear I'd stay in this pit forever. But I wasn't ready to give in quite yet.

Only a couple of people opted to accept the sheriff's invitation. Which was hardly a surprise. There were no songs and little cheering — just a general rumbling of resolve.

"They're testing the waters," Claude said. "Weekend visits by the sheriff are not routine procedure. They wanted to see how we'd respond."

"Well," someone said, "they just handed us a perfect opportunity to show where we stand."

Doc nudged me. "Sometimes just being present makes a difference," he said.

A smile stole across my face. "I guess I can still manage that much."

A while later, the shower-wagon returned. Camp etiquette dictated that those who'd missed the previous visit go first. I was among the first in line. Six of us were ushered into a green canvas tent with a wood-slat floor, where we disrobed under the watchful eyes of two guards.

I felt especially naked as we were steered through a flap and into a second, larger tent. I turned the knob and tested the water coming out of one of the six showerheads. Lukewarm. Oh well, better than cold.

Little cakes of motel soap were the only washing material. I washed my body hurriedly, then did my best to work up a lather and scrub it into my hair. The soap and oil congealed into a pasty film. How did our ancestors live without shampoo? I rinsed as best I could and cleared out so others could have a shot. I stepped back into the first tent. No towels. Of course. What was I expecting? I sponged off with my T-shirt and pulled my jeans over my still-damp legs. Not very satisfying.

I hardly made it back to my cot when dinner was called. About seventy-five people had fasted along with the hunger strikers for breakfast and lunch. Our numbers were noticed by the guards, but it didn't make much difference in the bigger scheme of things. For dinner, though, twice as many sat out the meal. We gathered in a big circle and shared our motivations for fasting. Some spoke of internal resolve, or of making a statement to the authorities. It felt good to speak my intent aloud: Solidarity with the strikers in my cluster.

Just before the evening talent show I got a letter from Holly. The lawyers operated a shuttle service, carrying missives, poems, and calls to action back and forth. Holly's letter wasn't very personal, mainly reflections on jail and its effects on the movement. But it felt good to hold it in my hand. Holly and I actually are sharing this experience. We're facing a lot of the same pressures. Sometimes it feels like we're in different realities. But maybe that's part of the experience. Maybe years from now we'll look back to this time as forging a deeper trust and love between us.

With the letter she included some drawings that Caroline had made of the women's camp, and asked me to post them on our bulletin board. Funny, I thought, I had no idea Caroline was an artist. Of course, since we met last June, when had she had any spare time to draw? Until now.

After the talent show, Antonio and Moonstone helped organize a full moon ritual. I declined their invitation to attend, but I liked hearing the fifty men singing together in the distance. One song, with a chant-like melody, especially reverberated in me:

We are the power in everyone,
We are the dance of the moon and sun,
We are the hope that will not hide,
We are the turning of the tide.

Some of the other parts, like when they invoked "the spirits of the four directions," were too new-agey for me. But the warmth of their singing and chanting pervaded the whole tent.

Later on, Holly and I talked on the phone. We chatted about odds and ends, sharing impressions more than feelings. Holly was in her usual upbeat mood, which I was finding harder to believe. Was the women's camp that different from ours? Something felt unreal. Still, I appreciated having someone outside my immediate universe to share the dramas of the day.

Before lights-out, I made myself jot a few notes in my loose-leaf journal. I had smuggled in blank paper, and the guards provided us with pencil stubs. I knew I'd regret it if I didn't write some jail-reflections. I tried to catch all the feelings, but the perfect metaphor eluded me, which seemed like a metaphor in itself. The lights were going down. I folded the paper and tucked it into my pocket. Maybe I'd be more inspired tomorrow.

After the usual tossing and turning and coughing and mumbling, people settled down. I was drifting into my own thoughts when I half-noticed Sid, the young punk I had met in the office a few weeks before, fidgeting around a few cots over. He propped himself up on one elbow. As lanky as he is, he probably can't ever get comfortable, I thought.

I lay back, grateful for the momentary calm before the snoring set in. Suddenly a shrill tone pierced the stillness. It took a second to place — a kazoo. It was Sid, serenading us with a slow, heartfelt rendition of Taps.

By the end, you could hardly hear the kazoo for the laughter. I made a mental note to smuggle a kazoo to all future protests.

The guards came in with big flashlights and made a fuss about knocking it off and getting to sleep. As I lay back, I yawned widely and smiled to myself. Score the final round of the day for us.

Had it been the final round, I'd have slept happily. But the good humor quickly gave way to malaise. Another day, another fizzle. What was the point in fighting my way through the wasteland of the day, if it came up empty in the end?

Sunday, June 26, 1983

SHORTLY AFTER lunch on Sunday, just as we were gathering for our parade, Sheriff Krieg arrived with his offering of cite-out forms. In keeping with the Gay Pride Day theme, Clustosterone gave him a special welcome. From each side of the tent, three Greek graces danced in, attired in mini-togas and sporting green paper wreaths around their brows. They pirouetted across the front of the tent, strewing invisible confetti as if welcoming a conquering hero. When they reached the center, they curtsied to the sheriff, who looked like he was struggling to keep from laughing.

Amid tumultuous applause the Clustosterone men danced back into the crowd. When the cheering subsided, Sheriff Krieg read his obligatory call. Not one person accepted the invitation, which led to a fresh burst of applause. The sheriff went away shaking his head, and we started lining up for the Gay Freedom march.

The participants — about two-thirds of the men in the camp — assembled in the open space at the front of the tent. Our route was down the left aisle, around the center cots, and back up the right side. The men not marching sat on cots lining the route, awaiting the procession. Clustosterone got ahold of a pad of "While You Were Out" office memos and tore them into pink triangles for everyone to wear.

Change of Heart, anchored by Enola Gay, was bringing up the end of the parade. As I waited for us to start, I looked out the front of the tent. A half-dozen guards huddled just outside the tent-flaps, looking perplexed and a little scared. I wondered if they would try to stop us. But on what grounds? So far, all we were doing was milling around in funny clothes. Not much they could do about that.

Finally we got rolling. The dancing graces led off the march, snaking around the front before starting down the aisle. They were followed by the rest of Clustosterone in togas and paper-plate tiaras, singing Bob Marley's "Get Up, Stand Up!"

The next AG fashioned dresses, skirts, and evening gowns out of sheets, with make-up and scarves courtesy of the legal team. As a chorus sang "Somewhere Over the Rainbow," four beefy, topless men carried aloft a cot bearing their "Queen for a Gay Day."

Scattered through the parade were contingents of teachers, union members, and health workers. A guy carrying a sign proclaiming "Just Came Out Today" got big cheers, as did an older couple whose sign read, "Twenty years and going strong."

One AG marched in jockstraps. Several groups fabricated harnesses and collars and other restraints from the scant materials at our disposal. Interspersed among the props and costumes were men walking hand in hand or with arms around each other, waving to the hundred or so "spectators."

One guy on the sidelines decorated a cardboard box like a TV screen, from within which he delivered a running commentary on the proceedings. And Hank, who had felt too sick to be in the parade, apparently couldn't resist. He donned his Nixon mask and walked stiffly around shaking hands with everyone in sight.

Enola Gay and Change of Heart thought it fitting that the parade culminate in a symbolic gay wedding. Moonstone was coaxed back into his still-pristine wedding gown for the occasion, and Doc borrowed a coat and tie from one of the lawyers. Rick was the best man, and the rest of us fitted ourselves as jacketed ushers or bedsheet-bedecked bridesmaids. Antonio, who had a valid mail-order minister's credential, was selected to officiate. "Of course, the courts probably won't recognize a gay wedding," he said.

"That's okay," Rick said. "We don't recognize the courts."

The parade wound around the back of the tent and started up the right-hand aisle. Cheers and shouts rang through the space.

The graces led us out the front of the tent, past where the guards were perched. They twisted and paced, caught on the horns of a dilemma. They couldn't turn away, or they wouldn't be guarding us. But neither could they risk appearing remotely interested. We weren't breaking any known rules, so they couldn't shut us down. We pretty well had them.

Paraders, inspired by the guards' predicament, turned them into a judging stand. Affinity groups did dance numbers, choruses sang extra loud, and all through the march people kissed and hugged as they passed in review.

The jubilant crowd circled around the portajohns and into the side yard, where we gathered in a celebratory circle. Gradually the catcalls and laughter congealed into a call-and-response chant. Half the circle would yell, "Shout it out loud," to which the other half answered, "I'm gay and I'm proud!"

A special edition of the talent show got underway in the side yard. I took a seat by Moonstone, but Rick, who had been on the phone getting a report from the women's march, tapped me on the shoulder as he passed. "Holly wants to talk to you," he said. I got up and walked over to the phonebank.

"How are you doing, sweetie?" she greeted me. Her voice sounded tinny, and the now-familiar sense of disconnect crept over me. The past five days had been our longest separation. It seemed like ages since I had seen her, and ages more till I would again.

Searching for some commonality, I asked her about the women's parade.

"Oh, it was amazing," she said. "So much creativity. You know how the San Francisco Gay Pride march is always led by the women's motorcycle contingent, 'Dykes on Bikes?' Well, the women leading the march here today rode piggyback, and they called it 'Dykes on Dykes!'"

I laughed out loud. "You should have seen the guards at our parade," I said. "It really flipped them out."

"Here, too. The way people were making out, the guards must think we're all lesbians. Angie and Jenny were marching together, they were really cute. I've wondered if they might get involved now that Jenny's single. And you should have seen Angie's costume. She made a sarong out of her sheet, with two tampons as earrings. She'll probably win a fashion prize at the talent show."

As usual, Holly said she was doing great, especially after the parade. I didn't want to worry her, so I said I was okay. It wasn't her fault I felt so low. We talked a bit longer, then signed off.

"I love you, Jeff."

"Me, too, Holly," I said as brightly as I could muster. "I love you."

The talent show went on for another hour, mostly gay-related music, poetry, dance, and even a couple of well-rehearsed skits. One song got the whole crowd singing, a new version of "Amazing Grace":

Yes, we've been queer ten thousand years,
Bright shining as the sun,
Our movement's progress has been great
And more is yet to come.

Toward the end, Doc and Rick did a presentation on a mysterious disease called AIDS that was especially affecting gay men. I didn't know much about it, and that seemed true for most of the straight men present. "It's no wonder no one has heard of it," Doc said. "Hundreds of men in San Francisco are dying of AIDS. But the media barely mentions it, and the President refuses to publicly speak the word."

The show wound up, and we gathered in a big circle. Someone announced that our solidarity statement had been read at the San Francisco rally, to the cheers of thousands of marchers. We applauded the news, then drew together, arms around shoulders, in a tighter circle. We're doing it. Amid all the pressure, we're holding together.

I headed back toward the tent to escape the sun, catching up with Doc, Rick, and Antonio.

"Great march," Antonio said.

Rick nodded vigorously. "That's a Pride Day I won't forget — especially the looks on the guards' faces. They had not a clue what to do."

"Yeah," I said as we ducked under the tent-flap. "I think we found the perfect way to one-up them."

Ahead of me, Doc paused. "We don't need to one-up the guards," he said. "They've become irrelevant. We're not trying to escape, and there hasn't been a single fight. What do we need them for?"

"So true," Antonio said. "We have our own institutions here — a spokescouncil, a food barter system, workshops, talent shows. The guards are superfluous."

"Not quite," Rick said. "They have ways of making their presence felt, by force if necessary."

We cut between some cots and reached the first aisle, right near my quarters. My legs felt heavy, and I sat down. Doc sat next to me, and Rick and Antonio perched on the edge of the adjacent cot.

Doc crossed his arms and looked at Rick. "Sure, the guards can try to impose their structures by force. But the moment they relax their grip, our model sprouts up again. Consensus, nonhierarchy, affinity groups — we're living it. If you ever needed proof that anarchism can work, this is it."

"Well, it works here," I said. "I can't see transplanting it to the real world. This is a special situation, where everyone is present every time a decision needs to be made. In the real world, we don't have that luxury, so we have to fall back on representatives. And that raises problems of coordination..." My voice trailed off, and I couldn't help laughing at my inexorable logic. Doc smiled too, as if in tacit agreement not to re-open that particular can of worms just now.

Rick leaned forward from the opposite cot. "In any case, we're seeing how an extraordinary situation can shatter our old patterns and show us what's truly possible."

Antonio nodded. "Precisely. We've created a model village, a living embodiment of our vision."

I surveyed our village. "The problem is, the urban design is off. These rows of cots are like suburban tract houses. The wide aisles are the highways. There's no internal common space. The only open area is up at the front. We should have a big plaza in the center, with a couple of smaller ones farther out. The cots would be in arcs and swirls around the plazas."

"Maybe we could landscape it so we have some hills and valleys," Rick said.

"That would be an interesting direct action, to reconfigure the tent," Doc said. "But there's no way the guards would allow it. These rows are a vital part of their sense of control. That's the first thing the military does when they go into a new region — build straight roads."

Doc was called away. Antonio picked up my copy of *The Fall.* "You're going for light reading during your stay here, aren't you? Did you finish Shakespeare?"

"Not quite," I said. "But I needed something with bigger print."

As he parted, I lay down on my cot, wanting some privacy but feeling good about the whole jail scene. Sure, I wanted out — the sooner the better —

but there was no desperation. After five days here, I seemed to have reached some sort of balance.

I let my mind wander, faintly tracking the chorus of voices surrounding me. My eyes traced the billowy curves of the red and white tent stripes, soaring to the peak and gliding back down the other side.

It was almost peaceful, but still something wasn't quite right. Maybe it was the tent itself. How was I supposed to relax in a bright red tent? Had they gotten this color on purpose? I wouldn't put it past them. I closed my eyes, but that made the voices around me louder and harsher.

Jailyard volleyball, with improvised net and ball.

The arrival of the legal team changed the equation. Lawyers on Sunday evening? A lot of men headed toward the front of the tent to check it out. Could it be another late-night arraignment? I stayed on my cot, but my ears were tuned to the legal circle. If something came down, I was ready.

Applause rose up front, but it didn't sound conclusive. Maybe an offer from the court? What if they'd dropped probation? What if we got out tonight? I'd walk out to the all-night grocery in Albany. I pictured the low branches hanging over the shadowy sidewalks on Sonoma Street, my favorite route.

Antonio walked by my cot on his way back from the legal briefing. "The lawyers just wanted to check with us before they meet with the judge tomorrow morning," he told me.

"So there's nothing new?"

"Not much. They said that a lot of people who were at Hands Around the Lab yesterday are going to call the district attorney Monday morning and demand that our charges be dropped. Public pressure might have some influence."

"Maybe eventually," I said dejectedly. Antonio moved on. I dropped back down on my cot. When was I going to learn — stop fantasizing about the outside.

Actually, I was surprised how seldom my thoughts strayed outside our confines. This was our universe. Nothing else mattered. Who people were or what sort of work they did on the outside meant nothing, as if our very identities were in flux as we groped for a new cultural lexicon.

Not that we were total beginners. The ongoing spokescouncil showed us well-prepared for some challenges.

But in other aspects, we were lost at sea. Like how to function without women for emotional support. Or how to survive with zero personal space. And most of all, how to pace ourselves when we had no idea how long the race was.

That evening, we didn't have the usual talent show. The one in the afternoon sort of took its place, but there was also a sense of conserving energy, of people bracing to resume the legal fight the next day. There could be a showdown first thing in the morning.

Toward the end of the evening, I stopped to talk with Craig on my way back from the watercooler. He'd been keeping to himself the past couple of days. I wondered what was going on for him, especially since I was no paragon of sociability myself. Was he just a step ahead of me on the pathway of despair?

He looked at me warily as I sat down on the cot across from him, and for the first time I realized that his discouragement might run deeper than our stalemate with the legal system.

It made me uneasy to see Craig wavering, and I tried to lift his spirits. "Three quarters of those arrested are still here," I said. "No one expected to be in jail for a week, but here they are. That must pick you up, as one of the main organizers."

"I guess so," he said with a shrug.

"How can you not see that as positive?" I didn't like the pleading tone in my voice.

He laughed dryly. "You want to know? A while ago I heard Antonio and Daniel going on about International Day, how it's going to abolish nuclear weapons and save the world. Their vision of the future is more of the same, only bigger. As if we have all the answers, and all we need is more people. There's no grasp of how little we have accomplished, or of what it might take to build an effective movement. International Day offers nothing."

I felt defensive not just for Holly, but for civil disobedience itself.

"Spreading the idea of direct action is a big step. International Day got a dozen groups around the country to do CD for the first time. That counts for something."

"Sure," Craig said. He spoke with no rancor, as if giving directions to a lost traveler. "But it also distracts us from deeper questions. Beyond appeasing our conscience, what have we accomplished? Does it matter that our numbers are growing? More people being ineffective isn't going to change anything."

I didn't see what to say. I wasn't going to abandon my belief in civil disobedience just because Craig was depressed. Whatever direction LAG and the movement grew, CD was surely the foundation. Still, it was hard to hear our whole program called into question by one of LAG's cornerstones.

Before we could say more, the guards came through the tent and ordered everyone back to his own cot. Bedtime. Craig and I awkwardly patted each other on the shoulder. Not a very satisfying encounter.

As I headed for my cot, I thought about what I should have said to Craig. It boiled down to one thing. "If you want to engage people's passion, you have to start with direct action, not talk. All the rest — education, community outreach, coalition work — are built on this foundation."

But suppose I'd said that? Craig wasn't going to listen. Save your breath. Talk to him after we get out. Maybe everything will look different. I tried to picture us playing pinball and drinking beer, but all I could conjure up were old, faded images. How far away that world seemed.

I stretched my body to the limits of the six-foot cot, trying to get less uncomfortable. The lights went down, and my mood sank with them. I tried to picture moments of color and light during the long day, but it all came out gray. Had I actually laughed because our parade outwitted the guards? Whoopee. Some triumph.

I rolled onto my side. I'd felt lousy most of the day, as far as I could recall. But evening was the worst. You'd think it might be getting easier by my fifth day.

Jailed in a circus tent. It felt like a deliberate insult. And there wasn't one damn thing I could do about it.

So what else was new? Futility — the watchword of my political life. What had I ever done that mattered? From my high school principal to Reagan and the Pentagon, authority was a monolith, impervious to my efforts. Why should this be any different?

Monday, June 27, 1983

I AWOKE MONDAY morning to thoughts of work. I knew that I had to phone both of my jobs that day. My boss at the apartment repair job would probably be cool, since she knew where I was. It was just a matter of asking for more time off.

But my night job at the little office building was a different matter. I barely knew the owner, a suit-and-tie guy who ran a small geological survey company. I doubted he'd have much sympathy for my plight. And thanks to Reaganomics, there were plenty of people only too eager to take my job.

Why hadn't I arranged a vacation before I got busted? I could have used a break anyway. Never count on getting out of jail, I was learning. The hard way.

Not like losing the job was the end of the world. Sure, I needed the money, but I could probably find something else. Anyway, it was my first offense. Maybe he'd show clemency.

The phones opened about nine o'clock. I got his number from information and reached him on the first try. I pitched right in. "I'm sorry I didn't do any cleaning over the weekend," I said. "I got arrested at an anti-nuclear protest and they're holding us in jail. I have no idea when I can be back at work."

He listened silently. When I finished, he answered in a brusque voice. "I know about the protest. Stay as long as you need to. I'll take care of the cleaning. I'm behind you one hundred percent."

Maybe it was my general level of exhaustion, but his response brought tears to my eyes. Despite the Hands Around Livermore crowd, it was easy to feel like it was those of us in the tents against the whole world. Not so. We had allies on the outside. I had proof.

The morning's Change of Heart meeting brought me back to Earth. Having hung tight through the weekend and shown our determination, we might have hoped for some movement. But the report from the legal collective was stark. Not only was there no change, but unlike the previous year, the two local judges were adamant in refusing to disqualify themselves. Our lawyers were filing papers to challenge them, but the process would take a couple of weeks.

"It's trench warfare," Doc said. "Both sides are dug in, and neither can dislodge the other. Confrontation gives way to endurance. Who will cave in first?" He looked around our haggard circle. "The adversary is no longer the guards or the court. It's an internal struggle. Are we strong enough to outlast the state?"

Other men nodded. That was the question, wasn't it? No reinforcements, no relief in sight. We're on our own. How long can we hold out?

We did a go-round to see how people were feeling about staying in. A few said they would have to leave by the next weekend, but most grimly committed to an open-ended residency. When my turn came, I vacillated more than most, committing only till the weekend but admitting it would be hard to leave.

Only Rick said he might have to leave sooner. He had been ordered to be back at work by Wednesday or lose his job. "I'm not sure what I'm going to do," he told us glumly. "It's only a waiter's job. I could find another one. But my rent's due Friday. I really can't afford not to be working." Everyone assured him that it was cool to leave, but Rick seemed torn. "I'll decide tomorrow morning," he said.

Daniel updated us on the hunger strike, which besides the seven core people had a couple of dozen solidarity fasters pledged for each meal. Daniel's eyes were sunk, and his unshaved beard showed streaks of gray. Give him a cloak and a staff, and I could picture him striding into the courtroom like a latter-day Jeremiah, crying down the wrath of God on Judge Lewis.

Not that the rest of us were looking much more chipper. With no mirror, I could only guess my own appearance, but around me I saw gaunt, sleep-deprived men. Clothes were grungy, faces unshaven. Voices were low and raspy, and laughs were getting fewer by the day.

As the meeting ended, we gathered in a weary circle. I'd come to the meeting only out of obligation, but in an ironic way I was glad I had. It reminded me that I wasn't alone in how demoralized I felt.

We did a quick check-out and set our next meeting for the following afternoon. Then Rick spoke up. "Since I may have to cite out, I have a special request. There's a song I really like, and I think most people here know it. It would mean a lot to me if you would join me."

His proposal was greeted by nods. We tightened our circle. Rick hummed the pitch. Then with a kick of his right leg he launched into the Hokey Pokey. At first we were laughing so much that we couldn't coordinate the motions. But eventually we danced our way through the whole body, and for good measure added a final verse: "You throw the jail guards in, You throw the jail guards out, You throw the jail guards in, And you shake 'em all about..."

Other men around the tent applauded as we wrapped it up, and I went back to my cot on a better note. That was the most I'd laughed since — well, since the previous day. I shook my head. How could some moments be so uplifting, and yet the gestalt so oppressive?

As I sat down, I thought of Rick leading the Hokey Pokey. He might be leaving, but he was making one last contribution by getting us all to laugh together. Good job. I wondered at my own contributions. Pretty minimal. I'd fasted one day, and sung a couple of times in the talent shows. I hadn't initiated anything since I got here.

What about a sing-along? That's a concrete step I could take. Find the folks who were singing the other day, announce it at a meal, and make it happen. I could do that, couldn't I?

I sunk back on the cot. The thought of organizing pressed like a weight on my chest, driving me down. Let it go, I thought. There's enough happening here already. Someone else will do a sing-along, and maybe I'll join in. Let it go.

Holly sent me another letter that afternoon. I rolled onto my side and opened it. From her opening sentence I could feel a difference.

"Today has been hard," she wrote. "I still haven't gotten over Caroline switching AGs. It makes me wonder about my relationship to organizing, if this is what comes out of the way we work together."

I thought about Craig and myself. At least we weren't avoiding each other. But it wasn't like we were sharing any personal feelings. Of course, we didn't share much on the outside, either.

I looked back at Holly's letter. "However much I've loved working on International Day," she said, "my life is out of balance. I never garden anymore, or meditate, or get out of the city. Sitting here in jail, I don't miss the LAG office at all. I miss you, but I wonder if this experience is pushing us apart? I wonder if we're growing in different ways."

It was a side of Holly that I rarely saw, and not at all since we got into jail. Reading her words made me want to talk with her. I got in line for the phone, and ten minutes later was connected with her.

"I got your letter," I said. "How are you doing?"

"Oh, I was just depressed when I wrote it," she said. "I'm better now."

I started to tell her that the letter was the most real she had sounded since we got arrested, but it didn't seem like a fair thing to say. We chatted for a few minutes, but my heart wasn't in it. "I guess I'm not feeling real talkative," I said. I paused, and she didn't speak. "What I really wish," I continued, "is that we could just be together. Not have to talk or anything, just be together."

"I want that so much, Jeff," she said. "I love you."

"I love you, too. I'll talk to you tomorrow."

What was happening with me and Holly? I hated phones. It's such a weak connection. Not being able to look into her eyes or touch her. Just a disembodied voice. Plus the alienation of jail. No wonder we felt so distant. Let go of it. It'll be different when I see her. Whenever that is.

When I got back to my cot, Hank met me. His face was an odd mix, wracked by cough and contorted in laughter. "Check it out," he said. He pointed to a cot back in the corner of the tent. "A little surprise for the guards."

Hank was sacrificing his precious Nixon mask to a higher cause. There it lay, propped up on a makeshift pillow. Below it, Hank had rolled up sheets to mold a body, then covered the whole thing with a blanket. Simple enough. Nixon in bed. With one twist. His arms appeared to curve down and grab his crotch. And right in the center, a ten-inch stick poked the blanket straight up in the air.

I'd barely had time to appreciate Hank's art installation when the guards launched their latest raid. "Everyone out in the yard," they ordered.

Hank could hardly contain himself at the prospect of the guards discovering his creation. "Tricky Dick's going out in style," he said.

We joined the crowd shuffling up the aisle. Ahead of us, Sid and Raoul began to "moo" like cattle. The crowd picked it up, and we dragged our feet, forcing the guards to herd us out.

In the yard, Hank regaled Craig and Claude with an account of the Nixondummy. He was laughing so much he had to stop and blow his nose. "It was a classic," I put in. "You should have seen it."

At that moment, four guards marched out of the tent carrying the cot like pallbearers. Nixon's head had fallen sideways and grinned grotesquely at us as it went past. One sheet-arm flopped limply off the side of the cot. But right in the center, Nixon's rod still shot straight into the air.

The guards hustled it away, but everyone who spotted it got a laugh. "Nixon wanking his crank," Raoul said. "You've got to love it."

When we got back into the tent, we discovered that the guards had confiscated more than Nixon. A couple of affinity groups had been folding paper cranes, an international symbol of the desire for world peace. Using every available scrap of paper, the AGs had folded over half of the thousand they were aiming for. Now, they were back to zero.

"Just the sort of stupidity you expect from jail guards," Hank said. "Anything to mess with us."

Nathaniel tilted his head philosophically. "Those cranes represented a threat to their system. Our whole presence is a challenge to their worldview. This is what they have been reduced to — stealing paper cranes."

The talent show seemed subdued that evening — more poetry, less comedy. I had planned to sing one of my anti-nuke songs, but my throat was feeling dry and tight, and I opted out.

After the show, I drifted back to my cot. I kept swallowing, trying to convince myself that the swelling in my throat was my imagination. Damn. Asking for medical attention was a good way to get isolated and force-cited by the guards. It had already happened to several guys.

I held my throat and winced as I swallowed. Well, at least I have something concrete to be dismal about, I thought. I guess that's an improvement.

How ironic, though, that I'd catch a cold right when I'd scored a second blanket. A neighbor who cited out that day bequeathed his to me. Two blankets. I could fold one underneath me to cut the cold that seeped through the canvas. What a difference that would make.

The legal team paid a surprise late-evening visit. Their arrival was so low-

key that my hopes weren't aroused. Walt stopped by my cot. "We're just checking to see how many people are citing out the next couple of days," he told me. "It gives us an idea of our bargaining position. Not that the court is budging. But it's our job to keep trying."

He told me that he was taking a packet of stuff down to Alby and Karina, who were doing their sixty-day sentences for the June Vandenberg action in prisons near Los Angeles. Walt told me they were holding up okay so far. I scribbled a quick note of encouragement to Alby. But I spent longer on a letter to Karina.

Karina had been flitting through my mind occasionally for the past week. Picturing her in federal prison strengthened my resolve. Her sentence dwarfed mine. How could I think about leaving? I felt a pang for her carefree spirit and dreamed of being together, planning our next adventure in the sunshine at People's Park.

That night, lying on my cot after lights-out, I found myself having sexual fantasies for the first time since my arrest. I tried focusing my attention on Holly, but it kept shifting to Karina and Angie. It didn't exactly put me in a good mood, since there wasn't much I could do about the longings within my present confines. But frustration was a welcome distraction from my usual brooding.

Tuesday, June 28, 1983

A SHARP ACHE in my throat greeted me Tuesday morning. I grimaced, trying to ward off the pain. The night had seemed especially cold, and I preferred the warmth of my two blankets to whatever miserly fare the National Guard could dish out.

Exhausted as I was, I managed to drift back to sleep for a while, and might have dozed away the whole morning if the guards hadn't ordered us all out of the tent for another in their continuing series of raids. The only contraband they ever found were things like nail-clippers or a jar of aspirin, but the show had to go on.

I made my way out into the yard. Dawn struggled for a foothold over the distant hills. A flat gray fog cloaked the valley sky, as if the sun itself were in prison.

I spotted Hank, shivering off to one side. "Just when I was finally getting some good sleep," he said. He coughed hard, then caught his breath. "Have you noticed how they're moving the barbed wire in? The yard is getting smaller."

I scanned the boundary. "I don't know. I think that's where it's been all along."

"No, I'm sure of it," he said. "They move it in just a little each day, to squeeze us. I can tell."

I didn't have the energy to argue with him. All I could do anymore was wait. And wait. And wait.

Someone announced that the morning spokescouncil would start at ten o'clock. To me, it sounded as remote as if they had been reading stock market quotes. I hadn't even been thinking about the spokescouncil, let alone sitting through the proceedings. It was hard to believe that the previous year I had found it so fascinating. I guess I'd filled my quota of meetings over the past year.

I'd hardly been to any workshops, either. There was a steady offering — yoga, organic gardening, consensus training, co-counseling. The latter sounded interesting. I could see where counseling might be helpful in jail. I wondered if I'd be less depressed at night. If it were offered again, maybe I'd do it. But for now, I felt more like reading.

I thumbed through *The Fall,* searching for my place. Hardly an inspiring book, I thought. But the narrator, having set himself up as Judge-Penitent at a local pub, had me in his grip. Endlessly confessing his own inexpiable guilt, he held a harsh mirror to all who heard his tale.

"Go easier on yourself," I wanted to say to him. "Just because you once failed to answer a cry for help doesn't condemn you forever. Maybe it will be different next time."

But Camus didn't seem to think so. What if he were right? Are moments of crisis really tests of character? Failing once, we're condemned to a life of futility. I felt the glint of the Judge-Penitent's mirror. Too many times I'd frozen in my tracks. I thought back to the Marshals at Vandenberg, how they grabbed Cindy and threw her against the wall — and how I sat glued to my seat until Karina started screaming and shook me from my stupor.

Yet it wasn't like I was incapable of action. Given a moment to collect myself, I didn't do too shabbily. The sheer fact of getting arrested proved that I could decide and take action. But spontaneity?

Anyway, what did it all mean right now? What could you do when the only effective action was inaction? "I didn't cite out today." That was my sole claim to fame.

But what was the alternative? Fasting with the hunger strikers left me empty. Confrontation with the guards seemed pointless. What else was there? Someone suggested that all of us simultaneously walk out of camp, refusing to acknowledge the token boundaries. But I doubted that it would get us anything except taller fences.

I got up and walked over to the watercooler, where I ran into a big guy named Kurt whom I remembered from Vandenberg. "What's happening?" I asked.

Kurt seemed to take me literally, and filled me in on the latest twist at the spokescouncil. "Someone proposed that we all cite out and demand jury trials. If we keep straggling out a few at a time, they're going to win. They're wearing us down. We'd be better off leaving together and taking the fight to the courts."

Part of me grasped at the idea. We were probably going to get stuck with probation anyway. It would be better to leave jail together, at our own initiative, than to trickle out till there were too few to fight. Maybe the threat of a thousand trials would force a compromise.

But I remembered what Antonio had said a few days before — compromise would be perceived as surrender. We'd committed ourselves to resistance. Citing out would be like giving in. They'd consolidate us all into one big trial. And if we lost — which protesters almost always did — they could give us all the probation they wanted.

It turned out there was a final twist to the tale, though. "Only a few spokes supported the proposal, and it was withdrawn," Kurt told me. "It's moot for now."

I walked back toward my cot. So most people were resolved to stay. In a way, it was a relief. I'd feel worse about citing out if a lot of men were leaving. If most were staying, maybe I could be spared.

I could be more help on the outside, anyway. What if I cited out, then signed up for legal work? Of course. Why hadn't I thought of that before? They surely needed help. That way I'd still be in the middle of the action, but I'd get to sleep at home at night.

Right near Craig's cot I ran into Hank, straggling back from the portajohns. "What miserable facilities," he said. He pulled out a wad of tissue and blew his nose. "You'd think there'd be a sanitation code or something."

Hank and I sat down opposite Craig, who put down the book he was reading. Hank leaned away and coughed deeply.

"You ought to cite out," Craig said. "You need to get some antibiotics."

"I know," Hank said when he regained his breath. His speech was slurred. "I keep thinking it's just going to be one more day. I don't want to break solidarity."

"Come on," I said. "You're sick. Nobody is going to hold it against you."

"No, it feels too weird to leave," he answered. "Every person who cites out just encourages them not to

The guard shack in the side yard, behind which one blockader planned an escape route.

compromise. But that doesn't mean I'm stuck here. I've been refining my plan."

"Your plan?"

"My escape plan."

Hank seemed feverish, so I figured it was best to humor him. "Do you really think you could do it?"

"Sure," he said emphatically. His eyes brightened, and his speech was suddenly quite crisp. "It'd be easy. I've been watching the guard post in the side yard. Most of the time the guards are facing toward the front of the tent. All I have to do is slip out the back of the tent and crawl behind their booth till I reach the barbed wire. It's only about three feet high. I'll throw a blanket over the wire, dive across, and hide in the ditch by the road. As long as they stay in their guard-shack, I'll be out of their sight lines. Then comes the tough part. I have to get across the road. If another guard comes into the side yard at that point, I'm dead. So I'll be counting on you guys to create a diversion in front of the tent."

He looked from Craig to me as if expecting a response, and I realized I was nodding my head. "It'll work," Hank continued, "I know it will. Our tent is outside the main Santa Rita security. There's probably just one more barbed wire fence, and then it's a straight shot toward Mount Diablo. I've heard it's a few miles to an outside road, but I can handle that. They won't know anyone is missing until they do their bed-check, so they won't be searching. By the time they notice, I'll be long gone." He looked at us triumphantly.

Long gone? I was at a loss for words. Craig glanced at me and then spoke slowly. "That's, uh, quite a plan."

"Yeah," Hank said as if he'd just received a ringing endorsement. "I already did a test run to see if I could make it out to the barbed wire, and it went perfect. It's only getting across the road that I'll need you to create a diversion."

I didn't want to seem unsupportive, especially when Hank had put so much effort into his plan. But if he got nailed, he'd be in deep trouble. Should I intervene? Or would I be crushing the dream that was sustaining him?

I wasn't sure. I'd have to talk with Craig about it later. In any event, there was no denying Hank's determination. He wasn't giving in. And as long as he was holding firm, how could I even think of citing out?

I made my way back to my cot. What now? Where did it leave me? Back to waiting for something to happen. I picked up Camus, but was in no hurry to finish it, since I hadn't seen anything else exciting in the book-bin. A copy of Alice Walker's *The Color Purple* was circulating, but there was a long waiting list for that one. I could re-read Shakespeare, but that would just reinforce my sense of being stuck in time. The Earth turns, the days pass — but I'd forever lie on this cot watching Hamlet delay his rendezvous with destiny.

Did I even want to be reading? Or was I just starved for stimulation, craving connection to the world beyond the tent-stripes? I was sick of struggling to fill the empty hours. If only something would happen!

Standing in line was a favorite occupation.

Something did. The spokescouncil I had been so assiduously avoiding came looking for me. Just before lunch, Doc and Antonio, Change of Heart's spokes for the day, stopped by my cot.

"Our cluster is responsible for providing one of the facilitators tomorrow," Doc said. "We want to know if we can volunteer you."

They sat down on the cot next to mine. "You facilitated spokescouncils this Spring," Antonio said. "We need somebody with experience."

"Thanks," I said, sitting up on the cot. "But I'm really out of the loop."

"That's not a problem," Doc said. "We need someone who isn't caught up in the conflicts."

"It wouldn't work," I said. "Facilitating takes an alertness I don't have. Not with forty spokes at my neck. I'm too worn down."

"That's exactly why you need to do it," Antonio answered. "You're feeling powerless. You need to assert yourself."

I gave a sad laugh. "What's the point? It's like Sisyphus pushing his rock up the hill. Will my facilitation bring us a single hour closer to getting out of here? We've stated our terms. It's up to the judge and DA now. All we can do is wait."

Doc leaned forward and jutted his jaw. His beard seemed to have grown grayer in the past week. "We can't build a movement by sitting and waiting," he said. "We have to keep the initiative. However futile it seems, we have to keep trying."

He and Antonio looked at me as if expecting a response, but I didn't see what to say that wouldn't be repeating myself. I studied a splotch of paint on my jeans. "It just feels kind of hopeless," I finally said.

Doc nodded and grew contemplative. "Do you know the story of Paul Revere? I've been thinking about him the past few days. Maybe because it's almost the Fourth of July."

I wasn't sure what it had to do with our conversation, but I couldn't help reciting the famous lines: "Listen my children and you shall hear, Of the midnight ride of Paul Revere..."

Doc settled back on the opposite cot. "When I was a kid in Boston, I wanted to grow up to be Paul Revere. Me and my friends used to race our bicycles from the Old North Church to Cambridge, like we were the modern version, saying, 'the Russians are coming!'"

I smiled, trying to picture him at ten. Doc looked past me, as if calling back the images. "Later I read about him and got inspired by how he acted in the face of huge odds. Even in Boston, there were only a handful of revolutionaries. And there was no guarantee that if Boston and Massachusetts rose against the King, the rest of the colonies would follow.

"Yet as hopeless as the situation seemed, people like Paul Revere kept organizing. He helped set up an emergency network of couriers. Other people formed militia at Lexington and Concord. Even at Boston's lowest moment, people were organizing, searching for some way to make a difference."

I tried to hold Doc's gaze. "I see what you mean."

He looked at me from under his heavy brows. "Think of it. The British army marches on Concord, not expecting to meet any serious resistance. But Revere's riders get the word out, and a bunch of farmers hiding behind trees and barns force the King's army to retreat. A few hundred people organize and act, and they changed history."

He paused, never taking his eyes off me. "The key player was Paul Revere. He and his network alerted the militia in time to respond. Without them, nothing happens. So consider — what if Paul Revere had insisted on knowing that his ride would launch the revolution before he jumped on his horse?"

I nodded. "Good point. I'm just not feeling real motivated right now."

Doc was silent. Antonio cleared his throat. "Jail is an easy place to feel hopeless. But think of it this way — hopelessness is actually arrogance. It assumes that you know everything."

I smiled slightly, but my spirit was heavy. I took a deep breath. Sisyphus' rock was inside me, weighing me down. As often as I clawed my way up from the depths, I'd slide back.

Antonio turned serious. He leaned forward on the cot. "Take the initiative. Make the world respond to you. Maybe your invincible adversary isn't as strong as you thought they were."

"That's a problem in my case," I said. "What if the adversary is myself?"

Antonio's eyes lit up, and he clapped his hands together like I had just clinched his argument for him. "That's precisely the reason to act. Even if it doesn't change the world, it might change you. Reclaiming our power, that's the real challenge. No government on Earth can resist an empowered people."

What was I supposed to say to that? Great words, but it's not like empowerment is there for the asking. It takes results. You feel empowered because you do something that makes a difference.

Suppose you can only take action if you already feel empowered. Catch-22. Which comes first, the action or the empowerment?

I wandered in a maze, groping for direction, groping even to keep my feet on the ground. I floated above the maze, and it morphed into a tangled knot. I groaned. Who could hope to unravel the mess?

Doc and Antonio stood up. Maybe they could tell I was on overload. I didn't try to speak. Antonio squeezed my shoulder in parting. "Think about facilitating," he said. "Let us know after lunch."

I lay back and heaved a sigh. Facilitating? I'd forgotten about that part. My mind was still enmeshed in the knot. I followed one thread, then another. Take action now. No, get out now. No, make a decision and do something here. No, cite out and join the legal collective. No...

The strands twisted around and around, a snarled mass. Then another figure materialized alongside it — Paul Revere. He seized the knot and grappled desperately, trying to get his horse free. The British are coming! The British are coming! He clutched at strand after strand, but it only tightened the knot. The British are coming! There's no time. Cut it! Cut the knot!

Suddenly it hit me. If I wanted to leave, this was the perfect set-up. I could facilitate the Wednesday spokescouncil and then — having made my contribution — I could gracefully cite out. I'd help Claudia in the office. I'd make phone calls. I'd join the legal collective and come back in to do support. But at the end of the day, I'd be sleeping at home.

Sign me up. I sat upright on my cot. Of course I could facilitate the meeting. I'd done it before. What was to decide, anyway? It wasn't like there was any sentiment in camp for modifying our position. No fines, no probation. Pretty simple.

And then — I could be out the following day. In time for the weekend. Fourth of July weekend, I realized. Just in time to watch the rest of America celebrate its precious freedom by getting drunk and blowing stuff up.

My excitement waned. It would feel weird to leave, I knew. Especially if Hank was still in.

But I wasn't ruling it out. And facilitating was the key to the plan. I got up off my cot, resolved to find Doc or Antonio. Better catch them before they ask someone else. I tracked down Doc by the watercooler and told him I'd do it.

He broke into a broad smile. "Great," he said. "Paul Revere would be proud. He probably facilitated a meeting or two in his day." Then he grew serious. "Anything you want to know about what's been going on at the spokescouncil?"

I thought for a moment. "Well, one thing I wonder is, how will people feel about someone so LAG-identified facilitating here?"

Doc weighed the question. "I haven't noticed much anti-LAG disposition. Everyone knows the LAG office isn't trying to run the show here. Besides, the co-facilitator will be a guy named Clem from up in Mendocino who helped start Abalone Alliance. So there's balance."

As Doc walked away, I filled a cup with water and drank it slowly. The die was cast. I opened myself to a wave of resolution, to an inner resonance that would affirm my decision. Unfortunately, the epiphany eluded me. It felt more like, "Sure, why not?"

Oh well, at least there were no second thoughts. Maybe something good will come of it.

As I got in the lunch-line, a guy named Norm from Sonomore Atomics introduced himself. I'd heard his name from Holly, who met him when he traveled down to the LAG office before the blockade. Norm was about forty, a high school teacher with an easy-going demeanor.

"Direct Action is a great paper," he said. "Holly tells me that you coordinate it."

The unexpected praise embarrassed me. "Well, Holly and I and a few others do," I said.

Norm nodded. "It's really important work. Especially the regional and

An AG meets in the circus tent. AG check-ins were a regular part of the day.

international news. It gives people a sense of belonging to a movement. It's easy for us to feel isolated up north. The paper makes a big difference."

I thanked him for the feedback. We inched up the lunch-line. Direct Action. Wasn't that a newspaper I used to work on? It hadn't crossed my mind since I got arrested. Maybe it was just a fantasy I'd always had of working on a radical underground paper.

What if they kept us in jail for a month? Maybe we could do layout here. That would be a hot issue. I'd seen a couple of guys with smuggled cameras — we could do our own inside report.

Lunch was classic fare — a balogna and cheese sandwich, grape kool-aid, and a shiny red apple. The swap-circle was doing a thriving business, but I decided to stand pat and have a balanced meal. I took a drink of kool-aid and looked around. Daniel. Moonstone. Norm. Craig. Claudia.

Claudia? What was she doing in our tent? She and Craig were sitting in a small patch of shade next to the tent. I went over to say hi, and they invited me to join them.

"I'm here as a legal aide," Claudia said. "I figured it was a chance to get out of the office."

"How's life on the outside?" I asked.

Her lips curled. "You don't want to know."

Her response chilled me. In my fantasy of the outside world, everyone was delighted with their work and brimming with purpose. How could anyone be depressed if they weren't in jail?

I'd have to cheer Claudia up, if only to get her to fit my fantasy. "Seems like your media work is going well," I offered. "We've been seeing the papers, and practically every day there's a front-page story."

"Oh, yeah," she said nonchalantly. "Maria and I have the media outreach together. Unlike some coalitions I know." She paused. "But where's it all going? So we get good media coverage. I don't see where LAG can go with this. Keep repeating the June blockade and watch it fizzle out? Change targets to keep action junkies excited?"

Craig looked directly at me. "There's no vision of a sustained campaign, no idea of what else might be involved besides the glamour of going to jail."

I couldn't help laughing at his choice of words. "Real glamour," I said, looking around the tent.

He smiled slightly. But his face clouded quickly. "LAG has to address the question of an overall strategy," he said, "or it's dead. We can't keep racing from action to action, or doing grandiose international networking when we aren't even part of a viable local coalition."

I reminded them of the October Euromissiles plans. "And that includes coalition work. That's a step forward."

Claudia grimaced. "We'll see how many people really work on the coalition, and how many just want to organize another protest. That's not the solution. We need to face the fact that our numbers here are smaller than last year. Maybe it's the wake-up call we need. We have to address issues like broadening our base, building new alliances. It all comes back to strategy."

Craig nodded slowly, seeming more relaxed with Claudia there to back him up. "That's what we were talking about when you walked up. We're working on a Strategy Proposal for the LAG Congress in August, to develop a long-range vision for our work."

Claudia nodded. "People have got to take a long look at where we're going. Because if all LAG wants to be is Dial-a-blockade, I'm getting out. Let VAC do that. Of course, you see what happens with that style of organizing. Sixty-day jail sentences."

"We might be here sixty days, too," I said in an attempt at humor. "Once people are out of here and rested up, there'll be interest in discussing LAG's future." My words didn't carry much conviction, but I was hoping Craig and Claudia would get the hint and slow down a little.

"The Congress in August is a great place to start these discussions," I said.

Claudia laughed coldly. "All people will want to discuss is the date of the next blockade."

Her tone grated on me. And Craig's wasn't much better. I didn't have a problem with strategy discussions. But it felt like they were going to ram through their proposal or quit if they didn't get their way. Like they weren't asking for input, but acquiesence.

The legal team was heading out, and Claudia said her goodbyes. I stood to give her a hug, but she was already moving away. I felt a twinge of sadness. Even if I was upset at her, I wanted to feel like we were working together. "See you soon," I called after her.

She looked back and gave me a wry smile. "For your sake, I hope it's on the outside."

Odd that she could smile, I thought. I couldn't imagine it. Sure, I'd been depressed for the past week. But my malaise hadn't extended beyond my narrow confines. Now, for the first time, the wider world was implicated. I could picture the August LAG Congress: Two hundred people, a dozen proposals, zero focus — and Craig and Claudia haranguing us to drop everything and debate movement strategy. By the time that's over, I may be nostalgic for jail.

As I shuffled toward the watercooler, a beautiful sight buoyed my spirits — a fresh shipment of books from the legal team. I dropped down and dug through the first box. It yielded nothing, but in the second I hit pay dirt: *The Brothers Karamazov.*

"Wow, Dostoyevsky," I said gratefully. I showed it to Antonio, who was sorting through the other box. "This'll keep me busy for a while."

"You'll probably have time to read the whole book," he said. "Too bad it isn't *Crime and Punishment,* though."

I laughed. "Or *Les Miserables.*" I returned to my cot pondering my existential dilemma: Finish Camus? Or plunge right into Dostoyevsky?

I was thumbing through my new book when Raoul and Sid stealthily approached the tentpole near me. Shhhhhh, Raoul gestured with a finger to his lips. Sid draped a bedsheet over his shoulder, grabbed ahold of the pole, and started shimmying up. I couldn't believe it. What if he falls, or gets caught by the guards? I clutched my book as Sid wormed his way up to the peak of the tent. He paused and looked jauntily down at us. Then he hoisted himself through the small opening. All we could see were his feet, gripping the pole.

Raoul scanned the tent for guards. "All clear," he called up to Sid. A small crowd was gathering. If a guard came in, the craning necks would give it away. Raoul tried to wave people away, but it was too intriguing a spectacle. "What's he doing?" people asked.

"He's putting up a peace flag," Raoul rasped. "We're declaring it the Santa Rita Peace Camp." The crowd broke into laughter and applause, which Raoul tried to quell. But it was too late. Shouts alerted us that the guards were on the way. Sid was just squeezing his wiry body back through the roof opening. "Come on!" Raoul yelled to him.

Several guards came barrelling back toward us. Sid was only halfway down the pole. He would have been nailed in the act if Les from Mustard Seed AG hadn't stepped directly in front of the oncoming guards. "What are you doing in here?" he cried out. "You have no right to be in this tent!" Accustomed as they were to taking orders, the contingent of guards actually halted for a moment before shoving Les out of the way. They kicked their way through a row of cots and arrived at the swelling crowd around the pole.

"What's going on here? What were you doing on that pole?" The guards glared at us. Reinforcements were on the way.

But instead of trying to grab Sid, the guards yelled at us again: "Come on, what's going on here? Who was that climbing the pole?"

They didn't know who had done it!

Sid's jocular demeanor practically gave him away, but the shouts and jostling of the rest of us covered for him. The guards were incensed, but there wasn't much they could do.

After a lecture on safety and authority and a stern warning not to try the same stunt again, the disgruntled deputies marched out empty-handed. A little later, a guard climbed onto the outside of the tent-roof. I followed the crowd out into the side yard, where we heartily booed as he used the guy-ropes to pull himself up to remove the peace flag. "It's still the Santa Rita Peace Camp," Antonio called out. "You can't kill an idea."

A while later, I was lying around reading and catnapping when a commotion erupted at the front of the tent. I couldn't tell what was going on, but I could see a row of baton-wielding guards lining the entrance to the tent. I joined the men moving that way.

"They just grabbed Darryl," Doc told me. I recognized Darryl's name, but couldn't put a face to it. "He was coming back from the portajohns and several guards grabbed him. Before anyone could do anything, they threw him into a patrol car and took off. Nobody knows where they took him."

A handful of men yelled at the guards, but most people seemed more puzzled than angry. "Why did they grab him?" Raoul asked. "I didn't see him do anything."

A tall, thin guy spoke up. "I heard that yesterday when the guards wouldn't let us go out to the portajohns, he whizzed in a paper cup and told one of the guards to empty it."

"Wait a minute," Moonstone interjected. Moonstone was still fasting, and spoke so seldom that his croaky voice startled me. "He never peed in any cup. I was with him. All he did was take an empty cup up to the guards and say, 'Do you expect me to pee in this?'"

The guy who had made the original remark looked embarrassed. "Why would they drag him away for doing that?"

"Just to mess with us," Raoul said. "Pure and simple, to mess with us."

"It was retaliation for the peace flag," another guy conjectured.

A few people were still jawing at the guards, who refused to let anyone leave the tent. There were only a dozen of them, so we could have swept past them if we'd wanted. But what would that accomplish? Darryl was gone. Someone suggested a hunger strike for dinner, but general grumbling shot that proposal down, and the crowd gradually dispersed.

My throat had settled into a dull swelling. If it would just stay there, I could live with it. Between Dostoyevsky, dinner, and a funnier-than-usual talent show, I got through the early evening in tolerable spirits. Maybe the decision to facilitate was paying dividends.

When the lawyers stopped by later that evening, they brought an update on Darryl. He had been taken to "Graystone," the maximum security section of the jail. Faced with confinement there, he had agreed to give his name and cite out.

That's one path to freedom, I thought. But as much as I wanted out, Graystone wasn't the route I was looking for.

Some men from Matrix AG came around announcing a ritual. I was actually tempted to join Moonstone and Antonio when they went. Part of me knew it might help break the isolation I was feeling. I'd come to jail expecting to bond with people like Craig and Daniel whom I worked so much with on the outside. Wouldn't it be ironic if the people I wound up connecting with were Pagans and gay men?

But I also craved private space as the day wound down. The tent grew quieter after the lawyers left, and Dostoyevsky won out over the ritual. I read for a while, then pulled out my journal. But writing felt like work. My throat stung every time I swallowed. How long was this going to go on?

How long? As if we were the first people to spend a week in jail for our beliefs. I set my paper down and closed my eyes. No, it wasn't the week that was the problem, but the uncertainty about how much longer. If I had a definite number of days to count, there would be some purpose to getting through another day. As it is, I straggle through, and when I get to the end, it's meaningless.

Wednesday, June 29, 1983

THE NEXT DAY dawned like lead. I went out to use the toilet thinking that it was still night, but the morning imposed itself in sullen grayness.

I swallowed and winced at the sharp pain in the back of my throat. Damn. Just what I needed. I returned to my cot and lay down, but I knew I'd never get back to sleep. Breakfast couldn't be too far off. If I was going to facilitate the spokescouncil, I better get whatever nourishment I could. And maybe I can get some salt to gargle with.

Doc, Rick, and I were among the first people in line as the National Guard set up shop. A cloud of steam rose from the vat of oatmeal as the lid was removed. We inched forward, awaiting permission to approach the tables.

But the guards had a new twist on the game. "Everyone has to leave the tent during breakfast," they announced. "No sleeping in. And no wearing blankets at meals. New policy."

Guards circulated through the tent, rousting sleepers from their cots. "No blankets," they said.

I wasn't cold, so I didn't mind. But Doc tied on his blanket like a cape. "They're probably going to confiscate our second blankets," he said.

"You think so?"

"Let's see what happens when I try to go to breakfast."

Nothing, I hoped. Couldn't we enjoy our oatmeal in peace?

Finally the chow line started moving. The first two or three people didn't have blankets, and went on ahead to get their cereal and toast.

Then Doc and I stepped up. The guard gave Doc a perfunctory look. "No blankets," he said. "No breakfast till you get rid of it."

Doc glared at him, then turned and stalked toward the back of the tent.

I looked past the guard to the buffet table. The oatmeal looked edible. But I was getting fed up with them yanking us around. I spun on my heels and followed Doc. "Come on, don't give in," I said to Rick, who joined us.

The next couple of men had blankets, and they followed suit. Then a blanket-less guy stepped forward. He paused in front of the guard and stood at attention. Then without a word he turned sharply and headed after us. The next man did the same, and the pattern was set. As each man reached the front of the line he paused, peeled off, and marched toward the rear.

Doc initially headed toward his cot, but Rick had a better idea. "Form a picket loop," he called out. "Everybody get a blanket. We'll go through the line again." I grabbed one of my blankets and joined the loop. Someone struck up our old standard, "Solidarity Forever." Soon two hundred men were trudging through the line, droning the words in husky morning voices. My hoarseness felt like a badge of resistance, and I sang through the pain.

A few people stopped to argue with the befuddled guards, although it was clear that they weren't making their own decisions. Someone higher up had ordered our blankets confiscated, and the orders couldn't be changed.

But they needed our cooperation to clear the tent. And if the authorities

"Solidarity Forever..." The old Labor classic was sung incessantly in the tents.

weren't budging, neither were we. Round and round we marched, clinging to our pride and our precious blankets. "Solidarity Forever" morphed into "Solidarity for Breakfast." The joke added a layer of delirium to my grogginess, and I wound up feeling more fortified by our bedraggled picket than I ever would have by their gummy oatmeal.

After breakfast, everyone carried a blanket around. I wore mine loosely draped over my shoulders as we launched the morning spokescouncil. The forty-odd spokes took seats on a circle of cots near the front of the tent. Behind the cots, fifty or sixty men had gathered to watch the proceedings.

I sat down on a cot next to Clem, the co-facilitator. The cot sagged, and I wished I'd sat on the ground, where I might find some back support. Maybe I'd move after Clem and I talked.

Clem had been the spoke for his cluster the preceding day, so he offered to facilitate the morning session. I was glad to have time to get acclimated. I moved down to the ground and leaned back on the cot, but it didn't offer much support, either. I tried to get comfortable. Don't rustle around too much, I thought. Facilitators are supposed to look grounded.

The opening check-in rang with the names of the AGs and clusters: Livermore Liberation League, Bombs Away, Radical Ions, Love and Rage, Cazadero Hill People, Low Priority Evacuees, Sane Franciscans, Lou Snit, Walnettos, Endangered Species, Cosmic Compost, The Ring, Nolo Comprendo, Clean Genes, Non-Nuclear Family, Acorn Alliance, Apocalypse Never, Chrysalis, Death and Taxes, Ozone Cluster, Gray Whale, La Paz, Lorax, Matrix, Oz, Fission Abolition, UC Students and Staff, Arms for Embracing, Shalom Mayom, Sangha for Disarmament, Critical Mass, Love is the Way, Atoms Family... And my favorite, the Crustacean Cluster, made up of people from Abalone and Clamshell Alliances and All Us Mollusks AG.

The blankets gave the morning's meeting an obvious theme. Right away a dozen men wanted to talk. People kept trying to make proposals, but Clem held them in check till all the ideas were on the floor — everything from a silent sit-in to wearing our blankets as capes and running around like Superman. The entire meeting could have been spent discussing the different ideas, but Clem deftly shifted the focus onto the immediate issue — what to do at lunchtime. "Based on what we've heard here, can anyone frame a proposal that they think could be consensed in the next forty-five minutes?"

A tall guy I hadn't noticed before raised his hand. "I propose that for the first fifteen minutes of lunch, we all sit or stand in silence in the tent-entrance..."

Murmuring rose around the circle. "I don't think that's going to be a quick consensus," Clem said diplomatically. "Anyone else?"

Raoul raised his hand. "I propose that one cluster remain in the tent at all times to prevent a confiscation. If the guards try anything, the cluster sounds the alarm and the rest of us get back inside."

"They'll never get my blankie," Sid popped off, setting off a round of laughter.

"We should all clutch our blankets and suck our thumbs like Linus," said someone else.

As the laughter subsided, Clem restated Raoul's proposal. After a few questions and comments, we reached consensus and chose the first few clusters to stand watch.

The meeting started to adjourn. "What now?" Sid said. "What are we doing about lunch? We should all carry blankets. Keep the pressure on."

Plenty of people agreed, judging from the blankets already in evidence. "Some people want to go ahead and eat lunch," Nathaniel said. "We should let them go first." No one objected, and a hundred men went to the head of the line.

I stayed back. I wasn't that hungry, anyway. Dinner might be harder, but skipping lunch wasn't that big a deal. I went back to my cot and grabbed one of my blankets, pulled it around me like a poncho, and joined the end of the line.

The lunch-eating crowd got their bag of grub. The first members of the blanket brigade would soon step forward. I couldn't see much from back where I was, but I figured we'd form another picket loop.

The line had moved ten or fifteen feet when it struck me that no one was heading back to form the picket. What was happening?

Word filtered through the line like a game of telephone. A guy in front of me passed the news back. "When the first men with blankets stepped up, the guards told them to go ahead, like they couldn't understand why anyone was hesitating. It's like they officially 'forgot' the rule."

Officially forgot? It sounded like *1984*. But it also showed that we weren't powerless. Our breakfast protest had an effect.

Most people seemed more amazed than jubilant. But Daniel drew his head back. "This is exactly what I knew would happen if they were faced with concerted action," he said. "If everyone were to join the hunger strike for even a day or two, they might give in completely."

Heartened as I was by our victory, I didn't share his analysis. The hunger strike felt like an alternate reality. As Daniel got deeper into his fast, we were communicating less than ever. It felt like he was on a solitary mission, a personal crusade. I didn't see where I fit into his vision.

After lunch, we took a break before re-convening the spokescouncil. I lay on my bed with my book open, but I couldn't concentrate. I'd be reading a sentence and my eyes would drift off the page, compulsively tracing the red and white lines to the top of the tent. And why not? They were the foundation of my consciousness. I'd always been staring at these stripes, and always would. I was going to be here for the rest of my life. Now and then someone would leave, but never me....

The idea of citing out after facilitating was still on my mind. In my heart I knew that it would gall me to leave before things were wrapped up, but I craved the outside. Hank's escape plan started to make sense. Sure, they might eventually nail you, but for a day, a week, a month, you'd be free.

I'd given up on Dostoyevsky and was retracing the tent stripes when the lawyers arrived for their afternoon chat. Around me people rustled. I figured I could skip the briefing. I'd hear a report about it when the meeting resumed.

But a burst of applause shook me from my meditations. People were shouting from the front of the tent. I sat up and fumbled for my shoes. Everyone was moving toward the legal gathering. I couldn't hold back a wave of hope. Was this the moment?

As I reached the enclave, the cheering reached a peak and "Solidarity Forever" broke out.

"What happened?" I yelled to Antonio.

He turned to me, wide-eyed. "They dropped probation!"

Around him other voices echoed the tidings: "They dropped probation!"

My heart pounded. Was it true? They dropped probation? I couldn't believe it. They had caved in? I looked around. People were yelling and hugging like they hadn't the whole time here. "They dropped probation!"

"Wow!" I yelled. Antonio and I embraced, and I cast my raspy voice into "Solidarity Forever."

Yet part of me held back. For once, I didn't let my hopes run away, and I wasn't shocked when the celebration subsided and a more sober picture emerged. Judge Lewis had indeed announced that he would not sentence people to probation, including folks who had already cited out. That was a major breakthrough.

But the prosecutor was demanding a fifteen-day jail sentence, which the judge supported. We still had five more days to serve!

For me, a late arrestee, it might be seven. I could be here another week. That took the luster off the bright tidings. Probation was a future threat. Seven more days was right now. I want out now, not in a week.

After the legal team left, the spokescouncil circled up. I took a seat on the ground with my back to a tentpole. Spokes filled the circle of cots, with a few on the ground. With the stakes suddenly raised, most of the other men gathered behind the cots, forming an amphitheater.

So here we are. I caught my breath. What now? Sure, we were united in our jubilation at the no-probation offer, but I knew we were a long way from consensus on our next step. I surveyed the ring of faces. Where to start? How was I supposed to know? Stall for time....

"How about if someone summarizes the court's offer," I said. "Once we're all clear on that, we can make proposals about how to respond, and then spokes can go back to their affinity groups and clusters and see what people think."

People nodded in a get-on-with-it way. Clem reiterated the prosecutor's latest offer: No probation, but five more days in jail.

I saw a chance to clear up something for myself. "What about people arrested in the Wednesday action? Do they have two extra days?"

"The lawyers said everyone would get five more days, regardless of how much you've already served. That includes people who've cited out already."

That's a relief, I thought. No extra time. I looked around. Okay. Refocus. Facilitate. Hands are up. "So let's take the next ten or fifteen minutes," I said, "and hear what people think. In twenty-five words or less. Will somebody keep time?"

The first couple of speakers gave lukewarm support to the five-day offer. "At least we'll know when we're getting out," one said.

"Plus," said the second, "we could probably agree to the deal, then get out of jail and come back later to finish our time. That could make a difference for a lot of people."

Raoul was next. He was planted on the end of a cot, which looked none too stable under his big frame. "If you come back later, they'll put you in general population. You'll be on your own, powerless. Being here together is our power. We shouldn't leave till we all walk out free."

"We could be free today if we go for a mass trial," Pilgrim said emphatically. "They would have to release us immediately if we plead not-guilty. And if we're acquitted, we're free."

"Right," interjected Claude. "But if we're found guilty, they can turn around and slap us with probation. It isn't worth the risk."

I was jotting down ideas as fast as I could, trying to see common threads, some way to weave the strands together. It was hard when I felt myself tugged in all directions. I pressed my back against the tentpole, trying not to get swept up in the emotional cross-currents. As facilitator, I wasn't supposed to be attached to a particular proposal. Well, no danger there. My problem was getting tossed around by every new wave.

Sid, squatting next to Raoul, raised his hand. He stood up and looked quickly around the circle. "We should up the ante. They're caving in. Why let them sentence us to another five days? Take it to them."

Raoul riffed off Sid. "Why not all walk out of camp? There's only about a dozen guards out front. By the time they got reinforcements, we'd be all over the place. What could they do?"

Well, I thought, they do have clubs and other implements of persuasion. But I liked the image of hundreds of men strolling nonchalantly into the barren fields while the guards frantically tried to corral us.

"What are we waiting for?" Raoul's voice rose in agitation. "Why not do it right now?"

Had there been a surge of support, I would have joined in. Great theater, if nothing else. But this was a spokescouncil, and no decision could be made without exhaustive discussion and at least one report-back to clusters and AGs. Raoul muttered something to Sid, but the meeting moved on.

A couple more people advocated accepting the court's offer. Then I called on Daniel. He was standing with his arms folded stoically across his chest. "If the goal is to escalate our resistance," he said with a nod at Sid and Raoul, "the hunger strike is the ideal tool. It puts pressure on the court and is undeniably nonviolent. If we all refuse to eat, the court might be compelled to set us free."

"Problem is, I'm allergic to masochism," someone behind me mumbled, and a general muttering suggested the fate of the proposal.

A spoke from Acorn Cluster raised his hand. "Why are we even discussing how to respond to their offer?" he said in exasperation. "Just ignore it, and say the only thing we'll accept is dropping all charges. I'll bet we'd get out just as soon."

The next speaker was back to lobbying for the mass trial idea, saying it would get as much media coverage as the blockade did. The following guy opposed escalating resistance because it might alienate the judge and drive him deeper into cahoots with the district attorney.

Around and around we went. Accept the deal. Take them to trial. Hunger strike. Walk out of camp. Do nothing. Accept the deal. Take them to trial...

The mid-afternoon sun radiated through the tent-stripes. Patience was running short. All the ideas seemed to be on the floor, but I didn't see much ground for synthesis. How did you mediate between those demanding a trial and those saying drop all charges? You can't have much of a trial if the charges get dropped.

Without a concrete proposal, it wouldn't usually make sense to break for report-backs to our clusters. But we needed a breather. Or I needed one, anyway. I tossed out the suggestion, and people seemed to agree. A couple of people raised their hands, but I waved them off. "Let's take the break right now," I said. "You can speak first when we come back."

The spokes left to meet with their clusters. I started back toward Change of Heart, then reversed my tracks. I'm not a spoke, I thought. I don't need to be there. I headed out into the front yard, which was almost deserted. The sun shone brightly. A slight breeze cooled the air. I gazed at the distant hills. The fog had cleared. A few wisps of cloud drifted past on their journey inland. I imagined myself wafting away on them. But Berkeley is the other way. I want to go home.

Go home. Yes! But first, I had to facilitate a decision on the court's offer. What to do with all these proposals? Go to trial, hunger strike, cite out, do nothing... What a mess. How were we ever going to reach consensus? Someone better have a stroke of genius, and fast.

When the spokescouncil reconvened, practically the entire tent had gathered around. Clem suggested that we do a straw poll of everyone present, to see which ideas had the most support. "Someone make sure the guards aren't listening," he said. A couple of guys volunteered for sentry duty, and we commenced the poll.

"Hunger strike for dinner?" Fifty or so men raised their hands. Daniel scowled — it wasn't a bad showing, but hardly a mass action.

"Walking out of camp?" Another fifty. And many who raised their hands seemed tentative. Same for me, I thought, although I refrained from voting.

"Mass trial?" A hundred hands went up immediately, followed by a smattering more. Pilgrim seemed pleased, and I wondered whether he even cared about consensus, as long as he had enough people to stage a trial.

"Do nothing and demand the charges be dropped." A dozen at the most. Clearly people had their fill of sitting around waiting.

That left about two hundred men in favor of accepting the proposed fifteen-day sentence. While they were the largest group, hands were raised with no alacrity. If someone came up with a solid idea for fighting back, a lot of these people might swing behind it. Maybe some of the trial people would, too. With the right proposal, consensus wasn't impossible. All it took was one inspiration.

But where was the straw to grasp at? What could galvanize four hundred tired, cranky men? Something that didn't take too much exertion. And preferably would make people laugh. I strained my imagination, but I drew a blank.

The tent grew hotter and stuffier. I called on a few people, and their comments ranged all over the map. The meeting was getting frayed at the edges. Something needed to happen.

Take another break? I couldn't think of a rationale. Another straw poll? Nothing would have changed. I looked over at Clem, who looked relieved not to be in my seat. You're on your own, his glance said.

People looked at me expectantly. What, did I look like a miracle-worker? The pressure built. Weariness muddied my brain. I took a deep breath and exhaled slowly, then was engulfed in a yawn so big that I didn't even try to mask it.

As my watery eyes refocused, Sid stood up. "Naptime," he called out in his high, clear voice. "Everyone get out your nap mat."

"I want milk and cookies," someone else said, and the spokescouncil devolved into naptime jokes and repartee. I shook my head, marveling at what my yawn had set off. I leaned back against the pole and let my shoulders relax a notch.

The next couple of speakers didn't shed much new light, and I started to despair again. This was going nowhere. What to do?

Claude was next. He'd been to a few protests in his day. Maybe he saw the magic solution. "A third of us want a trial," he said in a voice that both lectured and pleaded. "Half want to go with the five-more-days offer. That's a pretty even split. Maybe we have to admit that we don't have consensus. Solidarity doesn't have to mean that everyone does the same thing. If we take separate actions with mutual support, I don't think it weakens us. The key point is that we got rid of probation."

No one seemed thrilled with his assessment, but no one was leaping up to denounce it, either. I felt relieved that someone with Claude's experience would say that consensus was unlikely. It took some of the pressure off me.

Someone brought word from the phones that the women's camp was facing similar divisions. A few speakers made final pitches for their viewpoints, but there were no mass conversions, and the reality of non-consensus sank in.

Clem suggested a different straw poll. "How many people plan to cite out now that we've won on probation?" Hands rose slowly, but the trend was clear. Half or more of the men would leave. Some would plead not-guilty and go to trial. Others would plead no-contest and return later in the Summer to complete their sentence.

I looked around at the drained faces. This is no good, I thought. We can't leave like this. There has to be some way to pull us together. I groped for words. "Even if we can't agree on a unified tactic," I said, "we might want to consense that we're supporting each other's responses."

Scattered grumbling met my words, and I wondered if it was worth prolonging the meeting. I glanced across the circle and caught sight of Doc. He looked back at me and nodded. I wasn't sure if it had anything to do with my suggestion, but I took it as a good omen. Go for it.

"So that's a proposal," I said. "I propose that we declare full support for all of the options we've discussed. Any questions or concerns?" Somewhat to my surprise, the spokes went with the flow. After another half-hour of discussion and debate, we consensed that we were united in spirit, if not in tactics.

I sighed. A small victory, if not the most passionate consensus I'd ever had the pleasure to facilitate. Oh, well. All you can do is toss out an idea and see what happens. They can't all be gems.

As the afternoon session wound to a close, Antonio raised his hand. "This is our last meeting as a whole community," he said. "With the legal settlement and so many people leaving, tomorrow will be completely different. I suggest that we join in a circle for one last time and acknowledge our unity — in honor of each others' decisions, and in honor of our time together here."

Good idea. I climbed to my feet and followed him toward the big open area at the front of the tent. Most men joined right in, but some resisted. Especially the lefties. Hank and Craig were two of the obstinate ones. Come on,

I wanted to yell. It's not religion. It's about remembering we're all in this together.

Someone started an "ommmmm," and it spread around the group. Not the best recruiting song for Marxists. But gradually, almost all of the men joined in. Even Hank and Craig linked into the big oval.

I looked around the ring of faces. Fatigue, yes. Overlaid with irritation and impatience. But notes of satisfaction and relief were just as prominent. Here and there a pocket of laughter bubbled up, and a lot of men, like me, were scanning the circle as if imprinting the faces and spirits on their hearts.

People clasped hands or draped their arms around each other, swaying back and forth together. We did it. Against a system specifically designed to shatter and isolate, we held solidarity. They tried to shut us down with probation, and we outlasted them.

I gazed around, catching people's eyes. We made it, those tired eyes seemed to say. The end is in sight.

Relief and gratitude welled up in me. My nightly depression, my daily bouts of futility, paled next to memories of Moonstone's wedding dress, of Hank plotting his great escape, of Doc's words of challenge and inspiration, of Daniel's austere determination. I pictured Change of Heart, fifteen bedraggled men propping each other up for another day. We did it.

One by one, people cast thoughts into the circle: memories, inspiration, humor, appreciations. Once I'd heard a few, I knew I would speak, though I wasn't quite sure what I'd say. I waited for an opening, then spoke up. "This has been one of the most powerful experiences of my life," I said. My voice cracked, and I flushed. "It's challenged me in ways I never imagined. I'll be feeling the reverberations for a long time. Thank you all."

The man to my right, an older union guy, squeezed my shoulder. "Thank y'all," he echoed, the only words he spoke.

Someone started toning an "om" and once again it took hold of the whole group. I let myself ride the waves of tone as they rose and fell, rose and fell, finally trailing off into silence. Some men turned and hugged their neighbors. Others knelt and touched the ground. I spotted Clem nearby, and gave him a hug. Neither of us spoke, but I felt that our eyes telegraphed the same message — I'll never forget you.

The circle dissolved into a web of farewells. I hugged a few people who were heading out, but not many people I knew were leaving. Most Change of Heart men elected to plead no-contest and stay and serve their time now. Even Moonstone, whose fasting was entering the martyr zone, was

staying. "I need to get these five days done with," he said. "Looking at what happened to Alby and Karina, I'll probably have to go back and do time at Vandenberg later in the Summer."

Daniel was in the same boat, but I couldn't imagine him citing out, anyway. Antonio and Doc were staying on, as well as Rick, who had been fired from his job the day before. I hadn't quite made up my mind, but with my whole cluster staying, I might as well see it through.

Hank, still fighting the flu, decided to split. I went over to hug him goodbye, but he fended me off with a handshake. Ah, well, some things even jail can't change. "Hope you get some good drugs," I said. "Too bad you never got to try your escape plan."

"Yeah," he said. "It would have worked. Maybe next year. You know what I've been thinking about today, though?"

I shook my head, hoping he wasn't planning some courtroom prank that would get him a contempt citation.

Hank's eyes glowed, as if he were gazing into the future. "I have a bunch of super-thin sheets of plywood at my shop," he said. "They're so thin you can mold them around a curve. We take four of them and make a big canister, five feet across and eight feet tall. We mount it on a trailer, paint it white, and there you have it — a mobile nuclear reactor."

"That's perfect," I said, although I wasn't sure what it would be perfect for.

"We can haul it around Berkeley," Hank said. "We'll make a container for dry ice at the top, so it has smoke coming out of it. And a flashing red light and an alarm that keeps going off. And how about a couple of guys with radiation suits and push-brooms cleaning up behind it?"

"Great, finally a role for me," I said.

He looked at me curiously, as if sizing me up. "Yeah," he said thoughtfully. "Yeah, I could see that."

We shook hands again. "I'll call you when I get out," I said. "Play a game of pinball for me."

Just before dinner, the sheriff made his visit. With the confrontation over, the energy was slack. No arms were linked in defiance, and no songs were sung for Sheriff Krieg. When he read his invitation to arraignment, over half of the men in the tent raised their hands. They were accompanied not with songs and cheers but polite applause.

Every previous exodus had been a small group leaving the main body. Now, with over half the men preparing to leave, it felt like the main body was going, and we, the stragglers, were left behind. Someone tried to start "Solidarity Forever," but it faded after a couple of times through. The departing men began to filter toward the exit. It was a desultory moment till Moonstone called out, "Don't forget to write!" His croaky voice triggered laughter and imitation, and a flurry of farewell jokes filled the air.

Dinner was a subdued affair, although it was nice to get seconds on "stew" and Wonder Bread. The Santa Rita crash diet program had cost me an inch or more off my waist. Maybe I could beef up these last few days.

I talked with Holly after dinner, who told me that things had gone about the same on the women's side. "Angie left, but Jenny and Sara are staying through the weekend. I'd say most of Change of Heart is staying."

"I guess we just can't get enough of jail," I said. "What about Caroline?"

"I think she's staying," Holly said. "But we haven't really been talking much." I felt a tinge of sadness in Holly's voice. "Caroline has really stayed away from me and Jenny. We must remind her too much of the office and her job." But a moment later she was telling me that she had been meditating with a Buddhist AG, and was going to a Pagan ritual that evening.

When it was my turn to talk, I wasn't sure what to say. She asked about my facilitating, but it seemed long ago. "Overall, I think it went pretty well," I said.

The best news — that I hadn't felt so depressed the night before, or all day today, I couldn't really share. "I'm feeling better, and by the way, I was really depressed the past week." No, that wouldn't work.

It wasn't a very satisfying talk. As usual. But then at the end, Holly's voice grew quieter. "It's been hard not being with you," she said, "I'm glad we have the telephone, but you feel far away. I want to see you so much."

Her voice wavered, and I felt a pang in my heart. "I really miss you," I said. I pictured us hugging and kissing back in our apartment. I could almost feel her thick hair and see her blue-green eyes. "I can't wait to see you, Holly. I love you."

We parted in that spirit. The alienation of the past week seemed already to be fading. In just five days we'd be back home together and we could forget this whole episode.

I wandered over to the watercooler to get a drink. Claude walked past. "You did a good job facilitating today," he said.

"Thanks," I said, surprised by his compliment. "It was frustrating not to reach consensus."

"Sometimes it just isn't there. The main thing is that all the different opinions got heard without ripping the group apart. You did a good job of that."

His praise filled me with pride, like I'd moved up a level as an activist. And to think — I hadn't even wanted to facilitate the meeting. The whole tent looked brighter as I strolled back to my cot.

If only I could have hung onto that feeling. But as I sat down, a pall descended. After the exodus, only about one hundred and fifty men remained. Empty cots surrounded me, and I felt distant from the other men. I looked up at the stripes. Had they always been so drab?

The only consolation prize was that there were blankets to spare. There were so many that I even got a choice of colors: light gray or dark gray.

It was only with effort that a few die-hards got the talent show to happen that evening. I wasn't going to go, but Doc and Rick said that they had written a special song for the occasion, so I followed them across the tent and took a seat on a cot toward the back of the audience.

The day's developments cast a reflective air over the show. Songs and poems were more introspective, and low chuckles supplanted laughter. That was fine with me. Nothing too taxing.

Toward the end of the show, Enola Gay got up to take its turn. Rick stepped out to introduce their number. "As difficult as this experience has been, there are so many ways we have loved being here. We're going to miss you all, and especially the men from Change of Heart..."

As he spoke, I thought about our cluster. Antonio and his poetic vision. Moonstone and his airy good humor. Daniel, with his unwavering resistance. And most of all, Doc, Rick, and Enola Gay, with their steady modeling of how men can support one another.

"... So this is our going-away song," Rick concluded. "It expresses what to us has been the highlight of our time here. It's to the tune of 'We are the Power in Everyone.'" The crowd hushed. Rick hummed the opening note of the Pagan chant, and gestured like a choir director. The men sang out: "We like to shower with everyone / We like the dance of the naked buns...."

The assembled men erupted, and I was swept right along, laughing harder than I had in a long while. Tears pooled in my eyes, and I felt a little of the grayness dispel. Good riddance, I thought. Laugh it away. Enough, already.

That night as I headed to bed, I felt like I might fall asleep without depression. After eight days of stalemate, we had won. The court had backed down. And I'd been right in the thick of it.

But it wasn't quite that simple. Something nagged at me, unresolved. What exactly had I achieved? I pictured my obituary: "One of his great accomplishments was not getting probation."

And even if it was a victory, how much did I, or any of us, have to do with it? We didn't win — the state lost. It was like winning the World Series because the other team dropped the ball. Not a lot to cheer about.

Oh well, we're on the home stretch. Home. I closed my eyes. Images of my apartment, my guitar, and my books poured into my mind. I could smell the popcorn, taste the first toke off my pipe. Five more days? How would I make it?

Thursday, June 30, 1983

I WOKE UP Thursday morning and it was crystal clear. Get out now.

What was holding me here? With the legal deal struck, solidarity was no longer an issue. A breakfast rumor from the guards said that any men remaining that evening would be moved into general population for the weekend. Someone cautioned that it was probably just a ploy to get people to cite out, but with our shrinking numbers it seemed plausible to me.

If we're going into general population anyway, I figured, why not take a break, go home for a while, then come back in July and serve my last few days? My throat would sure appreciate the care.

I told Doc about my decision after breakfast. He peered at me. "Do you know what you're getting into?" he said. "It's one thing for fifty or sixty of us to go into general population together this weekend. It's another thing if you go in by yourself. I've been in general population. It's endless hassles and power games, with the threat of violence hovering over every interaction. Maybe it especially strikes me as a gay man, but I think anyone who is perceived as different or alone is targeted."

His assessment was sobering. But no logic was going to sway me. "Maybe I'll find some other men who want to go back at the same time," I said. "I don't have to do it alone."

Doc shrugged, then stepped forward and hugged me. "I'll miss you," he said.

Expecting the sheriff by mid-afternoon, I went around saying my goodbyes. Antonio looked disappointed that I was leaving, but gave me a warm send-off. "It's not too late to change your mind," he said as we parted. "Think about it."

I smiled sadly. "I'm about thunk out."

We parted, and I hunted up Craig. "Are you staying in?" I asked.

"Yeah, I'd just as soon get it over," he said matter-of-factly. He looked at me steadily, as if awaiting my next question.

Funny, I thought. On the outside Craig and I have an easy rapport, in the office or playing pinball at Hank's. Here, we'd hardly found anything to talk about. And yet once out of here, we'd probably get along fine.

"I'm taking off," I told him.

Craig nodded. "No reason to stay if you don't want to," he said. "I was thinking of getting out. But then I'd have to come back later and be in general population. I did it once before, and that's enough for a while."

We hugged gingerly. As we stepped back, I looked into his eyes. He held my gaze, then chuckled. Yeah, I thought. We'll probably pick up where we left off once we were out of here. "See you next week," I said.

Who next? I felt like it was my job to track down everyone I knew. But just then, Sid came loping toward me like he was dribbling in for an easy basket. "Hey, I heard you're taking off," he said as he pulled up short.

"Yeah, it's true," I said. I wondered if I was setting a bad example for youth. "I have to get out and start planning the next protest."

"My sources tell me you're one of the directors of LAG Central."

I rolled with the joke. "Uh, no, I'm just an assistant."

"I heard you were up for a promotion," he answered. We laughed together, and he told me that he was interested in working on Direct Action. We made plans to talk after he got out, then hugged goodbye.

I had to look around for Daniel, eventually tracking him down in a workshop on war tax resistance. I tried unsuccessfully to get his attention, and finally walked around the circle of cots and knelt down next to him.

He was still on his hunger strike, and his face was ashen. I felt pangs of guilt just looking at him. "I'm going to leave today," I told him. He nodded without changing expression. I put my hand on his arm. "Good luck over the weekend," I said.

He nodded again, then turned back to the workshop. I waited a moment, then quietly stood up and backed out of the circle. I looked around for someone I hadn't said goodbye to, hoping for a final connection. But before I spotted anyone, a guard came through the tent saying the sheriff would arrive in a few minutes.

The moment of decision had come. It wasn't too late to change... No, forget it. I'm out of here. Enough already.

I went back to my cot to get my stuff together. But once I got there, I figured, what's to take? My journal pages and pencil-stub are already in my pocket. My change of socks? No thanks.

The Brothers Karamazov? Now there was a tough one. What were the ethics of taking the book? Would I be stealing from the camp library? It wasn't like I needed more books on the outside. I could get a copy at Moe's for a dollar. But we'd probably have time to kill in court. What better companion than Dostoyevsky?

I stood there, perplexed, gazing at the book's tattered cover. Heads I take it, tails it stays. I flipped the book onto the cot. Heads. Take it. Phew!

Time to get in line. I had a concern that they might bring just one bus. If it was full, some people might get bumped. First come, first served. I picked up my pace. There wasn't exactly a line, but there was a clear pecking order of men seated nearer or farther from the front. Maybe thirty men in all. Not a full bus yet.

I was about to sit down in my allotted space when I remembered Caroline's drawings on the bulletin board. Damn! I'd probably lose several places in line. But I had to get them. Maybe I should leave my book to hold my space. But then someone might take the book. I gritted my teeth. How could I be thinking about petty stuff like this?

I walked back to the watercooler as quickly as I could without being conspicuous. An older man looked at me oddly as I took down the pictures. "Saving them for Direct Action," I said. He seemed satisfied. I gathered my stash and hurried back to the line-up. I'd lost just three spaces. Not bad.

The queue was mostly silent. No buzz of anticipation. No chatter about what we were going to eat when we got home. I sat alone on the cot, waiting, waiting. I had no idea what time it was. Asking someone felt intrusive. I thumbed my book. Too much work. Let me go. I'll walk home. Just let me out.

Finally, the sheriff arrived and gave his customary recitation. There was scattered applause as the forty of us took our leave and followed the sheriff out to the bus. We just fit, with a seat or two to spare. I looked around and recognized most of the men, but there was no one I especially knew. I should have left with Hank yesterday, I thought. I'd have had someone to hang out with.

People talked in low voices about what to expect from the judge. Someone rehashed the pleas: not-guilty if you wanted to go to trial, and no-contest to get five more days. "But we already served one of those days by staying till today," someone said. "So it's four more."

We were transported across the jail grounds to a little pre-fab office complex. Our first stop was in the cafeteria. Fluorescent lights glinted off the dingy white cinder block walls. A zig-zag row of banquet tables divided scruffy inmates from pristine guards. Behind the tables, the authorities searched for our files, matching us to our photos. I wondered how much I still looked like that long-ago portrait. Maybe they'll take another one now — before and after.

The process dragged on. I wasn't ready to open Dostoyevsky yet, not till I was sure they'd found my file. What if they can't find it? Do you get out of jail free, or do they throw you in the tank while they figure out what to do?

After what seemed like an hour, the guards found the last file. We were led down a narrow passageway with a low, curved ceiling that made me feel like I was inside a vacuum cleaner tube. The tube led to the rear entrance of a long, narrow classroom. The forty men squeezed into wooden chair-desks. Up front was a makeshift judicial bench, with a couple of lower tables for court functionaries. Much-erased chalkboards lined the right-hand wall. The windows, along the left, were dark and tightly closed. A whole row of fluorescent lights was burned out, and the room was about as vibrant as an early morning Summer-school class in statistical procedure.

Luckily, I got a back-row seat. My spirits hadn't improved since leaving the tent, but now that we'd reached the courtroom, I could settle in and read. Just listen for my name and say...

And say what? No contest? I should plead not-guilty and join the trial. If we won, I wouldn't have to come back at all.

But if we lost, they could give us probation. Forget that. I smiled to myself. Miserable as the past week had been, I insisted on my right to do it again.

The bailiff came in and warned us to remain silent in the presence of the judge. His vehemence made me wonder what had happened in prior hearings. "There will be absolutely no talking while court is in session," he said. "If you need to speak to your attorney, you will be allowed into the hallway, two at a time." He paused portentously. "There is to be no gum chewing. No laughter. And no reading."

No reading? How low could they sink? I flashed on grad school, surviving a tedious Kierkegaard class by sitting in the back row reading Hegel. Not here. No reading allowed.

After more sitting and waiting, we were graced with Judge Lewis's presence. He came in through a side door, grumbling to the bailiff about something or other. He took his elevated seat and rapped his gavel perfunctorily, then shuffled through some papers and spoke in a low voice to the prosecutors. If we hadn't been assured that the deal was settled, it wouldn't have looked good for us.

Without even acknowledging us, the judge droned into a painstaking reiteration of our charges and his interpretation of the deal that had been struck. People shuffled in their chair-desks. A few lined up to talk to the lawyers. Most looked like they were doing their best to tune it all out.

Perhaps inspired by the classroom setting, Judge Lewis soon broadened the scope of his discourse to include responsible citizenship, waxing eloquent on the privilege of living in a free country. How dare we criticize America! It was the old conservative adage: Prove that you cherish your freedom by not exercising it.

Any minute now, Judge Lewis would start blubbering about how different it would be if we had been arrested in a communist country. "Get on with it," I wanted to holler. "No one gives a hoot." But contempt of court would send me right back to jail. Keep cool.

On and on the judge prattled, expostulating on the duties of obedience to duly-constituted authority. Where'd this guy get his law degree, a Cracker Jack box? Finally I couldn't take it any longer. I let out a long, loud sigh, ending in "Hooo, boy!"

It reached the intended ears. Lewis grabbed his gavel and slammed it down. "That's enough! I'll clear this courtroom!"

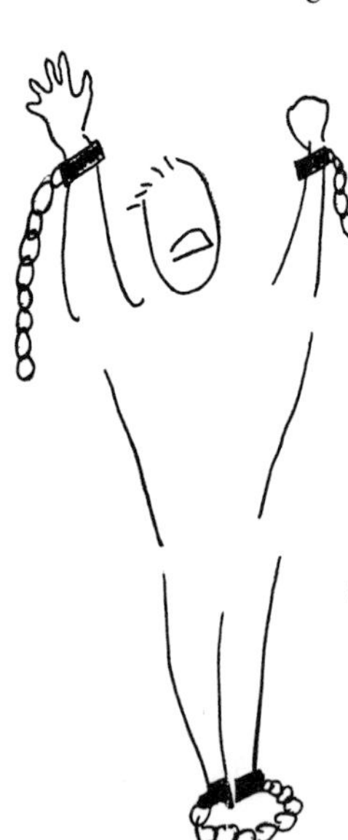

His vehemence took me aback. "That would be a blessing," I wanted to retort. But the threat of contempt gave me pause. I clenched my teeth, filled with consternation at being intimidated.

Maybe Lewis was chastened by the negative review, though, because he wrapped up his diatribe and got on with the business at hand. One by one, our names were called. It wasn't to the judge that we answered, though, but to a deputy seated behind a wooden table off to one side. "No contest," I told her. "Do I get to choose my own jail dates?"

She handed me a slip of paper. "The details of your sentence will be determined at a hearing in Livermore next week. This is not an optional hearing. You must attend."

Oh, great. Another wasted day in Livermore. We straggled out of the courtroom, too drained to celebrate. Any stray hopes for sense of release — for a glimpse of the exhilaration I'd known the previous year — dissipated as we reboarded the bus and rode to the edge of the jail grounds.

Outside the fence we were united with the women who were leaving that evening, about twenty in all. I hugged a few strangers, but didn't see anyone I knew. Fine. Just put me in a car and take me home.

On the ride back to Berkeley, I sat silently in the back of a ten-person van while some of the others talked over their experiences. The women seemed in better spirits than the men. Maybe women's camp really had been different. I thought of Holly and her buoyant moods.

Suddenly it hit me — I hadn't told Holly I was leaving. There was no way to call her now. How could I be so self-centered? What a stupid move. She'd figure it out, sure, but how alienating. Maybe I could get a lawyer to tell her. I couldn't believe it.

My ride dropped me off on Dwight Way at about ten o'clock. I made my way up the wide front stairs. A key. Oh yeah. I fished in my pocket and produced the little piece of flat metal. I studied it, then slid it carefully into the lock and eased the door open.

Old newspapers and magazines littered the lobby, as if no one had swept since I was last here. How many years ago was that?

I heard voices coming through the garage entrance. Clear out. The last thing I want to do is run into someone. I kicked into gear and took the stairs two at a time. The hallway was deserted. I unlocked the apartment door and stepped inside.

The curtains were open, and the low fog seemed to cast an orange light on the space. I went across and opened the sliding glass door to get some fresh air.

A shower. That was the first order of business. A drooping plant caught my eye. "I'll be right back," I promised. I peeled off my filthy clothes and stepped into the miraculous shower of hot water. This was why I came home.

Finally, hunger drew me out. The refrigerator wasn't very inviting, but in the cupboard I found a half-pound bag of peanuts in the shell and a couple of packs of Ramen. The freezer yielded a can of lemonade concentrate. Not the most elegant of homecoming dinners, but a good antidote to the National Guard's grub.

As I stirred the Ramen, the drooping plants called to me again. How strange they looked. The whole apartment seemed to have the life drained out of it. Tapes and books lay where I'd abandoned them. A half-empty beer bottle sat next to the stereo.

Music. But what? Nothing loud or jangly. I studied the shelves. How about Bob Marley? I seem to remember liking him.

I set the volume lower than usual and tended to the plants. None had died, although the fern plant that Holly and I had recently bought was losing needles. Hopefully they'd grow back by the time Holly got home. I shook my head. Why hadn't I remembered to call her? She'd probably have been happy for me.

I mixed the lemonade and ate some peanuts, then got out my pipe. It was half-full from nine days ago, waiting to be smoked. A living link with my own past. The thought amused me, and I finally got a little perspective. I really was out of jail! I could get high at the end of the day.

I took a toke and held my breath as long as I could, just for the kick of it. I let go and waited for the buzz. It came on quickly, and I welcomed the soft, billowy feeling. But something was off-kilter. I felt unsettled, slightly nauseous. I tried to blame my exhaustion, but it was more. I wasn't really free. All I had done was postpone the final reckoning. Sure, I was glad to be out now, but sometime soon, I'd have to return. And it wasn't going to be a circus tent with a bunch of other protesters. It would be the real jail at Santa Rita. What had I gotten myself into?

Enough of jail, already! Think about something else. I got out a book on Medieval painting and flipped through the pictures absentmindedly, trying to spin out on art-thoughts. But my imagination felt leaden, earthbound. I remembered the previous year, lying in bed after the blockade and reliving the whole experience. This was the opposite. The last thing I wanted to do was to relive what I'd just been through. I just wanted to escape....

I smoked a few more hits, but all it got me was light-headed. It was certainly a change from the ponderous moods of jail. But it wasn't especially liberating.

Finally I went to bed. Thick as my mood was, my body welcomed the feel of the old futon. I sprawled out on my back, luxuriating in a bed wider than my shoulders. I fluffed my pillow and reacquainted myself with the art-prints on the walls. By god, I was home. I'd stayed in solidarity till they met our demands. I had survived....

Sleep wasn't as easy as I had hoped. Lying in bed, my thoughts ran free. Whether I pictured events in jail or out, though, red and white stripes colored everything, as if my imagination hadn't yet escaped the tent.

I thought about people I hadn't seen since before the arrests. Karina, off in federal prison for another month. I felt a pang, knowing how long it would be till I saw her. Mort, who hadn't gotten busted. What did he make of the whole thing? Hank, hopefully on the mend. Angie with her whispery phone voice....

And Holly.... Once more I berated myself for forgetting to call her. Where were my priorities? It would be four days till I had any contact with her. All I could do was wait.

In October 1983, LAG joined activists in Europe and North America in a series of protests...

STOP THE EUROMISSILES!

OCTOBER 24, 1983

... against a new generation of nuclear-tipped "Euromissiles" — the Cruise and Pershing Two.

Top: Keith Holmes
Middle: Bob Thawley
Bottom: Unknown (see Appendix)

Stop the Euromissiles!

October 24, 1983

On October 24 LAG protested in the financial district. A dozen affinity groups did actions at war-contracting corporations.

Die-Ins, imported from London, increased disruption while lowering the risk of arrest. Even the nukecycle got into the act (top left).

Photos by Ted Sahl, except top right by Keith Holmes.

Any connections between the people pictured in the photographs and the characters in this book are purely coincidental. The characters are fictional. No photo should be taken as implying that an individual is in any way connected to a fictional character.

A youth AG blockaded Wells Fargo. Many other protesters wore costumes and face paint at the pre-Halloween action.

Protesters celebrated a successful action.

Top: Keith Holmes
Lower pair: Ted Sahl

Three / 1983

"You are deluding yourself about the Court," said the priest. "In the writings which preface the Law, that particular delusion is described thus: before the Law stands a doorkeeper. To this doorkeeper there comes a man from the country..."

— *Franz Kafka, The Trial*

Monday, July 4, 1983

A cloud of beige dust rose behind the old station wagon as it pulled away. I turned my head and tried not to breathe till it settled.

Had I ever spent an odder Fourth of July? And it wasn't over yet. I put down my guitar and shuffled to the right, trying to stay in the shadow of one of our cars. Out in the sun, it must be a hundred degrees.

Twenty of us held vigil in the parking lot of Santa Rita jail, waiting for the final Livermore protesters to be released. I looked at the barbed-wire encrusted complex. Santa Rita. If I had stayed in, I'd be a free man today. No more time to serve. Instead, I was looking at a return trip in three weeks. Right back here.

So I wasn't feeling especially nostalgic. Left to my own devices, I'd have skipped this visit. But I knew I needed to be here. Having forgotten to tell Holly I was leaving jail, the least I could do was welcome her when she got out.

I took a drink of water, then fiddled some more with my guitar, keeping to myself. Since I got out four days earlier, I'd found it hard to be around more than one person at a time. I kept my head low, watching my left hand fingering the strings.

I settled into a simple chord pattern, my mind alternating between dreading jail and fretting over seeing Holly. She probably knew by now that I had cited out. I pictured how our reunion might have been had I stayed in — stepping into freedom together. Instead, it felt like we would be living in separate realities.

The first taste of freedom.

My thoughts were interrupted by a van the size of an RV pulling into the parking lot. I had expected people to be released through the barbed-wire tunnel leading out of the jail's concrete command post. But the big van wheeled up behind us, and protesters began streaming out.

Antonio was the first person I recognized. The sun glinted off his silver hair. A huge smile lit his face. "Great to see you, old man!" he cried out. I welcomed him with a hug, envying his exhilaration.

A dozen others emerged. Then I spotted Holly. She paused in the doorway of the van, as if taking the full measure of the outside world. I pushed through the little knot of well-wishers. I paused for a moment, wondering how to greet her. Then her eyes fell on me. A beaming smile broke over her face. She stepped down from the van and threw her arms around my neck. She felt slight, almost fragile.

She trembled. How great it must feel to be out. To be finished. To have closure.

I felt a flicker of resentment. Did she have any idea how I was feeling? Did it occur to her that not everyone was so ecstatic?

But I pushed it down. It's not her fault that she's free and I have to go back.

As she beamed at me, though, I wanted to pull away. I reached out and hugged her again, to avoid having to look directly at her.

Friday, July 8, 1983

Holly was in the kitchen, making tea. I sat down on the living room floor, then got up and went over to the stereo. "What do you want to hear?" I asked.

"How about flute music?"

We'd set aside Friday evening to work together on the new Direct Action. It was seven o'clock already, and I was anxious to get going so we didn't have to work all night.

I sifted through my tapes and found a Peruvian recording. The haunting tones of pan-pipes opened the album. I sat down on the floor again and tried to get comfortable. The breathless flitting of the pipes sounded a little too close to my life over the past week.

I'd been out of jail for eight days now, and I hadn't taken a break yet. When I wasn't working extra hours to make up lost income, I was scrambling to pick up the pieces of LAG that lay strewn in every direction. With everyone out of jail, it was clear just how scattered we were. The second LAG Congress was planned for early August. I told Craig I'd help pull it together, assuming there would be a whole work group like last year. But most of my expected colleagues were missing in action. Mort was traveling a lot for his job. Craig and Claudia were focusing on their Strategy Proposal. I'd hoped Holly and Caroline would pitch in, but they were busy getting the office back on track. So it fell to me, Jenny, Artemis, Lyle, and a few others to organize the biggest meeting of the year.

To compound matters, the proposals for actions and projects were all over the map — another encampment and action at Vandenberg; a second International Day; October actions in solidarity with demos planned by European peace groups; an anti-nuke alert network; urban actions against corporate military contractors; and a peace camp at Livermore. How were we going to consense on a coherent plan?

Holly came out of the kitchen carrying a small teapot and a cup. She knelt and set them on the floor. She placed a cushion against the rolled-up futon and sat down. Then she stood back up. "I forgot my notes," she said, and walked back toward the bedroom.

I went over to the futon and sat down. It felt lumpy, and I shifted around, trying to get comfortable. I looked at my own notes, ten pages of ideas scribbled, scratched out, and margin-scrawled. I wished I'd had time to type them up, but I hadn't gotten to it yet. Maybe later.

Holly came back carrying a red file-folder and sat down next to me. She took a sip of tea, then started sifting her papers.

"Want to get started?" I finally said.

"I thought we already started," she said without looking up. Her voice was calm and bright, as if she didn't even detect my impatience.

Holly sifted through a stack of papers. "Angie said she can work on the paper all day tomorrow. And Sara will be around, too. With Karina in prison for another month, she has plenty of time on her hands."

Karina was halfway through her prison time for the Vandenberg action. "Have you heard anything about Karina?" I asked.

"Yeah. Sara talked to her and Alby this week. Karina is getting along okay, but Alby isn't. He's in the men's prison down at Terminal Island. It sounds like a pretty tough place, especially for someone as small as Alby. He's been threatened, and he figured it was useless to complain to the guards. He told one inmate that if the guy attacked him, he would scratch his eyes out. Can you imagine Alby saying that?"

"I guess you do what you have to do," I said. I thought about my upcoming sentence. In seventeen days I'd be in Santa Rita. A lot of my fellow inmates would come from inner-city Oakland, where violence was a fact of life.

My head shook involuntarily. I pulled my attention back to the newspaper. "We have eight pages for International Day follow-up, is that right?"

"Yeah," Holly said. "I'll write an overview article, and then we have reports from all over the place. Plus, we want to get people thinking about next year."

My mind clouded as I thought back to my jail-talk with Craig and Claudia. "Maybe we shouldn't be jumping right into another International Day," I said.

"If we want it to grow," she said, "we have to get going right away. People are waiting for word on next Summer. With a full year to work, we may be able to get a lot more groups interested in CD. We need to get the date out now."

"I think you need to wait to see if there is a new consensus."

She looked up in surprise. "International Day was conceived as an ongoing, annual event. We want to keep up our momentum. Is there something wrong with that?"

My jaw tightened. "You seem to think everything is like it was before the blockade. It's not." My voice felt thin and strained.

Holly set her notes down and looked at me. "What's wrong, Jeff?"

I clutched my sheaf of notes. "I'm really depressed about LAG right now, and I feel like you're oblivious. The Congress is in a month, and there's no focus at all. LAG is in a total shambles, and you just go on assuming that International Day will save us."

Her eyes flickered. "International Day inspired thousands of people to take action against nuclear weapons. It was a big success. The movement is growing all across the country."

"So what if people got arrested in Iowa or Florida? Is that going to help LAG figure out what to do next? We can't just blindly call another International Day. We need to stop and think about what we're doing."

To my surprise, Holly nodded. "You're right," she said quietly. She looked down, and the color seemed to drain from her face. "Most people in LAG don't care about International Day. It was obvious in jail, but I guess I haven't wanted to face it."

I reached out and put my hand on her arm. "I'm sorry, Holly. I didn't mean to be so harsh."

"No, that's okay. You're right."

"Yeah, but I didn't have to be so sarcastic." I took her hand. "I'm sorry. I'm under a lot of pressure."

She set aside her International Day folder and looked at me. "The paper can wait. Let's talk."

I took a breath. Why not clear the air? Tell her I'd been feeling on a totally different wavelength from her, and not just about politics. We were hardly communicating.

But what if she agreed that we weren't communicating? Then where would we be?

I grasped at a convenient straw. "It's the LAG Congress," I said. "It's not like last year. There's only a few of us even working on it. And to make matters worse, Claudia and Craig are demanding that their Strategy Proposal get top priority the first day, and everything else be put off till the second day. That's going to blow the lid off the Congress."

"I heard about that," she said. "At least Artemis said she would facilitate. She's good at pulling people together." Holly seemed to search my eyes for a sign that I shared her hope.

I tried to look encouraged. "Yeah, that's a plus," I said.

"And Caroline told me that finances are looking better. She said your blockade-a-thon brought in almost $3000."

That made me smile in spite of myself. "Pilgrim alone raised over $300 in pledges," I said. "And Mustard Seed AG just sent in another $250."

"That's amazing," Holly said. "Sounds like you and Jenny are getting the hang of fund-raising."

I nodded. "But I think Caroline is pretty fried. She was talking again yesterday about quitting the staff."

"I don't think she'll do it," Holly said. "She just wants to work on something besides fund-raising. Maybe Jenny will take on more of that."

Holly stretched her neck as if working out the kinks. I scooted over behind her and massaged her shoulders. I worked my thumbs deep into her shoulder muscles. Why had I been fighting with Holly? When would life get back to normal?

Sunday, July 24, 1983

As I walked along Dana Street, I picked up a spindly twig and tested its flex between my fingers, seeing how far I could bend it without breaking. My shirt felt sweaty. Six more blocks to Ashby House, to the newspaper, to my last day of freedom.

What else would I rather be doing today? Wasn't Direct Action supposed to be my dream project? Besides, we had to go all out if we were going to get it to the printer the next day.

The next day. The first day of the rest of my life in jail. Early Monday morning, Lyle and I would head for Santa Rita.

General population. Would we be kept together? Would we see each other in the cafeteria? Why hadn't I stayed in jail those last four days, when there were fifty men? Now it was two of us.

Three, actually. We'd heard that one other blockader would be there, a guy named Thad whom Lyle knew a little. With luck, we'd all be kept together, but it wasn't like we'd have any choice in the matter.

In a way, I was ready to go. Get it over with. A cloud of gloom had hung over me since I got out of the tents. It wasn't just fear of jail. It was a feeling of unfinished business. I craved some way to put the gloom behind me. I tried to recall the burst of empowerment I had felt the previous year. This year, life since my release felt like treading water. Or molasses. Hopefully finishing my jail time would give me a new perspective.

I crossed the street and headed up the front walk. Even though I'd been there the day before, the walls struck me as dirtier, the couches more broken-down. The room wasn't as crowded as I expected, considering it was the final day of production. Mort, Claudia, Daniel, and Holly. The thirties crowd. Mort looked up as I came in and offered me a beer, which I accepted but didn't open.

Holly looked relieved to see me. "Can we check-in? I really need a break."

My brow furrowed. I didn't want to pressure her to stay, but I couldn't see how we'd finish if she left. "Are you coming back later?"

"I'll come back in the morning to wrap it up." She stretched and yawned. "It'll be okay. Jenny and Angie said they'll stay late tonight, and Sara should be here soon."

I nodded and ran my hand through my hair. Maybe we could do it. Angie in particular had been a big help this issue, making a production chart that helped us organize the twenty-four pages more systematically than our old method of twenty-four separate scraps of note paper.

Where was Angie now? Maybe she and Jenny were getting something to eat. The two of them had just moved in together, in an apartment in central Oakland. That might have started the rumor mill churning if Jenny and Raoul hadn't hooked up about the same time. Somehow I didn't picture Angie joining them in a threesome.

Holly gave me a briefing. All of the stories were proofread, but several pages of layout hadn't even been started, and none of the 24 pages was finalized. We had our work cut out for us.

Sara arrived a few minutes later. She greeted Holly warmly, but her face clouded as they talked. I went over to join them.

"Sara just got another letter from Karina," Holly told me. "We were discussing whether to run it."

Karina. Would she ever get out of jail? "How's she doing?" I asked.

Sara's expression softened. "She's okay, considering she still has a couple of weeks to go. But I saw Madrigan, who got thirty days for a first arrest. She's out now, but she's pretty shaken up. She doesn't ever want to get arrested again."

My chest tightened. Neither would I, probably. Not for a long while.

Sara rubbed the letter between her fingers, as if savoring the texture of the paper. "The only sad part is, Karina is pretty depressed that they didn't stop the MX test. She thought if there had been more people, they could have stopped it."

"I agree," said Daniel from across the room. "And in the end, most of us got our charges dropped. The government apparently has its quota of sacrificial victims. It's a shame that more people weren't willing to put their bodies on the line."

Claudia had been working quietly at the main table. Just the previous week, she had announced her resignation from the LAG staff. Except for the Strategy Proposal, she seemed to be withdrawing from the fray. But apparently she couldn't resist a jibe. "Given how brilliantly-organized the action was, and given the sentences that some people got, I'd say we're lucky that VAC could only get thirty people arrested."

Sara flinched. Holly leveled her gaze on Claudia. "I think we should be proud of those who did the June action."

Claudia tilted her head. "Oh, sure. But after what happened with the March action, with people getting shipped to Arizona and no one having a clue where anyone was or what was going on, it was obvious that VAC wasn't credible. You can't do federal protests and think everything is going to come out right just because your process is pure."

"It's a tough call," I said. "Everyone wanted to stop the MX test, but people were exhausted by the March action."

Daniel folded his arms across his chest. "Surely we're more committed than that," he said. "If we're unwilling to make sacrifices, how can we expect to stop the arms race?"

GLOBAL ACTION

Mobilization for Survival Conference Sets 1984 Program

1984 ACTIVISTS CALENDAR

Spring

Summer

Fall

CAMPAIGNS

Nuclear Free Zone

First Strike Euromissile

Electoral Strategy

Deadly Connections

West Coast Mobe Affiliates Meeting Regularly

Strengthening Direct Action Network

NUCLEAR FREE

Evaluation

mobilization FOR SURVIVAL
853 Broadway, Room 2109
New York, NY 10003
212-533-0008

Following International Day, Direct Action continued devoting pages to international activist news.

"I hate to disillusion you," Claudia muttered, "but a bunch of anarchists running around on an Air Force base isn't going to stop the arms race."

Mort had been working in silence, but now he laughed caustically. "No more than a bunch of White middle-class peace groups holding coordinated protests on the Solstice. I hope no one is proposing another International Day for next Summer before we evaluate this one."

Holly sighed, as if to say she'd heard it all before. But Daniel turned to face Mort. "If we waited for some people to finish evaluating," he said dryly, "we'd still be debating whether to do International Day *this* year."

"Well, we need some debate," Mort said. "Are we going to remain a ghettoized peace movement, or are we going to build a coalition that might actually change something?"

Daniel rolled his eyes. "This idealization of coalitions, of trying to link existing groups, ignores the fact that there are millions of people who are opposed to militarism, but aren't involved in any group. The old forms don't attract them. They're waiting for a new paradigm."

"New paradigms," Mort sputtered. "What scares people about building a local coalition is, we would have to sit in a meeting with people who aren't exactly like us. That's the challenge, not sharing new-age psychobabble with people halfway around the world."

Daniel started to respond, but Holly cleared her throat and rattled the stack of production notes she was holding. "I need to get going," she said sharply. She gestured toward Sara and me. "Are you two clear on what needs to get done tonight?"

Sara looked at me and nodded uncertainly.

"We've got it," I told Holly. I followed her out onto the porch. Her face was blank, as if she had dissociated from the turmoil inside.

I put my arm around her shoulders. "Are you doing okay? You want me to walk you partway home?"

"No, I'll be fine. I just can't stand it in there." She shook her head and looked at me sadly. "I'll see you at home tonight. Don't stay too late. It's our last night together."

Our last night. I hadn't thought of it that way. "I won't stay past ten," I said.

She gave me a quick kiss and started away, then suddenly turned back. "Don't forget to call Tai about his photos of the blockade!"

"I already talked to him. Have a good walk home."

When I went back inside, the air felt stagnant. I walked across the room and opened a window. Of course I agreed with Mort and Claudia, politically. But did they have to drive such a sharp wedge between themselves and the International Day crowd? With Claudia promoting the Strategy Proposal for the LAG Congress, you'd think she might be a bit more diplomatic in her criticisms. Then again, having resigned from the staff, maybe she didn't give a damn anymore.

And Mort seemed out of touch. He'd just been heaping scorn on Holly's project. Now he came over to tell me he was leaving. "Let's get together for a beer later this week," he said like nothing had happened.

"I don't think that will work," I said. "I've got an appointment at Santa Rita."

"Oh, right," he said, patting me on the shoulder. "Hope it goes well. Give me a call when you get out."

When I get out? That seemed like a long way off. And I wasn't that excited about hanging out with him, anyway. People have feelings, I felt like saying. Don't you get it?

DIRECT ACTION

MID-JULY 1983

PUBLISHED BY LIVERMORE ACTION GROUP

WE MADE IT!

NOW WHAT?

LAG Congress Convenes Expected to Reject Nukes

M L KING RALLY AUGUST 27

"WE STILL HAVE A DREAM"

Coalition Forms for October Euromissiles Protests

Direct Action #8, July 1983

But I wasn't up for tackling it right then. "I'll talk to you next weekend," I said as he headed out.

I tried to get back to layout, but Claudia corralled me before she left. "Is the Strategy Proposal on page one?"

"Yeah," I said. "It's under my Congress story." I knew she wanted top billing, but I didn't think that was smart. "A lot of people see the Strategy Proposal as delaying decisions on actions for next year. If we put it first, people will say it's a conspiracy to stifle dissent."

"They'll get over it."

Unlikely, I wanted to say. The Congress was shaping up as a royal mess. Even among the action-faction, there was no consensus on *which* actions to call. Vandenberg? Livermore? Diablo Canyon? An urban focus on military corporations?

And hovering over the whole tableau was the likelihood that the Democratic Convention was going to be in San Francisco the following Summer. What a jumble.

In that sense, the Strategy Proposal was the answer — step back, take stock, and regroup. But the way Claudia put it, the proposal seemed more like punishment than perspective.

Luckily for my mood, as Claudia took off, Jenny and Angie returned, bringing Raoul with them. "Let's have some music," Raoul called out. "How can anyone work in this oppressive silence?" He pulled a reggae tape out of his pocket and popped it into the boombox, cranking up the bass till the speakers started rattling. "That's more like it. Now I can think."

Angie came over and gave me a warm hug. Her hair was done in a bunch of small braids that fell over my arm. "Aren't you done yet?" she said as she stepped back. "What have you been doing, standing around talking the whole time?"

"Not far from the truth," I said.

Angie sat down on the floor in front of her layout board. She was doing the front page, with my Congress story at the top.

"Think you'll be at the Congress?" I asked her.

"No," she said. She straightened the headline, eyed it for a moment, then pasted it into place. "I'm going backpacking up at Point Reyes. I'll be gone all that week."

I imagined her hiking across the coastal foothills, swimming in the ocean, sitting beside a secluded campfire. It certainly sounded more appealing than two days of meetings.

Jenny set her Bay Area pages down opposite Angie. "Shouldn't we say something about the October protests? We already consensed to do an action." Jenny glanced across the table at Raoul, then back at me. "Maybe we could talk about street actions in the financial district."

"I don't know if we should be so specific," I said. "Some people want to stay focused on Livermore. It's up to the Congress to decide where the October demo will be."

Raoul sat down in a folding chair and eyed me warily. "San Francisco is where we should be. A lot of people I know have been talking about a roving protest of military corporations in San Francisco, with street theater and autonomous CD actions. It's perfect for the Euromissiles demo."

I folded my arms across my chest and nodded. "I think we can float the proposal in the paper as long as it doesn't sound like a free-for-all. Melissa and Nathaniel will flip if they picture a mob running through downtown."

Raoul rocked back in his chair. "They're worried about losing control. In the City, it's harder for the pacifists to enforce their code of discipline, where everyone meekly submits to mass arrest."

"Well, if you put it like that, I guarantee it'll never get consensed," I said. "You have to emphasize that it's an AG-based action, and connect it to corporations that are developing the weapons that Livermore Lab designs. If you frame it right, people might go for it."

He squinted at me. Then a slow smile spread across his face. "Sure, we'll call it a street festival. It's the week before Halloween. People can come in costumes. We'll make it sound like a real fun action to bring your kids to."

I wasn't sure how serious he was, but I needed to get some work done on the paper. Raoul clicked the reggae tape off. "Mort left a Nigerian tape that's really good," I said.

"I want to put on this rap mix I made." For once, I didn't mind being one-upped by Raoul. I'd been wanting to get some rap records. Maybe I could make a copy of his tape.

We worked through the hip-hop mix, the Nigerian tape, and a couple more. By ten, most people were wrapping up. Sara, Angie, and I surveyed the progress: every page started, but a lot of loose ends. The two of them agreed to come back and help Holly the next morning, and Raoul volunteered to drive the finished boards to the printer.

They'd get it done, I knew. Still, it felt odd to walk away. It was the first time that I hadn't been present at the end of production.

"Want a ride home?" Jenny asked as we descended the front stairs.

"No, thanks. I want to enjoy the walk. It'll be my last for a few days."

"That's right," Jenny said. "You're going to Santa Rita tomorrow, aren't you?" She gave me a quick, tight hug. "I hope it goes okay."

"Thanks," I said, surprised not to have thought about jail for the past three hours. Score one for the magazine.

Global Resistance

Conflict in the Middle East : The U.S. Neither Neutral Nor Peacekeepers

Global Resistance

The U.S. in Lebanon

Rapid Deployment And Nuclear War

Who's Who in Lebanese Politics

What Can You Do?

In addition to activist news, Direct Action began carrying news and analysis on global hot-spots such as the Middle East.

I moved toward Raoul, but he fended off a hug by thrusting out his big hand to shake. "Good luck," he said. "Let's catch an A's game after you get out." He seemed unusually serious, and the reality of the next day started to hit me.

I looked at Angie, unsure what to say. She looked up at me soberly. "Remember — don't bend over in the shower!"

We all burst out laughing. Angie gave me a long hug. "Think of me," I said as we parted.

On the walk home, I tried to appreciate the shadowy trees and unkempt lawns along Dana Street. But my mind was shackled to jail. In twelve hours, I would be behind bars. What a waste. As if I'm a menace to society.

Holly was still up when I got home, seated at the table. She turned in her chair as I closed the door. Her face was somber. "Caroline is quitting."

"Quitting?"

She nodded slowly. "I just got done talking to her. She's turning in her resignation tomorrow night at Coordinating Council."

I dropped my daypack. "What a shame."

"She's just burned out," Holly said. Tears pooled in her eyes. I knelt next to her and put my arms around her. Was it the first time I had ever seen her cry? "Caroline was my best friend in LAG," she said. "It was hard enough when she pulled away in jail, but now I might never see her again...."

I groped for something to say. "Maybe she'll reconsider." But I didn't believe it myself. Still, it baffled me. How could anyone in such a powerful position — staffperson for the whole group — give it up? Take a sabbatical, or ask for different responsibilities. But why quit?

"It'll really be different in the office without Caroline and Claudia," I said.

"It's hard to imagine it without Caroline." She shook her head. "Maybe Jenny will pick up the slack. But it won't be the same."

For a moment, I was lost in Holly's sadness, and in the surprise of Caroline resigning. What would it mean for LAG to lose another of its key people?

But nothing could distract me long from Santa Rita. Ten hours. The clock was ticking, louder and louder. Would I be able to sleep tonight? What kind of dreams would I have? What time did I have to be up? My ride was coming at 6:30 a.m. Maybe I could sleep till 6:10. No, can't be late for jail. 6:00.

Holly looked at me curiously. "Are you okay?"

"Huh? Oh, yeah, I guess. Just thinking about what time I have to wake up."

"Too soon, probably," she said. "Let's go to bed." We stood up. She led the way down the hall.

In the bedroom, Holly lit three candles. I put on a tape of Renaissance lute music. The rippling notes wove a delicate tapestry around us. We lay down side by side. Our legs intertwined, and we gazed at each other. Holly brushed a strand of hair off her face. A slight smile rested on her lips. I'll be here for you, her eyes seemed to radiate. I'll hold you in my heart.

I looked at her steadily, trying silently to convey that my love would be unchanged by our time apart. But I had a hard time sustaining my focus. Not that I doubted I would still love Holly after jail. But I had a hard time envisaging a time beyond jail. Santa Rita was a looming vortex — time would whirl round and round, and only by chance might I someday be flung up on the far side.

Gradually Holly drew me away from my brooding. Making love was sweet, tinged with the sadness of parting. Afterwards we lay quietly, holding each other, not speaking a word. I ran my hand up the outside of her thigh, up her back, coming to rest on her neck, beneath her thick hair.

I held her to me, closed my eyes, and tried to memorize the feeling. Finally she faded off to sleep. I wished I could do the same, but my mind wouldn't let go of these last moments of freedom. I reached over and put on a Bach Cantata, took a toke off my pipe, and rolled over onto my back. I'd served time in a warehouse, a gymnasium, and a circus tent. At Concord, I'd even been in a cell-block, but it was protesters-only. This time I was going to jail.

Monday, July 25, 1983

Mort drove Lyle and me out to Santa Rita early Monday morning. We were quiet as we swung onto the freeway outside of Berkeley. Mort put on a South African jazz tape. My last music until I get out, I thought. I had the same album at home, and usually I loved it. But now the saxophones set me slightly on edge.

Lyle rolled his window partway down, and a welcome gust of fresh air hit my face. I didn't know Lyle very well. He was a friend of Mort's from Overthrow Cluster and came to pinball sometimes, but he was pretty reserved. Still, he seemed like a solid person, someone I could count on. He had three days left to serve, so I'd have one day by myself at the end unless we hooked up with Thad, the other protester serving time that week.

As we started through the Caldecott Tunnel, I fingered my personal library. Each entering inmate was entitled to three books. Lyle was taking action novels, to have something to barter for cigarettes or shampoo. But I wanted to use the time productively. After much inner debate, I chose a tome on Elizabethan drama to get me back on track with my history studies; a collection of essays by Lenin to sharpen my political perception; and in case the other two seemed too ponderous, *The Trial* by Kafka.

We passed out of the hills into the Livermore Valley and turned off the highway onto the jail access road. The sparse grass of the sprawling grounds was withered to a pale yellow, stretching toward the distant hills. Several perimeters of razor wire surrounded the core compound like cheap necklaces. Behind them were rows of dilapidated barracks.

We pulled into the visitor's lot in front of the concrete command post. In our anxiety to be punctual, we wound up getting there twenty minutes early. Of course they made us wait — no early admittance. We talked a little, but the conversation kept dying.

Finally at 8 a.m. the gate swung open. We bid adieu to Mort, stepped through the portal, and walked down a fifty foot open-air corridor. Chain-link fence formed the walls, with tightly-bunched coils of razor wire as the ceiling. Forget escaping from this sidewalk.

The guards at the front desk studied our IDs, double-checked our prints to make sure we weren't impostors, and confiscated our loose change, keys, pens, and paper. Once they checked our books for drugs and weapons, though, they handed them back.

A guard ushered us down a moldy concrete tunnel to a holding tank. As we stepped in, the steel gate slammed behind us, echoing off the walls.

The cell was fifteen feet square and ringed with locker-room benches. Urine and lysol mingled in the stale air. The shiny white walls had aged to a gray-yellow. A tiny slit window, permanently sealed, allowed a glimpse of a gravel lot and a plain white wall beyond it.

Another prisoner was placed in with us, a middle-aged man who greeted us in Spanish. Lyle returned the greeting. A minute or two later, the guard came and led the guy away. I wondered if we'd see him again on the inside. And whether he'd act like he knew us or not.

A while later, a young White guy was stuck in with us. He was clearly drunk, and with no prompting gave us a complete confession — he'd been busted trying to enter a freeway via the exit ramp. He seemed to plead for sympathy or absolution, but we didn't have much of either to offer.

A stumpy guard strutted by. He recognized us as protesters, and took a little jab. "You guys had it easy before, out in the tents. Now you're going to see what jail is really like."

"I hope so," I answered. "I'm sure it'll be educational."

He harumphed. "I'm sure it will be."

We were left sitting for what seemed like several hours. Finally, a guard fetched me, Lyle, and four men from other holding cells. I was glad to be on with the process.

We were led to the far end of the dank hallway. The other four prisoners were Black. None of them was talking. Lyle and I kept quiet, too.

The guard led us around a corner to a big roll-up window, where we received our jail garb. I had expected some sort of uniform or jumpsuit, but what I got looked suspiciously like what I was taking off — faded blue jeans and a T-shirt. One guy got a shirt stamped "Santa Rita," but mine was plain gray.

As we started to undress, several new guards arrived. I braced for a search, but they didn't even bother to pat us down. We got to keep our own socks and underwear, and no one seemed to notice that I was wearing two pair of each. I pulled on the jeans, which were a few sizes too big. I tried to tuck in my T-shirt to pad them out, but it was too small to stay tucked.

The worst part was losing my tennis shoes. I'd assumed we'd keep our own shoes, and had stuffed a couple of pair of earplugs into the toes. But now I was losing the shoes altogether. And for real junk. Although some guys got what looked like old bowling shoes, Lyle and I each got a pair of red plastic sandals.

Two guards lined us up and led us out a heavy metal door. "This way, gentlemen," one said, leading us up a gravel road. "Stay in line."

Gentlemen, he called us, as he treated us like errant children.

As we passed a compact concrete building off to the left, one of the other prisoners said, "That's Graystone." I recognized the name — the high-security solitary confinement stronghold.

A hundred feet up the road we approached a chain-link gate monitored by a guard booth. Up to that moment, I had been feeling more curious than apprehensive. As we filed past the booth, I saw several guards eyeing us like we were cattle being driven to slaughter. A chill ran through me. I felt vulnerable, naked to their power.

Inside the gate, a two-lane road stretched for about four blocks, where it seemed to dead end at a tall fence. To the left were four squat buildings made of cinder block and corrugated metal, which one of our comrades identified as the cafeteria, shower, weight room, and infirmary. A long row of barracks lined the right side of the road. Each cluster of three barracks was completely encased inside rusty chain-link grating.

The grating looked familiar. Where had I seen it before? Seventh grade gym class, of course. Seventh grade, when I changed schools and was the youngest kid at a strange junior high.

We were walking quickly, and a sweat broke on my forehead. I used my shirttail to wipe it off. I glanced over at Lyle, but he seemed lost in his own thoughts.

Our first stop was the commissary, where we got our check-in supplies. The area teemed with men, some buying stuff, others hustling or bartering. While we waited in the commissary line, I sensed the other inmates checking us out, which felt a little intimidating. I looked around at the fifty or so men in the vicinity. What stood out was the racial demographics. Three-quarters were Black. Most of the rest seemed White or Latino, with one or two Native Americans. Asian Americans were absent, which seemed ironic, given the compound's origins as a World War II interment camp for Japanese Americans.

Despite standing next to Lyle, I felt isolated. I was not only a White guy in a mainly Black neighborhood, but when I thought about the books I had brought, I got the feeling I wasn't exactly going to blend in with the Whites, either.

A short Latino man in a muscle shirt walked by and looked at us inquisitively. "You guys protesters?"

"Yeah, from the Livermore blockade," I told him, watching for his response. He nodded noncommittally and walked away.

We got our check-in supplies: a toothbrush, a comb, a motel-sized bar of soap, a pencil stub, a few sheets of paper, and two stamped envelopes. No sooner had Lyle and I received this bounty than we were accosted by an inmate beseeching us to give him the paper and envelopes. I wanted the paper, but gave him the envelopes. Another guy hit us up for soap, but I wanted to keep what I had. He went away grumbling over his shoulder.

Lyle and I were led back to the first barracks inside the fence, a nearly-empty transitional dorm. I was glad to be isolated. It seemed safe, outside the main social scene, and I hoped we'd just be left in there for the duration of our sentence. We staked out a couple of cots in the back. The beds had sheets, but no blankets. I knew from our time in the tents how cold it could get at night out here in the valley. We went outside and asked a guard, who informed us that we had received our blankets on the way in.

"No, we didn't get any," Lyle said.

"Well, then you blew it, gentlemen," he said. When we protested, he finally told us to check with the shift officer back at the booth.

The cage around our barracks wasn't locked, so we walked back out and told the gate officer our story. He looked bored. "Not much I can do," he said.

I turned away. "Jesus," I muttered, prepared to spend four nights freezing rather than beg. Lyle persisted, though, and the guard finally relented. He stepped outside his booth and pointed his finger like a pistol. "See that truck just outside the gate? There's a laundry cart right behind it. Run down there and get one blanket apiece."

I looked at him, then at Lyle. How stupid did he think we were? Was this some kind of rookie hazing? Were they going to nab us on escape charges and throw us into Graystone?

The guard looked annoyed at our hesitation. "The gate isn't going to close! Go on, hurry up." His irritation seemed so sincere that Lyle and I went for it. The cart was where he had said it would be. We grabbed a blanket each and hustled back to the gate. As we passed the guard booth, the officer didn't even look up.

We went back into the barracks. As we lay on our cots talking, two Black inmates, one tall and one stocky, came in and looked around. The stocky guy, who had dark, glistening skin, gave us the once-over and apparently decided we weren't a problem. They shoved a bunk bed out into the center of the room. The stocky guy went to watch the door, while the tall guy clambered atop the bunk and reached up into a light fixture. He pulled down a paper bag, took something out, and restashed the rest. They shoved the bunk back into place and exited, never speaking a word to us.

We were silent for a moment, making sure they weren't going to return. "Phew," Lyle finally said. "So that's how they do it."

"Could be useful knowledge," I said with a quick laugh. "Maybe we should stash our books for future blockaders."

We settled in to read for a while, till we were called to dinner by a trustee, a longer-term inmate who was something like a Resident Assistant for the barracks. He pointed us toward the cafeteria. "Are you guys blockaders?"

His tone was friendly, and I felt my body relax a notch. "Yeah, we were busted in June and have some time left to serve."

"That's good," he said with a trace of an accent. "I'm glad somebody is protesting."

As we followed him out toward the mess hall, I wondered whether he was Latino. I frowned. Why did it matter? Every person we passed, I found myself pigeonholing into a racial group. I wondered how much was the lack of other stimuli, and how much was due to my being in the minority.

The cafeteria, with a concrete floor and metal ceiling, looked like the mess hall at Boy Scout camp. Only here, everything was bolted down. The tables and benches were stainless steel, as were the food trays and the serving counters. At best there would have been a lot of clattering, but everyone seemed to take special joy in slamming metal against metal. Over this incessant racket, conversations were conducted in shouts, punctuated by fists pounding on the resonant tables.

We were the tail end of the chow line, although a few other guys straggled in. Some of them cut in front of us, but what could we do? New guys are at the bottom of the pecking order.

The food was served with great panache. The dispensary window was so low that we couldn't see the workers' faces. Two plastic-gloved hands would slam a partitioned tray on the counter. Big metal spoons splatted gobs of food onto the tray. A carton of milk and an apple were hand-dropped, and the ensemble was shoved out at the eager diner.

Lyle and I made our way to an empty stretch of table. We sat on opposite sides, and could barely hear each other.

Most of the inmates sat in racially segregated clusters. Near us, a table of Blacks and another of Chicanos were exchanging loud put-downs. Some of the guys were laughing, but others looked more aggravated. For once, I was glad there were plenty of guards around.

Here and there, I noticed a man eating alone. One guy stared blankly into space, but most of the solitaries kept their heads down. Probably to avoid accidental eye contact, I figured. I glanced appreciatively at Lyle, glad for his company.

The food was short on taste, but at least it was filling, in marked contrast to the National Guard fare in the tents. Still, all the clanging metal didn't make me want to linger. Lyle and I ate quickly. We tossed our trays into a bin, and under the watchful eyes of two guards returned our silverware.

We went back to our barracks, where we got a rude surprise. While we ate dinner, someone had pilfered our soap, combs, and toothbrushes, Lyle's sci-fi novels, and my spare socks.

Lyle seemed to take it in stride, but I felt rattled. Only my obscure taste had kept my books from being swiped, too. Was it the druggies? The guards? Surely not the trustee...

I let Lyle borrow Kafka, and we agreed we'd each carry one book with us at all times.

A bit later, our trustee came and told us we were being moved down to barracks number four. So much for our private barracks. We gathered our blankets and our scant supplies and followed the trustee down the road. At least we were being kept together. At the second-to-last complex, a guard unlocked the rusted metal grating and ushered us into our new home.

As we walked through the door, Lyle pointed to a tattered, hand-lettered sign: "No stealing!"

We had entered the barracks near the rear. The building was about a hundred feet long by thirty feet wide, with walls twelve feet high. A ring of windows which appeared to have no glass lined the top two feet of the walls. The walls and ceiling were painted in a dark green that reminded me of football bleachers.

Three steel picnic tables were bolted to the floor in the rear. Several guys playing dominoes barely glanced up at us. Beyond them, a wide opening in the rear wall led to a toilet room.

Arrayed along the two long walls were about twenty-five bunk beds. Between each bunk was a wardrobe cabinet. Across from the door, one cabinet stood open and glistened with shiny color. It took a moment for me to realize the wardrobe was lined with centerfold pin-ups.

Thad, the other protester we had heard about, came back to say hello. He was a short, thin White man around twenty-five years old. Lyle knew Thad a little, and I vaguely recognized him. He wasn't real friendly, and didn't seem thrilled when Lyle and I secured top bunks near his. I was surprised at first, then realized that he might have deliberately come to jail alone, as some sort of personal challenge. We might be spoiling his solo experience.

As I set my books on my bunk, I noticed several other inmates checking us out. Were we intruders, interlopers? Or a welcome distraction, a curiosity? Gradually, the others turned back to their own affairs.

Our new trustee, a Black guy about thirty, filled us in on a few details about barracks life. He also told us that we wouldn't get a work assignment, since we were in for such a short time.

A work assignment. I hadn't even considered that. I might have been put on a chain gang. I wondered if other inmates would resent our not having to work.

The trustee returned to watch the TV that was blaring in the front of the barracks. I'd been dimly aware of it before, but only then did I tune in to what people were watching: "Jeopardy." Twenty inmates sitting on a semicircle of cots were trying to outguess the TV contestants, without much luck. Not that I could do any better. The capital of Assyria? Got me. But there was something comforting about the familiar patter.

Lyle and I talked with Thad for a while, who told us that he hadn't had very many hassles in the two days he'd been in, and had gotten to know a few people. Thad was doing time for the Good Friday action, and had six days left to serve, so he'd be around a day longer than I would. That was a relief. Even if he wasn't overjoyed at my presence, at least I wouldn't be totally alone after Lyle left.

The barracks were lit by two rows of bare lightbulbs screwed into the twelve-foot roof. Some were burned out, but I was lucky to have one over my bunk, near enough to read by.

I stretched out on my back and opened the Elizabethan drama book. It was hard to tune out the TV, let alone the game table in the back of the barracks, where they were playing high-impact dominoes. No one slid their pieces into position — they slammed them onto the metal tabletop, interspersed with cursing and arguing, mainly in Spanish.

I turned onto my side and angled to catch the light better. I was facing the front of the barracks, and I looked past my book to see the twenty or so guys gathered on a ring of army cots watching TV. "Jeopardy" was over, replaced by a cop show. That my roommates would choose an action show didn't surprise me. But they seemed to be cheering for the wise-cracking cops. I guess everyone wants to back a winner.

One Black guy near the TV turned and looked back in my direction. I looked back at my book, but not soon enough. The guy stood up and made his way back toward my bunk. He was about my height, with short hair and an odd tilt to his head. I concentrated on my book, but he came right up to the side of my bunk. I leaned up on one elbow and met his eyes, which seemed sullen. He looked slowly up at the lightbulb, then back at me.

My chest tightened. Was a lightbulb thirty feet from the TV really causing a problem? Or was he just irritated that I was trying to read? Finally, without a word, he walked away. I felt relieved.

But a moment later he returned holding a long stick. He stopped next to my bunk and glared up at me. Was this for real? I put down my book, keeping my eyes on the stick. Lyle and Thad were somewhere else. I was alone. The guy gestured toward the light with the stick. I got the message. But somehow I knew I couldn't give in. I had to draw the line somewhere. Might as well be here. Anyway, if he tries to hit me, he has a bad angle. I stared back at him. If he wants the light off, let him climb up the next bunk and unscrew it himself.

He glowered at me, then jabbed at the light with the stick. I flinched, then realized the stick had a rubber cup on the end, which he used to unscrew the bulb. He stared at me again, apparently daring me to screw it back in.

I wanted to keep reading. Without the light it was impossible. I searched for some response, but I knew whose turf I was on. I took a deep breath, then looked at the lightbulb and shook my head, trying to convey my aggravation. But I made no move to screw it back in. I wasn't going to push my luck that far.

Apparently satisfied, the guy put the stick down and swaggered back to his cop show. I shoved my book aside and scowled. Gradually I realized other people had been watching the drama. Damn. Had our run-in been private, that might be the end of it. But a public confrontation, that was different. What if the guy pushed it further? What if I became a target to prove his toughness?

What a great start. One day, one enemy. Maybe he had a short attention span, and would forget it by the next day.

Soon after, the guards ordered everyone onto their bunks for bed-check. I felt a sense of relief as they went through and counted us. Did guards stay in the barracks all night? I wished they would.

As they finished their count, I reflected on my chronic end-of-day-malaise in the tents. Surprisingly, I hadn't even considered that it would return here. Tension, yes. But depression? So far, the drama of the day's events was keeping me from sinking too low. Besides, even if I still had several days to serve, I felt a distinct sense of accomplishment as the lights went down. I'd made it through my first day in jail. One down, three to go.

Tuesday, July 26, 1983

I SLEPT RIGHT through breakfast. Gummy oatmeal and cold toast couldn't match the extra hour of sleep I got after my fifty snoring roommates had gone off to eat.

I whiled away the morning reading and talking with Lyle and Thad. One inmate approached us to talk, but he wasn't very lucid, and we didn't try to detain him when he wandered away.

The phones were available any time the barracks were unlocked. But with all the cutting in line, it looked hopeless. And after the lightbulb incident, I didn't feel like another run-in.

I didn't really feel like talking with anyone on the outside, anyway. Holly and I had been distant enough when we were in the tents. This would feel even more remote. How could she or anyone on the outside begin to grasp where I was? They'd probably try to cheer me up. No, thanks. Being in jail seemed easier to handle if I wasn't reminded of the outside world.

The morning droned on. I'd almost reached the chapter on Shakespeare in my Elizabethan volume, which felt like the payoff, the climax of the book. But my attention was slacking as the day grew warmer.

Lunchtime finally rolled around. Everyone was sent back to their barracks, and we were summoned one compound at a time. Thad was ahead of Lyle and me, talking to another inmate. We joined the end of the line. But before we made it to the front, the next barracks came filing in. Half the guys cut in ahead of Lyle and me, scarcely acknowledging our presence. Oh well, there was plenty of food, and we'll get there eventually. Assuming yet another barracks didn't arrive before we got served.

A few more people cut in front of us. Where do you set the limit? Speaking up risked a fight. Was it worth a showdown?

But I remembered getting hazed in junior high, the same nonsense around lunch-line cuts, and how it didn't stop till I fought one of the instigators. Did I have to do that here? If I were around longer, probably. Maybe with a four-day sentence, I could sidestep it.

Luckily, the line moved quickly, and we got our food without further ado. We made our way over to our familiar table and ate in noisy peace.

Later that afternoon, Lyle and I were sitting by the road in front of our compound, when a White guy from our barracks approached us. "I'm Gabe," he said. "I could tell you guys were blockaders. I met another blockader a couple of weeks ago."

Gabe reminded me of street people I knew on Telegraph Avenue, but harder-edged. He was about thirty-five, I guessed, though his weathered face looked older. He was shorter than me, but his arms were more muscular, and were ringed with tattoos, professional and homemade. He readily confessed to having been in and out of jail all his adult life, for theft, marijuana dealing, or vagrancy. "I'm a public nuisance, you could say," he said with a smile.

I liked him right off. For his part, he seemed genuinely interested in why protesters would voluntarily go to jail. "Jail is okay," he said. "I've been through worse. But why would someone with a home and a job want to be here?"

I laughed. Lyle tilted his head back. "I wouldn't exactly say that we *want* to come here," he said. "We did the protest to draw attention to Livermore Weapons Lab."

That's right, I remembered. That's why I'm here. I knew there was some bigger reason than getting closure on my previous incarceration.

Lyle asked Gabe when he was getting out.

"A little over three weeks. I left a car down in Hayward that almost works. If it hasn't been towed, I'm going to get it running and get the hell out of California."

"Where are you going to go?"

"I'm not sure. Depends on how much money I have for gas."

I asked where he was from. "Well, I've moved around a lot," he said. "Never one place for long. I'm what they call a 'lumpen.'"

"A lumpen-proletariat?"

"Yeah, a lumpen. People like me, we never get a real job. We drift around, and finally wind up in the army or jail. Me, I'm too old for the army, so here I am." He shrugged. "At least there's regular meals."

There was something surreal about hearing this guy call himself a lumpen. "Have you read Marx?" I asked.

"No, not really," he told me. "I just heard some of the ideas."

I made a mental note to leave my Lenin essays behind with him. Our real bond, though, turned out to be music — specifically, Hank Williams. Somehow it came out that I was a folk singer, and he said he was, too. His repertoire was old country songs, and he sang me a few verses of Hank's "I'm So Lonesome I Could Cry." He had a rusty, mournful voice, and a poignant way, at the end of a line, of flipping up into falsetto and letting it trail off.

I sang him a number I'd written called "The Minimum Wage," which was set to the tune of a Hank Williams song:

It's lousy pay, but it's for the best
I'm sure if it was legal they'd pay me less
Than the Minimum Wage, yeah the Minimum Wage
You learn time's money when you earn it at the Minimum Wage.

He applauded when I finished. "That's it, exactly," he said. "If you're a lumpen, you're lucky to get minimum wage."

When dinner rolled around, Thad joined Lyle and me in the line. Gabe stopped to talk with someone else, and said he'd catch up with us.

The line was short, but immediately, guys started cutting in front of us. I tried to ignore them and pretend I didn't care. But then the lightbulb guy stepped up. He eyed me callously, then cut in front of me in a way that felt personal. My throat tensed up, and I knew I had to say something. It wasn't the worst of situations, with Lyle and Thad right there and guards nearby. In fact, I sort of wished a guard would walk our way. I would welcome a little show of authority right now. But no such luck.

"What's up?" I said in a shaky voice.

"What's up with you?" the guy spat back. "Got a problem?"

"Oh, just getting hungry," I said, trying to keep it light. "But I'm sure there's plenty of food."

He started to respond, but then hesitated. Something behind me seemed to have caught his eye. I snuck a look around — Gabe had rejoined us, and was glaring at the guy. Was I ever glad to see him!

"Got something to say?" Gabe said to him in a level voice.

The lightbulb guy turned his back on us. I was happy to let the matter go. Maybe he'd learned his lesson and would lay off.

But Gabe was just getting warmed up. "What's the problem? You have something to say? You can say it to me, I'm right here." A couple of other Black guys ahead of us turned around. Gabe's belligerence radiated in all directions.

Hey, it's all cool, let it go, I wanted to say to him. But maybe that would just aggravate him more. I looked at Lyle and Thad, who were staring at Gabe.

Luckily for us, the line was moving, and the lightbulb guy kept his back turned. The clatter of metal on metal made a long-distance argument impossible, and Gabe cooled off. But the whole situation had just gotten a lot more complex. It was hard enough having my own hassles, but now I was getting sucked into Gabe's. Who knew what past history he had with this guy? And now I was right in the middle of it.

The evening went quietly enough. I read for a while after dinner, but decided to unscrew the lightbulb on my own when the prime-time shows came on. I thought about going up to watch TV, but I still wasn't feeling confident about socializing. Maybe it was reserved seating. I stayed on my bunk.

Lyle and I talked a little, but that faded pretty quickly. He seemed absorbed in his own processes. I envied Thad, who seemed to have a knack for approaching other inmates. At the moment, he was off playing checkers.

At least there was enough light to write. I got out my pencil stub and paper and jotted down some notes. It seemed important to record my impressions while they were still fresh. Maybe someday I'd want to know what I was feeling. Bored, mainly. Like I'd never get to the end of the day, let alone get through two more.

At ten o'clock, the TV was turned off and the place settled in for the night. I pulled my army blanket snug. Two days down, two to go. I was surviving.

But the hardest part was still to come. Lyle was getting out the next day, and Thad didn't seem to want much to do with me. By mid-afternoon tomorrow, I would be on my own.

Wednesday, July 27, 1983

I SKIPPED BREAKFAST again and caught up on my sleep, which shortened the morning to a tolerable length. I'd had enough drama for a while, and turned to my Lenin essays. Maybe I'd develop a new revolutionary theory in prison. There was still time, if I thought fast.

The afternoon brought a special diversion — an Oakland A's baseball game on TV. Most of the guys spent the time outside anyway, but a few men stayed inside and watched.

I sat on the edge of a bunk, not saying much but sharing a few laughs with the other guys, especially a man named Eduardo. He was around forty, with thick arms and a missing front tooth. He kept making rude remarks about the TV announcers, peppering his jokes with Spanish idioms that I didn't understand but which still made me laugh.

During one commercial stretch he pulled out a photo of his kids to show me. It was smudged and dog-eared, but he cradled it in his palm like it was the Mona Lisa. "There's Eric, and Donnalynn, and that's Laurita," he said, pointing to the youngest. "She's three now." The kids smiled shyly at the camera, and Eduardo beamed back at them.

I looked at Eduardo — on the streets of Oakland, I'd probably feel too intimidated to speak to him. Yet here he was, showing me his kids....

Eduardo had been busted a year earlier for stealing a car. "I had to get my family to Bakersfield. I didn't even want the stupid car, I just wanted to get them to my parent's place before I went to Reno for a job."

"What happened?"

"I got caught and did six months. Then I got picked up again on a probation violation in June and sent here for the Summer."

"Are your kids still in Bakersfield?"

"Yeah. That's where I'm going as soon as I get out of here and get the money together." He looked over his shoulder, then smiled gently. "If I have to, I'll hot-wire a car. I miss my kids."

I nodded. It made total sense. Who could fault him for those priorities?

A while later, Lyle came over to say goodbye. We shook hands. He seemed embarrassed to be leaving me behind, and told me to call him when I got out. "Maybe I'll see you at pinball on Friday night," he said.

"Yeah, maybe so," I said, although Friday night seemed half an eternity away. Lucky guy, to be leaving now.

I walked out to the road with him and bid him adieu. Despite meeting Gabe and Eduardo, I still felt isolated. Well, at least I know a couple of people to sit with in the cafeteria, I thought.

Outside, the day was waxing hot. Stuck in long jeans, I was sweating, and my body itched all over. Could I really go another day without a shower? Even without soap and shampoo, it would feel good. Why hadn't I done it while Lyle was still here? Going it alone felt like a risk. But I decided to scout out the bathhouse.

As I walked by, I saw two White guys from my barracks head inside. I hated to admit it, but that made it seem safer. I could act like I was with them. I made a quick decision to go for it.

Inside was a chintzy locker room, with a row of old benches in the front, and five showerheads attached to the bare concrete of the rear wall. I bundled up my clothes and stuck them in a corner where I could keep an eye on them — all I needed was someone stealing them.

I spotted a sliver of soap on the floor. No one was near. Quickly I bent over and scooped it up. I rationed it out over my body, and coaxed a little lather for my matted hair. It probably just made it gummier, but even the idea of a shampoo was satisfying. The other White guys finished up, and I hastened to keep pace. Not having a towel shortened the process, and in no time, I was back outside, feeling refreshed and proud of my daring.

My luck lasted about five minutes. As I headed back up the road toward the barracks, who did I run into but the lightbulb guy and his pals. He strode away from them and approached me. I sucked in my stomach, ready to roll with the punches.

"Going somewhere?" he drawled at me. I saw no point in walking on, so I stopped and stared at him.

His companions stopped about ten feet away. For the moment, it was just me and him. He looked me up and down. "Pretty quiet, aren't you, White boy?"

"Give me a break," I said, not wanting to provoke him, but determined not to back down.

"Ain't gonna be no break, Whitey," he said. He made no move toward me, but I braced just the same.

"You got a problem with me?" I said, trying to keep my voice steady.

"Looks like I do, don't it?"

His friends moved in closer. My stomach churned. Should I run? The idea galled me. No way I'm moving until I have to. Not till I take at least one punch.

At that moment, two guards walked out of the nearby weight room. Would they intervene? They looked our way with no special concern, but one of the guys near me mumbled something, and several of the group started to move away. The lightbulb guy smirked at me as he turned to follow the others. "Looks like you escaped this time, Whitey."

Given a reprieve, I sputtered angrily at him. "You're real tough, aren't you? Do I look like I'm scared of you?"

He glared at me. His companions looked at me like I was crazy, but the guards were watching now, and my tormentors moved on down the road.

My stomach was tight with anger — at him, but even more at myself. What a stupid thing to do, try to show him up in front of his friends. Now he practically had to do something. And I couldn't count on Gabe or the guards being around to rescue me every time.

Even worse, it felt like the pressure had beaten me down. I had played right into the whole jailhouse game. Before I came in, I saw clearly how the system thrives on infighting. So what happens? I'm here three days, and I get sucked in just like everyone else.

I deliberately went to dinner late, hoping to avoid the guy, and it worked. I didn't even see him in the cafeteria. Back in the barracks, I decided to leave the lightbulb unscrewed. Lenin would have to wait. Hopefully I'd survive tonight, and then tomorrow I'd be out.

I hung out with Gabe for a while, which I figured gave me a little cover. Then midway through the evening a bunch of guards came in and ordered all of us to stand at the foot of our bunks.

The guards had been taking a head count several times a day. It felt like a formality, but this time, they actually came up short. At first I thought it was because Lyle had left, but then someone noticed that a shy, nerdy White guy who slept at the back of the barracks and kept to himself was missing.

The guards shut off the TV, the worst form of group punishment — as if it were our fault the guy was missing. We were ordered to sit on our own bunks, where we remained for the next hour. Well, at least I won't get hassled over the lightbulb, I thought.

Rumors circulated freely. Apparently the guy had been threatened by someone on his work crew, and it wasn't inconceivable that he had climbed over the inside fence and was hiding in the outlying field somewhere. Maybe he'd escaped altogether.

Finally we got word from the guards that the missing inmate had been discovered. The guy had been on laundry detail, and found a way to climb down an elevator shaft and hide. "He probably did it to get put in solitary," someone said. "At least he'll be away from whoever was threatening him."

Now there's a strategy, I thought. If I had more than one day to go, it might actually have appealed to me. But my getting out the next day was dependent on "good time." If I got put in solitary, they could keep me two more days. I'll take my chances with lightbulb dude.

By the time the head count was corrected, it was bedtime. As I lay back on my bunk, I felt a wave of relief. This was it! Get through tonight, and sometime tomorrow I would be out of here. For the first time in what seemed like weeks, I felt a lightness, almost a sense of release. My mind drifted forward to the next day. Up at the highway entrance was a McDonald's. That was probably the closest pay phone outside of the jail lobby. A plan formed in my mind. Get out, hike up the highway, eat a McBurger, and call Holly to tell her I was out and was catching a bus back to Berkeley.

One more day. I could make it.

Getting to sleep was hard. For the first time I thought of my friends back home. And one who wasn't at home — Karina. Sixty days in federal prison. How could she do it? I could barely do four without giving in to the pressure. I wondered when I'd see her again. Maybe I could write her a short letter the next morning, before I left. I turned phrases over in my mind as I drifted off to sleep.

Thursday, July 28, 1983

AFTER BREAKFAST the final morning, Gabe and I talked about my getting out. I felt awkward at being so excited, and it seemed to get him down.

Hanging out with Gabe was appealing, as a hedge against lightbulb dude. But our conversation was stilted. I got my copy of Lenin's essays and gave it to him. "I put my phone number in the front," I told him. "Call me after you get out." He said he would, then went off to use the toilet.

I paused beside my bunk, wondering what to do. At the front of the barracks, the TV was going full blast, and there were a dozen guys hanging out. Maybe I should join them. Even if the lightbulb guy showed up, he probably wouldn't pick a fight there.

Suddenly a shriek of pain tore through the barracks. A moment later, Gabe came staggering out of the toilet area. He clutched his face. Bright red blood streamed through his fingers.

Oh, shit. I took hold of the bunk bed for support. Someone must have jumped him. I stood frozen in my tracks as Gabe groped toward his bunk.

Two guards came running in. Their presence made me feel safer, and I started back toward Gabe. But the guards grabbed him and pulled him toward the door. Several more guards came running in. "Everyone stay where you are!" They ran into the toilet area. Who would they bring out? As if I needed to ask. Who did I know that might be laying for Gabe?

But the guards returned empty-handed. They looked at us accusingly. "What happened?" the head guard demanded.

"Maybe he fell and hit his head," someone ventured.

"Bullshit," the guard snarled.

No one was allowed to come or go. What if the loudspeaker called my name? I felt ashamed of my pettiness, and of having jumped to the conclusion that Gabe had been assaulted by Black guys. I was buying into the whole jail mentality.

Some of the other inmates talked about Gabe and what they thought might have happened. But none of it made any sense. I'd looked up as soon as Gabe screamed, and no one else came out of the toilet.

Our other barracks-mates were gradually allowed back in, and the story was retold. But no one could explain what had happened.

What with the blood and then my prejudiced reaction, I was feeling queasy, claustrophobic. Enough of this place. I needed some air.

Hoisting up my jeans, I headed out to walk on the road. Maybe my name would get called soon and I'd be done with this whole experience.

It was a balmy morning, with tufts of cloud occasionally hiding the sun. As I walked toward the gate, the main road was crowded with inmates. It felt odd to be walking through the crowd and not know anyone. I reversed my path and headed toward the deadend. I never had walked to the end of our little universe. Might as well see the whole place before I go.

I was still musing over what had happened to Gabe when I saw two Black guys walking directly toward me. I recognized them as companions of the lightbulb guy from the day before. I looked around for guards or some other support, but I'd gotten myself too far from the crowd. My gut tightened. Two on one — get ready.

One of them tilted his head back and squinted into the sun. "You're the guy who was hassling with Jerome yesterday."

No question who Jerome was. My mind raced. I spoke to the squinting guy, taking a step sideways so he wouldn't have to look into the sun. "Yeah, shoot, I didn't mean to be so hard on him. I'm sorry I called him a loser."

He flipped his hand as if dismissing my words. "It's bullshit," he said. The second guy nodded sharply.

They were right in my face. The second guy, who was shave-headed, poked his finger at me. "That stuff shouldn't happen. Jerome was whack, talking like that."

"What?"

"He had no reason to hassle you."

"Yeah," said his companion. "We know why you're here. It's cool. We told Jerome to chill."

I still couldn't quite believe what I was hearing, but I'd take any break I could get. "Tell Jerome I'm sorry for what I said, just the same. I won't see him, I'm leaving today."

"Good for you," the first guy said. "Where you from?"

"Berkeley."

"Cool. Maybe I'll see you at People's Park when I get out this Fall. I hang out there sometimes."

We shook hands, and they walked off. I smiled uncomfortably at my own assumptions — that because Jerome was Black, the other Black guys automatically took his side. That our lives outside would never intersect. And that I was the only one around here with any political awareness.

I went back to the barracks and looked around for Thad, just to have someone to tell the story to, but he was nowhere in sight. Shortly after, they called us for lunch, but even though the lightbulb hassle was resolved, I decided to stay behind and read. I'd save my appetite.

I was daydreaming about hamburgers when two guards escorted Gabe back into the barracks. He went to his bed and started to gather his stuff. He didn't notice me, so I climbed down from my bunk and went over to him. "Hey — are you okay?"

He looked up, startled. Across his forehead was a heavy bandage with bloody edges. He cast a nervous glance at the guards, but they weren't paying attention. Then he cracked a sly smile. "Yeah, doing great," he whispered. "They're putting me in the infirmary for a couple of days. You should have seen the babe who put this bandage on me!"

"So what happened?" I asked.

"I needed a break," he said. "I've done this before. You draw a little blood and they freak out. All I had to do was bang my head on the sink."

I looked at him dubiously, but he seemed so matter-of-fact that I finally believed him. "I gotta go now," he told me, reaching out to shake my hand. "Thanks for the book. I'll call you when I get out. We'll sing together."

I waved to him as he and the guards left, then shuddered. Cracking his head open to get himself put in the infirmary for a few days? Life must look pretty bleak if that's your option.

The barracks looked stark and cold. It was a beautiful day outside. I gathered my books and my note paper and headed outside. A spot of grass near the weight room beckoned. I stretched out under a scrawny maple tree. I thumbed Kafka, but I was saving him for the holding tanks on the way out. Seemed like a fitting transition back to reality. I tried to read about post-Shakespearean drama, but the subject seemed remote.

Lying there in the sun, I remembered nature, grass, trees. An ant crawled up my arm. Poor little guy. What crime had he committed?

I thought of my friends on the outside. Holly wondering when I was going to call. Hank plugging through the work week, counting the hours till Friday night. Mort buried in his computer. Angie — where was Angie, anyway? She might be sunning herself on a Marin County beach this very minute.

Their faces filtered by, especially precious now that I had been denied contact. I remembered how claustrophobic I had felt in the tents, how much I wanted to be alone. Now, it was the opposite. I couldn't wait to see people. Holly tonight. The pinball crowd tomorrow night. Even Coordinating Council seemed appealing.

A bird alighted in the little maple tree and looked me over. Amazing, I thought. It can leave whenever it wants. I wouldn't mind coming back as a bird in my next lifetime.

Yet look at me — coming and going in four days. I felt embarrassed as I thought of the other inmates, many serving six or twelve months. To them I must seem as flighty as a bird.

I studied the men milling about in the road and over in the playing field. What if I had to serve six months? Would I ever fit in? Or would I always feel like a privileged interloper?

The loudspeaker crackled. A short roster of names was called out — Jeff Harrison! At last! I grabbed my books and headed toward the gate. Farewell to all of you! I wished I'd spot someone I knew, to wish them well. But I didn't see anyone familiar.

Six of us were getting out. No one knew anyone else, but everyone seemed in good spirits. We followed the guards out the chain-link gate and back to the main building.

Inside, they gave us back our street clothes. My feet relaxed into their familiar tennis shoes. No one was watching us, and one of the men slipped his own shirt over the "Santa Rita" T-shirt he had been wearing. Lucky guy! I wished I had a souvenir.

A guard hollered for us to come down the hallway. Two of us were put into the first cell, the rest taken further up the block.

I looked around. There I was, back where I started, in a foul-smelling concrete holding tank. I peered out the slit window and remembered the little gravel lot and the white wall beyond it.

My cellmate seemed to settle into his own thoughts. I sat down on the wooden bench, leaned back against the cool cinder block wall, and launched into *The Trial.*

Kafka wasted no time on preliminaries. Within a page, the hero, Joseph K, had been arrested. Or perhaps detained was a better word. The details of his charges — in fact, any information whatsoever on why he was under suspicion, or perhaps already indicted — were unavailable at the moment.

Down the hallway, bars slammed. Judging from the tone of the voices, it was someone getting out, not coming in. Maybe I'd be next. It was only around one o'clock. At this rate, I'd be home by three or four.

The stumpy guard I had seen on the way in came and unlocked our cell. I closed my book, but he beckoned only to the other guy, then re-locked the gate. As they headed down the hallway, the guard turned back to me. "Well, what do you think about jail now?"

I smiled with satisfaction. "It was a learning experience."

He scrunched his face and walked away. I got up and tried to look down the hall, but couldn't see much through the grating. I went across the cell and looked out the slit window. The front of a blue pickup truck glinted in the sun.

I reopened Kafka and read another twenty pages before the guards brought a surly White guy and stuck him in the cell with me. He was clearly on the way in, and didn't even speak. Fine with me, I thought. You stay over there, I'll stay over here.

Every once in a while my roommate would spit on the floor, then mutter something about killing someone who was somehow responsible for his presence at Santa Rita.

I concentrated on my book. K had finally found the courtroom, which was packed to overflowing with a fractious crowd. Shoved in front of the examining magistrate, K appeared on the verge of overturning the entire prosecution, when a disturbance in the back of the room threw the proceeding into disarray and ruined his prospects for justice.

My cellmate spat again. I sucked a breath through clenched teeth. Don't take it personally, I told myself. It isn't me he wants to kill. So far, anyway. Still, I was relieved when the guards came and led him away.

No voices came from the other cells. Was I alone down here? I got up and peered out the window again. The truck was gone. Just gravel and the white building, which cast a shadow toward me now.

I read uninterrupted for another hour. Wandering through the offices of the administration of justice, K suffered a fainting spell which the Clerk of Inquiries, despite K's ardent denials, clearly interpreted as a sign of guilt. Why had K even gone to the offices? His own misguided attempts to exculpate himself were bringing him to grief.

A trustee came down the hall pushing a dust mop. I started to ask what time it was, but having seen Kafka's hero reduced to begging petty functionaries for information and assistance, I caught myself. Asking the time was admitting that the wait was getting to me. Don't give in. It must be nearly five, and they had to process me out by then.

On I read, now buoyed by K's renewed dreams of exoneration, now downcast by the perpetual dashing of his hopes. A door opened and closed down the hallway, but I heard no footsteps. It was probably a changing of the guard shift. It must be five by now. What was going on? Were they leaving me here to rot, just because I called their stupid jail a learning experience?

Oh, come on. It's probably 4:30. Chill out. I walked over and checked the window. The shadows were lengthening, maybe ten feet from the wall now.

I tried to get comfortable on the bench and trudged through another chapter without hearing a sound. I was alone in the dungeon. Even if I got out now, I might have to call someone to come pick me up. The last bus to Oakland was at seven. Maybe they had till eight o'clock to process me out. Had I misunderstood? No, it was five. I was sure of it.

Weren't the cops arresting anyone? If they would just bring a drunk driver in, I could get their attention. Could they really have forgotten me? Why not? Who was checking? I shivered. I tried to lie on the bench — too narrow. I thought of my cellmate's spitting — no way I was going to lie on the floor. Damn it! I should yell. No. They want you to give in, admit you can't take it. How could they get so upset over one little remark? Were the guards really that insecure? Come on, bring someone in. I could at least ask what time it is. No! I'll read Kafka all night.

I forced myself to read another half-dozen pages. But my concentration was flagging. I paced the cell again. Out the slit window, long shadows stretched toward me. I was spiraling into another round of despair when the door down the hall creaked open. Feet shuffled my way. A guard? Ask him. No! I am not giving in.

The trustee I had seen earlier ambled down the corridor and stopped in front of my cell. He pulled out a set of keys and started trying them on the door. Alright! Finally! Come on, hurry up! At last one of the keys worked. As casually as I could, I strolled after him up the hall, through the door, past the sewer-like receiving area, and up to the processing window. I was about to burst — I made it! So what if I'd missed the bus. I'll call Holly. She could borrow someone's car and meet me up the road at McDonald's.

As I waited at the window, I didn't mention the delay, refusing to acknowledge their pettiness. All that mattered was that I was free.

The receptionist pushed some papers toward me. "Sign these."

I scribbled my name illegibly. As she took the forms back, her phone rang. One sheet, with my photograph attached, slipped onto the counter. My eyes lit on the mug shot — a souvenir! The receptionist was looking the other way. No one else could see me. I slid the paper off the counter, folded it over, and stuffed it into my pocket. "Can I go?" I said in a thin voice.

She was already pushing a button. Two guards appeared from behind me. One of the guards stepped toward me. I froze. He reached out and opened the final door. I never looked back, bounding up a short flight of stairs and into the lobby. Free! I reeled at the possibilities. There's the exit — but there's a candy machine! Forget it, get out of here! Wait, there's a phone — call Holly. No, get out of this place! Call her from McDonald's.

I swung around and headed through the double doors, down the barbed-wire tunnel and into the parking area. I practically ran out to the access road, shooting a glance past the fences and barbed wire toward the jail barracks. The compound looked peaceful, almost quaint. Had I really just come from there? Or was that another lifetime?

I was steaming. Kafka felt sweaty in my hand. I peeled off my sweater without breaking stride. Get to McDonald's. I hadn't eaten a bite since yesterday. I didn't feel physically hungry. I just craved food.

I made my way up to the overpass and crossed the highway. Outside McDonald's I found a pay phone. I groped for a quarter. Three rings and she answered. "Holly — it's me. I finally got out! They left me in solitary all day because I smarted off to a guard. Can you come and get me?"

"Jeff? Is that you? Where are you?"

"I'm at the McDonald's up the road from the jail. I missed the last bus. Can you come and get me?"

"What happened to the bus?"

"The last one was at seven."

"But it's only five now."

"Really?" I peered up at the sun, still far above the horizon. Five o'clock. So that was their game. They held me exactly till the legal limit. Wouldn't you know it. They thought of everything...

"Jeff? Jeff?" Holly's faraway voice called me back. "Are you okay? Should I come get you? I'll borrow Daniel's car."

"No, no, it's okay," I assured her. "Nothing a hamburger won't cure."

Friday, August 5, 1983

GIVE JAIL credit for this — it rehabilitated my outlook on life.

After I got out, I felt as though I were rediscovering LAG, Berkeley, and Summertime. Best of all, rediscovering Holly. We made love my first two nights back, went for walks, ate late dinners together...

As I waited for her to get home from the office, I went out on the balcony and examined the pages of the new Direct Action. I remembered doing layout ages ago, before my sojourn at Santa Rita.

But flipping through the paper brought home what we had lived through in the past few months. Livermore, Vandenberg, International Day — it was all there, in print. It had really happened.

I paused, awaiting a wave of pride at our accomplishments. But something was off-kilter. I walked back inside and set the paper down, and paced around the room. All the stories about our glorious past basically drove home one point — except for a vague Euromissiles protest in October, LAG had no plans for the future.

The Congress was coming up fast, and positions were ossifying. Claudia and Craig, backed by Mort and a few others, were determined to ram through their Strategy Proposal and force LAG to stop in its tracks and do some long-term planning. Against this strategic consortium, a ragtag alliance of Livermore stalwarts, urban anarchists, suburban liberals, and religious pacifists were preparing an all-out defense of their right to call whatever protests they wanted, whenever they wanted.

A typical phonepole in South Berkeley.

It had all the ingredients of a disaster. The only hopeful note was that Artemis had agreed to facilitate the main session. If anyone could hold the Congress together, it was Artemis, with her twin powers of staying grounded and making people laugh.

She asked me to co-facilitate, probably because I knew the personal tensions that were rumbling under the surface. But I planned to leave most of it to her. Maybe she could magically transform the convoluted conflicts into a coherent strategy built around the very actions people were dying to do.

Realistically, the best I hoped for was a truce that allowed some concrete decisions to be made without anyone storming out of the Congress. Going into August, even if half of our staff had resigned, no one had totally walked out on the group.

But the list of potential defectors was growing.

HOLLY GOT home about seven o'clock, and we decided to get pizza. I waited while she got a scarf, then led the way down the stairs and out into the twilight.

At the corner of Telegraph, we stopped for a minute to listen to a saxophonist playing a Thelonius Monk song. A small audience applauded as he finished the number. Holly placed a dollar in his open case and we crossed the street.

At the next corner, a phonepole flyer caught my eye. "Look," I said. "It's BARF!" The second annual Berkeley Anti-Reagan Festival, sponsored by Berkeley Citizens' Action, was still a month away, but I had good cause to be excited. I scanned the list of performers and spotted my name in the fine print, right underneath Wavy Gravy, the Funky Nixons, and the Plutonium Players: "Jeff Harrison, Satirical Folksinger."

"There you are," Holly said. "That makes it official."

"I better start finding more time to practice," I said. I looked over the poster again. Playing at BARF felt like being an official part of history, part of the Berkeley-led vanguard of public opinion that would soon sweep Reaganism into the dustbin of American politics. True, Reagan's popularity had risen slightly in recent months, but once the 1984 campaign started, runaway military spending and decimated social services would wash him right out of office.

A hand-pasted flyer for the October protests.

We went into Larry Blake's and got a half-sausage, half-vegetarian pizza. I was hoping we'd get a window seat, but we wound up in the back along a dark-paneled wall adorned with photos of Berkeley in the 1950s. Muddy Waters played from a speaker behind the bar.

As we ate, Holly updated me on the peace camp proposal that she was co-sponsoring. "Our latest idea is not an open-ended camp, but just a couple of months. That way we can see how many LAGers will really come out there, and whether we can open a dialog with Lab workers. If it works, we'll reopen later for a longer period."

Pitching a tent in the fields next to Livermore Lab didn't fire me with passion, and I didn't put much stock in trying to dialog with employees. But Holly's eyes shone so brightly as she talked about the peace camp that I almost wished I shared her vision.

"The Lab workers are human beings," she said. "They have their own hopes and fears. If we want to change what they're doing, we have to be able to speak to those hopes and fears."

After dinner, we walked up to campus. As we crossed Sproul Plaza, her voice turned somber. "Jeff, there's something important I need to tell you."

"Oh yeah?" My response felt flippant, and I added, "What's going on?"

She looked back at me sadly, reaching out to touch my arm. "I've decided to resign from the LAG staff."

"No..."

"Yes. I just can't handle the office any longer. Even if we do another International Day, I want to be out networking, not stuck in the office answering phones. I'm so much happier when I'm out meeting people."

We walked on in silence. Caroline's resignation had been a blow, but Holly? I felt like the office, my most intimate link to LAG, was withering away.

I looked at her in the light of a streetlamp, studying her face in profile as we stopped at a corner. Her chin was jutted out, and her gaze seemed fixed in the distance. I thought back to the day I unloaded my own frustrations on her. Did I share the blame for her quitting?

We crossed a wooden bridge over Strawberry Creek. "I have a job offer preparing an experimental diet for a woman who's recovering from cancer," Holly said. "I'll earn as much as LAG was paying me, and have the rest of my time free for activism. I could work on Direct Action, International Day, the peace camp..."

My head felt light, and I sat down on a bench to collect my thoughts. "But what about the office?" I said. "You, Caroline, Claudia — that just leaves Craig."

"And Jenny," Holly said. "Plus, Sara says that Karina is interested. She'll be out of jail in just a few days."

I smiled slightly. "Karina would keep things hopping," I said. "I'd like to see her on the staff."

"And Daniel might apply," Holly said. "He wants to work on International Day."

My smile faded. "I can imagine Mort and Claudia's response to that."

"Daniel would be great," she said plainly. "There's no one more dedicated."

I tried to picture the office without Holly. Her desk had been my anchor, the calm center around which the chaos whirled. I imagined a tidal wave of paper flooding over her desk.

Holly's gaze wandered away, and she sighed. "I need a break. My life is out of balance." She paused. "Maybe I'll even have time to do some gardening."

I slid closer and put my arm around her. "That would be great."

"Yeah," she said. We sat quietly for a minute or two. I assumed she was thinking more about gardening. But when she spoke again, she was back to LAG. "Sara wants to join Direct Action."

I smiled, relieved to hear Holly talking about Direct Action. "Good," I said, "she'd be great."

Holly turned to face me. "And you know what? Norm, the new guy who has been volunteering in the office, invited the Direct Action collective to go canoeing on the Russian River. He has a house up there. He suggested the last weekend of August. Will you go?"

"I love canoeing."

"Maybe you and I could stay another night and go camping."

"Yeah," I said. "I'll do that."

She smiled. "Great, I'll call Norm and set it up." We stood up and resumed our walk. A canoe trip. For all of Holly's dreams and plans around International Day or the peace camp, she found time to think of something outside LAG. I wished something as simple as a camping trip could distract me.

Monday, August 22, 1983

"WHAT A waste," Claudia said. She peered at me through her black-framed glasses. "I knew people would never agree to strategy discussions. God forbid we should stop and think about what we're doing."

"Give it time," I said as we talked in the hallway during a break at the Congress. The meetings were held in a grade school in the Haight-Ashbury, and all the furnishings, even the ceilings, seemed shrunken. I flexed my shoulders, which felt hunched in the Lilliputian hallway. "People need time to talk it over with their AGs. The Strategy Proposal could still get consensed at the September spokescouncil."

Melissa stopped on her way back to the meeting room. "Assuming the sponsors actually want consensus."

"What's that supposed to mean?" Claudia said sharply.

"Whoa, this is break-time," I said. "Haven't we argued enough this weekend?"

"Yeah," said Melissa sardonically. She tucked a strand of graying hair behind her ear. "And where has it gotten us? Two hundred people, and we haven't decided anything."

My brow furrowed. "We've made progress. There's still room for consensus at the next spokescouncil. A month from now, we could adopt the Strategy Proposal and call some solid future actions."

Right. Did I believe it myself? Thank god it was the final afternoon. We had one last session, where my fondest hope was that we could struggle through to a consensus on the date for our next spokescouncil. Because we sure weren't going to agree on anything else.

Since getting out of jail, I'd had time for some late-night walks, time to reflect and make sense of the whole experience. Especially my time in the men's tent. If those desultory days taught me anything, it's that my role wasn't to be an inspirational sparkplug for the movement, but a low-key bridge-builder. One moment stood out — facilitating the spokescouncil. Particularly my concern that we consense on supporting diverse actions, not just go our own ways.

A nice image. Bridge-building was difficult, though, when everyone had a different idea of where the road should lead.

Karina, coming up the hall, distracted me. I'd hardly seen her since she got out of prison, and I'd been wishing we'd find time to talk. But this might not be the best moment. All weekend she had been walking the fine line between the buoyant charm of LAG's reigning jail-time champ and the agitated impatience of someone who expected the revolution to happen that very minute.

As Karina approached, Melissa took a step back. Claudia folded her arms across her chest. I took a slow breath and looked around our circle. No one had walked out of the Congress — yet. Let's not blow it now.

Euromissile Fact Sheet

What makes the Pershing II and ground-launched cruise missiles so dangerous? How do they compare to the SS-20?

Pershing II

Although it will replace the short-range Pershing IA missiles now based in West Germany, the Pershing II is a completely new weapon with vastly increased capabilities.

It will be able to hit targets inside the Soviet Union eight minutes after being launched. Its sophisticated guidance system, which photographs the target and makes course adjustments as the missile approaches, will give it higher accuracy than any currently deployed missile. As a result, the Pershing will threaten to destroy important Soviet military targets, including some missile silos, command and control centers, airfields and weapons storage sites, with very little warning time.

NATO's 1979 agreement called for deploying 108 Pershing II launchers, which may mean more than 108 missiles, since the launchers are designed to be reloaded. The Army currently plans to buy 384 Pershing II missiles, 226 of which will be operational and available for deployment, even though the West German government has never agreed to take more than 108.

Another Army plan is to build a reduced range version of the Pershing II, able to reach Eastern Europe, just in case U.S.-Soviet negotiations are successful. They may also turn it into an intercontinental missile by adding a third stage and extending the range, possibly as a replacement for the MX.

But testing problems have plagued the new missile, beginning with four embarassing failures in 1982. The Army claims a string of successful tests in 1983, but has admitted in congressional testimony that testing standards were lowered and costly engineering changes are still needed. The Pershing II, rushed into production ahead of schedule for political reasons, still doesn't work well, and will become even more expensive.

Ground-Launched Cruise Missile

The ground-launched cruise missile (GLCM) has the accuracy of the Pershing II, but is much slower. Its speed and flight path resemble a subsonic jet plane instead of a ballistic missile such as the Pershing. But it can reach its targets undetected, because the GLCM flies at low altitudes beneath radar and air defenses. Its targets will be similar to the Pershing II's — missile silos, nuclear storage sites, command and air defense centers — but it will be able to reach more of them, including the Moscow area, because of its greater range.

The GLCM shares with the air and sea-launched cruise missiles a high-tech guidance system called TERCOM (terrain contour matching). A map is stored in the guidance system's computer. The system then takes pictures during flight, matches those pictures to the map, and makes flight adjustments to stay on course.

However, at least the first set of missiles deployed won't work. Tests have shown that the guidance system can be confused by certain weather and surface conditions. The computer software for the GLCM's launch control still can't launch most of the missiles it controls. And production line problems caused the Navy to overhaul its cruise missile program, run jointly with the GLCM, in late 1982.

A total of 560 missiles will be built, with 464 operational GLCMs planned for Western Europe. Deployment is scheduled to begin in December 1983 and continue through 1988.

What is the SS-20?

Since 1977, the USSR has been upgrading its medium-range missile force by replacing 15-year-old SS-4 and SS-5 missiles with the SS-20. The SS-20 is the first Soviet missile to use solid fuel instead of liquid fuel (almost all U.S. missiles are solid-fueled), which means a quicker launch time, increased safety and better reliability. The range has been increased to 3,000 miles and instead of a single one-megaton warhead, the SS-20 carries three warheads of 150 kilotons each.

Unlike the new American systems, the SS-20 is not a nuclear warfighting weapon. Although it is more accurate than older Soviet missiles, its CEP of 1300 feet is no match for the Pershing II. This level of accuracy is not enough to allow the SS-20 to hit particular military targets.

By June 1983, at least 351 SS-20 missiles had been deployed, with 243 of them in range of Europe and the remainder in East Asia. The SS-20, like the Pershing II and GLCM, can be dispersed to secret sites to be fired. But its mobility is overrated — the missiles based in East Asia cannot be easily moved within range of Europe. According to defense analyst Alexander Cockburn, it has "the actual speed of movement of an oil rig."

The SS-20 is clearly more reliable and sophisticated than its predecessors, and has been deployed in numbers that go well beyond any necessary deterrent. Yet as former national security adviser McGeorge Bundy has pointed out, "the SS-20 did not and does not give the Soviet Union any nuclear capability against Europe alone that she did not have in overflowing measure before a single SS-20 was deployed."

excerpted from "Euromissile Fact Sheet"
LIVERMORE ACTION GROUP
3126 Shattuck Avenue
Berkeley, CA 94705

Phone: 644-3031
644-2028
Hours: M-F 11 a.m. to 5 p.m.

Leaflet passed out at the October protests. A readable version of this flyer will be available at www.directaction.org

Karina walked straight up to Melissa. "The Euromissiles protest should be in the City, not at Livermore. People are tired of the same old blockades. We need to break out. We need to take direct action to the heart of the City."

"That's hardly the sort of action that LAG needs," Melissa said.

Karina jutted her jaw. "For people I know, it is. And we need to decide today so we can start organizing."

Claudia leaned against a bulletin board and laughed drily. "Why are we even talking about CD for October? The European peace movement is counting on us to present a united front, to work in coalition with the Freeze and other mainstream groups. And they aren't going to go for direct action."

"Why not?" Karina said. "Civil disobedience has been a respectable tactic since the Civil Rights movement. Liberals love watching it on PBS, but they run scared in real life."

I smiled and propped my foot on a little chair. "I've been to a couple of October coalition meetings," I said. "Organizers from the Freeze aren't anti-CD. They're just worried that a lot of people won't come to a demo where arrest is a possibility. So instead of a huge crowd, all you'd get is the already-committed."

"Getting a big turnout in support of Europe is the essential thing," said Melissa, "They're the ones in the most danger if the U.S. deploys the new missiles. We need to dedicate that day to building the largest possible legal rally."

"Fine," Karina said. "We'll do our action another day. Then we're free to do what we want. We might as well get used to working on our own. When the Democrats come to San Francisco next Summer, I don't think we'll see the Freeze out in the streets with us."

Oh, no, I thought. Not the Democratic Convention. Weren't we fighting over enough already? The more we argued, the more people's opinions seemed carved in stone.

Luckily, Artemis came out into the hall and announced that the final Congress session was reconvening. Just get through this meeting, and we can all go home.

"Let's go," said Melissa, heading into the meeting room.

"Yeah," Claudia said. "Let's get started so we can get out of here."

Saturday, August 27, 1983

"I WANT TO ride three in a canoe," Angie said. "I don't want to have to paddle all the way."

People were pairing off for our journey down the Russian River. The Direct Action collective had accepted Norm's invitation, and a dozen of us made the expedition.

Holly and I started off together. Jenny and Raoul were a natural team. Angie joined them, "as a chaperone."

Mort hooked up with Norm, Craig with Lyle, and Karina, Sara, and their friend Ariel rounded out the venture.

The Russian River wound through Sonoma County, a mostly-rural region an hour or so north of San Francisco. Although much of the county was covered with well-manicured grape fields, the area along the river was relatively wild.

We clustered on a patch of gravel along the river's edge as Norm briefed us. "This late in the Summer, the river is only a few feet deep in most places. But there's some good swimming holes along the route, too."

I'd brought an extra pair of shorts in case I wanted to get in the river, but the day was cool, and the water didn't seem very inviting.

Norm wrapped up his talk, then reached in his pocket and produced a couple of thick joints. "Better burn these before we fall in the river and ruin them," he said.

"Smells like great stuff," I said as he passed it to me. "Grown in Sonoma?"

"No, up in Mendocino County," he said. "That's the best weed-growing territory in the United States. It's getting harder, though. Now that the Republicans are in office, they want to stomp it out. They hate this whole region, the hippie counterculture."

Canoes on the Russian River upstream from Healdsburg.

"No wonder," Mort said. "The money trickles down to groups like LAG."

We paired off and hoisted our canoes into the slow-moving creek. Craig and Lyle were the first to leave shore. They paddled toward a bend that went around a sandbar. As the river narrowed, the current picked up. Their canoe spurted forward. Craig, who had been sitting in the rear, rocked backwards. Lyle dropped his paddle and grabbed for the side of the canoe. In an instant they capsized.

They had no trouble getting to shore and righting their craft. But they looked stunned. I struggled not to burst out laughing. But Mort couldn't refrain. "Hey, watch out for that first turn," he called out.

Holly and I cleared the bend and settled into the slow flow of the river. The water was cold and clear, and shallow enough in some places to see the rocks lining the riverbed.

The Russian River was twenty or thirty feet wide in most places, with a bend every hundred or so feet. Holly and I glided along, out of sight of the others. I was in the rear, steering. She put her paddle down and slid back toward me. We kissed, then she leaned back against my knees. A heron took flight against the crystal blue sky. I bent down and nuzzled Holly's hair, which was warm from the sunshine.

Seeing Holly so relaxed and peaceful made me especially glad I'd come on the expedition. She'd been on a roller coaster ever since jail. One day she'd be elated about plans for the peace camp. The next, she'd be wanting a six-month break from even thinking about organizing.

As we drifted along, I heard stealthy laughter from starboard. I turned and took a direct hit as Jenny, Raoul, and Angie used their paddles to slap a volley of water at us. I grabbed my paddle and tried to return fire, but they glided out of reach.

Raoul thrust his arms overhead. "Victory is ours!"

"Onward, troops!" Angie cried, and they raced off.

Holly scrambled back into paddling position, but our tormentors had rounded the bend and were out of sight. We had to accept defeat.

But the river soon evened the score. We caught up with them a few minutes later — capsized along a sandbar.

"Mother Nature exacts revenge," I said as we cruised by. Angie shook her soggy fist at us.

After lunch, we shuffled our canoe assignments. Holly teamed up with Angie. I wound up with Craig and Ariel. I'd been looking for a chance to talk with Craig. Just the previous week he had quit the LAG staff, completing the Grand Slam of resigning staffers. It hammered home my sense of loss, and I wished there were some way to dissuade him. At the same time, I wondered whether Craig and Claudia were cooking up some alternative scheme that I should know about. Maybe they'd quit in order to start something new.

But with Ariel being a VAC stalwart, I doubted that Craig would open up. Oh, well. We're here to relax and enjoy the scenery.

Jenny and Raoul inaugurated the second half of the trip by tipping over within twenty feet. "That'll make those kisses juicier," Angie yelled.

"Oh, shut up!" Jenny answered, dragging the canoe ashore and shaking herself off. Angie threw back her head and laughed, then walked to the riverbank and hugged Jenny. She turned back to her canoe, a fresh burst of laughter escaping her, and I was sorry I wasn't paired up with her. I could use some laughs.

At one turn we found a rope that swung out over a deeper spot in the river. Raoul, already soaked, tried it and landed with a huge splash. It looked fun, but the sky was turning cloudy, and I didn't feel like getting wet.

Toward dusk we reached our debarkation point under an old bridge in Healdsburg. All the canoes except Sara and Karina's arrived about the same time. We circled around, waiting our turn to land. Holly and Angie were the first in. Norm, Lyle, and Mort were next. Norm, up front, stepped onto the gravel shore. As Lyle stepped out, the canoe slipped backwards and he went knee-deep into the water. Holly grabbed the front of the canoe and tugged it ashore just as Mort stood to move to the front. Mort grabbed desperately at the air. Then, arms flailing, he tumbled into the river.

He staggered ashore like a wet cat. Holly looked forlorn. I thought Mort might toss her into the river, but Holly saved the day by stepping up and giving him a hug. Mort held her long enough to soak her, and then they both laughed.

The rest of us made it safely onto dry land, but there was no sign of Karina and Sara. "Either they capsized, or they got into some heavy necking," Ariel speculated.

"Or both," Angie said.

Ten minutes later their canoe finally appeared. "Sorry to keep you waiting," Sara said sheepishly.

Angie eyed her sternly. "I certainly hope it was worth it."

"Oh, it was," Karina said in a tone that made Sara blush.

The two of them and Ariel headed back to San Francisco, but the rest of us spent the night at Norm's house. We stopped for a hot dinner, got some wine, and drove back to his place, thinking to spend the rest of the evening talking. But the day's workout caught up with people, and with the help of the wine, we were all nodding off before long.

Holly and I rolled out our sleeping bags in a private corner. I curled mine up behind hers and wrapped my arms around her, nestling my face into her thick hair.

She turned her head and kissed my lips. "I love you, Jeff," she whispered. "This was a wonderful day."

Saturday, September 17, 1983

"ARE THERE any objections to Bank of America?" Karina was facilitating the Change of Heart meeting and lobbying us at the same time. "B of A invests in everything we're against. It ties together all our issues."

She looked around the circle as if daring anyone to object. Was she like this before her prison term? Actually, yes. But she seemed to have turned it up a notch.

"Then do we have consensus?" People twinkled their fingers in assent. A few applauded, and Alby leapt to his feet. "Look out, B of A!"

THE PREVIOUS week, at the September 10th spokescouncil, LAG officially endorsed the October rally with the Freeze and other peace groups. Central America groups, social activists, and even a few labor unions had joined the coalition. It was shaping up as the biggest San Francisco rally of the year. Even though it was a non-arrest action, the endorsement was a fairly easy consensus.

Not so the next proposal. Karina, Raoul, and others proposed that on

Monday, October 24th, LAG do its own CD action: a traveling, decentralized protest targeting corporations involved with Euromissile contracts.

I liked the idea of a downtown protest. We'd reach bystanders in a way that a rural site like Livermore or Vandenberg never could. And we'd be challenging the whole corporate structure, not just one weapons lab.

But it didn't sound like the unifying action that LAG needed. Whether anything other than Livermore could reignite the group was questionable. But an urban action wasn't the answer.

As soon as the proposal was stated, Melissa's hand went up. "We shouldn't be doing City actions. There's no way we can be sure everyone is in an affinity group. It could turn into a mob scene. The police could send in provocateurs, or people without nonviolence training could jump in and start trouble."

Karina pounded her fist on her knee. "If we want to stop business as usual, we've got to push some limits. Our blockades have become a formula. We play our role, the cops play theirs, the media prints their stories — and the arms race goes right on."

Melissa looked at her incredulously. "After all the lessons of the 1960s, the senseless violence that derailed the peace movement, you want to have a rerun? No, thank you."

Finally Melissa and Monique stood aside after eliciting a promise that all participants would be encouraged to have preps and be in affinity groups. Ten minutes before we were supposed to be out of the meeting space, we reached a reluctant consensus.

Which was good enough to keep the action-faction satisfied. But it wasn't going to please many others.

And that was a problem. Coming off the Summer, it seemed to me that we had a long way to go toward building a community that could withstand the pressures of imprisonment. I felt like all we had done — at least in the men's camp — was survive. We had a lot of collective growing to do.

But how could we grow as a community if we started calling actions which drew only one subgroup within LAG? What if we lost the cross-fertilization that the big actions provided? How long till we were down to isolated cliques pursuing private agendas? And how long after that till we were all sitting at home alone?

Raoul and I folded up the chairs after the meeting. I figured he'd be happy with the outcome, but despite his proposal being consensed, his expression was sour.

"Hey," I said as I shoved a rack of chairs against the wall, "at least no one blocked the City action."

"No, they just tried to strangle it into submission."

"That's just people airing their usual grievances. In the end they consensed. Or at least stood aside."

He looked at me intently, almost suspiciously. "The point is to restrict every attempt at spontaneity. Nonviolence training, police liaisons, monitors — they're all control mechanisms."

Forget I brought it up, I thought.

Sid came over and handed me a flyer. "This is a leaflet I'm making for punk shows in San Francisco."

I looked over the crudely-pasted handbill. "You think punks will come to a LAG protest?"

"Why not?" He seemed to dare me to find a reason. "They already reject corporate music and fashion. Why wouldn't they want to join a protest at corporate offices?"

DIRECT ACTION

Published by Livermore Action Group

September 1983

STOP THE CRUISE & PERSHING II

Table of Contents

Stop the Euromissiles!
Legal Demonstration October 22: p. 1
Anti-Euromissiles CD October 24th: p. 1, 9
Euromissile Information Week: p. 3
Peace Camps: p. 10-11
The U.S. War in Central America: p. 6-7

REFUSE the CRUISE

Livermore Action Group
3126 Shattuck Ave.
Berkeley, CA 94705

Bulk Rate
U.S. Postage Paid
Permit No. 20
Berkeley, CA

Direct Action #9, September 1983

I nodded, but I was glad he hadn't passed the flyer around at the spokescouncil. Recruiting punks for the protest would hardly reassure Melissa or Monique.

Jenny offered me a ride home, but I was heading to the City on a music errand. And better yet, I was riding there with Karina.

As we parted ways, Raoul called back to me. "Hey, some guys from the print shop are having a softball game and barbeque next Saturday — want to play?"

"Yeah, that sounds great — no, wait, there's a Euromissiles meeting I need to be at. Too bad, it would be great to play."

"Yeah," he said. "Maybe next time."

Karina and I walked down to BART. I could hardly believe I had her to myself for the ride to the City. She had been in constant demand since her return from prison, not just by friends and clusters, but by church and school groups who lauded her stand against nuclear weapons and invited her as an inspirational speaker.

On top of that, she'd been hired — along with Maria, Daniel, and Jenny — as the office staffers for LAG for the coming year.

Whenever I'd seen her, Karina seemed to be thriving. So I was surprised that once we got settled on the train, she slouched down in the padded seat and frowned.

"How are you doing?" I asked.

She looked at me for a moment. "Up and down," she said. Her voice was unusually soft, and I leaned toward her. "Adjusting to being out of prison has been harder than I thought."

"Yeah? I guess I can understand, but you seem to be handling it so well."

"Oh, the public stuff, sure. It's the personal part that's hard." She paused as if weighing her next words. "You know that Sara and I moved in together? Or rather, I moved in with her, into her house in the Mission. It's wonderful in a lot of ways. But it makes it harder when I'm with someone else. Not that I'd bring someone home. But if I spend the night with someone else, well, Sara can't help but notice."

Change of Heart icon.

"I can see where that would be tough," I said. "I guess I thought you two had worked that sort of thing out long ago."

"I don't know if you ever reach a permanent solution," Karina said. "I completely love Sara. But a monogamous relationship would never work for me. I'd feel stifled. If I care about someone else, and we're attracted to each other, it's natural to have sex. It's more than physical pleasure. It's a way of feeling really close to people I love."

She had an almost dreamy look on her face. I couldn't help searching her eyes for a further meaning. Was she trying to tell me something? Or was I caught up in fantasyland?

Suppose it were true? Sure, Holly and I had an open relationship, on paper. But neither of us had put it to the test since she and Frank broke off a year before. I remembered how I had responded to Holly's non-monogamy back then.

I looked at Karina, who seemed absorbed in her own thoughts. I pondered our political differences, imagining us in bed making passionate love and then getting in a huge fight about working with the Freeze.

My reverie was broken when a man sat down across from us and pulled out a very aromatic hamburger. Eating is prohibited on BART, but he hunched down in his seat and unwrapped the burger.

"Oh, gross," Karina muttered. "Charbroiled cow flesh."

It made me laugh even as it reinforced my sense that she and I weren't the most sympatico couple in the world.

But as we parted at the end of the ride, she gave me a warm hug and looked into my eyes. "We should get together sometime."

How could I say no to that?

SO THERE WE were a week later, at the cluster meeting. Once we'd agreed on the Bank of America focus, Karina knelt on a cushion. Her black hair bounced as she spoke. "We have to disrupt the whole financial district, not just B of A. We should do street theater in the intersection."

Sure, I thought. Why not dance on top of cop cars while we're at it? Much as Karina could intrigue me, I had trouble with her constantly raising the stakes. No sooner are we in the City than she has us out in the streets.

Alby was perched on a couch-arm. "Downtown will be packed with traffic," he said excitedly. "If we block even one intersection, it could cause gridlock on all the side streets."

Nice image, but I didn't share his optimism. For one, I didn't want to get arrested. I'd had my fill of jail for a while. Which led directly to my second concern. I raised my hand. "The San Francisco police probably won't take too kindly to shutting down streets."

Karina almost jumped up. "First they have to catch us! And when they do, we get up and run out of the street. We can play mind games with the cops."

"Every AG is an autonomous unit," Alby said. "Every time the cops think they have us pinned down, another AG will start doing something down the street. Even if some get busted, others will keep snarling traffic."

Around the circle, people were nodding. I found myself intrigued by the tactical possibilities of sparring with the police. But realistically, we'd all get busted pretty quickly. And I wondered how many LAGers would even take part in such an action.

As people brainstormed further tactics, I thought of Holly, who wasn't at the meeting. I could imagine her reaction: "It's all so negative," she would say. "What positive alternatives are we offering to people who work all day in those awful high-rises?"

The cluster meeting was winding down. A subgroup including Angie and Antonio took on the street-theater aspect. Karina and Sara offered to put together a leaflet detailing the bank's nuclear crimes, to hand out to bystanders and media.

I didn't volunteer for anything, having told Hank I'd help with the nukecycle he still hoped to build in time for the action. Whatever action Change of Heart did, they'd have to do without me.

But still, as I looked around the ragtag circle, I felt glad to call Change of Heart my home. However confused the rest of LAG was, however discouraged I could feel, our cluster never seemed to lack inspiration.

After the closing circle, Jenny and Angie came over to me. "Hey, we're going dancing tonight at Ashkenaz," Jenny said. "It's a world-beat band, the African Rhythm Messengers. Raoul and Alby are going, too. Why don't you and Holly come with us?"

For a moment, I was tempted to say yes. I didn't doubt it would be fun to go dancing with them. But as inept as I felt dancing to rock and roll, I couldn't imagine moving to African music.

"Come on and shake it out," Angie said. She swiveled her hips, and I had to smile. Some people must have been born dancing.

"Let me check with Holly," I said. "Maybe we'll meet you there."

Friday, September 30, 1983

ANGIE AND I were the last two to leave Direct Action production that evening. With Holly out of town, and Sara at a Shabbat gathering, Angie had stepped up and done most of the coordinating that evening, which I'd appreciated because it gave me a chance to get some layout done.

She unlocked her bike from a post on the front porch. "I'll walk partway with you," she said. But a moment later she slumped. "Oh, no. A flat tire!"

"We have a tire repair kit at home," I said. "And I have some tools. Do you want to go back there and work on it?"

"That would be great," she said.

We headed up Ellsworth Street. Angie pushed her hobbled bike alongside. The night was warm, the low fog illumined by the glow of the city lights.

"I really appreciate your work on Direct Action," I told her. "It's made a big difference."

"Thanks," she said. She tilted her head as if considering what I'd said. Her braided ponytail fell across her shoulder. "I like the paper a lot. I hate going to meetings and sitting in a chair. But the newspaper is so tangible. Plus, I get high on the gluesticks."

"That explains why they keep disappearing," I said. We walked a moment in silence. "So what have you been doing besides the newspaper?" I finally said.

"Working and sleeping, that's about it the past week," she said. "No, not really. On Wednesday, Alby and I did a graffiti action on bank walls around Oakland and Berkeley. We made stencils with questions like, 'Whose future are you investing in?'"

"Wow, pretty elaborate," I said. I felt jealous of Alby. "That's a lot of words to cut out."

She nodded. "It was worth it. We wanted to get people thinking. They just block out slogans. But a question gets into your consciousness in a different way."

"Do you do a lot of graffiti?"

"Not really. If I get better, I'd like to do art-graffiti, like the subway artists in New York City." She paused as if recalling a favorite car. "I don't know if graffiti is really my medium. But it's a fun way to connect with someone. It's a lot more exciting than going to a movie."

We got back to my apartment and hauled her bike up the stairs. "Where's Holly?" Angie asked.

"She flew to Colorado for her brother's wedding."

"Oh, that's right. She mentioned that to me last week."

"You want some tea or a beer?" I said.

"What are you having?"

"Beer."

"I'll have one, too."

I got us a couple of Sierra Nevadas from the refrigerator. She declined the glass I offered, lifting the bottle to her lips and tilting her head slightly back as she drank.

We took the tire apart, but it soon became clear that a repair kit was useless. "The tear is right by the valve," she said.

"What are you going to do?"

"I'm too tired to walk all the way home. I guess I'll call a cab."

I knew that with her part-time job, she didn't have money for a cab. Besides, I was enjoying her company, and didn't want her to go so soon. "You can stay here if you want," I offered. "We have a futon out here. You could stay overnight and buy a new innertube in the morning."

She seemed to weigh my offer. "That would be a lot more relaxing. I should call Jenny and tell her I won't be back, so she doesn't worry."

I put on a reggae tape, and we sat down on the folded-up futon on the living room floor. She sat with her legs extended, crossed at the ankle. In her hands she cradled the bottle of beer. A strand of hair had slipped out of her ponytail and fell across her cheek.

We drifted into the sort of get-acquainted conversation that we had never really had — where are you from, what's your family like, why did you come to California...

Like me, she was a midwesterner, from Minnesota. She had come down to Indiana to go to school at Earlham, a well-known Quaker college across the state from my home in Terre Haute. Her family sounded a lot more progressive than mine. "I've told them all about LAG," she said, "and I sent them a copy of Direct Action."

"That must be nice," I said. "I've never told my parents about getting arrested."

"Yeah," Angie said, "Jenny's the same way. I feel lucky that my family supports me. Of course, they think it's a little odd. But at least they try to understand."

She was working a part-time job to pay her bills, clerking in a UC office. "I work nineteen hours a week," she said. "They can't let me work twenty hours or they'd have to give me benefits. UC does that to all their part-time help."

"I guess I'm better off," I said. "I can work all the hours I want at my maintenance job, and still not get any benefits."

She smiled. "I want to change jobs soon. Sometimes I think I want a real job, a career. But I'm not sure what I'd do. My college degree isn't very practical."

"What was it?"

"Comparative religions. It's ironic, because I'm not a member of any religion. I just studied them."

"I thought you went to Pagan rituals."

"Oh, sure. But I wouldn't say it's a religion. I just like doing rituals. They're a way to mark the cycle of the year. For Equinox, me and Jenny and our circle went up in the Oakland Hills and walked a labyrinth. It was a beautiful, overcast day that made me think of home."

She spoke so matter-of-factly of labyrinths and cycles and rituals that I found myself drawn in. "So what do you really believe?" I asked.

She leaned her head back against the wall, her eyes gazing slightly up. Her chest rose and fell slowly as she pondered the question. "I haven't really spelled it out. I believe the Earth is sacred. I believe that the way we treat other people and other living beings makes a difference." She paused, then looked at me. "And I believe in reincarnation."

"Is that part of Paganism?"

"Not really. But I like the idea. I want to come back as a bird. To me, that seems like the highest form of life, to be able to soar through the air."

I smiled, recalling my bird-thoughts as I waited to be released from Santa Rita. "When you think about it," I said, "reincarnation makes as much sense as anything."

She asked if I was going to the Spiral Dance in a few weeks.

"I don't think so," I said. "It's not really my style."

"In a way it's not mine, either. I like smaller, more personal rituals. The Spiral Dance is several hundred people, so it gets kind of impersonal. But I went last year, right after I got to the Bay Area, and it was a good place to meet people. That's what got me involved in LAG."

"That's funny," I said. "I don't think of it as a political event."

"It is, in its own way. It's about death and rebirth, so it makes sense to bring in things like nukes and war and clear-cutting forests, and to do chants about renewing the Earth. I like that part a lot."

She went to use the bathroom. The reggae tape was about over, so I switched to a tape of bands from Zimbabwe that Mort had made for me.

Angie smiled as she came back to the living room. "Here you are listening to African music, and you didn't come to Ashkenaz?"

"Well, I like listening, but I'm not the world's greatest dancer."

"What's there to it? Just move to the beat," she said. She was still standing, and began gently swaying to the rhythms.

"As if it were that easy!" I said. I was admiring the watery way the music flowed through her body, when she beckoned to me.

"Come on, let's see you do it." I tried to decline, but she insisted. "No one's watching, this is your chance to learn."

My face felt flushed as I stood up and faced her. She smiled at me, started swaying, and looked at my body as if expecting something to happen. I started shuffling my feet to the music, keeping careful time to the complex beat.

Angie watched for a minute, then made a simple observation. "You're dancing from your feet. You need to dance from your hips. Watch." She planted her feet squarely, then undulated her hips in time to the music.

I tried to follow. After a minute she came over behind me. "Keep your feet still." She put her hands on my hips.

Her touch sent a shiver through me. I took a breath and looked straight ahead. Little by little, under the gentle pressure of her hands, my hips loosened.

"Back and forth," she said, "back and forth. Don't think about it. Just follow me."

Slowly, unbelievably, I fell into synch with the music. The percolating drums and cascading guitars set off a vibration in my body that I'd never felt before. Move from the hips.

"Just keep it simple," Angie said, releasing my hips and dancing back in front of me. "The rest of your body will follow when you're ready."

We danced through most of the tape, stopping only to open another couple of beers. I was still a bit mystified about what to do with my arms and hands, but Angie assured me that would come around in due time. The main thing was, I was dancing.

After the tape ended, we went out on the balcony to cool off. The fog had lifted enough to see the lights of San Francisco glistening across the expanse of the Bay.

"Thanks a lot," I said. "All these years I never got the part about the hips."

"My pleasure. Next time there's African music at Ashkenaz, be there."

"Agreed," I said.

Back inside, I put on some quieter music. We sat down again on the futon, side by side. I was still wary of touching her, afraid that it would give her the wrong idea and spoil the mood. After a minute, she stretched out on the carpet, using the futon as a pillow.

"Tired?" I said.

"Getting there."

We talked for another half-hour or so. Finally she said apologetically, "I'm fading. I have to go to sleep."

"Yeah," I said. We rolled out the futon, and she lay down as if testing it out. Then she rolled onto her side and looked up at me enigmatically. A spark seemed to hover between us. What would happen if I... And what if she...

I coughed and looked away, embarrassed at my rambling imagination. "So," I said, "I guess you need some blankets."

She didn't move. "That would be nice."

I got up and fetched a couple of blankets. When I came back, she was lying on her back, eyes closed, hands folded across her stomach. She had taken the braid out of her hair, which fell loosely over her shoulders. I unfolded the blankets and spread them over her. She smiled without opening her eyes. I gazed down at her slightly-parted lips and smooth, untroubled forehead. Did she look so content every night?

I knelt next to her. "Do you have everything you need?"

"I think so," she said. She opened her eyes and met mine for a delicious moment. I reached out and touched her shoulder. "I'm really glad you stayed," I said. "It's been fun talking."

"Yeah," she said. "That's one flat tire I'll have a good memory of." She leaned up, put one arm around my neck, and gave me a long hug. "Good night, Jeff."

"Good night, Angie."

I headed down the hallway to my bedroom and closed the door. The room felt small, confined. I lay down on the bed and opened an art book, but my eyes strayed from the page. I hunted around and found a South African tape Mort had lent me. It was more jazz-flavored than what Angie and I had been dancing to, but it was close enough. I got up and opened the window, then dropped back in bed. I stretched out on my back and closed my eyes. Against the darkened lids I thought I could make out a glimmer of hope — about LAG, about changing the world — even about dancing.

Friday, October 21, 1983

I HAD TO work all afternoon. The building was a mess, and if I wanted Monday off, I had to finish a couple of plumbing repairs.

I got done around six, washed up, and headed over to Hank's shop. Tonight was the big night. The twenty-foot tube had arrived. A bunch of us were gathering that evening to turn Hank's dream into reality: LAG's own Cruise missile.

It was the eve of the Euromissiles demonstrations. October had flown by, and despite the impending actions, LAG still felt scattered. At the September spokescouncil, after much hand-wringing, we consensed to the Strategy Proposal. *It's About Times,* the Abalone Alliance paper, did a big story on how important it was. But Claudia hadn't been to a meeting since the Congress, and Craig drifted in and out. With the sponsors in withdrawal, the implementation of the strategy discussions — and LAG's future — was left in abeyance.

Meanwhile, the financial cushion we'd built up after June had frittered away. We'd mailed a fund appeal the previous week, but without a major CD action to focus attention, and nothing at all planned after October, a big return was unlikely.

It ran against the spirit of the Strategy Proposal, but I felt like we needed to call another action, pronto. Even if we got the strategy discussions going, it could take months to produce a coherent plan. If LAG was going to get through the Winter, we had to have something concrete to rally around.

October 1983
Issue # 10
DIRECT ACTION
Published by Livermore Action Group
Join the Human Billboard Oct. 22
Women's Peace Dragon in S.F. Financial District
Disrupt the Financial District Oct. 24

Direct Action #10, October 1983

Craig and I were the first two to arrive. We looked at each other awkwardly as we waited outside Hank's shop. Since he'd quit the staff, our talks were rare.

I felt like I owed it to Craig to run the future-action idea by him, despite my resentment at him and Claudia. When they got me to help facilitate the September spokescouncil that finally consensed on their Strategy Proposal, I trusted they were doing what they felt was best for LAG. But lately I felt like the whole proposal was just their way of saying goodbye with a vengeance.

Claudia, I'd about given up on. I'd talked to her a couple of times, and her cynicism grated in my ears.

But Craig could probably be coaxed back aboard. I had a sense that his retreat was more pain at how he'd been attacked over Vandenberg than political pessimism.

"Just be patient," I told him as we stood by the curbside in the fading sunlight. "People will finally listen."

"I don't think so," he said, then paused as a truck drove past. "Sometimes I feel like a prophet of doom." He chuckled, but immediately clouded. "Every passing day brings us closer to nuclear or ecological disaster. Most people can't handle the truth. They need to feel hopeful. I don't cater to that."

I scuffed the toe of my shoe against the sidewalk. "Cut people a little slack. You can't lay out some objective political line, some universal truth, and demand that everyone instantly see it your way. You have to start from where people are."

"No, we have to start from what the movement demands. And that's obvious — a long-term strategy."

"But that can start from where people are. Why can't we assume that we're going to do blockades at Livermore, and build a strategy around that?"

"You can't preordain your target and your tactic, and then say it's an open discussion. That's a joke."

My chest tightened. "No more of a joke than proposing strategy discussions and then disappearing as soon as they're consensed."

Craig took a step back. "If there was any point in my staying around, I would."

Just then Mort pulled up alongside the curb. "Where's Hank?" he called to us as he got out of his car.

"He's on the way," Craig said, walking over toward Mort. I let him end our conversation, but felt frustrated. After a year of working together, wasn't I entitled to some explanation of what he was doing?

Looking at the two of them, I felt distant. I had never cleared the air with Mort about his continual trashing of International Day. He didn't even seem to see it as a problem. With Mort, everything turned into a debate, a win/lose struggle where one side was in sole possession of the truth and the other a deviant tendency to be rooted out. Once the argument was over, it was all supposed to be bygones. "Why can't we debate ideas without all this emotional attachment?" he would say. "Why do people take political criticism like it's a personal attack?"

"Hey, here comes Hank!" Craig called out.

I pulled myself back to the present. It was Hank all right, driving a big flatbed truck with the tube lashed on back. "Check it out," he yelled. "What do you think?"

"Looks like a missile to me," I said, glad to get my mind off politics. "Want to hoist it off?"

"Are you kidding? This tube weighs a ton. It's reinforced three-quarter-inch cardboard. It'll take at least a half-dozen people to carry it. I asked Tai and Lyle to come by. Meanwhile, here's a six-pack to get us ready."

The others arrived shortly after. We set aside our beers and tackled the tube. It was heavier than I could have imagined, and the shape didn't lend itself to grabbing hold. But we finally wrestled it off the truck and into the shop.

"How are we ever going to move it at a demonstration?" Mort asked.

"Oh, don't worry," Hank told him. "It'll have wheels. The problem is what to do at the financial district demo on Monday. I won't have time to do the wheels, so we'll have to carry it. I'll cut away a lot of the top and bottom for people to stand inside it, so it'll be lighter."

Hank pulled off his gloves and flipped a couple of circuit breakers, filling the workshop with the multicolored lights of the pinball machines. Swatches of green neon glowed from one corner. Near the door was an old beer sign where a keg seemed to flow endlessly into a mug.

Once the lights came on, I let go of my earlier grievances. I shared a laugh with Mort, and was sorry when Craig took off. Hank popped the lid off a beer and handed it to me. "Is the jukebox working?" I asked.

"Yeah, go for it."

I punched some numbers, and The Who's "Magic Bus" started spinning. Hank and Tai set to carving the tube with skill-saws. The rest of us turned to pinball.

Lyle left for a few minutes. When he returned, he brought along a friend from Spain, a woman named Carmen who was involved in peace organizing in Madrid. She was about our age, but very professional-looking, with short, styled hair and matching slacks and jacket.

Having a woman around the Friday night scene was unusual. Hank's partner Judith, who was into Buddhism and meditation, rarely came by. Holly had come once, and seemed to have a good time for the short while she stayed. But I doubted she'd become a regular.

Carmen, on the other hand, seemed delighted by the games. "I never played because I was no good and didn't want to lose my money," she said. "But if it's free, how can I say no?"

She apologized for her English, which, other than being formal, seemed as good as anyone else's. "I read better than I talk," she said. "I've been reading the San Francisco newspapers since I got here, and I understand them well."

"That's cheating," Mort said, leaning back against a pinball machine. "With American papers, you already know what they are going to say before you read them."

Carmen laughed. "Es verdad — that is so true!" Then her brow furrowed. "No wonder most Americans are so ignorant of global politics. In Europe, the common people are much more aware. A man as stupid and self-centered as Reagan couldn't be elected in Europe."

"I know," said Mort. "Political leaders in Europe are expected to have a grasp of issues. They've worked their way up through the parliamentary system. A stooge like Reagan could never get a toehold."

I asked Carmen about European activists, how they were different from us.

Her hand fluttered in a flamenco motion. "You Americans are crazy, compared to Europeans."

Hank stopped working on the missile and joined us. "Wait, I want to hear this," he said. "Why are we crazy?"

"Oh, in many ways. For example, I've heard about Pagan rituals at protests. I can't imagine that in Europe."

Mort scoffed. "You're not alone. Outside of California, most Americans think it's pretty strange."

I winced at Mort's tone, but Carmen's response surprised me. "Strange, yes. But Americans are also more creative than Europeans. American people will try new things. Even if it's sometimes strange, this gives me hope."

LAG reps to the Euromissiles Coalition worked to get the coalition to do something more active at the Saturday event than the usual march and rally. The compromise was a "human billboard," which failed to excite most LAGers.

"I wish I felt some hope," Mort muttered, setting his empty bottle next to the jukebox.

"No, I see what she means," I said, looking directly at Carmen. "You never know how something will grow. What seems strange to us today might turn out to be the wave of the future."

She nodded. "This is the hope of America. In every other way, you're crazy!"

Hank brightened. "What a perfect transition to the missile. Let's try it out. We cut openings so we can stand inside and carry it on our shoulders."

We rolled it over on its side, but try as we might, we couldn't find an angle to lift it. "Wait," Hank said. "Lift the front onto the workbench, and we'll crawl under it."

Even lifting the front end was a challenge. We finally got it propped up, slipped underneath, and prepared to go airborne. "Okay," Hank called out. "One — two — three!"

Carmen cheered us on: "Come on, you strong American men!"

With much groaning we staggered to a standing position. "We could never walk like this," Mort said between gasps. We eased it back against the workbench and crawled out from under it.

Hank put his hands on his hips. "I'll have to cut away more."

While Hank and Tai took skill-saws to the tube again, Mort and I went back to talking with Lyle and Carmen.

"How many people will be at the rally tomorrow?" Carmen asked.

"Twenty thousand, maybe," I said, repeating a figure I'd heard at the last coalition meeting.

"If we're lucky," Mort said. He scraped at the label of his beer bottle with his thumbnail.

Carmen looked perturbed. "The rallies in Netherlands and Germany have drawn a half-million people."

"Half a million," I said. "I can't imagine that in this country."

Mort set his beer down. "Not without getting labor involved. That's the difference. In Europe, there's a historic bond between the left and labor that's lacking in this country."

"We have some union people coming to the Euromissiles coalition meetings," I said. "The Service Employees and the Longshore unions have endorsed it."

"SEIU and the Longshoremen, sure," Mort said as if I had stated the obvious. "Those are the last strongholds of progressive labor. But we have to reach out to the broader rank and file."

"Easier said than done," Lyle said. He pressed the start button on a casino-motif pinball game and fired the first ball.

Mort picked up his beer and turned to watch Lyle's game. "Getting working people involved means building alliances around issues that touch their lives. You aren't going to see most Americans in the streets because nuclear missiles are being stationed halfway around the world. We have to frame our nuclear protests in terms of issues like jobs, health care, or transit. We have to show how military spending means cuts in basic human services, and how it creates fewer jobs than investing in education or the environment."

"I think you're right," Carmen said. "Of course, it helps to have credible socialist parties to put that message out in Parliament."

Mort rang up the game next to Lyle's. "So what's happening in Spain?" he asked Carmen.

Lyle turned to her. "Tell them about your NATO action."

She smiled. "We did a direct action at the meeting of OTAN, or NATO, as you call it. The national coalition of Spanish peace groups was protesting at the

The Saturday, October 22 coalition rally drew about 15,000 people to San Francisco civic center for speakers and music.

OTAN meeting, directly in front of the building. At lunchtime, the diplomats planned to come out on the front stairs for newspaper photographs."

She took a sip of beer. "Before the protest, some of us had painted letters on our butts, one letter on each cheek, spelling, '¡OTAN Mierda!'"

Lyle gestured with his beer bottle. "Loosely translated, it means, 'NATO is Shit!'"

Carmen nodded. "As the delegates came out on the steps, we turned our backs to them, dropped our pants, and delivered our message."

We burst out laughing. "Now there's an action we haven't tried yet," Mort said. "I'd like to see the media coverage of that!"

"In Madrid, it got on the front page of *El Païs,*" Carmen said, then smiled sadly. "It's the only time my picture has ever been in *El Païs.* And it's my butt."

"Well, your butts were probably more photogenic than the diplomats' faces," I said.

Carmen laughed. "That's the American perspective."

We talked a while longer, and then she and Lyle took off. "We'll see you at the Euromissiles rally tomorrow," Lyle said.

Carmen bid us all buenas noches. As she was leaving, I caught her eye. "Hasta mañana," I said.

She smiled. "Si, hasta mañana."

Hank and Tai sanded down some rough edges on the missile, and we studied their handiwork. A friend of Hank's had fashioned a nosecone of blue plastic that exactly fit onto the tube. Tai added a couple of plywood fins at the back and a little windshield in front of the cockpit.

"This is practically a full-sized Cruise missile," Hank said. "You could hide one in a two-car garage."

"Or your shop," Mort said.

I had pictured the missile bright silver, with an American flag decal so it looked official. But Hank's aesthetic was a little different. On top of a coat of whitewash, he sketched lines and dots to make it look like the whole thing was riveted together out of scrap metal. Here and there was a jagged crack. Both sides were to be lettered with slogans.

"Can't miss a chance to get a message out," Hank said.

I shrugged. "You're the design engineer."

It was midnight by the time we finished painting the slogans and touching up all of the rivets. I'd told Holly I'd be out late, but I figured I better get going if I was going to be up early the next day.

"Aw, stay for one more game of pinball," Mort said. He passed me a joint.

"Well, when you put it that way, it's hard to say no." I inhaled the sweet smoke. I looked around our circle with a wave of appreciation. Nothing like a little weed and pinball to help us remember that we're all in it together.

A half-dozen games later, I finally headed for the door. Hank called out one last logistical detail. "Don't forget next Tuesday night. We're gonna hit that new building on Telegraph. I want to spray 'Cubeland' on it. That's what it is, a concrete cube."

"Count me in," I called back. "Sounds like the cultural avant-garde — architectural criticism, right on the offending walls."

HOLLY WOKE as I came in. "Hi, sweetie, how did it go?"

"We finished the missile. It's ready for Monday in the financial district. How are you doing?"

"I'm good," she said as I lay down and curled around her. "I talked to Caroline. She wants to ride BART to the rally with us tomorrow."

"So you're definitely going?"

"Oh yeah, I was just in a bad mood when I thought I would skip it. When I talked to Caroline, I knew I wanted to be there."

She rolled over to face me, and we kissed. "You can put on some music if you want," she said.

"I need to eat," I said. I caressed her hair. "Did you ever figure out a costume for Monday's action?"

"No, not really. Dressing up like an office worker seems so depressing, like I'd be punishing myself. How about you?"

"Well, I had an idea of doing something with the *Wall Street Journal*, but I haven't worked it out yet."

We kissed again. Then I headed back to the front room. I was still wired, and put on a Ramones tape, hard-driving punk to draw off my excess energy. I got out bread and cheese and settled in at the table to catch up on my journal.

I should write about the next day's Euromissiles march, my reasons for being involved in the coalition. But that seemed like work. If I was going to write about politics, the Monday action seemed a lot more interesting.

Monday, October 24, 1983

MONDAY'S FINANCIAL district protest gained a distinct psychological advantage from Saturday's Euromissiles rally. Namely, anything had to be an improvement.

Fifteen thousand people took part in the Saturday coalition rally, lining Market Street in downtown San Francisco with a "human billboard" of signs calling for peace and disarmament.

The hitch was, being a weekend, the office high-rises were deserted. Only shoppers, tourists, and panhandlers caught our message. After a couple of hours of standing around on the half-deserted streets, we marched up to civic center for music and speeches. The rally got a little blip on the evening news, a photo on page four of the Sunday paper, and disappeared.

Monday's protest could hardly do worse. I set my alarm for nine o'clock. I'd assumed Holly was coming, but she decided at the last minute to spend the day gardening. So I rode over on BART with Lyle, Tai, and several other Overthrow guys who were the crew for the LAG missile, which Hank and Mort were driving over on a flatbed truck. I'd expected to help carry the missile, but there seemed to be plenty of volunteers, and I wasn't sorry to be relieved of the burden. This was LAG's first City protest. Who knew what might happen? I didn't want to be trapped inside the missile if things got interesting elsewhere.

Affinity groups dressed as waiters and waitresses approached downtown café patrons with a platter of toy soldiers, tanks, and fighter planes, saying, "Did you order this? Well, you're paying for it!"

The proximity of Halloween brought out costumes at the October 24, 1983 Euromissiles protest in San Francisco.

We arrived at Embarcadero Plaza around ten o'clock and were greeted by a quiet crowd. My shoulders sagged as I did a quick count. Sixty people. Maybe we were early.

Mainly I saw familiar faces. Some were obvious — Jenny, Raoul, Sid, Karina, Sara, Alby. Others were no big surprise, like Doc or Belinda or Moonstone. But I hadn't expected to see Artemis from Matrix AG, or Nathaniel, my nonviolence prepper. Even Melissa and several others from Spirit had made the scene.

Of course, Melissa might just be keeping tabs on the action. At the previous week's Coordinating Council meeting, she went head to head with Karina and Raoul, insisting that the protest have monitors. Maybe she was checking up.

I wandered around, saying hi to a few people, but not getting any conversations going. I wished Angie would show up, so I could let my guard down, admit my disappointment at the turnout. She'd agree, and we'd share a pensive interlude before pitching ourselves back into the fray.

The protesters gathered in the center of the big plaza. Most others in the vicinity — business types, service workers, tourists — gave us wide berth.

I spied Raoul and Sid nearby and walked over to say hi. "Missed you Saturday," I said jokingly.

Raoul pulled back his head. "The World Series was on! Where are your priorities?" I laughed, but he turned serious. "What's the point in going to a protest that's completely pre-programmed? The organizers guarantee in advance that nothing spontaneous can happen. And then they wonder why more people don't show up. At least the outcome of a baseball game is an open question."

I nodded, then looked at Sid. "And what's your excuse?"

Sid bounced on his toes. "I don't go to legal demos," he said. "A hundred people disrupting traffic does more good than ten thousand getting a permit and marching up an empty street. If you aren't risking arrest, you're no threat to the system."

I smiled. "Hey, I never expected the coalition to threaten the system."

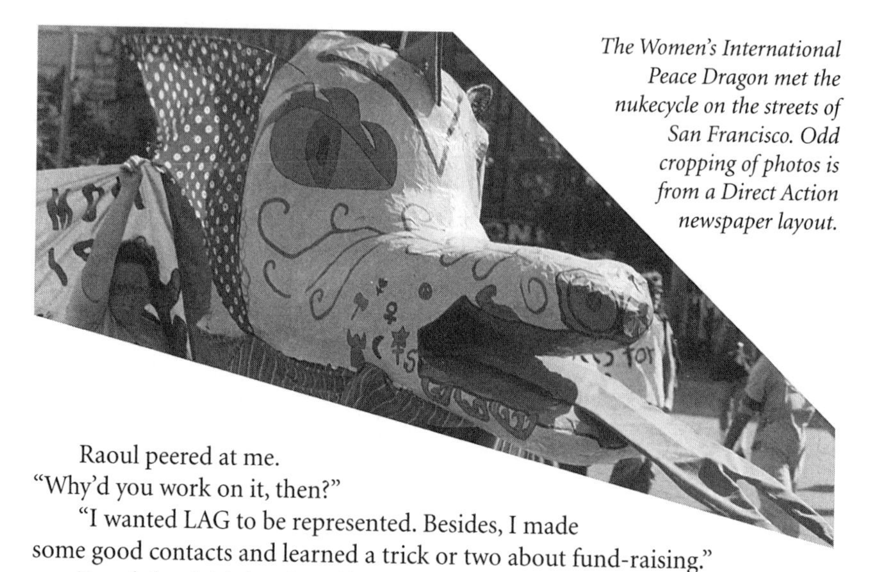

The Women's International Peace Dragon met the nukecycle on the streets of San Francisco. Odd cropping of photos is from a Direct Action newspaper layout.

Raoul peered at me. "Why'd you work on it, then?"

"I wanted LAG to be represented. Besides, I made some good contacts and learned a trick or two about fund-raising."

Raoul shook his head as if he were genuinely baffled. He and Sid walked off to find Jenny. I rotated my shoulders, trying to get loose. I surveyed the plaza. Now what? To the right, the old Ferry Building sported a tall tower with a dysfunctional clock. Beyond, the crisp blue sky shone through the steel arches of the Bay Bridge. To the left loomed the four towers of Embarcadero Center, heralds of the sunless, windswept streets of the financial district.

Hank and Mort pulled up, providing a distraction from counting the slowly-growing crowd. I helped hoist the missile off the truck. The white paint glistened in the sun. A crew of six slipped underneath and bore the missile aloft. Hank was up front, wearing an old leather aviator's helmet and a dashing scarf. The crew took a few tentative steps, then seemed to hit stride, taking the missile for its maiden voyage around the plaza.

A cluster circled up prior to the action. Above and right, a Freudian moment as the International Women's Peace Dragon met the mobile missile.

Other protesters laughed and cheered. Around the plaza, bystanders stared and pointed.

Meanwhile, Spiderwomyn AG had gotten hold of the International Peace Dragon, a big paper-maché dragon's head with a tail made of cloth panels painted or sewn by women's peace groups around the globe. Spiderwomyn stretched the tail to its full hundred feet, ending in the new LAG panel they had added.

The dragon's head was yellow, with a long, slithery red tongue. As Belinda lifted the big puppet, Artemis called out: "Don't get that tongue anywhere near the missile or we'll never live it down." I laughed, but Belinda scowled. I wondered whether she was more irritated at the heterosexual innuendo or the restriction on her movement.

The proximity of Halloween brought out a costumed crowd. One AG fashioned "warheads," silver hats shaped like missile nosecones. Next to them was a couple dressed as Uncle Sam and Betsy Ross. Several groups donned business suits with a twist — ties replaced by nooses, faces painted like skulls, or mouths drooling blood.

Nathaniel was part of a group of tax resisters dressed as waiters and waitresses. Carrying a platter decorated with toy soldiers, tanks, and warplanes, he approached a café table at the edge of the plaza. "Did you order this?"

The diners looked baffled and slightly amused. "No."

"Well," declared Nathaniel, "you're paying for it!" With a crisp gesture he presented them with a bill for $300 billion, the current military budget.

Beyond the café, a commotion erupted. A crowd of bystanders parted, and down the center strode a ragtag band of punks. A couple of dozen people, mainly in their twenties, had responded to Sid and Raoul's leafletting. They gamboled through the crowd, their spiked hair, shredded clothes, and nose-rings clashing with the pastel fashions and erect postures of the Embarcadero regulars.

The punks joined our protest, but stayed off to one side, talking among themselves. I'd heard from Jenny that the punks had formed two affinity groups, Domestic Terrorists and Gruesome Rebels. But she also said that most of them hadn't taken a nonviolence prep.

A moment later, Angie came walking across the plaza. I took a slow breath, and a smile crossed my lips. At last, someone to talk to.

Jenny spotted her as well, and reached Angie just before I did. I expected them to hug, but they greeted each other with a quick touch, like they'd just spoken moments before.

They were both dressed as office workers. Jenny's hair was pulled back in a taut bun, and she wore a gray skirt and vest over a white shirt. Angie opted for brown slacks and a matching jacket. Her auburn hair was gathered in a ponytail, and a touch of rouge colored her lightly-tanned cheeks.

I stepped toward her, and Angie threw her arms around my neck and hugged me. I held her for a long moment, then squeezed her tightly before letting go.

"What's your costume?" Angie asked.

"I have this idea to get a *Wall Street Journal* and dress myself from head to toe in stock market quotes."

"Let's do it," she said.

They walked with me to the edge of the plaza to buy a paper, then helped tape the sheets of newsprint onto me. I affixed a paper veil to a pair of sunglasses, and crowned the ensemble with a hat featuring the paper's masthead.

Tai, dressed and face-painted in military camouflage, came over with a can of poster-paint and splattered red drops on me. "Let's put a bloody hand print right over the heart," Angie said. She dipped her hand into the paint and pressed it onto my chest.

"There," she said as she toweled off her hand. "You're a walking Dow Jones."

Tai moved on, and Jenny went over to talk to Raoul, leaving me and Angie alone. I took off my sunglasses. Standing there with Angie, it was a lot easier to quit counting heads and appreciate the spectacle. Uncle Sam and Betsy Ross posed for a tourist-photo. A guy dressed as Gandhi stood talking to a couple of punks. A woman in a multicolored sarong blew soap-bubbles that wafted over the plaza.

Next to me, though, Angie

The International Women's Peace Dragon, with a tail made up of cloth panels contributed by women's groups around the world, tied up traffic as it wended its way through downtown.

seemed increasingly agitated as we waited for the action to start. I wondered whether it was pre-protest jitters or something else. I wished I could put my arm around her, but my costume got in the way. I rustled around, and Angie looked up at me expectantly. I fumbled for words. "So — are you getting busted today?"

The panels of the Peace Dragon's tail stretched for over a block.

She nodded. "I think so. I took tomorrow off work, just in case. How about you?"

"Not if I can help it. I've seen enough of jail for a while." I frowned, not liking the sound of my words. "But I'm here to protest, not sit on the sidelines and watch."

"That's good — it provides some cover for people who are getting arrested."

I smiled. "That's a good way of looking at it. The cops will see two hundred people coming up the street, and they'll have no idea how many will risk arrest. That'll give them something to think about."

Angie got called away to fetch Change of Heart's props. I thought about following her, but I wasn't in the skit, so I'd probably just be in the way. I looked around again. Still not much of a crowd. At the June Livermore action, there had been over a hundred affinity groups. Here, there were barely a hundred people.

Well, maybe a hundred and fifty. I'd heard that about a dozen affinity groups had planned actions. Where were the other ninety from Livermore? The day seemed tailor-made for AGs. Each group took a military corporation to research, prepared a leaflet about its complicity, and organized an action at their San Francisco office. So where was everybody?

Karina came past, trying to gather Change of Heart for a cluster circle. But as soon as she'd get a few people together, they'd melt back into the crowd again.

Her efforts to rally our cluster touched me, and I started to help. But Karina threw up her arms. "It's pointless, everyone is too scattered."

Melissa, standing behind us, spoke up. "What do you expect?" She cast an eye toward some skateboard punks warming up on the rim of a concrete fountain. "Affinity groups can't function in this setting. Once you get into the City, it's bound to turn into a mob."

"We're doing AG actions," Karina answered without looking at her. "You could at least wait until we get started before you pass judgment."

"It doesn't matter," Melissa said. "I've seen it before. This is a perfect set-up for provocateurs."

Karina turned around to face her. "Maybe the monitors will protect us," she said coolly. "The 'peace police.' Why do we need them? We can take care of ourselves."

"LAG always has monitors," Melissa said. "You need people who know the general plan of the action, who can answer questions or be ready for problems. It's especially important for new people. If new people don't feel safe, your movement stops growing."

Judging by today's crowd, it looked like we'd already stopped growing. In fact, we were shrinking. Where were Claudia, Craig, Pilgrim, or Caroline? They'd probably never missed a LAG demo before.

But maybe I was expecting too much from our first roving urban action. Maybe this was the cutting edge. We'd pioneer the new style, and next time hundreds more would join.

Walt, wearing a red headband that marked him as a monitor, pulled out a bullhorn and rallied the crowd together. The tinny sound grated on my ears and I stayed toward the back of the circle, touching up the tape on my costume. Walt gave a quick rap about the day's itinerary and the importance of everyone being in affinity groups. He called on any individuals not in an AG to gather over by the fountain and form a group for the day. No one moved.

"We were going to print up a route map," he went on. "But that would tip off the police. So we're going to let whichever AG is doing the next action lead the march to that site."

The tail end of the Peace Dragon flowed past the monstrous metal fountain at Embarcadero Plaza.

"Let's sing a song before we start," Melissa proposed.

"No, come on, we're already behind schedule," Raoul called out,

Only one fender-bender marred the maiden flight of LAG's nuclear missile, which weighed several hundred pounds and was carried by crews of four to six men.

and the crowd seemed to agree. Melissa looked frustrated, but rejoined her AG.

Cindy of the Commie Dupes took the bullhorn and led our ragtag procession out to Market Street. The wide sidewalks were bustling with business people and shoppers, and behind my newsprint veil I laughed at the bewilderment rippling through the oncoming faces.

I looked around for Angie. But she was talking intently with Jenny and Alby, probably fine-tuning Change of Heart's action. I adjusted my newsprint mask and fell in step with the march. Through the sunglasses, the street looked dusky. I felt removed, like I was doing my own action parallel to the main event.

Apparently I made a good sideshow. A man with a cane jerked his head and stared at me. Another guy started chuckling. A woman in a bright blue suit squinted as if she were trying to read the stock quotes.

The women's dragon moved into the lead, snaking through the sea of pedestrians and clearing a path for the rest of us. An AG in suits and bloody palms tried to shake hands with strangers, getting no takers. The punks hung together toward the back of the march, leering and making grotesque faces into the store-windows.

Hank and his crew brought up the rear. The missile glided forward gracefully, its blue plastic nosecone glinting like a warning light. In its wake it left a sea of puzzled, irritated, or amused faces. It was an auspicious debut for the missile. But one look at the grimaces on the crew's faces and I had to wonder how long they could shoulder their burden.

Up front, just behind the dragon, there was a flurry. I picked up my step. Karina and a guy named Jacey were several feet off the curb, calling to the crowd: "Into the street! Take the street!" Raoul and Jenny and Sid followed. A taxi coming up the side lane slowed and honked.

I made my way toward the front. Were they trying to get busted before we'd even done the first corporation? Didn't make sense to me. Still, if this was where the action was, I didn't want to miss it.

So far, only a handful were out in the street. The monitors were trying to keep the crowd moving on up the sidewalk. Karina and Raoul and Jacey yelled louder. A few more joined them. But most people shuffled forward, watching over their shoulders to see what would happen.

The instigators looked chagrined, especially Raoul and Jacey. I studied Jacey, whom I vaguely recognized from a couple of Berkeley demos. He was around my age, with curly brown hair and a chipped front tooth. He seemed disgusted with people's hesitation, and I thought he might storm away. But he stuck around. Which didn't thrill me. It was one thing to have Raoul or Karina pushing the limits. But someone I hardly knew? Wasn't this a LAG action?

Some costumes bordered on fantasy attire...

We turned onto Washington Street and halted in front of a nondescript high-rise that housed the offices of Boeing. As skateboarders did stunts on the corporate stairs, the Commie Dupes read a short indictment of the company for its nuclear profiteering. Then five AG members in business

...while other protesters chose especially realistic costumes.

suits climbed the stairs, sat down, and linked arms to block the main entrance.

Several motorcycle cops pulled up just as the Dupes were seated. But none came forward to initiate the arrests. We waited around for a few minutes, expecting more cops to show up and complete the action. The crowd grew restless. Three other members of the Dupes stayed behind to leaflet and observe the eventual arrests, but the march moved on.

Enola Gay, decked in vintage women's apparel, did a "Nukes are a Drag" skit in front of the Department of Energy. A third AG targeted McDonnell-Douglass Corporation. At both sites, the police again left the blockaders sitting in front of the doors. We marched on, leaving a few people behind to leaflet.

Were the cops really this unprepared, or were they messing with us? The arrests were supposed to be a highlight of the tour. When nothing happened, our morality tales lacked a climax. Maybe it was a new police strategy — bore us into submission.

The women's dragon turned off and went its own way. Hank and the missile crossed to the opposite side of the street, where they didn't have to dodge the rest of the march. The rest of us followed Spirit AG toward our next stop. The march stayed on the sidewalk, but the crowd had developed its own momentum. When the signals changed, people would keep going, stopping traffic till everyone had crossed the street. The motorcycle cops tailing us looked frustrated, but made no move to intervene.

The next stop was Dupont. Spirit and Mustard Seed AGs invoked a solemn tone by inviting people to join hands in a circle. Even the skate-punks paused and held their boards. Daniel, who recently had joined Spirit, spoke about Dupont's role in processing the fuel for the Hiroshima and Nagasaki bombs. Then he knelt on the sidewalk with Melissa and the others. After a moment of prayer, they approached the entrance, wrapped a length of chain around their waists, and padlocked it to the doors.

As they settled into position, a dozen foot-police came marching up the street. They wedged between the blockaders and the rest of us, but instead of

A die-in conveyed the aftermath of a nuclear explosion, shutting down a financial district intersection in San Francisco.

beginning the arrests, they turned to face us. The commander was talking on his radio. Was he calling for reinforcements?

People seemed fidgety, and we moved on. The march, despite losing blockaders, had grown to about two hundred and fifty people by picking up stray bike messengers, office temps, and other marginal downtown types. The mood was decidedly serious, as if everyone were straining to figure out why the cops weren't busting people.

Lunch hour was upon us. If the streets had been crowded before, now they were packed. Blow-dried functionaries squeezed past leather-and-chain punks with spiked mohawks. One AG held up hand-mirrors, mutely challenging the business people to take a look. Few did.

We crossed against another light and wound up on the same side as the missile, which stopped to let the crowd pass. As the last protesters moved past, Hank, still wearing his aviator's helmet, barked out orders. "Company, forward ho!" The six co-pilots lurched into motion. The missile careened down the sidewalk, threatening a first strike on unwary pedestrians.

Next on the itinerary was Change of Heart's Bank of America action. As we started up the slight hill of California Street, the effort seemed to drain the crowd. I took off my sunglasses and wiped my brow.

Then, as if by prearrangement, a late-arriving cadre of drummers joined us. A half-dozen men and two women, playing everything from congas to cowbells to snare drums, kicked into a rhythm.

Heads turned. Eyes brightened. Steps grew bouncier, bodies began to sway. Ahead of me, Angie skipped to the beat, the archetype of the liberated secretary. She called back to me, "Come on!" All around people were joining in, but I couldn't quite pick up the groove. Dancing in my living room was one thing. But dancing in the street?

"Go for it!" I yelled to her. She danced on ahead and caught up with Alby. I scuffed my foot on the concrete. Why hadn't I worn a more flexible costume? Why hadn't I practiced dancing more? Why couldn't I just go for it?

But it was hard to stay down for long. The missile-headed AG danced past me like a conga-line. People stepped off the curb, and the punk AGs, ignoring the pleas of the monitors, swept out into the street. Sid, Jenny, Raoul, and Jacey joined them. Traffic halted. Horns blared. Punks hooted and yelled back. The drummers pumped the beat. Angie danced out with a second wave. I stepped between two parked cars and followed, wishing she'd turn back and see me. Maybe I couldn't dance, but at least I knew how to block traffic.

Soon the entire march was in the street. The laughing and shouting reminded me of getting out of jail my first year at Livermore. People danced among the stalled cars. Sara and Karina waltzed up the center stripe of California Street. Moonstone twirled in circles, his tie-dyed gown fluttering in the breeze.

The motorcycle cops worked their radios overtime. A block ahead, a couple of squad cars and a paddywagon appeared, driving toward us. I moved for the sidewalk, but Raoul called out, "Come on! Up this one-way street! The cop cars can't follow."

The main crowd swung right onto Battery, leaving the paddywagon in our wake. Oncoming traffic on the narrow street backed up as we waded between the cars and trucks. Several motorcycle cops eked their way up the street in pursuit of us.

We passed Sacramento Street, heading toward Chinatown. I turned my *Wall Street Journal* hat so the masthead faced forward and wove around the stalled cars, savoring the mystified faces behind rolled-up windows.

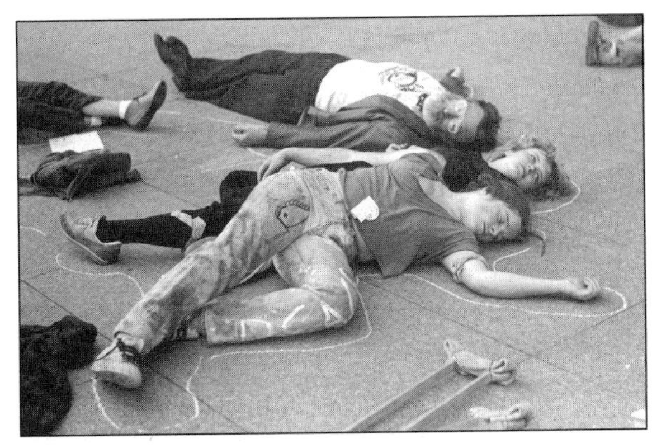

As some protesters lay motionless in the street, others traced their outlines in chalk.

At the next corner, a squad car was blocking the street. Officers were directing traffic away from the scene, but made no attempt to confront us. Jacey and Karina were up front, and steered the march left onto Clay, another one-way street. As the last of us cleared the corner, a smile broke across my face. We were outrunning the cops!

Up at Sansome Street, there were no police in sight. We gathered at the corner, a motley but jubilant crowd of two hundred. Protesters filled the intersection, bringing traffic on both streets to a standstill. I saw Angie with Jenny and headed over toward them. All around was shouting and chanting, but the punks were the loudest: "10! 9! 8!" They yelled like it was a missile countdown. "7! 6! 5!" Angie picked up the count. I joined in, wondering where it was going. "4! 3! 2! 1! Aaaaaaaggghhhhh!!!" Several dozen punks collapsed on the pavement, screaming as if they had just been nuked.

What a sight! As quickly as I could without tearing my costume, I lowered myself to the street.

As the screaming subsided, I rolled onto my side and looked around. Forty or fifty people lay strewn about on the concrete. Other protesters hung back, though, eyeing the "die-in" uncertainly.

A police van wormed its way up to the scene. A dozen riot cops debarked and brusquely lined up fifteen feet away, facing us.

Several protesters jumped up and hurried to the sidewalk. Others followed more slowly. Glad that I wasn't the first to retreat, I got to my feet. The cops weren't moving toward us. I stood there a moment eyeing them, then sauntered back to the curb. Traffic resumed its flow.

The crowd milled about. Office workers elbowed their way through the quagmire. Near me, Karina called out: "On to Bank of America!" I picked up the cry: "On to Bank of America!"

Change of Heart filtered toward the front and started down Sansome Street. Most of the crowd followed, but at Sacramento, the punk AGs peeled off and headed up the one-way street. Sid waved people out to block traffic, which was already stopped by the rest of us crossing against the light. An AG of high school youth turned down toward Wells Fargo headquarters to prepare for their action, which was scheduled after Change of Heart's.

The cops seemed confused by our splitting up, and didn't immediately follow. As we turned the corner at California, I dropped back to walk alongside Hank and the nuke missile. Chugging up the slight incline, the crew huffed and strained. Mort's eyes were tightly shut, and he winced with each step. He groaned in relief as they hit a level stretch. The missile picked up speed. As the crew approached the next corner, they veered left to cross the street.

Suddenly, a mailbox loomed directly in their flight path. I yelled to Hank, who reacted in alarm. "Stop! Stop!" he shouted. But it was too late. The momentum of the heavy tube sent them crashing into the mailbox. The

More people joined the die-ins, and traffic backed up.

nosecone shattered with a loud crack. The missile rocked crazily. Other protesters rushed to stabilize it.

Hank adjusted his aviator's headgear, then looked over his shoulder. "Don't abandon ship," he shouted. "Company! To the rear, ho!" The crew staggered into reverse. "Damage sustained," Hank called. "Resume mission!" The rest of us cheered, and the missile rounded the corner and resumed its flight.

Ahead of us, the protest approached the Bank of America building, a dark plate-glass monolith fronted by a large plaza. I speed-walked toward the front of the march, not wanting to miss Change of Heart's action.

Although we were being pursued by a half-dozen foot-cops, there were none between us and the entrance. As we swarmed toward the glass doors, the security guard inside the lobby looked panic-stricken. He scurried up to the doors and locked them. Some protesters heckled him and pounded on the glass. I felt sorry for the guy, who seemed shaken. Employees approaching the doors were turned away by protesters. "This bank is closed by order of The People!"

A squad of cops caught up with the protest, shoved a few people aside, wedged their way in, and formed a line between us and the door. The crowd was hollering and jeering, and the squad leader radioed for help. I edged up close. The line of cops planted their boots and gripped their nightsticks. I studied one officer, a young guy with a thin black mustache. He refused to make eye contact, but through his visor I could see discomfort playing across his face. Was he troubled by our message? Was he nervous? Scared? I laughed to myself — a scared cop. Of course, he had a club, and got paid to use it. Maybe scaring cops wasn't the best idea.

Change of Heart huddled off to one side. Then, with the row of cops as a scenic backdrop, Antonio stepped forward and declaimed a paean to Mother Earth in his rich, impassioned voice. As he waxed poetic, Alby led a solemn procession of business-suited "executives," their faces painted like skulls, across the plaza. The executives carried briefcases stuffed with money and splattered with blood, each stenciled with a lucrative investment sphere: "South Africa," "Nuclear Weapons," "Third World." They circled Antonio, throwing fistfuls of money over him like confetti.

A circle of downtown workers gathered around to watch. Some seemed scornful, but many seemed curious, and accepted leaflets delineating B of A's nuclear portfolio.

Two protesters in gray stepped out from the edges of the crowd, each holding a "mushroom cloud" made of helium balloons. Strung between the mushroom clouds was a sign reading, "Stop Banking on Nukes." Simultaneously they released the clouds, and the banner rose gracefully past Bank of America's windows.

Following a skit about Bank of America's nuclear portfolio, protesters stage a die-in on the Plaza.

As the balloons rose, Angie marched in waving a flag embroidered with the Earth and stars. She joined Antonio and Lifers AG in front of the bank, where they planted the flag and clustered round in a re-creation of the famous Iwo Jima photo from World War II. "In the name of the Earth and its people, we reclaim this land for peace," Antonio proclaimed.

Karina came forward carrying a length of chain and several padlocks. The original plan was for the cluster to chain themselves to the bank doors. But the row of cops closed off that option.

Karina looked at Sara, then cast the chains down in front of the line of police. "Out into the street," she cried, "Let's take the street!"

Planting the Earth flag — an AG re-created the famous World War II image.

Before the cops could regroup, eight Change of Hearters and a half-dozen other volunteers moved into the intersection and sat down in the face of oncoming cars.

Angie and Jenny were the first ones seated, with Moonstone and Alby not far behind. Sara, next to me on the curb, hesitated. Conflicted thoughts seemed to flit across her brow. Then she stepped into the street and joined the action.

The rest of us, plus assorted bystanders, filled the sidewalk in front of B of A, bearing witness to the drama. The cops, torn between the bank and the intersection, were spread too thin to arrest and detain the blockaders. A half-dozen officers lined up in the street and pulled out their batons. My eyes grew wide. Were they seriously going to attack peaceful protesters?

Luckily, they held off for a minute and reinforcements arrived — a paddywagon and a dozen more police. The new squad fastened down their helmets and quickly took the blockaders into custody.

Jenny and Angie were the last two arrested. I tried to catch their eyes as they were hauled away, with no luck. From inside the paddywagon came shouts and laughter. I pictured Angie laughing with Alby, and felt a twinge of regret. That could be me. I should be in there. Why hadn't I joined Change of Heart's action? What was the big deal about getting arrested?

I wondered whether the earlier AGs had been busted. And what about the rest of us — would the cops try to sweep us all up?

The paddywagon doors slammed, jarring me from my reverie and reminding me how glad I was not to be getting arrested. Besides, with Raoul and Jacey still at large, who knew what else might happen? Maybe the best was still to come.

We retreated to the plaza. What now? Somewhere in the crowd, a voice cried out: "10! 9! 8!" Jubilantly, people picked up the count: "7! 6! 5!" Dozens yelled together: "4! 3! 2! 1! Aaaaaaaggghhhh!" Hardly anyone held back. A hundred people dropped onto the pavement, screaming and kicking.

The cops fanned out as if to surround us. We scrambled back to our feet. "Down to Wells Fargo," someone called out. "This way!"

The mass of protesters moved as one, leaving the cops behind. I stepped aside to retape a page of my costume, watching the crowd flow past. Our numbers seemed down. Then I remembered that the punks and a couple of other AGs had peeled off. Hopefully we'd all rendezvous at our next site.

Wells Fargo, a block down the hill, was the final stop of the tour. The bank had investments in thirty-two of the thirty-six top U.S. nuclear contractors, making it a fitting climax to the day. An affinity group of Berkeley High students, Dr. Spock's Youth Brigade, had gotten to the bank's main entrance before the cops caught on. When we arrived, a dozen teenagers were blockading the doors.

The police had been called, and a row of riot cops stood in front of an open paddywagon. They seemed thrown off by our arrival — even more when the roving punk AGs rejoined us, pursued by their own personal squad of cops.

The protest spilled into the street. The police cordoned off the entire block to traffic. Some people cheered, but I wondered if it was really a victory to get isolated with a bunch of increasingly-irritated cops.

In front of me, Sid pointed to a clump of tough-looking men across the street. "Meet your friendly neighborhood narcs! Memorize their faces!"

The half-dozen undercover cops stared back at us. Despite their attempt to dress like protesters — flannel shirts, blue jeans, and headbands — they looked more like construction workers ready for a brawl. Next to them, even the punks looked soft and innocent.

I looked through our crowd. Were we already infiltrated? It wasn't like Livermore, where I knew everyone that I was in the street with.

A squad of helmeted police marched up to the blockade line. We jeered as they began arresting the teenage protesters.

Someone started counting off a die-in. Ten seconds later we were lying all over the sidewalk and street, moaning and groaning and generally making it difficult for the police to get the arrestees over to the paddywagon.

I lay on my back, crinkling my newspaper costume. I took off my sunglasses. My eyes ran up the old twenty-story high-rise. I squinted, and realized there were faces peering down — dozens of Wells Fargo employees were leaning out the windows of the old building, gawking at us.

Someone started a chant: "Corporate Killers! Corporate Killers!"

Even more workers leaned out of their windows, and a second chant gained momentum among the protesters: "Jump! Jump! Jump!" I shuddered and laughed. "Jump! Jump!"

A youth AG blocked the entrance to Wells Fargo headquarters as the final action of the day.

The cops gradually got the youth AG into the paddywagon. They slammed the back door and fired up the engine. With everyone arrested, the die-in seemed pointless. I climbed to my feet and moved back to the sidewalk with the rest of the crowd.

People looked around. Was the demo winding down? That was fine by me. It had been a good day, and I didn't see a lot more we could do. If we wrapped up now, we could call the day a success.

I assumed others felt the same. But as the paddywagon started to pull out, Raoul stepped directly in front of it. "Come on!" he hollered. "Take the street!"

Was he crazy? Did he really trust the cops not to run over him? "Come on!" Raoul yelled again.

Several officers came trotting toward the commotion. People yelled to Raoul, who slowly backed away from the approaching cops. A couple of them used their clubs to nudge him back, but meanwhile Sid and Jacey slipped past them and blocked the van again. Others spilled off the curb, and the van had to wait while the cops formed a line and forced everyone back onto the sidewalk.

Finally, the paddywagon made its escape, seeming to take with it the last lingering purpose of our protest. People were starting to leave. Jacey and Raoul looked exasperated.

I felt exasperated back at them. Over the course of the day, I had marched in the street, done die-ins, even gotten in the way of the cops arresting the youth AG. But every time I joined something, these guys went and pushed it further. Enough already!

Norm, still wearing his red monitor's headband, took the bullhorn. "Come on, let's march back to the Embarcadero and do a closing," he called out. A handful of people seconded the idea, but no one started the stampede. Jacey muttered to himself and stalked off with a few friends. Other people were filtering away.

I felt a dull pain building behind my eyes. What was the point in a closing circle? I looked at the dwindling crowd. Why not just head for BART? I felt like I'd come full circle, back to how I felt before Angie had arrived at Embarcadero. I wished she hadn't gotten arrested, so I had someone to ride home with.

Suddenly, back in front of Wells Fargo, a scuffle erupted. Two undercovers had grabbed a protester — Raoul! They forced him toward a patrol car. More cops converged. They formed a tight circle around Raoul and shoved him into the back seat of the cruiser.

I joined a knot of people yelling at the cop car as it sped away. Tai was the only person I recognized. "They got him for blocking the van," he said. "They waited till people were leaving and grabbed him!"

I sucked in a breath. What dirty players, nailing someone after the protest was done! Then I laughed coldly. Had I thought there were rules, and the game was officially over?

The undercovers had disappeared. The crowd, now fifty strong, yelled at the remaining cops, who gestured mockingly at us with their clubs as they backed away toward their cars. One seemed to point right at me, as if calling me a dupe, and I erupted. "Cowards! You wait until we're leaving and grab someone! Cowards!"

Norm hurried up to me. "What happened? That was Raoul? Damn! I told him if he got popped, I'd go, too." He pulled off his shoulder bag and thrust it at me. "Take this back to the office, I'll get it later." He fished around in his pockets and slipped me a small baggie of weed. "Get rid of this, too," he said.

I didn't have time to ask questions before he turned and strode into the street, blocking the path of a departing squad car. From the other side of the street, Sid and a couple of punks joined him. The cops got out, pushed the protesters against the car, clamped on handcuffs, and shoved all four into the rear seat of the cruiser.

I stood there, still holding the weed. The police turned toward the rest of us. A chill ran up my back. I ripped off the remnants of my newspaper costume, wadded Norm's bag of weed into it, and stuffed it deep into a trash container.

As I turned back, one cop seemed to be staring directly at me. I felt vulnerable, isolated. Where was everyone I knew? Oh yeah — in jail. How weird to be the only one on the outside.

I spotted Tai and headed over toward him. The rest of the protesters were filtering away. Lunch hour was over, and the sidewalks were thinning out.

I looked at Tai. "Think anyone went to Embarcadero for the closing?"

"Maybe. Hank said he was taking the missile over there."

At that moment, Hank and Mort came around the corner without the missile. Mort massaged his shoulder as they approached us. "What's going on?"

"Two undercover cops just grabbed Raoul," Tai said. "He wasn't doing anything, just standing there."

"Narcs," Hank said contemptuously. We looked around. The remaining cops seemed to be packing up shop. Hank turned to me. "Can you give us a hand getting the missile over to Embarcadero?"

"Where is it now?"

"We stashed it in an alley around the corner," Hank said. "Hopefully we didn't get a ticket for an illegally parked nuclear missile. Come on, let's get out of here."

I RODE BACK to Berkeley with Hank and Mort. Hank basked in the success of the missile. "People loved it. Now we have to get some wheels on it. Can you imagine their faces when we come peddling up the street?"

"Our whole protest got some pretty funny looks today," I said. "And we had the cops totally confused. When we split into smaller groups, they didn't know what to do."

"I wouldn't go that far," Mort said. "I think they were checking us out. The stakes were pretty low this time. I wouldn't read too much into it as far as how they'll be next time."

"Yeah," Hank said. "Cops don't like losing."

By the time we got back to Berkeley and unloaded the missile, it was 6:30. Coordinating Council had been called off for the week, so the two of them were heading to Hank's shop to play pinball. "We'll probably order a pizza," Mort said. "Why don't you come over?"

"Sounds like fun," I said. "But I told Holly I'd meet her around seven."

Holly, who was gardening at an Urban Ecology plot in West Berkeley, wasn't back when I got home. I made some popcorn and opened a book on Medieval economics, but my mind kept wandering off. The only subject I had attention for lately was art history. I was still pretty good at looking at pictures.

I fiddled around with my guitar, which I had been neglecting again since singing at BARF a month before. Maybe I'd have more time for music this Fall, since LAG didn't have anything planned...

Of course having no plans was hardly something to celebrate. We had to find a way to move forward. The Strategy Proposal was taking forever to get up and running, and I sensed our momentum grinding to a halt. There seemed to be just one option — call an action. Jenny and I were proposing a spokescouncil meeting in November to consider action proposals for the Winter and Spring. Something to tide us over until the Strategy discussions produced a new consensus. Unless we had a focus, it felt like LAG might fizzle out altogether.

A key turned in the front door, startling me out of my thoughts. Holly came in and gave me a quick hug. "I'm so cold," she said. Her face was pale except for the red of her nose. "I've got to take a hot shower."

As she headed down the hall, I opened a beer and put on a tape of The Clash. As the guitars crunched the opening chords, I suddenly wanted to tell Holly all about the protest — Hank's missile, countdowns and die-ins, the confused cops, marching down the center of the street, Raoul getting arrested... I grabbed a piece of paper and started listing things I should write about in my journal.

When Holly came back from the shower, she went in the kitchen and put some soup on the stove. I clicked off The Clash and walked over to the doorway. "You missed a really good action today," I said.

"Oh, yeah. How was it?" She opened the refrigerator and got some juice.

I leaned against the door frame. "Pretty exciting." The images came flooding back, but how could I put them into words? I thought of the people in jail — Angie, Jenny, Raoul, Sid, Karina, and the rest. They were still in the midst of the action.

"How many people were there?" she asked.

"Two or three hundred."

"Is that all?"

"Well, yeah." I remembered my initial disappointment with the size of the crowd. "But the spirit was amazing. People were marching in the streets, running up one-way streets to avoid the cops, blocking intersections. Raoul got grabbed by undercover cops, and then Norm and Sid got busted in solidarity."

She poured her soup into a bowl. "I'm glad I wasn't there," she said.

I looked at her in chagrin. She was looking down and stirring her soup. "Too bad Norm got arrested," she said. "We have a peace camp meeting tomorrow night. He's been going out to Livermore to look for land. If he isn't there, it'll be hard to move ahead."

"Norm might have other priorities than the peace camp right now," I said. "LAG had an action today."

She looked up in surprise. "The peace camp is LAG, too. There's a whole work group — Daniel, Melissa, Artemis, Monique..."

"Not the broadest cross section," I said.

"Was today any better?"

"A little." I ate a handful of popcorn, but it tasted stale. I wished I hadn't said anything about the peace camp. "How about some music?"

"Sure," she said. "Not too loud, though."

Nothing in the rows of tapes looked very appealing. I finally settled on an old bluegrass album.

Holly brought her soup out to the table. "I'm sorry I'm not more excited about the protest," she said. "How did Change of Heart's action go?"

I sat down with her and took a drink of beer. "It was good," I said quietly. "I didn't feel very involved with the cluster today."

"Yeah, sometimes Change of Heart doesn't feel like my group anymore. And with International Day postponed, I don't see those people much, either." She paused as if observing a moment of silence. "That's part of my dream for the peace camp. If we're living together on the land, maybe we'll build deeper bonds than at protests."

She scrunched up her neck as if trying to release a knot. I stood up, moved behind her, and started kneading her shoulders. She leaned her head back against my stomach.

"How about going out for a walk," I said, hoping the change of venue might shift our perspectives.

"I'm really tired," she said. "How about coming to bed with me? We haven't made love all week."

"Okay," I said, although a walk was what I really wanted. Maybe later I'd go out alone. My back felt tight as I followed her down the hall. I stopped and stretched against a door frame, then let go a yawn.

In our bedroom, Holly lit a candle. I put on a Thelonius Monk tape. We stretched out on the bed, still talking about this and that. I told her about Karina and Sara waltzing in the street at the protest.

Holly smiled. "I'd like to have seen that. Those two are so beautiful. Especially Sara. Don't you think so?"

I nodded. Holly was quiet for a minute, then asked in a calm, inquisitive voice, "Have you ever been in bed with two women?"

Her question caught me off-guard, and I had to think for a moment. "No," I finally said. "I guess I think of it like conversation — the deepest connections are between two people. It's hard to imagine that kind of intimacy among three."

Holly rolled onto her back. "Frank and I slept with a woman friend of ours one time. I liked it a lot. It's hard to imagine being physical with just a woman. I'd feel so awkward. But with a man and a woman, it was like I had permission to explore. I wanted to do it again, but Frank and I broke up shortly after that."

I tried to picture Sara with us in a threesome, but I had trouble imagining her being interested. Now Karina or Angie, well, my imagination definitely stretched that far. Not that I was going to initiate anything. But if Holly wanted to try it, well...

Holly leaned over and kissed my lips. We gazed into each other's eyes silently, then kissed again. I ran my hand down her back, down the length of her leg. She pressed her body against mine. As I ran my fingers through her hair, I imagined it was Karina's thick black tresses I was caressing. I felt a rush of excitement. I pushed the image away, but it kept coming back, and finally I stopped resisting.

Afterward, we lay together silently, side by side, holding hands. I felt guilty for my fantasies, and was glad Holly wasn't facing me. Finally she drifted off. I lay with her for a while, ruminating about our relationship and about LAG. In the flickering candlelight, the two seemed barely distinct. What would it take to rekindle the passion? What would it take to bring us back together?

Tuesday, October 25, 1983

Sixteen Americans were killed and seventy-seven injured this morning as the United States invaded the Caribbean nation of Grenada and deposed recently-elected Prime Minister Maurice Bishop. Bishop is an avowed socialist and leader of the "New Jewel" movement in Grenada.

A Reagan administration spokesman said that ensuring the safety of the approximately 1100 American citizens on Grenada was the goal of the intervention, which was supported by the Organization of Eastern Caribbean States.

— *from news reports*

THE NEXT DAY began as usual. I slept till noon, showered, and shuffled out to the living room to have a snack before I checked in on my job.

As I got to the end of the hallway, Holly was just hanging up the telephone. She turned her head slowly. Her hand remained motionless on the phone. "That was Caroline — Reagan has invaded Grenada."

"Grenada? The island? What did they do to us?"

"Elected a socialist government."

"So we invaded them? That's incredible." I looked out the window, then back at Holly. "The strongest country in the world invading a tiny island? You'd think we might have a little pride."

Holly nodded. "I wonder if there's a protest up at Cal?"

We decided to walk up to campus. On Telegraph Avenue, people were going about life as if nothing had happened. Did people even know? When we crossed Bancroft onto Sproul Plaza, though, a speaker with a portable mic and amplifier was giving a forceful speech about U.S. imperialism. He was flanked by a few people with hastily-lettered signs. A small crowd of students gathered to listen, but most people ignored him, or stared as if it were a historical re-enactment of Berkeley's glory days.

I felt like I'd awakened into an alternate reality. "Where are all the protesters?" I said as we walked home afterwards. "Hasn't anyone heard of Vietnam? Don't they know what intervention means?"

"People don't understand what's happened yet," Holly said. "The media is calling it a 'police action,' not military intervention. It'll take time for the truth to get out."

At the rally, someone had announced that CISPES and other Central America groups were calling for a march through downtown Berkeley that evening. I needed to work my job that afternoon, but Holly dedicated a couple of hours to phoning LAGers to let them know about the march.

We headed downtown about five o'clock. "A lot of people told me they'd be there," Holly said. "I'll bet there'll be several hundred people."

"I sure hope so," I said. The little lunchtime rally had left me unsettled and irritable. Another pint-sized protest and I'd have to wonder what was becoming of our movement.

I needn't have worried. When we arrived at the downtown Berkeley BART station, a couple of hundred people had already gathered. Handmade signs were everywhere, and the Inkworks collective had printed a bunch of red and black placards for others to carry.

Here and there I spotted familiar faces, but most were new to me. That's actually a good sign, I thought. Not just the usual suspects. As more and more people arrived, I could practically feel the tide turning.

A couple of leftist groups with dueling bullhorns each attracted a small audience, but the demo lacked focus. I wished I'd brought my guitar.

Sure enough, what brought us together was music. Country Joe McDonald, a hero of the 1969 Woodstock festival, showed up and sang his Vietnam-era "Feel Like I'm Fixin' To Die Rag," followed by "Give Peace a Chance." As Country Joe sang the final chorus, the whole crowd seemed to join in — except for one young woman in ragged black clothes who stalked the perimeter snarling, "Screw this! Let's march! Screw this!"

Hank and Mort showed up with a van-load of signs that Overthrow had painted for past Central America demonstrations. "These'll come in handy,"

Hank said. “Especially since Nicaragua is probably next on Reagan’s hit list.”

Karina and Sara arrived from the City. “There’s a march tomorrow in the Mission, but nothing tonight,” Sara said. “So we came over here.”

“Yeah,” Karina said. “I couldn’t miss this.”

Sara looked at the crowd, which overflowed the little plaza and stretched down the sidewalk. “Reagan has gotten away with covert intervention in Central America, hiring mercenaries and selling weapons. But people won’t stand for war. Didn’t the government learn anything from Vietnam?”

“I guess Reagan has to learn the lesson for himself,” I said.

All through the crowd I spotted LAGers — Pilgrim, Daniel, Claudia, Doc and Belinda with their son Jeremy, Artemis, Moonstone...

The one person I missed was Angie. If Karina and Sara were out of jail, Angie must be, too. I should have called and made sure she knew about the protest. Probably Holly left her a message. More people were showing up every minute, so there was still a chance.

One of the bullhorns finally rounded the crowd up. Five or six hundred strong, we marched away from the BART station, waving banners and chanting. For once, chanting felt good, like it focused our anger instead of squandering it. We started on the wide downtown sidewalks, but at the first intersection we swept out and took over the southbound lanes of Shattuck Avenue, clogging the southbound lanes. The Berkeley police ordered us out of the street, to no effect. Some people even crossed over the median strip and slowed oncoming traffic, but the police succeeded in herding them back onto the southbound side.

As we rounded the corner at Dwight, two young guys in leather jackets came marching toward us waving a large American flag. My eyes opened wide. Were they crazy? Then one of them whipped out a pocket lighter and flamboyantly torched the corner of Old Glory, which went up in flames so fast that his partner dropped the pole and jumped back.

Crowds shut down Berkeley streets in response to news of the Grenada invasion.

Most people cheered, although a few shook their heads. I stood transfixed till only embers remained. I'd just witnessed my first flag-burning — a rite of passage.

I found Holly, and we headed up Dwight toward Telegraph Avenue. "Right toward our building," I said. "Can you believe it, we're marching right past our apartment!"

Bystanders joined in. The fresh recruits fueled the chanting: "Stop the killing, Stop the war! U.S. out of Grenada!"

As we passed a row of three-story apartment buildings on Dwight, someone belted out another chant, which the crowd quickly took up: "Out of your houses and into the street! Out of your houses and into the street!" Faces appeared in the windows. Voices twenty feet above yelled their support. From every door people streamed out. Like magic, the crowd doubled in the space of a few blocks.

Holly and I clasped hands as we swept by our building. I gazed at the front steps and the little garden that I tended daily. They'd just become part of history.

We crossed Telegraph, where dozens more joined. "Looks like the truth is getting out," I said to Holly.

We must have numbered a thousand as we angled across People's Park and hit the first U.C. dormitory complex. We marched through the commons, raising a ruckus in the concrete canyons. Hundreds of students were out on their balconies, cheering and raising their fists in solidarity.

When we emerged from the dorms and turned onto Bancroft Avenue, Holly spied Caroline. She made her way through the crowd, and I lost sight of her. I looked downhill toward the front of the march. For a good three blocks, the wide street was packed with people. Chants and shouts resounded from the surrounding buildings.

The cops gave up challenging us for control of the street. Instead, they acted like parade monitors, stationing themselves at cross streets and ordering oncoming traffic to stop for us. Stalled motorists responded by honking in time to the chants. Everyone seemed to know they were part of something big.

As the march headed back downtown, I ran into Sara. I was walking fast, and she sort of bounded alongside me, her long hair fluttering over her shoulders. I remembered hearing that Sara had been a cheerleader in high school. Go team! Stop traffic!

"Unreal, isn't it?" I said. "This is the most people I've ever seen at a protest."

"Hardly," she said. "There were a lot more than this at the Euromissiles demo on Saturday."

I laughed. "That was different. This is the real thing!"

The cops continued to stop traffic for us. But one intersection eluded their patrol, and a couple of fraternity types in a sports coupe tried to force their way through a thin spot in the crowd.

Marchers exploded in rage. Fists and signs hammered down on the vehicle. People swarmed against the doors and started rocking the car, but others stepped in and shepherded the coupe back out of the jam. When the car turned and fled, a roar went up from those in the vicinity.

I stepped to the sidelines and watched the crowd stream by. People passing the spot even a minute later seemed to have no idea of the incident. The march was too dense for anyone to know what was happening a half-block away.

My part of the march neared the downtown Bank of America. Perhaps out of patriotic zeal, the bank had left its American flag flying on the corner pole. It would have been torched long before, except for one resolute protester, a short woman with glasses and graying hair. She stood with her back to the pole, begging the crowd to spare Old Glory. "Please don't burn it," she pleaded. "It alienates people from our cause."

A tall, skinny guy about my age jumped up on a trash container and started shrieking, "Burn it! Get the flag! Burn it!"

I stopped and stared at him. His fists were clenched, and the veins bulged out of his neck. "Burn the flag!"

Several people harried the flagpole, but the woman fended them off.

"Get the flag! Burn it!" His screeching set me on edge. Suddenly he leapt off the trash can and started for the woman. I stepped into his path. "Hey, buddy, cool off."

He froze for an instant, then whirled at me. "Narc! Cop! Get away from me! Pig! Get away from me!" With a wild look he darted into the crowd.

I staggered back a step and wished I could disappear. How mortifying, to be called a narc in front of all these strangers!

To my relief, I spotted Lyle and Mort coming past. I made my way over and took a deep breath, glad to be among friends. I looked back at the flagpole, where the woman continued to fend off all attempts on the flag.

We rounded the corner and overflowed the six lanes of University Avenue. Up front, CISPES and others argued over what to do next. The CISPES faction wanted to go to city hall and demand that the city council, which met on Tuesday evenings, pass a resolution condemning the invasion. Others wanted to march on through downtown.

CISPES' plan made sense to me. Success with the liberal city council was likely, and a resolution would be a good climax to the march.

Out in the center of the intersection at Shattuck, someone had gotten a small fire burning. I spied Jacey rifling a newspaper rack for fuel. "More newspapers," he yelled. "We need more papers."

The police, restrained up to that point, seemed agitated at the sight of the fire. Several cops near me bunched together and conferred. Over in front of McDonald's, a row of helmeted officers fidgeted with their billyclubs.

Across the street, a protester with long dreadlocks kicked in a *USA Today* stand and grabbed the papers. Onlookers cheered. A moment later, though, four cops pushed through the crowd and seized the perpetrator. They had him dead to rights. But in a flash, a dozen people surged forward. I watched incredulously as they grabbed the dreadlocked guy back. The cops melted, and slunk away like reprimanded schoolboys. A shout rose from the crowd, and more papers were heaped on the bonfire.

Gradually, the crowd drifted toward city hall, two blocks away. It was eight o'clock, still early enough to catch the council and demand a resolution.

The crowd overflowed the lawn and closed the street in front of the old domed building. I arrived just in time to see Mayor Gus Newport come out of the council meeting. He walked slowly to the top of the stairs holding a bullhorn. People were yelling and chanting, but finally the crowd quieted enough for the mayor to speak.

Newport was a burly man, with the presence of a fullback or a bodyguard. But his speaking manner, even through a bullhorn, was distinctly low-key. He calmly informed us that the Berkeley Citizens' Action majority on the city council had already adopted a proposal condemning the Grenada invasion as a racist attack on the predominantly Black Caribbean nation, and calling it a diversion of attention from the real war on the poor in our own country. The crowd cheered, and when Newport urged people to head home and return to the streets the next day, most seemed ready to comply. A few die-hards wanted to keep marching that night, but it made sense to me that a peaceful denouement to the first night's march would encourage more people to come out tomorrow.

I found Holly in the crowd and gave her a long hug. "Pretty amazing, huh?" My voice was hoarse from yelling.

"It's hard to believe," she said. "And this is just the first night."

All the way home, we traded stories and relived the night. I told her about the un-arrest of the dreadlocked guy. "I always think of the police as invincible," I said. "But when the crowd challenged them, they caved in."

"I think we were reaching a lot of the police," she said. "I loved seeing them stopping traffic for us."

Holly went to bed soon after we got home, but I stayed up for several hours, trying to capture every detail and nuance in my journal.

It was a great story. Somewhere along the way, though, my exhilaration abated. We take over the streets and yell and chant angry slogans — then we go home and have dinner and write in our journals. It seemed a little too easy.

Still, gripping images stayed with me. Thousands of people taking to the streets... Traffic brought to a standstill... Flags burned... The police powerless to stop us...

Friday, November 4, 1983

THE FOLLOWING afternoon saw a big noon rally on Sproul Plaza, followed by a march and die-ins around downtown Berkeley. The marches continued for the next several days, and Central America support groups called for an emergency coalition to do a rally on November 12th. Mort and Melissa and I went to the coalition meetings as LAG reps, and I volunteered to help coordinate fund-raising.

True to our word, we continued protesting until the war ended. Which was easy, since the fighting was over in a few days. The socialists were deposed, an acceptable regime was installed, and the conquering heroes headed home to a wave of patriotic fervor unmatched since the early 1960s. Aside from small protests in San Francisco and a handful of other cities, there was no visible dissent. Every day it was the same headline: "America Stands Tall Again!"

I was stunned. With our anti-nuclear protests, even if we numbered only in the low thousands, I always felt that huge numbers of Americans stood behind us. Now, far from being the vanguard of a new anti-war movement, the Bay Area looked like a dusty relic of a bygone era.

That first night, I thought we'd reached a crisis point — even moderates who had slumbered through the nuclear build-up and the social cutbacks of Reagan's first three years would finally wake up.

But where were they? Where were the legions who had stopped the

UC students and community members gathered for an anti-invasion rally on Sproul Plaza, historic site of the mid-1960s Free Speech Movement.

Vietnam War? Where were the university occupations and waterfront strikes? Did we have to wait till thousands were dead before war was worth protesting?

Even worse was the absurd outpouring of patriotism in middle America. As if attacking Grenada was something to be proud of! I pictured my family back in Terre Haute, good Christians every one. They took it on faith that America stood for righteousness and truth. If the president said we were fighting a just and necessary war against a ruthless enemy bent on our utter destruction, it must be so.

Doggedly, almost as a way of distracting myself from reality, I stuck with the organizing for the November 12th rally. The coalition meetings were stiff and uninspiring. But I felt appreciated for my work on fund-raising, and LAG, which older organizations seemed to have regarded as a flash in the pan, was becoming part of the progressive community. Maybe something good would come of it.

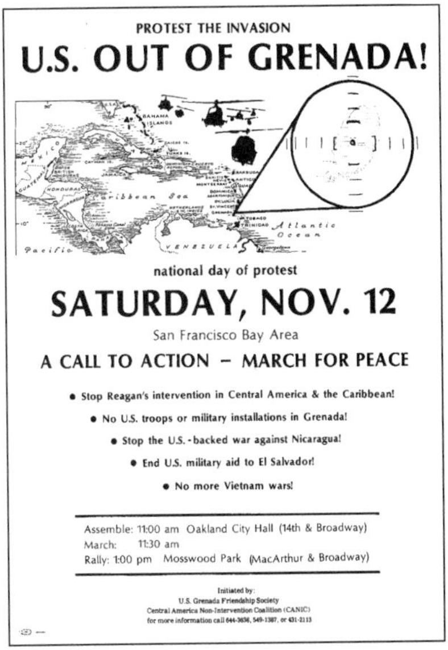

PROTEST THE INVASION

U.S. OUT OF GRENADA!

national day of protest

SATURDAY, NOV. 12

San Francisco Bay Area

A CALL TO ACTION – MARCH FOR PEACE

- Stop Reagan's intervention in Central America & the Caribbean!
- No U.S. troops or military installations in Grenada!
- Stop the U.S.-backed war against Nicaragua!
- End U.S. military aid to El Salvador!
- No more Vietnam wars!

Assemble: 11:00 am Oakland City Hall (14th & Broadway)
March: 11:30 am
Rally: 1:00 pm Mosswood Park (MacArthur & Broadway)

Initiated by:
U.S. Grenada Friendship Society
Central America Non-Intervention Coalition (CANIC)
for more information call 644-3636, 549-1387, or 431-2113

A hastily-formed local coalition called a November 12 rally, but by that time the "war" was over and the troops were heading home.

As I APPROACHED the office early Friday afternoon, I spotted Karina and Sara talking outside the door. I started toward them, then realized they were arguing heatedly. I tried to nod and slide past, but as I approached, Karina stepped over and welcomed me with a long hug.

I looked over her shoulder at Sara, who said a quiet "hello." She seemed to be staring at the back of Karina's head. As we ended our hug, Karina kept hold of my hand and asked how I was doing. Sara reached for the door. "I'm going back inside," she said curtly to Karina. "I'll see you tonight."

Karina squeezed my hand as if thanking me for extricating her from a tight spot. "I'm taking off. See you soon."

"Where are you heading?"

She looked both ways, then leaned close. "To buy spraypaint. We're doing a stencil that shows the outline of Central America, plus two lines of words, so we need three colors."

"On a Friday night? Why not wait till Sunday, so you only have to stay in jail one night if you get caught?"

She smiled slyly. "We're doing the same stencil over in the Mission on Sunday night."

I laughed. "Give me a call from jail."

"It's a collect call," she said.

"It'd be worth it. I've never gotten a call from anyone in jail." We hugged again, and I turned to enter the office. The door seemed to stick more than usual. Inside, it took a moment for my eyes to adjust to the light and spot the people amidst the clutter. Sara and Claude were working at a front table. Maria turned from her desk to say hi.

At a back table I spied Angie and Jenny and Raoul working on a mailing. Angie was seated facing the front, and waved to me. I needed to open the Direct Action mail and talk to Maria about the next weekend's spokescouncil, but then maybe I could go back and hang out with them.

As I checked the mail, I looked at Sara. What was going on between her and Karina? Was it a spat, or deeper problems? Her forehead was furrowed as she talked with Claude about the proposal for an Emergency Response Network. I pulled up a chair next to her.

"We need the ERN in place fast," Claude said. "Nicaragua and Cuba are prime targets. Reagan would love to wipe economic and social issues off the front page with war. We need to be ready."

"I think the spokescouncil will go for it," Sara said. "It would give LAG a whole new purpose."

I agreed. I'd heard some

Enola Gay AG led the Faggot Liberation Army and other Allied Forces in an invasion of Angel Island in the San Francisco Bay, in solidarity with the U.S invasion of Grenada.

concerns about process, like who could trigger the network and how to choose a target for an emergency action. But we could work on that. The key point was to be ready with a plan. Reagan's militaristic posturing was polarizing the country, forcing thousands more to take a stand. Soon, it might be millions. And LAG would be on the cutting edge, rallying the forces of dissent and resistance.

Then I thought about Holly. What if she were typical? After the initial frenzy of "emergency responses," the reality of our isolation and powerlessness seemed to overwhelm her. "All we do is rush around protesting the latest atrocity," she had said recently. "It's burning me out. I need to stay focused on positive projects like the peace camp."

Holly had been so depressed the past week that I didn't argue. If working on the peace camp helped stabilize her moods, good for her. But to me, the ERN held a lot more promise for rejuvenating LAG than did the peace camp. We needed an action.

Doc came in the door. "I've got the photos from yesterday," he said.

I went over and sat next to him on one of the front couches, glad for the respite from worrying. The previous day, Enola Gay AG had commemorated the Grenada invasion by leading Change of Heart and friends in an amphibious assault on Angel Island, a state park in the middle of the Bay.

Angie and Jenny, who had been part of the expedition, came to have a look. Jenny sat by Doc. Angie sat on the back of the couch, draping her arm loosely around my shoulder and leaning forward to see the pictures. Her hair brushed my face as she reached for one of the photos. It was a shot of her, Jenny, and Alby paddling a rubber raft toward the island. Jenny gritted her teeth as she worked against the waves. Alby was laughing, and Angie, wearing a camouflage beret, wielded her paddle like a bazooka aimed right at the photographer.

Why hadn't I done the action with them? I had convinced myself that the Grenada coalition rally, just a week away, demanded all my attention. And there certainly was plenty to be done. But seeing the photos, I doubted I'd made the best decision.

Doc held up a photo of the rafts landing on the island. An upside-down American flag fluttered in the breeze. Another showed Enola Gay planting the Faggot Liberation Army banner.

"When we landed," said Jenny, "there were some tourists on the beach, and they put up their arms like they were surrendering."

Angie laughed, which set me laughing, too. She put the photos in the graphics folder, then followed Jenny back to where Raoul was working on the mailing. I looked over my list of phone calls. Nothing seemed especially pressing. I put the list in my mail slot and made my way to the back of the office.

Just as I pulled up a chair, the phone rang for Angie. She went up front to answer, and I was left with Jenny and Raoul.

Jenny and I had gotten closer since Holly left the staff. She was my main co-conspirator at the office, and I supported her at Coordinating Council. But our relationship didn't have the lightness of Angie and me, especially when Raoul was around.

Raoul and I folded the letters and handed them to Jenny to stuff in the envelopes. I hadn't talked with him since his arrest at the financial district action, which seemed like ages ago. He and most of the forty men arrested had elected to stay in jail till arraignment.

"They threatened some of us with heavy charges," he said. "But most of the men held solidarity and refused to give their names. And after three days they let us all out with time-served. It was a great feeling, especially when Norm and Sid got busted in solidarity with me."

"Three days," I said. "What did you do for three days?"

"We spent a lot of time analyzing street tactics. Sid and I made up this board game called 'Gridlock,' where you try to block streets and stop traffic and outrun the cops."

I laughed. "Go straight to Jail — do not pass Go."

He squinted at me. "The point is to get people thinking in terms of small groups. There's an inertia in a large group of people that makes it easy for the monitors and cops to control. With small groups, the cops might thwart some of us, but other AGs would get through." He paused, and his eyes seemed to focus beyond me. "But at least we disrupted something. With just a couple of hundred people we created chaos. What if there were a thousand next time?"

Silently I took a new stack of letters and began folding. Good luck finding another eight hundred street protesters. Gridlock tactics weren't going to draw old-line LAGers. I could already hear Melissa and Nathaniel lecturing us about nonviolence and taking responsibility for our actions.

But I didn't bring it up. Raoul and I tended to get into a dynamic where he was the hip young dude into rap music, squatting, and street demos, while I was the stodgy old-timer who made phone calls for coalition rallies and worried about what Melissa might think.

This time, though, I had a trump card. Raoul's three days in jail meant that he missed the first Grenada march. I told him about the crowd taking over the streets, the cops stopping traffic, and seeing the dreadlocked guy get un-arrested.

I narrated the last incident in gripping detail, but Raoul just shrugged. "Oh, yeah, cops are total cowards if anyone stands up to them. They depend on us being intimidated by the mere threat of violence."

"It's sometimes more than a threat," I said.

He shrugged again. Too bad Angie was still on the phone. She'd find a way to prick Raoul's bubble.

Suppose he had been at the Grenada march. Sure, he'd have been in the street. But would he have grabbed the dreadlocked guy back? It wasn't just a question of courage or strength — it was speed. You had to act without hesitation. No time to think. I had little doubt about myself — I'd be too slow, too worried about the consequences, too much in awe of the police. That others were so unflinchingly defiant amazed me.

As we folded the last of the letters, Angie got off the phone and came back to join us. I gestured to the chair next to me. But she declined. "I've got to get going," she said. She leaned down and gave me a hug. "I'll see you soon."

DIRECT ACTION

November 1983

Published by Livermore Action Group

Table of Contents

GRENADA P. 1, 3, 12
OCTOBER PROTESTS
LOCAL P. 4, 5, 15, 16
USA P. 6-7
INTERNATIONAL RESISTANCE P. 8-9
LEBANON, SHARON DEMO P. 1, 11, 12
CENTRAL AMERICA P. 11, 13, 19
DECEMBER ACTIONS 1, 10
VANDENBERG ACTION COALITION P. 11
DIABLO CANYON P. 10
LIVERMORE LAB P. 2
LAG INFO, HOW TO JOIN P. 15-17
LEGAL P. 16-17
CALENDAR P. 19
--HOW TO JOIN LAG--SEE PG. 16--

WELLS FARGO. OCTOBER 24: ABOVE & BELOW

WELCOME TO THE FINANCIAL DISTRICT

Keith Holmes

Livermore Action Group
3126 Shattuck Ave.
Berkeley, CA 94705

Bulk Rate
U.S. Postage Paid
Permit No. 20
Berkeley, CA

Direct Action #11, November 1983

Just my luck, I thought. I work on the mailing, suffer stoically through Raoul's smugness — and still get no time with Angie.

Monday, November 21, 1983

"Damn it!" Claude said. His gray hair glowed under the flickering fluorescent light. "Either we provide a channel for the anger, or we're going to be swept aside. The ERN is our one hope to keep LAG relevant."

Across the twelve-person circle, Doc exhaled sharply through his teeth. "The ERN would destroy affinity group process. Why not set up a steering committee and quit pretending?"

The Emergency Response Network wasn't even on Coordinating Council's agenda. But the bad blood from the previous weekend's spokescouncil seeped into every discussion.

I was facilitating the meeting, trying to keep us on the agenda while allowing some opening for people to vent their frustrations about the ERN. I cleared my throat, which felt scratchy. Someone's folding chair creaked. I wished I had some water.

Claude, sitting with his back to a green chalkboard, didn't even bother to raise his hand. "You're condemning LAG to impotence," he said. "In a crisis, decisions are needed in an instant. If we wait to get consensus from a hundred affinity groups, history will pass us by. It's simple — is LAG going to take leadership, or stand on the sidelines crying about process?"

At the spokescouncil, Claude and Sara's carefully-crafted proposal had received strong support from most of the sixty people present. But consensus process meant that if even one AG objected, the proposal was delayed or derailed. Four AGs expressed concerns about how decisions would be made in a crisis. Three agreed to stand aside and allow consensus.

The lone dissenting voice was Enola Gay, which insisted that the ERN proposal go back to the work group and be amended to give affinity groups the final power in calling an emergency action.

Reactions ranged from resignation to exasperation, with Claude storming out of the meeting. People sputtered and pleaded and cajoled, but Enola Gay stood firm — send the proposal back to the work group.

Several members of Enola Gay had been at the spokescouncil to take the heat for blocking consensus. But at Coordinating Council, Doc was alone. He crossed his arms and glared at Claude. "We're not opposed to an emergency network. But we refuse to empower a central committee to call actions without consulting the spokescouncil."

Sara held out her hands beseechingly. "By the time the spokescouncil meets, the emergency might be over."

Exactly, I thought. Time is of the essence. In more ways than one. We needed the ERN approved before the next Direct Action went to press, so we could start preparing for the crisis the government was sure to provoke. Consensing to the ERN virtually guaranteed LAG a Spring action.

I called on myself, and twisted in my folding chair so I faced Doc. "Why doesn't Enola Gay have a member on the ERN work group? Anyone can be on it. If you want input, join the work group."

Doc spoke slowly and deliberately. "That's not the point. I'm talking about principle. The spokescouncil is the body that calls actions. We don't need a work group calling actions that they think the movement needs."

Sara slumped in her chair and looked away. Claude looked like he was about to speak anyway, so I called on him. "We're at a critical juncture," he said. "We could wake up tomorrow and find that the U.S. has invaded Nicaragua or Cuba. We have to be prepared to respond now."

"Crying 'crisis' is always the way democracy is subverted," Doc said. "Besides, why do we need a central authority? AGs can do actions in an emergency without a central authority."

Claude leaned forward. His fingers gripped the edge of his chair. "Of course AGs can protest. But for a major action, we need LAG's reputation and experience. What use is LAG, if not to call and coordinate actions?"

He seemed about to walk out again. I groped for some way to mollify Claude and Sara without pushing Doc further into a corner. To my relief, Melissa spoke up. "Can we move on? There's no decision we can make tonight. Let's get on with the agenda."

"Fine," Claude muttered. "LAG can stand on the sidelines when they invade Nicaragua."

I shared his exasperation , although as facilitator I couldn't say it. Sure, there were other groups that could organize a response. The Grenada coalition could be reformed if needed. But what about LAG? We were an action group without an action, and not even the ability to call one in an emergency. It made me wonder why we were sitting through a four-hour Coordinating Council meeting.

As we moved into work group reports, my attention wandered across the circle to Angie. She didn't come to many Coordinating Council meetings, but tonight she was the Direct Action spoke. Her head was down, and her braids fell across her face. She seemed to be doodling on her notepad. After a moment, she looked up at the clock, then caught my eye and smiled. I smiled back, drinking in the contact.

She stopped drawing to report on Direct Action. I was glad she was giving the report, so I could sit back and enjoy the good news. "The newspaper just celebrated its one year anniversary," Angie said. "And we're no longer losing money. There are enough subscribers to pay for it."

Murmurs of approval rippled around the circle. "We're working on the December issue right now," Angie continued. "We'll have some articles about the local response to Grenada, and four pages of international news. Plus, we're starting a section on organizing around the Democratic Convention."

The Convention. Finally, something definite! The Democrats were on their way to San Francisco next July to nominate an opponent to Ronald Reagan. Since Grenada, Reagan's popularity ratings had shot through the roof, and no one wanted to help him by undermining the Democrats. But at the same time, we couldn't ignore the fact that the Democratic-controlled Congress had rubber-stamped every aspect of Reagan's military build-up. We couldn't stand by and ignore their culpability while they partied in San Francisco.

Angie finished her report, closed her notebook, and stuck it in her daypack. Was she leaving? Damn. I tried to catch her eye, but she waved a quick goodbye to the meeting and headed out of the room. I watched her go, then looked back at our circle. A dozen people sitting on folding chairs in a dingy classroom. This was the revolution? No wonder Angie didn't stick around.

Next to me, Jenny suddenly jumped up and ran after Angie. Maybe we should take a break and I could go, too.

"What's left on the agenda?" Melissa stared impatiently at me.

"Huh? Oh, let's see..." I pulled my attention back to the final topic — a meeting space for the December spokescouncil. A meeting that would consense on the ERN proposal, call a Spring action, start organizing for the Democratic Convention...

Why not? We were due for a breakthrough. We needed a decision, now. Everyone seemed to accept that the Strategy Proposal was on hold. Unless we agreed on something quick, we could kiss the Spring goodbye.

Jenny came back in and volunteered to reserve the meeting room at the Unitarian Fellowship for the spokescouncil. We did a closing circle, put the folding chairs away, and closed up shop. Outside on Vine Street, I caught up with Doc, hoping to do a little low-key lobbying.

"Can't we find some compromise?" I said as I wrapped a scarf around my neck. "Most people want the ERN. There has to be some way to have good process and still get things done."

He shrugged. "Depends on what you're trying to get done. Is your goal to win a specific campaign, like closing a nuclear plant or saving an old-growth forest — or are you trying to challenge the entire way our society operates?"

"We can do both," I said.

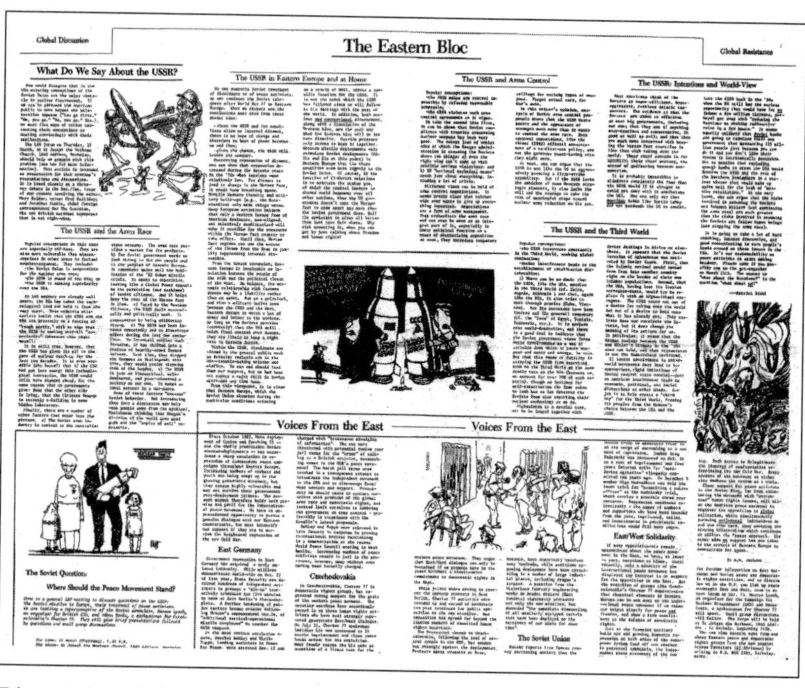
Global Discussion

The Eastern Bloc

Global Resistance

What Do We Say About the USSR?

The USSR in Eastern Europe and at Home

The USSR and Arms Control

The USSR: Intentions and World-View

The USSR and the Arms Race

The USSR and the Third World

Voices From the East

Voices From the East

The Soviet Question:

Where Should the Peace Movement Stand?

East Germany

Czechoslovakia

The Soviet Union

East/West Solidarity

Direct Action tried to keep readers abreast of emerging dissident movements in Eastern Europe — part of the changes which preceded the collapse of the Soviet bloc in 1989.

His eyes narrowed. "Not always. Good process isn't efficient. It doesn't produce quick fixes. That's why groups focused on 'winning campaigns' are usually hierarchical." He looked at me carefully, as if weighing how best to phrase his next point. "To build a movement for fundamental change, trust is the key. Over the long haul, you have to have good process to keep people together. Each person has to feel like their voice is being respected."

"Fine," I said. "But Reagan could invade Nicaragua tomorrow. We need an action in place."

"Why? Why is LAG suddenly putting its focus on responding to the government? That was the point of doing our blockades on the Summer Solstice — we were setting our own agenda, creating our own timeline. And didn't we learn at Vandenberg how, if we're in response mode, they can jerk us around by changing their dates? Why are we falling into that trap again?"

It was more than I wanted to hear. My head drooped.

Doc reached out and touched my arm. "Really, I'm not opposed to emergency actions," he said. "I just want accountability. If we sacrifice process to expediency, we're defeating ourselves. Political victory isn't enough. The problem is institutional. We have to change the entire social and cultural system. We have to challenge the whole idea of delegating decisions to 'experts' or 'leaders.'"

As he spoke of challenging institutions, my mind wandered off to a Lenin essay I'd read in jail at Santa Rita: "State and Revolution." Wasn't that Lenin's main point, that we can't simply rehabilitate the existing institutions, but have to create entirely new social structures? Was Doc turning Leninist on me?

It was time to let go. I hugged Doc goodbye, and Jenny and I headed for her car. With the meeting behind me, my mind drifted back to Angie again. "I guess Angie had enough of the meeting," I said to Jenny, fishing for some more specifics.

Jenny was searching her daypack for her car keys. "Yeah, she was meeting this guy named Jackson at ten. He was waiting on his motorcycle when she got outside."

A guy on a motorcycle? At ten o'clock at night? I felt hot. I clawed at my scarf, which was choking me. Jenny opened her door and reached across to unlock mine. A motorcycle. Well, what was it to me? I had plenty to think about with Holly. I didn't need to worry about Angie riding around on a motorcycle.

I climbed inside and rolled down the window. Jenny seemed lost in her own thoughts and said I could put some music on. I poked through the box of tapes on the floor, but nothing inspired me. I stole a look into the back seat, half-hoping Angie would suddenly materialize and transform my spirits. But all I saw was old newspapers.

I stuck in a reggae tape to have some sound besides traffic. So Angie was riding on a motorcycle with some guy named Jackson. Damn, I thought. I hope she's wearing a helmet.

Thanksgiving 1983

THE AIR FELT moist as we passed under the trees that marked the beginning of the fire trail through the Berkeley hills. The morning rain had blown over, and the sun was beginning to dispel the clouds.

Around a bend, the trail narrowed to the width of a jeep, and we began the winding ascent. The trees and underbrush, rising to our left and dropping off to the right, glistened as sunlight struck the wet leaves.

Holly and I were going to Caroline's for Thanksgiving dinner, but that left us the whole afternoon to hike. We strolled hand in hand out of the tree-shadows and into a stretch of sunlight.

Holly had shown signs lately of pulling out of her up-and-down cycle. She was mostly avoiding meetings, but the peace camp seemed to have awakened some of her former passion for organizing.

"It looks like we have land," she told me. "The owner could change his mind, but apparently he has his own feud with the Lab, so he's happy to see us protesting. We just have to agree not to use it as a base for illegal actions."

"That could be a problem if we call a Spring action," I said.

"The camp will close at the end of March. As long as the action is after that, it's fine."

I nodded silently and drew a long breath. It still felt like a distraction. Regardless of the timing, could LAG afford to divert energy into a peace camp?

And if the peace camp wasn't enough, Holly told me about Sara and Karina's proposal for a cluster action in late January. "I'm not sure of their exact plans. They want to do something around Central America."

"We could get that chance any day," I said tersely. "That's why we need the ERN. Who knows what Reagan is planning? We need to stay focused on a LAG protest, not siphon energy away into smaller actions."

Holly shrugged. "You should talk to Sara and Karina. They're presenting their proposal at the cluster meeting next week."

I looked to the right, where the hill dropped off sharply. Far below, a creek flowed past. Why was I arguing with Holly over Sara and Karina's proposal?

"I heard Daniel met with some Mobilization for Survival people from out east," I said, "and they want to revive International Day for next Fall."

Holly yawned. "Yeah, they might. They can use our contacts if they want, but it won't be International Day. I think they want to call it Days of Disarmament. It isn't the same."

We walked along silently. I remembered the previous year, how she'd lived for International Day and for LAG. What would it take to bring her back? What would it take to bring back any of the people who were drifting away?

I thought of Craig, who had just returned from a month of travel. "Do you think Craig will be at Caroline's?"

"Yeah," she said, her voice brightening. "And Claudia might come by, too."

"Wow, a regular office reunion," I said. Holly smiled, but I felt some agitation. "I never have cleared the air with Craig and Claudia for disappearing after we consensed to the Strategy Proposal. I feel like they planned to quit all along."

"I don't think they did it on purpose," Holly said. "They're just feeling burned out. I can relate. You get a burst of inspiration, and you think you have all of your energy back. But then there's a setback, and suddenly everything feels hopeless again."

As we climbed a steep section of the trail, my mind slogged back through the past few months. What a roller coaster. No wonder I felt drained.

We reached a level stretch. A rustic bench afforded a view down the canyon all the way to the Bay. I put my arm around Holly. Enough politics.

We took a deep breath together. Shafts of sunlight played off the waters of the distant Bay. A feathery breeze wafted through the trees, and a wave of thanks spread through me — thanks for Berkeley, for my friends, for the radical community of the Bay Area. Most of all, thanks for having Holly to share it with. Amid the swirling currents of LAG, she was my anchor. Even the peace camp was a blessing, if it kept her engaged.

I looked at Holly, who still gazed out at the tranquil Bay. Her hair, which glinted in the sunlight, rustled against her jacket. She slowly turned toward me, and our lips met in a kiss.

Tuesday, December 6, 1983

"COME BACK to our apartment with us," Jenny said. "We're going to eat dinner before the cluster meeting. Come on, it'll be better than staying here at the office."

I knew she was right. I'd been working on the newspaper all afternoon and would be at the Change of Heart meeting all evening.

"Take a break," Angie said. She came over and tugged on my arm. I didn't need much persuading. We closed up the office and headed for Jenny's car.

"You sit in the front," Angie said. I waited to get in while Jenny moved a daypack and a couple of paper bags off the seat. Angie cleared space in the back and buckled herself in.

On the ride home, they told me about a graffiti action they were planning. Jenny glanced at me as we waited for a light to change. "The idea is to have a garden bloom on the sidewalks over the next few months, leading up to Spring Equinox. The first round will be a stencil of some small green stems poking through the soil."

"Great idea," I said. "Where are you going to do it?"

"Oh, all around," Angie said from the back. "In our neighborhood, around the LAG office, up near Telegraph Avenue. Once we've made the stencils, we might as well get some use out of them." She paused as Jenny swerved around a stalled car. "After we do the first round, we wait for some rain. Once the pavement is dry again, we do a round adding taller sprouts and stems. The next round adds buds and little flowers. The last adds full-grown flowers."

"Plus we're going to do butterflies and other bugs," Jenny said.

"Wow, that's really ambitious," I said.

"Yeah," said Angie. "We'll see how far it gets. We already made the first two sets of stencils."

Jenny pulled into a parking area in front of their little building, a two-story number wedged between a big house and a bigger apartment complex. Angie unlocked the front door and we stepped in.

The living room had a low ceiling that gave it a box-like feel. On one side were bookshelves and a stereo, on the other an old tan couch. The only ornament on the white walls was a glossy Michael Jackson poster that had come unstuck at one corner. A bright overhead light illuminated the books, clothes, and cassettes strewn around the room.

"So, this is our place," Jenny said with a flutter of her hand. "Back there are our bedrooms."

The doors were open, and it was no mystery whose was whose. Jenny's room continued the living room decor, stark white walls highlighting the clutter on the floor. "I haven't had much time to clean lately," she said apologetically.

"You've been working overtime with Raoul," Angie said.

"Yeah, well...."

Jenny turned toward the kitchen. Angie went into her room. "Come on in," she said to me.

I stepped into a different world. Cloth hangings made the walls gently undulate. Neatly arranged bookshelves rose next to the door. On her bedspread, a deck of tarot cards lay fanned out. Rocks, leaves, candles, beads, goddess figurines, and the like were arrayed atop her dresser. "I like the stuff you have here," I said.

"Stuff?" She laughed softly. "That's my altar."

"Oh." I flushed. I was glad her eyes were on the altar and not on me. "It's nice. What kind of altar is it?"

"It represents the four elements," she said. "Earth, air, fire, and water." She straightened a circle of polished stones. "It helps me stay centered when I do rituals."

Jenny called to us from the kitchen. "I'm heating up some chicken soup, want a bowl?"

"Sure," I said.

"I'll be out in a minute," Angie said.

The kitchen looked like an annex to Jenny's room. Dishes filled the sink and counters. Papers covered the kitchen table. "Maybe you could wash a few bowls," Jenny said. "I'll clear us a place to sit." She scooped up a bunch of papers and deposited them on the living room couch.

I washed the bowls and set them out. Jenny poured us some soup. "Oh, I forgot to tell you," she said. "The spokescouncil got moved to the campus ministries building. And we have to be out of the room by six o'clock because there's a chorus rehearsal."

Jenny and I were scheduled to co-facilitate the upcoming spokescouncil. "I don't care if it gets moved to Siberia," I said, "as long as we call a Spring action."

"Well, there's plenty of proposals."

"Yeah," I said. "Too many. But only two have any support — Livermore and the financial district."

"Everyone I know wants the financial district," she said.

I nodded. "I'm fine either way, as long as we come up with a decision."

Angie came into the kitchen and held out a brown vest. "Can I wear this tonight?"

"Sure," Jenny said. "You can have it if you want."

"Thanks," Angie said. "I accept." Right in front of us, she pulled off her sweater. Under it she wore a black bra. I acted casual, but I couldn't keep my eyes off her. Her jeans hung low on her hips. The bra was trimmed with lace which followed the curve of her breasts.

I twinged with jealousy at the image of her riding on the back of Jackson's motorcycle, her breasts pressed against his back. What was up with that, anyway? Was it serious? She never mentioned him when I was around.

Jenny dished a bowl of soup for Angie, then went to her room to call Raoul.

Angie buttoned her vest and sat down at the table. There was an unaccustomed silence between us. She blew on her soup. I tried to think of something to ask, and thought of her altar. "Have you been to any rituals lately?"

She sipped her soup. "Mainly, I've been doing rituals by myself, trying to get clear on what to do with my life. I'm tired of sitting in an office typing and answering phones."

"I can see where that would get old," I said.

She glanced over her shoulder as if checking for eavesdroppers. "Don't tell anyone else this, okay? I haven't even told Jenny. But I'm thinking about enrolling in a cabinet-making class. I want to learn a trade."

"Really? Why cabinet-making?"

"I like working with wood. I've heard there's plenty of jobs. And it seems more artistic than regular carpentry. It's just an idea. But lately I've been casting a circle and doing tarot readings to help me see the bigger picture. Because whatever choice I make will close off other options." She tilted her head, then laughed. "I think I just figured that out, right now." She looked at me and laughed again.

I didn't quite get the joke, but I laughed, too.

Angie added salt to her soup. "So that's my personal rituals. As far as bigger ones, the next Reclaiming ritual is the eve of Winter Solstice out at the ocean. I've heard it's wonderful, that there's a bonfire and people go in the ocean and then come back and dance around the fire." She paused and looked at me intently. "Have you practiced dancing since our lesson?"

"Me? A little." I rubbed my neck. "I've been listening to a lot of African music, and I'm getting better at feeling the beat. But it's still hard to move to it."

"You need to hear it live. We should check the schedule at Ashkenaz."

Jenny came back and dumped her bowl in the sink. "We need to get going. Raoul is over at Tai's. I told him I'd give him a ride back to Berkeley."

I finished my soup and followed them out to the car. Tai lived close by. Jenny found a spot across the street and shut off the engine. "I'll be back in a minute," she said as she opened the door. She headed toward Tai's house. Angie got out and climbed in the back seat with me to make room for Raoul.

It was a small car, made even tighter by several boxes of books and tapes, plus an assortment of old *Bay Guardians* and other alternative media. I slipped my arm across the seat behind Angie. Her feet were propped up on a stack of papers on the floor on her side, and our knees touched.

Silence settled over us. I tried to remember what we usually talked about, but drew a blank. My chest felt tight, and our cramped quarters made it hard to get a deep breath. Groping for a topic, I asked her about cabinet-making.

This graffiti mural appeared on a vacant South Berkeley building in early 1984.

But she seemed reluctant to say more, as if I might hold her to her words.

Jenny and Raoul were taking their time. Not that I objected to being alone with Angie. If only I could think of something to say. I turned toward her, and she looked at me expectantly. At a loss, I lowered my arm around her shoulders. "I really like being with you," I finally said. My voice felt small.

"Thanks, Jeff," she said in a hushed voice. "I really like spending time with you. You're a special man."

I laughed involuntarily. "I don't usually think of myself as a man."

She looked me up and down. "Why? What are you?"

"A 'guy.' It comes with a lot less baggage."

"I guess I can understand that. Well, you're a really nice guy."

I laughed again, feeling lighter. She turned toward me and we hugged. I ran my hand up her back and squeezed her to me, feeling her warmth. "You're great," I whispered.

The car door wrenched open. "Hey, what's going on back there?" Raoul called. "Think you're at a drive-in movie?"

I flushed. But Angie shot right back: "Yeah! Where's the popcorn?"

We settled into our seats for the ride to Berkeley. My arm was still around Angie, and my chest still tingled.

I looked at her and wondered what she was feeling. Not as much, apparently — she was asking Raoul about the graffiti action he was doing with Tai later that evening. I felt a little disappointed, and made myself listen to Raoul.

"We have this wall in South Berkeley scouted out," he said. "It's really visible during the day, but at night it's dark enough that the cops probably won't spot us. Tai wants to do this whole big mural of Beetle Bailey, with Sarge chasing him and yelling, 'We're going to El Salvador!'"

Tai was good enough with a spraypaint can to pull it off, I knew. "I'll mainly be the lookout," Raoul told us. "But I've been wanting to do my name on that wall in wild-style. Tonight's the night."

We dropped him off downtown and headed for Alby's house for the Change of Heart meeting. It was almost eight when we arrived and made our way into the crowded living room. Holly looked surprised to see me come in with Angie and Jenny. I suddenly felt warm. I pulled off my sweatshirt and said an awkward hello to the circle, then went over, bent down, and gave Holly a hug.

She gave me a quizzical look. "Are you okay?"

"Yeah," I said. "Just running late."

Most people were on the two couches or sitting on the floor in front of them. I took a seat by myself in a high-backed armchair. I tried to get my attention on the meeting, but it was hard. Angie was sitting on the floor across the circle from me, and I had a tough time keeping my eyes off her.

Then I looked at Holly and felt queasy. I looked away before she noticed. I shifted around, trying to get comfortable in my chair, straining to keep my mind on the meeting.

Not like the meeting itself was exactly a model of focus. Karina read the agenda: "We need to evaluate the financial district action, then discuss the proposal for a cluster action. We have to talk about the Emergency Response Network. Plus, we need people to help wheat-paste some posters about Nicaragua around San Francisco."

Antonio offered to facilitate. We started with an evaluation of the October 24th financial district action.

I'd heard plenty of talk about the action in the past couple of weeks, some negative but most of it indifferent. The City action failed to excite the wider Northern California network that had developed around Diablo, Livermore, and Vandenberg. And even within the Bay Area, a lot of pacifists and Livermore stalwarts were unenthused about another roving action.

But at the Change of Heart meeting, speaker after speaker lauded the protest. There was only one criticism — it was too restrained.

Angie joined the chorus from her seat on the floor. "It's demeaning to have monitors making people stay on the sidewalks," she said. "It's like we're in third grade, and we need crossing guards."

"Yeah," Alby said. "If LAG wants monitors controlling every action, maybe it's time to do our own."

I looked at Angie. Was she thinking the same? I'd heard that Jenny and Raoul and Jacey were forming a new AG to do autonomous actions. Was Angie part of it, too?

We moved on to the cluster action. Karina, who had been sitting on the floor, got up and sat on the arm of the couch opposite me. "Sara and I have a proposal for an action next month," she said. She looked eagerly around the circle. "It's in the City. But we can't tell you the exact location."

A buzz ran around the circle. I looked over at Holly, who was smiling at Sara. Was she in on the secret?

"Can't you give us a hint?" Angie said with a trace of irritation in her voice.

"We want to get inside and disrupt things," Sara said. "So we can't risk letting the police find out."

People started talking about costumes and street-theater ideas, as if consensus on the basic proposal were a foregone conclusion. I seemed to be the only one not enthralled with the idea. And how could I be? LAG was struggling to pull together a Spring action — and Change of Heart was going off and doing its own thing. How was LAG supposed to survive if the most active clusters pulled away?

I looked over at Angie, hoping she would read my mind and offer some sympathy. But she was leaning toward Jenny, sharing a laugh.

My lips tightened. I felt like I was swallowed in the big armchair, that no one could even see me. Holly was saying something to Sara. What did she know? Holly wasn't the clandestine type. Karina, sure. And Sara made sense. But Holly? Why was she supporting this? Why wasn't she wasn't thinking of LAG, of the bigger picture?

As if to accentuate LAG's impasse, we moved on to the ERN. Doc had sat quietly at the end of a couch through the early part of the meeting. Now he leaned forward. "Enola Gay wants Change of Heart to support our block of the ERN until it's revised to guarantee spokescouncil input on all decisions."

Sara looked as if she'd been caught off-guard. "Block? You're blocking it?"

Holly quickly raised her hand. "Why can't the spokescouncil decide ahead of time what the target and type of action will be? Then all the work group does is set the date."

"But there's still the question of triggering the alert," Doc said. "Who decides what's a crisis? What if it's not an outright invasion, but a naval blockade or a bombing raid? I don't want to see some steering committee dragging LAG into an action without consulting the AGs."

"Then be on the work group," Sara snapped. "I'm sick of people acting like the ERN is a conspiracy trying to take over LAG!"

Several people came to Sara's support, and it was clear that Doc was outnumbered. "I can't believe how little we value process," he finally said. "Everyone gives lip service to consensus, but when the crunch comes, out the window it goes."

He stared blankly at the floor. I hated to see Doc isolated. I searched for something to say, some common ground. Holly, too, seemed to be groping in vain.

DIRECT ACTION

December 1983

Published by Livermore Action Group

Tax Day Livermore Action—See Page One

Direct Action #12, December 1983

Antonio called us back to the agenda, asking if there were any closing announcements. Alby and Karina said they needed people to wheat-paste Nicaragua posters, and several people volunteered.

To my surprise, Angie objected. "Plastering posters makes a mess. We should have more respect for the neighborhood."

"I don't think we need to respect private property," Alby said. "We're putting them on banks and boarded-up stores. We don't paste them on people's houses."

"It's still something everyone has to look at," Angie said, her voice rising.

"We're not asking you to consense to it," Karina said. "If you don't like it, don't do it. Anyone that wants to help is invited."

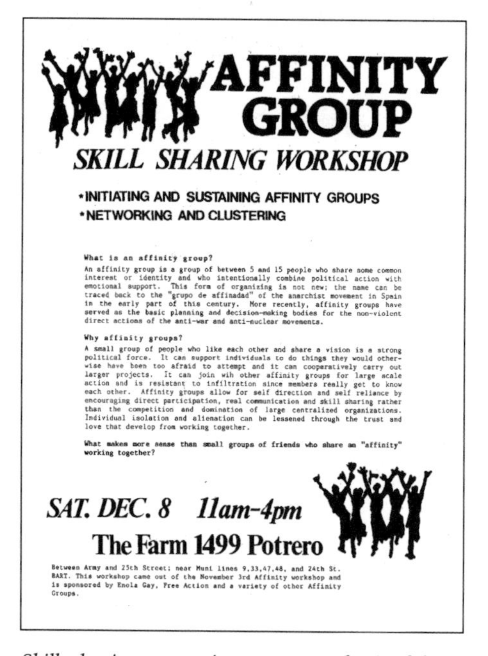

Skills sharing was an important emphasis of the 1980s direct action movement, either through workshops such as these or through informal internships with more experienced activists.

Finally we gathered for a closing. As we linked arms around shoulders, talk returned to the secret January action. Antonio and Karina talked about props. Holly and Jenny shared a laugh. I joined the circle, but felt out of the loop. Doc seemed withdrawn, too. I tried to catch his eye, but he was lost in his own thoughts.

As Karina laughed aloud, I felt irked. How could she, a LAG staffer, be pushing a non-LAG action? Didn't she have any sense of responsibility to the group?

Across the circle, Angie and Alby were talking together. I looked away, then took a deep breath and exhaled so loudly that people looked at me with surprise. I wasn't sure what to say, but Karina spared me the trouble. "Let's *all* take a deep breath!" she said. Most of the cluster obeyed, exhaling loudly and dissolving into laughter. I smiled in spite of myself. Did these people take anything seriously?

The circle broke up. I was pulling my sweatshirt over my head when Karina said loudly, "Angie, what's happening with your motorcycle honey?"

I paused with my sweatshirt half on. Several other voices clamored for an answer, and everyone looked at Angie expectantly. I braced myself for a dose of reality.

"Oh, it's nothing," she said. "Jackson is just a friend. We were going to hear a band that night, that's all."

No one else seemed to believe her, but I found myself urgently wanting to. I went over to give her a goodbye hug, holding her an extra moment and running my hand down the curve of her back.

She looked at me as we parted. "I'll see you soon?"

"Yeah," I said. "I'll be down at the office Thursday afternoon for sure. And you?"

"I think I'll be there, too."

I wished it were definite, but it wasn't like I could make her sign a contract. I reached out and rubbed her arm once more as we parted. "Until then."

Sunday, December 11, 1983

IT TOOK THE eighty spokes all afternoon, but finally we seemed close to a decision. But there was no time to spare. It was five, and a women's chorus had reserved the room for six o'clock sharp.

As the clock ticked down on our last hour, Jenny was facilitating the discussion of a financial district protest. All afternoon, I'd supported her trying to work through the objections and reach consensus, but it was obvious that we'd never get agreement on a City action without another meeting. We needed to move on to Livermore.

The clock hit 5:30. Something had to happen now. I whispered a hint that we should switch to Livermore and test for consensus as a fallback plan. Jenny shot an irritated glance at me and called on several more speakers about the City.

I tried to sit back and let her facilitate, but I had trouble staying still in my chair. Finally, with twenty minutes to go, Jenny called for discussion of Livermore. Even then, Karina and some others seemed upset that we didn't keep talking about a City action. I clenched my teeth. How were we ever going to reach consensus in time?

Melissa must have felt the same. She raised both hands for a process point. "We've discussed Livermore plenty, for the past two years. Everyone knows how they feel about it. We don't need more discussion. We should move straight to hearing concerns and objections. Are there any objections to consensing on an April action at Livermore Lab?"

I looked at her in appreciation. I knew Melissa really wanted another June blockade at the Lab, and that April was a compromise to avoid competing with the Democratic Convention in the Summer. Finally, someone was seeing the bigger picture!

Her eyes made a circuit of the meeting, as if daring anyone to speak out against a return to our roots. A few people questioned how big a Spring action would be. Several AGs said they would probably do autonomous City actions anyway, and one guy argued for doing both Livermore and a City action. But no one directly opposed Livermore, and that was the proposal on the floor.

I leaned toward Jenny. "We should test for consensus," I said. "I think it's there."

Her mouth tightened. She didn't look at me. "So if there are no objections, does anyone stand aside?" Several spokes raised their hands, but not enough to make a difference. "Does anyone block?" A moment passed. I looked at Jenny expectantly.

Finally she spoke. "Then do we have consensus?" She looked as if she weren't sure of the answer. Around the circle, though, people twinkled their fingers and nodded their heads. Someone clapped and called out, "Yeah!" That set off polite applause, which faded quickly. The women's chorus was already coming in the door carrying music stands. We hurriedly folded our chairs and stacked them in the corner.

I picked up my papers and squeezed out the door behind Mort and Hank. As we filed down the stairs, I wished I felt some excitement about our decision. But it was more a sense of relief. We got what we needed — an action to announce. The date was far enough away to give us time to do outreach and build momentum, but close enough to feature in our Winter fund appeal and in the upcoming Direct Action, which we'd delayed in hopes of such a front-page story.

I looked for Jenny afterwards, but she seemed to have disappeared. Karina likewise was nowhere to be seen.

Mort came over and asked if I wanted to have dinner with him and Hank and Melissa. We headed down to Villa Hermosa on Telegraph. The dining area was laid out like a plaza, with tables around a central fountain. We got a table near the windows. Ivy dangled from a trellis above. Along the side wall was a mural of Chicano history.

Melissa got a cup of coffee. Hank, Mort, and I split a pitcher of beer. "Phew," Mort said as we opened our menus. "I'm getting too old for all-day meetings."

"Well, that's the last one of 1983," I consoled him. "And at least we came out with some decisions."

In addition to the Livermore action, we had consensed to the ERN proposal. The work group made some concessions to AG input, and Enola Gay withdrew its block. But Doc, Belinda, and Claude all missed the meeting. "Seems like a commentary on their fighting," I said.

Melissa nodded. "When people tear at each other, no one wins."

The spokescouncil had also reached a vague consensus to "organize" around the Democratic Convention. It was a step in the right direction. But there was no agreement on what "organize" meant, and I envisioned endless debates over how far to challenge the Democrats.

The one surprise of the day had been an organizer from the Revolutionary Workers Party showing up at the meeting with a Call for a People's Convention, a counter-convention endorsed by Congressman Ron Dellums.

"A lot of people took the flyers," I said as I dipped a chip in the salsa bowl. "Think it's for real?"

Mort poured himself a glass of beer. "The RWP is credible," he said. "They've done good work on the east coast. This is probably an attempt to expand their base out here. We should check it out. A People's Convention could help us connect with Black organizers in Oakland and Latino activists in the City. Those opportunities don't come along every day."

Our dinner arrived. Hank unwrapped his burrito to the halfway point. "We should do something at the Convention that draws attention to Livermore. We'll have the nukecycle up and rolling by then. We could paint Livermore slogans on it and launch a strike on the Convention."

I smiled at the image of Democratic delegates dodging the missile. Even Melissa laughed. "If you have to do something at the Convention, that's the best idea I've heard." She paused and looked at me. "It's such a shame to abandon June at Livermore."

"We'd never have gotten consensus on an blockade a month before the Convention," I said. I poured myself more beer. "April was the only hope."

"I know. But it wasn't a very strong consensus. How many people actually joined the work group?"

"Me and Monique and a few others signed up," I said. I took a breath and held it. "A lot of people weren't at the meeting. Maybe they'll join later."

"I doubt it," Mort said. "People are burning out. Where was Antonio, or Walt, or Caroline? And where was Holly?"

I poked at my burrito. Holly was at work, of course. But why wasn't this meeting worth her time? Or Angie, who had opted for a poetry workshop. I set my fork down. At the meeting, I had convinced myself we were getting somewhere. But the reality was, action or no action, people were drifting away.

Hank changed the topic, and I tried to shake off my doldrums. Maybe the Livermore action would gain steam after the holidays. Maybe something would trigger the ERN and that would give LAG the burst of energy we desperately needed. But right now, those prospects seemed remote.

I finished my meal in silence. "Hey," Hank said as we parted, "next Friday is the Christmas party at pinball. You should come over, because I'll be in Boston visiting my family the week after that. Holly's invited, too."

"It'll be a good party," Mort said. "We should have a new shipment of buds from up north."

Even the thought of getting high didn't do much for my mood. I gave them a weak smile. "I'll try to make it."

A drizzly rain was falling as I bid the others goodnight. I turned my jacket-collar up. My shoulders hunched, and my whole body felt stiff. It wasn't even Winter yet, and already I was weary of it. I peered into the future and tried to envision Spring. But as far ahead as I could see, it was gray.

Small wonder. My pessimism wasn't just about LAG. In the aftermath of our demonstrations, the Euromissiles were being deployed, upsetting the balance of terror. The U.S. was harassing tiny socialist countries like Grenada and Nicaragua, almost daring the Soviets to respond.

Suppose they did? Suppose a nuclear showdown developed? Could Reagan be trusted not to push the button? He probably thought the whole thing was a movie, anyway. What were the odds that we'd live to see Spring?

Thursday, December 22, 1983

TEN MORE phone calls, and Angie and I could go over to the Starry Plough and have a beer. Stay focused. Keep dialing.

I'd hoped chance would throw us together sooner, but nothing had developed since going to her and Jenny's apartment two weeks earlier. Finally I suggested going to the Starry Plough, and we settled on Thursday.

As the day approached, I anticipated it like a holiday. I imagined questions I would ask, or bits of my past that I might share. What a relief from worrying about LAG all the time.

I made another couple of calls, trying to get AGs to commit to taking part in the April Livermore action. It was already almost five. I wondered whether Angie had the whole evening free. Maybe we could go for a walk. Maybe she'd get another flat tire...

It was just a coincidence, but Holly was gone again, spending the night in a farm field near Livermore Lab. She, Artemis, Daniel, and Norm were camping overnight at the prospective site of the peace camp to check the rhythm of the morning commute along the adjacent highway.

That left my Thursday evening open. My plan was to play guitar for a while, then do some writing. But spending a few hours with Angie would be a great start to the night.

I was down to six calls when Sara and Karina came in. I sucked in a breath. I'd hoped to avoid them and escape with Angie. But here they were, and we needed to talk. Not only had they gone off and organized an autonomous cluster action. Now I'd heard that they wanted LAG's April action to be changed from Livermore to San Francisco! Wasn't it obvious that most of LAG had no interest in City protests? Were they trying to undercut everything we had worked for?

I took a deep breath, then walked over to Karina's desk. "Can we talk for a minute? I want to check-in about the April actions."

Karina set down her daypack. "Sure. We've been doing a lot of thinking about them. The war-tax angle is perfect. We can visit all the nuclear corporations and talk about how they get millions of tax dollars to build weapons of doom. We'll end up at the main post office at the end of the day and do street theater while people are coming to post their last-minute returns. I'll bet we'll get a lot of media coverage."

I stood there in silence, unable to decide whether to be angry or laugh out loud at her presumption. Luckily, she talked long enough that I could collect myself. Challenging Karina head-on would just harden her resolve. I had to take an indirect approach.

I made myself speak slowly. "I'm all for another City action, but not in April. Livermore is our best bet to pull people together. We can do a financial district action later."

"We could do Livermore later, too," Karina said. "Most people I know will ignore Livermore, anyway."

"And a lot more will skip a City action..." My voice trailed off as it occurred to me that she and I weren't disagreeing. A lot of younger people, including most of my own cluster, had lost interest in Livermore. And people like the Walnettos and Turning Tide and Spirit AGs would boycott a City protest.

Sara looked at me tentatively. "Maybe we should do both," she said. "Why not do a tax-day action in the City on Monday, and move the Livermore demo to Tuesday?"

I leaned against a table and frowned. "With the peace camp and the ERN, we're already spreading ourselves thin." I looked at Sara, who seemed to be weighing my objection. I felt a wave of appreciation for her attempt to find a compromise. I smiled sadly. "Maybe two actions is the only way out."

"It works for me," Karina said jauntily.

Good for you, I thought. I'd probably be happy, too, if I got my way all the time. I looked the other way.

"I've got to get going," Karina said. "I just came by to pick up this folder." She held it out as if it were evidence, then put it into her daypack. Should I say anything else about the action? What was the point? Maybe Sara could talk some sense to her. Sara at least grasped the problem. Karina seemed to think it was all about adrenaline.

I turned back to my lists, which looked like a jumble of letters and numbers. Why was I bothering to make phone calls for the Livermore protest? All the creativity was heading to San Francisco. But having worked so hard for the Livermore consensus, I couldn't very well drop it.

Especially with a five-person work group. Even Jenny, who I assumed would work on Livermore, was staying away. In fact, she seemed to be avoiding me. She hadn't said anything, but I sensed she resented my pressure when she was facilitating the spokescouncil. And now the decision was coming undone, anyway. I'd alienated Jenny for nothing.

I made a couple more calls, but no one seemed to be home. Finally I closed my notebook and put it on the shelf. I wandered back to where Angie was organizing the Direct Action graphics file.

"Do you want to head over to the Plough?"

"Sure, let's do it," she said. She stuck the folders of graphics back into the box. She pulled an oversized brown sweater over her head and wrapped a purple scarf twice around her neck. I zipped my jacket and we took off.

The Starry Plough occupied the ground floor of an old apartment building on the corner next to La Peña. It took a moment for my eyes to adjust to the dim light. Several people at the bar looked up. To the right, a couple of women were playing darts. In the far corner, a band was setting up for the evening. An old Bob Dylan album was playing so loud that I had to shout our order to the bartender: "Two pints of Guinness and an order of home fries."

I followed Angie to one of the shadowy side-tables. The bench seats had tall backs, like being in a private booth. We sat side by side, the only way to carry on a conversation over the music.

I leaned toward her. "Jenny said you're going home for the holidays."

"Yeah. I'm really excited about seeing my younger sister. It's her last year of college. Then maybe she'll move out here." She paused for a moment, as if measuring a thought. "I'm glad I stayed here for Solstice, though. I doubt I could have found anything like it back home."

"Yesterday was Solstice, wasn't it?"

"Yeah. It was beautiful. This time I did the plunge."

"In the ocean?"

"Yeah. It's part of the ritual. Half of the people there did it, maybe thirty of us. In the middle of the ritual, just as the sun set into the sea, we stripped off our clothes and ran out to meet the tide. I thought I was being really brave by going into the water, but I saw Karina dunk all the way under. And Moonstone dove into the surf headfirst. His hair was all ratty, and he looked like a sea creature. I went in up to my knees, but then a big wave came and drenched me to my waist, like the ocean was coming to welcome me."

"Weren't you freezing?"

"Yeah. When you can't stand it anymore, you go back and dance naked around the fire. Those who plunge get to be in the inner circle. People were drumming, and everyone was chanting and singing. By the firelight you could see some people's faces, but those who were further back looked like a ring of ghosts."

I imagined Angie dancing naked around a bonfire and shivered. For once, I wished I had been at a ritual.

We talked a while longer. I was already light-headed, and didn't want to drink another beer. But I didn't want to say goodbye, either. "Do you want to go for a walk?"

"Sure," she said. "I'll walk you home and catch the Telegraph bus from there."

It was dark when we left the Plough. As we started up Prince Street, the top edge of the moon slipped from behind a cloud. Low-hanging trees lent a mysterious air to the sidewalk. We turned north on Fulton, a street of small houses and old trees. Cautiously, I put my arm around Angie's shoulders. She put her arm around my waist, letting her hand rest lightly on my hip. We walked along slowly, learning to match our steps.

The Starry Plough, conveniently located across the street from the LAG office.

Angie told me about the progress on the spraypaint garden she and Jenny were doing. "We've got the first buds opening now. There are four, two red and two yellow. Plus there's a caterpillar. It came out too big, in proportion to the flowers. But you still get the idea."

I looked at her. Her hair was pulled back in several thick braids, giving her forehead a high, open look. I was struck at how unperturbed her face was, even as she talked about spraypainting.

"We have one more stencil to do," she said, "with the flowers fully opened. We'll paint them right over the buds, like they bloomed. I wonder if people will notice?"

As we passed under a streetlight, she looked up at me. Was she checking my opinion about the flowers, or to see if I approved of her adventure?

We turned up Dwight and approached my apartment building. I felt torn. I wanted to ask her inside. And I had the feeling she'd say yes.

We stopped in front of the building, and I turned to her. The porch lamp shone on her face, which seemed clouded by unaccustomed doubt.

"I sort of want to ask you in," I said haltingly. "But I'm not sure it's a good idea."

"Yeah," she said. "Maybe we should say goodnight now."

I stepped forward and slipped my arms around her. "I don't really want to do that."

"I know," she said. She held me tightly, and ran her hand slowly up my back. "But I need time to think about what's happening, and I can't think clearly when I'm with you."

I leaned back to look at her, my arms still around her. "Will I see you again before you go on vacation?"

"That depends, I guess," she said. "I mean, no. I'm flying out the day after tomorrow. We shouldn't see each other again. Not till I get back. It's better." She disentangled herself from my reluctant arms. "I need to go. Really." She squeezed my hand and started away.

"I'll miss you, Angie," I called out.

She stopped and looked back at me, and I thought I saw tears glistening in her eyes. Then she turned and walked quickly toward Telegraph.

A light rain started falling. I looked up at the building. Should I go in? If inviting Angie inside seemed inappropriate, how much better was it to take my present thoughts into my and Holly's apartment? I turned away from the lights of Telegraph and lifted my face to the clouds. The mist caressed my cheeks. I fastened my coat, tucked my hands into my pockets, and set off into the night.

Livermore Peace Lab

January-February 1984

Livermore Peace Lab opened along Highway 580, about a mile from Livermore Weapons Lab. Leafletters distributed the Peace Lab News to workers each morning. Workers and townspeople visited the peace camp, sparking local organizing.

Issue no. 1

LIVERMORE PEACE LAB NEWS

Livermore Peace Lab Opens

On Sunday, January 29, the Livermore Peace Lab opened in the city of Livermore, California. The peace camp members knew we were off to a good start when many people turned out for the dedication ceremony, workshops, music and good food.

There have been many peace activities in Livermore over the past several years. What's different about this one is that it is here to stay for longer than a few days. There are a number of people who will reside at the peace lab, which will serve as a base for visitors from the town and for traveling peace activists.

The peace lab is envisioned as a site for exploring alternatives to the weapons research which goes on at Lawrence Livermore National Laboratory. It was not planned as a base for civil disobedience actions at the research lab. Peace lab residents will be visiting Livermore Laboratory in the hope of engaging in open dialogue with employees.

Residents and supporters of the peace lab are responsible citizens who are taking time off from our work to explore non-military alternatives for workers at Livermore Lab. We are responsible for one another's well-being in the peace lab. We want to have a continuous presence in Livermore. If the workers at Livermore Lab have to come here every day, we want to be here every day too. This signifies the depth of our commitment.

We come in peace to the town of Livermore. We do not want to be confrontational, but rather to talk openly with and listen to local residents and workers. We look forward to the personal growth and political discussions which will inevitably result from the interactions that will take place at our "laboratory of human experience".

Workers Invited To Visit Peace Lab

Employees of Lawrence Livermore National Laboratory are cordially invited to visit the Livermore Peace Lab. Feel free to stop by for dinner after work and chat with us. Or come by on a weekend.

Directions to the peace camp are: Take the First Street exit south off Interstate 580 in Livermore. Make the first possible right turn onto a little dirt road. The Livermore Peace Lab is right behind the Tri-Valley Tire Store.

Come talk to us! Members of the Peace Lab would like to schedule speaking engagements by Lab workers. To arrange a date for a talk or a forum, call the Peace Lab at 449-8308 or 449-8309, or stop by the camp. We will carry announcements about such talks, about film or video showings, etc., in future issues of this newsletter. We are eager to discuss the issues of peace, disarmament, and peace camps with you. And we promise we'll try to listen as much as we talk!

Brief History of Peace Camps

The Livermore Peace Lab belongs to a strong tradition of peace camps which have been established around the world to resist the increasing militarization of the planet and to look for peaceful options.

United States Peace Camps

The first two peace camps in the United States started last summer at the same time as the civil disobedience action at Lawrence Livermore Laboratory. On June 20, 1983, the Tucson Peace Camp opened outside Davis Monthan Air Force Base, where cruise missile personnel are trained. The camp received excellent local support, including endorsement by the Tucson City Council and both city newspapers, before the base forced the local sheriff to close down the camp on Nov. 28.

continued on next page

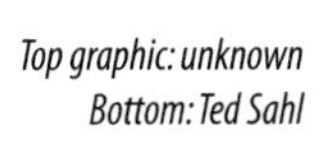

Top graphic: unknown
Bottom: Ted Sahl

Any connections between the people pictured in the photographs and the characters in this book are purely coincidental. The characters are fictional. No photo should be taken as implying that an individual is in any way connected to a fictional character.

Livermore Peace Lab

January-February 1984

All photos on these two pages by Ted Sahl, except top left by Ilka Hartmann.

Several dozen volunteers pitched in to build the camp, including a construction crew and a rotating squad of ditch-diggers.

Was it a peace camp, or a new subdivision going in?

The day's work complete, peace campers circled up, then shared dinner and a campfire to celebrate the opening of the Livermore Peace Lab.

All photos by Ted Sahl.

Four / 1984

In the aftermath of even a limited nuclear exchange, debris blown into the atmosphere would not settle for weeks or months. Sunlight would vanish. Temperatures would plummet. And most of life on Earth would perish in the "Nuclear Winter."

Saturday, January 7, 1984

"No one wants to protest at Livermore anymore." Karina slung the words as if she were being forced to state the obvious. "The real action is in the financial district."

I didn't feel like arguing with her. The first Change of Heart meeting of 1984 was at her and Sara's Mission District flat. Karina sat cross-legged in a big chair that was draped with blue and purple fabric. Her throne, I thought. No point in fighting with her on her home turf.

Jenny, seated on the floor across from me, raised her hand. "There are still a lot of people who want to do Livermore. We can do both, can't we?"

"Fine," Karina answered, "as long as I don't have to work on it."

I shoved my cushion further into the corner and scowled. Two actions. What a compromise. Bump Livermore back to Tuesday, and do City actions on Monday, April 16th.

Should I speak out against the change? As a rallying point for LAG, the City was a loser. But if I opposed the financial district, I'd just push Change of Heart further from LAG.

So where did that leave me? Livermore was being organized by people like Spirit AG, Monique and the Walnettos, Melissa, Daniel... Good people, sure, but when I pictured our meetings, I saw a circle of folding chairs in a fluorescent-lit church classroom.

I looked around Sara and Karina's living room. Mid-afternoon sunlight filtered through gauzy curtains. Hanging plants filled the bay window. Fifteen people were settled into couches or cushions on the floor. The meeting seemed small for Change of Heart, although the regulars were present.

Most of them, anyway. Holly was working her food-prep job. But she probably wouldn't have been at the meeting, anyway. Since Caroline left for Nicaragua, Holly seemed even more estranged from LAG than in the Fall. If not for the peace camp, she might be gone altogether.

And then there was Angie, who was still back east visiting her family. We hadn't talked since that night in front of my apartment. Once she'd been gone a few days, I felt thankful we'd parted that evening. What was I doing, risking my relationship with Holly for a fling? However enticing I found Angie, I couldn't imagine us long-term. We were meant to be friends and co-workers, not lovers.

Still, I wished she were here at the meeting. We could have gone out for a burrito afterward, then taken a walk over to Balmy Alley to see Claude's new mural.

Sara, who was facilitating, cleared her throat and looked around the circle. "The proposal is to do the City Monday and Livermore Tuesday. Are there any objections to our supporting the changed dates?" No one spoke. Sara's eyes stopped on me. I sighed, then shrugged my shoulders. Sara paused a moment. "Do we have consensus?"

Around the room, people twinkled their fingers. Doc and Walt leaned their heads together and exchanged a few words. Alby said something, and Megan and Moonstone laughed. Only Karina seemed genuinely excited. "That's great," she said. "Now let's talk about the Consulate action. It's only two weeks away."

Yes, even with the April financial district action in the bag, Karina was pushing ahead with a late-January cluster action. Word had leaked out within the cluster that the target was the Salvadoran Consulate, located in an office building in downtown San Francisco.

I couldn't argue with the target, given Reagan's support for El Salvador's pro-corporate government — a government which had killed fifty thousand of its own people in a decade of civil war with leftist guerrillas.

Alby, who was sitting on the arm of a couch, proposed that some people be peasants and others Salvadoran soldiers. "We'll pull out squirt-bottles of fake blood and do an execution right there in the office," he said.

"Why use fake blood?" Karina said.

Alby bounced up from his perch. With sweeping gestures he demarcated the room. "We can have three zones — real blood, fake blood, and no blood."

I smiled to myself. No wonder Sara and Karina had opted for an autonomous action. I could picture a hundred-person spokescouncil trying to reach consensus on real versus fake blood.

In truth, it didn't look like LAG was ever going to consense on anything meaningful again. The only action we'd agreed on in the past year — April at Livermore — was disintegrating. And the upcoming meetings to hammer out some sort of plan for July's Democratic Convention looked even more hopeless.

The only bright spot was the Emergency Response Network. Since the consensus at the December meeting, not a lot had been done. But at least we could use the LAG office and network as a basis if Reagan launched another invasion.

The meeting moved through the scattered agenda. Walt reported on plans for Spring protests at the Diablo Canyon nuclear power plant. Sara asked who was planning to make the six hour trip down to Diablo, and almost everyone in the room raised their hand.

"How about a mock-wedding ceremony?" Doc proposed. "Something like the People of California getting married to PG&E and having radioactive children."

Incredible. Why couldn't we put this energy into Livermore? I took a breath. It's only January. When April rolls around, people might be just as excited about the Lab.

We took a break, and someone opened a package of Oreos. In a minute, people were laughing and tossing a nerf football around the room. Alby pulled a copy of Orwell's *1984* off the shelf and commenced a dramatic reading, to much applause and encouragement.

I ate a few cookies, half-wishing I could share in the joking. But when I tried to join the laughter, my face felt tight.

The second half of the meeting kicked off with a bang, but soon faded into a post-sugar slump. Sara read an announcement about the Livermore peace camp, slated to open at the end of the month. With Holly absent, no one at the meeting was really involved, and silence followed the announcement.

The same low-key response greeted the report on the recently-concluded "representative trial" that wrapped up the previous Summer's Livermore blockade. Rick from Enola Gay had been one of the reps, along with Monique and nine others. The other two hundred defendants — the people who had pled not-guilty instead of no-contest the previous Summer — agreed to accept the verdict meted out to the eleven representatives. The reps and a team of lawyers developed a multifaceted defense strategy. But the judge disallowed discussion of international law or the "defense of necessity" — the claim that protesters committed their crime in order to prevent a greater evil. After that, the guilty verdict was a foregone conclusion. "We never denied that we blockaded the Lab," Rick said. "The only possible defense was the justice of our motive."

The judge handed down thirty-day sentences to second-time blockaders, meaning people might have to go back to jail. But Rick didn't look concerned. "The sentence will probably be reduced to time-served on appeal," he said.

An announcement about an upcoming spokescouncil to plan actions around the Democratic Convention brought some spark back to the circle. Several people volunteered to go to the meeting. Good. Let others be the spokes. If by some miracle there was a LAG protest at the Convention, I'd take part. But I was tired of wasting my time on deadends.

Besides, I had an alternative — work on the People's Convention. Get to know some different types of organizers. It might be a welcome change. And it might help LAG in the long run if we built some wider connections.

Sara crossed the last item off the agenda, then gave me a quizzical look. "We forgot the report on the April Livermore action, didn't we?"

Oh yeah... I appreciated her support, but I didn't sense much interest in the room. I mustered a few meeting dates and a perfunctory list of help needed. People nodded their heads dutifully, but no one volunteered for anything, and I was glad to let it drop.

As we gathered in a closing circle, my mind drifted off. Jenny had offered me a ride home, but I felt like being alone. Tension still lingered between us from the December spokescouncil, and I didn't feel like dealing with it now. Enough meetings for one day.

She walked up as I put my jacket on. Her teeth were clenched, and her hair frizzed out of its tight bun. "Ready to go?"

"No, I remembered an errand I need to run," I improvised. "I'll catch BART later."

She looked surprised and relieved at the same time. "Are you sure?"

"Yeah, yeah," I said. I felt guilty for making up the errand part, but I didn't want to go into my motives right then. There'd be a chance to talk with her soon and clear the air.

Balmy Alley, off of 24th Street near Harrison, an outdoor mural gallery coordinated by Precita Eyes — see resources page of the Appendix.

Karina came over and asked Jenny something. I took the opportunity to step away, said some quick goodbyes, and headed out the door ahead of the crowd. The recent rain left the air crisp and cool, like a Fall day in Indiana. I took a deep breath, glad to be alone. If

Angie were here, it would be different. I pictured us strolling through the Mission, dissecting the meeting, laughing away the tensions. If only...

Lacking that, I was grateful for the solitude. Other relationships felt heavy, something to be endured or, better yet, escaped. I picked up my pace, lest someone from the meeting drive by and offer me a ride. I couldn't go to BART yet, either, for fear of running into folks riding the train back to Berkeley.

Why not go see Claude's new mural? I knew it was somewhere off of 24th Street. I figured I could find it. I slowed my pace as I passed a group of kids talking in rapid Spanish. Rows of old Victorians lined Shotwell Street. Most of the tall wooden houses had two, three, or even four front doors, each leading to a separate flat. Some had steps going down to doors below street level, behind which I pictured subterranean studios with open-beam ceilings and rustic brick floors.

I turned on 24th and stopped for a burrito. Someone had left a sports page on my table featuring a story about off-season baseball trades. Several big stars had changed teams, but none were coming to San Francisco or Oakland. It was a long, slow Winter. And unless the Giants or A's — both of whom had losing records the previous year — got some new players, there wasn't much to look forward to in the Spring.

I finished my burrito and recycled my tray. I considered asking which way Balmy was, but didn't want to come off like a tourist.

I made my way up 24th Street. A small crowd clustered outside a storefront church. At the corner, the smell of fresh donuts almost drew me in, slowing me just enough that a bicyclist coming down the side street didn't decapitate me. Thank you for small coincidences, I thought as I collected myself and crossed Folsom Street.

Ahead of me, a man was yelling something in Spanish to a woman leaning out a window above. Her long black hair

Archbishop Oscar Romero of San Salvador, who spoke out for workers and common people, was assassinated by a military death squad funded by the U.S. His life and words inspired activists around the world. "Una Ley Inmoral," Balmy Alley, San Francisco, ©1996 by Juana Alicia.

fluttered in the breeze as she laughed and answered him. I stepped around the man and found myself at the entrance to Balmy Alley.

A rainbow covered the side of the one-story building at the corner. An Aztec medallion was mounted in the center like a golden shield. I turned into the narrow easement, which was fronted by rickety fences and small garages. A rusty basketball hoop was nailed to a phonepole. Ivy overgrew the first garage.

It could have been any alley in America. Only here, every available surface had been turned into a mural. I moved slowly down the alley, taking in the paintings. Kids had covered one long fence with gangly people, trees, and animals in a crazy-quilt panorama. Nearby, a picket fence commemorated the United Farm Workers' struggle for union justice. Across the way, a garage door was painted as if you were looking inside, where a couple of men tinkered under the hood of a low-rider.

Claude's mural was easy to spot, since I knew his style from Berkeley. He and several collaborators from Galleria de la Raza had done a collage-style depiction of life in the Mission. My favorite touch was a clothesline in one corner, with actual T-shirts glued into the mural.

On a garage door at the far end of the alley was a portrait of Oscar Romero, the archbishop of San Salvador who was assassinated in 1980 for his stand against government repression. Romero's gentle, determined face was rendered as if it were a multihued tapestry. Flanking the portrait, in Spanish and English, was a quote: "Una ley inmoral nadie tiene que cumplirla/No one should comply with an immoral law."

I stood there a long time, captivated by the painting. Finally a guy in a European car came putt-putting up the alley, stopping now and then to gawk at a mural. The fumes drove me toward the exit. What did he think this was, a drive-through museum? Have some respect for art.

As I departed from the alley, I thought again of Angie. She would love this. Maybe we could come back together sometime.

My steps were lighter as I headed for BART. I wanted to stay irritated at Change of Heart for its lack of commitment to LAG, and especially at Karina, a staff member with so little regard for the good of the group. But maybe I was smart to give in now. Maybe if I supported her, she would return the favor when the Livermore action rolled around.

One concern, though, I couldn't shake — how Karina kept raising the stakes. Getting inside the Salvadoran Consulate? That was a little more serious than blockading Livermore Lab. And it wasn't just Karina. The rest of the cluster seemed right in step.

The combination of smaller numbers and confrontational actions seemed risky. At Livermore, it was only our numbers that saved us from probation. What was to keep the authorities from hammering a small group of people with probation or a heavy jail sentence?

Or was that the point? Was Karina looking for a rerun of her Vandenberg sentence?

By the time I got to BART, it was seven o'clock. I stopped outside to phone Holly. We had tentative plans to go to a movie that evening. There was still time, if we met at the theater.

But when I reached her, she said she was tired from work. "Maybe we can go for a walk later, do some catching up. Maybe about nine?"

"Sounds good. I'm going to stop by the record store. I'll see you in a little while."

Friday, January 13, 1984

A LIGHT RAIN was falling as we left the auditorium. Luckily, Angie's umbrella was big enough for both of us. As we waited for the bus, I put my arm around her. She huddled closer, pressing against my side. I took a breath and held her to me, glad for once that the bus was late.

"Night rain is so beautiful," she said. "Look at the streetlight in the puddle, how it shimmers with every drop."

I studied the ripples of light. "It reminds me of Monet."

She nodded. "Don't you love it when nature imitates art?"

The bus pulled up. "This will drop us off a few blocks from my apartment," she said. "We can walk from there."

Our plan was to go back to her place for a while and listen to music. Then I'd catch a bus home from there. Or better yet, if the rain would let up, I'd walk back to Berkeley. Holly was spending the night with Daniel and Artemis out at the peace camp site, so I was in no hurry to get home.

We sat side by side on the bus. I looped my arm behind her seat, and she leaned lightly against me. I'd seen Angie once at the office since she got back in town, but this was our first real time together. We'd spent the early evening at a hip-hop show organized by the Federation for Afro-American Unity, one of the groups that was co-sponsoring the People's Convention. It was a good show, but I wasn't sorry when it ended and Angie and I headed for the bus.

Her apartment was dark and quiet when we entered. "Jenny must be over at Raoul's," Angie said. She picked up a stack of magazines cluttering the couch and tossed some stray clothes into the corner. "Put on whatever music you want. I'll heat some tea water."

I shuffled through the tapes and albums strewn around the stereo. One caught my eye. "Wow, Run DMC," I said. "I've heard they're really good."

"Raoul left that and some other rap albums here," she called from the kitchen. "You can put it on if you want."

I started to get it out, but somehow rap didn't suit the mood. I selected an old Joni Mitchell tape instead. Angie came in carrying two mugs of tea. "I hope raspberry is okay. It's all we've got."

I sat down on the couch. She sat to my left, about a foot away. I felt a twinge of disappointment that she wasn't closer. I wished there were more clutter on the couch, so I'd have an excuse to scoot over.

She took a slow sip of tea. Her hair was pulled back in a single braid, and she had put on a blue button-up sweater that looked like a hand-me-down from her father.

I took a drink of tea and tried to think of something to say. "Are you going down to Diablo Canyon next month?"

She nodded slowly, looking down at her tea mug. "I think so. At some point, I need to go over to Laney College and take care of the paperwork for the woodworking program. And I want to check out the options over at S.F. State. But I think I can get it all done before Diablo."

"State has a woodworking department?"

She shook her head. "Keep this just between you and me, okay?" She waited until I assented before continuing. "I'm thinking of applying to the film-making program at State."

"Really? That sounds great."

"I think it would be. Of course, I've heard that jobs in the film industry are hard to come by. Woodworking would be a lot more practical. And sometimes I think I should go into teaching or social work." She sighed and looked away. "I need to figure out some sort of career. I can't handle secretarial work much longer."

She seemed absorbed in her own thoughts, and I wished I could draw her out. "Is film what you really want to do?"

"I'm not really sure what I want," she said without looking up. "I mean for a career. I like working on Direct Action and organizing protests and street theater. But no one is going to pay me to do that."

"Some people get paid to organize."

"Yeah, but that's still office work. Anyway, I couldn't handle all the infighting. Yesterday at the office, it was all I could do not to strangle Karina. She always has to be the one true anarchist."

She paused for a moment, then yawned and stretched. Was she giving me a hint? "Do you need to head for bed?" I asked, wanting to be polite but wishing she'd find a second wind.

"Yeah, pretty soon," she said. "Sorry I'm so tired. If it's still raining, you can sleep here."

I cast a sideways glance at her. Of course she meant on the couch, which wasn't very comfortable. Anyway, I doubted I'd get much sleep knowing that Angie was in bed in the next room.

"Thanks, I should take off."

"Are you sure?" She touched my arm, and a tingle rippled through me. I looked at her. Was she being polite, or was I missing something? I took her hand in mine. "Yeah, I should go. It's not raining hard, and I'm not ready to sleep yet."

Her smile turned formal. "Okay," she said. She squeezed my hand and stood up. "I'll lend you an umbrella."

"Thanks, that would help."

I got my jacket, and she escorted me to the door. I stepped forward and hugged her. She seemed to press herself against me, laying her head on my chest. I closed my eyes and absorbed her warmth, holding her body to mine. Finally we let go and eased back a step. "It's been great seeing you," I said.

Her eyes seemed to search mine for an instant. Then she settled into a friendly smile. "I'll catch you sometime soon," she said, handing me the umbrella and opening the door.

I squeezed her arm. "I hope so." I turned and headed into the rainy night.

It was only a light mist, not as cold as I expected. Forget the bus. I buttoned my coat, opened the umbrella, and set my sights homeward.

Home. To the apartment I shared with Holly. Smart move to leave Angie's. That's a temptation I don't need. It's one thing to fantasize from afar, and another to spend the night twenty feet away.

A fantasy — that's where Angie needs to stay. Sure we have fun together. But how much do we really have in common? How long till the luster wears off? Stay focused. My future is with Holly. Our relationship means too much to jeopardize with a fling.

Hunched under the umbrella, I repeated the words aloud as if answering an interrogator. "How much do Angie and I have in common? How long till..."

But however carefully I enunciated them, they wouldn't quite take hold. A different question gnawed at me — what if Angie had come right out and said, "Sleep with me." Would I have left? Was it loyalty or fear of rejection that sent me out the door?

Holly and I had an open relationship, didn't we? Granted, neither of us had tested it in over a year, since she and Frank stopped sleeping together. But we'd never explicitly changed it. There was no need to feel guilty...

The memory of holding Angie swept through me. Why hadn't I kissed her right then? Why was I so scared?

Rejection. A sweat broke on my forehead. I slowed my pace and wiped my brow with the back of my hand, which was wet from the rain. Guilt over having two lovers, I could handle. But wanting Angie, and having her say no — that seemed mortifying.

But she wouldn't have said no. How could I be so slow? Why couldn't I seize the moment?

Reaching the corner, I turned and circled the block. Not quite returning to Angie's place. But not getting further away, either. Why not go back and say, "I changed my mind, I'd like to stay the night." So what if I end up sleeping on

The Chariot: motion (or not).

the couch? We might stay up and talk a while longer. Maybe we'd even go in her room.

But what if she's already in bed? Why not wait till the next time I see her? Yet what an opportunity lost! This was our night together. Holly wasn't waiting at home, so she wouldn't have to know until I talked with her. Jenny wasn't there, so the gossip factor was eliminated. This was my chance.

She opened the door, gazed up at me, and flung herself into my arms! No — she hesitated for a moment, and I swept her off her feet. No — we slowly came together in a long, sweet kiss. No — she stared at me in disbelief and I realized I'd made a terrible miscalculation. No — Oh, for god's sake, quit calculating!

I stood outside her apartment. The mist swirled around me. Her lights were still on. I shivered. There was never going to be a better moment. Go for it. Just act.

I knocked. A moment later the door opened. Angie stood there, still wearing the blue button-up sweater. Her braid lay over her left shoulder. One hand held the door open.

I fumbled for words. "It really was raining a lot."

"You can stay here," she said with a vague gesture.

"Thanks. Don't let me get in the way, if you were heading to bed."

"That's okay. I was going to lie down and write, or maybe do a tarot reading." She paused for a moment as I took off my wet jacket and hung it over a chair. Then she looked up at me. "Why don't we go in my room? It's a lot nicer in there."

I caught my breath as she shut the door, lit a few candles, and turned off the lamp. I ducked around a macramé hanging. The candlelight cast dancing shadows on the walls. Angie lit a sprig of sage. I sat down on the edge of the bed, studying her profile as she wafted the earthy smoke into each corner.

After she finished, she stacked up some pillows against the headboard and settled in. I joined her there, leaving a little space between us.

"Do you want to do a tarot reading?" she asked.

"Sure," I said. "I'll watch you."

"We'll each draw a card, to tell us — " She paused and looked at her altar for a moment. " — to tell us the inner truth of our lives." She smiled and shuffled the deck, then fanned them out on her bed. "You draw first. Use your left hand, it's more receptive." She showed me how to let my hand hover over the cards till one presented itself. "Leave it face down. Now I'll draw one."

At the same moment, we turned the cards up. Mine was the Chariot, hers the Five of Wands. Her brow furrowed. "Yours is easier to read," she said. "The Chariot is a card about power and control. Maybe too much control. The charioteer is all ready to go somewhere, he's in the driver's seat — but he isn't moving."

I studied the image and nodded. "What's yours?"

She looked pensively at her card, which depicted five young men fighting with staves. "The Five of Wands," she said. "Conflict. I drew this card last week, too, when I did a reading about me and Jenny. Seems to be a theme right now."

She leaned forward and placed the card, still face up, on the bed near the other cards. Our arms brushed, and as I placed my card next to hers, I shifted closer so we were touching. My whole body tingled. Neither of us spoke. She wasn't moving away, but she stretched her neck forward, as if to relieve some pressure.

Carefully, I reached over and squeezed the back of her neck. She let her head droop, and closed her eyes. I kneaded my way up her neck, then down onto her shoulders. "That feels great," she whispered.

My chest trembled. I turned so I could get both hands on her shoulders and massaged them, pressing my thumbs into the muscles.

She shifted toward me. "A little lower — yeah, right there..."

Her eyes were still closed, and an enigmatic smile rested on her lips. "Why don't you lie down," I ventured. "I could get more pressure on your back."

"Okay," she said. "But just a minute." She got up slowly and made her way out of the room.

I shook my head. Who could have guessed, an hour ago? To think, I almost went home.

When Angie returned, she was wearing a loose T-shirt and gym shorts, and had taken the braid out of her hair. "If I lie down, I'll probably fall asleep," she said. "I don't want to have to get up again."

She stretched out on her stomach, her face turned away from me. I knelt next to her and softly rubbed the full length of her back, savoring the curves and valleys. She had removed her bra. I played my thumb into her shoulderblade where the strap had been, leaning over her so I could see her better. Her eyes were closed, and her brow was knit. I paused a moment, then reached out and stroked her head, petting her soft hair. Her brow relaxed, and her lips parted slightly. She

Five of wands: conflict.

took a long breath. I did the same, drinking in the moment. I ran my hand over her hair again, then gently massaged her neck. She moaned softly, and shifted her body so it pressed against my knees. My voice quivered as I whispered, "How are you doing?"

"Scared," she whispered. She rolled over on her side, facing me. Her breasts were outlined against her T-shirt. Our eyes met in the flickering candlelight. I stretched out next to her and ran my hand along the curve of her back. She shuddered, then slid against me, her body melting into mine. I kissed her face, her lips, her neck, burying my face in her hair. My hands roved over every inch of her body, marveling and caressing.

We flowed into making love with an ease that made me wonder why I had ever hesitated. Making love with a passion I scarcely recognized. Losing all sense of time, all sense of place. Winding up on my back with Angie curled up beside me, fending off sleep for fear of never again knowing such a feeling. I wrapped my arms around her, and she stirred, nestling her head against my neck. I ran my hand down her body and gently squeezed her to me. Yes.

Saturday, January 14, 1984

HOW TO tell Holly....

There was nothing to feel guilty about, I kept telling myself. I hadn't deliberately misled her. And it wasn't like I was planning to break up with her. Angie was wonderful, but no way could I picture us together the way Holly and I were. I just needed some breathing space. Maybe Holly secretly wanted the same thing.

Get real. What if she moved out? Then where would I be? Why hadn't I talked to her before? Now I had to drop a bombshell.

When Holly got home from her overnight at the peace camp site, she dropped her daypack by the door and came over and kissed me. Then she went in the kitchen, washed her hands, and made a cup of tea. A couple of minutes later she joined me at the table. I reached out and took her hand. She squeezed mine, and a tranquil smile crossed her lips. A flash of guilt ran through me, not for having a fling, but for spoiling Holly's mood. Maybe I should wait? No, I had to do it now.

I took a breath and plunged in. "Angie and I slept together this weekend. It's not something we planned, but it happened."

She looked at me, the vestiges of her smile fading. "Okay," she said. She wrapped her hands carefully around her teacup.

"I'm sorry I didn't talk to you about it before," I said. "I guess I didn't believe it was going to happen."

She looked at me, but her expression was veiled. "So are you telling me that it happened, or that you plan to keep sleeping together?"

"Well, both," I said clumsily. It was the first time I'd explicitly considered the issue. Of course I wanted to sleep with Angie again. "Both."

Holly took a breath, but said nothing. I leaned toward her. "I'm totally committed to our relationship, Holly. That's not what this is about..."

Her eyes seemed opaque as I spoke. Was she really listening? She gave a tired smile. "I guess we'll just have to see where it leads. Maybe it'll be fine."

Fine? I could wish. But her flat tone wasn't very convincing. What was going on for her? I wished she would show some emotion, so I'd have a clue.

But I knew it wasn't fair to make her dwell on it. She stood and picked up a notebook from the table. "I need to stay focused on the peace camp right now," she said. "We have less than two weeks to get it all together."

I nodded. Standing and kissing her seemed clumsy, forced. I reached out and squeezed her hand. "I love you, Holly."

Her eyes softened. "I love you, Jeff. Let's give things time, and see where they lead."

Saturday, January 28, 1984

WHAT WAS IT exactly that was bothering me? Nothing Holly had said, nothing she had done. Not our sex life. We were actually making love more often the past couple of weeks.

No, it was a glimmer missing when Holly smiled at me. A slackness, ever so slight, when we held hands. A barely perceptible dimming of the love that radiated from her eyes.

And why? For the sake of a fling? What was I doing? Didn't I have enough to worry about? If we were going to keep the paper coming out, organize two April actions, and do something around the Democratic Convention, we needed focus.

Much as I loved being with Angie, I had to end it. Maybe it would be messy. Or maybe she would be in total agreement. But either way, I knew I had to act.

I saw Angie at the office later that week. She was wearing faded blue jeans and an oversized gray sweatshirt. We worked side by side for an hour on a renewal mailing for the newspaper. Then she winked at me and walked casually to the back of the office. I followed a moment later. She stepped into a little nook behind a couple of file cabinets, pulled out a drawer, and started rustling through the folders. A mischievous smile played across her lips. I slipped behind her and slid my arms around her waist. She stood, took my hands, lifted them to her breasts, and leaned back into me. I caressed her and kissed her hair. She turned and stood on her toes to kiss me. "I can't wait to be with you," she whispered. "How about Friday night?"

Whatever you want, I almost said. You name it. But I caught myself. I'd

Opening Day at the Livermore Peace Lab combined a construction brigade, dinner prepared in the half-built kitchen, entertainers, and a campfire.

already promised Friday to Holly, and Saturday to Mort and Hank. "How about Sunday evening?"

Her hands slid down to my hips. "Okay, I guess I can do that." She leaned forward and kissed my chest, then slipped away and went back to the mailing. I closed the cabinet drawer and took a breath. How would I survive till Sunday? And what was I going to tell Holly?

For the next few days, I tried to be especially sensitive to Holly, playing music I knew she liked, keeping my dishes out of the sink, even making dinner with her one night. But I couldn't escape the brooding malaise that plagued me whenever I thought of what I was doing to our relationship.

Once Angie and I were together that Sunday, though, my cares evaporated. We went to her room and made love, listened to Bach's cello suites, talked about performance art, read Rimbaud, made love, discussed the theatrical implications of urban direct action, looked at photos from her trip to Ireland the previous Summer, and made love. A night of pure beauty.

The next day was the El Salvador Consulate action. I showed up on about two hours of sleep, and never quite got my feet on the ground. Holly scarcely talked to me, and I was glad when we got put into separate paddywagons. Knowing she planned to stay in jail, I cited out. I needed an evening alone to regroup.

WHEN I IMAGINED the Livermore peace camp, I pictured a bunch of pup tents sprinkled along the highway. But what I saw when we arrived looked more like a new subdivision going in. A tool-belted construction crew erected a wood-framed kitchen complete with a propane stove. A dark canvas circus tent loaned by Greenpeace sprouted nearby. The smaller tents were arrayed in a graceful arc, and a fire pit marked the center of the little settlement.

The most elegant touch was the bathroom, featuring two flushable toilets and a solar-heated shower. All afternoon, pick-and-shovel brigades excavated a trench for the drainpipe, stirred on by the reggae beat of Raoul's boombox.

I pitched in on the drainage ditch, hoping to impress Holly with my ardor. But she seemed too busy coordinating volunteers to notice. Finally, as people got washed up for dinner, I tracked her down.

She hugged me, but kept looking around. "Are you doing okay?" I asked.

"Yeah, it's just hard to slow down," she said. She cleared her throat. "I'm guess I'm feeling a little overwhelmed. But it's so exciting, after all our meetings, to see the peace camp coming to life."

"Looks like a whole village," I said. "And a pretty upscale one, at that."

She smiled. "We want it to be an inviting place for local people," she said. "Somewhere they'll come to visit and dialog with us."

A dinnertime concert at the peace camp, in front of the half-constructed kitchen.

My skepticism flared, but I suppressed it. "I hope it all comes together for you," I said, then regretted sounding like I wouldn't be back.

Holly nodded, as if she hadn't expected more. She started away. "I need to check with Artemis and Antonio about the meeting tonight. Are you staying for dinner?"

"It depends on my ride."

"Say goodbye when you leave," she said over her shoulder. "I won't be home till Tuesday evening."

I nodded silently. Dusk was starting to set in. Out in the yard, Norm stoked the campfire. The volunteers gathered around. I thought back to the bonfire at Vandenberg, exactly a year earlier. I remembered how Craig and I stood in the misty rain talking, how dozens of us crowded into the big tent for the meeting, and how Holly and I huddled together in our sleeping bags later that night. I took a slow breath and sighed. What a long time ago.

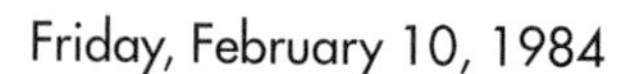

Friday, February 10, 1984

"IF IT WERE my city," Angie said, "I'd tear down all of the skyscrapers except the Pyramid."

"I don't know," I mused. "Couldn't we make them into high-rise artists' studios?"

Angie had come over to the City with me to run a People's Convention errand, and we decided to stay and do some exploring. We took a shortcut under the Pyramid, whose huge structural beams demarcated a shaded plaza area. "Not where I'd want to be in an earthquake," I said.

"Why not? What a great way to go — squashed by a pyramid."

I put my arm around her, drawing her closer to me, and we headed over a couple of blocks to Grant Street, the main artery of Chinatown. The narrow street, lined with ornately-decorated old buildings, was packed shoulder-to-shoulder with locals and visitors. The pungent scent of fish announced a seafood vendor sandwiched between a nightclub and an import shop. Outside the import shop was a rack of San Francisco postcards. "Let's send one to ourselves," Angie said. We picked out a prestamped one showing a cable car at Fisherman's Wharf, wrote ourselves a cheery message, and mailed it off to her apartment in Oakland. "Now, if there's ever any doubt, we can prove we were here," she said.

We continued up Grant Street. Chinatown gradually blurred into the old Italian neighborhood of North Beach.

Grant Street in Chinatown.

City Lights bookstore, ground zero for the Beat Generation in San Francisco. Vesuvio's pub is to left.

The streets were just as narrow, but the architecture grew less ornate. For a couple of blocks, chow mein diners alternated with pizza shops and garlic bistros, with the occasional bookstore or laundromat tossed in for good measure. The most famous of all San Francisco bookstores occupied the corner at Columbus — City Lights. "When I first moved to the Bay Area," I said as we went inside, "I came over here and bought a copy of Alan Ginsburg's *Howl.* It felt like a pilgrimage I had to make."

We browsed the poetry section. I thumbed a collection by Patti Smith. Angie opened a slim volume of Adrienne Rich's poems. She leaned against me, her eyes on the book. "In college," she said, "I wrote a poem called 'Howl.' I had no idea there was already a famous one."

"What a bummer."

"Yeah, and it's one of my best poems, too."

She bought the Adrienne Rich book. I scanned the art shelves and found a photobook of Tuscan cathedrals. Then we went across the alley to Vesuvio's, legendary watering hole of the Beat Generation.

We stepped in. It took a moment for my eyes to adjust. The front tables of the dark, oblong space were occupied. We made our way to the bar along the left-hand wall. Veils of smoke hovered around

Coit Tower on Telegraph Hill, home of the murals on the next two pages.

Tiffany lampshades. Stained wood paneling absorbed most of the light. Slides of ancient art were being projected high on the rear wall.

We got a pint of Anchor Steam to share and made our way up to the balcony, where we found a table with a view of the slide-show. Next to us an older man was intently writing in a black notebook. Across the aisle, a group enshrouded in smoke argued about what sounded like a street-theater performance. Angie got out her Adrienne Rich book, opened it at random, and read to me in a low voice.

Dusk was approaching by the time we got back outside. "We could walk up Telegraph Hill and watch the sunset," I said. "And we can see the murals in Coit Tower." We headed up the hill, which was so steep that steps were cut into the sidewalks. At the intersection, the tower was visible behind a row of houses. I paused for a moment, then took quick breaths as we started up the next block.

We circled up the last stretch of the hill to a grassy knoll at the very peak. Coit Tower was an off-white cylinder twp hundred feet tall and forty feet in diameter, with a classical loggia at the top. A couple of dozen people were in the parking area overlooking the Bay. The tower was closed, but we walked around the outside and peered through the windows at the illuminated murals inside.

Downtown San Francisco c. 1935. The Depression-era murals in Coit Tower have a leftist tint, evidenced by details such as the titles of the radical papers in the stand at lower left.

An idealized California farm, a dream that lured dust-bowl refugees like those in John Steinbeck's Grapes of Wrath.

The west side centered around an industrial scene, juxtaposing the cold geometry of pipes and gears with the supple forms of the humans. "The workers have such nobility," Angie said. "They look like they're performing a sacred act." She mimed the ritualistic posture of a man turning a wrench.

I shielded the glare with my hands. "Yeah, and look over there in the corner. It's a single figure, a welder or something, standing like a saint in the niche of a Medieval church."

The south mural captured downtown San Francisco in the 1930s, while the east side portrayed an idyllic California farm of the same era. To the right, harvesters worked in an orange grove. Off in the distance, the sun shown on a dairy farm. "This place must have seemed like paradise during the Depression," Angie said.

"For some people," I said. "Woody Guthrie's songs don't make it sound so great for poor folks."

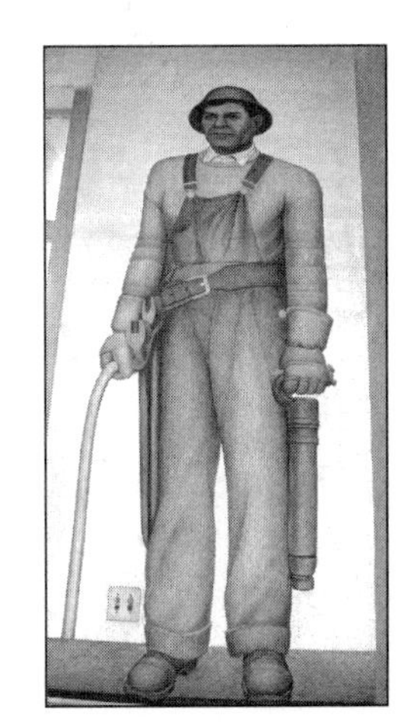

Solitary workers and farmers stand like saints in a Medieval church.

We stepped away from the tower. Clouds covered most of the twilight sky, but the quarter-moon appeared for a moment to the south, rising behind the Pyramid. I stopped to look, and Angie leaned against me. Her head lay on my chest. I put my arms around her and squeezed her close, then ran my hands down her body.

"Maybe we should head home," she said dreamily.

"Delighted to comply with your wishes," I said.

On the way down the hill she told me about a letter she'd received from an old school-friend, Isabel, who lived in Portland. "Isabel said that some friends of hers are planning an action later this month to blockade the weapons trains that run from Texas up to Washington state."

"Wow. We should cover it in Direct Action."

"Yeah. Isabel can probably get us photos. You know what else she told me? She's pregnant." Angie put her hands into her jacket pockets. "I want to go visit her. I love Portland. Sometimes I even think of moving up there. It seems way less stressful. There isn't the constant competition for who is the most radical. People have lives, not just meetings all the time. I could go back to school, take some art classes, all the things I never make time for here."

I cast a glance at her. Was this for real? Was she thinking of leaving, just when we got together?

But I couldn't say that. I took a breath, and in a quiet voice asked, "Are you seriously thinking about moving to Portland?"

"Oh, probably not. I have moments when it seems idyllic. Other times, I think how, when I was young, I wanted to grow up and be where the action was. And that's here." She shook her head. "I just wish I felt more connection with people. I hardly ever see Jenny anymore. When she was between boyfriends, she wanted to live together, but now that she's with Raoul, that's all she cares about."

I put my arm around her. "Maybe the Diablo Canyon action will feel different," I said. "Besides, think of all the good things you're doing with LAG, especially with the newspaper."

She nodded slowly. "It's not a unique contribution. Anyone could do it."

I wanted to disagree, but at that moment, a light rain started to fall. "Shoot," I said. "It was so nice."

"In Portland and Seattle it rains all the time," she said. "You get used to it."

"I'll take a drought any day," I said. "I hate getting my feet wet."

We walked along in silence, and I felt even more aggravated at the rain. We got only one night a week together — why did the weather have to come between us?

By the time we got to BART, it was already past nine. We had talked about going out dancing, but what I really wanted to do was go back to her apartment. I craved time alone with her. Time in bed. The silky warmth of her body. The sweet caress of her lips.

Fortunately, when we got off BART, without discussing it, we transferred to the bus to her place. The ride seemed to take forever, but finally we got there. All of the old clutter was still present, plus a huge pile of laundry on the couch and four boxes of books on the floor, one of which had been unpacked and its contents scattered around the carpet. Angie picked her way to the kitchen, got some juice, and led me into her room.

She lit a few candles and turned out the overhead light. As she stepped past, I reached out, put my arm around her waist, and pulled her to me. I wanted to drop onto the bed, but I could feel resistance. Take your time, I told myself. We're home. No need to rush.

She slipped away from me and lit a white candle on her altar. "This candle was blessed at the Brigid ritual last week," she said. "Brigid is the goddess of poetry and smithcraft. Now, whenever I relight the candle, the power of Her flame is rekindled."

She passed her hand slowly above the flame. I sat on the edge of the bed and looked at the flickering candle. "So there's power in the flame?"

She sat down next to me. "It's not really in the flame. The power is inside of us, lying dormant." She gazed at the altar. "The flame frees that power. That's what rituals do — get us in touch with our own power. Rituals and magical spells."

I slid across the bed so I was sitting with my back against the headboard. "'Spell' is a funny word," I said. "We talk about magical spells. But we also 'spell' words."

"Yeah," she said. "It's connected to the power of language."

I nodded. "There's another way we used the word back in Indiana. We'd say, 'Come on in and set a spell.'"

Still sitting on the edge of the bed, she spoke slowly, pausing between each phrase. "A magical spell. Spell a word. A spell of time. It ties together magic, language, and time." She looked past me. "At the ritual, each person made a pledge for the coming year. You stepped to the center, where there was a flaming cauldron, and made your pledge to Brigid. After you spoke, a priestess struck an anvil."

"What did you pledge?"

"My pledge was really a commitment to myself. I pledged to get some direction in my life. I asked Brigid's help with finding a focus. It was good to speak it in front of the whole community. Now I have witnesses."

She fluffed a pillow and propped it against the headboard next to me. "I wish you had been there," she said as she settled in. "At one point Artemis was talking about how Brigid is honored by both Pagans and Christians in Ireland. It made me think about you and your Medieval art pictures."

"Hey, we should look at my new art book," I said. I rolled to the edge of the bed and pulled it out of my daypack. I sat back against the headboard and she leaned against my shoulder as I opened the book. Each right-hand page featured a photo of a Medieval Italian cathedral. "There's Santa Croce in Florence, it's filled with great murals from the 1300s. And Pisa, with the leaning tower. But here's my favorite — Siena."

She sat up and looked at the striped stonework. "It looks like those circus tents we were held in last Summer, doesn't it?"

"You're right, I didn't think of that," I said. "What a wild design, stripes in a church. And it's not like it was a passing fad. It took over a hundred years to build."

"A hundred years," she mused. "That's four or five generations. So the people who started it never saw it finished. That's too bad."

"No, they knew it would take that long. They planned for it. They had faith that if they laid a solid foundation, their descendants would see it through to completion. They had to work with their great-great-grandchildren in mind. Can you imagine someone thinking that far ahead today? No way."

"They must have really believed in God," she said.

"I think what they believed in was their city, their community. They believed that their descendants would live in that city, and that they deserved the very best." I looked again at the cathedral, then thought of the nuclear missiles being deployed in Europe even as we spoke. "How weird to live at a time when we aren't even sure there will be a human race a generation from now. What an awful legacy we're giving to the future."

Interior of the Duomo, 13th-century civic cathedral of Siena. This magnificent building, a hub of urban life, expressed the pride of the independent Medieval city-state.

"I guess that's where the faith part comes in," Angie said. "Believing that we'll somehow survive, that future generations will pick up where we leave off."

She settled back against the headboard. I set the book down and leaned over to kiss her, but she didn't respond. "What's up?" I asked.

She looked away. "I wish we had more time together. One evening a week goes so fast." She paused a moment. "Are you going down to Diablo next weekend?"

I wished I could tell her whatever she wanted to hear. But I was already way behind at work. And what would I tell Holly, who had asked me to come out to the peace camp that weekend? "I can't do it. Sorry."

She sighed. "It's okay, I understand. I just wish we could do an action together."

"Why not do a graffiti action? We could do that on a Friday night."

"Sure," she said. She seemed to make an effort to shift gears. "I had this idea. You know how B of A is a big investor in South Africa? We could make a stencil of their logo and the words, 'Blood of Africa,' and stencil it in front of all their branches."

"I'll do that," I said. I'd probably have agreed to any proposal, if we could put the tension behind us.

A candle flared up, casting its dancing light on the ceiling. I leaned over and lay soft kisses on her forehead. Her breathing grew faster. Her hand caressed my knee and slid up onto my hip. She started to pull my T-shirt out, and I closed my eyes. But as her fingers grazed across my side, I flinched. A mischievous laugh escaped her. "Did that tickle?"

I tried to deny it, but she pounced, grabbing my ribs. A spasm propelled me backwards. She leapt on top, burrowing into me, searching for a vulnerable spot.

"No, no," I cried between fits of laughter. "Stop!" I grabbed at her arms, but she pulled free and went for my ribs again. I managed to get hold of her wrists and wrestled her down onto the bed. She giggled, which set me to laughing. As soon as I relaxed my vigilance, she pulled one of my hands up to her mouth and bit me hard enough to extricate herself. In an instant she was tickling me again.

Finally I pinned her to the bed. "Whoa," I said, coughing from the exertion. "I haven't laughed that hard in a long time."

"Okay, no more tonight," she said, but little bursts of laughter still escaped, and I wasn't going to let go yet.

I leaned down and kissed her, still holding her wrists. "Promise?"

She raised her head and kissed me. "I promise." She giggled again. "No, really."

Slowly I let go and stretched out next to her. She pushed me over on my back and crawled on top, pinning my arms to the bed. Then she leaned down and laced her tongue across my lips.

I gazed up at her, feeling at her mercy in ways she didn't imagine. How could I have dreamed that I could walk away from her?

She leaned down and licked my ear. Her breasts rubbed softly against my chest.

Anything you want, I sighed. Anything you want.

Saturday, February 18, 1984

EVERYONE ELSE seemed to think they were at a big party, laughing and swapping stories. I was the only one out of the spirit. And no wonder. I was practically the only one not getting arrested.

Not quite. Two days earlier, Angie had told me that Antonio was making the round trip in one day and persuaded me to ride down with them. I felt guilty for making a ten-hour round trip to Diablo when I hadn't been out to visit the peace camp since opening day. But this was a Change of Heart action. I owed it to my cluster to be there.

As we huddled in the blustery grayness outside the front gate, Alby and Karina regaled the cluster with their travel story. They had left from San Francisco a few days earlier and ridden the rails all the way to San Luis Obispo. "It was easier than we thought," Karina said. "The hardest part is getting off at the right place. It's not like there are any roadsigns. We overshot Stockton the first day and had to wait overnight till another train stopped long enough for us to get onboard."

Angie's eyes were wide as she questioned Alby. "Were you riding in boxcars?"

I studied her warily. Was she taking notes for an adventure of her own? What if she and Alby took off freight-hopping across the country?

Alby cocked his head. "Boxcars are too obvious. We found a flat car carrying construction equipment, and crawled under some bulldozers. It was freezing cold going through the central valley at night."

I shook my head. "Didn't you worry abut falling off?"

"Oh, you could," Karina said nonchalantly. "But the greatest danger was when the train went through a tunnel. It lasted forever. The whole tunnel filled with diesel fumes. If the train had been going slower, we probably would have suffocated."

Someone called Karina away, and the circle dispersed. I followed Angie away from the intersection, where a squad of cops were lining up. I put my arm around her shoulders. Angie put her hands in her pockets. "Riding the rails. That's pretty amazing, don't you think? I didn't think anyone did that anymore."

"I don't know," I said, wishing she'd focus more on us during our last minutes together. "Seems like risking your life for a cheap thrill."

Angie laughed sharply. "Everything can't be safe and secure. You have to take chances once in a while." She slipped from under my arm and walked away to help Alby and Megan with props for the cluster action. Damn. Why had I taken the bait? I hated to part on a sour note.

But I didn't want to be clingy, either. Wait a few minutes, then try again. I looked around for someone else to talk with.

Belinda and her partner Frida stood nearby, but I figured all I'd get from Belinda was a lecture on Coordinating Council and the evils of centralization. I could pass on that one right now. Finally I spotted Moonstone. "How's it going?" I called to him.

He greeted me with a hug, seeming to hang on my shoulders for support. "Just got out of jail this morning. I've hardly slept for five days."

Moonstone's affinity group, Deadheads for Peace, had come down the previous week.

"Did you get onto the site?" I asked.

"Yeah. We set out last Monday just after dark. We hiked all night and reached the ridge above the plant before dawn. We had this giant banner that said, 'Diablo: We Can Live Without It.' We fastened it to some trees above the construction site, where the workers could see it when the sun rose. Then we crossed the perimeter road and took cover along the security fence."

DIRECT ACTION

#13

February 1984

Published by Livermore Action Group

Livermore Peace Camp Opens—See Page 6, 7

Direct Action #13, February 1984

He crouched slightly, as if reliving the action. "By this time it was dawn. We worked our way along the fence till we came across a hole in the outer ring, probably left by construction workers taking a short cut. We slipped through and made it up to the second fence, where the gate was standing open. We couldn't believe it. Just then a guard comes ambling along, carrying a lunch pail and reading his morning paper. We duck, but he doesn't even look up, he goes on through the gate and up toward the construction zone. As soon as he gets past, we run through the gate and hide behind a shed to scope out the last fence between us and the reactor area. We start for it, but right then two more guards come through the gate."

"Oh, no," I said. "So close."

"Yeah. We tried saying we were workers, and it confused them for a minute. But finally they arrested us. On the police report, they wrote that they busted us outside the first fence. They wouldn't admit we got inside the site. But we'll bring it out at our trial."

"Assuming they don't drop the charges to shut you up," I said.

Moonstone nodded. "They may have to, since we just blew a huge hole in their security claims."

We hugged again, and he wandered off to get some rest. I looked around for Angie. She and Jenny were putting their costumes on. They leaned their heads together as if sharing a secret. I hesitated to interrupt their tête-à-tête, but Karina, dressed in a gorgeous white-lace gown, spared me the decision. "Let's go," she called out. "Now's the time."

"What's the rush?" Angie said in a chafing voice.

"There's a TV crew here," Karina answered.

"Why should that determine our action?" Angie said.

Karina jutted her chin. "Who else are we doing it for? There's no one here except other protesters and some cops. This is our chance to have an impact."

Sara stepped between them. "We spent so much time planning our action," she said to Angie. "We might as well get some media coverage out of it."

"Fine," Angie said with a wave of her hand. She buttoned up her long black robe and walked over to where I stood. "Sure you don't want to change

Affinity group action at Diablo Canyon, where hundreds of people were arrested in 1984 protesting licensing of the nuclear plant. This layout is from Direct Action, April 1984.

your mind and join us?" she asked. "We need more ushers for the wedding. It's probably just a four day-sentence."

I shook my head. "I've got to get home. I have all kinds of stuff to do for the Livermore action."

Angie nodded silently and hugged me, but there wasn't much passion. As I held onto her, I pictured myself sitting alone in the LAG office, hedged in by the clutter, tangled in the phone cords, the archetype of the anti-nuclear bureaucrat. What was I doing, passing up an action to make phone calls?

Angie gave me a last squeeze and stepped away. I reached after her and rubbed her shoulder. "Have a good time," I said wistfully.

"Yeah, I will," she called back. "I'll call you when I get home."

Change of Heart launched its performance, and in spite of my melancholy I couldn't help smiling. For an audience consisting of me, Antonio, Belinda, Frida, and a bunch of cops, the cluster celebrated the betrothal of the People of California (Karina, a bouquet of delicate blue flowers highlighted against her traditional white gown) to Death by Radiation (Alby, bedecked in a suit and top hat, his face painted as a skull).

Doc and Sara handed out programs, and we all sang the wedding hymn as Karina came down the aisle:

> Here comes the bride, soon she'll have died.
> From radiation, no one can hide.
> Here comes the groom, bringer of doom.
> Corporate profit is building our tomb.

When objections were called for, Jenny stepped forward. "As the Mother of the People of California, I beg you to reconsider..."

Reverend Angie, wearing a big gold dollar sign over her black choir robe, waved her hand sharply. "Shut Up!" She turned to Death. "You may irradiate the bride." Alby planted a long, deadly kiss as Karina collapsed in his arms. Kazoos took up the recessional, and the big wedding cake stood up and led bride, groom, and wedding party in a dance across the no-trespassing line. Doc proposed a toast to Diablo Canyon, and the whole party dropped dead in the road.

The cops shook themselves into action. Next to me, Antonio seemed as agitated as I. We edged toward the intersection, and I tried to make eye contact with people as they got busted. Doc gave a tight smile. Karina blew kisses. Angie waved just before her arrest, but I couldn't tell if it was to me, or our little crowd in general.

Antonio and I didn't talk much on the ride back, and I found myself with altogether too much time to ponder when I might see Angie again. It was hard enough saying goodbye to her anytime, seeing her as seldom as I did. But to part company when we weren't bonding in the first place, that really hurt.

Wednesday, February 29, 1984

BACK AND FORTH, up and down. One day I'd get an encouraging phone call and think that the Livermore action was finally coming together. The next I'd get smacked in the face with someone's indifference.

Six weeks to go. Shouldn't more be happening? Where were the arguments over jail solidarity, or the debates over blockade tactics? Did we really have it all figured out? Or was Karina right? Was Livermore passé?

Not that the April financial district action was catching on, either. I might be aggravated at Karina and the others for siphoning off people from Livermore, but that didn't mean I wanted the City action to flop. We needed something to go right. If neither of the protests went anywhere, what was left? What was the meaning of Livermore "Action" Group if we never did anything?

The only positive note was the Democratic Convention. True, there hadn't been any specific decision about what to do. But at least people cared enough to show up at meetings and fight over it.

"We just need to be patient," Sara said as she and I sat stuffing envelopes at one of the long worktables in the middle of the office that afternoon. "There's still plenty of time to reach consensus on the Convention. People just need a chance to express their concerns."

"I hope you're right," I said. A spokescouncil was planned for the following weekend to discuss the Convention. Sara and Alby and a few others were submitting a proposal for a LAG protest. I admired their perseverance, but I wasn't sorry that I had a People's Convention meeting the same afternoon. Let other people hash it out. "It's going to take some work to get people like Melissa or the Walnettos to stand aside," I said. "They're so worried about sabotaging the Democrats and helping re-elect Reagan."

"We're proposing that we target military corporations who donate to the Democrats, not disrupt the Convention itself," Sara said. "Someone needs to hold them accountable."

"I'll say we do." Raoul boomed through loud and clear from halfway across the office. He pulled himself up off the couch and ambled over to the table where Sara and I were working on the outreach mailing. "What do the Democrats have to say about disarmament? Nothing! And the liberal groups with their peace rallies sure aren't going to hold them accountable. We've got to shake things up. If we shut the City down during the Convention, that'll get their attention."

I started to say something about toning down the rhetoric in order to get consensus, but just then a paper airplane crash-landed on the table in front of me.

"Airmail! Special Delivery for Jeff Harrison!" It was Sid. I hadn't seen him come in. He did a hop-skip-jump across the office and pulled up just short of our table. "Getting high licking stamps?"

It was hard not to laugh, even though I felt vaguely put down. Sid wouldn't be caught dead working on a mailing. If there were flyers to deliver, he'd go straight to the nearest punk concert and hand them out in person. "Hey, somebody's got to keep this group afloat," I said.

"Yeah," Sara said. "We have to pay for this office for you guys to hang out in."

Sid looked at Raoul. "Did you tell them about our plans for inciting mass riots at the Convention?"

Raoul frowned. "It's serious. Just because some people are scared to rock the boat, we can't back off. We have to assert our right to the street."

"The main thing is to keep moving," Sid said. "Don't submit to arrest. That's how you're going to reach younger people, people with more spirit of rebellion."

Ouch, I thought. I'm not *that* old, am I? "I'm all for mobile protests," I said. "But some people in LAG are going to have trouble with hit-and-run actions."

Jenny had joined us as I spoke. She looked at me as if testing the waters. "We're not necessarily thinking of this as a LAG action," she said. "If LAG doesn't want to protest the Democrats, somebody has to."

Sid started to echo her, but I was still staring at Jenny. Was she, the anchor of the LAG staff, drifting off?

"We'll try to work out a consensus," Jenny added quickly. "There's probably some common ground."

Democratic Convention

Bohemian Grove Protest Planned for July

People's Convention Planned for July 14-15

Jesse Jackson

Limitations and Possibilities

What's In It for LAG?

The newspaper devoted many articles to dialogues about how to respond to the Democratic Convention coming to San Francisco. Most proposals involved protest, with disagreement over how much to work in coalition with other groups.

"I doubt it," Raoul said moodily. "It's all about control. If it's a LAG action, Coordinating Council will want to control it."

How was I supposed to answer that? Of course Coordinating Council would want input on a LAG action. I stared at the floor, trying to think of a new angle.

"There are a lot of other things LAG could do at the convention," Jenny said. "There will probably be consensus on joining People's Convention, don't you think?"

I looked at her glumly. "LAG might join," I said. "But who is actually going to coalition meetings? Me and Mort...."

"I thought Claudia was working on it," Jenny said.

"Yeah. But she doesn't consider herself a LAG rep."

Sid picked up a piece of string and made a cat's cradle. He gestured at Sara. "Are you coming to the planning meeting for the May 22nd action?"

An affinity group prepared these mock transit passes for Tax Day actions protesting the military budget.

"What's May 22nd?" I asked.

"We're planning a financial district action in late May to try out some roving tactics," Sid said. "You should check it out."

"Why not just do it at LAG's April 16th action?" The irony of my pleading for the City action wasn't lost on me, but at least it was part of LAG. The last thing we needed was another autonomous action.

Raoul cleared his throat. "It wouldn't work at a LAG action. We want to get inside the corporations and disrupt them. There's only so much you can accomplish by blocking doors and streets."

"You could go inside at a LAG action," I said.

"No, we'd have monitors herding us around like we're a bunch of sheep," Raoul answered. "And then you get people saying that when you do civil disobedience, you have to sit down and accept the consequences. To hell with pacifism."

"What?" Sara said sharply. "I'm a pacifist, and I resent that stereotype."

Raoul's big shoulders slumped. "Sorry. You know what I mean. I get sick of that submission model. If you can get away, you should. Don't give in. Keep protesting as long as you can."

Sid nodded vigorously. "I already made up a flyer for May 22nd that says, 'Avoid Arrest.' I'll pass it out at the Dead Kennedys show this weekend. There's a lot of punks who won't come to protests if they think they have to surrender to the police."

And there's a hell of a lot of LAG people who won't go anywhere near your protest, I thought. Did any of you ever consider that?

I was relieved when the office door swung open. It was Cindy from the Commie Dupes, dropping off artwork for the paper. Raoul and Sid followed Jenny back to her desk, and I turned my attention to Cindy. She reached into her handbag and pulled out what looked like a playing card. She snapped it down on the table — a Muni Fast Pass altered to read, "Blast Pass."

"We're going to pass them out during the Tax Day action," Cindy said, "and at the main post office that night when people are dropping off their last-minute returns. There's a war tax resisters rally all evening."

"It looks great," I said. "We'll get it in Direct Action."

"Thanks!" She headed for the door. "Gotta go. I'm double-parked."

As she departed, Sara and Norm came over to take a look. "Speaking of Direct Action," Norm said, "I want to write a story about local people visiting the peace camp. Two more stopped by yesterday. One woman wants to push for a study of groundwater contamination near the Lab. That's the sort of thing a nuclear facility is vulnerable on."

"Especially if the initiative comes from local people and not 'outside agitators,'" Sara said as she turned back to addressing envelopes.

Norm nodded. "We're going to write it up in the next Peace Lab News. That reminds me, Holly asked if you would mind pasting up the new issue — I have all the stuff. If you can do it tonight, I can get it xeroxed tomorrow and take it out there."

"Sure," I said. I had plenty else I needed to do, but the idea of manual labor sounded appealing. Besides, pasting up a flyer was a way to support Holly and the peace camp, even if I hadn't been back out since opening day.

Norm got a manila folder from his desk and handed it to me. "So, when are you coming back out? Come spend a night."

"Yeah," I said apologetically. "I'm planning to."

"The food's great," he said. "And there's always chocolate on hand, not just Bit o' Honey."

I smiled. It was an inside joke. Literally. Back when we were in jail for the Consulate action, before I cited out, we got moved upstairs to a larger holding cell with a bunch of regular inmates. Norm and I sat together scoping out the scene. Every so often, one of the prisoners would kneel down by the back door of the cell and slide some change under the door. A minute later a candy bar would slide back through. I pointed it out to Norm.

"There, see? He got two. Both Bit o' Honeys. That's what the guy over there got, too."

"I'll try it," Norm said, fishing in his pocket for change. "You want one?"

"Yeah," I said, handing him a quarter. "But see if they have any chocolate. A Snickers bar would be great right now."

Norm strolled over toward the door and leaned toward an older man chewing meditatively on his Bit o' Honey, flat squares of sugary caramel that gave good time-value for your money. A few words were exchanged, and then Norm tapped on the cell door. He held up two fingers to the little window, and slid our change under the door. Sure enough, a minute later, he came walking back with the goods. "There's a trustee out there," he explained, "and a candy machine."

The Peace Lab News was a serial flyer for leafletting at Livermore Lab. A new edition was produced at least once a week during the Spring and Fall peace camps.

"Thanks," I said, trying to mask my disappointment as he handed me a Bit o' Honey. "Is that all they have?"

"No," he said, peeling back the wrapper and working the first square loose. "But that's the only kind that will fit under the door."

Standing there in the office, we laughed again. "LAG should campaign for wider spaces underneath holding cell doors in all future jail construction," I said.

"That could make a big difference," said Norm, "considering all the new jails they're building."

Sara pulled on her sweater and walked toward me. "Are we going to finish Direct Action this weekend?"

"Yeah, I think we can." I surveyed the twenty-four pages in my mind — our best issue yet, I thought. "Carmen sent a great story on the impact of the Euromissiles on European peace groups," I said. "And Angie said she'd get the Bohemian Grove story done by tomorrow."

"Good. I can be there all day Sunday, and I'll stay late if it looks like we can finish. What about the Middle East pages?"

"Mort said he'd finish them Saturday."

Sara looked skeptical. "He always says he'll finish things, and then you or Holly wind up doing it."

"Yeah, well... Maybe you could finish it this time?"

Sara scowled. "Just because you're willing to pick up after Mort doesn't mean everyone else is. That's the sort of thing that's burning people out."

I flushed. "I was just kidding."

"It's not a joke. The production process is really sloppy, and it's getting hard for me to keep working on it."

Tears welled up in my eyes, and I was glad that she turned to pick up her daypack. I'm doing the best I can, I wanted to say. We're all volunteers here. Do you have to be so critical?

Sara said a short goodbye and headed out the door. Raoul and Sid followed soon after. I welcomed the quiet. But my mind was still racing. I restlessly scanned the conversations of the past two hours, searching for some sign of hope. Something must be going right. The Blast Pass. But that was about it.

I stared at the table. A hundred unstuffed envelopes stared back. I sighed, louder than I intended. Jenny looked my way. "How are you doing?" she asked tentatively.

"Okay, I guess. Getting jumped on by Sara didn't help."

"Yeah," Jenny said. "Don't take it personally. Karina has a new lover, and Sara's really stressed. Especially because Karina is so open about it. Not everyone is into non-monogamy..." Jenny's voice trailed off, and she looked at me sheepishly.

I scrutinized her eyes. When I wasn't around, did she say the same thing about me and Holly? Had we become gossip-fodder?

Jenny looked away. "How's, uh — how's the mailing going?"

"Okay, I guess." I looked at the table again. The stack of letters wasn't getting any smaller. But I didn't have it in me to stuff another envelope. Why not go home? I needed to put in some hours around the apartment building, anyway. Smoke a pipe and vacuum the halls. Do some singing. Let my thoughts wander.

I gathered my jacket and the Peace Lab News paste-up folder, said goodbye to Jenny and Norm, and headed toward the door. I took a deep breath and yearned for release, the satisfaction of a hard-worked day about to give way to more relaxed pursuits.

But as I stepped outside into the grayness of a week-long overcast, my anxiety lingered. I searched back through the frayed encounters of the day, looking for the cause. Raoul? Sara? Jenny? No, it was vaguer, less tangible. A feeling that Winter would never end. Not here. Somewhere bands were playing, and somewhere hearts were light. Why, down in Arizona and Florida, baseball was in the midst of Spring training. That must count for something.

Not with me. All I knew was fog and rain and more of the same.

Sunday, March 4, 1984

It seemed like weeks since we'd gone for a late-evening walk. Holly and I held hands as usual, but our feet seemed out of synch. I kept shuffling, trying to get in step. We headed for the Cal campus. Get under some trees, I thought. Get away from all the concrete.

We took turns talking, but our usual flow of conversation was missing. Holly was the one to suggest a walk. Was there something particular she wanted to discuss? We never had talked much about my and Angie's affair, or what it meant to our relationship.

I had been thinking lately about what I'd do if Holly insisted on a choice. One moment I'd be grieving my relationship with Angie. The next, I'd be struggling over how to say goodbye to Holly.

The Campanile at UC Berkeley, descendent of civic belltowers which served as lookout points and alarm signals in the days before electricity.

We were still chatting when we crossed onto campus. As we passed Harmon Gym, Holly fell silent. She seemed to be staring intently at the pavement ahead of her, as if she were trying to figure out the best way to say something unpleasant.

We passed under a streetlight, and I looked at her. Maybe I should initiate the conversation, I thought. Before I could make up my mind, she spoke. "Caroline's coming back at the end of March."

Caroline? Was that what she was thinking about? I felt embarrassed for assuming all of Holly's thoughts were about me. "Did you hear from her?"

"Well, I got a postcard that she wrote several weeks ago when she visited Managua. So I'm assuming that her plans haven't changed." She fell silent again for a moment. "I hope she comes back soon. I really miss having someone to talk to."

I nodded silently. We walked along a cobblestone path toward the Eucalyptus Grove. I looked down at the patchwork of stones, struck by the seemingly random pattern. Did someone plan this? Or did they just sit there with a big stack of rocks and try to get them to fit?

We crossed a small footbridge and came to a stop under a eucalyptus.

Holly tilted her head back and looked up at the soaring trees. Overhead, a dark web of leaves and branches traced a tangled pattern against the lighter gray sky.

"Are you going to the People's Convention meeting next Saturday?" Holly's voice sounded disembodied, like it was coming from a loudspeaker.

"Yeah, probably," I said, lowering my head. "Why?"

"I was thinking of going. Now that the peace camp is over, I'll have more time for things like that."

"Really?" I looked at her, then gazed out across the grove. If Holly got involved, maybe Craig and Daniel and Caroline weren't far behind. Maybe the Winter had been a fallow period, and people would return to the fray rested and refreshed. My advance work on People's Convention might yet bear fruit.

"That would be great," I said. "People's Convention needs more LAG people involved. It's a lot of old lefties, with a handful of direct action people to try to balance the load."

I couldn't make out her reaction, but I sensed that my sales pitch had missed the mark. "Have you thought about doing a workshop on the peace camp?" I added quickly. "There are workshop slots on Friday and Saturday afternoons."

"That's a good idea," she said as we made our way across the Eucalyptus Grove, which was illuminated by old-fashioned streetlamps. "We're hoping to find land for the Fall, so we need to be making contacts and getting more people involved."

We headed out of the grove, and Holly fell silent again. Did we used to have these sort of lulls when we talked?

We paused on an old wooden bridge over Strawberry Creek. A gnarled tree cast its shadow over us. Holly leaned against the railing. She looked at me, but didn't speak.

"What are you thinking about?" I asked.

She looked at me intently for a moment. "I've been thinking a lot about our relationship the past couple of weeks. It's crossed my mind to move out of our apartment."

I grasped the bridge rail and said nothing, lest my voice betray me.

"I haven't wanted to make a decision without talking it over with Caroline," Holly continued. "Sara has been a big help, but she doesn't know me as well. Caroline would understand things no one else would, and help me see whether I'm making the right decision."

I nodded. My head felt light, and I gripped the railing more tightly. I took an audible breath, and Holly looked at me expectantly. My words came out slowly. "Are you feeling like you have to decide now?"

She took my free hand. "Right now? No." She looked at me carefully. Then her eyes softened. "Everything is so confusing right now. I don't know how much is about you and Angie, and how much is feeling discouraged about LAG. And how much is just wondering what to do with my life."

I breathed a little easier. We stepped away from the railing and resumed our walk. We angled uphill toward the Campanile, the old bell tower in the center of campus. I tried to relax and enjoy the night air.

But a knot remained in my chest. How long a reprieve could I expect? It wasn't like clarity lurked around the corner. What difference was another few weeks going to make? Why did I think I'd be any closer to a decision?

The Campanile bells pealed. The metallic strokes echoed off the stone buildings and reverberated in my head. I let loose of Holly's hand and sucked in a breath, trying to hold the clanging dissonance at bay until the hour had tolled.

Friday, March 16, 1984

FINALLY — an action. And a journalistic one, no less.

I arrived early at the Berkeley BART station. I pulled a *Bay Guardian* out of a news rack and looked over the music listings and ate a candy bar till the rest of the group showed up around seven o'clock. Half were from Change of Heart, but there were some Overthrow guys, several people who worked on Direct Action, and a few others.

Two dozen of us huddled together. A couple of cops strolled across the plaza and gave us the eye, but they seemed more interested in the nervous-looking guy hustling pirate bus transfers out by the street.

Karina knelt and unfolded a map of the city. She handed one side to me, and I knelt next to her in the center of the circle.

"There are four quadrants," she said. "Downtown, North Shattuck, Telegraph, and West Berkeley. Most of us should focus on downtown and North Shattuck. West Berkeley should take a car and cover the other BART stations too."

Alby and Sara passed out stenciled signs the size of the top half of a newspaper. A broken television set was framed by the words "Sorry: TV On the Blink."

"We have a couple of rolls of quarters," Sara said. She and Karina doled the money out.

"I brought a bunch, too," I said. I reached into my pocket and jangled the coins.

Angie had postponed our usual Friday date till Sunday so she could take a workshop at Berkeley Women's Health Collective, and Holly wasn't interested in the action. So I was glad when Mort beckoned to me. "Let's do North Shattuck with Lyle," he said.

The rest of the crowd divided up the town. "Does everyone have the legal number?" Karina said. "Walt said he'd stay by his phone till ten o'clock in case someone gets busted."

I wrote the number carefully on my wrist, even though I planned to be extra careful. The West Berkeley crew set off to get their car. The rest of us started away from the plaza in our respective directions. But Sara called us back. "One more thing — who's going to do the box on the plaza here?"

Now there was a challenge. Sure, the cops were ignoring us. But to pull it off right under their noses?

Karina gestured at Alby. "You set up a diversion," she said. "I'll nail the box."

Alby strolled across the plaza to a Chronicle newsstand, pretended to drop a quarter in the slot, and when it wouldn't open, started rattling the door and berating the machine. The forces of law and order zeroed in on the commotion. Across the way, Karina popped open the *USA Today* box, slipped the "TV" sign into the display window, and squirted superglue into the coinslot. Mission accomplished. As she strode away, Alby gave his machine one last angry tug, then turned to the approaching cops and loudly proclaimed his dissatisfaction with modern technology.

Stencil from an action targeting USA Today stands.

"That's an inspiring send-off," Hank said as we parted.

"Yeah," I said. "After tonight, no more McNews in Berkeley."

"Hey, don't forget pinball later on," Hank called after me. "We'll meet back at my shop around nine."

"I'll be there," I promised, then glanced over at the cops. "Knock on wood!"

The evening was warm with a light breeze. Lyle and I were in T-shirts and jeans. Mort wore his usual button shirt and slacks, but his shirttails were half untucked. We strolled across Shattuck and came to our first stop. Mort and I stood lookout while Lyle went to work on the newsstand. Thirty seconds later, we were on the road again. "The only risk is the glue," Lyle said. "Otherwise, it just looks like you're buying a paper."

We crossed over to Bank of America plaza. After Mort glued the news box, I proudly pointed out the spot where Angie and I had recently done our Blood of Africa graffiti. The bank had painted over it in gray, but you could still see the outlines of our B of A logo. "They've actually preserved it for future archaeologists to excavate," I said.

The next intersection had a whole herd of stands clustered around the stoplights. "If we have enough signs," I said, "we could do the *Examiner* and *Chronicle* boxes while we're at it."

Mort shook his head. "No, not the local papers."

"Why not? It's all just big corporations controlling the news."

"It isn't that simple," he answered. He took off his glasses and wiped them on his shirttail. "With local corporations, we have other means of access. We might influence them via local actions, if necessary right at their offices. If it's a multinational with headquarters who-knows-where, how do we hold them accountable?" He put his glasses back on. "It's in our interest to play local corporations against an outsider like *USA Today.* Capitalists fight among themselves, and we can affect the outcome of the fight."

We approached another box. Lyle gave the all clear sign, and I took my turn on the glue-gun. "Local papers or not, I don't suppose we'll get any media coverage for this. You have to blow something up to get in the news."

"Well, maybe we could escalate next time," Lyle said. "I tell you, I have it in for USA Today. It's the victory of style over substance."

"Just like LAG," Mort said. "All style and no substance."

"That's a cheap shot," I said. "Livermore Lab is on the map because of our actions."

"Sure," Mort said without looking at me. He stretched his back and grimaced as we waited for the light to change. "Direct action can focus media attention. But people get sucked into a trap, doing flashier actions trying to get press coverage. Things like education and coalition work that don't excite the media get ignored. Look at the Democratic Convention. Who's doing outreach or coalition work? All people care about is where to protest."

The light took forever to change. "Maybe we need to start from where people are," I said. "The Democrats deserve to be protested for caving in to Reagan."

"As if a protest is going to have any effect on the Democrats," Mort scoffed as we finally got the green light. "If we'd already built a cross-issue movement which could effectively pressure the Democrats to challenge Reagan, and then they waffled, that would be the moment for a big protest. If we were the direct action wing of a broader movement, we could be the voice of conscience for liberals. But it's naive to think that protests by themselves are going to have any effect on politicians who spend their lives isolated in Washington or Sacramento. They don't even know we exist."

I jumped in as soon as he finished. "What better way to reach them than CD? If we disrupt the Convention, that'll get their attention."

Lyle gave me a funny look, and I had to wonder myself at what I'd said. Disrupt the Convention? Was that really the logical outcome of my views?

But Mort seemed to take it in stride. "That's just what I'm talking about," he said with no rancor. "You get sucked into fringe actions that most people in LAG won't support. You get a smaller and smaller base of people doing outrageous actions to make themselves feel important. It's dramatic. But is it building a movement?"

We walked along in silence. It was frustrating debating with Mort. Couldn't he at least go through the motions of considering what I'd said?

We were approaching Cedar Street, and spotted a *USA Today* box in front of Andronico's grocery. "I think it's my turn," Mort said, taking the glue from Lyle. I glanced up Shattuck — a cop car! "Ssssst!" I hissed at Mort. He looked at me in alarm. The patrol car pulled to a stop right near us. Mort thrust his hands into his pockets — a sure giveaway. Lyle tucked the signs under his arm and acted like he didn't know Mort.

But the cops never even looked our way. The light changed, and they cruised on down Shattuck. My chest was tight, and I gave a sharp laugh. Mort looked pale beneath the streetlights. He started away from the newsstand. Lyle caught his arm. "Come on, the cops are gone. We can't skip a box."

I nodded. I checked the street, pulled out a quarter, and held the door open as Lyle slipped a sign in. Then I took the glue-gun from Mort and shot a bead into the slot. "See? We've got to start with direct action."

Mort gave a laugh, and we headed north at a more relaxed pace. "The problem with the way we're doing CD," he said as if thinking out loud, "is that there's no analysis of how to expand our base. Who historically has done direct action? Partly it's been activists and students, young people acting at a privileged moment of their lives, before they take on responsibilities like careers, houses, families. But that hasn't accounted for the major movements of the past century — Labor and Civil Rights. Both have been far more broadly-based. They've involved working people who have a lot more at stake. We've got to connect our work to these constituencies. And we won't do that by organizing self-indulgent affinity group actions. It's going to take economic and social analysis, a grasp of class dynamics that I don't see LAG undertaking."

True, it was hard to imagine most affinity groups engaging in class analysis. But did that mean we should disband? "A group like LAG can do other things," I said. "We can break new ground that later groups will expand on. That's the justification for smaller, flashier actions."

"That might occasionally work," Mort shrugged. "But unless you see a potential mass base for what you're doing, you just attract more people like yourselves. Look at the actions in the financial district. What's that laying the groundwork for? All they reach is anarchists who won't subordinate their egos to a group process. Those kinds of actions won't build a movement. You end up escalating your tactics until everyone burns out or winds up in prison."

Before I could think of an answer, we reached Walnut Square, a yuppie shopping enclave at the foot of the North Berkeley Hills. "Keep an eye out," Lyle said, "I'll get this one."

Mort and I checked the street. "All clear," I said.

Lyle approached the newsstand. Suddenly he halted. "Whoa — check this out!" Mort and I abandoned our posts and went over to look. The box's face was melted into a warped mass of plastic. Black soot stained the upper edges of the front door. Lyle dropped in a quarter and gingerly opened the door. Inside, ashes and charred newsprint bespoke an earlier visit. "Looks like someone else got here first," Lyle said.

"Think it was someone with us?" Mort said.

"No," I said, shaking my head at the gutted stand. "I think we have competition."

We admired the handiwork for a moment longer. "I don't think we should leave a stencil," I said. "It's too incriminating if we get busted somewhere else. And wipe your fingerprints off the door."

Lyle complied, then shot a stream of superglue into the coin slot. "Might as well slow down the repair crew."

That was pretty much the end of the Shattuck commercial district. "We still have to cover the area north of campus," Lyle said. A semi-trailer rolled by, drowning out the rest of his words. But once it passed, the night was still. We headed up Cedar toward Northside. A slight breeze rustled through a row of small trees.

Mort was silent, and I couldn't tell what he was thinking. But I thought I spied a flaw in his logic. "The problem with what you're saying," I said, "is that it's CD that pulls people together in the first place. It's fine to talk about education and coalition work, but it's protests that get people involved. You can't just write that off, or you don't have any movement, period."

"I'm not saying don't protest," Mort said. His breathing was heavy as we walked uphill. "But it exhausts people. It can highlight injustices or throw a monkey wrench into the system, but it can't be a permanent tactic in any struggle. The enemies we're fighting — government, corporations, the military — have bottomless resources compared to us. We can't fight them forever. We have to build alliances with liberals who can consolidate the gains we make via direct action. Look at labor. Unions initially won their rights by wildcat strikes, sabotage, and outright battles with the cops and military. But they couldn't fight those battles indefinitely — they had to get their rights consolidated by 'legitimate' channels, by Congress and the courts. There's a time and place for direct action. We need to use CD when it can be effective, and recognize when it isn't."

I didn't know enough Labor history to contradict him. Still, something nagged at me. I looked at Mort. "Where does that leave us? LAG was built around CD."

As we reached the top of the hill, Mort paused and put his hands on his hips, catching his breath. "You can't build a movement around a tactic. The question is whether LAG can grow beyond mere tactical unity. We need to analyze the role of direct action in a broader strategy. We have to broaden our focus to include environmental and social issues that speak to working people and people of color. That's the value of People's Convention — it offers a starting point. Of course," he added with a dry laugh, "it's not a protest. So nobody in LAG has any interest."

DIRECT ACTION

#14

March 1984

Published by Livermore Action Group

Autonomous Decentralized Actions April 16

See Page 1

Brian Crowley

Direct Action #14, March 1984

Real funny, I thought. Was it a laughing matter to mock the most active people in LAG, just because they didn't want to go to coalition meetings? Maybe we needed to figure out how to work with younger anarchists, not force them into a leftist mold. If they wanted protests, give them one. People's Convention had talked about doing a march from Embarcadero to the Democratic Convention to deliver our People's Platform — why not latch onto that idea and try to get LAGers involved? It didn't have to be an ordinary march. We could make it what we wanted. With a little imagination, it could be a highlight of the week.

I was tempted to share the inspiration with Mort. But not quite yet. He'd counter with ten reasons why it would never work.

We reached Northside, a little commercial strip just north of the UC campus, where we found two *USA Today* boxes. By this time, we were a well-oiled machine, and in a couple of minutes we had finished our work and stood outside La Val's pizza house. "Let's stop in for a beer," Mort said.

"Why not get a six-pack and head over to Hank's shop?" Lyle answered. "It's nine-thirty. Pinball's probably open."

"Assuming Hank got home okay," I said. "I wonder if anyone got popped? Maybe the others weren't as lucky as we were."

ALTHOUGH EVERYONE was invited to Hank's shop, it didn't surprise me when we got there and it was all guys. It had been a month since I'd been to pinball, and I felt out of synch with the scene. No one but me was working on the April actions. I wasn't sensing much involvement around the Convention, either. Wasn't that the whole point, to party *and* rabble-rouse? If we weren't organizing together, was it just another place to drink and smoke weed?

Well, it isn't just any old place, I had to admit as my eyes took in the row of glistening machines. The jukebox cranked out "My Generation" by the Who. Tai was playing an old pre-flippers game with a circus tent and a bunch of clowns on the back-glass. Craig was leaning against another machine, watching Hank fiddle with the wiring on his latest rehab project, an Americana number called "Crossroads."

"It's a real beauty," Hank said as he emerged from under the machine. "Just needs a little cleaning up."

Lyle stashed the beer in the corner fridge. Hank pulled out a thick joint and fired it up. "I was up in Humboldt last weekend for an Earth First! gathering, and I made a pit stop on the way back at a friend's farm outside Willits. He gave me a big bag of tops as a 'disarmament dividend' and said to make sure people from LAG enjoyed the harvest."

"Harvesting in March?" I said.

"Yeah, he grows year-round in a greenhouse. It's a great set-up, with natural and artificial light. You practically get high walking in the door."

"Nice of him to make an in-kind donation," Lyle said.

Soon a smoky haze hovered over our little circle. "How was the Earth First! meeting?" Mort asked.

"Pretty good," said Hank. "They're organizing to stop a logging road up near Headwaters Forest. People figure it's either stop the road now, or get ready to sit in the trees."

I accepted the joint from Craig. "Were there any people from Livermore or Vandenberg?"

"A few," Hank said. "But I didn't know most of them. They're too adventurist for me, doing backcountry actions into logging areas. But they're really dedicated people. They decide what to do, and they do it. They spend a hell of a lot less time arguing than we do."

The door opened, and Walt entered. "Hey, it's the legal team," Hank called out. "Anyone phone from jail?"

"No, it was a boring night. I watched the Knicks' game and played dominoes for three hours." Walt took off his jacket and accepted a beer from Lyle. He leaned back against a machine. "Looks like almost all the men are here. Is Norm coming over?"

Tai shook his head. "I don't think so. He had something else going on after we finished."

Hank took a long toke. "Who is this Norm guy, anyway? Where'd he come from? Am I the only one who's nervous about someone that no one knows volunteering full-time in the office?"

"Aw," I said, "Norm's been around since last Fall. He does a ton of work."

Mort scowled. "That doesn't mean anything. When Alliance for Survival down in L.A. found out they were infiltrated last year, it turned out to be some of their staff people."

"Yeah," Hank said. "If the FBI is paying you, you have a lot of time to volunteer."

I tried to picture Norm as an infiltrator. Were most FBI informants so laid-back? And did they all jump in and help with the messiest jobs the way Norm did? I looked from Mort to Hank. "All I can say is, if Norm's an agent, I hope they send a few more like him to help in the office."

Walt laughed. "Yeah, I'll take a few more like Norm." He looked around at us. "So how did the action go?"

Mort lit another joint and passed it to Lyle. "Tell them about the burned-out box," he said.

Lyle took a hit and passed it on to Hank. "Oh, yeah, we saw this one box that somebody had torched. The whole front was melted, and the inside was full of burned papers."

"We saw something like that," Hank said. "Somebody had dumped a can of red paint inside the box, like the papers were dripping blood." Hank wiped his hands on a cloth tucked into his belt, then rang up a game on Queen of Diamonds. "Better get your fill of playing tonight," he said. "I'll be gone the next two Fridays. Next week I'm going to a pinball tourney in Sacramento. And the week after that, me and Lyle and Tai are heading up to the redwoods. You guys want to go?" He looked at me and Mort.

"Camping?" I asked.

Lyle took a drink of beer. "Yeah. We're gonna do some target practice along the way, too, if you're interested. Do you have a gun?"

"No," I said, surprised at the question.

"The way this country is going, you're crazy not to," Hank said.

Craig gestured at Hank with his beer bottle. "You think owning a gun is protection against the U.S. government? They'll just bring out the tanks."

"Sure," Hank said, "in an all-out confrontation, we're screwed. But if it comes to death squads, like in Guatemala or El Salvador, a gun at least gives you some chance."

Mort exhaled a long stream of smoke. "Face it, the right wing has us outgunned. Our only hope is to keep the conflict in the nonviolent arena as much as possible. That's the political challenge, to define the terms of the struggle."

Lyle eyed Mort suspiciously. "I don't know if it's ours to define. If we're attacked, aren't we going to fight back? You've got to have at least the threat of resistance, or you get walked on."

Mort leaned back onto a machine. He seemed to be gazing at a purple lava-lamp perched on top of a tool cabinet. "It's a question of context, of the relation to a mass movement. Take the Black Panthers, who formed a Black militia to 'fight back.' The Panthers didn't spring up in a vacuum. In the Sixties, there was already a huge Civil Rights movement. There was rioting in a lot of American cities. The establishment knew that the Panthers might be the vanguard of a larger uprising. They were crushed, but the government also had to let off steam by expanding civil rights. Even in defeat, the Panthers and their rhetoric had a major impact." Mort took a drink of beer. "But outside of the context of a mass movement, talk of violent resistance has the opposite effect. The government and media portray it as lunacy or terrorism, and use it to discredit a movement."

Lyle laughed sharply. "So we're supposed to wait for a mass movement before we learn to fire a gun?"

Mort fidgeted with his beer bottle. "I'm fine with target practice. But if you start talking guns, you've got to be aware of the implications. Yeah, sometimes a radical threat can force the government to compromise with liberals. It's a plausible strategy. But watch out, because the liberals will strike their deal, cut you loose, and let the government crush you. That's what happened to the Panthers, and that's what happens to most armed radicals around the world."

I had been standing behind Mort, listening carefully. Now I stepped forward. "I don't want to come off like a pacifist," I said. "But is it really the threat of violence we're talking about here? Or is it the threat of disruption? If we can shut down business as usual, close financial districts, or shut down highways, we could cause just as much havoc as an armed uprising in other countries."

Mort actually stopped and thought about what I'd said, which I appreciated. But Hank scoffed. "If you really disrupt the machine, they'll cut you down whether you're armed or not. Nonviolence isn't going to save you."

"It all comes back to the political struggle," Mort said. "Whatever we think of 'democracy' in this country, public opinion does play a role. If the government tries to repress us, we have to have mainstream allies. And that's hard if you use extreme tactics. I'm not just talking about violence, but the sort of mindless disruption that people are talking about at the Democratic Convention. You can't ignore the implications of your tactical decisions."

"Or lack of decisions," Hank interjected. "The spokescouncil for the Convention last weekend was hopeless. Five hours of arguing, and not even close to a consensus. The idea of a LAG protest at the Convention is dead."

"That's not how I heard it," I put in, frustrated with the direction of the conversation. "We consensed way back in December to do something at the Convention. You can't just throw that out."

"The meeting was split down the middle," Hank said. "A protest at the Convention would be totally divisive." He turned to change the music. I wanted to pursue the issue, but Tai was clamoring for Hank's attention on a broken pinball machine. I'd have to wait till later.

I joined Craig and Lyle for a game on "Old Chicago," my favorite machine. As Lyle took his turn, Craig leaned onto the adjoining machine, his eyes following the trajectory of the ball. "This whole Democratic Convention thing is irresponsible," he said. "Talking about CD at the Convention makes us look like the lunatic fringe."

"So we're supposed to sit and do nothing?" I said. "I'd rather be a futile protester than a passive bystander."

Craig seemed oblivious to my jab as he stood in for his turn. "We can't be everywhere at once," he said.

I wasn't going to let him off that easy. "The Convention is what's happening. Somebody needs to light a fire under the Democrats' butts."

He shrugged as his ball drained. "I don't see it inspiring many people."

Speak for yourself, I thought as I took my shot. Quit if you want. Some of us aren't ready to give up yet.

I almost said as much to Craig. But I was still hoping he'd come work on People's Convention. I didn't want to push him further away. I jammed the flippers hard and fired the ball back to the top of the machine.

Behind us, Hank finished fixing Tai's machine. "Ah, yes, pinball surgery was successful, and the patient has revived."

"Do you ever think about doing this as a business?" Craig asked, turning away from me.

"Naw," Hank said, "I love it too much for that. But sometimes I restore a game and then trade it for a couple of fixer-uppers. That's how I get new ones."

Mort gestured at the machines lining two walls of the workshop. "You're going to overflow your shop pretty soon."

"Yeah, it's time to buy a house, isn't it?" Hank said. "Judith and I are actually saving money for a down payment. Can't you see a whole basement full of these things? I'd have the jukebox in one corner, one of those big old bowling machines in another, and the electric train running around the whole place." His eyes glazed over for a moment. Then he shook his head. "It's just a dream. Even with both of us working, it's hard to afford anything in the Bay Area."

He lit a roach and passed it on to Craig. "Hey, I almost forgot — we need a test crew for the nukecycle tomorrow. I just about have it up and running."

"No kidding?" Craig said. "Pedals and all?"

"Yeah. The frame is welded together, with four motorcycle wheels. The steering is a little off, but I'm working on that. It should be ready for the financial district next month. We'll have to cart it across the bridge on a trailer, but then we can pedal it down Market Street."

Craig chuckled. "What sort of license do you need to drive a nukecycle?"

"Type N, I reckon." Hank looked around at us. "But there's altogether too much talking going on. We're here for pinball therapy, not another meeting. Who's up for a game of Old Chicago?" He punched out some Rolling Stones songs on the jukebox and put on a tape of the Three Stooges in the background.

Well, so much for talking. I considered going out for a long, quiet walk. But there was no time to waste. Matters had to get settled. Just stick around, play some pinball, and hopefully later I'd have a chance to talk with Craig about the next crisis meeting. And with Hank about the December consensus to protest the Democrats. And with Mort about the People's Convention meeting this weekend... Things had to get moving.

Friday, March 23, 1984

"YOU DON'T want to hear anything negative," Angie said. She wrapped her scarf tighter. "I can't say anything about LAG or you get defensive. And if I'm mad at someone, you don't want to hear about it."

I just don't like it when you trash someone, I wanted to say. But I wanted to put the argument behind us. It was my one night seeing Angie all week. "I can see your frustrations about living with Jenny," I said, trying to be sympathetic as we walked stiffly down the dark sidewalk.

"It's beyond frustration," she answered, looking straight ahead. "Jenny and I never even talk anymore. She spends all her time with Raoul. When they formed their

Ashkenaz dance club, fabled West Berkeley home of World Beat music.

new affinity group with Jacey, they didn't even ask me if I wanted to be in it. I guess I'm not radical enough for them, just because I don't want to run around in the streets at the Democratic Convention."

"I can relate," I said. "There's more to the Convention than street demos."

She let out a loud sigh. "The whole Convention is such a bore," she said. "I'm so sick of hearing about this protest or that coalition. I'll be glad when it's all over."

And I'll be glad when we get to Ashkenaz, I thought. We were walking down to the north Berkeley club to hear the West African High-Life Band. I was plenty nervous about dancing to African music, but it seemed like a piece of cake compared to fighting with Angie.

Was it blowing up in our faces? How much longer could we take the pressure? Angie had been talking more about a trip to Portland to visit her pregnant friend Isabel, and I wondered if she might just decide to stay.

I groped for some way to engage her. "There's a lot of other things happening," I said. "We have the next issue of Direct Action coming up. And there's the Livermore action in April that really needs energy."

She growled her response. "Nothing LAG is doing is going anywhere."

"Well, it sure won't if people don't work on it," I snapped. "Sometimes we have to work on things that are good for the movement."

"So now LAG is the movement?"

"Until we figure out something better. We can't give up. Times will change, and we need to be ready."

"Maybe we need to be ready to let go when times change," she muttered.

Damn, I thought. Why had I taken the bait yet again? I put my arm around her shoulders. I could feel her bristle. "Nothing I'm involved in is going anywhere," she said. "Something has to give."

Was that something LAG, love, or life? Was she quitting LAG? Was she getting ready to break up with me?

And what could I say if she did? Was I going to beg her to stay? Sad as her leaving made me, I also felt relieved that she might be the one to call it quits. Let her initiate the break-up, and I'd graciously accept that we needed to say goodbye. Time for us to move on. Time for me to re-commit to Holly. Time for a fresh start for all of us.

South African music really is easier to dance to than rock and roll. Somewhere amid the polyrhythmic drums and guitars I found a beat that had always eluded me. I welcomed the escape from trying to converse with Angie, and we were on the floor through two entire sets. On the last song, with the eight-piece band in high gear, I found myself bouncing up and down, casting off my worries about Angie, about LAG, and even about dancing — simply surrendering to the buoyant music.

We left Ashkenaz barely in time to catch the last train back to her place in

Oakland. I hoped that the spirit of our dancing would carry over, but once we got outside the confines of Ashkenaz the cloud descended again. All it took was a phonepole flyer announcing a protest at an electroshock facility which I made the mistake of stopping to read.

"Not another protest," Angie said. "Is that all anyone knows how to do, protest?"

"There's a lot that needs protesting," I said, feeling my fists clench.

She thrust her hands into her pockets. "Well, I'm tired of it. It's so one-dimensional. Even if we're against nukes or intervention or Reaganism, I want to be creating something, not just protesting."

My hands gripped again, then loosened. Whether it was the dancing or the beer or both, I felt lighter on my feet. "Speaking of Reaganism, you know what I heard? BCA isn't going to do the Berkeley Anti-Reagan Festival this year — they're too busy with the city council campaign to do another BARF."

"No BARF? You'd think they'd do it as part of the campaign. What better way to get their message out than a festival?"

"They're probably stretched too thin," I said.

Angie suddenly bounded a step ahead and turned to face me. "We should do BARF! I bet we could get a great work group together to do it. There'd be dance bands and game booths and clowns — and there has to be a Reagan piñata."

"Sure," I said. "That's a great idea." Already I was fitting the festival into our Fall fund-raising plans. But even more, it was a chance to work with Angie on something that excited her.

Once we got seated on the train, she leaned against me and closed her eyes. I put my arm around her and held her close, leaning my head down so it rested on hers.

It was nearly two when we got back to her apartment. We went into her room. I took off my jacket and tossed it on the floor. Angie lit a few candles and pulled back the sheets, then sat down on the edge of the bed. I sat next to her and kissed her on the cheek, letting my hand glide over her breasts. She didn't resist, but there was no answering touch. I leaned back. "Is something the matter?" I asked. She looked at me silently, and a chill ran through me. I braced myself for the worst.

She reached out and took my hand. "There's something we have to talk about," she said quietly. Her finger traced a spiral on my palm.

I took a breath and held it. Was this goodbye? Would she ask me to leave? Please, no. Let us have one last night together...

She looked at me intently. "We have to start being more careful, Jeff."

I didn't follow her. "Yeah?"

"Jenny is pregnant."

"Oh..." So that was what was on her mind. I almost laughed in relief, and had to feign a cough to cover it up. "Wow. How's Jenny doing?"

"I think she's doing okay, besides being sick a lot. I think she's going to have the baby. She and I haven't talked much about it. She's mainly been over at Raoul's." Angie looked at me again. "Anyway, we have to be more careful. I can't risk getting pregnant. Not now."

I nodded. "You're right," I said. "I'm sorry."

"It's my responsibility, too," she said, looking down. "I had an abortion when I was younger, and I don't want to go through that again."

I wasn't sure what to say. I kissed her cheek. She didn't look up. "Can we just be together tonight? Without sex, I mean?"

"Sure," I said. I was so relieved that she wasn't breaking up with me that a night of celibacy seemed like a minor inconvenience. We lay down and nestled together. Her hair caressed my cheek. I wrapped one arm around her. She took my hand and pressed it to her heart.

She soon drifted off, and I felt her grip on my hand relax. I leaned up on one elbow, watching her in the candlelight. She looked peaceful, almost childlike. Awake, she was so restless, brimming with challenges and doubts and dreams. And sure, I treasured that about her. But now as I gazed at her untroubled brow, her slightly-parted lips, the lock of hair falling over her cheek, I felt more in love than ever.

As I lay down, though, the unease crept back in. Sure, the evening had ended gracefully. But how long could I expect Angie to be content with a once-a-week lover? And how would I feel if she ended our relationship?

Yet surely it had to end...

But maybe it was ending only because I wasn't offering a commitment. What if I were to leave Holly and pledge my love to Angie? Was I throwing away my opportunity?

I rolled onto my side, away from Angie. Come on, get real. We'd never last. And if we didn't end it soon, who knew what Holly might decide. There was the real pressure. How long did I expect Holly to sit and wait?

Time to get my priorities straight. Do what had to be done. Now.

I just wanted to be sure I got it right.

Monday, April 2, 1984

It was not where I wanted to be.

The April actions were just two weeks away, though, and there was no way I could skip Coordinating Council, even if it meant a trip into the City. Mort offered me a ride, but I made an excuse and took BART, just to get some time alone after a hectic day working on People's Convention and the Livermore demo.

On BART, I opened a history book for the first time in a week, a collection of essays on Baroque music. But though I managed to turn a few pages, my mind never stopped reeling off lists of urgent phone calls, last-minute mailings, and a hundred unattended details. It was a relief when I finally got to Melissa's house.

I was one of the later arrivals, and I walked into a roomful of familiar faces, none of whom I was overly delighted to see. There were Doc and Belinda, all but absent from the April organizing... Over in a corner sat Jenny, avoiding eye contact... Karina, primed to fight anyone who didn't jump on board every wild proposal she came up with... Monique, whom I was seeing plenty of at the April Livermore meetings... Mort, increasingly dismissive of anything to do with the Democratic Convention...

Conspicuously absent was Holly, who had been coming to Coordinating Council as the spoke for the peace camp. It was our one shared meeting each week, and I felt irked that she'd gone and made dinner plans with Caroline, who was just back from Nicaragua. Couldn't they have chosen another night? A year earlier, they'd both have been at the meeting.

Actually, as far as Caroline, I wasn't sorry she was absent. I'd seen her once since she got back, and I could feel her silently judging me for my relationship with Angie. I didn't need an evening of her frowning at me. Still, it bugged me that Holly considered Coordinating Council expendable.

We gathered as usual in the front room at Melissa's, which might have been some comfort. Not tonight. The house was being remodeled, and a gaping hole yawned where once a wall separated the living room from the kitchen. Dusty tarps were strewn behind the couches, and paint-trays were stacked in front of the fireplace. I took a seat on a couch next to Sara, where I didn't have to stare directly at the hole. But it loomed over my shoulder just the same.

Artemis offered to facilitate, which was a plus, since she wasn't caught up in any of the feuding. The agenda was imposing: the April actions; finances, which were looking worse and worse; what to do about the stalemated Democratic Convention meetings; and a dozen smaller disasters that demanded attention.

All of this I was prepared to sit through. But before we could get started, Craig and Claudia walked in the door. Some of the others seemed to know they were coming, but it was a jolt to me.

"Can we go first?" Claudia asked. "I don't want to stay for the whole meeting." People assented, and I silently acquiesced.

"What we came to propose," Craig said as he passed out copies of a densely-typed letter, "is that Coordinating Council call a series of meetings later this month to discuss the crisis of LAG."

I stared at him, but he didn't look my way. Craig paused as if to let his words sink in, then continued. "It's time we face the fact that LAG has lost its direction. Since last June's blockade, we've consensed to nothing of substance. And with the Convention coming to San Francisco, the situation is getting worse."

Around the room, people were nodding. "We need to act while we can," Claudia said. "LAG still has the credibility to bring a hundred people together. If we wait another six months, even that may be lost."

I twisted in my seat. Here we are, two weeks before our biggest actions of the year, and what are we discussing? Not how to make them a success, but how to deal with their failure. Where were Craig and Claudia when we were trying to figure out what actions to call? Where were they when we split over Livermore versus the financial district? Missing, ever since their Strategy Proposal didn't get everyone's unquestioning devotion.

DIRECT ACTION

April 1984

15

Published by Livermore Action Group

1040 U.S. Individual Income Tax Return 1983

PROTEST WAR TAXES!

APRIL 16-17

See Pages 1-9

Direct Action #15, April 1984

Claudia looked around. "LAG dropped the ball on the Strategy Proposal last Fall. That might have spared us the mess we're in now. But we need to do what we can. We're proposing two all-day meetings, a couple of weeks apart. The first will deal with the crisis, and hopefully the second can come up with some concrete steps to move forward."

"It's an excellent idea," Belinda said. "There needs to be wider input. We need to reach out to all the old affinity groups, try to get as many people as possible together. Coordinating Council can't deal with the problems alone."

I folded my arms across my chest. As if it were Coordinating Council's fault that no one was working on the April actions! Yet once again, everyone seemed to be nodding.

After a moment, Melissa spoke up. "I'm not opposed to having these meetings," she said, looking at Claudia. "But I think it's ridiculous to call them 'Crisis' meetings. LAG has been one of the most successful grassroots groups in the country the past two years. Just because we're in a slump after the Euromissiles and Grenada is no reason to despair. We need to have more faith in ourselves than that. We need to look at what has worked for us in the past — blockades at Livermore — and have the courage and conviction to stick with it."

Claudia let out an exasperated sigh, but before she could speak, Artemis stepped in as facilitator. "This is not the time to debate the future of LAG," she said. "What we need to consider is whether or not to call the meetings that have been proposed. Are you objecting?"

"I suppose not," Melissa said.

"Does anyone else object?"

I looked around. Wasn't there anyone else who felt how outrageous this was? Not a soul spoke. I looked at Artemis, who peered back quizzically. Now or never, I thought.

Artemis took a breath. "If there are no objections —"

I scowled and looked away. I could drag the discussion out, but what was the point? We could spend all night hashing it over, and still come to the same morbid conclusion. Let's just get on with the meeting.

" — then we have consensus."

Craig looked triumphant. "We'll pin the dates and location down, and call the office later in the week," he said. "Now if you'll excuse us..." The two of them left so quickly they seemed to suck the air out of the room. People slouched in their seats, and no one spoke.

I looked down the hall after them. Thanks a lot, I thought. Glad you could drop in. Come by again when you're in town.

Artemis took a deep breath, and I emulated her, letting out a sigh on the exhale. Consensing that we were in crisis wasn't a very inspirational opening, and LAG finances were next on the agenda.

Jenny lurched to her feet. She shuffled her notes, dropped a paper, and retrieved it. I hadn't heard directly from her that she was pregnant, but Angie had mentioned it again, and told me that Jenny and Raoul were planning to have the baby. LAG finances were probably the furthest thing from her mind.

She ran down the grim figures: $3000 in debt, with no relief in sight. The Spring mailing, calling for support for the April actions, was barely bringing in enough to keep up with current expenses. And even if LAG could agree on an action around the Convention, it could hardly be expected to raise much money.

Jenny folded up her papers and glanced around the room like a trapped animal searching for an escape. "So that's it," she said tentatively.

"Are there any questions?" Artemis asked.

"Yeah," Melissa said. "What ever happened with those bumper stickers about not voting?"

I cringed for Jenny. The infamous bumper stickers, which read, "Don't Vote: It Only Encourages Them," had been Karina's idea. But Jenny had been the one to okay the funds for printing them.

"So what happened?" Melissa demanded.

"I thought we agreed that they couldn't be used," Mort interrupted. "That's a stupid message to put out when we're trying to build coalitions around the Convention."

"So we had to destroy $300 worth of bumper stickers?" Melissa said scornfully. "As if our finances aren't bad enough already."

"No, no," Jenny said hurriedly. "We didn't destroy them. We just cut LAG's name off the bottom." She glanced around the circle beseechingly.

Melissa looked incredulous. "You're still going to sell them?"

"Why not?" Karina cut in. "You never said we couldn't sell them. You just said it couldn't go out with LAG's name on it. Anyway, it's true. Voting is a fraud. Why are people so afraid of the truth?"

Melissa was on the edge of her chair, but Walt intervened. "Come on, we sell all kinds of bumper stickers and buttons. No one thinks that we endorse every slogan on them. We need the money. As long as LAG's name isn't on them...."

"Let's talk about the April actions," Sara pleaded, and no one contradicted her. Jenny looked relieved, and retreated to her corner.

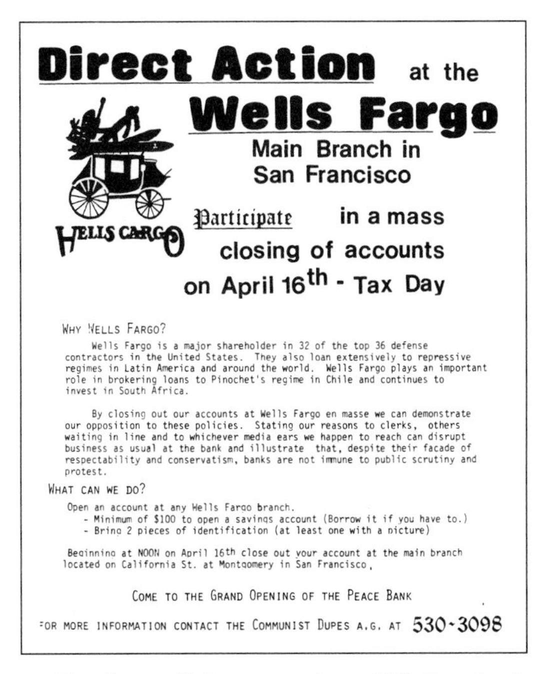

Direct Action at the **Wells Fargo** Main Branch in San Francisco

Participate in a mass closing of accounts on April 16th - Tax Day

WHY WELLS FARGO?

Wells Fargo is a major shareholder in 32 of the top 36 defense contractors in the United States. They also loan extensively to repressive regimes in Latin America and around the world. Wells Fargo plays an important role in brokering loans to Pinochet's regime in Chile and continues to invest in South Africa.

By closing out our accounts at Wells Fargo en masse we can demonstrate our opposition to these policies. Stating our reasons to clerks, others waiting in line and to whichever media ears we happen to reach can disrupt business as usual at the bank and illustrate that, despite their facade of respectability and conservatism, banks are not immune to public scrutiny and protest.

WHAT CAN WE DO?

Open an account at any Wells Fargo branch.
- Minimum of $100 to open a savings account (Borrow it if you have to.)
- Bring 2 pieces of identification (at least one with a picture)

Beginning at NOON on April 16th close out your account at the main branch located on California St. at Montgomery in San Francisco.

COME TO THE GRAND OPENING OF THE PEACE BANK

FOR MORE INFORMATION CONTACT THE COMMUNIST DUPES A.G. AT 530-3098

Flyer for an affinity group action at Wells Fargo bank, planned as part of LAG's Tax Day protest in April 1984.

Karina, with one last glare at Melissa, launched into a report on the San Francisco Tax Day actions set for Monday, April 16th. "The big news is that Henry Kissinger is coming to town the same day. The Central America groups have called a rally at the Hilton for noon. We're moving our starting time back so we can be part of it, and then we'll march to the financial district for our actions. Probably a lot of people will come with us."

I was lukewarm on the Kissinger protest. Celebrity demos were usually a bore, a bunch of people marching in a circle chanting slogans. Just our luck to have it fall on the same day as the action we'd been planning for months. "How many AGs are doing financial district actions?" I asked.

"It's looking really good," Karina said. "We have eight affinity groups confirmed, and several more possibilities."

Whoopee, I thought. As if eight AGs was some phenomenal number. The big Livermore blockades had a hundred or more. I knew better than to say that out loud, though, because the April Livermore demo was next on the agenda. And if it drew eight AGs, it would be a miracle. Hardly anyone had been showing up at the spokescouncils. And to complicate matters further, Daniel and Melissa had been pushing the idea of doing part of the action at Site 300, Livermore Lab's non-nuclear test area. Sure, it was still part of the Lab. But it meant that our blockade at the Lab gates would be even smaller.

Walt gave the Livermore report, which I appreciated, since I'd been giving it every week. As I expected, no one was very interested, except for one item. The previous day, Walt told us, Imagine affinity group had done its third annual April Fools Day action at the Lab. It was a routine action until the cops came for Pilgrim, who was taking the forty-second bust of his career. Ordered to stand, Pilgrim didn't budge. The arresting officer tried a wrist-lock, got it wrong, and fractured Pilgrim's seventy-year-old wrist in two places.

I flexed my arm involuntarily as Walt concluded his report. "We'll bring a lawsuit against them," he said. "But folks doing the April action need to realize that the police are upping the ante out at the Lab."

"Not just at Livermore," Hank said. "It'll be the same in the City. With the Convention coming up, you know the pigs have orders to keep things under control."

What a perfect segue into the next part of our agenda. Another spokescouncil had met the previous day, trying to break the logjam around the Democratic Convention. To my relief, agreement had been reached to endorse People's Convention as well as the Freeze's "Vote Peace in 1984" rally.

But discussions of a LAG protest had stalemated again. Half of the people were determined to protest in the City, the other half insistent that LAG should steer clear of the morass.

I sank into the couch. How could I be holding onto any hope? As if Melissa was going to budge. As if Karina was going to temper her rhetoric. As if Raoul was going to bother showing up at a LAG meeting again.

But without a Convention protest, we had nothing. Oh, there was some vague talk about a September action at Livermore. But given how thrilled everyone was with April, another Lab protest seemed like a dead letter. The Convention was our only hope.

Hank shuffled in his chair. "What more is there to talk about? The meetings have been split right down the middle. There's not a hell of a lot more we can do..."

Sara took a sharp breath. "We can't just drop it. There was a decision in December that we would organize something."

"There was obviously no consensus yesterday," Hank tossed back.

"Oh, I see," Sara said petulantly. "We're just dropping the previous decision?"

Melissa's jaw jutted out. "There was never a consensus on a specific action. And there clearly won't be. We have a responsibility to everyone in the group, not just the action junkies."

"Just as I thought," Karina said with a toss of her head. "People are getting scared. We're finding out who really believes in direct action."

Several hands went up. Before anyone could speak, Artemis held up both of her hands for silence. "This is getting personal. Could we all stop for a moment and take a breath together?"

People followed her request, but the exasperated exhales hardly sounded encouraging. I raised my hand, more to preempt Karina and Melissa than because I had something particular to say.

"Consensus requires patience," I said. I looked around the room. "We aren't that far apart, are we? No one wants to sabotage the Democrats. We just want to hold them accountable." I glanced over at Jenny. She seemed lost in her own thoughts, but I tried to draw her in. "Some people are working on protests exposing the corporate connections, the War Chest Tours. Can't LAG get behind that?"

Jenny at least looked up, but Melissa jumped in. "A message about corporate connections will get lost," she said. "The media would never grasp it."

"The point isn't the media," Sara said. "It's a question of integrity, of seeing an injustice and protesting it. That's what LAG should be doing."

Melissa looked pained. "I'm getting sick and tired of people trying to hijack LAG's name for every protest they think up. LAG was formed to do protests at Livermore Lab. Fine, go run around in San Francisco. Just keep LAG's name out of it."

Not this debate again, I thought. I glanced at Jenny, who was staring at the floor. What was dragging her down? Her condition, the meeting, or both? Why wouldn't she speak up about the War Chest Tours? Had she and Raoul and Jacey already decided to dump LAG and organize separately?

And what about Karina? She must have some plan for protesting the Democrats. Was she writing off LAG too, going on some adventurist spree and leaving us in the cold? I couldn't believe it, two LAG staffers completely ditching the group.

As if that weren't enough, Belinda chose that moment to offer up her unique perspective. "Why is Coordinating Council even discussing this? No decision can be made here. It's for the spokescouncil to decide —"

"Or not decide," Karina interrupted.

"— or *not* decide." Belinda glowered. "We have that prerogative."

"Coordinating Council is empowered to set up meetings," I pleaded. "We can call another spokescouncil to try to reach consensus."

"Oh great," Karina groaned. "Another useless meeting."

I shot a harried look at her, but she was staring off into space. Around the room, heads hung in discouragement. For a moment, no one spoke. I looked around at Jenny, Karina, Sara, Doc... Come on! Someone back me up! Are we going to let it all slip away?

It was Artemis who broke the silence. She wasn't a hardcore pacifist like Melissa, but she struck me as more likely to get arrested hugging a tree than shutting a street. She sat up in her chair. Her gray-black hair tumbled over her shoulders. "I want to take a moment and acknowledge the passion in this room," she said. "I'm hearing strong commitment to direct action at the Convention, and equally powerful concerns about the safety and the political wisdom of street demonstrations. I want to be especially sure these concerns get heard."

Flyer for the April 1984 Livermore Lab action.

A knowing smile crossed Melissa's lips. But her satisfaction evaporated as Artemis continued. "Sometimes, though, a situation cries out for action. Even if we don't see what it will accomplish, even if there are risks involved, we are compelled to act." She looked around the circle. "When we plant the seeds of truth, we don't know what fruit they will bear. Months or even years later our actions may fire the souls of people we've never met. That's the enduring power of direct action. If we fail to act, that possibility is lost forever."

As Artemis paused, I almost applauded. Walt nodded silently. Sara twisted a strand of her hair. Belinda looked troubled, Mort pensive. Melissa scowled, while Karina smiled to herself.

After a moment, Doc cleared his throat. "It's a moment like this that's the true test of consensus, isn't it? How do we formulate a proposal that takes everyone's concerns into account?"

Hank folded his hands and rolled his eyes heavenward. "Pray for a miracle?"

I laughed, but Melissa didn't seem amused. "So what are you proposing," she challenged Artemis. "That LAG organize a protest in the City?"

"I'm not proposing anything," Artemis said calmly. "I'm just saying that when so many people are inspired to act, maybe the rest of us need to sit up and listen."

Here at last was an opening. If only someone would take it. I considered speaking up myself. But the initiative needed to come from someone who was already organizing street actions. One of them needed to take the lead, and I'd be right behind them. I looked at Karina, Jenny, Sara — none spoke.

Finally Doc raised his hand. "I think we're making a mistake by looking to a spokescouncil to come up with the answer," he said in a troubled voice. "Large meetings are great for airing concerns, and for ratifying final proposals. But as far as synthesizing ideas into a concrete proposal, we should delegate a smaller group to do it."

"Good suggestion," Artemis said, facilitating again. "It sounds like you're suggesting that people with strong feelings set up a meeting, formulate the various ideas into a proposal, and bring it to the next spokescouncil."

Amazing, I thought. A voice of reason. Maybe we could work this out after all. Maybe I'd been demanding too much, too fast. Just be patient. Give us a little more time, and we might yet pull off an action.

Around the room, people nodded. Even Melissa seemed to grudgingly accept the idea. For a moment no one spoke. I settled back in my seat. Good job, Artemis. Now change the subject. Let's get through this meeting without another fight.

Next to me, Sara raised her hand. "I'm fine with setting up a work group. But whatever we do, it needs to be direct action. Direct action defines LAG. If we have a message to convey, it isn't going to be done by giving speeches or drafting a 'People's Platform.' We need to be out in the street."

Several hands shot up. Oh, no. Couldn't we have left well-enough alone?

Monique, who had barely spoken all evening, was first. "There is no way my affinity group is going to agree to that," she said. "The Walnettos may endorse a rally, but we are not going to authorize a street protest."

"Thank you," Melissa said in a loud voice. "If LAG really wants to be radical, we should just ignore the whole Convention."

"Well, then stay home," Karina said.

"Try that yourself," Mort muttered.

A half-dozen more hands went up. I slumped in discouragement. Even Artemis seemed dismayed. "Let's all stop and take a breath," she urged. "Let's remember why we're here."

People did pause for a moment, and after more grumbling agreed to move on with the agenda. It was nearly eleven, and amid the general grousing about the late hour, it wasn't clear whether we had consensed on setting up the smaller work group to synthesize a proposal. We'd have to deal with it next week.

We trudged through the last few items without incident. After a few announcements, the meeting broke up. No blood was shed as we parted, but the farewells lacked their accustomed warmth.

I was hoping to hitch a ride home with Jenny. We needed to talk. Time was running out, and with Raoul and Sid unwilling even to attend Coordinating Council, Jenny was the key to keeping the War Chest Tours in LAG. Why had she been so quiet at the meeting? Had she given up on LAG? Or was it because by the Convention, she'd be five months pregnant? I wondered how much she'd even be involved in the protests.

I tried to catch her eye as she hugged Karina. But she turned and started a conversation with Doc. I thought about interrupting to ask for a ride, but Mort came up and invited me to ride back with him and Hank. I hesitated a moment, then picked up my jacket and followed them out the door.

As we trailed Mort toward his car, Hank looked at me with a worried expression. "So how are you doing?"

"Fine," I said, surprised at his concern. "Why?"

"I heard about you and Holly splitting up."

I stopped in my tracks. "Huh? Where did you hear that?"

He looked embarrassed. "Gee, I don't remember. Maybe I misinterpreted something...."

"Probably," I said, none too sure of myself. "At least as far as I know."

"Yeah, yeah, I'm sure it was my mistake," he said hurriedly.

Was it? Maybe Holly had confided in someone who didn't keep the secret. Was she just waiting for an opportunity to tell me? I felt a sinking in my heart. I never meant for it to go this far. Would she be at home when I got back? Hopefully she'd be awake, and we could talk right then. Maybe it wasn't too late.

"Hey, don't take it hard," Hank said. "Really, I'm sure I misinterpreted something."

I wasn't so sure. But Mort had come to a halt in front of us. "Where did I park?" he asked Hank. "I wasn't this far down, was I?"

Hank stopped and looked around. "No, we didn't even park on this street."

Mort scratched his head. "Then where were we?"

"I think we were over on Sanchez."

We retraced our steps and eventually located Mort's car. I got in the back seat. Up front, Mort and Hank talked about the nukecycle, which they had taken for a test ride over the weekend. I tried to put aside my worries and follow their discussion.

But I couldn't stop thinking about what to say to Holly when I got home. I cracked my window as we started across the Bay Bridge. The cold air streamed across my forehead. Focus. This might be my last chance. I folded my hands in my lap. I gazed down at them then out the window. I better be clear on what I wanted.

Friday, April 13, 1984

I TARRIED AT the LAG office till almost eight, making last-ditch phone calls for the April 17th Livermore demo. I got a beer at the corner store and walked the long way home, swinging all the way up to Hillegass Street. Holly still wasn't back when I got home.

We needed to talk. Hank's rumor about her leaving turned out to be a false alarm, but it showed how out of touch Holly and I were. With the endless barrage of meetings, we hadn't spent an evening together for a week, and I had little idea what she was feeling.

Which was a worry. She was having dinner again with Caroline. If Holly were wavering, Caroline wasn't going to urge her to be patient. In fact, with Caroline house-hunting, they might decide to find a place together.

I opened the beer and ate some peanuts. Everything seemed up in the air. How to get people to the actions in the City and at Livermore next week? What to do at the Democratic Convention in July? Where to go with my relationships with Angie and Holly... Something had to be done. I just wasn't sure what.

I straightened up a stack of cassettes, watered the plants, and got the recycling together. I even tried to think about what I might say when Holly got home, but with no idea what she was thinking, it seemed pointless.

Why hadn't I talked with her earlier in the week? Not just to know what she was feeling, but to share my thoughts with her. My relationship with Angie seemed headed toward its natural end. Any day now we'd probably call it quits, at least as lovers. I should let Holly know it was her I wanted to be with for the long-term.

Was it, though? If only it were that simple. That's what I needed to figure out. A pang of guilt struck my heart — guilt for my vacillation, guilt for not having the answers, guilt for expecting Holly and Angie to wait around for me to make up my mind...

As I cracked a peanut, it occurred to me that there might be a baseball game on the radio. Baseball. I'd hardly thought about it all Spring. The season was already two weeks old. I flipped on the tuner and scanned the stations. Sure enough, the A's had a night game. I sat down and ate some more peanuts, picturing the white of the uniforms and bases against the deep brown of the infield dirt. I didn't recognize most of the players, though, and the slow pace aggravated my restless mood. When the commercials started, I switched it off.

I picked up my guitar and fiddled with a few chords, but a plant that I'd overlooked distracted me. It was a fern that Holly and I had bought up on Telegraph the previous Summer. Its stems drooped. Needles fell off when I touched it. I got the water jar, and was telling myself I should be giving the plants more attention when I heard the lock turn in the apartment door. My chest tightened. I saw Holly, jaw set, packing her bags. I set down the water jar and leaned against the living room wall. The door swung open and she stepped in.

Her back was toward me as she pulled her key out of the door. I stood rooted in the living room. "Hi," I said. "How was your dinner?"

She turned toward me with a slight smile, and I was relieved that she looked happy. "We had a great time." She gave me a quick hug, then went to the kitchen and poured a cup of juice. "Caroline was telling me more about her trip to Nicaragua. She's decided to go to nursing school, get her degree, and go back down there. There's a real shortage of medical people."

I took a breath and put on a Bessie Smith tape. Had I just imagined all the tension between us? Maybe there wasn't so much to worry about after all.

Still, why not talk now and clear the air? Maybe this was the time to air our concerns, when it wasn't a crisis. Why delay?

Well, maybe it will go away altogether. You never know. Why stir up the muck if you don't have to?

Holly came into the living room and took a seat at the table. "I forgot how great it is to have someone who knows me so well," she said reflectively. "Caroline and I decided to do the Site 300 action together. We're going to hike in on Sunday night and occupy the test area. If we can find a place to hide in the underbrush, it could take them all day to find us, and they couldn't do any testing. A handful of people could shut the place down all week."

I paced behind her. "Sunday night? I thought the idea was to do Site 300 later in the week. You'll miss the financial district action Monday."

"Yeah," she said, turning in her chair so she could see me. "But if we do Site 300 on Sunday, we'll catch them off-guard and have a better chance of getting onto the site. I wasn't excited about the San Francisco action anyway, especially since I heard about the Kissinger protest happening the same day. It's just not my style."

"What about Livermore on Tuesday?" I felt a tinge of desperation in my voice. I still clung to the hope that on April 17th, as if by sheer force of tradition, the old guard would show up at the Lab and save the day. But if I couldn't count on Holly, who could I count on?

Count on Holly? The irony sank into my heart. Trust was a two-way street.

She turned back to the table. "Oh, I'll be at Livermore," she said matter-of-factly. She took a drink of juice. "I'll cite out if we get arrested at Site 300. I want to be at Livermore so we can keep leafletting the workers. We want to let them know that just because the peace camp closed, we haven't gone away."

I sank into the chair next to hers, straining not to show my relief. Holly would be at Livermore.

Okay, so she was using our demo to promote the peace camp. The key was that she would be there. Maybe the demo wasn't hopeless after all.

"I heard the peace camp found some land for the Fall," I said.

Holly yawned as she nodded. "Yeah, Norm met with the owner, and it looks like we may be able to reopen in September."

"That's great, Holly," I said. "I know how much you want that."

Her brow furrowed. "It's the only thing I've done since International Day that has mattered," she said. She gazed at her empty cup. "What I want more than anything is to feel like my work is touching people. At the peace camp, I could see it, especially when local people stopped by. I could see how isolated they felt, and that we helped bring them together."

I reached across the table and took her hand. I chided myself for the times I had argued with her about the peace camp, hammering away at some obscure political point. What did that have to do with Holly's reasons for being there? Why couldn't I trust her inclinations and give her my undivided support?

I squeezed her hand just as the tape player snapped off. An echo of Bessie's blues lingered in the air. Holly squeezed my hand back, but didn't look at me. Should I say something?

But what? This was hardly the time to interrogate her about our relationship.

Well, just tell her how I feel. Tell her how important she is to me. Here's the chance.

At that moment, Holly stretched and stood up. "I need to go to sleep," she said. She yawned. "Will you come tuck me in?"

I got up and started down the hall after her. Okay, I guess we weren't meant to have the conversation tonight.

But was Holly deliberately avoiding it? Maybe she sensed I was going to ask something, and went to bed to escape having to discuss it. Was she holding something back?

Surely not. That wasn't Holly's style. If she and Caroline were making plans, she would tell me....

She sat on the bed and took off her shoes. "I'm getting together with Sara tomorrow morning," she said.

"What are you two doing?" I asked. I didn't mean for it to sound like a challenge, but Holly looked up in surprise.

"Just hanging out," she said. "I think she's feeling pretty depressed over Karina, so I want to give her some support. She's been there for me when I've needed a friend this Spring."

She slipped off her slacks and pulled back the covers. "Are you going over to Hank's tonight?"

"Hank's? No, I don't think so." I had totally forgotten about Friday night pinball. "I need some personal space. I've got a People's Convention meeting all day tomorrow."

Holly pulled the covers up to her shoulders. Her thick hair tumbled over the pillow. I sat down on the edge of the mattress and stroked her head. She smiled, then closed her eyes. "Have a nice evening," she said.

I bent over and kissed her lips. "You mean so much to me, Holly."

She opened her eyes. They glistened in the dim light. "Thanks, Jeff. I love you." Her eyes closed, but a soft smile settled on her lips.

"Goodnight, sweetie," she whispered.

"Goodnight, Holly. I'll join you in a while."

I left the room carrying a faint glow of peace. But by the time I reached the living room, it had dissipated. The finance report I had to make the next day at the People's Convention meeting weighed on me. But in truth, my mind was stuck on Holly and Angie. I filled my pipe and went out on the deck. A misty fog shrouded the city, punctuated by the orange glow of streetlights. I gazed into the night, trying to discern the usual landmarks, but nothing stood out clearly.

What to do? I searched for a way out, but every road seemed blocked. Damn. I wasn't cut out for this sort of doubt. All I was getting from two relationships was two sets of worries: Who was I hurting? Who was I shortchanging? Who was going to dump me first? The way things were progressing, it might happen simultaneously.

I looked over my shoulder into the apartment. So much of my stuff, but so much of Holly's presence. I pictured her sitting on the living room floor, teacup at her side. I imagined her watering the plants near the living room window. I thought of her lying in bed, her blonde hair billowing over the sheets.

I shook my head. I remembered my first meetings with Holly, how sure I'd been that she was the one for me. How empty the past two years would have been without her. A raindrop flicked my face, then another. The fog melted into a light, cold mist. I shivered. It was time to make a decision.

"Angie, I have to stop seeing you." "This has to end, now." "It just isn't working for me..."

It wasn't going to be easy, however I phrased it. But it had to be done. I shivered again and turned to go inside. It was time to act.

Wednesday, April 18, 1984

WASH THE hall windows. Had to be done. Get a clearer view.

I'd been working all afternoon, polishing the plate glass, but it wasn't like I was giving it much attention. The past two days, I had a one-track mind, obsessing over Monday's Kissinger demo. Images of the demo leapt incessantly to my mind. Arriving with Angie. Arguing and going our own ways. The crowd, a thousand strong, packed onto the sidewalk by the row of riot cops.

The horse cops assembling at the corner. The chants that kept fading. Raoul and Jenny's AG going into the street. Skirmishes with the cops. More of us get in the street. Angie and I dodge the cops. The horses paw the concrete, poised to charge. And then the punks march in, black flag aloft, throwing the police into confusion! Occupying the intersection with a die-in. Clearing out when the cops charged. Retreating around the block — then standing by myself as Angie went off to get arrested.

A chill ran through me as I bent down to get the squeegee. I pictured Angie turning and walking away. Over and over, the scene played before my eyes. Turning and walking away. I'd coax the story forward. On to the arrests. Sara getting clubbed in the head by the cop. Sid getting beat up by undercovers. Hank coming up from behind and scaring the daylights out of me.

But try as I might to reach the end, the reel kept rewinding to Angie. Turning and walking away. Turning and walking away.

Friday, April 20, 1984

He came closer to the city, and when he saw it he wept over it, saying, "If you only knew today what is needed for peace! But now you cannot see it."

— Jesus of Nazareth, quoted in Luke 19:41-42

"No, no, don't nail the cross there!" Hank yelled as he ran toward the flatbed truck.

"I'm just trying to stabilize it," answered Les, a Mustard Seed AG stalwart. He knelt at the foot of the big wooden cross on the back of the truck.

"Use this rope — we can't go nailing crosses to the truck bed."

I tried not to laugh. There was irony in Hank even being present, let alone having such a central role in the Good Friday demo. Hank had spent his early years in a Catholic school, and still nurtured a smoldering resentment toward religion in general and Christianity in particular.

And this was a Christian protest, to be sure. Good Friday was a "traditional" date at Livermore Lab, predating the big blockades. I'd never been to one, so when Hank and Mort got recruited to drive the rented flatbed out to the demo, I told them I'd come along.

A couple of hundred people were scattered around the gravel parking lot across from the southwest corner of the Lab. Many carried homemade crosses, and several nuns in full regalia added a touch of color. Off to one side, a twenty-foot replica of a Cruise missile lay on the ground.

I looked at Hank, who had just handed the rope to Les. "How come you didn't haul the nukecycle out here?"

He cleared his throat and looked away. "I don't know what we could have done with it. It can't be carried, and it can't be pedaled."

"Still the problem with the chain?"

"Yeah. It was actually up and running outside my shop last weekend. But the damn chain keeps snapping. I have to find some way to ease the pressure."

"Maybe if we pushed it first, so it had a rolling start," I said.

"That would help. But as soon as we hit an incline, it would break." He shook his head, then lowered his voice. "Speaking of breaks, I need one. Want to smoke a joint?"

I didn't think getting high was going to enhance my enjoyment of the Good Friday action. "I'll watch the truck," I said. Hank wandered off to find Mort.

I turned back to the crowd, which seemed subdued. Here and there a small circle prayed or sang. Across the street, a couple of dozen state troopers put on their helmets and gloves and lined up along the chain-link fence of the Lab. I wondered how many people they would have to arrest. Maria had told me she expected about thirty, but hoped that other AGs would join at the last minute.

However many it was, it wasn't going to change the outcome of our week of actions. So far there had been a grand total of eighty arrests at Livermore, counting fifteen at the Site 300 Test Area. Good Friday would push the week's total just past one hundred — a blip on the radar. Reagan and his cronies weren't losing any sleep.

And LAG's financial district action had been even smaller. Of course, there was a reason — the near-riot at the Kissinger demo. With almost two hundred arrests, it siphoned off most people who planned to get arrested that day.

The Kissinger protest gave us an alibi for our small numbers, so I guess I should have appreciated it. But as often as I remembered Kissinger, I'd feel my jaw tighten. What was to celebrate? The biggest action of the year and I watched from the sidelines.

Folks who got busted at Kissinger suddenly seemed like a caste apart — the true radicals, willing to defy the state on a moment's notice. The rest of us were relegated to tending the home fires, maintaining our dutiful presence at Livermore Lab.

Actually, Jenny and Sid, two of the Kissinger elite, were at the Good Friday demo. I walked over to where Jenny was staffing a literature table. "Hey, thanks for bringing Direct Action," I said, straightening the stack on the front of the table. I looked over the flyers, most of which were for non-LAG organizing around the Democratic Convention.

Jenny looked at me suspiciously. I stepped around the table, reached out and rubbed her shoulder. "Glad to see you here. I was feeling a little out of place."

She nodded but didn't say anything. Did she think I was going to pressure her about the Convention? Or was she feeling guilty about drifting away from LAG? Maybe if I showed some support for the War Chest Tours without lobbying her, it would ease the tension between us. But how to start?

Luckily, Sid came jogging up and broke the ice. "Jeff Harrison, ace reporter for Direct Action, on the beat."

"Just call me Scoop," I said. A shaved patch on the side of Sid's head caught my eye. The shaving might be the latest punk fashion. But the row of stitches probably wasn't. "How's your battle scar?"

"I'll live," he said offhandedly.

Jenny reached out and touched his head, carefully examining the wound. "Yeah, it's healing."

My brow furrowed. "I heard you had to go to the hospital. What happened?"

Sid's eyes squinted for a moment. Then he cocked his head back. "After the cops started herding people into the trap behind the hotel, some of us, mainly punks, circled back down the far side. We were dragging newsstands and stuff into the street, creating obstructions. The cops were cordoning off Taylor Street, and they had left a line of squad cars unprotected. I couldn't resist. I got behind a car and started letting the air out of the tires. I wasn't trying to damage anything, just playing a joke on them. All of the sudden, two plainclothes cops came charging toward me. I tried to run, but they tackled me. Some punks ran over and tried to pull me away, but one of the cops had his arm around my neck, and I just about passed out."

Flyer for the War Chest Tours. Planning meetings took place all through the Spring.

"So they busted you?"

He shook his head sharply. "Not then. A bunch more punks came running up, people who had stayed out of the arrests. The plainclothes guys panic and let me go. The punks are trying to revive me, and I'm staggering along, when some cops come running up and pull guns on us! I'm still only semi-conscious, and then one of the cops whacks me in the head, and I'm totally out. Next thing I know, I'm in the hospital getting stitches. Then they take me back to jail and slap me with a felony for assaulting a cop." He looked at Jenny and they smiled as if at a private joke.

Props, crosses, and missiles adorned the procession on Good Friday at Livermore Lab. At right, an AG deployed an early form of lockdown technology.

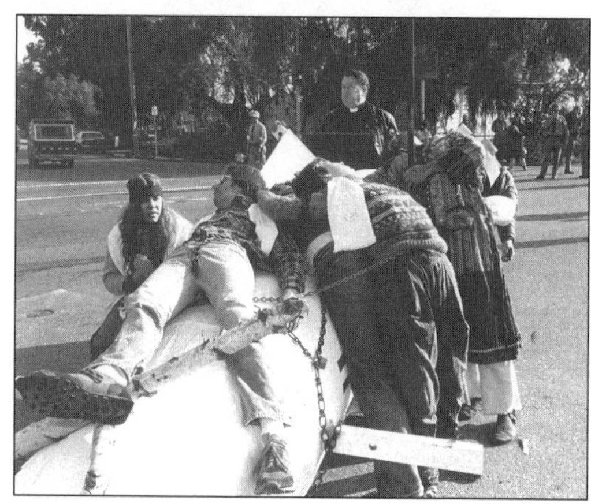

Christian groups have continued Good Friday protests at the Lab. For more information on upcoming actions at Livermore Lab, visit www.directaction.org

"A felony," I said. "Bad news."

"Not really," Sid said. "The lawyers say they'll get dropped to misdemeanors."

I looked at his shaved patch again. "Was it worth it?"

"Sure," he answered without missing a beat. "In some ways we got our butts kicked. Six people ended up in the hospital. But we took the streets. The police had to go to brutal lengths to restore control. Three months before the Democratic Convention, we forced them to lay bare the real basis of their power."

Jenny was focused on Sid, and I felt a twinge of jealousy. I thought about Angie, remembering her chagrin when I bowed out of the Kissinger demo. I scuffed my shoe in the gravel. For once, couldn't I have dropped my worries and joined the crowd? Sure, I'd have been flaking on my obligations at Livermore the following day. Major responsibilities, etc., etc. Great excuse. But I'd spent the past four days feeling like I couldn't pull the trigger. The clarion of revolution had sounded, and I'd rolled over and gone back to sleep.

Enough brooding, already. I picked up a flyer for the War Chest Tours that bore Sid's cut-and-paste imprint. "Nice design," I said. "How is the Kissinger demo going to affect your organizing?"

"They're raising the ante," Sid said. "We have to respond."

"Which means...?"

He bounced on his toes. "We've got to keep on the move. At Kissinger, we fell into their trap, fighting them for control of a single block. We played right into their strength."

I nodded. "Doc was saying the same thing."

Jenny glanced at Sid, then looked at me with more enthusiasm than I'd seen from her in a long time. "Last October, we showed what we can do by staying mobile. The point is to disrupt the whole downtown, not to capture a particular street. That's what May 22nd is about, a chance to try out new tactics."

"May 22nd, right," I said. "I'll be there." I made a mental note to talk to Angie about it when I saw her later that evening. Hopefully we could go together. With Angie, I'd feel like I belonged. And this time I'd clear my calendar so I could get arrested.

The Christians had gathered their crosses and formed into a loose circle. Led by a half-dozen clergy, the crowd bowed their heads in prayer. Jenny, Sid, and I hushed our conversation. Hank and Mort had come back from the van, and stood at a respectful distance. Even the cops stopped their shuffling about and observed a moment of silence.

The prayer ended, and a ragtag procession moved into the street. Several people carried the big Cruise missile right to the center of the intersection. Maria rolled her wheelchair alongside it. Les pulled out a length of chain and bolted the two of them to the missile. Melissa and a couple of her Spirit AG friends secured themselves to the opposite side. Around them, other protesters knelt and commenced a call-and-response litany.

The cops filed in, bolt cutters at the ready. But the arrests proceeded slowly as the officers seemed embarrassed about interrupting the Good Friday liturgy.

I turned to Sid and Jenny. "Now there's how you capture a street," I said.

For once, Sid was standing still. His eyes were glued to the protest. "Yeah," he said. "I'm taking notes."

THE SOLEMNITY of the action stayed with me all day, and I drew strength from having witnessed it. As I rode out to Angie's apartment that evening, it was clear what I had to say. We need to end this, now. The moment had arrived. However difficult, I had to do it.

The way things went when I arrived at her place, you'd have thought breaking up would have gotten easier. The front door would only open partway due to a big heap of stuff that looked like rejects from a garage sale. We cleared a space on the couch, sat down, and picked up right where we left off at the Kissinger demo — arguing.

The only thing was, we'd switched sides. After talking to Jenny and Sid at the Lab, I'd adopted their view that we had to respond to the Kissinger arrests with fresh tactics, show the cops that we couldn't be suppressed.

But Angie responded in a detached voice "I'm tired of the whole us-against-them mentality. They arrested us, so we lost that round. Now we have to go back and win the next round. It's totally reactionary."

A lightbulb with no shade glared at me. "So we should let them get away with beating people?"

She laughed dryly. "As if our protests are going to stop them."

"We have to do something!"

"Then how about something more creative than another protest."

I looked away in frustration. This was not how I pictured our last night. I'd seen us going for a walk, talking things over under the moonlight, reluctantly agreeing that it was best to end our relationship, coming back to her apartment, going into her room, and making passionate love one last time...

I reached out and took her hand. "This is our first night together in a week," I said. "Is this how we want to spend it?"0

She looked down. I paused for a moment, then suggested we go into her room.

She shook her head without looking up. "No, we need to talk, Jeff."

"We can talk in your room, can't we?"

"We can't have a serious conversation in there." Her eyes rose and met mine, as if challenging me to accept her terms of negotiation.

Miffed at her businesslike manner, I one-upped her. "If we're going to talk, then let's go out for a walk." I picked up my jacket to underscore my point. She went silently to her room, returned with a sweater and scarf, and led the way out the door.

We headed away from the freeway, up the Oakland Hills. I was feeling stretched about as far as I could go, and I had a notion to blurt out, "Let's just call it quits. I'm going home right now."

But as we found ourselves retracing a route we had walked one night back in January, back when things were so different between us, my exasperation dissolved in a wistful sigh. I pulled a leaf off a bush and tore it into little pieces.

Angie lit a cigarette. She rarely smoked, but when she did, she did it with a vengeance. She stared straight ahead, blowing out long streams of smoke that curled around her head as we strode uphill. Her hair was pulled back in two thick braids that fell across her shoulders. She turned and looked up at me. "I'm leaving," she said in a low voice. "I've decided to go to Portland."

My head felt thick and heavy. I barely registered her words as she told me that she and Jenny were planning to move out of their apartment anyway, that she'd been wanting to quit her job, that she wanted to spend time with her friend Isabel while she was pregnant — so she'd given everyone two weeks' notice and was leaving for Portland in early May.

I could hear the words, but it was hard to grasp. My knees felt weak, and I must have wobbled a bit, because Angie reached out and put her arm around me. I pulled her close, steadying myself. Was it my fault? Did my ambivalence drive her away? Was it too late to speak up? Yet what would I say?

"You're moving to Portland?" I finally managed.

"I don't know if I'm moving there or not," she said. "I just need to get away for awhile, see someplace different, do some thinking. I don't want anything to do with the Democratic Convention this Summer. And I need to get out of this." She gestured at me and herself, then took a long draw on her cigarette. "When Holly and I went to the Equinox ritual, it was so clear. Holly's been my friend as long as I've been in LAG. She's the one who got Jenny and me involved in the newspaper."

I nodded, and she continued in a contemplative voice. "At the Equinox ritual, we got into small circles. First we passed a bowl of salt water counterclockwise, and each person told of a time they felt powerless. Then we passed pure water clockwise, and spoke of a time we felt powerful. At the end, we sprinkled some of the water on our heads and said, 'I bless my power.'"

She took one last draw on her cigarette, knelt and stubbed it out, then flicked it into a trash can. "Being in my power means doing what would be best for me and the people I love. Whatever happens between you and Holly, I don't want to be part of it."

She looked up at the sky as if searching for a special star. I put my arms around her again, and she laid her head against my chest. We rocked gently back and forth. Tears trickled from my eyes and trailed down my cheeks. She'll never return. This is the end. I pictured her climbing into a car and disappearing forever.

This was the only way out. I belonged with Holly. If I had any hope of saving that relationship, it had to be now.

Then why was it so hard? Angie and I had always known it wouldn't last. It wasn't exactly a big shock.

But now the end was real. I felt a wave of nostalgia for our time together — working at the office, spraypainting, making love, looking at art, going to actions... Would I even know her in a year?

War Chest Tours

July 16-19, 1984

photos by Keith Holmes

War Chest Tours • July 1984

The War Chest Tours at the 1984 Democratic Convention protested corporate control of the Democratic Party. Several "dress rehearsals" were organized that Spring. These photos are from various 1984 actions.

Above, a roving protest crosses paths with a group of Hare Krishnas in downtown San Francisco.

Some actions got into the lobbies of corporate offices, where they did die-ins, then moved on before police arrived.

All photos by Keith Holmes

Any connections between the people pictured in the photographs and the characters in this book are purely coincidental. The characters are fictional. No photo should be taken as implying that an individual is in any way connected to a fictional character.

The July 1984 War Chest Tours resulted in several hundred arrests.

Some Spring actions successfully avoided arrest, staying a step ahead of the police.

Top: Keith Holmes

Bottom: Sam Perkins

Five / 1984

...for example, in the system of general elections. It might have been thought that the government could have spared itself the trouble and expense of these performances, the absurdity of which was obvious to all; but they were important because they turned every citizen into a participant and co-author of the same fiction, the official "reality"' which, by that very fact, ceased to be completely spurious.

—*Leszek Kolakowski, writing on the Stalinist era, Main Currents of Marxism*

Tuesday, May 22, 1984

YOU'D THINK by this time I'd have known better than to come to a demo alone. It didn't matter how many people I knew. If I didn't connect with some of them beforehand, I felt out of synch. But I'd done it again, not making any arrangements and riding over alone on BART.

Jenny and Raoul were probably riding with their AG. Karina and Sara already lived in the City. Hank? Mort? Craig? Holly? None of them were even coming.

I emerged from the BART station and headed for Embarcadero Plaza. Under a patchy gray sky that seemed to merge with the looming skyscrapers, thirty people had gathered — hardly critical mass. It looked like a parody, a scale model of a protest. I spotted a few other Change of Heart folks in the crowd. But we weren't doing a cluster action, and there was nothing drawing us together. I ran into Alby and a friend of his named Megan, a Cal grad student with curly black hair and sad eyes. We talked for a couple of minutes about possible police responses. Then I drifted away, looking for someone else to stand with.

If only Angie were still around. In the three weeks since she left, we'd only talked twice. She'd settled into a sublet up in Portland, found a job in a café, and was exploring schools for the Fall. Most of the time, our relationship was a receding memory. But at a moment like this, how could I not miss her?

Fifty or sixty people had gathered, still a poor showing. Maybe I was wasting my time. I'd seen today as my shot at redemption. For a month I'd lived with the odium of missing the Kissinger arrests, of having ducked out at crunch time. Today, I was determined to be in the middle of the action.

Raoul, one of the prime organizers, wandered by. He looked as lost as I felt. I approached him, thinking to commiserate, score a point or two for showing up, and drop a hint that working within LAG might attract a few more people.

But Raoul preempted me. "Been out to any A's games yet?"

"Uh, no," I said. "How about you?"

"Yeah. I went to one last week. Looks like they're gonna be terrible again this year."

The Oakland A's. Baseball season. An alternate reality. Lately I barely looked at the sports pages, and the thought of going to a game was remote. Who had the time, or the spare brain cells? But talking with Raoul, I felt a little less out of place, even if it was about baseball instead of the fine art of street protesting.

Jenny came over our way. Her left eye, in fact the whole left side of her face, was squinched up. Was it the sun, or was she warding off pain? I still had never heard from her that she was pregnant, but from Raoul's solicitous expression, I didn't doubt it. They gave me an awkward look. I took the hint and moved off.

Karina was trying to round up Change of Heart people for some adventure. Alby seemed on board, but otherwise, people were shaking their heads apologetically. Ask me, I thought. I walked over her way, but she seemed so exasperated that I veered off to talk with Sara instead.

Sara's eyes betrayed exhaustion. She'd been through a lot lately. Getting belted by the cop at the Kissinger demo left her with a week of headaches and slurred speech. Then she and Karina broke up. It wasn't quite final yet, which probably made it even tougher for Sara. But I'd heard that Karina was moving out, and the fact that Sara wasn't part of Karina's latest scheme didn't bode well.

She smiled wanly as I approached. "How are you doing?" I asked. She shrugged and said nothing. Not that I needed her to tell me. What if Holly moved out on me?

Actually, Holly and I had been doing better since Angie left. Despite the ups and downs, I felt committed to working things through. We were looking into couples counseling, and had set Saturday nights as a regular date. But Sara and Karina's demise was sobering. Even a "perfect couple" can break up.

Sara and I stood together, surveying Embarcadero Plaza. Around two hundred people were gathered by now. There were more punks than in October, and a contingent of rather serious-looking types who, Sara told me,

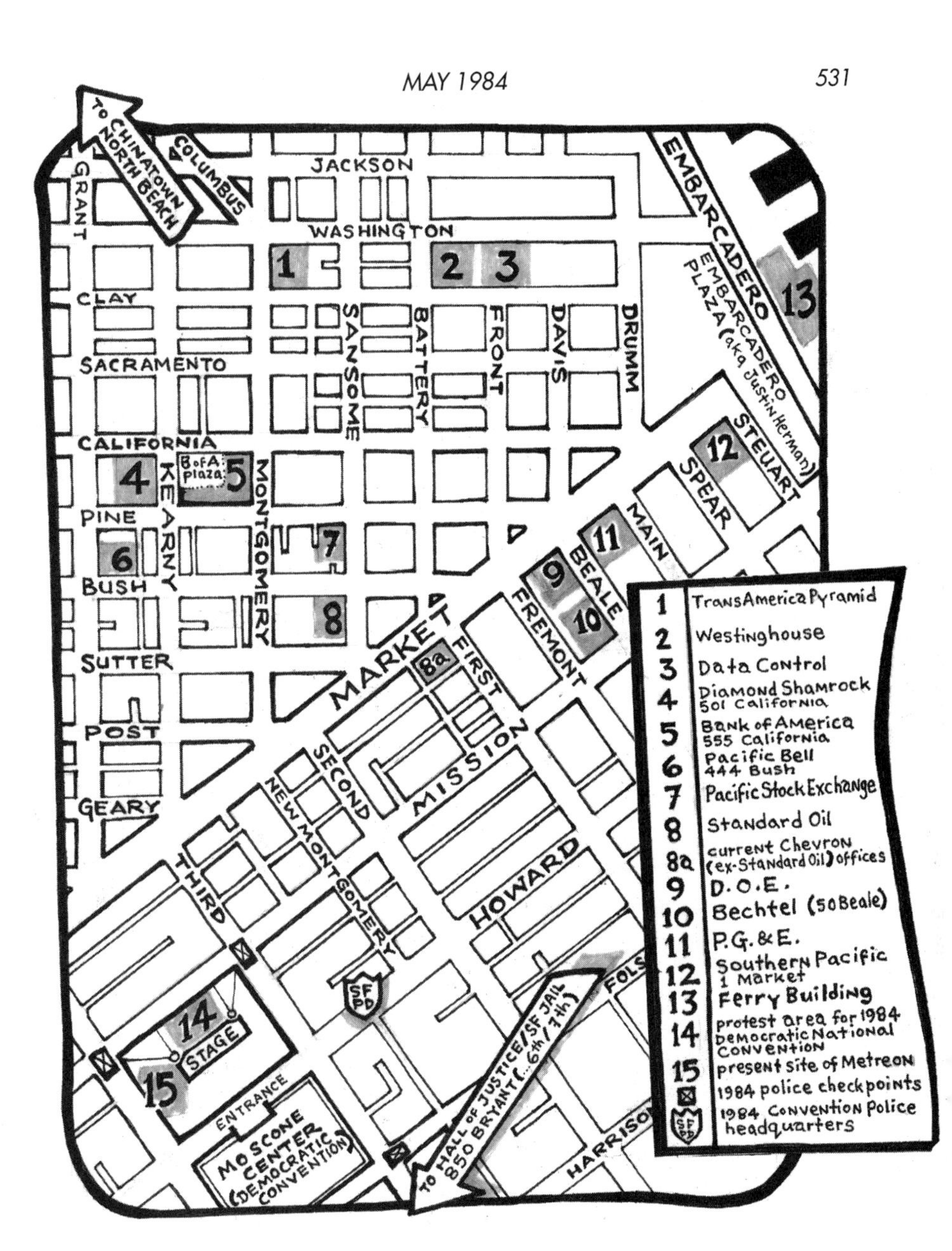

The San Francisco Financial District and South of Market areas, nerve centers for corporate domination of the Bay Area. In the early 1980s, a style of decentralized, mobile protests evolved, based partly on tactics borrowed from London anti-nuclear actions. The model was used in numerous protests of the 1980s, with mixed results as far as actually disrupting the operations of downtown. Lessons learned from those actions rippled out to Seattle in 1999, Washington DC protests since 2000, and back to San Francisco, where thousands of people paralyzed the financial district for two days following declaration of war against Iraq in 2003. Map by America Narcoleptic.

were the collective that ran Bound Together bookstore in the Haight. Some drummers tested a rhythm on a small throng of dancers. Doc and Moonstone carried a ten-foot paper-maché missile. Ronald McReagan wandered through our crowd, a clown in a Reagan mask with the McDonald's logo stenciled on his forehead.

Winston and Jürgen, members of LAG's recently-formed "International Group," came past us. They were attired in white radiation suits, complete with makeshift helmets and gloves. Winston was carrying a box-like contraption labeled "LAG-a-Tron." Jürgen held a vacuum cleaner hose that came out of the box, with which he scanned the briefcases of passing business-types for radioactivity. Every minute or so, a siren inside the box would go off, and the two of them would run around in panic-stricken circles.

Why hadn't I thought of something like that? I had to start planning ahead.

The organizers clustered together, arguing over whether to start or wait for more people. Sid and Karina were impatient to get going, but Jenny, Raoul, and Jacey wanted to wait.

I hadn't seen Jacey since the Kissinger demo. I studied him carefully. Maybe it was his chipped front tooth, or maybe the vaguely haughty look in his eyes. Something didn't sit quite right. He didn't seem to know who I was, but given his attitude toward LAG and nonviolence, I figured he'd be hostile.

As Jacey and Karina conferred, I felt jealous. It wasn't like she was all over him, but I noticed the way she would say something, then look to see his response. I wished I had someone who cared so much about what I thought.

A wave of Angie-nostalgia wafted me back to the October financial district action — hanging out with her beforehand, doing the die-ins together, seeing her dance up the street outside Bank of America. I fast-forwarded to her arrest at the Kissinger demo, the cop choking the air out of her as I watched helplessly from the sidelines. I'm here this time, Angie. No turning away.

"Want to help me with this?" Lyle startled me out of my reverie. He pointed to a cardboard box labeled Radioactive Waste. "It has holes punched in the bottom. I'm going to fill it with flour, and we can leave a trail of waste behind us wherever we go."

"Sure," I said. I appreciated the invitation. But Lyle wasn't part of the organizing team. Walking with him exiled me to the periphery of the action. Why couldn't Karina or Jenny have asked me to help with something? Damn, I thought. What a great mood to start the day.

Sid clambered on top of a trash container and yelled to the scattered masses. "Let's get going! Let's gather over here!" Sid was one of the chief instigators of the demo, touting it as the cure to all the movement's ills. Forget LAG's morbid dwelling on its "crisis." Forget LAG's stalemate over what to do around the Democratic Convention. Forget LAG altogether. Just get out in the street and protest.

Frustrated as I was with Sid's lack of concern for LAG, I leapt at the chance to be part of the new cutting edge. Get arrested today, and I'd be back in the swing of things.

"There are no monitors," Sid announced. "It's up to each person here to take responsibility for this action. We've planned a route, which will be directed by different people each step of the tour. But there's room for spontaneity, too. No one is in charge."

I looked around the plaza. So far, no cops in sight. Thanks to a timely coincidence, several Labor unions had called a protest of a manufacturers' conference across town, and the police must have considered that more of a threat than our ragtag event.

How long would that last, though? The previous Friday night at pinball, when I told Hank and Mort about the demo, they'd laughed derisively. Mort's words still echoed in my head: "How far do you think you'll get? The Convention is in six weeks. The cops aren't going to allow any trouble now. You're walking into a set-up. They could crack down hard and intimidate everyone just before the Convention."

"If they try to crack down, it's all the more reason to keep on protesting," I had answered. But Mort and Hank remained skeptical, and it was no surprise that neither was present.

Sid jumped down off the dumpster. Lyle and I hoisted our nuke-waste box, and we headed for Market Street. On most marches, you'd expect a banner and signs letting bystanders know what we were protesting. Not today. There was one American flag with something about "Amerika" written in black on the white stripes. But no banners, no bullhorns. And what would our chant be, anyway? "Screw the system!" Onlookers surely got that message loud and clear.

At each stop of the financial district protest, an AG would read an indictment of the corporation or government department, followed by theater or direct action.

We started off on the sidewalk, heading up the south side of Market Street. Most of the shoppers and business types gave us wide berth, as if we were carriers of a contagious virus that caused the holes in our clothes. Seeing their reactions, I smiled for the first time all day.

Some of the punks fanned out, making grotesque faces in boutique and restaurant windows. Two women wearing hooded sweatshirts followed behind the march unraveling a big ball of red yarn, weaving our trail around signposts, streetlights, and the spindly potted trees growing along the sidewalk.

Lyle and I jostled our nuke-waste box, leaving a ragged trail of flour behind. "Careful, watch your step," I warned pedestrians. "It's radioactive." Most people avoided stepping in the white powder.

A half-block up, the march veered off the sidewalk and into the mall-like ground floor of the One Market building. We cut a fine figure, urban riffraff traipsing through the halls of commerce. We waved and hollered at the curious bystanders, a few of whom shyly waved back.

Up ahead, a little knot of protesters bowed and scraped on the mall floor. To what? A big statue of the Grim Reaper. What it was doing there, I had not a clue. But I set down the box and joined in the bowing and moaning. Raoul yelled to the suited onlookers: "Bow down! Bow down before your God!" None joined us.

As we worshipped the Reaper, building security arrived, two flustered guards who busied themselves

The mobile protest stayed one step ahead of the law all afternoon, occupying corporate offices, dancing and doing die-ins in financial district intersections, then moving on before the police arrived.

with their walkie-talkies. To their evident relief, we wrapped up our little ceremony. With a cheer we headed out the far doors.

After the sterile air of the mall, the breeze on Mission Street was a welcome reprieve. We trekked a couple of blocks east to the Bechtel building, where the Wiccan affinity group Matrix was brewing a foaming cauldron of toxic waste. Artemis, adorned in a black cape and Witch's hat, delivered a spiel on Bechtel's sordid history of exporting nuclear technology.

"And don't forget, they're building Diablo Canyon," Moonstone put in. As the Matrix Witches stirred the cauldron, someone started chanting, "What's the smell? Bech-tel!"

Building security closed the main doors right away. Off to the side, Jacey and Raoul eyed a second set of doors. Were they thinking of going inside? It looked like it. But the guards caught on and quickly locked the entire entrance. Thwarted, Raoul turned back our way and bellowed: "10! 9! 8!" Instantly the crowd picked up the countdown, and a moment later, two hundred of us were sprawled on the concrete, screaming and moaning Bechtel's name.

It was good theater, but there wasn't much else we could do. As the drummers started a rhythm, people straggled to their feet. Lyle and I took up our waste box again, and the march filtered up the sidewalk away from Bechtel.

The sun was breaking through the clouds as we rounded the corner onto Market Street and came full tilt into the lunchtime crowd. Jacey, just ahead of me, looked like he wanted to get out in the street and block traffic. But Sid and Karina called him back. "We should wait till after Bank of America," Karina said, and Jacey relented.

The downtown regulars eyed us suspiciously. Even the panhandlers seemed upset at our invasion of their turf. Near me, a well-coifed woman remarked on someone's torn-up jeans. "We're not here to shop," the protester shot back, and it quickly morphed into a chant: "We're here! We're mad! We're not going shopping!"

Partway up the block, Alby drew our attention to the next site: McDonald's. A hundred of us squeezed into the lobby of the long, narrow Market Street franchise. The rest of our crowd peered through the plate glass. At a table next to me, a mother with three kids dressed all in blue gave me a troubled look. Not much I can tell you, I thought. I don't have a clue why we're here.

"Clear an aisle," Alby yelled out. Through the front door came a punk carrying a sign: "We've Got a Beef with McDonald's." Behind him, a gangly cow loped along, mooing deeply and nodding its paper-maché head at the patrons. The kids in blue laughed with delight, pointing and trying to pet the cow as it passed us. Their mother nervously held the youngest back.

Last down the aisle came Ronald McReagan, waving to the kids. "Nice cow," he cooed. "Nice cow." He reached out and patted the beast, which fawningly bowed at his feet. "What a nice cow."

Protesters crossed paths with an evangelizing band of Hare Krishnas.

I was wondering where this was going when someone stepped out of the crowd and handed McReagan a cardboard axe. With one swoop he seized the axe, raised it high, and came slicing down on the cow's neck. The skull cracked open, and bright red blood poured onto the shiny tile floor.

We laughed and cheered. Horror and fascination mingled on the kids' faces. Their mother cast a foul look our way, and I heard muttering from other patrons as the lobby emptied. Oh well, punks were never going to win a popularity contest.

We crossed Market against the light, but mainly within the crosswalk. The drivers seemed more perplexed than annoyed.

A couple of blocks north of Market, the march stopped at the Pacific Stock Exchange for a tax resisters' skit on military funding. The actors, in the center of the fifty-foot-wide stairs, weren't disrupting anything, but a couple of squad cars cruised up. Four cops got out and looked us over. When we marched away, they got in their cars and disappeared.

I surveyed our crowd, still two hundred strong. The drummers kicked into a beat, and people danced up the California Street sidewalk, weaving in and out of the suit-and-tie brigade along our route. At Sansome Street, we crossed paths with a bunch of Hare Krishnas out evangelizing the financial district. They welcomed us, and for a moment we melded together in one big happy dance.

The next target must be Bank of America, I figured. And judging from what I'd overheard, the goal was to get inside, not just demonstrate on the plaza. How was that going to work? Wouldn't the guards see us coming and lock the doors?

Raoul, Sid, Karina, and Jacey conferred as we walked along. I wondered why Jenny wasn't part of the parley, then saw her and Sara at the rear of the march. Jenny's face was contorted, like she was fighting off a bout of nausea. I considered abandoning Lyle and the nuke-waste box to drop back and check on her. But maybe she wanted to be left alone with Sara.

As I was meditating on Jenny, we unexpectedly turned off California Street. I wondered what side-target someone had chosen, but nothing was announced until we rounded the next corner. "Shhh!" came the word. Apparently there was a small back entrance to the Bank of America building. As we streamed up the narrow sidewalk, a half-dozen business types scurried out of our way.

Jacey was the first to the entrance. He swung the door open and leaned against it as our crowd of punks and misfits surged into the huge bank lobby.

The desk-bound employees to our right gaped at us. The stunned tellers along the left wall reminded me of targets in an arcade game.

"B of A — Blood of Africa!" Jacey called out.

"Yeah," Sid yelled. "Bank of America invests more in nuclear weapons than they do in San Francisco neighborhoods."

Doc and Moonstone hauled their big paper-maché missile up to the counter and tried to deposit it. When the teller waved them away, they marched the missile over to the desk area and plopped it down in front of a manager. "We hear you deal in nuclear weapons," Doc said. "We'd like to open an account."

Over by the tellers' stations, Winston and Jürgen took their LAG-a-Tron from window to window, the siren going off at every stop. "Aaaagh!" they yelled at the last window, "the money's all hot!"

Lyle and I got into the spirit, shaking our trail of

The march converged on the headquarters of Bank of America.

radioactive powder across the carpet. "Nuclear waste coming through!" we called out, finally plopping the box down on a business-loan desk. I wasn't sorry to be rid of it, especially if the cops showed up. Better to be free to move. I smiled to myself. Here I was in the center of the action, ready to maneuver.

At the far end of the lobby stood a pair of escalators, with a stainless steel ramp between them. People reacted as if seeing the magical moving stairs for the first time. Soon dozens of us were riding up and down, around and around, laughing and waving at those going the other direction. At the top, a punk with bright green hair stepped onto the ramp that divided the two escalators, plopped onto his butt, and went careening down the shiny steel. In a moment, there was a line of people waiting their turn on the slide.

A couple of late-arriving security guards tried to convince us to leave, to no avail. Gradually people gathered on the upper level, which looked into the desk-filled pit below. "Hey, hey, B of A, how many people did you kill today?" people chanted, pointing at the chagrined employees.

"The cops are on the way!" It was only a rumor, and someone remarked that we weren't really breaking any laws, but we had about exhausted the entertainment possibilities of the bank lobby. We did a quick die-in, then moved out to the plaza and back down California Street, leaving the alleged cops in our dust. I found myself with Karina at the front of the ragtag procession. Still amped by the bank scene, I put one arm around her and squeezed. She responded by wrapping both her arms around me and hugging me even as we

Deposit tickets lay scattered like confetti around the Wells Fargo lobby immediately after the festive protest. The Wells Fargo stagecoach can be seen in the background.

continued walking. I could feel her elation flowing through me, and breathed it in. "On to Wells Fargo!" she said. I didn't want to let her go, but she bounded on ahead, yelling over her shoulder, "Let's go ride the stagecoach!"

We were the first two people through the front door. We were greeted by alarmed stares, and I passed close enough to the line of customers to see the fear in people's eyes. It took me aback — did we look like their idea of a threat? Couldn't they tell we were nonviolent?

Like B of A, Wells Fargo had a huge lobby, but no escalators or second-story balcony. Without that diversion, people had to come up with new ways to protest the bank's voluminous nuclear portfolio. Sid grabbed a handful of deposit tickets and fired the stack into the air. Up they flew in a neat bunch, then burst apart like fireworks and confettied down around us. I grabbed a stack and joined the fun. Protesters were whooping and yelling like a pep rally before the homecoming game.

In the center of the lobby stood a beautiful old Wells Fargo stagecoach. There was only one guard on duty, a portly older man with sweat-stains under the armpits of his too-tight button shirt. He didn't try to stop our celebration, but focused on one mission: "Please! Please stay off the stagecoach! It's an antique!" He pleaded so eloquently that even Karina, who looked like she was dying to climb right up into the driver's seat, backed away. Amid the melee, word quickly spread to leave the stagecoach alone.

After a while we ran out of deposit tickets, and the revelry wound down. As we exited the bank, chanting and clapping, the fog was rolling in. I shivered at its damp chill. At that moment, a couple of police cruisers pulled around the corner. "About time!" someone yelled to them, and a chorus of taunts filled the air. A paddywagon swung up to the curb.

I sucked in a breath. My resolve to be part of the arrests had dimmed a bit. I hadn't eaten all day, and a bowl of hot popcorn on my balcony sounded a lot more appetizing than a cold bologna sandwich in jail. If I had to get busted, I was ready. But if there were a graceful way out...

Most people appeared to share my feelings. There were several more potential sites, but a lot of people seemed ready to call it a day. Sara proposed heading back to Embarcadero Plaza for a final circle.

Not so the other organizers. "Let's keep moving!" Sid yelled out. The crowd drifted along, but when Jacey tried to pull us into the street to block traffic, he met resistance. I had to agree. What was the point? Why this particular street? Especially with the paddywagon in clear view. Was there something here we were trying to disrupt? Or was Jacey just trying to provoke the cops into busting the whole march? It probably wouldn't take much.

I could have written Jacey off. But when Karina joined him, it got tougher. "Come on!" she yelled, gesturing in my direction. "Take the street!"

How could I say no? Wasn't this the moment I'd come here looking for? And with Karina, no less. I edged off the curb, joined by Alby and Sara. The cops eyed us, but didn't make a move. Emboldened, I stepped out further. A taxi had to slow and swerve around us. But only a few more people joined us. Others were drifting away.

Karina threw up her arms in exasperation. I tried to catch her eye, but she was commiserating with Jacey. I looked away, wondering where Raoul and Jenny had been through this interlude. I spotted them off to the side. Jenny was staring at the ground. Raoul hunched down to catch her words. A moment later he put his arm around her, and the two of them headed away.

Protesters sang and raised their arms in a "cone of power" following a spiral dance at the end of the protest.

The crowd was thinning out. Who could I leave with? One more reason I should have come with other people. The waning protest took on a dull aspect, and I couldn't fathom how I had been having such fun ten minutes earlier.

Sara still advocated returning to Embarcadero Plaza. Sid, never down for long, joined her. I preferred their plan to leaving alone. A hundred or so people straggled back to our starting spot. Although Jacey left in disgust, Karina stayed with us.

At the plaza we circled up, arms around tired shoulders. I felt relieved not to be in jail, and glad still to be with the others. Apparently no one had worked out an ending. Sid announced a planning meeting for Democratic Convention protests. Someone suggested a song. I searched my brain for an appropriate number, but drew a blank. People looked around.

"Let's do a spiral dance," Karina called out. "Everyone join hands. Sara, you lead."

People looked at Sara expectantly. She seemed embarrassed, but nodded and started winding to her left, leading us like a ribbon in a slow spiral toward the center of the circle. Karina started a chant-like song that others of us picked up:

We are the flow, We are the ebb
We are the weavers, We are the web

After a couple of circuits, Sara reached the center. The rest of us formed three rings around her, still holding hands so we formed a spiraling snake. Sara glanced around, then made a turn and led the head of the snake spiraling back outward, looping past those of us coming in so we passed each other face to face. "Look into each others' eyes," Karina called over the song.

As my part of the line reached the center, we pivoted and headed back out. Eyes flowed past me — Sid, Karina, Moonstone, Doc... The contact was awkward and beautiful, difficult and the easiest thing in the world. "We are the flow, We are the ebb...."

We spiraled out and back in, twice, three times, the familiar faces revolving against the silvery skyscrapers. Our steps grew lighter, and the song sped up. Faces passed more quickly, glowing with the exhilaration of the day. Voices harmonized the simple melody. "We are the weavers, We are the web!"

Finally Sara stopped spiraling, let loose the hand of the woman behind her, and started clapping and dancing in the center of the circle. Alby and Karina skipped into the middle and joined her, dancing and singing. "We are the flow, We are the ebb...." A couple of drummers grabbed their instruments and drove the spirit higher and higher. Moonstone twirled through the crowd. Around me, people waved their arms in the air, bobbing up and down.

I lost sense of time, singing the hypnotic lyrics over and over. "We are the weavers, We are the web!" Maybe it was five minutes, maybe ten or fifteen, before the energy crested. The drummers released the rhythm, and the words gave way to simple toning, at first discordant, but gradually tending to harmony, a hundred voices floating toward the sky. Some people raised their arms toward the center, forming a cone-shaped pattern around the circle. "Ommmmmmmm....."

As the harmony grew richer, I flashed back to the chanting circle during my first arrest at Livermore, hundreds of men toning together. How much richer today, with men and women joining voices. Our vibrant chord rose and fell, rose and fell, finally fading to silence. Arms slowly descended, and around me some people knelt and placed their palms on the pavement. Returning the energy to the Earth, I remembered, and knelt down. As my fingers touched the ground, though, I paused. Returning it to the Earth? No way. I need this energy! Hold on to it.

As if in response, Sara spoke up nearby. "Ground the energy," she called out. "Complete the cycle. Remember, when you need it, it's always there. For now, ground it."

Right, I thought. I placed both my hands on the ground. As I did, Angie glimmered through my mind. How I wished I were sharing this with her! I pressed my palms onto the brick of the plaza. The warmth of the day's sun radiated into my skin.

I'm getting it, Angie. One step at a time, I'm getting it.

Friday, June 8, 1984

PERSONALLY, I could live with a few typos. Pasting in corrections was my least favorite part of producing Direct Action. But Holly hated typos. And since she'd spent all afternoon coordinating production, it seemed like the least I could do when I took over at seven.

Just to be nearing the end of our June issue — Summer Solstice, we were calling it, since we were already a week late — was an achievement. We'd missed the May issue altogether. I hated to admit it, but maybe our momentum was running out. The money sure was.

Still, here were a half-dozen people giving up their Friday evening for the last push. We were at Ashby House, taking over the big living room as we had for the past two weekends. Raoul had moved in with Jenny after Angie left, so no one living in the house worked on the paper any more. But they seemed fine with us using the funky space.

I surveyed the ever-evolving diorama. Someone had stenciled a half-dozen black fists on the walls. Near the door a rusty muffler sat on a Grecian column. Across the room, Zairian pop played from a paint-splattered cassette deck.

Over in the corner, as if a department unto herself, Claudia was working on the local pages. Daniel likewise had staked out his own turf to paste up the national actions. I was glad they were around, since I wanted to talk to Claudia about People's Convention and Daniel about the Bohemian Grove protest. But I was more interested in talking with Raoul, Sid, and Karina, who were working at the center table on a two-page spread covering the recent street protests.

The layout was Raoul's idea, but as soon as he suggested it, I got behind the proposal. What better role for Direct Action than to be a forum for tactical discussions, a place where all the different tendencies came together? Whatever our differences, we still could share a common journalistic voice.

Not that I'd completely given up on us being involved in a Convention action. True, I'd abandoned the idea of LAG endorsing the War Chest Tours or any other CD action. The best we were going to do was a legal rally. But it could be a parallel effort, raising the same issues as the Tours. The important thing was to present a united front.

Of course, it took two sides to unite. And the War Chesters weren't showing much inclination to cooperate, beyond using LAG's telephones and electric typewriters. I wished that Jenny were around more. She was the bridge. But Jenny had taken the past few days off from the office. Given her pregnancy,

I wondered how much part she was going to play in the Convention actions.

Sid propped one foot on a chair and arched precariously over the table, pointing at the layout. "We can cover the May 22nd tour on our pages, too," he said. "I'll write something that fits the space." He looked at me excitedly. "You saw it. We outran the cops. They can't keep up. Now we need to leave more room for people to plan autonomous actions."

"That would make a difference," I said. "Do you think many AGs will?"

"Some people might do it," Raoul said with a scowl. "But face it, most people prefer to have leaders making the decisions. They like having monitors, so there's someone to blame when nothing happens."

"Yeah," Karina said, looking up from her layout. "When we came out of Wells Fargo, it was like everyone wanted some leader to announce the next step, instead of just taking the street and shutting the City down."

Behind her, Claudia laughed derisively, but said nothing.

"It might have been different," I said, "if there had been some discussion ahead of time."

Raoul made a face. "Can't people be more spontaneous? Does every detail have to be planned out like it's a LAG demo?"

I felt stung, but I knew Raoul's jab was probably more at Karina than at me, referring to her support of LAG's rally at the Democratic Convention. At first glance, it didn't seem like Karina would have much sympathy with the rally, either, since there was no CD. But she was, after all, still a LAG staffer. Was she finally thinking about what was good for the group? Or just backing up Sara and Alby, the main planners?

I wished she and I had some time to talk, for reasons personal as well as political. Earlier, she'd told me about a War Chest Tours meeting the following week. With luck, I'd run into her at the office that day and we could ride to the meeting together.

I turned back to my layout,

N. America ...A Forum

No Democratic Convention

Response to Democratic Convention

Independent Action and the Democratic Convention

The Left Must Be Prepared for a Reagan Victory

Discussions of how to respond to the Democratic Convention became a forum for airing divergent strategic visions of LAG.

but after a long silence, Karina abruptly responded to Raoul. "Just because LAG wants to control everything," she said, "why do we have to give in? Fight back."

Raoul's head drooped. "Why bother? They're so stuck, repeating the same tired formulas. You can spend all your energy fighting it, or you can spring free and do something creative."

"Not everyone's stuck," I said. "But if everybody with a fresh idea quits, where will we be?"

"We're not quitting," Sid cut in. "But the kind of actions we're planning, affinity groups can do a lot better than LAG."

How could I answer when I didn't even know what Sid was planning? I looked at Karina, but she was putting on her jacket. Raoul stretched and yawned. "I need to get going, too," he said.

That was that. End of conversation. I watched Raoul lazily pull his jacket on. Must be nice to feel so relaxed, I thought. No worries about deadlines or printing bills.

Sid was leaving with Raoul. "Do you know about the meeting next Tuesday?" he asked me. "It's over at Bound Together."

"Yeah, Karina was telling me about it."

"You should come."

"Thanks," I said. Sid might have no use for LAG, but at least he treated me like I was part of the alternative. I turned to Raoul. "Tell Jenny I hope she's feeling better."

"Yeah, I will," he said over his shoulder.

The Zaire tape had ended. I flipped it over, but it sounded too perky for the mood in the room, and I turned it down. I looked around. Me, Daniel, and Claudia. The Friday night hardcore. I felt warm, and went to open a window, but it stuck. I gave it a shove and opened it wide.

I picked up a sheet of corrections and tried to focus on the minutiae of Direct Action. Claudia came over to get the corrections for her page. "Well, that's one solution to the crisis of LAG," she said. "Just declare all organizations irrelevant and get on with the action of the week."

I smiled ruefully. "Yeah, what can you say?"

"You can ignore them and focus on the real problems of building a movement. I assume we're giving the crisis discussions major play in this issue."

"We have an article," I said. "But mainly this issue is focusing on the Convention organizing."

"And on the Fall actions," Daniel interposed in his deep, measured voice. He stood up from his layout table across the room. "I wrote a piece on the action at Livermore in September."

Claudia looked at him incredulously. "What's the point in doing another Livermore blockade with a hundred people? We need to step back and understand why we're in this slump, not keep beating our heads against the wall."

"One lackluster period doesn't constitute a slump," Daniel said. "Nationwide, civil disobedience is thriving. *The Nuclear Resister* reported over eight hundred arrests around Tax Day. That scarcely constitutes a crisis for the civil disobedience movement."

"The crisis isn't about how many are arrested," Claudia said. "It's about a lack of a coherent direction for the movement. It's about a total inability to look beyond the next action."

Daniel rolled his eyes. "You might recall," he said, "that this was precisely the problem International Day attempted to address. We set forth a vision of an annual action in which each year would build on the previous year's work, locally and globally. Moving beyond one-shot actions was the essence of International Day."

"All International Day did was institutionalize the 'next action' mentality," Claudia answered. "It had nothing to do with creative thinking."

Daniel folded his arms across his chest. "The Crisis meetings are scarcely a model of creative thinking."

"Isn't there room for both?" I tried to intervene. "Why can't we plan our next action while we're discussing long-term strategy?"

"It's a waste of time," Claudia said.

"On that point," said Daniel, "we are in complete agreement." He placed his proofreading into a folder and picked up his coat. "I'll return the corrections tomorrow afternoon," he said to me, then turned to leave.

I caught a whiff of fresh air as he shut the door. I wished I could leave, too. Enough of this. Wouldn't it be great to get high and go for a long walk? Play some harmonica, maybe work on a new song.

But I'd told Holly I'd meet her at home after her peace camp meeting. Even if she and I were communicating pretty well lately, I felt like I had to be on my toes. I didn't want to complicate matters by being high.

So I stuck around with Claudia, who was putting the finishing touches on her pages. She seemed happy to quietly co-exist, but it felt awkward to me, especially since we were supposedly working together on People's Convention. I tried to think of a way to bring it up, but I had trouble remembering why I'd been so excited about it in the first place. Sure, to connect with activists outside our usual White-middle-class-anti-nuke circles, et cetera, et cetera. Maybe if I could talk about the experience with people like Claudia, I'd be more excited.

Claudia wasn't excited about much of anything these days. Searching for some point of mutual interest, I asked what she'd thought about the "Crisis of LAG" meetings.

"They're about what I expected," she said as she poked around at her layout. "A hundred people, and you couldn't ask for a better cross section. So where did it get us? Nowhere. There was absolutely no collective vision."

That part I couldn't argue with. The dissonance still rang in my ears: Doc and Belinda decrying bad process. Daniel and Antonio heaping derision on opponents of International Day. Monique's phobia of anything that smacked of radicalism. Raoul calling us all control-freaks. Melissa scolding us for not being pacifists. Pilgrim's tunnel vision around Livermore. Karina scorning those who wouldn't continually up the ante.

Claudia looked away. "People talked all day and got nowhere," she said. "But I already knew that. Once the Strategy Proposal died last year, it was just a matter of time till LAG collapsed."

"If you knew the crisis meetings were futile," I said, "why did you waste your time?"

"I guess I had to convince myself one last time," she said. "I was hoping for some shared analysis. But a lot of people are just using LAG as personal therapy, like a bunch of two-year-olds crying, 'Gimme what I want!'"

"That's hardly fair," I said, chagrined to be put in the position of defending the meetings that she had called.

"Where was the common purpose?" she asked as she pasted down a headline. "To build a solid movement, you have to articulate a common

EUROPE

Global Resistance

AROUND THE WORLD IN 80 LINES

Great Britain:

Sweden:

Finland:

Scandinavia & N. Atlantic:

Republic of Ireland:

The Philippines:

December Actions:

Switzerland: Rising Dissent

CALENDAR OF INTERNATIONAL EVENTS: JANUARY TO JULY, 1984

• JANUARY

• FEBRUARY

• MARCH

• APRIL

• APRIL OR MAY

• MAY

• JUNE

• JULY

Sicily Human Chain

Austrian Teenagers Request Peace-Oriented Pen Pals

East German Peace Activists Need Help

New Directions for the Netherlands?

Direct Action's international pages covered many parts of the world, but gave special coverage to European peace groups, with many articles written by LAG activists originally from European countries.

strategy. You need a shared vision for people to rally around, to say, this is what the sacrifices are for. Direct action has to be part of a broader strategy. For LAG, it's the be-all and end-all of our group. No wonder people are burned out." She shook her head slowly. "Maybe we've done all we can. Other issues are rising, like forest defense or ending Apartheid in South Africa. Sure, there's some sense of loss, but we did what we could."

It was rare to see Claudia dejected. I set down my gluestick. "If you're feeling burned out, maybe it's time for you to step back," I said.

Claudia's eyes flared. "This isn't about personal depression. Ever since the last big blockade, LAG has floundered from one useless action to another."

"Useless?" I glared back at her. "Maybe it seems that way to people who aren't doing anything."

She peered at me through her glasses, seeming astonished at my challenge. "So what should we be doing," she said sardonically. "Protesting the Democrats?"

"Why not?"

"Oh, I'll bet they're shaking in their shoes."

"Do you have a better idea?"

"Sure," she said caustically. "Let's blockade Livermore again."

If she was trying to get my goat, Livermore wasn't the key. I leveled my eyes on her. "The Democrats are coming to town. Livermore Lab is still designing nuclear weapons. If you don't want to be part of the resistance..."

My voice trailed off. She stared at me, and her eyes seemed to redden. Then she stiffened. "Clearly we differ," she said. "Here's my pages, that's all I have time to do." She turned and pulled on her sweater. I felt an impulse to apologize, but I was getting tired of always being the one to smooth things over.

With a cursory goodbye, she headed out the door, leaving me alone with the newspaper. Somewhere in the house I could hear other voices, but none I recognized. I tried to put the argument out of my mind. Couldn't I just have let her have her say? Why did I have to fight with her? I looked down at my layout board. Maybe I should pack it up, too. Someone else would have to paste in the corrections.

Anyway, Holly would probably be home by now. Why not spend the rest of the evening with her?

The walk home was a rehash session. Worries over alienating Claudia. Anger at Raoul for his haughtiness. Frustration with LAG for letting the War Chest Tours slip away. And not least, the question of where Holly and I were headed. All woven into one tortuous knot.

As I STEPPED into the apartment, the aroma of vegetable soup greeted me. "Wow, smells great," I said.

Then I spotted Caroline at the table. "Oh, hi," I said. She greeted me from her seat. Even with Angie gone, Caroline still seemed upset at me whenever we met.

Holly, who was sitting at the table with Caroline, stood to give me a hug. "Caroline was at the meeting. We're just hanging out."

As Holly sat down again, Caroline reached out and touched her arm. "I need to get going," she said. "I'll see you Sunday and we'll do some gardening." She stood and picked up her daypack.

"Wait," Holly said. "Before you go, tell Jeff about the national anthem."

Caroline brightened and sat back in her chair. "When I was on the harvest brigade," she said, "we went out one night to an encampment of harvest workers and soldiers, mostly Nicaraguans, but also some Salvadorans. We were singing around the campfire for hours. Late that night, the Nicaraguans sang their national song, 'Nicaragua Nicaraguita,' which makes me cry whenever I hear it. Then the Salvadorans sang theirs, which seemed sort of odd to me. I mean, here's people who are in a civil war with their government, and they're singing their national anthem? It's certainly a different relation to their country than we have."

She shook her head slowly. "Then they asked us, the Americanos, to sing our national anthem. So we're thinking, sing the 'Star-Spangled Banner'? No way. We talked it over, and what we decided to sing was, 'This Land is Your Land.'"

"Woody Guthrie," I said in a hushed voice. I thought how little music I was playing lately, and felt sad. "Good choice."

She smiled. "Yeah, we thought so." Caroline radiated a confidence that I had never seen in her before. What a difference her trip had made. And what a difference from anyone else around LAG these days.

She hugged Holly goodbye, then turned to me. We looked at each other awkwardly, then ventured a cautious hug. "Nice to see you," I said.

"Yeah, it was nice," she said, waving to us as she stepped out the door.

Holly stood there for a moment watching her go. Then she shut the door. "How was production?" she asked.

"Oh, we made some headway," I said, trying to remember what had actually gotten done. "I got in an argument with Claudia about the Crisis meetings. It was kind of ironic. I wound up defending them." Holly looked at me with tired eyes. She probably didn't want to hear about an argument over a meeting that she'd skipped in the first place. "How was your peace camp meeting?" I asked.

Her eyes seemed even more tired. "Not so good. The land we thought we could use in the Fall is being sold."

"That's too bad," I said. "Any other leads?"

"Not so far." She poured herself a bowl of soup. "Want some?"

"Yeah, sure," I said.

She poured me a bowl. "Did you hear about Jenny?" she asked as we sat down.

I stirred my soup. "I heard she's been sick."

"She had a miscarriage," Holly said. "She asked me to tell you."

My spoon hovered over the bowl. "Really? How sad for her."

"Yeah. I think she had mixed feelings about being pregnant. But it's really upsetting for her. She says it's hard to care about anything else."

I set my spoon down. No wonder Jenny had avoided the office all week. I pictured her holding a baby with deep brown eyes and wavy hair. "That's so sad for her."

"Yeah, I think she realized how much she wants kids."

"It's amazing," I said. "How is it that people ever decide to have children? I mean, with the world in such lousy shape, Reagan threatening to blow us all to kingdom come, the environment falling apart... It's incredible that anyone dares to do it."

"I can't imagine it," Holly said. Her attention seemed to drift away again.

"What are you thinking about?" I asked.

"Oh, something Sara said about defending women's clinics. She was at newspaper production this afternoon. She wants me to go camping with her and some friends from the Berkeley Women's Health Collective."

"That sounds great," I said. "Think you'll do it before the Convention?"

"If Sara has time. I'd like to go the weekend before Solstice and do a ritual." She finished her soup and went to rinse her dish. I had still barely touched mine, and made an effort to eat some of it. Holly came back into the living room drying her hands, still pensive. "I'm going to go to bed and read," she said. "Do you feel like coming with me?"

My feet were itching for a walk, but I knew I should stay and spend the time together. I pulled out a book on music history and followed her into the bedroom. "How about if I put on Palestrina?" I searched for my favorite Renaissance tape.

Holly picked up a book called *The Spiral Dance* and settled into bed. "It's a handbook for doing rituals," she said, then looked at me curiously. "Would you do a ritual with me?"

"Now?"

"No, but sometime soon. I was thinking of doing a spell for new beginnings."

"Sure, I'll do that." Maybe it was just what Holly and I needed. A fresh start. Maybe the problem was that I was expecting us to recapture our old bond around LAG, which seemed less and less likely. What if we discovered other connections, new ways to weave our lives together?

I looked at her. She set down her book and gazed at me with the same steady love I had seen for almost two years. Through all the tumult, that had never wavered. But beyond the love, her eyes held no hint of wanting or expecting anything from me.

Why should that be a surprise? How long since I'd been totally present for her? Could she count on me? I lay back on the bed, and a sadness came over me. I needed to make a decision. Now. Because if I didn't commit to rebuilding our relationship, time was eroding it fast. I needed to let her know how I felt.

She was lying on her back. I rolled onto my side and curled against her. The book rested on her chest. Her eyes were closed, and a smile graced her lips. I closed my eyes and nuzzled into the curve of her neck, kissing her gently. "You mean so much to me, Holly," I whispered. I held my breath for her response. But she was already asleep.

Tuesday, June 12, 1984

Everything has to be changed — the way of thinking, the way of governing, the whole way of life, the family, how to go about one's work — the whole technical/economic complex — yes, how we laugh, love, and cry, and even how we dream — all this has to change.

— Gabriele Dietze, Overcoming Speechlessness: Texts from the Women's Movement

KARINA AND I left the office at six, giving us ample time for the trip over to the Haight. I was glad for the time with her. But I couldn't have said what I wanted from her. After the turmoil of my time with Angie, starting something with Karina was the last thing I needed. And face it, we were an unlikely pair. Yet something always drew me back to daydreaming about Karina. A fantasy of the ultimate fusion of political and sexual passion. A promise of standing in the eye of the hurricane.

As we walked from the office to BART, she told me about a clandestine action she and Jenny and some other women were planning for Concord. The idea was to slip onto the weapons depot at night, spraypaint disarmament messages, then get back off the base by dawn.

Part of me laughed, but another part wanted to grab her by the shoulders and yell, "Don't be crazy! Sneaking around on a weapons depot at night? Ever heard of trigger-happy guards?"

But I knew that cautionary pleadings would just divide us and make her even more determined to defy every authority. I made a mental note to take it up with Jenny. Dissuade the others, and surely Karina wouldn't do it alone.

We found a couple of seats at the back of the BART car, side by side. She sat on the inside and curled into the corner, facing me. Was she trying to keep a distance?

Right away she pulled out an avocado sandwich. "Want some?"

I declined. "Just knowing that it's against the rules would make me too uptight to really enjoy it," I said. "I'd feel like I had to hide it."

Karina took a bite and brushed the crumbs off her jacket. "It's good for your spirit to break laws like this, things that don't hurt anyone," she said. "Doing it on little issues makes it easier to stand up on big ones. People are so intimidated by authority."

I nodded silently. I thought about how often I broke the law by smoking weed. But I did it surreptitiously. No way did I want to get caught.

"So, how are things with Sara?" I asked as the train got rolling. I wondered how open Karina would be.

"Okay, I guess," she said, casting her eyes down. "I was hoping we'd keep living together, but she doesn't want that. So I'm going to sublet over at Urban Stonehenge for a while."

"That's convenient that they had a room."

"Well, it's really just a corner in the basement," she said. "They'll always make space for one more person."

"Do you think you'll get back together?" I persisted.

"It's up to Sara," Karina said sadly. "I'd like to, but I'm always going to have other lovers." She looked up at me. "What about you and Holly?" she asked. "How are you doing?"

Bound Together, an anarchist collective bookstore on Haight Street, was the site of planning meetings for the War Chest Tours and other actions.

"Pretty good," I said. Truth was, Holly and I were getting along fine, and could probably keep going indefinitely. But it had been two weeks since we made love, and neither of us seemed to mind. "I guess we're still sorting it out since Angie left."

Karina arched her brows at the mention of Angie. "Is Angie coming back?"

"Maybe to visit. We talked on the phone last week. She's getting pretty settled up in Portland."

"Do you miss her?"

I looked into Karina's eyes. I'd never noticed how steely-gray they were. "Well, yeah," I said. "It's hard not to miss Angie. But we'd about run our course, I guess. Something had to change."

Karina nodded and looked out the window as the train came above-ground amid the warehouses of West Oakland. We rode silently for a minute, but I didn't want to waste the opportunity to talk with Karina. It didn't happen every day.

"Kind of sad that Change of Heart isn't meeting anymore," I said. "Have you thought about calling a cluster meeting about the Convention actions?"

She turned to me. "Not really. I miss the cluster. But lately, whatever I want to do, everyone thinks it's too radical, or it's going to get us into too much trouble."

I looked at her expectantly. "What is it you really want?"

Her eyes drifted away again, but as the train went down into the transbay tube, she leaned closer. "I'm tired of symbolic actions. I want to put a monkey wrench into the gears of the system." She looked at me as if searching for a sign that I already intuited her deepest desire. "Sometimes I think about forming an affinity group and going back to Vandenberg, going on the base at night, getting right up to the MX command building, and cutting a bunch of wires to short-circuit the computers."

She had a dreamy look. I wished I could say, Me, too. Let's do it! But a five-year jail sentence sort of defeated the purpose of getting close to Karina in the first place. "Sounds like a Plowshares action," I said, "where they break into weapons plants and hammer on missiles."

She nodded, losing some of her élan. "I met with some people from Jonah House, the Plowshares support group on the east coast, when they were out here on a speaking tour last month. It's different, as far as their being heavy into the religious thing. But I learned a lot about the support system you need for that kind of action."

I looked at her carefully. "Would you plan to turn yourself in, or try to get away?"

The mural on the side of Bound Together depicts a visionary gathering of anarchist writers.

"That's something we'd have to figure out," she said. "It's just an idea, anyway."

The train pulled into San Francisco. We made our way to street level and transferred to a Haight Street bus. Bound Together bookstore, where the meeting was being held, was on upper Haight near Ashbury, right in the heart of the old hippie district. "When I moved to the Bay Area," I told Karina, "I came over to the Haight the very first weekend and went to the old Shady Grove. I heard that's where the Grateful Dead got their start. Then later I was in a band that actually had a couple of gigs there. I thought I'd hit the big time."

"Hey," Karina said, "did Sara talk to you? She said they were going to ask you to sing at the LAG demo at the Convention."

"Wow, I'm really out of practice," I said. "That would be like hitting the big time, singing at a protest in front of the Democratic National Convention."

I arrived at the meeting ready to join the grand conspiratorial protest planning group. But my euphoria dimmed as we entered the bookstore and I saw a roomful of strangers. Karina waltzed off to say hi to someone else. Mort was coming to the meeting to help make a presentation about People's Convention. But he wasn't there yet. Although I recognized some of the faces, no one greeted me.

The bookstore provided some distraction. A stack of postcards on the checkout desk reproduced the mural on the side of the building, which portrayed a couple of dozen famous anarchists accompanied by the caption: "History remembers two kinds of people — those who murder and those who fight back."

The store itself was anything but anarchic. Scuffed floors gave ample space between the neatly arranged shelves, each labeled by subject: Labor History, Women's Issues, Collectives, Latin America....

Turning to the magazine rack, I discovered a small cache of Direct Action. I smiled to myself, and wondered if Sid, who volunteered at the store, had brought them over.

People were gradually making their way into the back room for the meeting. It was a motley bunch — VAC-style anti-nukers. Bike messengers. A few more intellectual-looking types who I figured were part of the Bound Together collective. Several young punks, and one guy with a Mohawk who looked to be in his forties. A couple of staffers from *It's About Times*, the Abalone Alliance paper.

In front of me, Ariel from Urban Stonehenge checked in with Moonstone, who had just arrived with a couple of other Deadheads. Raoul was talking with Sid and some of the peace-punks from the financial district action. Off to one side, Karina gave Sara a welcoming hug. Sara's face mingled desire and sadness.

Jenny was studiously writing out the agenda on a piece of butcher paper. Her hair was freed from its usual bun, and frizzed down across her face. It was the first time I had seen her since her miscarriage. She looked up at me with a harried expression, as if she expected me to start lobbying her for something.

"Can I give you a hand?" I asked.

"Sure," she said, relaxing slightly. "Help me hang this agenda on the wall." As we pressed the tape into place, I was distracted by a rustling at the entrance. The punks stepped aside, and in strode a coiled bundle of tension. "It's Flint," Jenny said. A worried look crossed her face.

Flint removed his beret and shook his Ché Guevara hair. He scanned the room with the hardest pair of eyes I had ever seen outside of Santa Rita jail.

"Is he a problem?" I asked her quietly.

"No, no," she said hurriedly. "I just didn't expect him." Flint nodded to her from across the room, then turned to engage Raoul, who leaned back and eyed Flint warily.

"We've met him at some squatters' meetings," Jenny told me. "He's pretty famous in that crowd. He got charged with torching a police motorcycle at a riot a few years ago, and barely got off with a split jury."

"Looks like he hasn't relaxed since," I said, eyeing Flint as he spoke intently to Raoul. "Do you think he really burned the cycle?"

"I've never heard him say so, but everyone assumes he did," Jenny said.

I shook my head slowly. "That's a little different style of protesting."

As we took seats, Mort came in. He stood awkwardly in the doorway, his shirttail half out. I stood to greet him and pulled a folding chair up next to mine. He muttered something I didn't catch and didn't especially want to. I looked away and smiled to myself. Mort's fidgety discomfort actually helped me unwind. I know some of these people, I thought. I'm not totally out of place.

Jenny and Ariel were facilitating the meeting. Once everyone got seated in a ragged circle, Jenny welcomed us. I was struck by her humored tone as she announced the opening go-round. "Let's have each person say their name, what group they're from if any, and their favorite animal noise. Ariel will start."

There was a good deal of squirming as Ariel set the tone by imitating a crow's cawing. Most people entered into the game, although a few, including Flint and Mort, abstained. A tropical bird-whistle got a round of applause. I chimed in with a wolf-howl. But the real crowd-pleaser was Karina, who sucked in her cheeks and puckered her lips like a fish. "Sorry, goldfish don't make any sound," she said.

As the last "mooooo" faded, Ariel held up a sheaf of papers. "The main thing we want to do tonight is hear all the events around the Convention and make sure that the times aren't conflicting," she said. "Here's what we have on the agenda so far: the War Chest Tours, the Moral Majority demo, Stop the Sweep, the Bohemian Grove, Vote Peace, the LAG demo, and Rock Against Reagan. Plus, we need to go over legal support and jail organizing."

"It's too much," Karina said. "Do we have to talk about Vote Peace?"

"It's only an announcement," someone told her.

I raised my hand tentatively. "Is this the time to add things to the agenda? Mort and I want to announce the People's Convention plans." I looked around the room, trying to gauge whether there was any hostility to the topic, but I couldn't tell.

"Alright, then," Jenny said. "The idea is to have a short report on each item, and make sure things aren't scheduled at the same time. Then we'll form work groups around the ones that people want to focus on. Is that okay?"

"No, it's not," Flint said in a metallic voice. "What do we even need a meeting for if everything is already decided?"

"It's not decided," Jenny said quickly. "Just the dates are set."

"It sounds like everything is already in place," Flint said.

Raoul shuffled in his seat. "It's a month before the Convention. People have been making plans all Spring. The whole point of this meeting is to get input from the wider community, so we're not calling all the shots."

"That's noble of you," Flint answered coldly. "I didn't come here to rubber-stamp your pre-fab proposals. Nothing we have done in the past ten years is worth preserving. We have to tear down every existing project, every existing group. We have to get back to absolute zero."

Raoul looked like he'd heard the line before. He squinted. "You can talk about ground zero," he said. "But what's the point in even being here if we aren't going to plan anything for the Convention?"

Seeing Raoul take a dose of his own ultra-radical medicine gave me a secret kick. But when I thought about giving the People's Convention report with Flint glaring at me, I felt like a Boy Scout who had strayed into a Green Beret briefing.

Ariel suggested that Flint convene a group to discuss his ideas when the meeting broke into small groups. He acquiesced with a flip of his hand, and the meeting lurched forward.

It was the first time I had heard about some of the demos. The Moral Majority, a fundamentalist Christian group crusading against Gays, atheists, communists, and liberals, was holding their bash the week before the Democrats. A loose coalition of lefty groups had called a demonstration, which I figured would be the usual march-in-a-circle-and-chant variety.

"Stop the Sweep" was more promising. A network of groups was denouncing Mayor Feinstein's plans to "clean up the City" by jailing or harassing street people, prostitutes, punks, and anyone else who didn't fit the corporate mold. "Maybe we'll have sit-ins on the sidewalks, or in the doorway of Macy's," said a woman with short red hair. "The more of us that are out in the street, the less the cops can target their usual victims."

"Rock Against Reagan" was a punk concert on the afternoon of the final War Chest Tour. The Dead Kennedys and MDC were heading a lineup of local hardcore bands. "They're doing the same show in Houston for the Republican Convention in August," Sid reported.

"Vote Peace" was a rally sponsored by the same coalition of peace groups that had done the October Euromissiles demo, minus LAG. Actually, LAG had endorsed the rally, but no one was going to meetings. And no one from the coalition was at our meeting. "It's mainly speeches and folk music," Sara said. "They're calling on the Democrats to stand up to Reagan and cut military spending."

"Why not call on the Democrats to dance naked in the streets?" Moonstone put in. "You'd have about as much luck."

After Vote Peace, anything would sound lively, so I raised my hand and asked to announce the People's Convention events. "The idea is to have progressive groups get together the weekend before the Democratic Convention and draft a People's Platform," I said, looking out at a roomful of blank faces. In fairness, Moonstone, Sara, and a few others at least paid attention. I cut to the climax. "Then on Monday, we're going to march down Market Street to Moscone Center and present our demands to the Democrats. There's a farmer's group that's going to drive tractors right into San Francisco to lead the parade."

"Wait," Sid said, "Monday is the first War Chest Tour."

"That's at noon," I said. "Ours is at three o'clock. People could come from the War Chest Tour to our march. We timed it that way."

Mort cleared his throat. "The People's Convention is a diverse group," he said in a remarkably level voice. "The march will probably be the most multicultural event of the whole week."

"So is there anything else?" Jenny asked, tapping her fingers.

I looked at her with frustration. Can't you give us some support?

But Mort seemed not to take offense. "People here should turn out for the march. It's a chance to connect with communities of color, which might be smart for this group."

His dig hit home for at least some of the people there. Sara was nodding, and Raoul seemed to be listening carefully. I settled back in my chair as the reports continued, sensing that we'd gone up a notch in their estimation.

That left only the War Chest Tours and the LAG demo on the agenda. The Tours didn't require much explaining, since practically everyone in the room was already involved. Jenny, sitting on the edge of her chair and speaking quickly, outlined plans for a corporate tour each day of the Convention.

As she talked about affinity group actions, Flint got increasingly agitated. He raised his hand sharply. When Jenny seemed to ignore him, he glowered at her and finally interrupted.

"What's the real threat here," he said. "That traffic gets backed up? You're playing right into their hands. You cause a little disturbance, they throw you in jail for a few days, and then they say, 'Look, we live in a democracy, where people aren't executed for dissenting.' They can totally co-opt your protests. The only threat to the system is the possibility that things might explode."

Raoul's mouth hung open as he groped for words. "Any time you disrupt business as usual, it sends ripples through the whole system. And anyway, we're not trying to control the War Chest Tours. There's no permits, and no monitors. It'll be whatever people make it."

Karina jumped in as he finished. "The point is, how much can we disrupt? They think we're going to focus on the Convention itself. Forget that. I'm sick of protests where we know we're going to get arrested or beat up, and we're supposed to sit and take it. We should keep moving, and not let them arrest us without a fight."

Without a fight? Was she serious? Or was she trying to out-radical Flint? I studied her face. She looked pleased at the murmuring her comment had set off. And why not? If the point was to stir things up, why settle for half-measures? But knowing the cops' response at the Kissinger demo, it wouldn't take much before they clamped down. Escalating our tactics would escalate our arrest.

Sid raised his hand. "The War Chest Tours are going to be mobile," he said with uncharacteristic reserve. "We aren't planning to sit around and get busted. If we keep moving, the cops can't deal. They have to wait for orders to move, and we'll be gone."

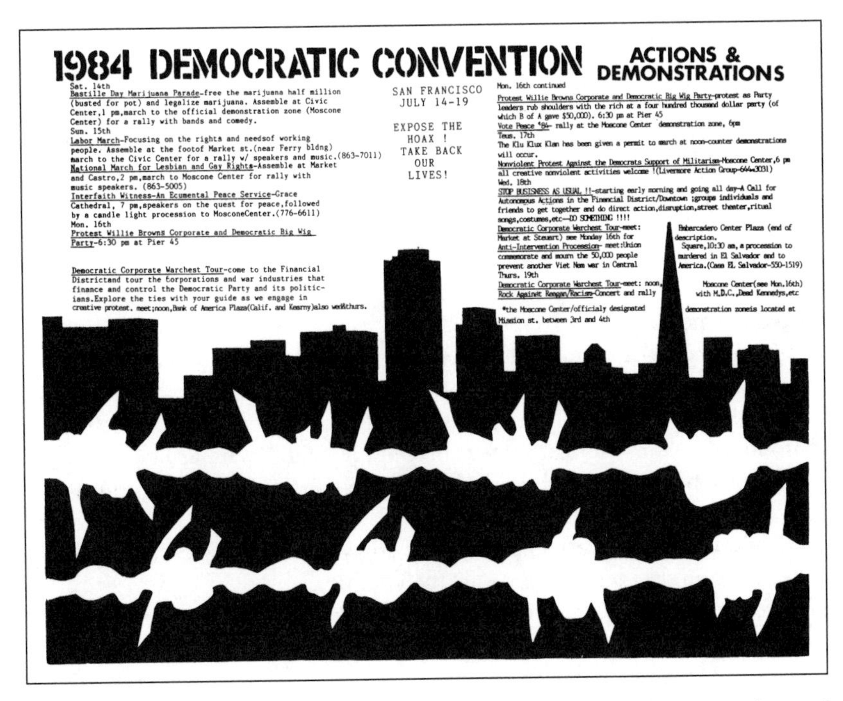

Groups planning direct actions around the Democratic Convention met to share plans and coordinate calendars for the week of protests.

"It's not just about moving," Karina answered. "A parade moves. It's about disrupting. Take that away, and you're nothing."

Flint nodded sharply. He pulled his beret off. "Here's what it comes down to," he said. "If you want to get your message out, get over your hang-ups about property. A few broken windows speak louder than a hundred bullhorns."

Sara's jaw dropped. She slowly turned to face Flint. "I don't think the Democrats care one bit whether windows get broken."

Flint leveled his eyes at her. "No, but local business does, and they'll raise hell at City Hall. It flips them out. They're afraid once it starts, where will it end?"

Jenny glanced at Raoul, then spoke carefully. "As facilitator," she said, "I'm wondering if we really need to go into this?"

"Yes, we do," Flint snapped. "If I'm going to stick my neck out, I want to know where we stand. Are we prepared to mix it up with the cops, or is this just one more pacifist anti-nuke protest?"

My teeth clenched, but I didn't see what to say.

Raoul looked at Flint. Sweat glistened on his brow. "There's a lot of gradations between blockading at Livermore and trashing the City," he said. "Look, if you want to form a planning group when we split up, you're welcome to. Can we move on?"

Flint tossed his beret in the air and let it drop at his feet. I took a breath. What was he getting at? Was he seriously advocating riots, or was he just trying to stir the meeting up?

I surveyed the circle. Not much eye contact. Next to me, Mort folded his arms across his chest and twisted his goatee, looking torn between jumping into the fray and throwing his hands up in disgust. Raoul glared at Flint, resentment playing over his face. Karina seemed lost in her daydreams, while Sara looked at her longingly. Sid slapped his knee, as if he'd belatedly figured out the perfect thing to say. Jenny and Ariel gave each other a relieved look and moved the meeting along.

For most of the room, the final report on the LAG demo was anticlimactic, but I was glad for the update. Sara took a breath and looked down at her notes, then filled us in on the rally in the official "free speech area" in front of the Convention. "Some people in LAG didn't want any CD," she said, "so it'll be speakers and music focusing on the corporate connections of the Democrats."

I nodded. If LAG wasn't getting on board with the War Chest Tours, this at least put us on the map. Better a rally than nothing.

Sara wrapped up her report. "We're hoping a few thousand people will show up. It's a way to communicate the War Chest Tours' message in a venue that a lot of people will find safer."

Sid leaned forward in his chair. Flint's assault seemed forgotten, and he was back on the offensive. "Are you getting a permit?"

"Yeah," Sara admitted. "The only way to get anywhere near the Convention is to use the free speech area."

Jacey, who had just arrived at the meeting and was standing in the doorway, didn't waste any time offering his opinion. "I heard Utah Phillips say that free speech isn't something you get a permit for. It's something you do. And if the state tries to stop you, you find out just how free you're willing to be."

Sara seemed to bristle. "Right now," she said in a clipped voice, "the War Chest Tours are completely isolated from the rest of the movement. We're organizing a rally to try to bridge that gap. If you don't want to be part of it, you're welcome to stay home."

Next to me, Mort humphed in agreement. But his face clouded as Karina interjected: "This isn't Vote Peace. We're not going to have a bunch of monitors herding people around. If people at the LAG rally want to go on a march, we're not going to stop them."

So that was the plan. No wonder Karina was working on a "legal" rally. Not a bad strategy. But with people like Hank and Melissa already upset that LAG was doing *any* demo, I could picture how this latest twist was going to play out at the next Coordinating Council meeting.

I glanced sideways at Mort to catch his response, but he stared off into space as if Karina's words meant nothing to him.

Ariel steered the report to a conclusion. The rest of the evening was set aside for focus groups. Mort and I scratched People's Convention from the list, figuring no one would come to that group. Sara took the LAG demo off. "We're meeting Thursday night in Berkeley, for anyone who wants to help plan it," she said.

Most people opted to talk about the War Chest Tours. But a small cadre joined Flint for his "ground zero" group: "This is for people who are serious about challenging every existing structure," he said as the group retreated to a corner. I was tempted to join Flint's group, just to see what he had in mind. I wondered if he was a loner, or the tip of an iceberg.

As I wavered, though, Jenny gestured to an empty seat in the War Chest circle. It had been a while since she'd invited me to do anything, and I figured it was smart to accept.

The group was too large to have a real discussion. Various ideas bounced around for forty-five minutes, everything from likely targets to the latest refinements on die-in tactics. But nothing really jelled, and I was glad when the meeting drew to a close.

Mort wanted to take off, but I had a few people I wanted to check-in with. I complimented Jenny on facilitating a tough meeting, and she seemed pleased. "Whose idea was the animal-sounds intro?" I asked.

"Oh, that was mine," she said. "I figured it would flush out the infiltrators right away."

Sara joined us. "Do you really think there were infiltrators?" she said.

"For some folks' sakes, I hope not," I said, eyeing Flint, who was arguing with Jacey.

"Well, it's a compliment if the government thinks we're *worth* infiltrating," Sara said.

Just beyond Sara, Flint turned away from Jacey. I hadn't planned on talking to him, but on the spur of the moment, I stepped in front of him. "Why don't you write something for LAG's paper, Direct Action," I said quickly. "We're carrying debates about the Convention protests."

His eyes narrowed. "What's the point in writing for pacifists?"

"LAG isn't just pacifists," I rejoined. "And besides, the paper circulates wider than LAG."

His expression didn't change, but he nodded crisply. "I'll think about it."

As he walked away, Karina came past. I reached out and caught her hand. She stopped and hugged me. "It was really nice talking to you on the ride over," she said.

I looked into her eyes as we parted. "See you soon," I said, not quite sure what I intended.

I would have liked to talk with Raoul, to see his reaction to the meeting. It was the first time I'd ever seen him outflanked, and it gave me some perspective on his views. He, Sid, Jenny, and Jacey were clustered off to one side, deep in conversation. I hesitated for a moment, wondering whether it was okay to join them. But Mort was jangling his keys, and I took the hint and followed him out the door.

As we headed out to his car, I wanted to tell Mort about recruiting Flint to write for Direct Action. To me, having Flint write would confirm us as "the" radical newspaper, the voice of dissent in the San Francisco Bay Area. That was a title worth pursuing.

But I knew better than to say that to Mort. He'd dismiss it and lecture me about the lack of analysis and strategic thinking in the paper. Fair enough. Sara had been saying the same thing at our last meeting: we needed more depth. I was open to that. But wouldn't it be nice if once in a while Mort were equally open to my vision?

He stopped in front of a strange vehicle and fumbled with his keys.

"Oh yeah, you got a new car, didn't you?"

"Yeah. As much time as I spend commuting out to Concord every day, I needed something more dependable," he said. He grabbed a stack of papers from the passenger's seat and threw them into the back, which was already a recycling bin of Direct Actions, flyers, and half-finished crossword puzzles.

"Looks like you're starting the mobile LAG archives back there," I joked as we got in.

"I'm going to clean it out this weekend," he said with no resolve. He flipped on the sound system and stuck in a John Coltrane tape.

"So, what did you think?" I asked as we headed out of the Haight.

"About what I expected," he said. "A bunch of self-involved anarchists without a clue as to the larger context."

A rush of frustration welled up inside me. Here are people actually trying to do something, and all they get from Mort is sarcasm. Why even bother talking about it with him?

At least he was at the meeting, I reminded myself. That was a lot more than the rest of LAG's old guard.

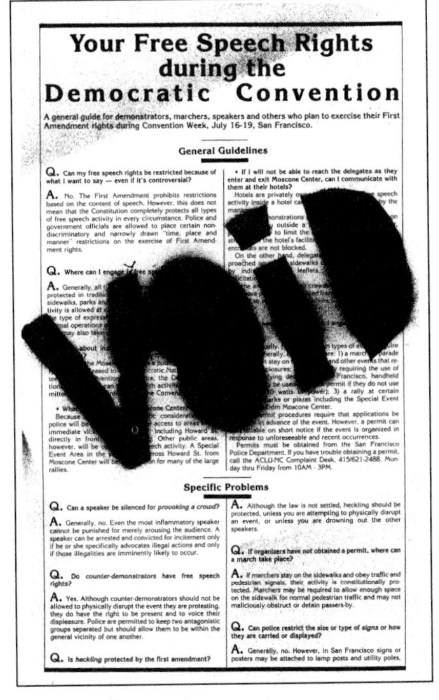

Your Free Speech Rights during the Democratic Convention

A general guide for demonstrators, marchers, speakers and others who plan to exercise their First Amendment rights during Convention Week, July 16-19, San Francisco.

General Guidelines

Q. Can my free speech rights be restricted because of what I want to say — even if it's controversial?

A. No. The First Amendment prohibits restrictions based on the content of speech. However, this does not mean that the Constitution completely protects all types of free speech activity in every circumstance. Police and government officials are allowed to place certain non-discriminatory and narrowly drawn "time, place and manner" restrictions on the exercise of First Amendment rights.

Q. Where can I engage [illegible]

A. Generally, all [illegible] protected in tradi[illegible] sidewalks, parks an[illegible] tivity is allowed at [illegible] type of express[illegible] mal operations [illegible] may also take [illegible]

[illegible] about ins[illegible]

[illegible] Because [illegible] c considerat[illegible] police will be [illegible] access to areas [illegible] immediate vic[illegible] including Howard St. directly in front [illegible] Other public areas, however, will be o[illegible]ech activity. A Special Event Area in the [illegible]ross Howard St. from Moscone Center will be [illegible]n for many of the large rallies.

• If I will not be able to reach the delegates as they enter and exit Moscone Center, can I communicate with them at their hotels?

Hotels are privately o[illegible] speech activity inside a hotel ca[illegible] by the mana[illegible]

[illegible]onstrations [illegible] on [illegible] outside a [illegible] to limit the [illegible] the hotel's faciliti[illegible] entr[illegible]es are not blocked.

On the other hand, delega[illegible] proached [illegible] sidewalks [illegible] by indi[illegible] leaflets [illegible]

[illegible]n types of e[illegible]uire [illegible]erally, [illegible]re: 1) a march [illegible] parade [illegible] stay on [illegible] and other events that require [illegible]closures; [illegible] requiring the use of [illegible] Francisco, handheld [illegible] be used [illegible] permit if they do not use [illegible]0 watts [illegible]power); 3) a rally at certain [illegible]arks or plazas including the Special Event [illegible] Moscone Center.

[illegible]mit procedures require that applications be [illegible] in advance of the event. However, a permit can [illegible]ailable on short notice if the event is organized in response to unforeseeable and recent occurrences.

Permits must be obtained from the San Francisco Police Department. If you have trouble obtaining a permit, call the ACLU-NC Complaint Desk, 415/621-2488, Monday thru Friday from 10AM - 3PM.

Specific Problems

Q. Can a speaker be silenced for *provoking a crowd*?

A. Generally, no. Even the most inflammatory speaker cannot be punished for merely arousing the audience. A speaker can be arrested and convicted for incitement only if he or she specifically advocates illegal actions and only if those illegalities are imminently likely to occur.

Q. Do *counter-demonstrators* have free speech rights?

A. Yes. Although counter-demonstrators should not be allowed to physically disrupt the event they are protesting, they do have the right to be present and to voice their displeasure. Police are permitted to keep two antagonistic groups separated but should allow them to be within the general vicinity of one another.

Q. Is *heckling* protected by the first amendment?

A. Although the law is not settled, heckling should be protected, unless you are attempting to physically disrupt an event, or unless you are drowning out the other speakers.

Q. If organizers have not obtained a permit, where can a *march* take place?

A. If marchers stay on the sidewalks and obey traffic and pedestrian signals, their activity is constitutionally protected. Marchers may be required to allow enough space on the sidewalk for normal pedestrian traffic and may not maliciously obstruct or detain passers-by.

Q. Can police restrict the size or type of *signs* or how they are carried or displayed?

A. Generally, no. However, in San Francisco signs or posters may be attached to lamp posts and utility poles.

The original leaflet was produced by the National Lawyers' Guild and widely circulated before the Democratic Convention. With a touch of spraypaint, it became a great phonepole flyer.

"Like it or not, they're practically the only people protesting the Democrats," I said.

"Protesting," he said disparagingly. "I don't think anyone in that room except maybe Sara sees what a place of privilege their whole conception of protest comes from. Who besides White middle-class people could get away with what they're talking about? What if a bunch of Black teenagers marched through the City disrupting traffic? They'd be shot."

I nodded, but he didn't seem to notice. His eyes were fixed on the road. We headed onto the Bay Bridge. "And this whole thing of not having any monitors at the LAG protest. Who are they kidding? LAG always has monitors. A work group can't just make its own rules. They're getting more and more marginalized. No wonder our protests are shrinking. If Karina has her way, pretty soon she'll be protesting alone."

"At least she's doing something," I said tersely.

"But who is she appealing to? Can you honestly see most LAG blockaders coming to the War Chest Tours?"

"If they don't, other people will," I answered, rolling down my window to get some fresh air. "More and more people are fed up with the system."

He arched his head back. "Being 'fed up' is not much of a

recommendation. Social change isn't going to come from a bunch of White middle-class dropouts. It's going to come from organizing within materially-oppressed groups. You have to study the class base, the relationship to the social and economic system. Look at the most successful movements of the past century: Labor and Civil Rights. For unions, they were confronting economic exploitation, and how that translated into social oppression. For Black people, it's racial oppression turning them into a permanent economic underclass. It wasn't a matter of 'disaffection.' It wasn't a choice. They were stuck in those relationships. A factory worker can't say, 'I think I'll join management now.' A Black person can't say, 'I've changed my mind, I think I'll be White now.' Their only hope is collective action."

Mort paused to mutter about a slow driver ahead of us on the bridge. Swinging a couple of lanes over, he settled into the faster flow and resumed his monologue. "Marginals — what solidarity do they have? It's a phase people pass through. Look at radicals from the Sixties. Sure, they may still hold progressive views. But how many are activists? In the short run, you might mobilize these people around a particular issue, like Vietnam or nuclear weapons. But to build a movement, you need a more cohesive base."

Who appointed you the expert on movement building, I thought. Not that I could disagree with his ideas. But why did it always come back to dumping on LAG? "So you're just writing us off," I said.

"No. But if we're serious about changing society, we have to be allies to oppressed groups, not marginal purists on our own crusade. Allies are critical to radical movements. Black liberation wouldn't have gotten so far without White allies. But making allies means reaching out to middle America, not focusing on the fringes."

As we came off the freeway into West Berkeley, I looked out the window at the shadowy warehouses. I thought about the people organizing the War Chest Tours and the LAG demo, how passionately they fought for their right to protest. "Those are the only people that aren't sitting on their asses while the Democrats sell us out," I said. "Sometimes it takes a small group doing something radical to spur the larger group to act. What seems marginal today might inspire the mainstream tomorrow."

"That's not what was going on tonight," he said. "What I heard wasn't radical. It wasn't even just stupid. It was dangerous."

"I'm glad you can tell the difference," I said with a sarcasm that Mort seemed to miss.

"Sure. Stupid is when you get yourself hurt. Dangerous is when you get other people hurt."

Clever, I thought. Reduce the whole meeting to one clever phrase. What was the point in arguing? "Why don't you drop me up here at the corner," I said, trying not to let on how upset I was.

"Are you sure? I'll drive you home."

"No, that's okay. I could use the walk," I said. He pulled to the curb, and I climbed out of the car.

He leaned over. "See you at pinball Friday night?"

"Not this week. Thanks for the ride." I shut the door and watched as he drove off. Someone I'd worked with so closely over the past two years. But now we were heading in totally different directions. Would I even see Mort at any of the upcoming protests? If not, what was the point in just "hanging out?" It felt like the end of an era. I wondered if we'd even know each other in a year.

THE MOON, almost full, shone over my shoulder as I trekked the half-dozen blocks home. It felt good to be outside. Enough of cars and buses and trains. Enough of offices and stuffy meeting rooms. Maybe I could just let it all go. Stop in and say hi to Holly, then go out for a long walk.

Holly had been at a peace camp meeting, and when I greeted her, she seemed more animated than usual. Maybe they found land for the Fall, I thought.

"Can I talk to you about something?" she asked.

"Sure," I said, glad to hear the sparkle in her voice.

She sat down on the rolled-up futon in the living room, and I joined her. I didn't have to wait long to find out what was up. "I think I want to sleep with Norm," she said.

My breath caught in my throat. Was this why Holly's attention seemed unfocused when we were together lately? I tried to read her eyes, but they were inscrutable. Well, not quite —I didn't detect any doubt. "Yeah?" I finally said.

"Yeah. He asked me a couple of months ago, but I wasn't ready then. I don't know if it will be something we want to do regularly, or just once or twice. But I really like him, and it feels right."

Numbness washed through me, and I had trouble telling what I felt. In a way I was relieved, as if this retroactively justified my having slept with Angie. But it was hard to see Holly so buoyant for the first time in ages — over someone else.

Yet what could I say for myself? Did I light up when I saw her? My mind drifted off to my ride with Karina earlier that evening. Maybe this was all for the best.

Norm had other lovers, so it was probably just a fling. Maybe Holly and I needed this, to take the pressure off our relationship. We could be roommates and primary partners, but have other lovers from time to time.

I looked at Holly again, and realized she was waiting for some kind of response. The numbness swept through me again. "Uh, sure," I said. "I'm not sure what to say. I mean, it's okay with me..."

"I wasn't asking if it was okay," she said plainly. "But if you want to talk about it, if you have feelings you want to share, I'll listen."

I looked away. If I acted too nonchalant, it would seem like I didn't care about her. "It's kind of hard to hear," I said after a moment. "It's great, for you. But it's hard to see you so excited over someone else."

"Yeah, I know that feeling." She nodded slowly and looked into my eyes. "I care about you so much, Jeff. I really want us to be together. That's not what this is about."

I leaned over and we hugged. I closed my eyes and remembered our first hug, in the park the day before the Livermore blockade. I thought of our first night together, and about how jealous I was over Frank, her old lover. I'd probably be jealous with Norm, too.

But then, Holly and me alone didn't seem like a solution, either. I looked into her eyes. "You mean so much to me, Holly," I said. "I want to be happy for you. It's just hard to hear, that's all."

She took my hand in hers and kissed it. "I'm going to bed. Will you come with me?"

I followed her to the bedroom and put on a tape of Andean music that she had recently bought. I slipped off my shorts and got under the sheets with her. We lay down side by side, holding hands, just breathing and listening to the music. I matched her slow, steady breathing. But I couldn't shake the tension in my heart. Things were changing too fast. I'd already lost Angie to Portland. LAG was threatening to implode under the pressure of the Convention. And now Holly?

Should I say something? Do something? I wanted time to stand still. No one move, and let me think this through.

Right. As if thinking were going to solve the problem. It's not about thought. It's in the heart. Listen to your heart.

But what my heart was saying wasn't exactly clear. I'd be daydreaming of Angie, or Karina... And then I'd get a flash of Holly moving out, and tears would well up in my eyes. Tears of sadness for an inevitable parting? Or tears of relief that we were still together, that it wasn't too late?

Holly yawned and rolled over toward me. "I love you, Jeff," she said sleepily. "Thanks for being understanding."

I wasn't sure that "understanding" quite captured my mood. But now wasn't the moment for details. I turned and wrapped my arms around her, holding her as she settled in. "I love you, Holly."

Friday, June 15, 1984

GEORGE BUSH. The Vice President. Not one of the more visible criminals in the Reagan regime.

"Don't let it fool you," Hank was saying. "The guy was director of the CIA under Nixon. He's in the loop. Drug trade, weapons dealing, death squads — he's a player."

Bush was speaking at some corporate wingding at the Saint Francis Hotel, right on Union Square. The adjacent streets were crawling with tourists and shoppers, and the cable cars ran right in front of the protest. "What a difference from a Livermore blockade," I said to Hank as we joined the lunchtime protest.

"Some things don't change," he said, pointing across the street to the row of cops lining the front entrance of the hotel. Another squad patrolled the barricade set up along our side of the street. The barricade looked like the world's longest bicycle rack, twelve-foot tubular steel sections held together by the ever-popular plastic handcuffs. The contraption stretched over a hundred feet, fencing us onto the ten-foot-wide sidewalk.

By noon, hundreds of protesters had gathered. Those of us in the center were wedged in between the barricade in front and a concrete abutment behind us, the backside of the elevated, manicured park.

In the wake of the Kissinger demo a month before, the cops seemed more jittery. The officers lining the barricades slapped their long black batons into their leather gloves. I looked at the cop across from me, who avoided my eyes. The paint on his baton grip was worn to bare wood.

As if by way of contrast, a cable car rolled by, laden with tourists gawking and snapping photos of this quaint San Francisco scene. Great, I thought. Glad we're doing our part to boost the local economy.

I looked around. Hank was talking with a couple of CISPES monitors. Down at the left end, Raoul, Jenny, and Jacey were huddled with their AG. Jacey and some of the others had on gloves. In June? Well, if the cops could wear them them, why not us? Maybe it was protest fashion. The bandannas around their necks sure looked that way.

Up at the right end, Sid and some of the punks from Gruesome Rebels and Domestic Terrorists AGs caucused. Flint, sporting his black beret, was standing near them with a few partisans. LAGers were few and far between. Sara and Alby were nearby, and I'd seen Doc and Karina

Religious activists at a 1984 protest hold photos of Salvadoran Archbishop Romero, murdered by U.S.-funded death squads for his outspoken views on social justice. Note the "bicycle-rack" police barricades, used to control crowds at many demos.

earlier. But that was about it. I looked around for Karina, thinking maybe she had a plan I could join. But I didn't see her.

Periodically, bullhorns rang out a chant: "George Bush, you can't hide! We charge you with genocide!" There was no room to form a picket loop, though, and the chants didn't take hold. An occasional crumpled flyer was tossed at the police, along with the usual taunts and mockery. So far, pretty tame. But I figured the AGs out at the two flanks had something up their sleeves.

Up at the far right, beyond the barricade, there was a fluttering. Heads turned, and people started pointing. Even the cops seemed curious, although they maintained their positions. I slipped through the crowd to where I could see. From around the corner came a half-dozen big pink noses, painted on cardboard and stapled to poles ten feet tall. Each nose had a name stenciled on the nostrils: Bush, CIA, Noriega, Contra, Mafia. The noses soared over the crowd, which parted as the proboscis-bearers made their way through our amused but uncomprehending ranks.

Behind the noses followed a ten-foot packing tube striped like a barber's pole. Finally came two women in business suits. Each had a burlap bag over her shoulder leaking a powdery white substance. "Cocaine delivery for Mr. Bush!" they shouted. "Stand back! Mr. Bush's cocaine coming through!"

Aha, the Bush-CIA-cocaine connection. The crowd eased back to clear a space in the center of our sidewalk. The cops craned their necks to catch a view. With much ceremony, the cocaine bearers emptied their sacks onto the ground. A man in a gray suit and dark sunglasses stepped forward with a big cardboard razor blade. Carefully he shaped the powder into a long line. The striped tube was plunged into the end of the line, and the noses began a frenzied dance around the top of the tube. A cheer rose from the crowd, and someone struck up the perfect chant: "Bush Nose! Bush Knows! Bush Nose! Bush Knows!"

A policeman breaks ranks to order a protester back across the street with the rest of the crowd.

Photographers crowded

in, and the rest of us turned back to the demo. The cops, amused by the skit, got a little lax. Up at the right flank, the punks started rattling the barricade, grabbing the waist-high steel contraptions and rocking them back and forth to make a clatter on the concrete. Flint, a step behind the punks, urged them on. The cops on the other side of the barricade rushed over and whacked at the culprits' hands with their billyclubs, scoring a few hits. I winced, understanding why some people were wearing gloves.

Billyclubs notwithstanding, the punks kept going after the barricade, rattling and jumping back. What a different tone from our recent financial district march, I thought.

Hank approached and said, "I'm heading back to work. You want to go?"

"No," I said, looking past him at the barricades. "I want to see what happens here."

He started away. I felt like I'd been dismissive and called after him. "Hey, how's the nukecycle?"

Hank turned back, his face brightening. "I think I solved the chain problem. Now I'm trying to get the steering worked out. I put it all together last night, but it wound up backwards, so when you steer left, the wheels turn right."

"What a great metaphor for our times," I said.

He laughed, which brought a smile to my face. The first smile of the day, I thought. Would there be another?

Hank headed out. I moved toward the punks at the right flank, not intending to join in, but wanting to be closer to the action. People continued rattling the barricade. Suddenly, a racket went up from the far left. I stood on my toes and saw that Raoul and Jenny's AG, bandannas pulled over their faces, had grabbed the end of the long barricade and dragged it ten feet out into the street.

With a loud screech, an oncoming cable car ground to a halt. I felt a rush of pride. Success!

Not that the riders seemed to mind. Out came the cameras. The protesters yelled and flipped them off, and everyone seemed happy.

Everyone except the police, who sent a detachment down to restore order. A couple of officers went around the end of the barricade and waved their batons menacingly at the crowd, which pressed back toward the center. The cops pulled the barricade back into position, and the cable car rolled past. A lot of people jeered at it. But up front I spotted Karina blowing kisses to the tourists. Good move, I thought. That's a lot more likely to win us fans.

The cops bolstered their patrols on both flanks, and I wondered how anything new could get started. It was nearly one o'clock, and folks started drifting away. From a distance I spied Raoul, Jenny, and Sid leaving, talking avidly among themselves. I envied their camaraderie and thought about catching up. But it was probably a private conversation. That would feel weird, to barge in.

As I pondered leaving, a scuffle broke out at the right end of the line. I worked my way up there and saw that the cops had grabbed a punk and were dragging him toward a paddywagon. Other officers squared around to form a defensive front, clubs at the ready.

"What did he do?" someone asked anxiously.

"He was rattling the barricades," said a tall, thin man. A punkish woman next to him gave him a sharp look, and he didn't say more.

The crowd yelled at the cops for a few minutes, then gradually lost its focus. More people left, while others stood around talking. I wondered if the cops would make another attempt. Best not to be right in the front, I thought.

Sure enough, not five minutes later, several cops charged into the narrow space behind the barricades and grabbed a woman with short, matted hair. They got her in their grasp. But before they could take a step, a dozen members of the crowd jumped forward, jostling one another and the cops. I craned my neck, watching for the outnumbered cops to beat a hasty retreat when they met resistance.

Not this time. They held their grip. More cops waded in, clubs jabbing, and grabbed another of the resisters. The front line gave way and a crush of bodies staggered back into the rest of us. "Shit," I heard someone say amid the general yelling. "They'll charge those guys with resisting arrest. That's a felony."

Damn. A felony, just for refusing to be grabbed by the cops? Or for trying to protect your friends? Even if the charges were reduced, they'd be facing jail time plus stiff probation for what was probably a spontaneous reaction.

The crowd retreated further behind the barricades. I stayed well back from the front. The cops reformed their line and smirked. And why not? They'd walked on us, and we had not a clue how to respond. I felt a flush of shame for having stood and watched.

The protest was fizzling out. People filtered away, muttering and shaking their heads. "Don't leave alone," someone called. "Stay in groups." I saw Winston and Jürgen ahead of me and hurried after them. Not a very inspiring finale.

Monday, June 18, 1984

I'D FORGOTTEN how whispery Angie's phone voice was. "The house where I'm subletting is really nice," she was telling me. "And there's a permanent room available in the Fall. I'd like a quieter place, but the location is great. I can bike everywhere."

"So what are you doing?" I was aware of a challenge in the question.

"I've been checking into schools. I think I can get into Portland State for the Fall semester. I'll probably take some social work courses, see if that's what I want to focus on."

"What about woodworking or film?"

She was silent for a moment. "I don't know," she said. "Woodworking is a tough field for women. And I wonder if I'd really feel challenged intellectually."

"What about film?" I said. "That would be a challenge — writing, filming, producing."

She was quiet again. "It just doesn't seem very practical," she finally said. "I probably wouldn't be able to make any money, not with the sorts of films I'd want to make. It's time to get serious."

"Have you checked into Bay Area schools? Cal must have a social work program." The urgency of my words surprised me. She'd been gone a month, and I thought I was getting over her. But now, hearing her on the other end of the line, I pined for her return. "Are you going to apply to schools down here?"

"No," she said without hesitation. "If I'm going to school, Portland is the place. Or maybe Seattle. San Francisco is just too distracting. The Bay Area was never what I dreamed it would be. I never found my niche."

"And so you're giving up?"

I could feel her bristle right through the phone. "It's time to get started somewhere else. There's nothing there pulling me back."

"Nothing?"

"It wasn't working," she said. "Not just between you and me. With Jenny, with Karina, the whole scene. I've had enough."

Now it was my turn to be silent for a moment. "I'm wondering if I'll see you again," I said awkwardly.

"Oh, you will," she said. "I have to come back and get the stuff I left in storage, close my bank account, that kind of thing. I'll be down in late July or August. After the Convention is over."

"Well, I'll probably have more attention then," I said. I thought glumly of how Angie used to make me laugh, how light our friendship once had been. Now, it seemed like weeks since I'd even cracked a smile.

As if she'd read my mind, Angie adopted an airy tone. "So tell me what's new with you," she said.

"Oh, not a lot," I said. As if she could understand a thing that was going on here. What was the point in even trying to explain it? "I got invited to sing at the Convention," I finally said.

"At Rock Against Reagan?"

"I wish," I said. "No, it's at the LAG demo."

"LAG decided to do an action?" she asked in a perfunctory voice.

"Well, no, not an action. Just a rally. But it's something."

"So Jenny and Raoul and Sid aren't doing street actions?"

"Oh yeah, they are. The War Chest Tours. They're not part of LAG, though. They're tours through the financial district, like we did in October."

"I heard there was another one in May."

"Yeah," I said, perking up. "I was on it. And you know what? At the end of the action, we did a spiral dance. There were a hundred people, with Sara leading it. We were singing this song about weavers and webs, faster and faster. It was a great ending."

"That sounds neat," she said, a wistful note creeping into her voice. "That's something I haven't heard about up here, public rituals. I'm sure there must be a Solstice ritual somewhere. But when I think of people in San Francisco building a bonfire and running into the ocean, I'll miss that."

"I thought that was at Winter Solstice," I said, picturing her running naked across the beach.

"Winter and Summer. It's actually harder in the Summer, because you expect the ocean to be warm. It's more of a shock. But I still wouldn't miss it if I were there."

Neither would I, I thought. Come back down for it, I wanted to say. But I didn't want to come off like I was pressuring her. And besides, I didn't want the rejection.

We wrapped it up on that note. She said something about talking again around the Fourth of July, I said sure, and that was it. I shoved the phone aside and lay back on the living room floor. So that was my friend Angie. My late great former lover Angie. Less than six months ago, we were hot and heavy. I remembered how she would crawl on top of me and let her body drop onto mine. How she would grab and pinch and bite until I pinned her to the bed. How she would press her lips to my ear as we made love, breathing her passion into me... Once more... Just once more...

Monday, June 25, 1984

"Orgasm!"

Not exactly the slogan you expected on LAG's front window. But there it was, in letters three feet tall, along with a smaller script reading, "Every Day I Break the Law." That slogan at least made sense, although spraypaint wasn't the usual medium for our window signs.

I stepped back to the edge of the sidewalk and took in the full fifteen-foot span. The lettering wasn't as flamboyant as some graffiti I'd seen around town, but it wasn't a bad job for one night's work.

The identity of the artists was no mystery. Raoul, who had been devouring a Wilhelm Reich book lately, must have done "Orgasm." And Tai's hand was evident in the cartoonish characters around it. I could picture them working feverishly to cover the big window, then stepping back and having a good laugh. And expecting everyone else to laugh along.

As I stood admiring the painting, Melissa barged out of the office door. "Can you believe this mess?" she said to anyone within half a block. "Who would be so stupid?" She had a package of razor blades, and set to work scraping the paint off, beginning with the word Orgasm. Slowly, inch by inch, the letters yielded to her painstaking labor. She groaned. "This is going to take all day!"

I didn't offer to help. I had enough issues with Raoul, without trashing his mural. I excused myself and started in the door just as Jenny came out. She said a quick hello, then took a blade from Melissa and started scraping. Must feel funny, I thought, scraping off Raoul's handiwork. To compound the indignity, Melissa lectured her as if she were the culprit. Guilt by association.

I went in and found the office deserted. Just as well. It would make it easier to stay focused with Doc. I was meeting him to talk over a flyer I had volunteered to paste up for Enola Gay. But I also had a further agenda — to recruit him back onto Coordinating Council. As the Convention loomed, the meetings were getting more and more divisive, with a core of younger anarchists squaring off against wizened veterans like Melissa, Maria, and Daniel. What we needed was someone older than the vets whose politics meshed with the street crowd.

Doc was the key. The idea was Holly's — approach a few old-timers and ask them to commit to Coordinating Council for six months. Long enough to get us through this fractious period. Cindy was another candidate, and maybe Claude. Beyond that, I was stumped. But Doc was definitely the starting point.

I checked my mail slot. Not much. A few more endorsements for People's Convention, along with a $25 donation. Finances were abysmal all around. I almost wished no money would come in, so as not to remind me of how much more we didn't have.

Somehow we had to limp through. The Fall could be completely different. We'd get beyond the Convention, refocus our efforts, and get back to fighting over things that really mattered. If we could just make it through the Summer.

Doc. He was the starting point. Bring back the voices of experience. Engage the old guard. Restore the balance and depth.

Right on cue, the office door swung open. Doc paused and took in the office with a sweeping gaze. I walked up and welcomed him with a hug. "Hey, it's been a while," I said. His beard was grayer than I remembered. "How's life?"

His lips tightened. "Not so great. My lower back went out last week, but I still need to work with the rent coming up. I'm taking today off, though. How's it going for you?" He looked at me intently, like he really wanted to know.

"It's been rocky," I said hesitantly. I felt how much I wanted to tell someone about missing Angie. But I couldn't bring myself to say it. Not out of embarrassment, but out of a sense that if I were to speak the words, I'd be summoning the shadowy feelings into full light. Not a good idea. Stay focused.

I pulled two chairs up next to the worktable. "Show me what you're thinking for the flyer," I said.

"It's for the Moral Majority protest," he said, pulling out a hand-drawn mockup of the flyer. "Enola Gay is helping organize it, as our Convention action." He stared down at the page. "I wish LAG could have gotten something together. But we finally had to make our own plans."

"Yeah. Hopefully this Fall is better," I said, sensing an opening for recruiting Doc to come back to Coordinating Council. "The Convention has thrown everything out of whack."

Doc shook his head. "It isn't just the Convention. It's been a year since our meetings had any focus."

"It's been a hard year," I said. "But that can change."

"I don't know. LAG may have seen its day. I wonder if it's worth fighting to keep it alive. Some projects might have ongoing value. But why pour resources into an office and a staff when there's no clear focus? It's time to move on."

"LAG can move on," I answered defensively. "Whatever projects people are working on, there's going to be a need for an organization that holds the strands together. Why not LAG?"

Doc's heavy brows furrowed. "A movement doesn't need to be coordinated from above. That model's been tried. The Communist Party ran schools, athletic groups, newspapers, and magazines — a complete radical culture directed by a central committee. They were really strong in the 1930s. But in the 1950s, McCarthyism destroyed the C.P. They've never been the same after that."

"You can't blame that on the C.P.," I said. "McCarthyism was an exceptional period. It doesn't disprove the model."

"Sure it does." Doc's eyes hardened. "A centralized structure can be destroyed by a direct strike at the heart of the organization, at its leadership. If you're at all effective, you have to anticipate these attacks. Not just from the police and the FBI, but from the universities and the media and the churches. Any successful alternative movement will be targeted." He paused for a breath. "Gays and lesbians have dealt with this for centuries, these concerted attacks. You're not just called illegal, but immoral, inferior, undesirable...."

He peered intently at me. I nodded, following his thoughts but not quite seeing the point.

"Gays had to learn how to organize in the face of incessant repression," he continued. "Any central organization would be smashed. The only possibility was invisible networks of friends, small circles having only informal connections with parallel groups. Even in San Francisco, the most open city in the country, the Gay community is a network of smaller groups — ad hoc coalitions, bars, gyms, political clubs. There is no central coordinating body. And who can deny its effectiveness? When one group is attacked, others go on, and maybe even gain members."

"Okay," I said, finally seeing what he was driving at. "Maybe it's better to do away with an umbrella organization. But it still makes sense to have resource centers, places like the LAG office with phones, meeting space, work space. Someone has to take responsibility for that."

He shrugged. "If that's really what you want to work on, I can't tell you not

DIRECT ACTION
#16
Summer Solstice 1984
Published by Livermore Action Group
San Francisco Summer 1984—See Pages 1-6
San Francisco Spring 1984—See Pages 8-9

Direct Action #16, June 1984

to. But why not take the threads that are still growing — the peace camp, Direct Action — and weave them with other threads outside of LAG? Trust that we've made valuable contributions that won't evaporate just because the group no longer exists. LAG was an experiment. We tried different ways of organizing, of working together. We'll keep experimenting until we're ready to build a new society, not just undermine this one."

"That's taking the long-range view," I said with a touch of irony that Doc missed or ignored.

"It is," he said. "If we're serious, we have to look way down the road. We have to ask what groundwork we're laying for future generations to build on. We'll have done well if twenty years from now, people are organizing civil disobedience around dozens of issues, and it's not seen as extremism, but as one tactic among many. It'll mean we took the torch from the Civil Rights movement and passed it on. It will take generations to change the world. Our job is to move the cause forward."

I nodded my head dutifully, but I must have looked pretty glum, because Doc grew concerned. "We've done a lot," he said quickly. "LAG drew more out of people than we knew we had to give. Our protests empowered thousands of people, and that will ripple out into the world. Not just as more actions, but in the way people work together. Consensus, collectivity, nonhierarchy — these are our contributions. And these aren't lost, even if LAG dissolves. People will carry these ideals back into their daily lives, and forward to new movements."

I had already given up on asking Doc to come back to Coordinating

Council. I mean, take a hint. Why bother asking when you already know the answer? I laughed with no humor. "It feels like you're writing us off already."

He smiled sadly. "Maybe I am. I can get pretty pessimistic these days. You think it doesn't bother me to see LAG fall apart? I poured two years of my life into it. But it isn't working for me anymore. I need to look elsewhere for inspiration."

He took a breath and exhaled audibly. "You know, I'm getting along in years. Fifty isn't so far ahead. One thing that gives me hope is younger people. Watching Jeremy grow up, seeing how he challenges my authority, how he won't accept my answers — that's inspiring." He looked at me adamantly. "There's a current of creative energy that runs through the planet, through every living and breathing thing. Even in a society as hell-bent on destruction as our own, it constantly bubbles up, in artists and dreamers, in children and youth, in ecstasy and pain. It's swirling around us all the time. Occasionally, miraculously, it crystallizes into definite forms. And then it flows on, leaving behind an empty shell..."

War Chest Tour organizers put together this eight-page handbook mixing urban protest tactics with articles on corporate funding of elections.

I was caught in his web of words, knowing exactly what he meant by the bubbling of energy. But when he reached the bit about empty shells, I sank again. So that was his point. Empty shells. What more was there to say?

With a sudden flurry, Melissa and Jenny came back into the office. "That's all I'm doing," Melissa said. "Raoul and Tai can get down here and do the rest."

Jenny seemed thoroughly beleaguered. I looked at her for a moment, then turned to Melissa, hoping to defuse her exasperation. "Thanks for tackling it," I said. "I guess it had to be done."

Melissa looked at me suspiciously, then picked up her daypack and stalked toward the door. "I still can't believe anyone would be so inconsiderate!"

With clenched teeth, Jenny watched her leave. Then she shivered. "Aaaagh! I'm going to kill Raoul!"

It wasn't what I expected to hear, and I almost laughed aloud, which probably wasn't the most tactful response. Fortunately, the office door opened again and distracted us. It was Spider, Doc's lover. "My car's still running, should I turn it off?"

"No, I'm ready to go," Doc said. He turned and gave me a hug. "Thanks for doing the flyer for us. Good talking to you."

"Yeah," I answered with no conviction. So much for getting any help from that quarter. I watched him go through the door. So much for the plan to lure the veterans back to Coordinating Council. If Doc wouldn't touch it, why would Cindy or Claude?

I looked up, and realized that Jenny, teeth still clenched, was looking at me. I walked over and sat down next to her desk. "What an afternoon, huh?"

She let go a long breath, and her jaw relaxed. "I can't believe I stood there and took that," she said. "A solid hour of guilt-tripping. That's Melissa's whole worldview — guilt. And it's not just her. That's all we ever do, go out to Livermore or the financial district and scream, 'Shame on you!' As if they're going to slink away and stop building nuclear weapons because of us."

"Well," I said, "we have to let them know how we feel."

Jenny pulled a clip out of her hair. "Guilt doesn't change anything. Sometimes I wonder about the whole idea of protesting, of always being against something."

"Famous words from one of the War Chest Tour organizers," I couldn't resist kidding her.

"Well, yeah," she said with a half-smile. "But for me, it's not really about protesting the Democrats. The point is to get closer to people. Doing intense stuff like street protests or graffiti pushes the usual limits of friendship. That's why I did the Concord thing with Karina."

My ears perked up. "So that action happened?"

"Yeah, didn't you hear about it? Four of us went onto the base last Friday night and spraypainted anti-war slogans on the bunkers. Karina wanted to go up to the buildings and do it there, but we could see people in them, it was too risky." She looked embarrassed to admit her own hesitation. "It was still fun, though, sneaking onto the base and back off without getting caught."

I had to smile. "So you think you'll get that sort of connection from the War Chest Tours?"

"I don't know. It's worth a try. Nothing else is working right now." A worried look passed over her face, as if she feared stepping on my toes. But she didn't take her words back. "I feel like I glommed onto LAG a couple of years ago to fill some void in my life. It used to be that working in the LAG office was almost satisfying, but never quite. Then being in an affinity group with

Raoul, I thought that street protesting was what I was looking for. But now..." She looked away and tugged at a strand of hair.

I guessed she was thinking about being pregnant and miscarrying and wanting kids. Should I ask her about it? Probably better to give her space and see if she wants to bring it up. I leaned back in my chair. Even if Jenny was down on LAG, it felt good to talk with her again. Maybe we were moving past the friction of the past few months.

But before we could say anything more, the office door opened and in blew Sid. His eyes bounced back and forth between Jenny and me. "You guys made fast work of the painting," he said, seeming to look especially at me. "I came all the way over from the City to check it out, and it's practically gone."

"It wasn't me," I said. "I'd have coated it with varnish to preserve it for future generations. But Melissa had a little trouble with it."

"Too bad," he said, then looked at Jenny. "Wanna come over to Jacey's with me? We're going to write a flyer on street tactics for the meeting this weekend."

"Pronouncements from the central committee?" I joked, half wishing he'd invite me, too.

Sid was more serious than I was used to seeing him. "It's a flyer to get people thinking about street theater and autonomous actions. Otherwise the herd instinct takes over."

"Yeah, that's a funny thing about urban actions," I said. "In the backcountry, or even at Livermore, people operate in affinity groups. But in the City, it turns into one big crowd yelling at the cops."

"We've got to be more mobile," he said. He traced a zig-zag on the table with his finger. "Hit a site and move on. Show up where we're not expected."

I leaned forward in my chair. "That's fine. But face it, no matter how well we maneuver, we're still going to lose. Downtown San Francisco isn't that big. It's not like we can avoid the police forever. We need to plan for that moment, to arrange safe retreats, to learn how to keep an exit open so people don't get trapped."

Sid drew his spindly frame to its full height. "We don't have to lose. We fall into this pattern of fighting the cops head-on. They catch us on a narrow street, when we're all packed together, so when twenty or thirty cops come at us, they don't have to deal with anyone except the front row. We're getting outmaneuvered."

"That's inevitable in a street demo," I said. "Cops don't have to stop to get consensus. They'll always move faster than us."

"Not if we break into smaller groups," Sid answered. "The cops can't deal with small groups. Like at Kissinger, when we marched in with the punks. The cops weren't ready. We came up behind them, and they totally backed off."

"But in the end, people still got arrested," I said.

"That doesn't mean we lost," Jenny put in. "I figure we'll get arrested at the War Chest Tours. If they don't try to arrest us, we must not be disrupting much. But if we have some control over the arrest, so people can choose whether to stay and take the bust or leave, that's a lot better."

"And maybe the first day, we won't even get arrested," Sid picked up. "Like at May 22nd, when we ended with the spiral dance. There's three days of War Chest Tours. We don't have to get busted the first day."

As if you'll have a choice, I thought. But I didn't say it. I was frustrated with myself for arguing with them, letting myself get set up as their adversary.

"I need to get going," Sid said to Jenny. "You want to come over to Jacey's?"

"Yeah," she said. "I've had enough of this office." She looked at me uncomfortably. "We need to talk about finances," she said. "I'm not sure there's enough money to print Direct Action."

Great, I thought as I watched them leave. One more crisis falling in my lap.

LAG's finances (along with most other grassroots groups') sank in the morass of 1984, prey to political reaction and economic stagnation.

Sunday, July 1, 1984

Back and forth, up and down the interminable halls, the ancient vacuum cleaner droned. Not like it was making much difference on this stained excuse for a carpet. I leaned into the vacuum. Out, damned spot! Out, I say!

Sunday afternoon. Payday was coming up, and I needed the hours. But why did it have to be a drudge? Why couldn't I be singing along with the hum of the motor like I usually did, rehearsing for my upcoming gig at the Convention? There were only a couple of weeks left. But try as I might, all I could focus on was my crumbling reality.

Angie gone. Holly drifting away. LAG evaporating in the heat of a hundred conflicts.

"You'll never act in time, you'll always be waiting for more clarity." No one had spoken the words, but I could hear them just the same. I tried to think of examples to refute the voices, times I had dared to act or speak, but they seemed lame. My sole refuge was a stoicism in letting events take their own course. Trusting that LAG would weather the storm and coalesce again after the Convention. Trusting that Holly and I would find our way to a new commitment. Trusting that Angie... well, trusting that Angie would continue to be Angie.

As I passed a hall window, I noticed my own reflection. I stopped and stared at the dim spectre, searching the eyes for a spark of hope.

Quit procrastinating. Walk out of LAG. No, throw yourself wholeheartedly back into LAG. Recommit to Holly. No, drive to Portland and beg Angie to come back... Of course, I didn't have a car. But that was a minor detail. Get one and go.

A tug at the vacuum jerked me back to reality. End of the cord. End of the line. Angie wasn't coming back. She'd said so, clear as day. Give it up. As I trudged down the hallway to the next outlet, hopelessness swamped me. Dump it all. Commit to something new. People's Convention. Some of the alliance building was taking root. Fertilize that soil, and who knew what might grow?

As I got going on the last stretch of the hallway, I tried to follow through on the inspiration. Stop obsessing about all the rest of it. Do some constructive thinking about People's Convention.

But something was out of whack. It wasn't just the rushed decisions and the pushiness of some of the organizers. What gnawed at me was the back room dealing. Some people from the Revolutionary Workers' Party had connections to Jesse Jackson's populist Presidential campaign. If we played our hand carefully, Jackson — expected to be a power broker if the Democratic Convention was deadlocked — might come and speak at the People's Convention. That would guarantee huge press coverage. Maybe he'd even join our march to the Democratic Convention and personally deliver our "People's Platform."

Great plan. But the process felt weird. The couple of times I had expressed reservations, there wasn't much support. "You can't have everyone involved in these sorts of negotiations," people said. "It would take too long. Time is short."

It left me feeling out of synch and a little distrustful. I tried to remember how it was with LAG when I first joined. It wasn't all fun and games. I was probably idealizing how great LAG was. Or had been.

And besides, I had met Holly right off. That colored my whole experience of LAG, sharing the ups and downs. I sighed. How great it had been. Back then.

Back in the apartment, I put on a Clash album. As the distorted guitars kicked in, I got the last beer out of the refrigerator and stationed myself in front of my typewriter. Time to knock out a letter to the Direct Action mailing list, calling on people to take part in the People's Convention and the LAG demo. And to send money so we could publish the next issue of the paper. One last appeal. From the heart.

I stared at the stark white page, but my mind drew a blank. I opened the beer, took a swig and waited for the sizzle. Squinting at the bitter aftertaste, I swallowed. It was beer, alright. But something was missing. I took another drink, and played it over my tongue. No fizz. I swallowed it distastefully and set the bottle down. Flat. Inspiration was getting hard to find.

Wednesday, July 4, 1984

For one cool, foggy day, it felt like Summer in San Francisco. No meetings. No mailings. No phone calls. No appointments. Maybe it took a national holiday to get a day off. At any rate, it was good to know it was still possible.

Holly and I had come to the City to see the Mime Troupe's new show, "1984," in Dolores Park. Afterward we stopped at Modern Times, where Holly got a book of essays on feminist psychology. I bought a thick biography of Queen Elizabeth, symbolic of my resolve to get back to my history studies after the Convention. Then we cut over to Mission Street to catch BART back to the East Bay. Our itinerary was pizza in Berkeley, followed by a movie perfectly timed to drown out the fireworks. All in all, a fine Fourth of July.

"What did you think about the Mime Troupe?" she asked as we got settled in our train seats.

I laughed. "I loved when the homeless guy had the crowd doing shopping-cart calisthenics."

"I liked that they tied in the tax issue — that we're all supporting war when we pay our taxes." Since starting her food-prep job with its steady paycheck, Holly had been talking about tax resistance. "We should do a story in the next Direct Action," she said. "People need to think about tax resistance now, not next April when it's too late."

"A story would be great," I said. I was glad to hear Holly use the words "we" and "Direct Action" in the same sentence. Maybe there was hope. Maybe our whole disjointed Spring was just a bump in the road. I got the feeling that Holly and Norm weren't catching fire.

Of course, she and I hadn't had sex for a while now, either. But our path was clearing. Get past the morass of the Democratic Convention, and maybe we'd rediscover the shared political passion that once fueled our relationship.

Was that so far-fetched? I could almost see the light at the end of the tunnel. Two weeks from now, the Convention would practically be over. The slate would be wiped clean.

Monday, July 9, 1984

Jenny and Alby were driving over to the Coordinating Council meeting, but I wanted to walk. I'd been cooped up in the office all day, and this was my one shot at some fresh air.

Actually, it wasn't all that fresh. No breeze stirred as I trudged across town, fretting over LAG's dwindling finances. I wiped my brow. Maybe we could slide on the rent for a week or two. But even so, would there be enough money to publish Direct Action — assuming we could even pull an issue together?

By the time I got to the meeting, my head felt fuzzy and my shirt was sticky with sweat. I got a low-key greeting from Mort and Hank as I entered the classroom behind the Friends Meeting House. I let my eyes adjust to the long windowless box with worn carpeting and too many chalkboards. Everyone's face looked wintry pale under the fluorescent lights. Melissa, Maria, and Daniel were talking in front of a bulletin-board display on South Africa. Jenny, Walt, and Alby gathered a dozen metal folding chairs in a tight circle.

I went over to say hi to Maria, whom I hadn't seen in a while. She leaned up from her wheelchair to give me a hug. We weren't working on any projects together, though, and there wasn't a lot to say.

Sara, who had just arrived, walked over our way. "Did you hear that some religious groups are starting their own Emergency Response Network? They're calling it the Pledge of Resistance."

"Yeah," Maria said. "I'm working on it. We're signing up people who pledge to do CD if the U.S. attacks Nicaragua or El Salvador. We already have over five hundred people. If we have thousands, maybe it'll make Reagan stop and think."

Sara peered at Maria. "Why did you go and start a new network when LAG already consensed to it?"

"I didn't start it," Maria said flatly. "But once it got going, I could see that it would be a lot easier and more flexible to start a new group than to try to get consensus in LAG."

"Why?" Sara put her fists on her hips. "You can't avoid the problems by starting a new group. Anyone who organizes direct action will run into the same things, sooner or later."

"Probably sooner," I tossed in.

"Right," Sara said. "Besides, we were already signing up affinity groups."

Maria gripped the arms of her wheelchair like she was going to spring at Sara. "It's not a competition!"

"No," I said. "But the Pledge makes the ERN superfluous."

Melissa, standing behind Maria, folded her arms across her chest. "It wasn't going anywhere. You can't expect the whole world to stand and wait while we get our act together."

To my surprise, Sara nodded. "It's true. We dropped the ball."

Dropped the ball? Not again. Every time I turned around, we'd dropped the ball. Emergency Response Network. International Day. The Strategy Proposal. Livermore. Vandenberg. We were leading the league in fumbles.

Maria turned her chair and wheeled away from us to join the meeting circle. I looked at Sara, whose eyes seemed to say, "Why am I doing this work?" I silently pulled up a chair next to Hank.

Agenda ideas were tossed out. With the Convention looming, most of the items concerned the upcoming demonstrations. I wanted to make one last pitch for the People's Convention, even though I knew no one in the room had any free time. Mort had a report from CISPES's Central America solidarity march. Daniel brought news of the Bohemian Grove organizing. Sara was the spoke for the LAG demo at the Convention, and I figured Jenny would update us on the War Chest Tours. Walt scribbled it all down on a legal pad.

"What about Livermore?" Melissa demanded. "Aren't we going to start planning for the September action?"

"And we've got to make room for finances," Jenny said in a somber voice. It looked to be a long evening. Oh well, I thought as I looked around the circle, at least we're in it together. After all the fights and feuds, here we are under one roof, a week before the Convention.

I waited for a pause in the agenda-setting, wanting to volunteer to facilitate. With a little dexterity, I might steer us clear of a major confrontation. Just keep it together one more week, and all the conflict around the Convention would be history.

But before I could speak, Walt piped up: "I'll facilitate." I sank back in my chair. Walt was a good facilitator, but he was more inclined to let people talk about whatever they wanted.

I frowned, not liking the sound of my own opinions. But if we could just avoid a fight for one more week...

We did a round of check-ins, and were making headway on the reports when the meeting room door burst open. Karina entered with a flurry and took a seat by Alby. I tried to catch her eye, but she was gesturing to Walt, wanting him to add something to the agenda.

Karina's thick black hair was uncombed, like she'd been to one too many meetings that day, and was probably running to another appointment after this. With whom, I wondered. I glanced at Sara, who was biting her nails. Probably not her.

I hadn't talked much with Karina since our BART ride a month earlier. Every time I saw her, she seemed more frazzled. I figured she was involved in the War Chest Tours, but I didn't know what she was planning. I studied her profile as she whispered something to Alby. What was going on? Why was she so agitated?

Walt interrupted my ruminations by calling on me for the People's Convention report. I gave a rundown on the itinerary, which aroused no passions. Not surprising. It wasn't arousing many, even among the organizers. But I noticed that Melissa and Maria spent a while studying the schedule of workshops I passed around.

Bohemian Grove took longer. Daniel filled us in on the protest at the Grove, where every Summer several hundred corporate and government bigwigs — all male, mostly WASP — gathered in an idyllic setting in the Northern California redwoods for rest, relaxation, and back room sleaze. Legend had it that the Manhattan Project, which created the first atomic bomb, was hatched at the Bohemian Grove. Reagan and Bush and their cronies were members in good standing, along with the heads of just about every corporation we had found cause to protest in the past year.

Talk about a natural target. The Bohemian Grove Action Network had held small protests and vigils in years past, but this Summer was on a bigger scale. "We're planning a blockade of the only access road," Daniel said. "We're going to blockade them *in*. We're declaring a quarantine, saying that these men are too dangerous to be let loose."

Sara and Alby quizzed Daniel on the blockade specifics. "I heard there's a stream that runs right through the Grove," Alby said. "What about getting innertubes and floating down it?"

Daniel drew back his head. "I believe that a variety of tactics are possible. My concern would be for jail solidarity among people arrested for different actions."

"We dealt with that at Vandenberg," Sara said.

Well, yeah, I thought. And some people got two-month sentences. I looked over at Karina, one of those people. She seemed lost in her own thoughts. Maybe she'd done enough jail time for a while.

We moved on. Jenny nervously updated us on the War Chest Tours. She leaned away from Melissa, as if expecting a rotten tomato. I cast a glance at Melissa, but she seemed disinterested. Maria and Daniel also sat silently. The Tours weren't part of LAG, so I figured the critics aren't concerned.

Not so the next item: LAG's Convention demo. People rustled around in their chairs as Alby and Sara outlined the plans: a rally on the small stage in the free-speech area, with singers, poets, and speakers, the whole event to have a distinctly anti-corporate flavor.

Immediately Maria raised her hand. "I assume we got a permit for this protest?"

"We had to," Sara said. "It's the only way they'll let you use the free-speech area." She looked embarrassed at the admission, but it pacified Maria.

Alby pressed on with the report. "We're still looking for a good generator, but everything else is in place."

"What about monitors," Melissa asked. "Do you have enough monitors?"

Alby tossed his head. "We're not having monitors. We're going to make announcements from the stage reminding everyone that we're all responsible for each other's safety."

Hank looked incredulous. "Wait a minute. Last time I checked, this was a LAG event. Since when do we not have monitors?"

Karina had been ignoring the discussion, but now she looked laconically at Hank. "What's the need? It's not civil disobedience."

"That's not the point," Melissa said scornfully. "LAG always has monitors. We're not stopping now."

Karina turned sharply on Melissa. "You never wanted this protest to happen, and now you're trying to undermine it!"

"Wait," I said, leaning forward in my chair. "No one is trying to undermine anything. People just want input, if it's a LAG action."

"Well, they're trying to control the whole thing," Karina said, slouching back in her seat.

"Damn straight," Hank cut in. "If you want to use LAG's name, Coordinating Council has the responsibility to oversee the action."

Karina and Hank glowered at each other. Several hands went up. Walt quickly called on Sara. Good choice — she was more likely than most to search for a middle ground.

"The problem with monitors," Sara said in a restrained voice, "is that they encourage people not to take responsibility for themselves."

"Not just that," Karina cut in. "As soon as you have monitors, they start acting like 'peace police,' putting out the idea that there are proper ways to protest. Then the cops and media start expecting us to police ourselves."

Alby perched on the edge of his chair. "What's the big deal," he put in. "It's only a rally."

"Any time you get a crowd of people together," Maria said with a sweep of her hand, "there's a potential for the unexpected."

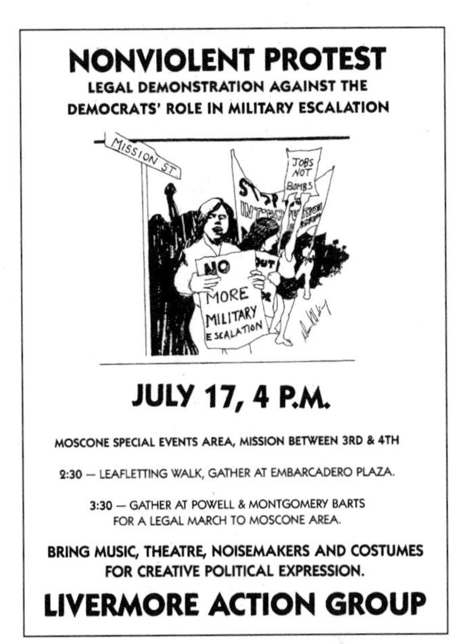

Caught between those advocating street actions versus those favoring a return to Livermore, a small work group organized a legal rally at the Democratic Convention.

"Everyone should be prepared for that, not just a few leaders," Karina answered.

"This isn't an anarchist utopia," Mort said. "We're talking about reality."

"You're talking about a police state," Karina said in a patronizing tone. "One where we provide our own cops. No wonder the War Chest Tours quit LAG. You really *do* have to control everything, don't you?"

"Oh, grow up," Melissa said. "It's about safety, not control."

"No, it's not," Karina shot back. "It's about trying to keep people from getting out in the streets. You're afraid the rally will turn into a march, and you'll lose control of it. You're scared to death of spontaneity."

"Spontaneity," Mort scoffed. "The anarchist cure for every problem. What is this, the Vandenberg Action Coalition?"

Karina practically jumped out of her chair. "What do you know about Vand — "

"Process," I pleaded, trying to drown out Karina. "Process. This is getting into a personal fight. The issue is monitors."

Walt held up his notepad, as if invoking the agenda. He looked imploringly at Karina as he spoke. "Can't we refocus? I understand why the planning group doesn't want monitors trying to control the demo. But LAG has always had monitors. It would take a new consensus not to have them."

Karina stared off into the distance, which was preferable to her launching a new diatribe. Walt looked at Sara again, as if begging for a suggestion. But Sara looked achingly at Karina.

Walt's eyes ran around the circle and stopped on me. Just hold people together, I thought. Get through the Convention. I ventured a proposal I thought might accommodate both sides. "Maybe the work group can choose the monitors, so they're more in tune with what the planners want."

"That's ridiculous," Melissa said. "As if we can trust them to do it."

Karina snapped to attention. "As if we can trust you!" She stuffed her papers into her shoulderbag and stood up. "Don't you ever get tired of being an obstruction? Have you ever supported anything positive? The protest is happening. If you don't want to be there, then stay home and watch it on TV!" Without waiting for an answer, she turned and stormed across the room and out the door.

"Karina!" Walt called, and I echoed him: "Karina!" But she was gone.

"Let her go," Melissa said. "Maybe we can actually get something done."

But that was the furthest thing from my mind. What was the point in meeting without Karina? Should I go after her? Right — for what? So she could vent her exasperation at me before storming off? Forget it. But wait. Maybe she *wants* someone to follow her. Maybe she's looking back right this moment. Should I go? I stole a glance at Sara. Her face was pale and drawn. I sank into the metal chair. If Sara thought it was pointless, what better hope did I have?

But maybe... Forget it... It's moot. She's a mile away by now. Damn. I'd missed my chance. Why didn't I go after her? What was there to lose? At least she'd have known I cared. Too late now.

I dragged my attention back to the meeting. Hank bemoaned the fact that the Convention demo was even being sponsored by LAG. "Do whatever you want, just don't call it LAG, and no one would object."

Sara turned toward Hank. "We need LAG's name to get people to the protest."

Melissa looked at her haughtily, as if scoring an easy debate point. "So to get people to a demo with no monitors, you're using LAG's name and reputation."

"Our great shining reputation," Sara said. She closed her notebook. Was she walking out too?

I looked from one to the other. Arguing with Melissa was pointless. I turned to Sara, leaning forward so I obstructed her view of Melissa. "What about the idea of the planning group choosing the monitors?"

Sara stared blankly at me for a moment, then with an annoyed expression said, "Sure, if that's what it takes to make people happy."

Melissa leaned around me. "Are you going to call people yourself?"

Sara's mouth dropped open. "Yes, I am," she said in a hurt tone.

"Do you want any help?" Melissa looked right at her.

Sara turned her head away. "I said I'd do it."

"Okay, golly, I was just trying to help." Melissa turned to me as if expecting absolution. Forget it. I had nothing to offer. She'd driven Karina away, and I wasn't going to try to make her feel okay about it.

We stumbled through the rest of the agenda with no major explosions, and finally headed out the door around eleven. What a relief, to step into the night air. The fog was rolling in, and the temperature had dropped twenty degrees. I shivered in my T-shirt.

"Hey, want a ride?" Mort called. "Hank and Walt and I are going down to the Albatross for a beer."

"No, thanks," I said. Mort and I had never cleared the air since the ride back from Bound Together. Not that he had a clue. It was my gripe, not his. But I didn't feel like getting into it tonight, and I had no interest in sitting around biting my tongue while he dumped on LAG and anarchists and anyone else trying to do anything.

What I wanted most was to be alone. Holly would probably already be asleep. I could go home and have the place to myself. Play guitar, or maybe read some history. Get my mind off LAG.

HAMLET CALLED TO me that evening. Shakespeare's circa 1600 play didn't fit in with my current studies, which were mired in the religious civil wars of the later 1500s. Catholics, Lutherans, Calvinists, Anglicans, Presbyterians, and Zwinglians fought each other across the length and breadth of Europe. It made my head spin. Maybe I wanted some sort of reprieve, some belief that history does in fact move on, and the gloomiest periods of conflict finally give way to the flowering of new creativity.

But *Hamlet*? Was that going to pick my spirits up? Nice writing, sure, but I'd read half the play, and the hero hadn't done much of anything yet except speechify. I set the book down, and my mind roved back to the evening's meeting.

To LAG? Or not to LAG? That is the question. Whether 'tis nobler in the end to suffer the slights and scornings of my erstwhile comrades, or to wash my hands of all these troubles, and by opposing end them.

To quit, to try no more. Thus by a simple word I'd end the headaches, and the myriad strains and burdens LAG bespoke. That was a dream worth pondering.

To quit, to embrace the unknown. Ay, there's the rub. For in the following moment what might come to take the place of that which I disdained? Images filtered through my tangled mind of hopeless times before the birth of LAG. Would I risk return to that despair in doubtful hope of finding something more? There's a thought to sap the firmest will.

Here is the inertia, the treadmilled path that binds our steps in place. For who would bear the burdens and the worries, the phone calls unreturned, the pleas unanswered, the two steps back for every one step fore, when but a simple word would end it all? Who would sit through endless anxious meetings whose sole result was yet another meeting, but that the fear of facing the unknown — of venturing to that realm from which no assurance returns — thwarts our resolve, and makes us rather bear the ills we know than fly to others we know nothing of?

Such pondering must paralyze us all. Thus the silvery glow of resolution is covered with a dull veneer of brooding. The gossamer visions of a fairer world with this regard do falter in their course, and lose the name of action.

Tuesday, July 10, 1984

ANGIE WAS coming back.

I'd been missing her all afternoon, and finally I sat down and called her. Mainly, I wanted to hear her voice, at least on her answering machine. I half-intended to tell her how much I wanted her in my life, to plead with her to move back. What did I have to lose?

She picked up the phone on the second ring. She seemed surprised and delighted to hear from me, and before I could even think whether and how and when I should mention her returning to the Bay Area, she told me she was coming back.

Sure, it was only for a few days, and not until right before the Democratic Convention. It didn't matter. She was coming back. In less than a week, I would see her, talk with her, hold her...

"I know it's where I need to be," she said. "I left a lot of unfinished business down there. Especially with Jenny. She was my best friend for over a year. If we're going to have any sort of closure, I need to come back for the War Chest Tours."

"Now there's a novel excuse for joining an action," I joked. How could I not feel buoyant? The prospect of holding her in my arms was reason enough. But just as importantly, her return validated my work around the Democratic Convention. Let Craig and Melissa and Daniel boycott it. Let even Holly be indifferent. If Angie was coming all the way from Portland, I had proof that it mattered.

"When will you get here?" I asked.

"Sunday. I'll stay till the end of the week. I called Ariel over at Stonehenge, and she said I could crash there."

I smiled to myself. After months of insisting she would not be part of the Convention morass, here she was, stepping right into the thick of it. Maybe she'd even come to the last day of People's Convention. Wouldn't that make a difference. I was feeling more and more estranged from that project lately, with its lackluster meetings and closed-door politics. If it was going to come to anything, there would have to be a showdown around process. It would be great to have Angie's support at crunch time.

"Wow," I said. "So you're staying in the City?"

"Yeah, it makes sense. That's where the actions are. But I'll come over to Berkeley, too. We'll have time to get together. Actually, I was hoping you would help me pack up the stuff I left in storage. I'm borrowing a van to take it back to Portland."

The idea of helping her make her final move put a damper on my elation. But a quick plan formed in my mind. Pick up her stuff, drive back over to Stonehenge, find a little private space... "I'm really looking forward to seeing you," I told her.

"Yeah, me too," she said. "I've missed our time together."

Thursday, July 12, 1984

If any form of pleasure is exhibited / Report to me and it shall be prohibited
I'll put my foot down, so shall it be / This is the land of the free!

— *Groucho Marx as President Rufus T. Firefly in Duck Soup*

"WE'RE SLIPPING in style," Doc said as we stood to the side of the crowd.

It was true. Instead of our usual gatherings in front of the Hilton or the Saint Francis, this protest was at the downtown Holiday Inn. The target was a conference sponsored by the Moral Majority, a right-wing Christian group dedicated to "family values" — patriarchy, sexual repression, and homophobia.

Doc was holding a hand-lettered sign that read, The Moral Majority Is Neither. "Where will we be next," he said, "Motel 6?"

We surveyed the crowd, hundreds of demonstrators clustered behind the row of bicycle-rack barricades opposite the hotel. The sidewalk was wide enough for a picket loop, and bullhorns hammered out the usual chants. Assembled across the street by the hotel entrance were several dozen riot cops. Down at the corner, an officer wearing a bright orange flak jacket diverted traffic. Up closer, a row of riot police stood watch along the full length of the barricade.

Doc and I were standing toward the left end of the demo, out of range of the bullhorns. "Honing their plans for the Convention," he said, gesturing at the cops. "They learned from the Kissinger demo not to give us a chance to get in the street."

"Yeah," I said, folding my arms across my chest. "They used barricades at the Bush demo, too. Must be their new game plan."

Off to one side, Raoul and Jenny and Jacey were conferring with their affinity group. Did they have a plan, or were they improvising? Hopefully they would come up with something soon, or it might be too late. Word had it that there was a separate protest against something else over at Union Square, and people were murmuring about ditching this scene and marching over there.

I was scoping out the row of cops in front of the hotel when suddenly Karina and Sara and two of their friends, wearing fancy evening dresses, emerged from behind police lines. The cops were as startled as us, but stepped aside as plainclothes officers escorted the four women through the cordon. When they reached the center of the street, one of the officers tried to deliver a lecture, but the women turned their backs and sashayed over to join us.

Doc and I stepped out to greet them as they came around the end of the barricade. "Looking sharp," Doc said.

"We wanted to blend in," Sara said. She bit her fingernails as Karina and another woman struck a glamorous pose for Doc and me.

"Were you inside the convention?" I asked.

"Yeah," Karina said. "But we just got booted."

A small crowd had gathered, and Karina was prevailed upon to tell the story. "We heard several months ago that the Moral Majority was coming," she said. "So Sara went and reserved a room in the hotel as a base of operations. The past two days, we did lesbian graffiti in the halls and restrooms, letting them know we were there. But we waited until today at their keynote speech to 'come out.' There was all sorts of security, but with these dresses, no one even asked us for ID when we went into the ballroom. We got seats right in front, all four of us. We waited until the speech was going, and then we stood up and yelled, 'We are your daughters, and we are everywhere!'"

Doc applauded. "And that got you thrown out?"

"Not right away. After we got their attention, we started kissing and making out, right in front."

"Oh, I bet they loved that," I said, picturing the scene.

Sara blushed. "Not exactly. People were yelling at us, calling us sluts, and making gross-out sounds. I thought some of them might physically attack us, but luckily, building security got in there and pulled us out."

Doc nodded. "Doesn't surprise me. A wanton display of love, right in the midst of a Christian gathering? What did you expect?"

"From the Moral Majority, nothing," Karina said. "But the stupid part was, there was a reporter there from the *Village Voice,* the big liberal New York paper. He called us hooligans and said that we should be dialoguing, not disrupting. Screw that!"

I laughed along with her. My sentiments precisely. And so succinctly stated.

A roving TV camera appeared. "Are you the Kissing Feminists?" asked the reporter. It didn't take much prodding to get Karina to recount the story for the press. How great to see her and Sara in action together. Like old times. And in just a couple of days Angie would be here. Like old times...

Doc wandered off, and I looked around for familiar faces. Raoul and Jenny and Sid seemed to have something up their sleeve, so I drifted over toward them. "We'll circle the block and catch them off-guard," Raoul was saying. "Then we'll come right down the middle of the road. If it draws the cops away, other people will jump the barricades, and we can take the street, just like at Kissinger."

I studied the odds. There were more cops than at the Kissinger demo. A squad of horses was poised off to one side, and a bunch of motorcycle cops were idling at the left-hand corner. Even if we succeeded in taking the street, arrests were likely. It was a tough call. People's Convention began the next day, and whatever my lack of enthusiasm, I couldn't flake on my commitments. But I hated the idea of staying behind if Raoul and Jenny started something.

Twenty or so of us, mainly punks and younger people, set out toward the left end of the protest. We stayed on the sidewalk, in groups of three or four, trying not to attract attention. Sid and Jacey, up front, steered us around the corner. Across the street, engines gunned. Before we'd gone a block, a half-dozen motorcycles tailed us. So much for the element of surprise. Would they try to bust us out here, away from the action? Our pace picked up.

"Take the next left," Raoul called to Jacey. "It's one-way." But the motorcycles followed us around the corner, ignoring the oncoming traffic.

Drivers slowed to gawk at the spectacle, and people razzed them. Without any verbal cue we went left again at the next corner. A minute later we took one more left, and we had circled the block. Up ahead at the barricades, the cops seemed unaware. Raoul and Jacey stepped into the deserted street. Others followed cautiously.

I took a couple of steps out, then turned to check the cycle cops shadowing us. They made no attempt to corral us back onto the sidewalk. But the revving of their engines alerted the barricade cops. Nightsticks snapped to attention. Instead of coming after us, though, the cops remained stationary, trapping the rest of the demonstrators behind the barricades.

As we approached the end of the barricades, a cheer went up from the crowd. "The streets belong to the people!" Sid hollered, and a dozen voices shouted it back to us.

The horse cops down at the corner got the signal to advance. A dozen mounted officers cantered up the street. Twenty feet from us, they pulled up, waved their clubs, and pointed to the sidewalk. One officer rode his mount up close. The horse's eyes were wide open, and both animal and rider wheezed for breath.

The cop turned his opaque visor toward us. His mouth was a grimace. "You are ordered to get out of the street!"

A few people jeered, but most were quiet. I thought it would be smart to obey, but I didn't want to be the first to move.

Raoul stepped further into the street. "Horses won't step on you," he yelled, and started a countdown for a die-in. At "zero," the little knot of protesters hit the pavement. I followed suit, sticking close to the curb. In a pinch, I could make a run for the crowd behind the barricades.

The sight of twenty bodies blocking the street seemed to confuse the horses or their riders or both. Behind us, though, the motorcycle cops revved their engines and rode their bikes right through the supine crowd. I staggered up and got on the sidewalk. The cops turned their cycles and rode back at us. "Idiots!" I yelled as they roared by. "You could kill someone!"

A squad of foot troopers headed our way. This was getting serious. I turned toward the barricades, but there was no escape in that direction — the whole crowd was coming right down the sidewalk at us. As they reached the end of the barricade, they spilled into the street. "March to Union Square," people shouted. "Take the street!"

The foot police, who were spread along the block, seemed taken aback by the sheer chaos. They stood and watched as we marched past. Then, as if on silent command, twenty cops came running beyond the end of the barricades and formed two lines along the flank of the departing crowd. They snapped to attention, paused for a moment, then charged directly into the crowd, clubs flailing.

Fear gripped my stomach. Which way to turn? People on the sidewalk were just as likely to get hit as those out in the street. Near me, a cop knocked a guy to the pavement. A woman in a white and red medic's jacket reached out to help him to his feet. As she straightened up, a horse cop rode over and struck her across the back with his club.

My fists clenched. "You stinking coward!" He jerked his horse around. I backed away, groping for the store wall behind me. At that moment, the medic let out a sickening shriek. The horse had kicked her in the head. Blood flowed from the wound. The cop wheeled around and rode away. Several of us ran to her aid, pulling her onto the sidewalk.

Another medic ran up and started first aid. I stepped away. My heart was pounding. The cops had backed away and regrouped their lines. Much of the crowd was retreating toward the barricades, as if that were a safety zone. I was closer to a small group which found an outlet toward the right-hand intersection. "Let's go to Union Square," someone shouted.

Jacey jumped in. "No, let's do a die-in at the next corner!" He ran on ahead, beckoning us after him. "10! 9! 8!" he shouted. Jenny and Raoul picked it up. "7! 6! 5!" I was swept along. "4! 3! 2! 1!" Thirty people screamed and sprawled in the street.

Once again, I stayed near the curb, ready to bolt. But no cops responded. "I bet they have orders to stay and guard the Holiday Inn," Sid said as we propped ourselves up on our elbows. Around us, traffic backed up. Horns honked, and heads thrust out of windows to yell at us. We yelled back, castigating the drivers as if they were to blame for the state of the world. Minutes ticked by. Cars did U-turns to escape our blockade. We sat up, marveling at the authorities' slow response.

Finally a squad of police marched our way, followed by the motorcycles. We scrambled up and headed onward. The cops halted, and a half-block later we did another die-in. This time the law moved more quickly. As we hurried out of the street, a couple of guys grabbed a trash can and rolled it into the path of our pursuers. Others dragged newsstands into the street. The cops stopped to remove the debris, and we continued our slow retreat.

Union Square was only a couple of blocks away. Hopefully the second protest was tamer. For once, I'd be glad to see a picket loop. Enough risking arrest for one day.

Suddenly, a bunch of burly construction workers charged out of a construction site and into our midst. What the hell? Next to me, two of them grabbed a punk and dragged him back toward the police. Another got a woman in a choke hold, forcing her away from our crowd. "It's the undercovers!" Jenny yelled. "Look out!"

Undercovers! I jerked my head around, trying to see all directions at once. Everyone was confused, and the narcs picked off a half-dozen people. A punk who'd dragged newsstands into the street got nailed. Had they targeted him, or was it random? I hustled over to where Raoul and Jenny were standing. Safety in numbers. Especially when the numbers were as big as Raoul.

Others clustered around us, and I realized that we were sitting ducks for a circle-and-surround arrest. Well, better that way than to be grabbed by a narc. But having lost the element of surprise, the undercovers faded behind the line of the approaching uniformed officers. Beyond them, we could see clumps of other protesters coming toward us, oblivious to our plight. "Let's get to Union Square," Jenny said, and we headed that way.

People were chattering around me, but I stayed to myself. That was a close call. Maybe I should get out while the getting out was good. But with undercovers on the prowl, it was best to stay with the group. Anyway, I wasn't quite ready to let go.

We turned onto Powell and headed toward Union Square. From a block away I could see a small demonstration up at the Saint Francis. The crowd marched in a picket loop, and the cops stood at ease.

Our little band reached the intersection at Post. Along the north side of Union Square, out of sight of the cops, a row of white limousines sat idling. It got under my skin, and apparently Sid's, too. He jogged down Post a quarter-block, turned toward us, and sprinted toward the last limo. With a leap he landed on the trunk. "Yeah!" Raoul bellowed as Sid bounded across the roof, down the hood, and hurdled across to the next trunk. The shiny white sheet metal resounded with every step. The chauffeurs standing nearby seemed frozen in place as Sid sprang onto the third limo, cleared the roof in three long strides, and landed on the hood. He thrust his fists into the air in triumph, a grin splitting his face. Then he jumped down, trotted on up to our crowd, and melted into the picket loop.

Compared to Sid's show, the demo was pretty dull. The crowd was thinning out, and people I knew were leaving. Raoul and Jenny were staying in the City to meet with Sid and the punk AGs. I looked around, but didn't spot anyone else familiar. I knew it was risky to leave alone, but I figured I could blend into the downtown crowd.

A slight headache was coming on. But overall I felt good. We'd fought them to a draw. They busted a few people, but mostly we hung together and outran them. And I'd been right in the middle of the fray.

I was approaching BART when a big white stretch limo pulled around the corner. Whether it had anything to do with what we were protesting, I didn't know. And I didn't care. As it stopped at the light, I bounded out into the intersection. No words came to my lips, but with both hands pumping I flipped off the tinted windows. I couldn't tell if there was anyone in the back seats, but it didn't matter. I pranced around the front, blocking its path, then circled to catch the driver's side. "Ha!" I called as the chauffeur rolled down his window.

He leaned out, squinting at me. "Is this some sort of political statement?"

"No," I yelled as I regained the sidewalk. "It's personal."

I wasn't even sure what I meant, but it felt good that the guy couldn't think of an answer. Heedless of the stares of bystanders, I headed down into the train station. As I went through the turnstyle, the station agent eyed me from inside her control booth. I reined my energy in, feeling suddenly vulnerable. Had the cops called ahead and put her on alert? But she didn't budge. I stifled my laughter as I rode the escalator down to the platform. Flipping off a limo in broad daylight. Maybe I was making progress. Of some sort or another.

Saturday, July 14, 1984

SIT. WHAT DO you expect to do at a Convention, anyway? Even at a People's Convention.

Sit.

People's Convention was shaping up as a decent networking event with no impact whatsoever on the Democrats preparing to gather across the Bay. Oh, sure, there was a lingering hope that Jesse Jackson would make a surprise appearance at the People's Convention's Saturday evening program. But any formal link was out of the question. The Revolutionary Workers Party's wheeling and dealing had fallen through. I felt bugged at myself for not having objected more loudly to the closed-door process back in the Spring.

So here we were at the main event, held at Laney Community College in downtown Oakland. I had just come from a steering committee meeting. The Jesse Jackson fiasco cast a pall over the RWP clique, and their response was to circle the wagons. I settled for voicing my one overriding concern: that no one from the RWP — and particularly not Lionel, their head honcho — "facilitate" the final plenary, when the People's Platform was to be adopted. I addressed my objection directly to Lionel and a couple of other RWPers. It felt good to make one last stand for democracy.

"No problem," Lionel himself told me. "I don't want to do it. We'll ask someone from the Federation for Afro-American Unity. How's that suit you?"

Great, I thought. A nice tokenistic touch. But it beat having Lionel railroading the RWP agenda.

Having delivered myself of that burden, I left the meeting. I walked out into the lobby and got a drink of water. A poster on the wall listed afternoon workshops. Nathaniel was doing a slide show on the history of nonviolent resistance. CISPES had a report from the front lines in El Salvador. Daniel was helping facilitate a workshop on the upcoming action at Bohemian Grove.

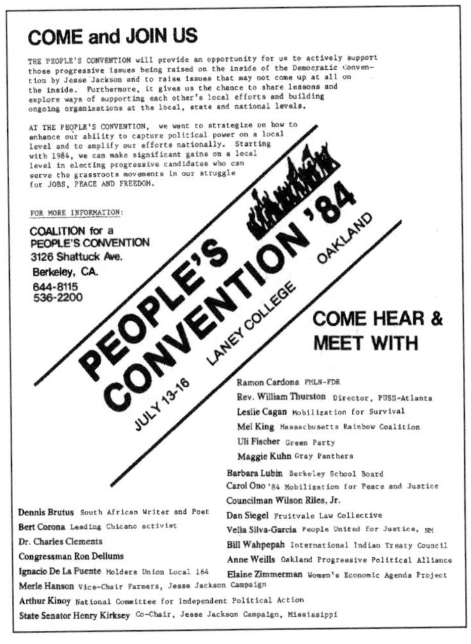

People's Convention was a leftist-inspired alternative gathering aimed at bringing together the left wing of the Democratic constituency with radical non-electoral groups.

Holly would probably be at the Boho Grove workshop. The previous day she'd been on her way to an overnight date with Norm, and even though she stopped long enough to tell me that she and Norm weren't lovers any more, it seemed like she was generally avoiding me. She had plans that evening with Sara, and had talked about spending the night in the City. Was it Angie's return, or a deeper malaise? How weird it would be if we ran into each other at People's Convention, former friends meeting by chance.

I looked back at the schedule. Claudia was co-facilitating a panel discussion on alternative media that I knew I should be at. I wanted to show her there weren't hard feelings about our argument a few weeks before. What better way than sitting through her panel?

Then I looked out the lobby windows at the central plaza. A big swath of the plaza was bathed in sunlight. If I had to sit, it could at least be in the sun. Why not set up a LAG table? Get some of our own alternative media out to the masses.

The plaza was a concrete square punctuated by steel benches and potted trees. Bland buildings of brick and glass abutted all sides. I found a picnic table in the sun and set up shop, laying out a half-dozen issues of Direct Action and a tray of buttons for all and sundry causes. Our bright red "Blockade Livermore" bumper stickers went up front, while the "Don't Vote" ones, with LAG's name neatly trimmed off the bottom, got tucked behind the buttons.

Conventioneers — mainly lefties from the Bay Area, with a smattering of visitors from around the country — drifted past the table for an hour or so, occasionally stopping to ask a question or offer an opinion. Nothing too taxing. I pictured a low-key afternoon, following which I might skip the evening plenary and benefit concert. If Jesse Jackson made the scene, he'd have to get along without me. How about a long walk around Berkeley? Later on, I could get high and look at art books, maybe play some guitar. Come back refreshed the next day.

A drop of sweat fell into my eye. I wished I had some cold water, but I didn't want to go look for it. Why didn't we have strolling vendors, like at a baseball game? Baseball. For all I knew, the A's might be playing just down the freeway, two BART stations away. Was there ever such a gorgeous afternoon to be out at the ballpark? Midway up the right field bleachers, beer in hand, gazing down at the vast expanse of fresh-mown grass.

I looked out across the barren plaza. Even Santa Rita jail was greener than this place. I remembered my last day in jail, a year earlier, how I lay in the little patch of grass waiting for my name to be called over the loudspeaker. If only it were that simple today: "Jeffrey Harrison, thank you for your contribution to global revolution. You may now go home with a clean conscience."

The plaza seemed to undulate as the heat rose from the parched pavement. The potted trees drooped like they were melting. Off in the distance, I spied two figures heading my way. Against the glaring backdrop they were silhouettes, one tall and massive, the other short and wiry. Like Raoul and Jenny. Was I hallucinating? Raoul at the People's Convention? What for, to tell me that Melissa was leading the War Chest Tours?

As the spectre drifted closer, I ventured a few words: "Hey, you guys, what's up?"

"We've come to relieve your watch, soldier," Raoul called out. "At ease!"

"Wow," I said, unable to contain my surprise. "What's the occasion?"

Jenny brushed her wavy hair back over her shoulders. "We were down at Raoul's print shop, and decided to see how things were going here," she said. Her eyes fell on the "Don't Vote" bumper stickers, and I felt bad about hiding them.

"So when does People's Convention nominate Jesse Jackson?" Raoul said.

I smiled wanly. "I'm not sure. It's a back room deal."

"Not surprising," Raoul said.

"Not really," I said hastily. "People's Convention is about networking, not nominations." I felt irritated at Raoul for making me defend People's Convention. I cast for another subject. "So, how's the War Chest Tour plans?"

Jenny looked concerned. "It's hard to say. The meetings have been amazing. There's a whole community forming around this, people I never met before. As far as the Tours themselves, well, I'm trying not to worry about how many people show up."

Raoul's eyes narrowed. "We've covered the bases. Word is out. We'll see who has the guts to be there when it really matters."

I thought of having to miss the Monday Tour because of the end of People's Convention. "I'll be there Wednesday, for sure," I said. "And Thursday."

Raoul took a seat at the picnic table and flipped through the box of buttons. Jenny looked at me carefully. "Have you talked to Angie?"

I looked up quickly. "No, have you?"

Jenny shook her head. "I probably won't be the first person she calls," she said.

I wondered if I would be. "I think she gets in late tomorrow," I said. "I'm hoping to see her Monday." It surprised me that I hadn't been thinking more about Angie. Maybe I'd let go more than I realized.

I accepted a dollar from Raoul for a button, then looked up and saw Melissa walking our way. I'd heard she was around, but it was the first time I'd seen her. I looked from Melissa to Raoul. There you have the two extremes of it, I thought. Their presence felt like an affirmation, not so much of People's Convention, but of my conviction that we were all in the struggle together. I'd be at their events, and here they were at mine.

Then I remembered the graffiti on the office window. Oh, boy. I stepped out to intercept Melissa with a hug, hoping she would say hi and continue on her way to a workshop. But she came over to the table and set her daypack down. "Hi, Jenny," she said. "Did you ever talk to Raoul about who had to clean up the mess he left at the office?"

Jenny shuffled her feet and didn't answer. Melissa continued to act as if Raoul weren't present. "I wish I got paid for every time I had to pick up after someone so immature."

Raoul stood up. "You can say it to me," he said. "I can handle it."

Melissa slowly turned to face him. "Maybe when people grow up and stop spraypainting and running around in the streets, we might actually accomplish something."

Raoul stiffened. "So what are you accomplishing?"

"I'm staying focused on what really matters," she said. "Not chasing after every new fad that comes along."

"Great," Raoul said, exchanging a knowing look with Jenny. "Let's go back to Livermore where we can be completely safe and totally irrelevant."

I winced, thinking of the April Livermore demo. Melissa put her hands on her hips. "You act like street protests are this great moment of freedom," she said impatiently. "But what's free about everyone following the person with the biggest mouth? How's it different than the Democrats following the corporation with the biggest checkbook?"

I had to admit she had a point. At City protests, I never got that feeling of shared decision-making, of direct democracy, that we'd had at Livermore and Vandenberg.

Raoul frowned. "If people come to a protest and act like sheep, you can't prevent it. You can't force people to be free. All you can do is create opportunities."

"Opportunities for what?" Melissa said, her eyes widening. "That's the whole point. For what?"

Big chance of agreement on that question, I thought. Yet it wasn't like the two of them were miles apart. Neither one had any use for the Democrats. Both believed that direct action was the only way to change the world. What we needed was a middle voice. An anarchist feminist pacifist street protester. Sara! Where was she when we needed her?

I tried to get between them. "We're talking about two different types of actions here. It's not a contradiction. There's no reason we can't be doing both."

"No reason except nonviolence," Melissa scoffed. "You're not going to see me trying to start a riot."

"We're not going to see you, period," Raoul shot back. "If you're scared to be where the action is, stay home."

Melissa stuck her face right in his. "What do you know about courage? You'll go start trouble with the police, then run away. So what will the police do? They'll go and take out their frustration on homeless people who can't run away. That's real brave."

Raoul took a step back, and I tried again to intervene. "This isn't accomplishing anything. What good does it do to trash each other's work?"

Melissa turned on me. "Work, I respect. Running around like a bunch of kids, seeing what sort of trouble you can cause, I don't respect."

"Melissa," I said sharply, "it isn't about age. There might be something happening that you don't understand."

"Maybe there's something *you* don't understand," she snapped back. "Like principles." She slung her daypack over her shoulder, gave me one last aggravated look, and stalked off.

I watched her go, retracing my words. Was I that offensive? I felt an impulse to call after her. But the words stuck in my throat. I'd spoken the truth. I wasn't going to apologize for that. If she didn't like it, was it my problem?

Raoul turned to Jenny. "What a mother hen! Did you hear what she said about kids? That's how she sees it. Kids are unruly, and adults have to keep them in line."

Now I felt like I had to cover for Melissa. "She has good intentions," I said. "She's trying to do what's best for LAG."

Raoul eyed me coolly. "Yeah. It's 'for our own good.' Where have we heard that one before? It's all about control. Fear of spontaneity." He turned to Jenny. "We need to get going if we're going to be at Jacey's by five," he said.

Jenny cast an apologetic look at me. "We'd stay longer, but we have a meeting."

"Sure," I said. I stood up and gave her a one-armed hug. Raoul leaned back as I turned to him, so I just bid him goodbye. "Thanks for coming by," I said. "Hope to see you Monday at the People's Convention march, after the War Chest Tour."

"Yeah, we'll try," Jenny answered.

As they walked away, I surveyed the plaza. Although it was only mid-afternoon, the shadows of the faceless buildings covered most of the area. I wished I had a sweatshirt. Was it too early to go home?

Damn. Why not go find Melissa and ask her to sign a permission slip?

I stood there a while longer, debating what to do. Finally, I started packing up the buttons and newspapers. As I did, weariness washed over me. I leaned one hand on the table and tossed the rest of the papers in the box. What a relief it would be to get away from all this.

Sunday, July 15, 1984

SHE WAS back. Well, at least as close as San Francisco. She called from Stonehenge around nine that evening. I wanted to get on BART and go straight over there, but Angie seemed to be hanging back.

"What's going on?" I finally said, hurt that she wasn't just as impatient to see me.

"I want to see you, too, Jeff," she said. "But not tonight. I thought about it a lot on the drive down here, and I just don't know about sleeping together while I'm here."

"Why not?" I hadn't even considered this possibility.

She sighed. "It doesn't feel right. I mean with Holly. To come into town and sleep with you."

"Oh, no," I said, "Our relationship is definitely open. It's different than in the Spring. Holly just had a fling with Norm last month."

Angie was silent. "It doesn't matter," she finally said. "It still feels the same to me."

My heart sank. I was glad we were on the phone and not in person. "So," I said quietly, "when will I see you?"

"Let's make plans," she said, lightening her tone. "How about Thursday, after the War Chest Tour?"

Thursday? What's wrong with Monday, Tuesday, and Wednesday? But I held my tongue. No pressure. Just go along with Thursday. Probably something else will materialize along the way. "Okay," I said. "Thursday night, too?"

"Yeah," she said hesitantly. "I'll keep it open. Let's see how it feels then." I didn't say anything. After a moment, she picked up the thread. "I'll see you a lot this week. Starting with the War Chest Tour tomorrow."

"No," I said, wishing she were more tuned in. "It's the closing day of People's Convention."

"Why don't you skip it and come on the Tour?" A challenge lurked in her voice.

"I'm one of the core organizers," I said testily. "I can't just skip the final session."

"Sure, I understand," she said. "If you change your mind, that's where I'll be. Otherwise, I guess I won't be seeing you tomorrow."

"We have the People's Convention march at three," I said. "You should come to it after the Tour. That's why we set it for later. Do you want to meet up before the march?"

She was silent for a moment. "Let me get some sleep and I'll know better how much I can do. Right now, I'm exhausted from the drive down. I don't want to get sick. I'll have to see how I feel tomorrow after the War Chest Tour. But probably I'll be there."

"Great," I said with no conviction.

Her voice regained a little vivacity. "So, I want to get to bed now. I'll see you tomorrow, or Tuesday for sure."

I grasped at the possibility of seeing her the next day. "It'd be great if you made it to our march," I said. "I'm really looking forward to seeing you."

"Me, too," she said. "I'll talk to you soon."

Click. That was it. For a few minutes after she hung up, I just sat there on the living room floor with the phone dangling in my hand. So it all came to nothing? What was the point in seeing her Thursday afternoon, if she was just going to send me packing that evening?

But even in my gloom, something else was poking through. After all, what about last week when she told me she was coming back? Her voice had been all whispery then, and she'd told me she loved me. Something was out of whack. How could she have changed so much? Once we saw each other, it would be different.

Monday, July 16, 1984

Everything that is wrong-headed, cynical, and vicious in me today traces straight back to that evil hour in September of '69 when I decided to get heavily involved in the political process.

— Dr. Hunter S. Thompson, "Fear and Loathing on the Campaign Trail '72"

I LEFT EARLY for the People's Convention march to get away from People's Convention. All morning I'd run errands, avoiding the final plenary. I could picture it: two dozen work groups getting up and reading their platform planks, to be debated and adopted by the larger group. What drama. What suspense.

But what really happened was worse. When I finally dropped in around noon, the ill-lit auditorium was half empty. Most people slumped in their seats, scarcely paying attention. The platform planks were being read, but it wasn't the various work groups that were making presentations. It was Lionel, ensconced behind the rostrum, a John Deere hat on his head to show his solidarity with the rustic masses. He read each platform plank and called for a voice vote of acceptance. RWP ringers in the crowd guaranteed compliance.

"What's going on?" I demanded of one of the other organizers near the back door. "Groups were supposed to read their own planks. And Lionel wasn't supposed to be facilitating at all."

"Yeah," she said, avoiding my eyes. "We decided it would be too time-consuming to have each delegation go up and read their plank. And besides, the debates could get messy. So Lionel's doing it. It's more efficient."

Efficiency? This was what I worked all Spring for? Efficiency?

I glared at Lionel, who droned on, never looking up. I simmered. Should I challenge the process, or just walk out? I looked around the auditorium for familiar faces. But between the dim light and the lowered heads, I saw no one I could count on. Disgusted, I turned on my heels and marched out, giving the door a hard shove behind me. Without speaking to another person, I headed straight for BART. Get to the City. Find the War Chest Tour. Maybe it's not too late to join the real action.

I caught a train within minutes, but it wasn't quite the escape I had hoped. Riding through the transbay tunnel, I chastised myself for not speaking up at the plenary. If Lionel was going to out and out lie to me, I had a right to disrupt him. Set the record straight.

For what, though? So a bunch of people could gape at me like I was some loony who had wandered in off the street? Would even one person have supported me?

Was that the point? What about simply speaking the truth, plain and simple, and letting the chips fall where they may?

Too late now. Always too late. Probably too late to find the War Chest Tour. Why wasn't I part of it all along? I thought about all the fights over the Tours, how angry and polarized people had been, to the point of walking out. But however deep the misunderstandings ran, I knew in my heart that no one in LAG had lied to me. Right now, that seemed like a big deal.

I made it to the City by two o'clock and hurried into the financial district looking for some sign of the Tour. Hopefully I could find Angie in the crowd. Maybe we could skip the People's Convention march and go off, just the two of us.

But block after block looked like business as usual. I made it as far as B of A, and there wasn't so much as a cop in sight. Maybe I should ask the security guards if they knew. I went up to the big plate-glass doors and peered into the lobby. A guard slouched against a planter-box. He eyed me suspiciously, and I decided against knocking.

I meandered through the district, feeling more and more alienated. No one made eye contact, not the business-types, not the drivers, not even the

The nukecycle was rolling for the People's Convention march, but the pedal and chain assembly wasn't completed. So the nukecycle was hitched to the back of a tractor and towed in the march down Market Street.

bike messengers. I stopped and got a soft drink, and even the clerk didn't look up.

I ended up back on Market Street around quarter till three. I didn't want to go to the gathering spot for the People's Convention march yet, or I'd just wind up standing around for another hour. Maybe I should wander down south of Market and find a gallery or some good graffiti.

But who did I run into as I crossed Market? Hank, driving an old flatbed truck right up the street. "Hey, come help me find parking," he hollered, and I was hooked in again. For the best, I figured. Just see the march through, get some closure. Anyway, Angie might well be there. If she showed up, it would be worth the effort.

"Where's the nukecycle?" I asked Hank.

"I unloaded it back at Embarcadero Plaza. Mort and Lyle are watching it."

"So it's up and running?"

His grip on the wheel tightened. "No," he said in a low voice. "Never could get the chain to hold. We'll have to tow it."

"Oh." It wasn't that big a deal to me, but I could see that Hank was really depressed about it. "Too bad," I said.

"Yeah." He didn't look at me. "How many chances do you get to drive a nukecycle right up to the Democratic Convention?"

"Not many," I sympathized. "But there's still a few days left."

"No, this was it. This is the one day I'm taking off work."

"So you're not coming to any of the War Chest Tours?"

"No way. I'm not getting my head beat in for the Democrats. What's it gonna prove? Maybe I'll go to Rock Against Reagan, but not the Tours."

He wheeled into a gravel lot, and I let the matter drop. I'd about had my fill of politicking, of trying to persuade people to work together. If he doesn't want to be where the action is, fine. I'll find people who do.

We left the truck and hiked back to Embarcadero Plaza. Mort and Lyle stood guard over the nukecycle, which gleamed in the afternoon sun, replete with spoked wheels and a blue tailfin. In lieu of actual pilots, Hank had strapped in dummies wearing every mask he could lay his hands on — Reagan, Bush, Maggie Thatcher... Along the tailfin, he had painted "Livermore Action Group" in bold letters. "Had to let the Democrats know we were here," he said.

I smiled, but my eyes wandered from the nukecycle to the growing crowd, searching for Angie or any of the War Chest Tour people. Nothing so far. Relax. There was still time. They were probably on the way.

Mort came around the nukecycle and clapped me on the shoulder. I scowled. I was still upset with Mort, not just for being negative, but for being oblivious to boot. But this was hardly the place to hash it out. "I thought you'd be at the plenary this morning," I said by way of conversation.

"No, I had to work. Anyway, it wasn't like there were going to be any surprises."

I laughed ironically. "Well, not the sort you'd wish." I told him about Lionel's duplicity.

Mort shrugged. "Doesn't surprise me. I thought the RWP had a little more integrity than that, but that's the story on those sectarian groups. They may have good politics, but if you're not a member, they don't owe you anything."

"Least of all the truth," I said.

Five hundred people had gathered. I scanned the lineup. As promised, two big tractors were up in front. Hank worked with one of the farmers to hitch the nukecycle to a towbar.

Earth First!, who hadn't come near the People's Convention itself, lined up with a banner protesting clear-cutting. Abalone Alliance brought a bunch of signs about Diablo Canyon. There was a cluster of nurses in uniform, a student group from S.F. State, and small contingents from several Labor unions — a more diverse mix than you'd see at a peace march. Now if only the War Chesters would show up to appreciate what we've got here. Surely they weren't still marching, or I'd have seen some trace of them. Maybe they couldn't be bothered. Could I blame them? I could think of places I'd rather be. Most of them involving Angie.

I sighed. Our Thursday night date seemed ages away.

A little after three, the monitors started lining us up. Fine, I thought. Someone has to get us going. Just don't embarrass me by trying to keep us on the sidewalk. Especially if the War Chest Tour joins us. We'd take over Market Street with ease.

The arrival of the RWP honchos, fresh from hijacking the plenary session, dampened my mood. Naturally, they paraded right to the front with their

Sista Boom, a women's marching drum corps, enlivened many marches around the time of the 1984 Democratic Convention.

The People's Convention march coming up Market Street? Well, probably not, given the umbrellas. But this shot from the same period shows what the People's Convention march looked like.

banner. Lionel hoisted himself onto the back of one of the tractors and grabbed a bullhorn to tell us that the goal of the march was to deliver the People's Platform directly to the Democrats. I appreciated his insistence that we were marching to the Convention, but then he started into a speech on how the Platform represented the voice of "The People."

I groaned. Lionel still had the John Deere cap on, and I debated walking over behind him and making a comment about urban agriculture. I looked around. Was I the only one with no patience for this?

Apparently not. "Let's go!" someone yelled. "Let's march!"

For the first time all day, a smile broke across my face. "Let's go!" I yelled. Through the crowd, other voices picked it up. "Let's march!" Signs were hoisted, banners pulled taut.

Lionel looked chagrined, but acquiesced to the will of the masses. The tractors lurched forward, and we were underway. It looked odd, the tractors and the nukecycle being out in the street while the rest of us marched on the sidewalk. Hopefully that would change soon enough.

Bullhorns pumped out the usual chants: "What do we want? Justice! When do we want it? Now!," "Hey hey, ho ho, Ronald Reagan's got to go," and the ever-popular, "The people, united, will never be defeated!"

Leafletters roamed the periphery, and I was struck by how many people seemed willing, even eager, to accept a flyer. Chalk that up to the tractors.

I filtered through the crowd. Several motorcycle cops cruised alongside of us, acting like an escort, while making it clear where the boundaries lay. Still, there were five hundred of us. If we decided to take over the westbound lanes of Market, there wasn't much a handful of cops could do.

How to get it started, though? I was wishing the War Chesters would show up and lend support, when a construction zone solved the problem. Up ahead, scaffolding and a bunch of sawhorses blocked most of the sidewalk. "Into the street!" someone yelled, and a cheer went up as the march swung off the curb and fell in step behind the tractors, filling the right-hand lane.

"Yeah!" I hollered. "Take the street!" The cops on their cycles glided over a lane, as if they had expected it all along. I looked behind us. A couple of patrol cars brought up the rear, shielding us from any lunatic drivers who might try to get through. I pointed it out to Mort and Hank. "For once, the cops are doing their job," I said.

But wouldn't you know it, several monitors decided to fill the authority vacuum. Using bullhorns and hand signals, they tried to herd the march back onto the sidewalk as soon as we passed the construction site.

"What the hell," Hank said. "Is this for real?"

Up front, some people got back on the sidewalk. I looked around, exasperated. But before I could think what to do, the Earth First! folks got in gear. Raising their banner higher, they yelled out, "Keep the street! Keep the street!" That was all I needed. "Keep the street!" I echoed. Dozens of other voices picked up the cry, followed by cheers as the monitors relented and we marched on down Market Street.

As the chants took hold again, Mort and Hank and I drifted further back. A TV van wheeled past us in the far lane, filming as it went.

"Not bad," Mort said. "This'll probably get decent coverage."

"Yeah," Hank said. "We should have tractors in every march."

"And nukecycles," I said. Now that we were underway, I was feeling better. Angie and the War Chesters would join us soon enough, and get to see that we were already in the street. "This will be the only memorable part of People's Convention," I said.

Mort nodded. "Luckily, it's the part that the media will focus on."

"There's a lesson there somewhere," I said.

"Yeah — stick with our strength," Hank said. "We've got to get going on BARF. I'm a lot more psyched about that than anything happening at the Convention. Let's go after Reagan."

The Berkeley Anti-Reagan Festival. I'd hardly given it a thought lately. It was true, compared to the Convention, BARF was a breath of fresh air.

Mort looked at Hank. "I think you're onto something. We need a way to participate in the electoral arena without compromising with the liberals. BARF might do it."

As he spoke, I drifted off to thoughts of Angie. BARF had been her inspiration. At least she'd been the one who kept bringing it up back in the Spring and making people laugh until Coordinating Council approved the seed money. I smiled wistfully. Now I'd be doing it alone. Well, not alone. But it wasn't going to be the same without Angie.

Lost in thought, I bumped into the person in front of me. I started to excuse myself, when someone stepped on my heels. "We've got a logjam," Hank said.

I waited a minute, figuring it was a bottleneck as we turned the corner toward Moscone Center. But up ahead, people were striking their banners. I made my way toward the front. The farmers driving the tractors had stepped down and were conversing with a couple of cops. "Just keep marching," I said to no one in particular. "The cops won't stop us if we just keep going."

"Oh, the cops didn't stop us," a guy from Abalone Alliance said. "Some flunky from the Democrats came out to meet us."

"Wait a minute," I said, pushing to the front where Lionel and a couple of other RWPers were conversing with a guy in a suit and tie. "We were marching to the Convention."

Lionel elbowed me away from the Democrat and eyed me coolly. "Change of plans," he said. "A couple of us are going with this delegate to deliver the Platform in person."

"No way," I said in disbelief. "The whole point was to march to the Convention." I looked for Mort or Hank, but neither was to be seen. Around me, people were drifting away.

Lionel spoke tersely. "There's no way they'd let us march to the Convention. It's cordoned off. The delegate came out to head off a confrontation."

I stared at him. "Do you really think they would have tried to stop us? Or could have? How would it look, arresting farmers on tractors?"

He cast an imperious glance around. "It's moot. The march is over. People are leaving."

They were. I turned away. Enough of you, I thought. I'm getting out of here. What a fizzle. Where were the War Chesters? They wouldn't have stood for this. I'd have had some allies.

But maybe it was better that they hadn't showed up. They never cared about this march. Maybe they were right. I stepped back and looked around one more time, wishing Angie would make a last-minute appearance.

I didn't feel like leaving alone. I hunted up Hank and Mort, who were with the nukecycle. "The tractors are going over to the Vote Peace rally," Hank said. "We're going to hitch a ride. Wanna go?"

"Vote Peace?" I shook my head. I wanted company, but not at the price of listening to a bunch of speeches about peace. "No, it's been a long day," I said. "I think I'll head home. Call me if you're going to Rock Against Reagan."

I COULDN'T SHAKE it. Sure, I'd see Angie at the LAG demo the next day. But it stung that she didn't show up at an event I'd worked on all Spring. One lousy hour out of her life. Was it too much to ask?

I wished Holly wouldn't be home when I got back, so I could have the apartment to myself. But she was there. I tried to tell her about the day. Although she listened, I could tell none of it mattered to her. And why should it? A fraudulent plenary, a boring march — why should she care? Politics as usual.

Holly looked at me with concern. "How are you doing? You look upset."

"Me?" I felt awkward, exposed. What was I supposed to tell her? That I wished she weren't home, so I could be alone with my disappointments? That if only Angie had shown up, it would all be different?

"I guess I'm angry over People's Convention," I said, sticking to externals. "I put so much of my life into it, and it came to nothing."

She looked at me consolingly. "That's too bad. That must be tough to deal with."

Holly went to bed early that evening. I lay down with her for a while, but had trouble keeping still, and got up again before she fell asleep.

I opened a beer and took my guitar out onto the balcony. It was a warm night, and the breeze wafted a faint scent of the Bay toward me. I picked out a pattern on the guitar, planning to run through my songs for the next day's rally.

Hopefully Angie would be there. I really needed to see her. Ask her to move back, the impulse came. As soon as you see her. Take her aside and speak your heart.

Wait, slow down. Scope out her mood first. Was she open to discussion? Or would it come across like an attack on her new life up north? Relax. She's here for five days. There'll be time to talk.

On and on my mind spun, till a cramp in my arm called me back to the present. I had been sitting with my hands poised on the guitar, ready to play, but not making a sound. I shook my head, trying to remember what I had been so intently pondering.

The phone rang, breaking my reverie. What now, I thought. Probably logistics for tomorrow. Let it go. But wait — what if it was Angie, trying to reach me? Maybe there was some good explanation. Maybe she was in Berkeley, and wanted to get together...

I hurried inside. "Hello?"

"Jeff," came a whispery voice.

"Angie — where are you?"

"Home, now," she said. "I've been in jail all day. They busted the whole Tour, didn't you hear?"

"No," I said, awash in relief. She had an excuse for missing our march. "What happened?"

"Hardly anything, really. I went down there with Sid and Ariel. When we got to B of A, where we were meeting, there were riot police, motorcycles, horses, everything. There were barely more protesters than cops."

"Many LAG people?" I asked.

"Some — Jenny and Raoul, Sid, Sara, Alby, Moonstone. But Karina wasn't there, that surprised me. I think she was doing some other action. Mainly it was punks and squatters, those types. We started with a die-in at B of A. We were on the plaza, so it was legal. There were cops all around us, though. After that, we moved across the street to some corporation called Diamond Shamrock. Everyone was staying real close together, yelling at the cops. But people were pretty scared, you could tell. We got on the sidewalk again, in front of the building, and Sid got up on a trash can to give a rap. All the while, this line of cops is marching back and forth, hup-two-three-four. People started moving away, but the cops swung around and trapped us against the wall. They got on a bullhorn and announced we were under arrest."

"And they busted all of you?"

"A few people got away," she said, "but most of us just sat down. That was smart, because a lot of the punks weren't used to dealing with riot cops. Raoul started chanting, 'Democracy in Action,' and we all picked that up. They arrested about a hundred of us. We were actually lucky. Some other people were doing die-ins up the block, and I heard they got beat up by undercovers."

"I'm surprised they let you out of jail," I said.

"They wanted to hold us," she said. "We heard that they wanted to stick us with felony conspiracy charges and keep us in jail till the Convention is over. But the National Lawyers' Guild went to some judge and got him to sign an order saying that because we hadn't actually disrupted anything, they had to let us loose."

Well, I thought, there is a little justice. Or a loose wheel in the judicial grinder. Whatever, Angie was free. "Will I see you at the LAG demo tomorrow?" I asked.

"Oh, sure. I want to hear you sing."

That's what I needed to hear. "Are you going to the Central America march before?"

"Probably not. I need to catch up on sleep. But I'll meet you at the LAG demo."

I nodded to myself. "Good, I'll see you there," I said. I paused for a moment. "I love you, Angie."

"I love you, too, Jeff," she said. "See you tomorrow."

Tuesday, July 17, 1984

It was sometime in the middle of the night that it struck me — LAG should issue a press release, condemning the War Chest Tour arrests. I could go down to the office first thing in the morning, type up a statement, call some Coordinating Council people for approval, and send it off to the local media. LAG's name would get far more attention than a statement by the War Chest Tour organizers. And it would be a way of rallying support for them. Whatever people's concerns about the Tours, I was confident I could overcome dissent in the name of unity against police repression.

Central America support groups organized a solemn funeral march through downtown San Francisco at lunchtime on the second day of the Convention. Several thousand silent marchers bore signs, coffins, and flowers through the streets.

But I didn't figure on getting to the office and finding Claudia thinking exactly the same thing. I tried not to act too surprised, but I had to ask what inspired her.

"I heard about the arrests on KPFA last night," she told me. "It's an attack on all of us. It isn't about supporting this or that faction. If we don't speak up now, we have no credibility."

We? That wasn't a word I expected to hear coming from Claudia. But I'd take her help any time. We hammered out a quick draft. I called Raoul and Jenny to check a few facts, and Claudia wrote a paragraph denouncing the arrests:

"Apparently the protest, directed at the role of the Democratic Party in the wars and military buildup of the last few decades, was intolerable to the authorities. Those arrested were not doing anything illegal. This was a preemptive strike by the police to prevent people from participating in other political events during the week. Its sole purpose was to create an atmosphere of intimidation."

Maria came in while we were writing and okayed it. Doc happened to call, and gave it his approval. I called Mort at work and Daniel at home, and both signed on.

Claudia undertook the toughest call: Melissa. I could only hear one side of the heated exchange. But Claudia never wavered, insisting that we had to stand together, and Melissa finally gave in.

"That's enough, I think," Claudia said as she hung up. "We should get it out to the media today, while it's news. Rebecca has a computer at home that I can use to send it out."

I gave Claudia a big hug as I prepared to leave. She looked at me with surprise as I started away. "Thanks a lot for your help," I called to her, then headed home to get my guitar. If I made good time, I could be in the City in time for the Central America march. Then on to the LAG demo.

A WAILING FIGURE from Picasso's "Guernica" soared like an icon near the front of the procession. Hundreds of silent mourners dressed in gray, black, and white filled the street. Some carried coffins bedecked with flowers. Others held photos of the disappeared, or white crosses inscribed with the names of those killed in the civil wars. A brass band played a dirge that echoed off the high-rises.

The Central America march ended with silent theater at the Powell Street transit plaza, a major downtown hub. As hundreds looked on from above, death squads executed dissidents to the beat of a solitary drum. Many LAGers took part in the procession, which was organized by groups like CISPES (see glossary).

The Central America march wound its tortuous path through downtown. It was lunch hour, and the sidewalks were packed with workers and shoppers. All gave the funeral procession wide berth. I hadn't heard about wearing black and white, so I didn't join. I stood back and stared with the same awe and disquiet as the rest of the bystanders.

The march reached the multilevel plaza at the Powell Street cable car turnaround and filed down to the lower level, a concrete-bounded semicircle that made a perfect stage. I found a spot along the upper railing and watched as most of the marchers formed a ring around the plaza. Ten peasants, including Antonio and Claude, stepped forward. They were flanked by soldiers wearing red bandannas over their faces.

The eerie silence of the protesters cast its cloak over the spectators around the upper rim. Some whispered. A few snapped photos. Most mutely observed. The soldiers held their pistol-fingers against the heads of the peasants, and to the stark beat of a snare drum executed their victims. After the demo ended, the area remained hushed as the crowd filtered away.

The LAG demo wasn't till four. I planned to go over to the site early to check out the sound system and loosen up my voice. But after watching the executions, it was hard to shift gears. I wound up walking out around the piers at the Embarcadero for a couple of hours. Between reflections on the somber march and thoughts of what it would be like to see Angie, I didn't get much singing done.

Finally I turned my steps toward the assembly area. I reminded myself one last time to stay cool when I saw Angie. Don't overwhelm her. Just let her know I'm glad to see her.

As I approached the vacant lot where the rally was to be held, I spotted her standing alone near the back of the crowd. I headed straight that way. My chest trembled with anticipation. She saw me just before I reached her, and welcomed me with a warm hug. "Great to see you," she said as she stepped back and looked at me. I smiled awkwardly. Would we go off and spend time alone after the rally? Or was this it — "great to see you?"

There wasn't much chance to think about it, as Sara signaled to me that my set was coming up. I hadn't played a gig in several months, and I felt clumsy in front of the microphone. Luckily, my slot was after a couple of speakers, so music was welcome. I did "Minimum Wage," followed by a new song I'd written that Spring, "Screw the Rich." The performance was rusty, but people laughed and sang along. On "Screw the Rich," Moonstone came twirling out of the crowd and started dancing in front of the stage, his tie-dyed robe shimmering against the dull gravel. And for my finale — "Jailhouse Rock," dedicated to the War Chest Tours — Angie, Alby, Karina, and a few others joined Moonstone in the dance pit.

For me it was a kick. But all in all, it was shaping up as a lackluster protest. Raoul, Jenny, Jacey and Sid didn't even show up. Karina at least was there, emceeing the show. But there was only so much you could do when you've been granted an official permit to exercise your Constitutional rights in a designated parking lot a block away from the Convention.

The demonstration area was only a portion of the parking lot. An arbitrary barricade, topped by yellow "Police Line — Do Not Cross" ribbon, defined the outer limits of free speech. The barricade was imposing, but the yellow ribbon had a short lifespan. "It's the perfect souvenir," Angie said as she rolled up a strand and put it in her pocket. I looked for a stray bit, but every inch had been pilfered.

We walked over to look at the Trojan Donkey, a big wooden prop built by Abalone Alliance folks as a warning to beware the Democrats' promises. "What they need is some people in business suits who pop out of it and try to sell us life insurance," Angie said.

Music, speakers, speakers, music. Angie was talking about leaving early, which made me edgy. Not that I expected us to go home and jump in the sack, but I was hoping we would at least hang out afterwards. Maybe her talking about leaving was a hint that I should make a proposal.

We were standing at the back of the rally, near Howard Street, when we heard shouts from the end of the block. I looked past Angie and saw three people marching toward us carrying an odd sort of flag. Already, protesters were hustling down that way, jeering at the trio. Angie and I started toward the action, but were herded back into the gravel lot by a line of police that formed a wall between us and the interlopers. Three men were coming into focus. It wasn't a flag they were carrying, but a banner featuring Ronald Reagan's grinning face.

LAG's legal rally at the Democratic Convention failed to generate much excitement among organizers or participants.

More people were pushing toward the street, pressing the row of cops back. A second police squad came marching our way double-time, and I saw a row of horse cops forming up at the corner. From our crowd angry voices were raised, more at the cops than at the Reaganites, who had been corralled and escorted away from us. "Screw the police!" someone yelled. Here and there, a cop jabbed into the crowd with a billyclub.

I sucked in a breath. Was this a set-up? Did the cops stage the Reagan thing just to have an excuse to attack? I looked behind us. No cops there. Just the entire crowd. I caught sight of the singer on the stage, looking forsaken. Ouch. Glad that's not me.

The horse cops pulled into formation facing us. I could see their tactics unfolding. The two rows of foot cops would peel to the sides, and the horses would charge right at us. I caught Angie's arm and tried to pull her to the side. "We should move back."

She didn't budge. "They can't attack us here. We have a right to be here."

A lot of good that's going to do, I thought. But I wasn't going to leave if Angie wasn't.

As if on cue, the foot cops turned and marched to the sides. The horses snorted restlessly. I braced for the assault.

Suddenly, from out of nowhere, a group of men sprang in front of the horses. One thrust a long pole toward the mounted cops. Another hoisted a metal contraption to his shoulder. Channel Seven News to the rescue! The cops looked dumbfounded. Emboldened, other photographers rushed into the gap. Click! Click! Click!

The absurdity of the scene cut loose the tension. In a moment, we were laughing and waving to the cameras like it was all a game. The cops recovered and patted their horses like good zookeepers. Onstage, Sara implored the

LAG standard-bearers consult with the operator of the famed LAG-a-tron, capable of detecting nuclear profiteering in passing briefcases.

crowd to turn their backs on the cops and come back to the rally, which most of us did, leaving a few die-hards to lecture the police on civil rights.

As we turned back to the stage, Angie let out a big yawn. "Sorry," she said. "I'm really glad I got to see you sing. But I've got to get home and sleep. After we got out of jail yesterday, we went back to Stonehenge and stayed up half the night talking." She stepped forward and gave me a hug, resting her head on my chest. "I'll see you at the Tour tomorrow," she said. "And I'm looking forward to our time together Thursday."

I squeezed her to me, savoring the way our bodies molded together. It was such a sweet moment that I forgot to be upset about her leaving early. Finally I let go and watched her walk away. Okay, so I didn't get what I wanted today. There's always tomorrow.

Wednesday, July 18, 1984

Since the writing of the Constitution, the U.S. government's main interest has been to protect the rights of property owners. From slave owners to oil companies, government has been primarily influenced by the rich... Elections cost money and lots of it, and it is quite obvious who has the money to give (or should we say 'invest'). Not you, not I, but the large corporations...

— *from the Democratic War Chest Tours Handbook*

"I BET THERE'S five hundred people," Sara said as we clustered at our home-away-from-home, Embarcadero Plaza. "That's way more than Monday."

I looked around the sunlit plaza. Shadows of potted trees and benches were etched sharply onto the pavement. Familiar faces dotted the crowd. If most of LAG had sat out the first Tour, it apparently wasn't for fear of getting busted. Once word spread about the Monday arrests, people came out in droves. Winston and Jürgen from the International Group, Cindy and two other Commie Dupes, Les from Mustard Seed, Artemis from Matrix, Lyle and Tai from Overthrow, Doc and Rick from Enola Gay, Belinda and several others from Spiderwomyn, and just about everyone who'd ever been in Change of Heart. Sure, most of those folks were predictable. But Nathaniel? There he was, standing calmly off to one side. And Claudia? She had just read our LAG statement at an impromptu press conference, and looked like she was sticking around for the action.

And of course, the best news — Angie. Maybe my "no pressure" policy was paying off. She greeted me with an exuberant hug when she arrived at the Plaza. She took my arm and looked around the plaza. I got the feeling that despite her Monday arrest, she still felt out of the loop, and was glad to hang with me as the organizers made their final preparations.

Standing with her, I felt more like I belonged than at the past several street actions combined. Finally, a comrade. Angie wasn't afraid to get right in the thick of things. Right where I wanted to be.

Of course, the thick of things might include jail, where I had no great desire to be. I hadn't eaten anything that day, and once in the tank, my only hope would be Bit o' Honeys. Worse, I'd be separated from Angie. What was the point in doing something together if it meant getting split up in the end?

But look at it this way. Whenever we got out of jail, Angie would have to spend that night at Stonehenge before driving back to Portland. So we'd have our date, regardless.

I could risk it.

I checked out the cops. There were a few at the periphery, and I spotted a couple more up on a balcony watching us. But compared with the hundred that met Monday's Tour, this was distinctly low-key. Was it a trick? Were they luring us into a trap? Or were they backing off, cowed by our numbers?

People from It's About Times newspaper built a giant Trojan Donkey to symbolize the empty promises of the Democratic Party, and hauled the beast around to the various Convention protests.

People milled about restlessly. Sid and Karina were talking nearby. I tried to listen in, to get a sense of the game plan. I caught a few names like Bechtel and Wells Fargo, but couldn't make out the details.

Beyond them, sullen, stood Flint. He was isolated from the main crowd, surrounded by a small coterie. I remembered his "back to ground zero" rap at the planning meeting, and couldn't help smiling at what it had come to: zero. It wasn't just LAG that never figured out what to do.

Jenny and Sid climbed up on a trash dumpster, and the crowd gathered round. Angie took my hand and we moved up closer to hear. Sid, who was wearing a tattered gray T-shirt with a spraypainted circle-A, welcomed us and gave a quick recap of the Monday Tour.

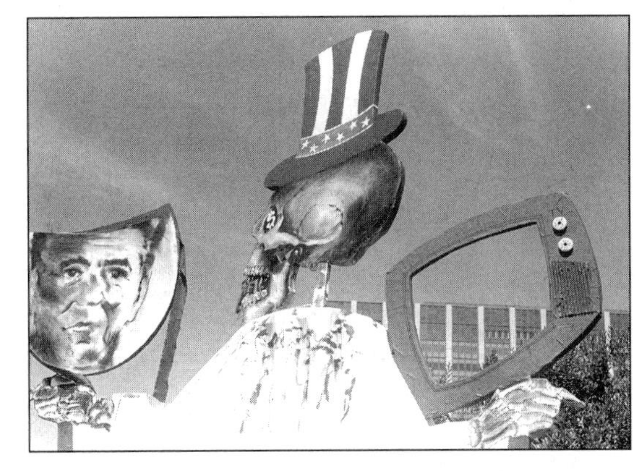

Props and giant puppets were not as common in early 1980s protests as they were by the end of the decade, but this media puppet joined the 1984 actions.

Jenny followed with a short talk about the Democrats' corporate connections. She looked out at us from her dumpster-perch. "We're all in this together," she said in a loud, pleading voice. "Look around. Recognize the people around you, and watch out for them. If you get arrested, try to stay in solidarity. The Lawyers' Guild will be there to help out, so don't agree to go to court for arraignment until you talk to them." She looked at Sid. "Anything else?"

"Yeah," Sid said, gesturing at the dozen or so cops scattered around the perimeter of our crowd, "we've hired armed monitors to accompany us on this march. You'll recognize them by their blue uniforms."

People laughed, and Sid jumped down from the dumpster. Jenny made a few more comments about die-ins and dealing with horses. I noticed that there was no mention of nonviolence. Maybe it was taken for granted, but with Flint and Jacey hovering in the wings, I doubted it.

"One last thing," Jenny said. "We're not going to travel as one big group today. It's too easy to round us up. We'll leave here in three or four tours and take different routes, to confuse the cops."

Jenny climbed down, and several people stepped forward to guide the routes: Ariel, Sara, Jenny, and Raoul. I was surprised Sid wasn't leading one, then realized that the punk AGs probably had their own plans.

I squeezed Angie's hand. "Want to go with Jenny?"

"Let's go with Sara," Angie said quickly. She tugged me away. When we were out of earshot, she spoke just above a whisper. "I know it's ironic," she said. "A big reason I came back was to support Jenny and reaffirm our friendship. But I get the feeling she's uncomfortable with me around, that she feels like I'm judging her, or that I think she's judging me, or something like that."

I put my arm around Angie's shoulders and we joined Sara's group. Karina had gone with Jacey to join Raoul's group, and Sara looked happy to have us.

A lot of Change of Heart seemed to be in our group: Alby, Antonio, Megan, Walt, plus Doc and Rick and a couple of others from Enola Gay. "It's like a cluster reunion," I joked to Antonio.

He turned a serious face toward me. "This was the only possible response to Monday's arrests," he said. "In Central America, our brothers and sisters stand up at the risk of death. The least we can do is risk arrest."

My smile faded. "I hadn't thought of it in those terms," I said.

"We have this right because people have fought for it," he said. "When we stand up against repression, we're keeping free speech alive."

A woman who looked like a downtown secretary walked through our crowd passing out little yellow business cards. I accepted one and looked at the print: "Get Out of Jail Free." I laughed aloud, prompting people around me to take a card. "Hope we don't need this," I said to no one in particular.

A hundred or so protesters followed Sara away from the Embarcadero toward the financial district. We walked in a loose clump up the wide sidewalks, with a half-dozen skateboarders riding alongside. Right away, a squad of motorcycle cops swung in behind us, working their radios. Probably calling ahead for reinforcements, I realized. Could be a short day.

When playing "Spot the Narc," try the hippie who looks like he's on the way to a barroom brawl.

We hiked two blocks north, sticking to the sidewalks. Then Sara suddenly reversed direction and led us back a block, where we came to a halt in front of Dupont's California Street offices. A guy with a long blonde ponytail got up on a concrete bench and spoke about how Dupont had built and operated the world's first nuclear plant, which fueled the bombs dropped on Hiroshima and Nagasaki. He finished his talk with a countdown. The crowd joined in, dropping on the sidewalk and sprawling up against the doors. As I lay there moaning, I caught the eye of a woman trying to enter Dupont. She looked unnerved, as if she might just turn around and go home.

After a couple of minutes, we got up and headed back toward Embarcadero Center. The motorcycle cops were still with us, but if they had tried to alert other troops ahead, our backtracking fooled them. We did another stop at General Electric, a major weapons player and campaign contributor, then headed toward Market Street, where we did a die-in outside IBM's headquarters in protest of their work on missile guidance systems.

Our hit-and-run tactics seemed to be holding the police at bay, and the crowd was exuberant. But compared with previous protests, there were no AG actions, no street theater. I had figured that with all the meetings for the War Chest Tours, something creative must have been planned.

Angie wandered off to talk with Alby as we headed away from IBM. Not like they were getting all smoochy, but I still wished she'd stayed with me a while longer.

A business-type walked past, looked me up and down, and made a remark about "getting a job."

"Doing what," I snapped, "building nukes with you?" He ignored me, and I didn't feel much release.

As we rounded a corner we ran into one of the other Tours. I spotted Moonstone and went over to say hi. The two groups melded into one, and our momentum carried us on to Bechtel. We paused in front of the entrance and heard a rap on Bechtel's corporate crimes, which were mainly of the construction variety, nuclear power plants being a particular favorite. As we paused, a squad of cops marched up and lined the entrance. There weren't enough to threaten us, but people pulled in closer just the same. "We should keep moving," I said to Moonstone.

"Yeah," he said, then turned to the crowd: "Let's march! Screw the cops, let's march!"

Behind us a voice echoed, "Let's march!" The cry resounded through the crowd. Two hundred strong we headed down Beale Street, leaving the cops in our wake. I looked at Moonstone, who surveyed the crowd with a big smile. Amazing. He got the whole crowd in gear. And with my idea. I sensed when it was time to move on. I was in the flow, part of a mobile disruption squad outrunning the cops and snarling the downtown.

Truth-in-labeling.

As we rounded the corner onto Mission, a chill ran through me. Directly across the street stood a dozen thuggish men in blue jeans and sweatshirts. Some were unshaven, some sported baseball caps, and most wore dark glasses. They cocked their heads as if taking our measure. I knew in an instant who they were, and anger rushed through me. "Narcs!" I exploded. I turned back toward the crowd coming around the corner. "Get a good look at them — your friendly neighborhood undercovers!"

Others joined in my jeering, and I felt proud. But Antonio caught my arm. "Watch it," he rasped. "You're making yourself a target if they come after us."

"Yeah, thanks," I said, following him on toward the next corner. "It ticks me off how they pretend like we can't tell they're cops."

We circled around to Bechtel's back entrance. The cops hadn't immediately followed, and some punks ran up to Bechtel's rear doors and tried to get inside. Thwarted by security guards who had already locked the doors, the punks started banging on the plate glass. Flint pushed his way up near the doors and yelled, "Bechtel, Go to Hell!" The crowd picked it up. "Bechtel, Go to Hell! Bechtel, Go to Hell!" The punks banged out the rhythm on the doors, and the whole street reverberated with the racket.

I spotted Angie up close to the doors, and worked my way in by her. We could see through the windows, where a handful of men in business suits, safe behind locked doors, were yelling back at us.

"I wonder what their chant is?" Angie said.

Suddenly there was a fracas behind us. A squad of riot cops forced their way into the crowd. Angie and I got elbowed aside as the cops tunneled their way toward the punks. "Looks like arrests," I said. I looked at Angie, wondering what she was thinking. But instead of grabbing anyone, the cops shoved the punks away. Amid much yelling and jostling, they set up a cordon in front of the Bechtel doors, holding their batons ready to strike if anyone ventured too close. I felt claustrophobic, afraid people in the back might shove us into the cops.

For much of the day, police let the crowd march in the street.

Luckily, people in the back were yelling for us to march away. "Screw the pigs, let's go!" Almost as a bloc, the punks headed out, and the rest of us followed, leaving the agitated cops behind.

We had been mainly on the sidewalks up to now. As we headed back toward Market, we ran into another Tour coming toward Bechtel. The collision spilled us out into the street and filled half the block. We persuaded the newcomers to reverse direction and join us, and we all headed north, several hundred strong. Traffic backed up behind us. Two punk women ran along shoving parked cars, setting off their alarms. A tall guy whapped his skateboard against a "No Parking" sign, and people yelled and laughed as we came up to Market Street and spied the fourth Tour.

Held back through most of the march, frustrated riot police finally got orders to move into position.

A squad of cops met us there, but they backed away. We poured across, tying up traffic at the three-way intersection. A few people grabbed newsstands and dragged them into the street, but no one strayed too far behind.

We filled all three lanes as we started up the incline of California Street. The crowd looked smaller, like we'd lost people along the way. People's feet were dragging. I remembered Angie dancing along this route back in October. I wished there were a troupe of drummers to inspire us this time as we trudged up the hill.

The only cops were the cycle squad, still tailing us. I found myself walking near Raoul and Antonio. "Looks like they're going to let us get our exercise," I said.

Raoul squinted. "Yeah, they'll wear us out and surround us at the top of the hill."

"I don't think so," Antonio said. "I think that the order to release people on Monday showed them that they have to respect basic civil rights."

Raoul laughed derisively. "That's one lesson your typical cop won't ever learn." He peeled off to talk to Jenny and Jacey. Final battle plans, I thought. I wished I had someone I was scheming with. I looked for Angie and spotted her with Alby. I clenched my teeth and dropped further back in the crowd.

Luck was with me. I spotted Karina walking by herself. Her eyes looked heavy, like she hadn't slept much lately. She smiled sadly. On an impulse, I put my arm around her, and she slumped against me. I let my body mold to hers and breathed deeply. "You doing okay?" I asked.

She glanced at me furtively, then looked away. "Yeah, just really tired," she said. "I'm not sure what I'm doing here."

I nodded. "Me either." I brushed my face against her thick hair and pictured the two of us slipping away, going off alone and just forgetting the whole mess.

As we crossed the last street before Bank of America, though, Karina straightened up. I let go of her shoulder and she walked away toward Jacey. So much for that daydream.

On the plaza, the crowd was bunching up. Was someone doing a theater piece? I moved in closer, and saw what the show was: fifty riot cops lined the far end of the plaza, batons at the ready.

"Go arrest the real criminals inside," someone yelled over the general jeering. Ariel climbed up on the edge of a tree-planter and gave a quick rundown on B of A. I'd heard it before, and moved to the side to get a handle on the police. To our right, on Kearny Street, fifty officers. Down at the intersection, horse cops. Behind us on California Street, several paddywagons pulled up.

With the bank building closing off the south, we were just about hemmed in. A few people slipped away while they had the chance, but most of us pulled in closer. I saw Angie with Jenny and Raoul's AG, which huddled off to one side. Angie waved me over. "We're going to go around the block and start a blockade at the next intersection," she whispered. "Come on. If we can shut down California Street, it will set off gridlock all down the hill."

My heart jumped. This was what I was looking for. Not just an improvisation like at the Moral Majority, but a plan. A way to outwit the cops.

A dozen of us filtered out in twos and threes, and the cops didn't seem to catch on. Jacey was up front with Raoul and Jenny. Sara and Alby were next, and a few people I didn't know. We circled around three quarters of the block to California and Grant, directly uphill from the B of A intersection.

"Are we ready?" Sara's voice drew me back to the present. I looked down California toward B of A, where I could see the horse cops. They seemed oblivious to us. What now? Jenny and Sara were the first off the curb. Raoul started waving his arms to stop traffic, and I picked it up. A smile broke across my face as cars came to a halt. One suit-and-tie guy was enraged, screaming out his window at us. But others seemed more confused than angry.

"We need a chant," Angie said. "Something to tell them why we're here."

I looked at her, then at the rest of the blockaders. Why *am* I here, I thought. Why this intersection at this moment? What exactly am I protesting?

Raoul, the loudest voice among us, turned to face the cars. "Shut down the war corporations! No business as usual!" Fine sentiments, but not exactly a ringing chant. Others yelled out similar ideas to the stranded drivers and curious pedestrians. I called out "No business as usual" a few times. Cars were backing up.

Downhill at B of A, either the cops heard us, or they were alerted by the traffic jam. One looked up toward us and pointed.

"Let's go," Raoul shouted. "Let's get back to B of A." Before the cops could get in gear to come after us, we disappeared, retracing our steps around the block to the plaza. We blended in with the others, congratulating ourselves on our deft maneuver.

The rest of the crowd, hemmed in on the plaza, milled around restlessly. No one had been arrested, I learned. But where were Sid and the punk AGs? Had they marched off somewhere else?

Alby tapped me on the shoulder. He and Karina were rounding up Change of Heart people. Another plan? I found Angie and we joined Sara, Moonstone, Antonio, and half a dozen others, arms around each others' shoulders. I took in the familiar faces, thankful for the ease and trust I felt in this circle.

Karina knelt in the middle like a quarterback and diagrammed the movements on the concrete. "The punks are down in the next block. If we go out in the intersection here, it will draw the cops to us. Then the punks will close California down the hill."

"There's a hundred cops," Angie said, "and horses ready to go. There's no way we can take the intersection."

Karina looked annoyed. "When they come for us, we get back out of the street. It's just a decoy."

Angie scowled but didn't respond. The plan didn't seem very plausible to me, either, but I wasn't backing out. If we got arrested, so be it. At least I was in good company.

We edged toward the corner, acting nonchalant. The horse cops, who I

Cops and protesters squared off in the financial district.

figured would be our toughest adversary, were in a loose line on the opposite side of the intersection.

"Go!" Karina yelled, grabbing Alby's hand. Angie grabbed mine and we streamed out into the street, forming a diagonal blockade. Traffic, already congested by the cops, halted. This time, the drivers seemed to grasp what was happening even without a chant. A gray-haired man in a Lincoln rolled up his window.

Karina, at the front of the line, thrust her free fist into the air. "No business as usual!"

I looked at the driver of the Lincoln, who gripped the steering wheel with both hands and muttered to himself. What if he rolled down his window and asked why I was blockading him? Nothing personal, I'd say. We're just trying to stop business as usual.

The horse cops got their order and pranced out toward us. They reached Karina's end of the line first, and she jumped away. The rest of us, still holding hands, followed around like crack-the-whip. I clung to Angie's hand as we lurched across the intersection. The tug seemed to fire her spirit. "Come on!" she cried to the mass of protesters who had come down to the edge of the plaza. "Take the street!"

She squeezed my hand, and electricity surged through me. "Yeah, take the street!" I called. "Come on!" More people stepped out, but the horse cops managed to coordinate their efforts and force our whole line back onto the sidewalk.

We huddled again, still watching the horses. Next to me, Megan bit her nails. Her wavy black hair fell across her face. Two squads of cops marched down our way. Not much chance of us taking the intersection now.

But off to the right, California Street looked invitingly empty. Sort of odd, I thought, no traffic in the middle of the day. Then I realized — the punks must be blockading down below. I helped make that happen! Two squads of cops trotted past us, heading downhill. A paddywagon did a U-turn and followed.

Police corralled protesters onto the sidewalk.

The dispatch of the cops left a vacuum in the intersection. Alby called out. We linked hands and swept into the street again.

With California blocked below, the horse cops took their time moving into formation and forcing us out of the intersection. By that time, the punks, who had ended their blockade and eluded the police, were filtering back toward us. Angie and I wound up across the street from B of A. Jenny was with us, and Sid jogged up. "Around the block," he whispered excitedly. "They're focused on the intersection. We'll come down the alley, catch them off-guard, and close the street."

Angie took my hand and we followed Sid and Jenny. I cast a quick look back at the cops. They didn't seem to be paying attention. The plan might work. If we surprised the cops at mid-block, others might take the intersection. For the first time, I understood, "why *this* street." It was a laboratory for an on-site social experiment — could we, in the face of repression, spontaneously organize ourselves to accomplish a simple logistical task?

We walked quickly up to Sacramento Street, turned the corner, and found the mid-block alley that ran back to California. So far, so good. But what if the cops got wind of the maneuver and trapped us in the narrow alley? Angie walked silently beside me. I reached out and took her hand. She squeezed mine in return. A warm glow suffused me. Bring it on, I thought. Whatever happens, I'm ready.

No one spoke as we approached the end of the alley. Were the police waiting to strike? We edged out onto the sidewalk. They didn't have a clue! Our ruse had worked. But traffic was flowing again. I looked toward the corner. At the edge of the plaza, a long row of cops formed a cordon, fencing off the intersection. People were drifting away, and the demo looked kaput.

Jenny cast a doleful look at Sid. A couple of cops looked down our way. I stepped back away from the curb.

Sid craned his neck and surveyed the scene, then turned to Jenny. "What a waste," he said. "All these people, and we didn't disrupt anything."

"Sure, we did," I said. Sid didn't respond.

Angie pointed to the far side of the B of A plaza. "There's still a lot of people over there. We should join them."

Jenny took one more look at the crowd. "No," she said quietly. "It's better to call an end today and come back tomorrow. We're not going to accomplish anything more here. And if we get busted now, they may hold us overnight, especially second-timers."

Angie eyed them intently, as if about to speak. Was she going to argue for rallying the crowd? Surely that would mean arrests. When we were out in the street, I was ready to go to jail. But now it looked different. If the demo ended here, maybe Angie and I could do something together besides ride in a paddywagon. Don't blow it now.

Before Angie could speak, Raoul walked up. "It's over," he said in a desultory tone. "Let's have our meeting. We've got to come up with something new for tomorrow." Jenny and Sid nodded, and they turned to go.

I smiled to myself. For once, Raoul and I were in synch. I looked at Angie. "How about going over to the Mission and getting something to eat?"

A troubled look crossed her face. "Jenny and I are having dinner after this," she said. "So I'm going to go with them." The others had started away, and she gave me a quick hug. "I'll see you tomorrow. We'll go on the Tour, and then Rock Against Reagan is in the afternoon."

I nodded glumly. "Sure. I'll be there." I watched her skip after the others. Let her go. We have tomorrow. Whatever that was worth.

I turned and started away. Over at the edge of B of A plaza, a TV news crew was trying to film a segment, using the dwindling protest as a backdrop. The anchorman was a pudgy White guy with a sweaty brow and what I hoped was a toupee. Flint and a couple of others were watching the crew.

I hadn't spoken to Flint all day, and I walked over toward him. "Hey, how are you doing?"

He jerked his head around to look at me for a moment, then abruptly refocused on the TV crew. Well, I thought, this will be a short conversation.

Just as the anchor began his spiel, Flint erupted. "News whores!" He glared at the anchor, whose eyes wore a "really, now" expression.

"News whores!" Flint shouted it again, and a couple of others picked up the line. The camera crew looked amused. The anchor clenched his teeth and turned his back, apparently hoping Flint would disappear.

A detachment of police was heading our way. Flint yelled once more, then walked off with a few people down California.

I followed them toward Market Street. Once we got away from the cops, my mind drifted back to Angie. Sure, her leaving without me was disappointing. But maybe everything was developing just as I'd hoped. Being around Jenny and Raoul and Sid would remind her what it meant to be in the center of the action.

But I couldn't count on other people to do all the work. It was time to step forward myself. The next day was ours.

We reached Market. Flint headed for the Muni trains. I boarded an escalator down into the sanctuary of BART. As I bought my ticket, a train pulled in. I double-timed down the stairs and through the doors.

As I took a seat, exhaustion swept over me. I leaned against the armrest, glad not to have to talk to anyone. I was running on fumes. One more day of this. Then I'm taking a long break.

Thursday, July 19, 1984

THE ALARM RANG louder than I remembered. I slapped it off, rolled over, and read the time: nine o'clock.

I rubbed my eyes. Holly was already up and had gone to work, then was to have brunch with Caroline. Brunch during the War Chest Tour, I thought. There's a different agenda.

I pushed the snooze button and lay back. Images from the day before, of Angie walking away, pressed upon me. Was I the only one who cared? It didn't feel like she was making any effort to see me.

The phone rang, jerking me back awake. Who was calling at nine in the morning? Then I flashed — it might be Angie. I stumbled out of bed and grabbed the phone. "Hello?"

"Hey Jeff, it's Hank," came the voice. "Still going to Rock Against Reagan? I got the afternoon off from the sweatshop. Wanna meet at BART?"

I bent over, feeling dizzy. Why not skip the War Chest Tour and go with Hank? The Tour would probably be a rerun of the day before, so I wouldn't miss much. And maybe my absence would deliver a message to Angie — I'm not going to be at your beck and call. I could meet her at Rock Against Reagan, and we could have our date with a better power balance.

"Good plan," I said. "Noon at BART." I climbed back into bed and pulled the covers up to my neck. Two more hours of sleep. What a relief.

It was harder than I expected to get back to sleep. Stray memories of the previous day's Tour kept flitting through my mind. But eventually I drifted off. I forgot to reset the alarm, and it was almost noon when I woke again. I sat up with a start, rushed through a shower, and speedwalked down to BART.

I was ten minutes late. Hank wasn't there. Had he already gone? I could wait, but if the Tour ended early and Angie didn't see me at the concert, she might just go home. Punk rock wasn't her favorite music.

I decided to wait five more minutes. I stared at my fellow commuters,

Several thousand people showed up for Rock Against Reagan in front of the Democratic Convention, whose flags fly in the background.

mostly office workers and Cal students, sunk in their daily grind. What was the Democratic Convention to them, I wondered. A few headlines? An evening telecast? Did they care any more than I did who got nominated as the sacrificial lamb to the increasingly popular Reagan?

Still, their indifference irked me, and I chastised myself for passing up the final War Chest Tour. So what if nothing dramatic happened? Sometimes you just had to protest.

As the clock ran out, Hank hurried into the station. "Sorry, I had to call the bank," he said as we headed for the train. "Did I tell you that me and Judith made a bid on a house? It's on Grant Street, right in the middle of South Berkeley. It's a fixer-upper that we can probably afford if we both keep working full-time. Now we just have to jump through the bank's hoops. If they approve the loan, we've got it."

"That's great," I said, trying to summon interest in what felt like a distant reality. "When do you find out?"

"Not for another week. It's driving me crazy. I can hardly think about anything else."

When we got to the City, Hank had yet another phone call to make. "I'll meet you at the concert," I said. I started down to the Rock Against Reagan show, a block south. The sun had been shining in Berkeley, but here the sky was dull gray. The air felt heavy, as if a freak Summer storm might burst out and soak us all.

The Trojan Donkey caught my eye as I approached. The concert was on the same gravel free-speech lot where the LAG demo had been. But the demographic had shifted: in the place of hippie-ish anti-nukers were hundreds of punks, goths, scraggly teenagers, skateboarders, and a bunch of ragged adults whom I lumped together as squatters. Onstage a guy with massive dreadlocks bounced up and down as he sang to a ska beat.

I didn't see Angie or Jenny or any of the others. In fact, in a crowd of a couple of thousand, I didn't see anyone I knew. That must mean that the Tour was still going. I was shuffling around on the sidelines, thinking of going out for a sandwich and coming back, when I saw Sid and Raoul running up the street. "What's up?" I called, suddenly alarmed.

They pulled up in front of me, huffing for air. "The cops busted half the Tour," Sid said between breaths. "Right at the end, at B of A — they surrounded us and busted a bunch of people!"

Angie? That was my first thought. Was she in jail?

"I'm going to go make an announcement," Sid said. He ran toward the stage. I felt embarrassed for thinking only of Angie and myself. I turned away from Raoul. Damn. Who better than Raoul to inform me that I had once again missed the action? Why was I never in the right place? All I had to do was wake up earlier, and I could at least have gotten arrested with Angie.

I shivered. Was that what I wanted? A sleepover in jail with a bunch of

Crowd participation at Rock Against Reagan.

punks? Well, it might have been entertaining. But not compared to spending the night with Angie.

Up front, Sid talked animatedly with the stage manager. The reggae singer was wrapping up his set. The stage manager nodded to Sid and pointed to the stage. As the applause died down, Sid bounded up the steps and took the microphone. "A hundred of our brothers and sisters were just arrested for daring to criticize the corporate system," he declared. "They're being taken to jail right this minute. And that's where we're going, too. As soon as the concert ends, we're marching to the Hall of Justice!" The crowd applauded, but it wasn't exactly a roar of approval.

"You've got to wonder," Raoul said as he looked around, "how many will do it? These people skipped the Tour in the first place. So what if they like punk music? How political are they in the final analysis?"

"I guess we'll find out," I said. I liked Raoul's logic, with its implication that going on the march would redeem those of us who skipped the Tour. We could still be "political" by the end of the day.

Of course, half the point of coming to Rock Against Reagan was to meet Angie. With her arrested, I was less thrilled about staying. Good music, yeah, but a little punk went a long way.

But I knew I couldn't leave. Angie was in jail. If solidarity meant anything, I had to stay for the march.

The warm-up bands were done, and it was down to the twin headliners. The Dead Kennedys kicked off their set with "California Über Alles," their college radio hit. Dozens of people slam-danced in front of the stage, sending up a cloud of powdery white dust from the dry gravel. I moved across to the upwind side, and thought again about lunch. There was still one more band, MDC, so I had an hour before the march.

I started in search of refreshment when I spied a group of people hurrying up the street. Moonstone waved, and right away I knew who they were — survivors from the War Chest Tour! My heart jumped. I headed toward Moonstone to see if he knew about Angie, when I spotted her in the crowd behind him. "Angie!" I called out.

She cut over and threw her arms around my neck. I squeezed her tightly. "Wow," I whispered. "I'm so glad to see you."

"So what if they like punk music? How political are they in the final analysis?"

"I am so glad to *be* here," she said breathlessly. "They tried to surround everybody, right at the end, but some of us got away. We thought we were out of danger. But we forgot about the undercovers. We got a block away, and a bunch of them jumped out and grabbed people and dragged them away. They got a guy right next to me. It was awful."

I hugged her again. "Sid already announced it onstage," I said.

"Oh, good, I'm glad he's here," she said. "I didn't see him after the first arrests."

"Yeah, he announced a march to the Hall of Justice after the concert is over."

I expected her to be excited, but she looked away and drew a breath. "I just escaped one arrest," she said. "Now I'm supposed to march into another one?"

A flash went through me. We could leave. Be alone, just the two of us. But my fantasy evaporated as Angie continued. "Of course we have to do it," she said. "We can't let them get away with this."

I knew she was right. Going on the march was the least I could do. Maybe there wouldn't be any more arrests. Why should the cops care about a couple of hundred people marching to the jail on the last day of the Democratic Convention?

After the Dead Kennedys finished, Sid and Jacey got up and exhorted the crowd to stay for the march. Again people applauded. A moment later, as if in response, a squad of police assembled back by the street. I wondered if a march would even be able to get underway.

Hank finally showed up. "I had to get something to eat," he said. His eyes narrowed as he sized up the police. "What's happening?"

"Well," I said, "You're just in time for the action. We're marching to the Hall of Justice."

Hank stiffened. "Marching where?"

"Didn't you hear? The War Chest Tour got busted. Right at the end, they arrested a bunch of people. So we're marching to the jail after MDC's set."

Hank laughed contemptuously. "For what? So they can throw us in the slammer, too? If we're lucky, maybe they'll crack a few skulls while they're at it."

His laughter annoyed me. Leave if you want, I thought. I've got to do it. But then I thought of Angie, of our night together. What was I doing, walking into an arrest?

MDC plugged in their amps and tore into the final set of the day. The singer screamed anti-capitalist-militarist-corporatist rants over screeching guitars and thrashing drums. I could catch only a few words here and there, but they were enough to explain the band's name. Multi-Death Corporations. Millions of Dying Children. Multitudes of Damned Christians. But the most popular song was their finale, the one that Angie told me first gave the band its name: "Millions of Dead Cops."

Dead cops. I turned and checked out the response of the officers lined up behind us. Apparently they had tuned out the cacophony, because they seemed unfazed by the song.

Sooner than I anticipated, MDC left the stage. They returned for a quick encore, and the show was over. The feedback from the final song still reverberated in my ears as Jacey took the mic and urged people to join the march that was forming at the back of the gravel lot. "Take the streets," he shouted. "Shut down the jail!"

Sid, Jenny, Karina, Raoul, and others were rabble-rousing among the crowd. I watched Jenny approach a group of young punk women, her face a picture of nervous ardor as she pled with them to join the march.

Some people were leaving, but most stood looking at the growing contingent of cops out in the street. Hank came over to where Angie and I were standing. "Punks get hassled by the pigs all the time. No wonder they don't want to join a march to the jail."

Sid found a wooden pole and tied a black T-shirt to it. Waving it like a flag, he paraded out to the sidewalk. The cops in the street drew their riot batons and formed a line, but made no move toward us. Jacey, still on the stage, yelled into the mic: "Let's march!" Angie took my hand. No turning back now. We joined the cluster forming around Sid. Yeah, I thought, let's do it. Those that are on board, let's go.

There weren't a lot of LAGers present, and I wondered whether others were arrested earlier at the Tour, or if like me they had skipped today after the previous day ended tamely. Leave it to LAGers to stay home if there were no arrests in sight. Still, scattered through the little crowd, I saw Moonstone, Karina, Alby, and Sara. Up front, Jenny, Raoul, and Jacey joined Sid.

"Alright!" Sid yelled, hoisting the black flag high and stepping into the street. A smattering of shouts answered him.

Angie and I were about twenty people back from the front. As we started out of the parking lot, the row of police braced. The commanding officer barked an unintelligible order. The squad snapped to attention, then stood stiffly as we paraded past and took over the left lane. It felt good to hit pavement after two hours of gravel. But the cops' acquiescence seemed odd. Were there more police ahead, waiting to surround us? I turned back to check on those we'd just passed, and couldn't believe what I saw. A river of people was filing past the officers. I looked over at the concert site. Except for a few stagehands, it was deserted. The entire crowd had joined the march, followed at the rear by the Trojan Donkey.

With ease we took over the four lanes of Howard Street. Cars on the cross streets gave us wide berth as punks taunted them. Here and there people yelled out, "Take the Street! Free the Tour!"

The crowd stretched for a couple of blocks. With no signs or chants, we looked like a couple of thousand people who just happened to be strolling down the middle of the street on a Summer afternoon. A few people carried bottles or rocks gleaned from the concert site. Must be their idea of being prepared.

Angie squeezed my hand. Then, leaving me with Hank, she bounded up toward Jenny and Raoul. I felt a bit abandoned, but I was glad to see her talking with Jenny, their heads leaning together. Old times, for sure.

I took in our surroundings. Cars of all shapes and colors sat watching us pass. White and yellow stripes were painted down the middle of the street, as if it were a playing field for some obscure competition. Traffic lights changed colors with no relation to our movement. What a strange city.

The colors seemed brighter. Was the fog lifting? I searched the sky, but could only see a faint hint of blue out toward the East Bay.

A dark shape flitted past the nearby buildings. I looked up to see a police helicopter hovering above us. Through the crowd, people yelled and flipped off the copter. A guy ahead of me pantomimed firing a bazooka.

It made me laugh, but Hank didn't look amused. "This is insane. It's a set-up. There's probably provocateurs all through the crowd, to give the pigs an excuse to attack. As if they need one."

"Come on," I said. "The cops wouldn't attack a crowd this size."

"No, but they'll find a way to split us up, then go after a smaller group. It's stupid to think they won't."

I turned away, weary of his attitude. I carried enough ambivalence of my own, without Hank compounding it. I searched for Angie, wishing I was walking with people who were more dedicated.

Sara came past me, and I caught her eyes, which were a mix of fear and determination. Good, I thought. I can relate to that.

Sara was dressed all in red, and I couldn't resist commenting.

With few signs or banners, the march looked like a thousand people who just happened to be walking up the middle of the street.

"It's for my initiation," she said. She seemed relieved to have someone to talk to, and we fell in step. "I got a challenge from my coven to wear each color of the rainbow for an entire week. This week it's red."

"That must tax your wardrobe," I said. "What's the initiation for?"

We were turning a corner, and the crowd bunched up. Sara looked around, then said in a low voice, "It's to become a Witch."

A Witch. I tried to take it in stride. "So there's a series of challenges you have to meet?"

"Each person gets a unique set, lasting for a year and a day. The toughest one came from Artemis. She challenged me to go rappelling."

"Rappelling? Like jumping off a cliff?" A queasy feeling rose in my gut.

"Yeah. I once told her that my worst fear was heights. So she challenged me to go rappelling with her. I didn't see how I could say no. We rented the gear, went to the edge of a two-hundred-foot cliff up the coast, and jumped off."

I felt a wave of vertigo. "Did you overcome the fear?" I asked in a weak voice.

She looked at me thoughtfully. "I wouldn't say 'overcome.' I was terrified.

But I learned that being afraid doesn't have to render me powerless. I can act in the face of my greatest fear."

I nodded, turning Sara's words over in my mind. At that moment, someone called to her, and she said goodbye and moved off through the crowd. We were turning another corner. I felt lost. Where had Angie disappeared to? Why she wasn't looking for me? I felt irritated that she'd dumped me and gone gallivanting off with who-knows-whom.

The protest stretched over several blocks, and I was toward the end. Our section had fallen behind the main body, and I picked up the pace. As I strode into an intersection, a car lurched forward, slamming to a stop just short of my legs. I flared with anger. "Open your eyes, damn it! Watch where you're going!"

I could see the driver through the glare of the windshield. He was a big guy, but I was ready for him. Get out of the car, jerk. Let's go. Right here, right now. Me and you.

In my mind, it *was* just me and him. But the driver was staring beyond me, stark fear in his eyes. I looked over my shoulder. Other protesters were gathering around. "What's going on?" a leather-clad punk yelled.

I looked from him back to the driver. Suddenly I felt a flush of embarrassment. I shooed the car away. The driver jerked into reverse and hightailed it. "He almost hit me," I explained to the leather-punk. "Guess I lost my temper."

The guy gave me an odd look, then turned away. I took a breath, glad my outburst hadn't touched off a riot. Gotta watch what I say around here.

Alone again. Where was Angie? I blended back into the crowd, wishing I'd see a familiar face.

Who I spotted was Flint. He was wearing the same black beret as always, with dark sunglasses. My eyes went to his hands, expecting a rock or bottle, but they were empty. A couple of other guys walked alongside him, talking conspiratorially. I tried to listen in, but the noise of the copter drowned it out.

Hank overtook me again, and greeted me with a look that said, "Why the hell are we still here?" I reached out to rub his shoulder, and he flinched. "I'm sticking with this up to the Hall of Justice, but then I'm getting out of here," he said.

Great, I thought. Then I'll be totally by myself. Maybe I'll leave too. What was I doing here, anyway? Screw it all.

Up ahead, the march had come to a standstill. Then I realized — we're here. That's it, that gray monolith set back from the sidewalk by concrete stairs — the Hall of Justice. In the middle of the bleak facade was a row of glass doors fronted by riot cops. Other officers hastily erected a long string of bicycle-rack barricades to keep us from getting near the building. Maybe they're scared of us, too, I thought half-seriously. You stay on your side, we'll stay on ours.

People were shouting all sorts of slogans. Gradually it jelled into, "Set them free! Set them free!" I chimed in: "Set them free!" It felt good to have some outlet, even if it seemed unlikely that our demand would be met.

Overhead the helicopter still circled. I caught sight of Raoul and Sid. Both looked slightly dazed. "Shit," Raoul exclaimed as they flitted past. "Every cop in the City must be here. We should have marched to the Convention. They'd never have been ready. We could have pushed right on in."

I pictured us barging into the Convention. What an image for middle America, sitting at home in front of their TVs. Let's go, I thought. Let's race the cops to the Convention. We certainly travel lighter.

The cops finished the row of barricades. As they stepped back to admire their handiwork, Sid jumped forward. Grabbing the top of the waist-high barricade, he gave it a hard shake. Steel scraped on asphalt, setting my teeth on edge. Other people leapt in and set up a racket.

Without waiting for orders, several officers whacked with their batons. In front of me a woman yelped and shook her hand. People backed off, but down to the left, Jacey and some others lifted the end of the barricade and dragged it forward a few feet before the cops stopped them. The crowd yelled its approval, and the cops moved in tighter.

I dropped back from the barricades and filtered through the crowd, sort of looking for Angie, but mainly getting my bearings. We filled the entire block and then some. I thought about the Kissinger demo, how the cops maneuvered to surround the protest, but I didn't see how they could do that here, with the

Marchers were met at the Hall of Justice by rows of riot police.

Protesters took over Bryant Street in front of the Hall of Justice. Squads of riot police, accompanied by mounted officers, faced the crowd on three sides.

crowd spilling down the side streets. Too many escape routes to close off.

The biggest threat was the contingent of cops forming in the next block to our left. I could picture them forming a wedge to force us out of the street and trap a small group against the barricades. I was ready for that. We had several lanes to work with. All we had to do was drop back when they charged, and regroup behind them.

I saw Raoul again, right up by the cops, and went to tell him my thoughts. But when he turned toward me, he looked scared. "The cops are losing it," he said. "It's gonna get ugly." He scanned the crowd. Looking for Jenny, I realized.

Where was Angie? Had she gone home? Or maybe she was with Jenny. No, because right then, Jenny walked up. She honed in on Raoul. "What do you think?" she asked him hurriedly.

"The cops are losing it," he said, hunching over toward her. "They're getting ready to thrash people!"

What to do? I flashed back to the Kissinger demo, when the punks had marched in and disrupted the cops' plan to attack us. Not this time. The punks were already here, part of the morass.

Jenny's eyes darted around the scene. She looked at Raoul for an instant, then abruptly said, "We've got to sit down." She turned to the people around us. "Sit down, sit down!" she called in a beseeching tone. Raoul, still hunched over, gaped at her. Then he stood up and bellowed: "Sit down!"

It was the best plan, I knew right away. What could the cops do if we were all sitting down? It would take away their pretext for hitting us. Around us, people began to settle to the ground. I dropped to the concrete with them. "Sit down!" we yelled. "Sit down!"

The intent rippled through the crowd. Twenty feet away, Sara called out, "Sit down!" She squatted and took a seat. Alby was close behind, and Sid with him. "Sit down!" Dozens more joined us on the pavement. I saw Moonstone, eyes closed, chanting to himself. Grounding the energy, I guessed.

Flint, on the other hand, looked terminally disgusted. He stalked along the perimeter of the crowd, glaring. Sit down? We come all this way, I imagined him thinking, and now finally, finally, here's our chance to mix it up with the cops, and you sit down? He yanked his beret off and stormed away.

Off to one side, I spied Angie. In the midst of the chaos, she stood alone and still. She seemed to be looking at the police. I jumped to my feet and made my way through the crowd to her. "Come on," I said. "There's a bunch of LAG people over there."

She remained immobile. "I don't know," she said. "After not getting arrested this morning at the Tour, I thought I was done with jail for a while." She looked up at me. "I'm surprised *you're* thinking about getting busted."

I laughed nervously. "I hadn't actually thought beyond the sitting down part. I guess if we don't move, they'll arrest us, won't they?"

As if in response, a bullhorn blared out: "This is an illegal assembly. If you do not disperse immediately, you will be subject to arrest." The crowd raised a chorus of jeers, drowning out the cop's attempt to repeat the ultimatum. But the message was clear. Here and there, someone stood up and moved to the sidelines. Those seated on the pavement shuffled closer together. Some linked arms. One guy pulled a bandanna over his face. The rest of the crowd backed up to the sidewalks.

Which way for us? I put my arm around Angie, who showed no inclination to move. I sighed with relief. My sentiments exactly. There's no reason to get arrested here. We could stay and support those getting busted, then leave with a good conscience. I looked at her. "What do you think?"

She looked out at the crowd in the street and took a slow breath. "I have to do it," she finally said. "This was the whole point of my coming down here, to reaffirm my connection to these people. To Jenny more than anyone. This is her action. I have to see it through."

My chest felt heavy, and I stared at her blankly. Was it all about Jenny? Did I count for nothing?

She slipped out from under my arm. Still holding my hand she took a step toward the street. "Are you coming?"

It wasn't a challenge, but it wasn't an invitation either. What could she invite me to? As soon as we got busted, we'd be separated. Over her shoulder I spied a punk with orange hair. That's who I'll be spending tonight with if I get arrested. "I don't think so," I said. "I don't see the point."

Her eyes roamed over the seated crowd. "The point is knowing that I did all I could."

"Yeah, well, I don't see what getting arrested here proves." I scuffed my shoe on the curb, wishing she'd change her mind.

She looked up at me, shielding her eyes from the glint of the sun. "Sorry about our plans for tonight. I'll call you when we get out." She rose to her tiptoes and kissed me quickly, then made her way over to join Jenny and Raoul in the street.

I sighed and gazed after her. Maybe she'll get out tonight. What reason was there to hold people in jail once the Convention ended? Maybe all isn't lost...

My reverie was broken by a policeman's bark. "Back on the sidewalk!" He poked at me with his riot stick. I retreated, but resentment flushed through me. Was I causing trouble? Was I not under enough control?

I looked through the crowd seated in the street. Just about everyone I knew at the action was out there. Well, not Hank. He'd probably left. It clearly wasn't his scene.

Not like I really belonged, either. I leaned against a lamppost at the edge of the crowd. Why did I think I would ever fit into this picture? What was I doing here?

Suddenly my heart jumped. There was Karina, not ten feet away, standing with her shoulders slumped. She must be feeling the same as I was. I started that way. Just what I needed — someone to share my frustrations, someone to think beyond this quagmire.

Then I saw that she was talking with someone — Jacey. I froze in my tracks. The two of them were leaning together, not quite touching. Jacey looked thoroughly disgusted at the sight of two hundred people seated in the street, and seemed about to stalk off.

Karina looked torn between her distaste for surrender and her passion for being in the middle of the action. She must know where she belongs, I thought, and I felt awkward at my own reticence. If only Jacey would leave, I could go offer Karina support, whatever decision she made.

But it was Karina who turned away from Jacey. She cast a glance at the blockade, sighed deeply, then picked her way through the crowd to where Sara and Alby were seated. Sara reached up and took her hand. Karina shook back her hair and took a seat.

A pang of guilt hit me. I couldn't just walk away. I looked around for Jacey. Little as I wanted to follow him, I figured he'd have a plan.

He and a few other people wandered out to the right end of the bicycle-rack barricade, well beyond the seated blockaders. I trailed a little behind. The line of cops had relaxed, apparently thinking they were on break till the arrests began. Jacey drifted up close to the barricade, then suddenly grabbed the end of the metal rack and shoved it forward several feet. A cheer went up from the nearby protesters.

The cops reacted with alarm. The closest officer slapped at the barricade with his baton. Another rushed over and shoved the end of the barricade back in place.

Jacey, meanwhile, ducked back into the crowd spilling off the sidewalk, hissed a quick "come on!" to us, and reappeared at the barricade about fifteen feet closer to the blockaders. He wasn't alone. Several others jumped forward. I gulped, and in a flash I saw the challenge we faced — can a group of relative strangers spontaneously organize and execute a simple logistical task in the face of potentially violent opposition? We weren't just closing a street — we were revolutionizing social relationships.

On-the-spot sketch of the stand-off at the Hall of Justice.

Spotting an opening, I grabbed hold of the barricade. With a shout we dragged it several feet forward. The vibration of steel on concrete rippled through my arms and chest. A helmeted cop lurched toward us, baton raised. I stepped back quickly, scared and proud. I shot a glance at Jacey, wondering if he recognized me. If he did, he didn't betray it.

We melted back into the crowd. Suddenly, out at the end of the line, a couple of men in business suits grabbed a woman by the arms. They dragged her behind police lines, jerked her around, and clamped handcuffs onto her.

"Fascists!" Jacey yelled at them. I wanted to yell, but my throat clenched. I'd forgotten about the undercovers. I looked around quickly. Had they seen me rattle the barricade? Boots scraped behind me. I jerked around. Hank looked back at me with surprise. "Hey, easy there," he said. "Just came to see if you were thinking about leaving. I'm getting out of here before they decide to do a sweep of the whole street."

Another squad of riot police marched up to the barricade. "You're probably right," I said. I craned my neck, looking for Angie. Down at the far end, a squad of cops was starting to arrest the seated protesters one at a time. Behind them, several paddywagons pulled up. Nice touch, I thought. What are they going to do, drive people all the way across the street to jail? Or were they taking them somewhere else?

I cast a final look at the crowd, but didn't spot Angie. Not much I could do even if I saw her, I thought. Not a lot to do, period, except go home and wait by the phone, hoping she gets out tonight.

"Yeah, let's go," I said to Hank. I felt glad for having someone to leave with. We made our way over to Gilbert Street, a two-lane alley leading away from the Hall of Justice. We weren't the only ones taking the back exit. Scattered along the block were little clumps of protesters, along with a few stray cops maintaining order. I even saw Jacey behind us. If he's leaving, I thought, the action really must be over.

Two armed officers, with plenty of backup, managed to arrest this protester.

Something bugged me, though. Sure, I'd have been separated from Angie as soon as we got to the jail. But at least we'd have gone in together. And I'd know that I'd done all I could to be with her. Why had I walked away? Too late now. She's probably already in the paddywagon.

My musings were interrupted by a commotion behind us. A cop pointed at Jacey and yelled. As the officer started toward him, Jacey backpedaled toward Hank and me. Another cop was closing in from the side.

"Hey!" Hank hollered. "Look out!"

Jacey turned the wrong direction. Hank pointed and yelled, "No! Behind you!"

Jacey jerked around and almost ran into me. The cop grabbed him by the shoulder. An arm flew past my face. I ducked and jumped back. The other cop was running our way. Jacey tried to pull away, but the cop had hold of his jacket. No time to think. I reached out, grabbed Jacey's free arm and pulled for all I was worth.

Had I expected a struggle? A test of wills? A desperate tug-of-war with the forces of law and order? Nothing of the sort. Faced with resistance, the cop melted. Jacey and I staggered backwards, and I fell on my butt. I scrambled away from the cop like a crab. Hank caught my arms and hoisted me to my feet. The second cop reached his partner. They shook their leathered fists and yelled at us. Another protester ran over and thrust a stocking cap into my hands. "Put this on, they'll be watching for you." I put it on, but it made me feel even more conspicuous, and I pulled it off.

Jacey had disappeared. "Come on," Hank said. "Let's get out of here before they come back with reinforcements."

Get out? How could I leave now? I thought of Angie back at the protest. She'd be thinking I'd abandoned her, that I never did anything spontaneous. Well, she was wrong. "I'm going back to the blockade," I told Hank. "I have to do it."

He looked at me like I was crazy. "If those cops recognize you, they're gonna go straight for you."

I started back toward the Hall of Justice. "Then the crowd will have to unarrest me," I said. "I've gotta do it."

He stood with his hands on his hips, shaking his head. "At least go around a different block," he called after me.

"Thanks, good idea." I circled back to Bryant Street without incident. The arrests were about half over. A couple of paddywagons pulled out, and another was filling up fast. I scanned the scene. A hundred people were still in the street. Bystanders jeered at the authorities and hollered about civil rights, but no one seemed to be pushing things further.

I spotted Sara. "Have you seen Angie?" I called to her.

"Yeah, she's over there."

I pushed through the spectators and sighted Angie just as she was arrested. The cop clamped the handcuffs tight behind her back, led her over to the paddywagon, and shoved her in. I yelled to her, but I couldn't tell if she heard me or not.

Picking my way through the remaining blockaders, I spied a cop getting out a fresh set of handcuffs. Without breaking stride I stepped right in front of him. He looked at me quizzically. "I'm ready to get arrested," I told him.

He grunted at my presumption. Then he swung a gloved hand out and jerked me around backwards. I crossed my wrists, and he cranked the handcuffs down hard. "Into that van," he directed, apparently trusting me to follow orders. I clambered in and greeted Angie with a big smile.

I figured she'd be surprised. But it felt even better when she welcomed me with a loud "Alright!" It made me feel like I was expected all along. I plunked down next to her. Hands behind our backs, without another word, we kissed as the next arrestees got on board.

I didn't know any of the other people, but each new face added to the energy cooped up inside the vehicle. "Let's rock the van," one guy yelled. Angie and I pitched in, throwing our weight back and forth to set the paddywagon rocking crazily. We rocked and laughed until a cop stuck his face in. "You want to get teargassed?"

That cooled us down. A couple of guys jawed at the cop, but I felt dizzy. I wanted to tell Angie about unarresting Jacey, but it seemed like bragging, especially in front of ten other people. It would have to wait.

The cop started to close the door. "Wait," someone yelled. "Here's one more for that van." The doors reopened and a tall guy with long dark hair was pushed in — Hank!

Forgetting Angie's tactful greeting, I welcomed Hank, "Holy cow, I didn't expect to see you here."

"Yeah, well, I followed you to watch out for those cops. Once I got in the crowd, I figured, what the hell, it's probably only a night or two in jail." He squeezed in on the far side of Angie. "Did Jeff tell you what he did?"

"No," she said, looking around at me. "What?"

"He unarrested a guy that the cops were trying to grab."

I felt a wave of pride. What a lucky break, to have Hank tell Angie.

"That's really great," she said. She held me in her gaze and nodded her head. "Wait. I have an idea." She stood up as best she could, hunched over in the paddywagon. "Reach in my pocket," she instructed Hank. He worked his arms around so he could reach into her pocket. After a few tries, he fished out the roll of yellow police-line ribbon Angie had gathered at the LAG demo a couple of days earlier. She took it from him, her hands still cuffed behind her. Turning her back toward me, she unfurled the roll over my shoulder, then draped it around my neck like a military sash.

She sat down next to me. "With this ribbon, I do hereby commend you for meritorious valor above and beyond the call of duty."

Hank laughed loudly. "Yeah, we hereby pronounce you Most Valuable Protester of today's demonstration."

I looked at them, then down at the ribbon. "Wow, thanks," I said, struck by the turn of events. "I always wanted to be MVP."

The back door was still open. Thirty feet away, the support crowd waved and hollered encouragement. "We need a chant or a song," Angie said. "Something to show our spirits." She looked at me expectantly.

I turned to Hank. "What's a good song?"

"Uh — how about that Monty Python song, you know, at the end of *Life of Brian,* when they've all been crucified?" He took a breath and launched into the chorus: "Always look on the bright side of life!" We joined in, singing even louder as the van doors were slammed shut. "Always look on the bright side of life!"

I glanced at Angie. Her head was thrown back in laughter and song. Yeah, we'll be separated soon enough. But right now, we're together. And right now, that's all that matters.

Epilog / 1984

*Para bailar La Bamba, se necesita una poca de gracia.**
— *traditional Mexican song, recorded by Ritchie Valens*

Thursday, July 26, 1984

RITCHIE VALENS was playing on the old cassette deck in the workshop. We were heading into the hot season, and I was repairing screens for the hall windows. Measure, cut, seal, trim — not a bad way to make a buck. My hands were occupied, but my mind was roving free.

I wasn't in bad spirits, considering all that had come down — down being the key word — in the past few months. Not just with Angie and Holly. Politics was a bust, too. People's Convention was a dud, and LAG was hanging by a thread.

The September Livermore action was drawing a bigger response than April had. But it wouldn't be anywhere near the scale of the previous two June blockades, and more than a few people talked about it as LAG's swan song.

I could think of all that and sink into pessimism. But then I'd flash on the Hall of Justice action, and it would all fall into perspective.

Not like it cured everything. But it alleviated my sense of lagging behind in the radicalism sweepstakes. I'd passed the initiation.

It didn't matter that hardly anyone knew. Jacey probably didn't even know my name, so Raoul and Jenny and Sid would never hear of it. Hank told Mort and Craig about it one night at pinball as part of his general narrative of our adventures, but it seemed unlikely to go further.

* *To dance La Bamba, one needs a bit of grace.*

And the only other person in on the secret, Angie, had left for Portland a day later, never to be seen again.

Well, practically. She had promised to come back the weekend of the Berkeley Anti-Reagan Festival. But BARF was two months away. Better not to think about her too much now.

I rolled the sealing tool along the last side of a screen, trimmed the overlap, and stacked it with the others. Four down, four to go. As I stood and stretched, my mind drifted back to my last night with Angie.

Following the Hall of Justice arrests, we were cited out that same evening, not too late. Angie and I were the first two back to Stonehenge, and retired to the basement. Her "room" was a corner enclosed by two dark curtains which didn't quite meet. A futon propped up on milk crates filled half of the floorspace. On a rickety nightstand sat a lamp with no shade and an old clock radio stuck on an AM classical station.

But being alone with Angie, it was all beautiful. Maybe it was because she was leaving the next day, but her reservations about us sleeping together seemed to have evaporated. To the tinny sounds of Haydn and Brahms we kissed, talked, read tarot, and made love till a sliver of dawn shown through the gap in the curtains. Finally she fell asleep, curled against me with her head tucked under my chin. I lay awake as long as I could, holding onto her, holding onto my hope — please don't let this be the last time...

Somewhere I dozed off. When I awoke, Angie was across the room packing. She was kneeling in front of her backpack, wearing only an oversized blue T-shirt and short white socks.

This is the moment, I thought. Ask her. This is the last chance. Ask her to stay. My mouth opened, but I feared the sound of my voice would startle her. I shuffled the blankets. Still kneeling, she turned to face me. "Just packing up," she said. She smiled, but in an it's-been-nice-seeing-you way. I lay on my side looking at her. She's gone. She made up her mind long ago. What's the point in asking her to stay? Why ask a question when you know the answer?

She put some clothes in the pack, then got up and came over to the bed. She stood there looking down at me, the blue T-shirt hung loosely around her. She smiled cryptically. "I'm meeting my old boss in Sausalito at noon," she said. "It takes forty minutes from here. That leaves..."

"Twenty-seven minutes," I said, glancing at the clock radio. She hovered over me. Should I ask her to stay? I closed my eyes. I could waste precious time asking futile questions, or I could answer her overture and leave us with one last memory. Clear enough. I arched up to meet her with a kiss. She lowered her body onto mine, pressing me down onto the bed. I drew her to me and felt her breath on my neck...

Twenty-seven minutes later she sat on the edge of the futon, tying her shoes. I lifted her T-shirt and kissed her on the back. She didn't respond. Okay, I won't beg you to stay. Just tell me when I'll see you. Don't make me ask.

But her words were elsewhere. "I'm driving as far as Arcata tonight. Unless I feel inspired to drive all night."

"Right," I said. I bent over to tie my shoes to avoid looking at her.

She picked up her pack. "Would you get the door?" I followed her out to the street. One of Sid's housemates was riding with her to Sausalito. He hoisted her pack into the van as Angie turned to face me. She stood on her tiptoes and kissed me gently on the lips, then put her arms around me. "I'll miss you," she said.

I squeezed her to me. "Angie, I'll miss you a lot," I said, my voice nearly breaking. "When will I see you?"

She stepped back, holding both my hands. "Unless you take a bus up to Portland, I guess it will be at BARF in September."

I stepped back onto the sidewalk and watched as she climbed into the van. She honked as she rolled away. I waved after her, but couldn't tell whether she noticed. There she goes. Off to Portland. And what about me? A bus to Portland? Why not? I could afford it. But what was the point? If she didn't care enough to stay here, why would it be different there?

Time to let go, I knew. Brooding wasn't going to make any difference. Back to work. Back to life.

I laid out another screen on the workbench. Actually, I wasn't as depressed as I thought I'd be. It was more a wistfulness, like waking from a beautiful dream to a dreary Monday morning. Life looked gray. But that probably stemmed as much from endless afternoons in the LAG office as from losing Angie.

If she was in fact "lost." Sure, the evidence pointed that way. Her first postcard said she'd been accepted at Portland State for the Fall semester. Plus, a permanent room had opened up in the house where she was subletting.

But my heart resisted the message. Almost subconsciously, I had been nursing a daydream: maybe tomorrow, I'll walk into the office, and there she'll be. We'll make plans to go over to the Starry Plough... Maybe tomorrow.

And what about our time together when she came back for BARF? It wasn't that far off. We'd take a nighttime hike to the top of Corona Heights, a rocky peak overlooking the Castro and Mission districts. We'd nestle together under a blanket, kissing, caressing...

Would she work on Direct Action that weekend? Would we sleep together? Was it too late for her to change her mind and move back?

The screen tool slipped and I scraped my hand. I clenched my teeth, warding off the stinging pain. Pay attention, I hissed. And not just to work. What was I doing, fantasizing about Angie? How long till she met someone in Portland? Stop living in dreamland. If it were ever going to work, it was back in the Spring. Hard as it was to let go, I needed to cut my losses, learn a lesson, and move on.

Thursday, August 2, 1984

WE PASSED THE Campanile, tall and silent, and turned toward the philosophy building in the center of campus. Holly had asked the night before if we could talk, and we'd made a date for this evening.

We walked under a brick archway that led to Strawberry Creek. The sun filtered through the leaves of the trees. We made our way into a little glade alongside the creek and sat down on a rickety wooden bench, half-facing each other in the dappled shade.

She took my hand between hers. Her eyes were veiled. She breathed in, then let it out slowly. I gazed at her steadily, ready for anything. What was the worst that could happen? Another lover. I could deal.

"I've decided to move out," she said plainly. "At the end of August."

"Move out?"

"We're drifting apart. We've hardly talked for a month. And it's not like the past year was all that different."

My hand felt limp and clammy in hers. I looked down at the weathered wood of the bench and felt alone, drifting. I started thinking about how inconvenient her decision was. Now I had to find a new roommate. I kicked myself for being so self-centered, and groped for something to say. "Where are you going? Do you have another place?"

"Not yet. Caroline and I might try to find a house. Or I might go traveling for a while. I'm not sure. I need to move on." A note of sadness played across her face. "I really wanted this to work. I guess my dream is that I'll meet someone to spend the rest of my life with. For two years I wished that was you. Now I know it's not."

I looked away. What could I say? I'd let her down. Not by falling in love with Angie, but by not being aware enough of my own feelings to see them developing and be open. That part I'd messed up. No wonder she was leaving. How could I expect her to trust me?

"Holly, you're really — " My voice broke, and I continued in a shaky tone. "You're really important to me."

She squeezed my hand. "Thanks, Jeff. I hope we can stay friends."

Wednesday, August 8, 1984

"KARINA did what?"

"At Vandenberg," Jenny told me. "On Hiroshima Day. She smashed up some computers or something. She's in jail right now."

I couldn't believe what I was hearing. "She's in jail? Down there?"

An odd look, almost of guilt, crossed Jenny's face. Did she know more than she was letting on? "I'm not sure where," she stammered. "Probably Walt does. He's coming by later."

Jenny and I were at Ashby house, the first arrivals for the evening's Direct Action session. The news about Karina was unsettling, but I was glad to have some time to talk with Jenny. With the Convention over, with Angie gone, and most of all, with Jenny having resigned from the LAG staff, our interactions were a lot less laden than they had been all Winter and Spring. It looked like she'd keep working on the paper, and maybe help with some action organizing in the Fall. If Jenny was plugged in, Raoul and Sid might stay on board, too. Slowly the dust was clearing. Give us a little time, and maybe we'd find a way to work together again.

"How is it between you and Holly?" Jenny asked as we settled in at the ping-pong table we were using for layout. "Must be hard to keep living together."

"No, not really," I said. "We're doing okay. I've been sleeping on the futon in the living room, though. I guess it would feel odd to keep sleeping together."

I paused. I wanted to say that the hardest part wasn't cohabitation. It was feeling like a loser, with Angie gone and Holly leaving. But I sensed that Jenny didn't want to hear about Angie, so I stuck to Holly. "In a way it's been easier," I said. "We don't have all that unresolved tension hanging over us anymore."

Jenny looked at me skeptically. "What are you doing about a roommate?" she asked.

"I found a sublettor for September and October," I said as I straightened a column of type on my page. "So that buys me some time. Long-term, Winston is interested, and Lyle might be. That's a relief. Who I live with makes such a difference."

GLOBAL ACTION

Central America Week, March 18-25th

The week of March 18-25 marked a dramatic escalation both of U.S. involvement in the war for Central America and of domestic opposition to Reagan's interventionist policies. The protest and lobby activities of national Central-America week took place against a backdrop of the continued Americanization of the war in El Salvador. As the situation in El Salvador continues to deteriorate the Reagan administration's support for the Salvadoran army is moving beyond providing military aid, to the direct intervention of U.S. combat forces.

El Salvador's recent presidential elections have provided the pretext for more conspicuous involvement of U.S. troops in the history of Salvadoran civil war. Under the guise of protecting democracy Reagan is establishing a permanent U.S. military presence in Central America without public or Congressional approval.

Reagan's open-ended and deepening commitment to a military victory for Salvadoran rightists is being reinforced with more and more firepower each day. U.S. military advisers have taken responsibility for directing Salvadoran combat operations for many months; Reagan has now given them approval to carry M-16's and small arms into battle areas.

U.S. pilots are currently flying reconnaissance flights over El Salvador, aiding government forces in "spotting" guerrillas. The CIA and the Pentagon have drafted a proposal calling for U.S. pilots to begin flying combat missions in El Salvador. The U.S.'s more active military role is not restricted to El Salvador, as Central America and the Caribbean are rapidly becoming one vast U.S. training base.

The Defense Department has announced plans to carry out two large-scale exercises in April. The Granadero I maneuvers will begin April 1, 2 months earlier than was originally proposed, and will involve troops from the U.S., El Salvador, Guatemala, Honduras and Panama. These maneuvers are scheduled to take place in Honduras, but the strong possibility exists that they will include a US-led amphibious landing in El Salvador at the Gulf of Fonseca. Upwards of 30,000 U.S. Marines, pilots, soldiers and sailors will participate in Ocean Venture 84, the largest maritime exercises of the year, beginning April 20 in the Caribbean. Presently five U.S. warships are stationed off the coast of Central America, including the nuclear-powered cruiser Virginia.

In addition to these publicly announced exercises, the Reagan administration has been steadily, but quietly, airlifting paratroopers and infantry units to the Honduran-Salvadoran border as well as introducing Special Forces Green Berets into its training programs for the Honduran military. Such concentrated and direct use of U.S. combat troops is unprecedented since the Vietnam war.

Reagan's insertion of combat troops into the volatile Honduran-Salvadoran border area has been accomplished through the use of "no notice" exercises, officially known as Emergency Deployment Readiness Exercises. Through continuous use of military alerts and "no notice" maneuvers Reagan has been able to insure a sustained combat presence in Honduras while claiming all the while that these exercises are routine and no cause for alarm. As long as the Pentagon labels these military moves "exercises" they are not subject to Congressional approval as defined by the War Powers Act.

- by Mike Zielinski
S.F. CISPES

Residents of Bombed Berkeley Sister City Try to Rebuild Their Lives

It's disheartening to witness knee-jerk reactions by cynical media sources and individuals to the tragic bombings of the 1,200 residents of San Antonio Los Ranchos, El Salvador, Berkeley's sister-city.

The people of San Antonio Los Ranchos had to evacuate their town when massive bombing occurred leaving their homes in rubble, as nearly a million other Salvadorans have been forced to do since the escalation of war with U.S. involvement. They live now in surrounding hamlets using the same fields to grow their food collectively.

It would be easy to give up hope in their situation if they did not have and maintain a sense of community. That is why they still utilize their local popular government system, with all members having a say and representatives being selected from members of the community.

Because of the war, mail service and communication with others is almost non-existent. Since most of us are not able to see proof of human rights violations -- 43,000 civilians murdered by government forces -- in commercial media sources, the people of San Antonio Los Ranchos felt it important for North Americans to see the results of our government's involvement in the war.

A video was filmed while a local representative of NEW EL SALVADOR TODAY (BERKELEY SISTER-CITY PROGRAM) visited the residents in December and learned the tragic fate of the town. Many lives were risked to get the film to the U.S.; the film only arrived a few weeks ago.

The people of San Antonio Los Ranchos encourage us to continue our struggle here so they are allowed to continue their lives in El Salvador--governing, educating, and feeding themselves collectively, and democratically with monetary and emotional support from us.

We must transcend our priviledged positions here, while our government is exporting death to Central America. A sister-city relationship is a good start for a NEW EL SALVADOR TODAY.

For more information, or to help with N.E.S.T. work, call 549-2114.

--by Hope McDonnell

Salvadoran Walk For Peace in Central America

It was a sunny day in San Salvador as Dr. Juan Peras stood in the doorway of a Church medical clinic. Army trucks pulled up slowly and stopped. Then soldiers opened fire with machine guns. He was hit in the head and arm and foot. Others died. Afterward, he was tossed into the bed of a truck and taken to prison where he was tortured for 24 days.

Peras, like many doctors and medical personnel, was marked for death for serving the poor. It was while in jail that Peras decided to come to the U.S. and "tell the American people what their government is doing to my country with their tax money."

Juan was one of about 20 refugees and 10 American supporters who marched from San Jose to San Francisco in a Walk for Peace. The march is to protest U.S. military support of the Salvadoran government, to demand peace through negotiations, no to deportation of Salvadorean and Guatemalan refugees, to stop the gross human rights violations, to stop the forced relocation of Salvadorean and Guatemalan refugees in Honduras, to bring to trial the assassins of Archbishop Romero and the 50,000 Salvadoreans killed.

Virtually all of the refugees on the march could be deported at any time. It is estimated that one out of ten deportees are murdered by the death squads upon arrival at San Salvador. The U.S. government deports about 1,000 Salvadoreans a month. There are about 1 million Salvadorean refugees in the world. 200,000 live in the Bay Area and 300,000 in L.A. Many churches are awakening to the terrible problems of the refugees and are offering sanctuary to them. The marchers stayed in sanctuary churches along the route. Each night there was a public forum where one refugee gave testimony. The stories are of shocking and brutal treatment, cruel murders. Stories of relatives bodies cut into pieces, eyes gouged out, testicles crushed, family members disappearing, later to turn up by the roadside a mutilated corpse.

Instead of terrorizing people into mute obedience, opposition grows. From these life and death situations springs a commitment and discipline that white Americans need to learn from. We cannot imagine the poverty and oppression people are forced to endure. We also do not know the strength that arises. The refugees want to know us, to share their lives with us, and want us to share with them. We are the only ones who can stop the U.S. invasion of Central America. It is up to all of us. I urge you to become more active. The refugees will come to A.G. meetings, house meetings, whatever. Their lives have already been threatened and they have escaped for now. Our efforts, much less risky, are the telling ones now. For more information, call Paul Dosfer, 848-3949.

LAG Prepares Response If US Invades Again

What are we going to do if U.S. troops invade El Salvador or Nicaragua as they so neatly invaded Grenada last fall? We are going to respond immediately by shutting down a few government buildings through LAG's Emergency Response Network.

The working group which is building LAG's Emergency Response Network has compiled a phone tree and identified ten affinity groups to consult about activating the network in the event of a foreign policy emergency. If you or your affinity group want to be added to the phone tree, fill out and return the coupon below.

In case of an emergency, the response plan is to rally on the evening of an emergency, when people will be encouraged to join in nonviolent direct actions the following day. People wanting to participate will be offered workshops in nonviolence preparation, legal and other kinds of support work that night. On the day following an emergency, people will blockade or occupy an appropriate, pre-designated site.

Part of National Network

At the same tim this plan was being worked out in the Bay Area, the Honeywell Project in Minneapolis, Minn., independently agreed to participate in a similar scenario. It is an idea whose time has come. Other groups prepare to act in coordination with us all over the country. LAG's Emergency Response working group is working closely with them.

By publicizing the network, and by gathering in advance commitments from people to disrupt "business as usual" at government or military installations, we hope the network will serve to prevent foreign policy crimes such as invasions or significant military escalation by the U.S. or one of its proxies. Your help is needed:

(1) on the Emergency Response Network working group, to keep the phone tree up-to-date, publicize the network, and decide on tactics. Call Lee Diamond at 731-1222 or 654-5481 to join the work group.

(2) As a participant, prepared to act quickly and decisively in the event of a foreign policy emergency. Discuss who will do what with your affinity group, then fill out and return the coupon below.

— Add my name to the phone tree for LAG's Emergency Response Network.
— I could help call people on the phone tree in the event of an emergency.
— You can publicize my name as someone who is willing to commit civil disobedience in the event of another U.S. invasion.
— I would like to join the working group organizing LAG's Emergency Response Network.
— Send me a copy of the National Emergency Response Network Proposal

Name ______
Phone ______
Address ______

Central America news and activism became a key focus of Direct Action's global pages.

Jenny nodded and brushed her hair out of her face. "Me and Raoul want to start a collective house. Caroline and Tai might be part of it."

I wondered if Holly would join them, and felt a little jealous. "Are you staying in Oakland?"

"Or South Berkeley. If I'm going to have kids, I want a house with a nice yard."

I looked up from my layout board. "So you're thinking of having kids soon?"

"Yeah," she said with as much certainty as I'd ever heard from her. "Raising kids in a new way is one of the most radical things you can do. Of course, that means dealing with my own patterns. That's why I had to get out of the LAG office. It was the perfect way to avoid my feelings — staying immersed in endless phone calls and meetings and actions."

I pursed my lips. "What are you going to do about it?"

"Well, for starters, I'm taking a co-counseling class."

I nodded without quite grasping it. "Co-counseling?"

"Yeah. If I'm really committed to not passing my patterns on to my children, I have to get in and do the personal work. Right now."

"That's great," I said, but I wasn't quite following her plan. Before I could ask, we were interrupted by the door. It was Sid and Raoul, coming to work on the centerspread about the Convention actions.

"Did you hear about Karina?" Jenny asked them. Sid and Raoul were as surprised as I had been. Jenny filled them in on what little she knew.

A couple of minutes later, Norm arrived with an update. "I heard she's over at the Hall of Justice in the City," he told us. "Alby said they didn't arrest her till she got back home."

Sid bounced on his toes. "We should organize a solidarity rally in front of the Hall of Justice."

Raoul shook his head slowly. "I just hope she knows what she's gotten herself into," he said. "What was she trying to prove?"

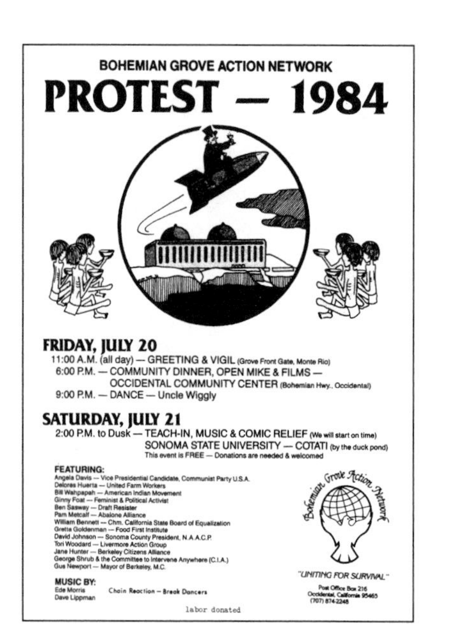

Bohemian Grove Action Network organizes protests of the annual July gathering of corporate and governmental bigwigs at the Bohemian Club in Northern California. See Fact and Fiction Appendix for info.

Probably nothing to you, I thought, feeling suddenly protective of Karina. If she did smash a computer, she must have had a good reason. Raoul's attitude made me think of Mort, who was over at Hank's shop working on the nukecycle. I was glad he wasn't coming to production that night. The last thing I needed was Mort gloating over Karina going off the deep end. Or whatever she had done.

ARREST THE BOHOS

Non-Violent Civil Disobedience
At Bohemian Grove

Sunday, July 22   **Monte Rio, Sonoma County**

EVERY FOUR YEARS, THERE ARE A COUPLE OF CONVENTIONS IN THE CITY THAT GET ALL THE ATTENTION...
BUT THE REAL CONVENTION HAPPENS, EVERY YEAR, AT THE BOHEMIAN GROVE 75 MILES NORTH OF SAN FRANCISCO ON THE RUSSIAN RIVER...
THE AMERICAN MALE POWER ELITE GETS TOGETHER FOR TWO WEEKS IN JULY--- NO WOMEN AND VIRTUALLY NO MINORITIES ADMITTED.
IN SECRET, INSULATED FROM HUMAN CONCERN, THEY BEGIN THEIR SUMMIT CONFERENCE BY "CREMATING CARE"-- AS IF THEIR DAILY BEHAVIOR HAS NOT BEEN CARELESS AND UNCARING ENOUGH.
THE "MANHATTAN PROJECT" WAS BORN IN THE GROVE IN 1942--NOW THEY'VE MOVED ON TO FIRST-STRIKE, AND "STAR WARS"...
THE LIVERMORE ACTION GROUP AND THE SONOMA COUNTY DIRECTION ACTION COALITION ARE CALLING FOR A NON-VIOLENT BLOCKADE OF THE GROVE ON SUNDAY, JULY 22ND
A PEOPLE'S QUARANTINE WILL TRY TO PROTECT THE WORLD AGAINST THE LETHAL HABITS, LETHAL ATTITUDES, LETHAL VALUES AND LETHAL POWER OF THE MEMBERS OF THE BOHEMIAN CLUB.

WE MUST DRAW THE ATTENTION OF THE WORLD TO THE FACT THAT...
THE ESTABLISHMENT EXISTS
ITS MEMBERS MEET AT THE GROVE
THEIR DECISIONS AFFECT ALL OF OUR LIVES--AND MAY SOON END THEM...

THE DAY OF THE ACTION

All participants in the July 22 non-violent action at the Bohemian Grove (CD ers and support people) will gather between 10:00 and 11:00 in the parking lot adjoining the north end of Monte Rio Bridge. A check-in and short orientation covering the action scenerio, law enforcement picture, and legal coordination will take place from 11:00 -11:45. Shortly before noon, we will walk the 1/2 mile to the front gate of the Grove and present a demand for changes in specific club policies and a peoples' platform for action.

Following this presentation, autonomous affinity groups will place the Bohos under citizens arrest (or quarantine them) by blocking their exit.

Protesters are expected to follow non-violence guide lines and bring food, water, signs and banners.

FRIDAY 7/20, Greeting and Vigil at the Grove, followed by a community Dinner (6-9 pm) with open mike and dance (9-12 pm). Call (707)874-2193 for reservations.
SATURDAY 7/21, Teach-In held by B.G.A.N. on the Role of the Demo & Repub. Parties in the Economic Roots, Military Expansion, nuclear proliferation and the subjugation of Women and Minorities. Speakers include:Ginny Foat of the Natl. Org. of Women, Bill Wahpepah of the American Indian Movement, Dolores Huerta of the United Farm Workers, Ben Sasway on Draft resistance, and others.
COME TO Sonoma State University in Cotati, 2-8 pm. Admission is free, tho Donations are welcome! Call (707)887-2364 or (707) 874-2248 for information.

RELAX The Russian River is a wonderful place to be in July, that's why the Bohemians are there. The river is refreshing and the beaches are numerous. The ocean is only a short hop from Monte Rio and Armstrong Redwoods State Preserve is nearby. Camping is available in many places and the weather should be excellent. Bring your swimsuit. Attend the many activities at the front gate, community dinner and dance in Occidental on Friday 7/20, and the Teach-In at Sonoma State University in Cotati on Saturday 7/21. Free camping is available with local residents and landowners; for reservations or information call (707) 874-2193.

L.A.G. (415-644-3031), SCDAC (707-664-8187)

In July 1984, LAG cosponsored the Bohemian Grove protests, helping organize a blockade of the only access road into the summer camp of the rich.

We rehashed the news a few more times, then settled into production. I started working on the calendar page, while Jenny tackled Sara's article on the Bohemian Grove action. Sara might have done it herself, but she and Alby had an extended commitment up north.

Alby and Sara were actually lucky their jail sentence wasn't worse, given how it looked at first. The whole incident had gotten blown out of proportion. It wasn't like they'd killed a cop. I couldn't believe that anyone had seriously said, "no solidarity."

Most of the fifty people busted at the July 22nd Bohemian Grove quarantine had either done a sit-down blockade, or woven "webs of resistance" across the road, trapping the bigwigs' cars in the Grove until Sonoma County sheriffs could make the arrests.

But Sara and Alby, fresh from the War Chest Tours, must have been thinking mobile tactics. When the sheriffs arrived to tear apart their web and take them into custody, the two of them took off running. The sheriffs gave chase and proved the better athletes, tackling Sara and Alby within a hundred yards.

The police slapped the two of them with resisting arrest, a much heavier charge than the other blockaders got. Immediate jail solidarity might have gotten the extra charges dropped, but some blockaders felt that running violated the nonviolence guidelines. No consensus was reached, and people cited out with the charges standing. Now the only hope was a courtroom showdown, and no one was pulling it together. Were people really cutting Alby and Sara adrift, or was it just lack of organizing?

The initiative needed to come from someone who did the action. Most participants lived up north. Daniel, the main Bay Area organizer, seemed like the only point of leverage.

I had stalled for a week or so, till the day before their hearing, then approached Daniel at the office and asked if I could talk with him about Bohemian Grove.

He looked up slowly, his fountain pen poised above a densely-worded sheet of paper. "About Sara and Alby, I presume?"

I nodded. "It's not like they're strangers," I said. "These are our people."

"They also broke the nonviolence agreements," he answered. "I don't think we should make exceptions just because they're our 'friends.'"

A flush of anger rose in me. "Well, if I were one of the organizers, I wouldn't want people saying I abandoned someone just because they tried to get away from the cops. They're facing six months in jail."

Daniel drew his head back. "I'm quite aware of that," he said. "I don't believe I need a lecture on solidarity."

Maybe you do, maybe you don't, I thought. Better not to push him into a corner. If I argued more, he'd never give in. Give him time to think about it.

When the day rolled around, I rode up north for the hearing, even though I knew I'd have no leverage as a mere observer. When we arrived, I hoped to have one last word with Daniel. I was curious what he intended to do. If he hadn't made up his mind yet, maybe I could make the difference.

Busted for wading in a fountain at the 1984 Republican National Convention in Dallas.

But when we arrived, he was already in a defendant's meeting. Maybe he'd give a ringing solidarity speech, urging people to stand firm with Sara and Alby and demand equal sentences. We took our seats in a small, wood-paneled room. As the defendants filed into court, Megan, who had been at their meeting as a legal assistant, came and joined us in the spectators' seats. She whispered to those of us close enough to hear: "Sara and Alby are going first. Daniel made a great speech about solidarity and how we can't abandon those we're protesting with. So the other protesters told the lawyers to tell the judge that Alby and Sara would be the first two arraigned and sentenced. No one else will cooperate until then. If Alby and Sara get outrageous sentences, the others will refuse to enter a plea, or plead not-guilty and demand separate trials."

The legal team passed that information on to the judge, who weighed the matter with troubled visage. Staring down at Sara and Alby, he informed them that he personally was inclined toward a ninety-day sentence for their egregious offense, but to expedite justice would settle for giving them thirty days. Then he launched into the old "work within the system" spiel. As he prattled on, a murmuring arose from the courtroom audience. The judge rapped his gavel for order. "I'm warning you, I'll cite you all for contempt of court!"

As if by prearranged signal, Daniel stood up and faced the bench. "Your honor," he declared, "I have nothing but contempt for this court."

Direct Action #17, September 1984

Before the judge could collect himself, four more defendants stood up, including Tony, the plumber from my first affinity group. The quintet received a five-day contempt citation and were led away.

"You never know who is going to step forward," Jenny said as she pasted down the drawing that Alby did afterwards. "I'd never have guessed Daniel."

I smiled to myself. With a little prodding.

Jenny pasted down a drawing for another story on the page, a scruffy man in boxer shorts standing in a puddle of water holding a dress and high heels — Moonstone in action at the Republican National Convention in Dallas. Now we just needed his story.

Which he obligingly dropped off about ten minutes later. "Good to see you," I said. "I heard about your bust. I'd hate to see you get six months for protesting in Texas."

"Aw, I don't think they minded us that much. We were sort of free entertainment. We did a drag-queen fashion show downtown. The Sisters of Perpetual Indulgence organized it, and a few more of us joined in. It was really hot, especially in the polyester dress I had on, so I thought I'd escape the heat by wading in the Southwest Life fountain. Unfortunately, I didn't escape the 'heat.'"

"They busted you?"

"Yeah. But they let me go after a few hours."

"That's lucky. I'd hate to be facing charges so far away."

"Well," he said, "I do have charges. I got busted again the next day on a War Chest Tour."

"You did a War Chest Tour at the Republican Convention?"

"Yeah. Over a hundred of us got arrested. Maybe it will catch on and people will do them at every Convention. But it's a drag having charges that far away. Hopefully the ACLU will get them dropped."

Shortly after Moonstone took off, Walt came in. All production ceased, and we crowded around. "What happened with Karina?" I asked.

"Pretty simple," he said, shaking his head. "She went down to Vandenberg and paid a visit to the Navstar computers."

Sid leaned toward Walt. "Is she at the Hall of Justice? We should do a march. We should start calling people right now."

"Probably not the best idea," Walt said. "We're posting bail tomorrow. She'll be free till her trial in November or December. After that, well, we may not see her for a while."

"What exactly did she do?" I asked.

Walt took a breath. "As her attorney, I can't elaborate on that. You'll have to ask her if she wants to talk about it." He paused, then added with a weak laugh, "which she probably does..."

Wednesday, August 29, 1984

"Wow," I said as I stood and hugged Karina. "Federal felony charges suit you well."

We took our seats in the small Vietnamese restaurant on Valencia Street. It was the first time I'd seen her since her Vandenberg action. Her hair seemed longer and thicker than before, and her dark eyes glowed warmly.

"Walt says you're out till November," I said.

She opened her menu. "As long as I don't get arrested. Then they could revoke my bail. But I'm being careful. If I get busted again, I'll make it count."

I frowned. Make it count? Where was she headed? Since hearing of her arrest, I'd done my best to stay nonjudgmental. But if she had a further escapade in mind, maybe I needed to speak up.

Regardless, I'd never seen her looking more enchanting. I gazed at her as she perused the menu. Her movements seemed almost stately. Even when she flipped her hair back, she did it with gravity and purpose.

Why had I always been so sure we were a bad match? I pictured us together in my apartment, talking and kissing. Was it out of the question? Of course, I'd heard that she was sleeping with Sara again, and probably Alby as well. That didn't leave a lot of spare nights. But I could be flexible.

I realized she was looking at me, as if waiting for me to start the conversation. Let's go back to your place, I wanted to say. Who needs lunch? Well, I didn't need to be quite that blunt. I closed my menu. "I want to hear about the action."

She looked away. I wondered if I had asked the wrong question, dredging up visions of her impending prison sentence.

But then she began speaking. "I wanted to do something at Vandenberg ever since Alby and I got the sixty-day sentences last year. I wanted to let them know once and for all that they weren't going to intimidate us." She nodded to herself. "Originally, I wanted to do it with an affinity group. When I met with Plowshares people this Spring, that was the first thing they asked, why I wasn't doing it as part of a group. But then I thought about all the meetings, if we wanted to have a true consensus. If I had to spend hours and hours in meetings talking about it, it would have been too hard. I needed to just jump in and do it."

Smart, I thought. Lately, meetings seemed like the best way not to do anything.

The waitress came back. "They have a great vegetarian platter," Karina said. "And how about some lemongrass tofu?"

"Fine with me," I said. I figured if it wasn't filling enough, I could get a burrito later.

She took a drink of water and resumed her story. "Once I decided to do it," she said, "I gave notice at the temp job I'd been working since I quit the LAG office. I told a few friends that I was going away for a while, because I assumed that I'd get busted and be in prison for the next few years. Alby and Sara knew something was up, but I didn't tell them exactly what I was doing, so they wouldn't be implicated if they got picked up for questioning.

"I rode a bus down to San Luis Obispo, then hitchhiked out near Vandenberg that evening. I had a daypack with my tools, a bagel, spraypaint and markers, and my Teddy Bear. For jail, I brought a copy of *Les Miserables* by Victor Hugo, one of those thick books that's really hard to read unless you just aren't going anywhere.

"By the time I got there, it was almost midnight, which was perfect. They weren't expecting anything, so I had no trouble getting onto the base. It's those same low fences that we saw in our earlier actions. I hiked right in, following the roads. I was making pretty good time, although I had to go behind bushes and pee every few minutes because I was so scared."

"I can imagine," I said with a nervous laugh.

The waitress brought our dishes and arranged them on the little table. I suddenly felt hungry, and filled my plate. Karina did likewise, took a few bites, then set her fork down and continued.

"It was so beautiful," she said, looking into my eyes as if searching for a sign that I could feel the beauty, too. "I remember a slight ocean breeze.

Crickets making a racket. And more stars than I'd ever seen in my life." She raised her eyes. "I looked up at the Milky Way and tried to imprint it in my mind, so I could visualize the stars when I was locked away in a cell."

I looked up, too. Could I visualize the Milky Way? Or hear crickets sing? I pictured Karina hiking through the woods, strolling resolutely toward — toward what? "Are there signs that tell you where you are?" I asked.

"Not many. But folks at earlier actions had reconnoitered the Navstar installation, and I had a Geological Survey map to go by. It only took me an hour to get from the edge of the base to the building." Her voice trailed off, as if the scene were rising before her eyes. "The building wasn't very big. On top was a white spherical drum about fifteen feet across, which I figured held the satellite dish. That's how I knew I was at the right place. It was surrounded by a tall barbed wire fence. But the gate was unlocked and I didn't see any guards.

"I'd brought a bouquet of red-white-and-blue flowers and a box of Mrs. Field's chocolate chip cookies. I left them outside the gate with a poem I wrote:

> I have no guns, you must have lots,
> Let's not be hasty, no cheap shots.
> Have a cookie and a nice day!
> Love,
> Karina

She smiled. "Then I closed the gate behind me, put a kryptonite lock on it, and put epoxy in the lock to slow them down. Plus, I figured they'd have to stop and disarm the box of cookies before they came in."

I nodded appreciatively. "I bet you're right."

"So there I am, sometime around one in the morning," she said, "I'm standing in front of the Navstar building. First thing, I get out my spraypaint and giant markers, and on the outside of the building I write 'International Law' and 'Nuremburg Principles.'"

That made me laugh. Here she is, trespassing on an Air Force Base with a bunch of breaking-and-entering tools, and she stops to spraypaint. "That's true dedication to the art," I said.

Karina beamed at the praise. "Mainly, I was thinking about my legal defense — how to prove my mental state while doing the action. I wanted to show that I was enforcing international law, by which we're bound. We've signed treaties at Nuremburg and Geneva that say we won't use weapons of mass and indiscriminate destruction, that we won't commit crimes against humanity. I was enforcing those treaties. But how do I prove what my thoughts were at that moment?"

"Of course," I said. "What better way than graffiti?"

"Exactly," she said. "You fix your mental state to the scene." She paused, as if refining a detail of her defense strategy. When she spoke, her voice was hushed.

"Then I had to break into the building. I was standing in front of the door, psyching myself. Once I broke in, the alarms would go off, and I would have seconds to accomplish anything. I had all kinds of tools: a crowbar, a hammer, a cordless drill, bolt cutters. It was like a little *Mission Impossible* kit. I even had the *Mission Impossible* music in my head. Half the time, anyway. The other half of the time I had this nursery rhyme: 'Going on a Lion hunt... I'm not afraid!'"

"So I'm at the door. I'm back to the *Mission Impossible* theme, trying to drill through the lock. But it's a dinky old drill, we're not getting anywhere, and guards could come by any minute! Then I realize, the door has this big plate-glass window. And I think, Karina, wake up! I take out the crowbar and tap at it, and it shatters. I reach through and open the door, and I go, oh my god, you're committed now."

I felt an impulse to reach across the table and grab her and say, "No! Get out of there!"

But I could see there was no dissuading her. Her eyes gleamed as she continued. "Now I'm inside, and I'm walking down the hall with the cordless drill in one hand and the hammer in the other, looking for the computer room, and the music is still going in my head, really fast!" She burst into laughter.

I pushed aside my worries and laughed with her. "That must have been so scary!"

She stopped for a bite of tofu. "Yeah. I was afraid of getting shot. But I was even more afraid of getting caught before I'd done anything. That would be the worst. I knew the alarm must have sounded when I opened the door. But the building seemed totally empty. Finally I found the computer room. The door was unlocked — I was in! Even though the soldiers could come any second, I knew I'd get in a few whacks. I felt so much better!

"First I smashed the monitors," she said, pausing as if savoring the memory. "Then I found the computer — a mainframe, not some mini-computer. It was in five big cabinets, row after row of circuit boards, probably two hundred in every cabinet. I couldn't believe it. I jabbed at them with the crowbar, like some kind of Aikido exercise. I was raking out whole batches of circuit boards, piling them on the floor and dancing on top of them. One of the cabinets was locked and I couldn't get into it, so I went and filled a wastepaper basket full of water and poured it through the vents on top and flipped the switch, and it sizzled and made sparks.

"After that, I wrote more international law stuff on the outside of the computers. And still no guards! Then I noticed that there was a big alarm box on the wall, so I opened it and it was full of switches. A bunch of them looked tripped, so I figured I better get back to work.

"I decided to go after the radar dish on the roof. I found the room underneath it, with a trap door way up in the ceiling. I made this pile of furniture, one desk on top of another, and a chair on top of that, until I could reach the trap door.

"I pulled myself up through the opening and into a little room. There was the satellite dish, as big as a king-sized bed. I whacked at it with the hammer and the crowbar, trying to dent the surface, but it turned out to be really hard. Then I tried to drill holes in it. I spent half an hour and barely gave it a case of acne, let alone warping it." A troubled look crossed her face, as if she were puzzling once more over how to damage the dish.

"So I gave up on that and climbed back down," she said. "And still no soldiers. Which was not at all what I expected. I sat down and ate my bagel. I tried reading my book, but I was too jittery for that. So I went to the bathroom and primped for a while. You want to look nice when you're arrested."

"Or shot," I said.

"Yeah, for sure." She took a drink of water. "Finally I was so restless that I decided to start walking back out. I had to climb out of the Navstar area, because I'd kryptonite-locked the gate. I still figured I'd get busted any minute. But I hiked all the way out and reached the edge of the base just before dawn. A delivery truck was driving by. I put my thumb out..."

She shook her head in wonder. "What was really weird was, the truck was actually going *into* Vandenberg. He dropped me off by the front gate, right where we did that first action. I was so excited and scared, and I had to pee and there was nowhere to go. Finally, I got a ride from a civilian employee leaving the base. The whole time I was expecting to get arrested. It wasn't till I was changing rides near Salinas that my heart finally stopped pounding."

Mine, too, I thought. I took a deep breath as she continued.

"I got back to the Bay Area late that night and called Sara and Alby. They were amazed to hear from me. They figured I was long gone.

"The next day, I phoned down to Vandenberg and said, 'I heard your computer got trashed last night.' And they said, 'That's a false rumor, it never happened.' And I said 'Yes it did — I did it!' But they had their party line, that it never happened.

"Next I called the U.S. Attorney. But they said that it wasn't their department, that I should call the U.S. Marshals. I'm thinking, what do you have to do to get arrested around here?

"I called the Marshals and said, 'I smashed these computers, and I'm having a press conference tomorrow at noon.' And they said something like, 'Call the FBI,' but I'm thinking, I've had enough of you people.

"At noon the next day, we called a press conference at the Hall of Justice. Walt was there as my attorney. Sara and Alby were present, of course. And word had leaked out, so there were a few other supporters in the courtroom, too. All sorts of media came, and we did a long interview. Finally, after about forty-five minutes, the FBI showed up. Their offices were in the same building, but they were clueless. They didn't even bring a tape recorder. They could have gotten all kinds of incriminating statements.

"Partway through, the Marshals came and confiscated my tools, which I had laid out like show and tell. They seized them as dangerous weapons that never should have gotten into the Hall of Justice.

"At the end of the conference, I was pretty hungry. Some of us talked about going to Chinatown for lunch. But then the FBI says, come hang out with us. I refused. Finally, just as I was leaving, they came and handcuffed me.

"I was in jail for several days before people got the bail money together for me. But now I'm out for a couple of months till the trial. I hadn't planned for this, but it's been amazing. I've been getting asked to speak all over the place. It's like my action is touching the world in ways I never imagined."

I nodded. It sure is.

"So that's my life," she concluded, "until the trial. After that, who knows? Maybe I'll be acquitted, or there'll be a hung jury. I only have to convince one juror. That's all it takes."

She was right. And if anyone could do it, it was Karina. She'd win her acquittal. And then she wouldn't be gone. Maybe we did have a future.

The waitress stepped up and laid the check on the table. Reality. With a cold flush, I knew acquittal was impossible. Not if the Feds wanted her.

She got up to use the restroom, and I gazed after her. Yeah, it was possible that we might sleep together in the next month or so. But what was the point? A quick fling that would just alienate me from Sara. And for what? Karina was as good as gone. And not just her. With her went Change of Heart. How could it be the same without Karina and her latest adventure?

She returned and picked up the check. I handed her my share, then watched her talking to the waitress, all warmth and good cheer. Karina at her best.

But it was out of context. Where were the police? Where were the solidarity meetings? Was this our life together, sharing lunch in a little Mission diner?

At that moment I knew it wasn't Karina I wanted, but something far more. Something that Karina had always pointed to — a sense of being at the very center of a vast conspiracy to change the world. That's what was slipping away. Not just a potential lover, but our entire reality.

We stepped outside and said a few parting words. If only we could roll back the clock and sit with Change of Heart in the warm grass of People's Park, planning our latest action. Karina scheming, Sara fretting, Alby clowning, Doc furrowing, Angie pondering, Moonstone daydreaming...

Gone. Karina and I hugged and said something about talking soon. It was the end.

Saturday, September 22, 1984

"What a charming amusement for young people this is, Mr. Darcy! There is nothing like dancing after all. I consider it as one of the first refinements of polished societies."

— *Jane Austen, Pride & Prejudice*

I LOOKED out the window. The sky was a solid sheet of gray. But it looked like fog, not rainclouds. Just stay that way. The last thing LAG needed was a month of work and $1000 in expenses washed away by a fluke September downpour.

BARF. That's how I felt, getting up at eight in the morning. I tried to think of the last time I'd done it. Livermore the previous Summer? Even once a year was hard to stomach.

I showered and headed downtown toward the park. My mind was thrown askew by the unfamiliar morning shadows. But soon I honed in on the most pressing matter at hand. Seeing Angie.

Seeing her for the first time in two months. She'd come into town the night before and stayed over at Urban Stonehenge. We had a date that evening, after BARF. Naturally, I was hoping to sleep with her. I wasn't dating anyone else. Probably she wasn't yet either. So why not? Casual sex between old lovers.

Right. "Move back," I still wanted to say. As soon as I saw her. She hadn't started school yet. Ask her today.

Was it impossible? Not on my end. Holly had moved out a few weeks earlier. In fact, she wasn't even in town, having gone with Sara and some of her friends to a women's Equinox retreat. I wasn't sorry. One less complication to deal with today.

Holly and I had gotten together a couple of times since she moved out and talked about where our relationship was heading. Not like we were going to drop out of each others' lives. But we were fumbling for ways to stay connected.

For my part, I was getting clearer on what I wanted from Holly. I wanted her to be happy. Not just satisfied, but vibrant, like she was when we met. I wanted it for her sake. But I wanted it for me, too. I had the feeling that until Holly was happy, I wasn't going to feel like I could forgive myself and relax.

Relax. What a concept. When I was about to see Angie for the first time in two months? What was I going to say when I saw her? "How was your trip down? How'd you sleep last night?" Forget it. Just get right to the point: "Move back!"

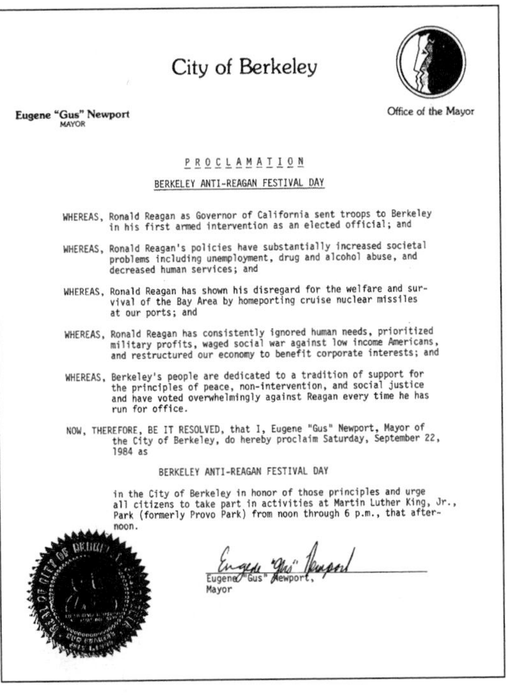

City of Berkeley

Eugene "Gus" Newport
MAYOR

Office of the Mayor

PROCLAMATION

BERKELEY ANTI-REAGAN FESTIVAL DAY

WHEREAS, Ronald Reagan as Governor of California sent troops to Berkeley in his first armed intervention as an elected official; and

WHEREAS, Ronald Reagan's policies have substantially increased societal problems including unemployment, drug and alcohol abuse, and decreased human services; and

WHEREAS, Ronald Reagan has shown his disregard for the welfare and survival of the Bay Area by homeporting cruise nuclear missiles at our ports; and

WHEREAS, Ronald Reagan has consistently ignored human needs, prioritized military profits, waged social war against low income Americans, and restructured our economy to benefit corporate interests; and

WHEREAS, Berkeley's people are dedicated to a tradition of support for the principles of peace, non-intervention, and social justice and have voted overwhelmingly against Reagan every time he has run for office.

NOW, THEREFORE, BE IT RESOLVED, that I, Eugene "Gus" Newport, Mayor of the City of Berkeley, do hereby proclaim Saturday, September 22, 1984 as

BERKELEY ANTI-REAGAN FESTIVAL DAY

in the City of Berkeley in honor of those principles and urge all citizens to take part in activities at Martin Luther King, Jr., Park (formerly Provo Park) from noon through 6 p.m., that afternoon.

Eugene "Gus" Newport,
Mayor

Progressive Berkeley Mayor Gus Newport issued this city proclamation in support of BARF, and spoke at the festival.

When I reached the park, Angie wasn't there yet. I wandered over to the stage to check-in with Hank, who was bolting together the scaffolding. "How's it going?"

He turned toward me wide-eyed. "We did it. We closed the deal yesterday. Judith and I bought a house."

I tried to follow him. "A house? The one on Grant? That's great."

"Yeah, can you believe it? Two working stiffs beat the system. Landlords want to keep you a tenant for your entire life. They'll suck you dry. It's a major victory to get even one piece of property away from them." He cast his eyes in the direction of Grant Street. "Judith gets the upstairs to decorate however she wants, and I get the basement. It's huge, I can get thirty or forty pinball games down there, easy. We signed the papers, it's ours on October 1st."

"Couldn't have happened to a nicer pinball restorer," I said.

"As soon as I get some machines set up, we'll have a dedication." He picked up a wrench and tightened a bolt on the scaffolding. "This stage is taller than I thought. I hope there's a good crowd, or it's going to seem weird to have it so high."

Walt asked for my help setting up a sun-awning for the backstage area. I looked up at the gray sky. Rain seemed more of a threat than heatstroke.

Off to the left side, Raoul and Norm were rigging a volleyball net. Raoul stood up, pulled out a joint, and fired it up. He passed it to Norm, who took a toke, then held it up between his thumb and forefinger and beckoned in my direction. I savored the rich scent as it drifted my way, but shook my head. No way I wanted to be high while coordinating the show.

An unexpected face passed in front of the stage: Melissa, carrying a big stack of leaflets. I wondered if she was dropping them off, or staying for the day.

Angie came walking across the park, stopping here and there to say hi to people. Her hair was longer, pulled back in twin braids, and she was wearing a baggy sweatshirt. I wondered what she had on under it. Come on, sunshine!

She greeted me with a hug, and for an instant, the world felt fine. But she quickly let go and surveyed the park. "We've got to get going," she said. "This place could be packed with people in two hours." She looked at me, her eyes all business. "I'm going to focus on the game booths."

I watched her walk away. She's right. Stay focused on the set-up. I have all day with her here at BARF, then hopefully all night at my place.

Work areas were scattered around the park, and booths, awnings, and tables sprang up. The only downer was that PG&E, the utility monopoly, had chosen the same afternoon to host an "Energy Fair." They were setting up a display in the parking lot of their branch office across the street from the park. "Freeloading off our event," I said to Hank. "Trying to look all community-minded."

The nukecycle crew put the finishing touches on the missile in preparation for its first unaided flight.

"Don't sweat it," Hank said. "I heard that COMA affinity group is planning something. They didn't publicize it because they want to surprise PG&E."

I nodded and turned back to our work. Alby, looking none the worse for his recent three-week jail-stint for Boho Grove, climbed a tree to the side of the stage and anchored the rope for the Reagan piñata. Moonstone pedaled up on a recumbent bicycle with a bag of donated bagels. He reached in the bag, grabbed several, and tossed them to people like frisbees. He started to toss one to me, but I waved him off. "In a while," I said. "Once we get settled here."

Partway down the left side of the park, Angie worked with Walt on my favorite game booth: "Smash Nancy's China." First Lady Nancy Reagan, oblivious to the mounting homeless crisis, had just spent thousands of tax dollars to buy a new set of the finest serving ware for the White House. Walt's response was to go to Ashby Flea Market and buy up all of the plates he could find, collect a few baseballs, and charge people a quarter a throw.

I walked over that way. "Let's test it," I said when the canvas backdrop was secured. Angie handed me a ball. I went into a windup and uncorked my heater. Wham! Right past the dish and into the canvas. I put my hands on my hips as Walt retrieved the ball. I studied the plate carefully, then unleashed a second pitch. Wham! Canvas again.

"Relief pitcher!" Raoul's voice came booming from behind me. He stepped over and picked up a ball, working it between his hands. Then he held one palm up near his mouth and pretended to spit into it. "Spitball," he said. "This one's for you, Nancy." He limbered his throwing arm, took aim, and fired. Crack! Shards flew in every direction. I joined in the applause, only a little annoyed at being upstaged.

A truck pulled up alongside the stage. "Ah, the reinforcements," Hank yelled. It was the staff of the Starry Plough, whom we had invited to set up a barbeque pit as one of the food booths. They unloaded a couple of big grills, barrels of ice for drinks — and then, unmistakably, several kegs of beer. "Uh-oh," I said to Hank, "that wasn't part of the plan. We don't have an alcohol permit."

"Aw, it's no big deal," Hank answered. "The cops won't mess with us. We've got Congressman Dellums and the mayor speaking. We're covered."

"Yeah, I guess so," I said, embarrassed that I was worrying about permits. "How's the nukecycle?"

Hank lit up. "All systems go. We parked it around the corner, behind the PG&E building. Craig's keeping an eye on it."

"So what's the plan?" I felt a little out of the loop.

"We want to do it around five o'clock, as the climax of the day. Wavy Gravy is going to announce it from stage." Hank's eyes got a faraway look. "Right when the Looters finish their set, when everyone's up and dancing, we'll launch."

"Sounds great," I said. "So you finally solved the chain problem?"

His face clouded. "I hope so. There isn't room in the frame for a heavier chain. But we test-drove it last night and it held."

While we were finishing the stage set-up, a commotion over on the side street caught our attention. Coming right down the center of the street was a flat trailer being pulled by a half-dozen huffing people. A sign identified them as "PG&E Ratepayers." Atop the trailer was an eight-foot cylinder labeled "Diablo Canyon." White-coated scientists with green and orange clown-hair scurried up and down a stepladder, throwing large wads of money and plastic baby dolls into the reactor, which spewed white smoke.

When energy monopoly PG&E tried to co-opt a community event by hosting an adjacent "Energy Fair," protesters constructed a mobile nuclear power plant which they paraded around downtown Berkeley on the day of the event.

"It's COMA," Hank said. We dropped our tasks and headed out toward the street, waving and applauding the rolling reactor. The scientists waved back, but directed the "ratepayers" to keep pulling the trailer down the street.

"Why don't they bring it up here by the stage," Mort said. Then we saw why. Over in front of the PG&E display was a wide-open driveway. As COMA closed in on their target, the PG&E types caught on and scurried to stop them. But COMA had momentum on their side, and deftly maneuvered the trailer into the slot, completely obscuring PG&E's visibility.

"Yes!" Angie yelled, and all of us cheered. PG&E threatened and cajoled COMA, trying to get them to move, but to no avail. The participants posed for a group photo, and the PG&E flacks wound up in some of the pictures, too.

Various lefty groups set up literature tables in a ring around the grassy central area of the park. Over by the game booths, a group called Food Not Bombs set up a free soup and bread table. The group had started in Boston/Cambridge a few years earlier. Recently, a San Francisco chapter had formed, and traveled over to Berkeley for the festival. Moonstone stirred the soup. "We're going to start a chapter here in the East Bay," he told me. "We want to serve free meals in People's Park."

"Sounds like a good place," I said, picturing a soupline stretching around the Park stage.

"Yeah. We'll see if the cops let us do it. Over in San Francisco they've busted people for serving food at civic center."

"Unbelievable," I said. "Busted for serving free food. It makes the government look so inhumane."

Moonstone nodded. "That's the great thing about Food Not Bombs. If they harass us, they betray their heartlessness. If they ignore us, hey, we're serving free food. Either way, we win."

It was almost noon. Knowing we were about to start, I went out front and looked for Angie. I wished we could share one last hug before things got crazy. But I didn't see her anywhere.

The crowd was disappointingly small as Wavy Gravy did a welcome, followed by Cris Williamson with a set of folk music. Mort and I were doing the backstage coordination. So far, there wasn't much to coordinate. Where was Stoney Burke, the comedian who was to go on next? Or Zulu Spear, the next band? The only performers around were members of the Funky Nixons, the closing act that included several LAG blockaders. Maybe we'd have to send them on for an impromptu acoustic set.

I walked around to the side of the stage. The sky was still overcast, and the sparse crowd was scattered across the grass. I felt sorry for Wavy, struggling valiantly to build some musical energy.

Off to the left I spotted Angie with Megan over by the game booths. With no customers, they looked a little forlorn. At the Starry Plough's bar and grill, a small line imbibed. Damn. Not like we had to make a fortune off BARF, but we had sunk almost a thousand dollars into advertising and equipment. It would be an ill omen for LAG if the festival was a dud and we lost money.

A couple of performers showed up, giving me a distraction from crowd-counting. Neither was happy with their timeslot, and while we haggled, a couple of speakers showed up and insisted on having more time. Where was Mort? How did I get stuck with this job? The one saving grace was that all the complainers got to hear each other, and gradually canceled one another out. I held firm on the lineup, and eventually everyone accepted it.

The leaky Diablo Canyon reactor later found a convenient parking spot directly in front of PG&E's "Energy Fair" booth.

The next several acts went smoothly. Around two o'clock, the "Ron-Off" got underway. With moderator Stoney Burke egging them on, two Reagan impersonators vied in reciting the Great Communicator's greatest hits:

"Ketchup in school lunches counts as a vegetable."

"Trees cause air pollution."

"The right-wing Nicaraguan rebels are freedom fighters."

"The MX Missile is a 'Peacekeeper.'"

"Cow gas causes global warming."

Whenever one of them got off a whopper, the big Bullshit-o-Meter in the center would tilt into the red zone. The cow-gas lie, which both Reagans mouthed simultaneously, sent the meter spinning wildly. The Reagans creaked to the middle of the stage and grabbed each other's necks, collapsing in a strangled heap. A swell of applause rose from the crowd. I walked over to the edge of the stage and looked around the park. The grassy area was half full, and the line at the Plough's booth was a dozen people long — a promising sign.

Hank walked past, adjusting the strap on his aviator goggles. I smiled at the sight of the old leather headgear, which usually hung above one of the pinball machines.

Comedian Stoney Burke moderated the "Ron-Off," in which dueling Reagan impersonators vied in repeating the Great Communicator's biggest prevarications and slips of tongue.

"Getting ready?"

He nodded curtly. "I wish we'd get it over with."

"Visualize a perfect flight," I said dreamily, hoping to get him to laugh.

He gave a grimaced smile. "I'm visualizing a cold beer after we park the thing next to the stage."

The sun came fully into play as Dave Lippman performed his George Bush impersonation. Native American poet John Trudell did a set. The San Francisco Mime Troupe sang and danced an excerpt from their classic "Armageddonman" shows. Then, as the "keynote," Ron Dellums made a short speech congratulating Berkeley on being itself. Hard not to applaud.

I was standing backstage with members of Family Nitoto, a Richmond hip-hop group I'd met during People's Convention. "This is down," said Marcus. "This is what People's Convention should have been."

"Amen," I said. "Live and learn."

As Family Nitoto's set kicked in, Walt wandered backstage. He was one of the nukecycle co-pilots, resplendent in a tan officer's cap and a long, flowing scarf.

"How's it going," I welcomed him.

Armageddonman (left) menaces Factwino, hero of San Francisco Mime Troupe's early 1980s plays.

He laughed dryly. "Well, I met with Karina this morning, so it's hard to feel too optimistic."

My smile faded. "What do you think? Does she have a chance?"

"At what," he said. "Acquittal? No way. Two to four years? If she's lucky."

"Are you representing her?"

"Well, about as much as anyone can represent her," he said with a sad smile. "Then I'm done with the law."

"Really?" I looked at him as if he were joking, but he nodded soberly. "I've had enough of it. I'm going back to grad school in political science. Time for a change."

What a loss, I thought. Here was a lawyer who understood direct action from the inside, a person all of us counted on. "What's going on?" I asked.

He took a deep breath. "I'm not cut out for losing all my cases, defending people I know are going to be found guilty. Especially when they're my friends." He lowered his eyes. "When Karina and Alby got sixty days last Summer, I couldn't sleep for the whole two months."

I thought back to the previous Summer. I remembered how depressed Walt had been at the time, but I hadn't thought about it since. I reached out and rubbed his arm. "I'm really sorry," I said.

He nodded, still looking down. "Yeah, thanks."

"So, political science?"

Armageddonman reigns supreme — will Factwino recover in time to save the world??!!?

"Something like that," he said, turning back toward the crowd. "I'm going to get something to drink before we do the nukecycle."

I watched Walt walk away. We're all losing something, I thought. Some more than others.

Following Family Nitoto's set, the kids' program got going to the left of the stage. It started with a water-balloon toss at Alby and Doc and Megan, who were prancing around in Reagan and Bush masks. I spotted Angie in the kids' line, a bow tied in her braided hair. It made me smile, but my old jealousy of Alby cropped up as Angie took special aim at him. Come backstage and talk to me, I thought. I felt neglected, but tried to set it aside. I'll have her to myself later. Let her hang out with Alby now.

As the Looters started into their world-beat set, Mort came over and tapped me on the shoulder. "Could you keep an eye on things here? We're going to get the nukecycle ready."

"Sure," I said, wishing I were part of the crew. Especially when Hank stopped by. "We're going to be waiting around the corner," he said. "When the Looters finish their set, Wavy will announce that LAG is about to make a first strike on BARF. That's our cue." He and Mort disappeared to round up the rest of the crew.

I was reviewing the clipboard and making sure the next speaker was ready to go when I spied Angie coming around the stage. With the sun out, she had taken off her sweatshirt, revealing a loose tanktop that ended just above her navel. I stood up to give her a hug, but she took my hand. "Come on, you're missing the Looters. Everybody's dancing."

I resisted. "Hank and Mort went to get the missile. Someone has to keep an eye on things back here."

Her brow furrowed. "It'll be fine for ten minutes. Nothing is going to happen. Come on."

I felt torn. I hated to lose a chance to be with her, and I hated to seem stodgy when everyone else was dancing. But I really was the only organizer backstage. If a later performer showed up, someone should be there. And besides, dancing? In broad daylight? Ask me to go to the game booths, or play volleyball. But dancing?

"I need to stay focused on backstage," I said, wishing she'd stay and keep me company.

But she dropped my hand and turned to go. "Okay, I'll talk to you in a while." I sighed as she walked away. This wasn't how I'd imagined BARF.

Another speaker showed up, a member of the Ohlone tribe, the original inhabitants of the Bay Area. I welcomed her, then walked over and looked at the crowd, which filled most of the central grassy area. Not bad, I thought.

Off to the left, Melissa was leafletting around the perimeter of the crowd. Even though we'd been at Coordinating Council meetings together, we'd hardly talked since the day she walked out on me and Raoul and Jenny at

People's Convention. It wasn't like she was holding a grudge, but more like she expected me to offer an explanation or apology. Not something that I felt like doing these days.

I caught Melissa's eye, and she started toward me with purposeful stride.

I nodded to her as she approached. "Hi, what's up?"

"Who told the Starry Plough they could sell beer?" she asked. "The nonviolence guidelines say 'no alcohol.'"

"They just set it up on their own."

"Well, I sure hope there are no problems about permits."

I smiled to myself. You worry about that. I'm trying to give it up. "What are you leafletting for," I said in hopes of drawing her attention away.

She handed me a flyer about a meeting for an action at Nevada Test Site. "Sounds like a worthy target," I said. "But do you think people will go all the way to Nevada to get arrested?"

Can you ever have too many Reagans?

"Sure," she said, her eyes growing large. "It's the nation's nuclear test site. What more obvious place to protest? If they can't test new weapons, we've stopped the arms race."

"I don't know," I said. "I wonder how many people will drive twelve hours for a protest. Not when there's so much to protest right here."

"People will do amazing things when they think it makes a difference," she said. "The Nevada Desert Experience has done Lenten actions at the Test Site for years. I'm going to go next Spring."

I made a note to get something in Direct Action about it. Melissa started back to her leafletting, then turned for a final word. "Are you getting arrested at Livermore Monday?"

"No," I said, and started to offer an explanation. But the words caught in my throat. "I'm not getting arrested," I told her, "but I'll see you there."

"Okay," she said. "I'll see you there."

As she walked off, the Looters were finishing their set. Wavy made his way to the mic. "We have just received word," he proclaimed, "that Livermore Action Group is about to launch a first strike attack on BARF. We've picked up the missile on our radar — there it is now!"

The crowd turned toward the back of the park. From behind the PG&E building the nosecone emerged. Slowly, the nukecycle came into full view. There was Hank in the driver's seat, looking like the Red Baron. Behind him Mort, Walt, and Craig huffed and pedaled. The missile, gleaming white in the afternoon sun, started up the incline into the park. A ripple of applause rose from the crowd. "This must be ground zero!" Wavy yelled, and the applause turned into a cheer.

The only known photo of the nukecycle moving under its own power.

I abandoned my backstage post and went out to welcome them. Most of the crowd was standing. Dozens of people fell in line behind the nukecycle, and others crowded around the sides, escorting it toward the stage. Despite the strain of pedaling, Hank's face shone in a broad smile. "Finally," I could practically hear him thinking. "Two years of shlepping, and finally a moment of glory!"

The nukecycle was fifty feet from the stage, gliding smoothly toward its target, when a loud crack silenced the applause. The missile teetered precariously as the crew struggled to regain their balance. "Oh, no," Hank groaned. "The chain broke again!"

People gawked as Hank clambered out of the cockpit. He stood with his hands on his hips, staring in disbelief at the immobilized missile. I went over and patted him on the back. "Bummer," I said. "So close."

He nodded, speechless. The crowd was sitting back down, but Wavy called out, "Come on, we'll finish this job by hand!" He rallied a dozen people to push the nukecycle up the incline to the side of the stage. Then Wavy bounded back up to the mic. "Let's hear it for the nukecycle! It probably works better than most of what the Pentagon designs."

The audience gave another loud round of applause, but Hank seemed oblivious. He wandered backstage in a daze. "So close," he said. "The damn chain just can't carry that much weight."

I nodded sympathetically. "What more can you do?"

His eyes narrowed, and he studied me. "What else *can* you do," he finally said, "except try again." A smile inched across his face. "Back to the drawing board."

I laughed. "Yeah, back to the drawing board."

The Reagan piñata was getting underway, and I walked over that way with Hank. Alby was up in a tree dangling the big paper-maché head. Angie blindfolded the kids one at a time and got them headed in the right direction. As they took their allotted three whacks, Alby bobbed the piñata up and down. The crowd cheered as one little girl landed a solid blow that sent Reagan reeling.

But the piñata remained unbroken until a teenage boy adopted a freestyle-thrashing method and cracked the gnarled caricature along one jowl. Candy and toy animals spilled onto the ground. The crowd whooped, and the kids scrambled for the treasure. Angie jumped right in with them, snagging a handful of candy.

The show was drawing to a close. A couple of speakers gave short talks, and then the Funky Nixons, wearing army helmets and waving little American flags, kicked off the day's final set. I took a deep breath and folded my list. The end. I wished I felt a wave of satisfaction, but relief was about the extent of it. And clean-up still remained.

The aroma from the Plough's barbeque pit lured me around the right-hand side of the stage. My head felt light, and I realized I hadn't eaten all day. I sized up the line, at least a dozen people long. My stomach groaned. I looked at the other food stands — burritos, falafel, veggie-kabobs, Korean BBQ — but their lines were just as long. I thought about going over to the game area and looking for Angie, but in the center of the park, a big crowd was dancing, so I'd have to walk all the way around.

I was mulling my options when Mitchell, the manager of the Starry Plough, beckoned me back behind the counter. "Something wrong?" I asked.

"No," he said. "You look like you need something to eat."

"That would be great," I said. "How about a hamburger?" A minute later, he handed me an oversized burger and pointed me toward the condiments. I reached into my pocket, but he waved me off. "It's on the house," he said. "Great festival."

I let out a surprised laugh. "Thanks a lot." I turned and looked out at the park. People dancing, lolling in the grass, playing volleyball, basking in the late afternoon sun. I nodded to myself. This was the point, wasn't it?

As I finished the hamburger, I saw Angie waving to me from the dance circle. "Come on," she called.

She had me this time. I tossed my plate in the trash and moved out toward her, trying to put a bounce in my step. There was a big enough crowd on the lawn that I didn't feel too self-conscious. But it was still hard to cut loose. I couldn't shake the feeling that this was the last time we'd ever dance together. I drifted ahead to the evening, Angie and I alone. Was I really going to ask her to move back? It didn't take a psychic to intuit her answer. She was gone. Why even bother asking? It would just make the rest of our time awkward.

I made an effort to focus on the Funky Nixons' song, which was about Reagan being a big fish in a little pond. Stay present. Here we are, together, me and Angie. The sun is shining. The band is playing. Let go. Tune in. Dance.

Easier said than done. I tried my best, but it never stopped feeling like work, and I was relieved when the Nixons finally wrapped up their encore.

I put my arm around Angie. She was sweaty, and spun away from me like a swing dancer. I squeezed her hand and let go, hoping her bright laughter would carry over into the evening. And on into the night...

The crowd filtered out of the park. The organizing crew and other LAGers drifted together in the center of the park. Raoul came over my way. "What a great day," he said, finishing off a beer. "A kegger in the park, that's style."

Sid, whom I hadn't seen previously, loped up next to Raoul and thrust a hand-lettered flyer at me. "A bunch of people from the War Chest Tours are putting this together," he said. "You should come."

"The Anarchist Coffeehouse," I read. "Where's that?"

"It's not one place," he said. "It's going to rotate around a bunch of collective houses over in the City. The first one is at Stonehenge in a few weeks. Sara's house is doing the next one. We already have houses signed up for the first five months."

"Sounds like a good idea," I said. It actually sounded like an alternate reality. Who had time for cultural projects when LAG was teetering on the brink?

Sid pointed to the fine print. "We're going to have an open mic. You should bring your guitar and sing."

"Thanks," I said, touched by the invitation. "I'll try to make it." I carefully folded the flyer and put it in my pocket as they started away. "See you guys later."

"Yeah," Raoul said. "Hey,

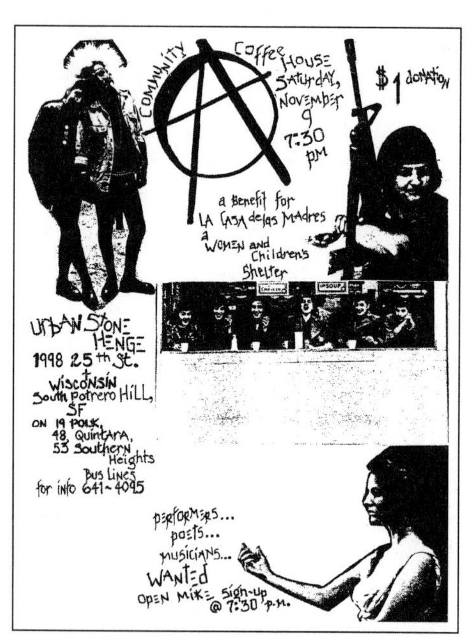

Flyer for an early Anarchist Community Coffeehouse. The monthly events rotated among collective houses in San Francisco and occasionally Berkeley or Oakland for five years, providing a regular meeting ground for radical artists and activists.

Wavy Gravy joins Tricky Dick and the Funky Nixons onstage.

I'm going to the ballgame on Thursday night. A's versus Boston. Let me know if you want to go."

I thought for a moment. "Count me in," I said. "See you Thursday." I smiled to myself. Back to real life.

Moonstone came over my way. "Hey, Jeff, we're doing a circle, come on."

I followed him over in front of the stage. A couple of dozen people who had worked on the event were standing with hands linked, sharing tired smiles. Hank, joking with Wavy, seemed already to have forgotten his disappointment over the nukecycle as they schemed how to climb the dome of city hall and hang a banner for some cause that I didn't catch.

Mort caught my eye. I remembered how bent out of shape I'd been at him over the Summer, feeling like all he did was criticize. Now we'd pulled off LAG's biggest success in a year. Of course we'd keep working together. On to the next project.

And Angie. I looked across the circle at her. The spirit behind BARF. Behind her, all of Nancy's china lay smashed, and pieces of the piñata lay strewn on the grass. Why couldn't it always be like this? She and I and a bunch of friends doing actions and festivals and graffiti and a newspaper... Why did she have to go?

Her arms were draped around Alby and Doc's shoulders. "Let's clean up and go out to eat," she called out to the circle.

Nods and sounds of approval greeted her proposal. "Let's go to La Peña," Hank said.

Good idea, I knew. I tried to shake off the rest of my doldrums. Sure, I wanted to be alone with Angie, the sooner the better. But maybe the perfect antidote to her wanting to move away was an evening reliving our success. Maybe a post-BARF dinner was just what the doctor ordered.

THE EVENING was warm. We pulled together several tables on the patio at La Peña. A row of potted palms separated us from the sidewalk. I sat next to Angie, with Craig on my left side. I hadn't been clear on who was coming, but it looked like about ten people, mostly men.

"Pitcher of beer?" Craig said to me and Doc.

"Not for me," Doc said. "I'll have a soft drink."

Craig's face seemed to redden. He turned to me. "Should we split a pitcher?"

"Sure, someone here will help us with it."

A couple of waiters brought our first round of drinks. Craig poured us each a glass, and we clinked the rims together.

"A toast!" called out Hank. "A toast to BARF!"

"To BARF!"

"And to the nukecycle," Angie said.

"To the nukecycle!"

I wished someone would toast LAG. After all, who had sponsored BARF? But I felt funny doing it, and no one else picked up the slack. We settled into smaller conversations. I turned to Craig. I hadn't talked to him in a while, and tried to think of something to say. "Glad you made it today. Mort said you'd started a new job."

"Yeah, I got hired on a construction crew," he said as if daring me to doubt him. "I've never done it before, and it's taking all my time trying to get up to speed."

"No time for organizing?"

His eye twitched. "Not anytime soon. My idea is to work for a few years and get construction skills, then buy some land and build my own house. It's something I've always wanted to do, and now feels like the time."

Well, maybe so, I thought. But what a loss to LAG. What a loss to the movement. Maybe he'd take a break and come back refreshed. But in the short run, I wouldn't bet on seeing him.

I couldn't think of anything more to say, and I was glad when our food came. As I focused on getting the correct proportions of beans, rice, cheese, and salsa onto a tortilla, Angie leaned toward me. "I never asked — can I spend the night with you tonight?"

I paused in mid-burrito and looked at her. "Yeah, that would be great."

She smiled. "Good, I just wanted to be sure." She gave me a puzzled look. "How are you doing?"

"Good, I think." Should I tell her how relieved I was to hear she was coming home with me? Now wasn't the time. I deflected the question. "I'm doing fine. I just wish all of us were having a real discussion instead of small talk."

Angie picked up her glass, held it aloft, and rapped it with a spoon. "Hey, everybody, Jeff has a proposal."

I shuffled in my seat. "Well, my idea is that we all say — that we go around the table and each of us says one thing we learned from working on BARF."

"Then we'll vote on whose is best," Hank said.

"No," Angie rejoined, "we'll synthesize them into one giant proposal and stay here till we reach consensus."

Hank started up from his chair. "Let me outa here!"

After a few more jokes, the proposal was adopted with the proviso that we go in random order. People shifted around to get comfortable. Craig poured us another round of beer.

Hank rocked back in his chair, beer in hand. "I'll start. I learned a lot about how to have an impact on local politics. Today probably swung some votes toward BCA. But the main thing I learned is, if your nukecycle is going to launch a first strike on BARF — make sure your target is downhill!"

Everyone laughed. "To the nukecycle," Mort toasted, and we all echoed his cry.

Megan brushed her hair out of her face. I was glad she'd come along, glad for her unjaded perspective. "Mine is easy," she said. "BARF taught me that we have to create our own ways of participating in electoral politics. It's usually so bureaucratic — phonebanking or stuffing envelopes. We have to cut our own path."

Doc nodded seriously. His eyes looked almost troubled. "What if we did that — simply did things our own way? That's the real revolution, when we take direct control over our lives. When people do this — whether it's Food Not Bombs, AIDS support, childcare co-ops, or neighborhood watches — when we organize and act for ourselves, nothing can stop us."

Good point, I thought. The trick is to convince people that their lives would be richer this way than by having more money.

A couple of others spoke. Then Mort set down his bottle. "The biggest thing for me was, BARF shows that we know how to throw a good party. We need all kinds of approaches. No one tactic is going to change the world. We need voting, big marches, educational work, letter-writing, protests — and we need festivals like BARF."

"Maybe we've found our role in coalitions," Hank tossed in. "We'll do the Reagan-bashing."

"It's an important role," Mort said, picking up his beer. "We need this kind of inspiration."

There was a moment of silence, perhaps in shock at hearing Mort say the word "inspiration." I took a breath. "I want to build off Mort's point," I said.

"I've been thinking about how sometimes we work in parallel with other groups, and sometimes in series. When we work in parallel, the liberals handle one function, like the electioneering, and we handle another — like BARF. That's good. But we have to learn how to organize in 'series,' so that each group can build off others' work. Not just add to it, but use it as a foundation for the next step."

People were listening attentively. Mort nodded his head slowly. "We already do this in street actions," I continued, "when one group draws off the police so that another can strike at a different site. Now we have to apply it to our broader work, so each protest builds off the preceding ones."

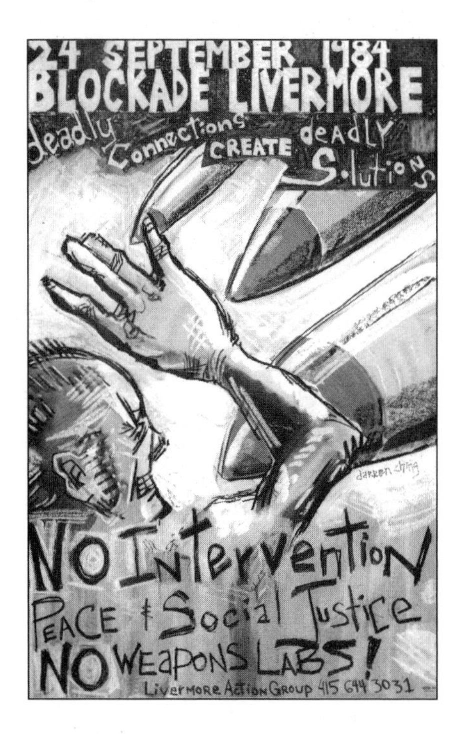

"I think that's called a strategy," Craig said sardonically.

I started to scowl, then felt it slide off. "Well, yeah. But it has to take into account what people are already doing, not impose some abstract scheme on the group."

Craig took a drink of beer and settled back in his chair. "If we're going to talk strategy, here's what I think. There are two broad levels of strategy. The first is how to organize before the revolution — how we gain power. The second is how to organize *after* the revolution — how we change society once we've gained political power. Most of what LAG does, our blockades and actions, are stuck in the first level. They won't mean much after we gain political power. Why I liked BARF is, festivals are the kind of events that cross over. They'll be just as important in the new society."

Well, at least he sees some value in what we're doing. Mort started to say something, but I held up my hand. "There are still some people who haven't spoken." I looked at Angie, who was leaning back in her chair.

She leaned forward so her arms rested on the table. "What I liked best about BARF," she said in a pensive voice, "was taking art into the streets. Or at least into the park. The games, the nukecycle, the piñata, the dancing — that's what's going to reach people, not yelling and finger-pointing." She paused and took a sip of beer. "BARF was great, but it still had an 'anti' focus.

We're anti-nuke, anti-war, anti-Reagan. I wonder if we really reach people that way."

She paused and looked down at the table. Then she leaned back and gazed out toward the foggy horizon. "What excites me isn't negativity. It's creativity. It's art and magic."

Her final words hung in the air. People looked around. Had everyone spoken?

Doc cleared his throat. "It's a mystery, isn't it — what causes change? What tips the balance? It could be our smallest act." I followed Doc's words carefully, but Mort and Hank fidgeted. "We never know exactly how our work fits into the larger picture. We may have far more impact than we realize."

"Hey," Hank said as soon as Doc finished, "BARF may just have launched the revolution, and we don't even know it yet. Speaking of impact, you know what I've noticed? Ever since our *USA Today* action last Spring, their boxes have been disappearing from Berkeley."

"Yeah," I said, "I noticed that! Adios, *USA Today.* We had a hand in that."

Hank raised his bottle. "Success!"

I raised my glass and clinked his bottle, joined by Angie and several others. "Success!"

We paid our bill and headed out to the sidewalk. A round of hugs ensued, a graphic reminder that we'd spent the whole day together and no one had walked out. Maybe we really were moving beyond the Convention and its strife.

Angie and I bid goodnight to the others and started our walk back to my place. We rounded the corner at the Starry Plough, then stopped in the shadows. I leaned down to kiss her, grateful for the day we'd spent together, grateful for the night we were about to spend. Worries about the future, regrets about the past, all faded. For one long, sweet kiss, I almost succeeded in forgetting that this might be our last night together.

Monday, September 24, 1984

LIVERMORE LAB. One more time.

Angie had left the previous day, after a wonderful, nearly-sleepless night together. Now, getting up at five in the morning for a demo, I was pretty well exhausted. Hopefully the protest wouldn't last too long, and by noon I'd be back home, settling in for a long nap.

It was still dark as we gathered at the intersection of East and Vasco Roads. The crowd wasn't much, a few hundred people. Even counting Holly, Caroline, Daniel, and some others out at the Site 300 test area, it was a mere shadow of the previous two Summers. Hank and Mort weren't there, and I knew I wouldn't be seeing Craig or Claudia. Karina was steering clear of further arrests, and Sara and Alby had probably seen enough of jail for a while.

Still, I spotted plenty of familiar faces in the pre-dawn conclave. Some were Livermore stalwarts, like Melissa, Daniel, and Nathaniel. Monique and the Walnettos were out in force, as were Maria and Spirit AG. Change of Hearters like Moonstone, Doc, and Megan didn't surprise me. And Imagine AG, with Pilgrim taking the forty-fourth bust of his illustrious career, could certainly be counted on.

But the sight of Jenny, Raoul, and Sid was unexpected. Maybe after the dismal performance of affinity groups at the War Chest Tours, they were seeing the virtue of LAG. "Turning over a new leaf?" I couldn't help saying to them. "I didn't figure to see you at a LAG action."

Military laboratory Sandia's local offices were located directly across from Livermore Lab. In September 1984, an affinity group entered the public gate and poured blood on the sign.

"We aren't thinking of it as a LAG action," Sid answered. "Our AG wanted to try out some new tactics."

Melissa walked by as he spoke. "Just be sure your 'tactics' are nonviolent," she said without stopping for an answer.

Raoul turned slowly toward her and jutted his chin. "Just make sure your tactics aren't stuck in the mud."

Melissa halted in her tracks. "Who's stuck in the mud? What's so new about your ideas? You think you're the ones who invented running around in the streets yelling? That's been tried for a thousand years, and it hasn't changed anything yet."

"Oh, yeah?" Raoul shot back. "I haven't noticed Livermore Lab closing down on account of your pacifist blockades."

Before Melissa could answer, I stepped between them. "Come on," I pleaded, looking first at Raoul and then at Melissa. "The Lab has four different gates. Everyone can do the action they want. Why do we have to tear each other apart?"

Melissa stopped glaring at Raoul and shifted her eyes to me. She gazed at me like a doctor deciding what medicine to prescribe. Then she reached out

The first policeman on the scene tried to corral two protesters.

and patted me on the arm. "Don't worry," she said in a reassuring voice. "We're just having a fight."

I stared back at her, then looked at Raoul, whose mouth hung open. Then a slow, rolling laugh rose from him. "That's it," he said. "We're just having a fight." I had to laugh, too. Just fighting. Even Melissa started to smile, but at that moment, Belinda called to her.

Raoul and Jenny's AG headed out for the West Gate. I was going to follow them, figuring that whatever they did would be a good show. But as I started away, Melissa called to me. "Jeff, will you take some photos of our action?"

"I don't have a camera," I said.

"Use mine." She came over and handed me a small camera, as if I had already accepted the assignment. "We need someone who isn't getting arrested."

Well, that's me, I thought. Not today. Not if I could help it.

I followed her down toward the South Gate, where the Walnettos, Matrix, Spirit, and Mustard Seed AGs were circled up, discussing who would blockade first. "While they're blockading the gate," Melissa told me, "a few of us are going to do an action at Sandia." Sandia Laboratories were located across the street from Livermore Lab.

Police circle in on the Sandia protesters.

Melissa signaled to Maria, Artemis, and Belinda, who joined her off to one side. With the cops focused on protecting the Lab, the four women had a clear shot at Sandia. Artemis and Belinda paired off and headed toward the entrance driveway, with Melissa pushing Maria's wheelchair behind them. "We're doing a blood action," Melissa said to me in a low voice. "Wait till we get up by the sign, and then start shooting."

The first rays of dawn lit the east as Artemis and Belinda approached the big Sandia sign about a hundred feet past the entry. So far, no cops. Belinda pulled a tall plastic jar out of her coat and popped the lid off. She glanced at the other women, then flung the thick dark liquid toward the sign. It splattered over the big letters and dripped onto the manicured entrance lawn. I adjusted the focus and started clicking.

Artemis flung her bottle at the sign. A half-dozen state troopers came trotting our way. Melissa opened a second bottle and hurled more blood onto the sign. Artemis and Belinda walked toward the cops, who quickly handcuffed them and took them into custody.

I figured the action would be over quickly. But as Belinda and Artemis were led away, Melissa grabbed the handles of Maria's wheelchair and started carting her away across the parking lot. The cops looked confused, and so was I. What is this? Mobile tactics? A page out of Raoul's book? Did they really expect to get away?

Who could tell? After a moment's lapse, the cops regrouped and corralled Melissa and Maria. I shot most of the film, trying to stay on top of the action. It hadn't occurred to me that I, too, was trespassing on corporate property, until a couple of officers started gesturing at me. I looked around, abruptly aware of my predicament. I was on Sandia property, behind a chain-link fence — with cops between me and the exit.

Just stay still, I thought. No sudden moves. Maybe they'll go away. I cast a glance over at Melissa, holding up her camera. She nodded to me, then called out to the troopers. "He's not with us. He's a press photographer."

The cops turned to me, and I couldn't resist a jaunty wave, almost a salute. "Just taking some pictures," I told them. They looked at each other, mumbled a few words, then headed over toward the paddywagon. I waited to make sure they really were leaving, then sauntered back to neutral ground.

Once I was back on the public road, I laughed. A narrow escape. I started around to the West Gate, thinking it would be funny to use the rest of Melissa's film to shoot Sid and Jenny and Raoul's action. But someone coming the other direction told me that the AG had gotten swept up right away, before they got to try any of their new tactics.

We drifted back to the intersection at East and Vasco. Our old familiar meeting place. There had been about a hundred arrests, I heard. Not an embarrassment, but nothing like former years. Was this our last hurrah? I thought of Melissa throwing blood, of Pilgrim racking up another bust, of Sid and Jenny and their new tactics. Could it be the end?

Surely not. Was Livermore Lab going to stop producing weapons of mass destruction? Was the administration suddenly going to direct the weapons labs to focus their research on alternative energy or environmental restoration?

Unlikely. I doubted that we'd seen the last of the Lab.

Tuesday, October 16, 1984

HOLLY AND I were meeting at Café Mediterraneum on Telegraph Avenue. In our two-plus years together, I couldn't remember a single time we'd sat together in a café. Even this afternoon, I'd give it fifty-fifty that she'd come in and propose going for a walk.

I picked a table toward the back of the lower level, got an orange juice, and sat facing the door. Out on the street, people filtered back and forth, familiar faces among them. There went Moe, the cigar-chomping owner of my favorite bookstore. And Julia Vinograd, the berobed street poet who carried a bubblewand with her wherever she went. Julia stopped to talk to someone, then came into the Med.

I pulled out the sheaf of paper I lately had taken to carrying in my back pocket. Never know when inspiration might strike. Maybe I should write a song about LAG. What rhymes with "civil disobedience?"

I looked up to see Holly approaching, wearing as bright a smile as I had seen in a long while. "Hey, Jeff."

I stood to hug her. "Want to sit down here, or go somewhere else?"

"This is good," she said. "I need to sit down. Let me get some tea."

As she moved through the serving line, she bantered with the woman behind the counter. Was Holly always so outgoing? Had I forgotten, or was this something new?

She sat down and pulled a sketchbook out of her pack. "Want to see the drawing I did for the peace camp flyer? I thought it might work in Direct Action, too."

Holly had taken art classes in college, but during the whole time I'd known her, I'd never seen her draw anything. Her sketch showed tents, a table, and a teapot, with Mount Diablo in the background. "That's great," I said. "I like the shading. Why not make it the cover of the next issue, for the reopening of the peace camp?"

She smiled. "I think it would look good."

I studied her as she put the drawing away and took a drink of tea. Why was she in such good spirits over art? I wished I felt as excited about my writing or music.

She looked at me. I wondered if I should ask her about her art, or something more personal. "So what's been happening>" I finally asked.

Holly beamed. "I slept with someone new this weekend, and I'm really excited about it."

I tilted my head slowly. "This weekend," I said. "I thought you went camping with Sara over the weekend..." Slowly it dawned on me. Sara. I felt dense for not catching on sooner. True, I wasn't expecting Holly to get involved with a woman. But when was the last time I saw her so bright?

I felt a pang in my heart, stronger than anything I'd let myself feel all Spring and Summer, a pang for Holly's buoyancy, for her belief that anything was possible. When we met and fell in love, when she moved in and we shared a home, I'd practically believed in those possibilities myself. The past year had tested us, as our paths diverged and our dreams faded. Yet I'd always trusted that her optimism would revive, I'd be reinspired, and we'd be swept back together.

Now she'd discovered a fresh source of hope. But it wasn't something we could share...

Holly was still telling me about the weekend. "I'd met her before," Holly said, "but this time it was different, being together all weekend. Her name is Louisa, and she's been 'out' since high school. She works with Sara at the Berkeley Women's Health Collective..."

Louisa? Wait. Not Sara? I'd never met anyone named Louisa. Jealousy crept over me, jealousy that someone would pull Holly's attention away from what we shared. Sara was part of LAG. She was safe. But who was Louisa?

I groped for something supportive to say. "What's it been like?"

She looked at me blankly, as if she had no idea where to begin. "I've hardly slept for three nights," she finally said. "When I was with Louisa on the camping trip, it was wonderful. But then last night, by myself, I was lying awake feeling nauseated and paranoid. I wondered if I was falling apart. The 'me' I've known for thirty years was disintegrating. I never did get to sleep. But Louisa called me this morning, being all sweet, and I'm going to see her in an hour, so now it feels great again."

She stopped and took a breath. "I'm not sure how much more I want to say. I guess I'm still sorting it out myself."

Watching Holly recount the ups and downs, I felt a little scared for her. At the same time, in spite of a tinge of jealousy, I felt a blossom

The Livermore peace camp, drawn by a participant.

Telegraph Avenue near Dwight, with Café Med to the right.

of hope, hope that she had embarked on a new pilgrimage, that she was moving on with her life. Maybe we both could turn a new page.

Face it, I was ready for a whole new chapter. I thought about how I'd seen Holly as my anchor, the unshakable foundation of my commitment to reshaping the world. Through the Spring I'd worried that my indecision was jeopardizing our relationship. But Holly was changing, too, in ways that even she couldn't predict. Time to give up my illusions — not just about Holly, not just about us as a couple, but about finding an unshifting anchor, period. Let it go.

Angie, too. Enough pining after someone who had moved away. Let her go.

And Karina. Enough daydreaming about someone who was going to prison.

Even LAG. Maybe LAG would continue, and I'd be part of it. But enough clinging, enough trying to stem the tide of dissolution. It wasn't up to me or anyone else to save the group. It was time to step back and let events take their course.

We finished our drinks and left the Med. Standing there on Telegraph Avenue, I wished Holly well. I was heading home and she was going toward campus, so we hugged and headed in opposite directions. As I stood at the corner of Dwight waiting for the light to change, I wondered when I'd see her. I had no guarantees. I'd just have to be patient and trust that our paths would intertwine.

Saturday, October 27, 1984

IT WASN'T YET dusk as we came out of the 16th and Mission BART Station on our way to the Spiral Dance ritual. I was disoriented, but Angie saw our mistake. "We're east of Mission," she said. "We need to cross back that way."

The air was warm and crisp, wonderful to breath after being on the train. The wispy clouds over Twin Peaks were taking on a pink tint. We made our way up a block and turned south onto Valencia. "I love this street," Angie said, and I could see why. We peered into windows as we passed: a tattoo parlor, a liquor store, a bookstore, an appliance repair shop, a thrift store filled with junky treasures, a burrito joint grilling slabs of beef over an open fire, a Middle Eastern restaurant with live belly dancing...

Angie paused in front of the belly dancing club and perused the schedule. I stood behind her, ruminating. She was probably missing San Francisco right this minute. Should I ask her to return? Or give her time to let the feelings sink in?

Oh, no. Not another night of now-I'll-ask-her-now-I-won't. And anyway, now wasn't the moment, as Angie picked up the pace. We made our way down the crowded Valencia Street sidewalk to 18th Street, where we swung west. Just ahead, an imposing puddle loomed in our path. I started around it, but Angie

A small portion of "Maestrapeace," the incredible three-story mural on the San Francisco Women's Building portraying the contributions of women of many cultures.

took my arm and steered us right through the water. "A cleansing," she said. I wasn't sure if she was joking or not, but I was thankful for having bought a new pair of shoes the week before. I'd hate to start my first ritual with wet feet.

I'd never been to the Women's Building, our destination. Angie told me it was covered in murals, and I expected a small community center like La Peña over in Berkeley. I was unprepared for what greeted me. Even in the fading light the four-story building was stunning. Flowing patterns of color leapt from the walls. Women of every age and race were woven around the mullioned windows.

We crossed the street for a better view. Atop the north facade, breaking through the line of the roof, a pregnant woman in Earth-tones channeled crystalline energy to the child in her womb. From her belly flowed a river teeming with life, twisting downward in multicolored ribbons cascading to the ground. At each end, as if guarding the corners of the building, was an aged woman, the left one African and the right one Native American. In the center, amidst the streaming ribbons, their care-worn hands reached toward one another.

I drew Angie to me, and she leaned back onto my chest. Above the building, the crescent moon hovered in the darkening sky, as if pouring down its blessings on us.

Being here with her was a blessing in itself. She'd called the week before to say that she was coming down for the Spiral Dance and asked if I wanted to go. I'd jumped at the prospect.

I had to laugh. Me, excited about going to a ritual? I'd heard plenty about them. Here was a chance to see one, up close. Not to mention spending the evening with Angie.

Angie had briefed me on what to expect that evening, but it was still mostly a mystery. What did you do for three or four hours? I mean, how much invoking and singing and meditating can you do?

But I was committed to participating, to doing whatever it was that everyone else did. Even dancing. "Several times during the ritual, everyone gets up and dances," Angie told me. "The best place is right in the center, where it's really hot." I wondered if I'd have the nerve to follow her into the center. I wasn't ruling anything out.

As we stepped into the lobby, masked and painted faces bobbed past. A woman in a velvet gown and golden tiara anointed people with her magic wand. Behind her, a woman in the traditional garb of a Halloween Witch cackled as she blessed people with a handmade broom.

The people near us in the line looked innocent enough. But further ahead was a man with a very hairy chest, wearing sheepskin leggings and two small horns on his head. "The god Pan," Angie said. "He was here last year, too."

We paid our donation and were starting in when I spotted Karina across the lobby. I tugged on Angie's arm. "Let's go over and say hi."

Angie tensed under my touch. Oh, yeah, I thought. Maybe not the best pairing. But she relented and followed me through the crowd.

Karina was talking with someone, but Sara, standing next to her, saw us coming. She seemed surprised to see Angie, down from Portland, but even more surprised to see me, period. Still, she welcomed me with a warm hug.

Karina finished her conversation and turned to us, glowing. She even smiled at Angie, and the two of them hugged like old friends. Wow, I thought, magic works. Maybe it's just a truce for the evening, but that's magic enough.

Karina told us about her upcoming trial. "The problem is how to introduce the issue of my motivation. We know the judge won't allow international law defenses, but we're hoping the prosecution introduces photos that have my graffiti in them. Then we can use them to explain my motives to the jury."

Her delight as she described the graffiti made me wonder if she really expected to be acquitted. I glanced at Sara, who followed Karina's every move. Her eyes looked tired and care-worn.

"What's realistic," Angie asked. "Assuming you get convicted?"

Karina scarcely blinked. "Two or three years, maybe five," she said. "Walt's been checking into it."

Two or three years, I thought. Or five. In federal prison. I could almost hear Sara ticking it off in her head. Two or three birthdays. Or five.

"When is the trial?" I asked.

"Early December," Karina said. "Till then, I'm free. I'm leaving next week on a speaking tour around Oregon, and after that I might get flown to the East Coast for some events."

Angie nudged me. "We should go inside." She looked at Karina. "I hope this all goes well for you," she said. "I really do."

Karina stepped forward and gave her another hug. "It already is."

Well, I thought, if anyone could handle it, it was probably Karina. I hugged her again, holding her tightly. When we let go, she stepped back, smiling radiantly. "I'll see you before the trial," she said.

"Definitely," I said, then followed Angie toward the entrance.

As we stepped through the doorway into the dimly-lit ballroom, two "graces" in white robes ushered us through an Autumnal portal. Over our heads arched branches, leaves, dried flowers, and wild berries. At the far side, two more graces welcomed us. "You are now entering sacred space," one said as the other sprinkled water on our heads with a rosemary branch. "You are now entering sacred time."

I felt like I'd stepped into a cave. The room was a rough square about eighty feet across, with a two-story ceiling. A small balcony stretched along two walls. The other two walls were hung with dark fabric. The only light came from candles in the four corners and a dim chandelier above the center. Maybe two hundred people milled around, some in costumes, some in fancy dress.

But a lot of people were in street clothes, and I didn't feel out of place in my usual jeans and sweater. Several drummers played a slow, loping rhythm while a few dozen people moved and stretched.

Around the room I picked out familiar faces: Moonstone, Megan, Alby, Doc and Belinda. Walt came by carrying a box of candles, and off to one side I saw Sara meeting with Artemis and Antonio. "They're the 'guides' for the ritual," Angie told me. "Some people call them 'priest' and 'priestess.' But I think that we're all priestesses. So I like the word 'guides.'"

In each corner was an altar, aglow with candles. East was a simple affair, a small table draped with white veils and feathers, symbolizing the element Air. "Why are there knives on the 'air' table?" I asked Angie as I eyed a shiny blade.

She studied the knife. "I think of them as signifying sharpness of intellect and imagination," she said. "And cutting away the past to make a new beginning. That's what East means."

New beginnings. I could use some of those. On all fronts.

Flaming red and orange cloths adorned the South altar. From amid the folds burst a fiery painting of a Goddess dancing and shouting. On the altar burned a small cauldron. Angie passed her fingers above the quivering flame, then touched them to her breast. "South is for passion and creativity," she said. "The flame that burns in our hearts." I passed my fingers over the flame and touched them to my chest.

West was a rich blue cloth on which were placed dishes and bowls of water. A large glass bowl sat in the middle, and people were dipping their fingers and anointing themselves. "It's salt water," Angie whispered. "For purification. Think about things that you want to let go of, or worries and cares that you can set aside this evening. Visualize them moving out to the tips of your fingers, and let them go into the salt water."

My hands clenched. I looked down at the water. Letting go? Of what, exactly? If I cared about something — or someone — why would I let go?

Still, I was determined to enter into the spirit of the ritual. Let it go. For one evening. All the worries over Angie, over the future of LAG, over what in the world the past two years added up to. Let it go. I looked down at my hands, as if I cradled the cares in them. Then, following Angie's lead, I dipped my fingers into the salt water and breathed out. As I removed my hands from the bowl, Angie touched a wet finger to my forehead. "Welcome to sacred space," she said.

I smiled. But in truth, there was one care I hadn't let go of. Whether to talk to her about returning. And what to say. And when...

We moved on to North, which was built on a different scale altogether. The altar, draped in black and gray, filled the entire corner. Stacks of old wooden boxes and crates formed a latticework of nooks and cubbyholes sheltering faded photographs, driftwood, bones, pieces of old lace, rusted metal, and the like. "This is the ancestors' altar," Angie said. "This is their ritual, too." I studied the old photos. Faces of the once-living gazed back at us in the candlelight, and I could almost feel them present.

To the left of the altar, a black-draped bulletin board was filling up with small white paper skulls, each with a name written on it. "I'm going to add my grandmother," Angie said, "even though she's been dead for several years." She took a paper skull, wrote her grandmother's name and fastened it onto the board. I wondered if I had a name to add, but none came to mind.

Shhhhh. The wispy sound began to fill the room. Some people spread blankets and even cushions on the hardwood floor. Shhhhh. Others of us found space between them to form a circle around an open middle. Shhhhh. The chandelier lights were dimmed till only candlelight from the altars remained. Silence.

From the balcony above, a chorus of voices held forth a mysterious tune: "This very night, this very night..." Slowly, a solemn procession led by Artemis and Antonio filed down the stairs to our level, singing all the while. "This very night..." Each singer bore a white candle. They circled our space, then took up a station near the East altar and finished their song: "Fire and sleet and candlelight, May Earth receive thy soul."

Silence reigned for a moment. Then Artemis stepped into the circle. She was wearing a long black gown, with a gauzy scarf draped over her shoulders. Specks of glitter sparkled in her hair. "This is the season of Halloween," she proclaimed. "The time when the veil is thin that divides the worlds."

She turned slowly, the sweep of her arms encompassing the entire circle. "Tonight we journey into the darkness of Winter and through to the promise of Spring. For Halloween is our new year — the new year of the Witches."

Around me, people nodded and twinkled their fingers as if consensing to Artemis' words. I was surrounded by Witches. Was I the only novice in the room?

"This is the night that we mourn our dead." Artemis paused, letting the words sink in. "This very night, when we sail to the island beyond time and dance the spiral, the ancient symbol of rebirth, we perform an act of magic and turn our culture back toward balance. And when we remember what has passed and renew ourselves, we do it to reclaim the future." She swept her arm around the circle again. "So join with us now — the spirits are gathering..."

Doc, wearing a turquoise robe that glistened behind his gray beard, stepped to the middle and beckoned us to stand and close our eyes. "Imagine your spine as a cord passing through your body, down through the floor, down into the Earth below," he said in a measured voice. "Imagine the love of Mother Earth pulling that cord down, down to Her heart. Down through the topsoil, down through the rocks. Down past the fossils of past ages, past the streams that run beneath the Earth, down, down through the bedrock, until we can touch the molten core at the very center of the Earth, still pulsing with the energy of the sun and stars. The molten, living core, still alive and pulsing. And as we reach that core, feel how the roots of all the others in this room are there with you, weaving, winding, binding us together."

The root metaphor was making me a little queasy. I took a deep breath. Then, following Doc's words, I slowly pulled the molten energy back up through the Earth and into my body. I let the fire swirl through me, rising higher and higher, till it flowed out of my head and showered down around me.

Some people raised their arms as if releasing the Earth's fire to the heavens. Finally people knelt and touched the floor. "Grounding the energy," I remembered, kneeling next to Angie and placing my palms on the floor. Hey, I'm not a complete rookie.

People stood, and a woman I recognized from the Vandenberg spokescouncils came forward. With both hands she grasped a dagger in front of her. In the center, she paused, as if pointing the knife toward an imaginary cauldron. Then she turned and strode toward the North altar. There, at the outer edge of our circle, she inscribed a star in the air, then proclaimed loudly, "By the Earth that is Her body."

She gestured to the right with the dagger and circled around to the East altar. "By the air that is Her breath," she said, inscribing another star.

"Why a star?" I whispered to Angie.

"It's a pentacle. It's a sign of power for Witches. She's casting the circle."

I nodded. The woman moved on to the south. "By the fire of Her bright spirit." And to the West. "By the waters of Her living womb." She circled back to North, then came to the Center, where she drew two final pentacles: "By all that is above... And all that is below..." Then she stretched out her arms to embrace the entire room. "The circle is cast. We are between the worlds. What happens between the worlds changes all the worlds."

Between the worlds. I liked that image. And the part about changing all the worlds.

Most people sat down, and Angie and I joined them. An open space fifteen feet across was left in the center, with a three-foot aisle out to each altar. "Now we invoke the directions," Angie whispered. She rotated toward the east altar. I cast a glance at her. Just do what she does, I thought.

Do what she does? Sure, so I should move to Portland? Hardly. Well, then how can I expect her to move back here? I shook my head sadly. Let it go. Stay present.

A fluttering sound came from behind the East altar. An angelic figure appeared, draped all in white, with gauzy wings and a fairy wand. "Spirits of the air," the angel said as she glided toward the center. "Feathery ones! Fill us with your gift of breath, the mystery of life." She inhaled deeply, and I followed suit, letting the air stretch my lungs. "Grant us clarity of vision," she said. "Grant us sharpness of thought and insight. And as the wheel turns again to the new year, bless our fresh beginnings. Spirits of the East, be here now."

"Be here now," echoed voices in the crowd. "Blessed be."

Eyes turned toward the South, where Sara, Karina, and several other women in red and yellow tights clustered. They reached out and linked hands, then leapt toward the center of the circle. "Passion!" Sara shouted. "Bright flames!" yelled another woman. "Sparks! Creativity! Blazing! Forging! Fire!"

At the final cry, a dancer clad in black stepped up to the South altar. She held a stick out to the candles and it burst into a flaming torch. The crowd gasped as she skipped into the center. The red-robed women danced around her, still shouting, "Passion! Creativity! Fire!" They ended with the torch held aloft and the dancers raising their arms to the sky. "Powers of the South," called Karina, "be here now!"

"Be here now!" people called back, and a cheer filled the room.

As the fire invokers left the center and the cheering subsided, a woman and man dressed in blue sarongs entered from the West. The man carried a basin, the woman a pitcher, which she bore aloft as if consecrating it. Reaching the center, she looked into his eyes, then began to pour the water into the bowl.

"Hail, guardians of the watchtowers of the West," she intoned as the water swished against the bowl. "Watery ones, mysterious ones, spirits of the ocean depths. Flow through our emotions, visit us in our dreams. Touch us with grace and fluidity. Teach us openness to the deep. We beseech you, spirits of the West: be here now!"

"Be here now," we answered.

To the North we turned at last. From the shadows around the altar emerged four Earthen creatures wearing elaborate rag-dresses. Dirt was streaked on their faces, moss ratted through their hair. They stooped low to the ground, swaying as they moved. When they reached the center, they faced one another, dropped to their knees, and pounded their hands on the floor three times. Still kneeling, they faced out and began chanting:

Cycles of the moon, the stars, the Earth
Secrets of the path from death to birth
Keeper of the flame, the source, the light
Presence of the deep, the dark, the night

The crowd picked up the chant. Voices rang through the room, then faded into silence. The Earth creatures pounded on the floor three more times. "Spirits of the North, be here now!"

"Be here now," we responded. I had to smile. Earth, air, fire, water. The classical elements. Where were we, ancient Greece?

As if answering me, Angie whispered, "Next is the invocation of the Triple Goddess — Maiden, Mother, and Crone." Three women — a teen, a parent, and an elder — danced in from different directions. Meeting in the center, they joined hands and promenaded in a circle like graces from a Renaissance fountain, singing:

"There is no end to the circle, no end,

"There's no end to life, there is no end."

Two men whom I recognized from the street demonstrations of the past year invoked the "Horned God." They did a slow, sinuous dance, twining together as the chorus sang:

"There is no end to the circle, no end,

"There's no end to life, there is no end."

As the song finished, one of the men sprang into the arms of the other, who cradled him like a newborn son. I placed my right hand on my heart as if anchoring the impression. Angie reached out and squeezed my left hand.

The final invocation, of the ancestors, ended in the drumming and dancing that Angie had told me about. I could see it coming as the drummers picked up the beat, and I braced myself. But oddly, Angie remained on the perimeter as the center dissolved into dancing. I was happy to stay with her. Was she feeling alienated, out of the loop? Or was she realizing how much she missed this?

As the dancing wound down, people backed out of the center and took seats. Some people were even laying out their jackets like pillows. Angie stretched out on the floor near the West altar. "Get comfortable," she said as she settled in. "This part lasts a while."

I stretched out on my back, hands folded across my chest. What was going on for Angie, I wondered. I tried to catch a glimpse of her face, but the light was wrong. Let it go, I told myself. Stay with the ritual. There's time later.

"Breathe deeply," came Artemis' voice, pulling me back to the moment. She began a simple, hypnotic rhythm on a Middle Eastern drum. I pushed aside thoughts of Angie. Focus. Listen to the drum. Think of something else. Think of the elements. How does it go? East is air. South is fire. West is water. North is Earth. East, South, West, North. And again, East, South...

The resonant tones of the drum pulsed through the room. The voices of the guides floated above the rhythm. "Breathe in the night air," Antonio said. "Move forward into the darkness... Feel yourself approaching the shores of the sunless sea... Breathe in the salty scent... Hear the water lapping against the beach... And look now as a ship comes out of the fog..."

I was lying with my eyes closed. In the hazy grayness, I pictured the outline of a wooden ship. "Let your breath guide you," Antonio said. "Step on board the ship. Leave behind all worldly cares, and journey to the Isle of Apples, the land of the ancestors... Step aboard the ship, and set sail, set sail..."

As the drum continued its entrancing rhythm, a flute joined in, and the chorus sang a haunting ballad.

Set Sail, Set Sail,
Over the waves where the spray grows white
Into the night, into the night

Set Sail, Set Sail,
Pass in an instant through the open gate
It will not wait, it will not wait

Set Sail, Set Sail,
To the Shining Isle where your heart is led
To meet the dead, to meet the dead...

The song faded and the trance drum was heard again. I remembered what Holly said once about talking to ancestors at rituals. Maybe this was my chance to talk to Leonardo. Although if I had to choose one person, maybe it should be Ben Franklin. Or St. Francis. Do you get a choice? What if someone else chooses that spirit first? Hopefully they'd worked out these details at previous rituals.

Artemis' voice wafted through the air. "Look! There through the mist. We approach a sandy beach. Our ship washes gently ashore. Coming to greet us are the spirits of the ancestors. Listen as they speak to us..."

From throughout the room came whispery voices, welcoming us, cautioning us, calling us to take heed. "Listen," Artemis intoned. "The spirits are here with us. Listen, they call to us."

I was hearing the voices more as whispery music than as distinct words, when suddenly discordant shouts rent the room. "Stop! Listen! Hear us!"

My eyes snapped open, but aside from the two guides in the center, I saw nothing. "Listen!" cried voices that seemed to come from all around me. "Hear our stories!"

"Behold the unquiet dead," came Antonio's steady voice. "Spirits whose conscience gives them no peace, even in death. They will not let us continue until we have heard their stories. Listen! Listen to the voices of the unquiet dead!"

At his summons, white-veiled spirits rose among us. They wandered aimlessly through the room, wringing their hands and lamenting:

"With these hands I set fire to the Witches' pyres..."

"With these hands I sold my brothers and sisters into slavery..."

"With these hands I cut down the ancient forests..."

"With these hands I gave the Indians blankets infected with smallpox..."

"With these hands I hit my children like my father hit me..."

A chill permeated the air. These weren't the ancestors I thought we were going to meet. I took a deep breath. Near me, I could hear someone sobbing quietly as the voices continued:

"I hoarded grain while children starved..."

"I rounded up Jews and sent them to the gas chambers..."

"I evicted a family on Christmas eve..."

"I knew my orders were unjust, yet I obeyed them."

"I knew it was wrong, yet I would not stop."

"I saw the truth, yet I did not speak."

The voices paused. An eerie silence filled the room. Then, like a Greek chorus, they cried in unison: "Hear us! Acknowledge us! We are your ancestors!"

"No!" Artemis swept her arms as if banishing the spirits. "You are not my dead! You are not my people! I disown you!"

The restive spirits wailed. "Hear us! Acknowledge us! Who we are and what we have done — you inherit!"

Their words hung in the air. Antonio looked around our circle. "The unquiet dead belong to us all," he said. "Feel their presence. Feel your own past. When we deny the dead, they rule us invisibly from the depth of our being."

Within me I felt rise my German heritage, which I usually ignored. But I'm a good German, I wanted to say.

Artemis held out her hands toward the spirits. "What do you want from us?"

"Perhaps they need us to undo their sorry legacy," Antonio answered. "Perhaps there is something that we, the living, can do to ease the misery they left behind."

That's it, I thought. That's what has to be done. But what exactly? How did you know where to begin?

"Feel the power of our circle," Antonio said. "You are not alone. Feel the power here, and let the spirits speak to you."

I groped for an answer, but none was forthcoming. Hey, I'm new at this, I thought. Give me time. I'll get it....

But Artemis' voice drew the ritual on. "Breathe deeply now, and listen," she said. "Other spirits are crowding around us. Listen!"

Again, veiled spirits rose and roamed through the space. This time, instead of wringing their hands, they gestured lovingly, as if offering a gift.

"With these hands, I ran a station on the Underground Railroad..."

"With these hands, I openly loved other men..."

"With these hands, I stole bread, that my children might survive..."

"With these hands, I protected the forests from destruction..."

The spirits drifted toward the center of the room, where they linked hands in a circle around Artemis and Antonio.

"I prepared food, that the hungry might eat..."

"I stood watch, that refugees might sleep..."

"I did not hit my children like my father hit me..."

"I refused to obey unjust orders..."

"I learned the truth, and would not keep silent..."

Then with a single voice, they called out, "Hear us! Acknowledge us! We are your ancestors, too!"

That's more like it, I thought. Here were the ancestors I expected.

"These spirits also belong to us," Antonio declared. "They are in our thoughts, our bodies. What do they ask of us? Which of their traditions will we carry on? Which of their dreams can we bring to fruition?"

Before I had time to reflect, the drumbeat swelled through the room.

"Breathe deeply," came Artemis' voice. "Look ahead, through the mists. More spirits come to greet us. Look carefully. Who reaches out to you?"

She paused, and her drum carried me forward. Lying on my back, I peered through the haze. Coming toward me I beheld a stocky man in rough peasant garb. Somehow I knew that his name was Benvenuto, and that he was a stonemason in Medieval Siena. He stood before me, gazing back, and I had the feeling that I was just as much his vision as he was mine.

Artemis' voice seemed far off as she beckoned: "Listen to the voices of the dead, who have wisdom for us..."

I strained to listen... and a voice, faint at first, came to my ears. It was Benvenuto speaking, although it seemed almost to come from inside my own head. I implored him to speak up, and finally grasped a single word: "Dance."

"Dance?" It wasn't exactly what I expected to hear from a Medieval stonemason. "I don't know how to dance," I felt myself answer.

Benvenuto nodded knowingly. "I used to think that." He tossed his arms into the air and spun a circle on his toes. "Just do what you feel," he said, and spun again.

I took a step back. "I can't do that. I'd look all uptight."

"Then dance that way," he said. "Make your own statement. Dance your own truth." He pointed off to the side, where a wiry Morris dancer was twisting his body into a series of grotesque poses. "Cousin Wilhelm over there once Morris danced all the way from Frankfort to Mainz." From across the road, Wilhelm waved to me, then continued his contorted peregrination. "Of course," Benvenuto told me, "they had to put him on the rack afterwards to straighten him out."

"That's fine," I said, sensing our time slipping away. "But what about your stonework? I've seen pictures of the cathedral you built in Siena."

Benvenuto swept his arm as if parting a veil. I thought I was ready for anything, but as the haze lifted and the outlines of the cathedral emerged, I shook my head in wonderment. My eyes soared up the striped spires, then played back down over the marble saints and prophets adorning the facade. "Which part did you work on?" I asked.

"The foundations," he answered, pointing. "Look closely. Look at the foundations."

As if the building were translucent, I gazed into the pavement and saw the massive stones that lay at the base of the cathedral. What labor it must have taken to drag those stones into position. What skill to carve and lay them precisely level.

"The foundations had to be perfect," Benvenuto said. "They would carry columns, arches, walls, and roof. This was my generation's work. We knew we would never see the finished building, that it would take a century or more to complete. But our work had to be perfect. One misplaced stone and the entire edifice would be threatened."

The Duomo, civic cathedral of Siena, Italy. The building, which was more a communal center than a church in today's sense, was begun in the early 1200s and took nearly two centuries to complete.

"It's stood for seven hundred years," I said.

"Seven hundred years," he echoed. "Look to the foundations that you lay."

"What?" I said.

"Look to the foundations." A cloud of mist washed around him. "What stones will you lay for future generations to build upon?"

"Foundations? Like what?" I groped for his meaning. Then suddenly it was clear. "Consensus? Nonviolence?"

His eyes strayed off into the distance, and I wasn't sure that he was hearing me anymore. "Lay them most carefully," he said. "The future looks to you."

"Nonviolence. Collectivity. Solidarity." I spoke the words as if stating a vow. "That's it, isn't it?"

The mists swirled, and he receded without taking a step. "Wait," I called, "one more question!" But he smiled benignly and waved farewell. I gazed after him as he faded from sight.

"Foundations," I said to myself. I wondered if I would ever see Benvenuto again, or if every trance was unique. "Look to the foundations."

Around me I felt a stirring, not of spirits, but of bodies. From across the room, Artemis' voice floated through. "Soon we must bid farewell to the spirits. The time is short, and we must prepare to return through the veil...."

"Remember the ancestors you have met," Antonio said. "Remember what you have learned from them, and the message you bring back. In these words there is power. And by that power we commit ourselves to create a future in which all people, all cultures, all races can live with respect for one another. So mote it be."

"So mote it be," Artemis echoed. She beckoned us to stand and form a circle around the outside of the room. I was still a bit dazed from the trance. I looked around for Angie, but didn't see her. Somehow it wasn't surprising, as if the journey to the Isle of the Ancestors had transported us to different parts of the room.

I wound up between two strangers in the circle. "As we take hands," Artemis said, "we feel our neighbors as our allies. We are not alone in this struggle. Perhaps you have discovered a truth, or made a commitment. Imagine that truth, that commitment, as a flame burning in your heart. Feel it warming your spirit, flowing out through your hands, flowing around the entire circle. Feel our flames join together here in the center, burning on a hearth which all people can call home. This hearth will be our center as we dance the sacred spiral."

Foundations, I repeated silently, gazing into the center. Collectivity. Solidarity. Community. Look to the foundations.

I let my eyes play around the circle. Didn't I recognize that man from jail? And that woman from a spokescouncil? Or was it another lifetime?

A mandolin plucked the opening notes of a melody. Hand-drums laid down a stately rhythm, and the chorus began a song that the crowd picked up:

Let it begin with each step we take
Let it begin with each change we make
Let it begin with each chain we break
Let it begin every time we awake

Artemis stepped to her left, still holding the hand of the person behind her. Slowly, majestically, the line began snaking inward. Once, twice, three times we spiraled toward the center. Candles cast a flickering light on the faces opposite me. It was beautiful, but not quite right. Wasn't there something more?

Artemis turned and led the head of the snake spiraling back out, passing face to face with the inbound dancers. That was it! My heart jumped as the first faces passed me on their way out. Our eyes met in quick flashes. Artemis. Doc. Sara. Alby. Antonio. My part of the line reached the center and started winding back out. The drums picked up the rhythm. Our steps became quicker. The tail of the line streamed past me. Karina. Ariel. Moonstone. The guy from jail — yes, he recognized me, too!

We reached the outside and turned back in. Faces flowed past a second time. I drank them in. But one face was missing. Angie. I watched carefully as we wended our way into the center — not a sign of her. We wound back out, and I peered into the dark recesses of the perimeter, where a few figures lurked. If she was out there, she was well-concealed.

My spirit sagged. How could she desert me at the climax of the ritual? I felt an impulse to leave right then. Even if she were still around, we weren't in this together. What was the point in staying? Quit clinging to the past. I'd missed my chance. Time to get on with life.

Yet I couldn't just walk out of the spiral. I felt my neighbors' hands gripping mine. My lot was cast. Stay with the flow. She must be here somewhere. Maybe it was a test.

The chant was picking up momentum, and I threw myself into it, reaching for the high harmony. "Let it begin with each step we take..." In we spiraled and out again. Faster and faster the drummers drove the rhythm. "Let it begin with each change we make..."

Artemis reached the center once more. She let loose her neighbor's hand and raised both of her arms in the air as if summoning all the spirits. "Let it begin with each chain we break..." Throughout the circle others joined her. Louder and louder we sang, as if sending our voices through the roof and out to the stars. "Let it begin every time we awake!"

People near the center were dancing ecstatically. I was a few rows back toward the West altar, singing over and over, "Let it begin now, let it begin now." Voices sailed free of the words, pouring out long, melismatic tones. I felt myself leaning toward the vibrant center. I closed my eyes and chanted the words like a mantra, blocking out all other thoughts: "Let it begin now, let it begin now."

Finally I let go of the words. The drums slowed the rhythm, then released it, leaving a medley of freely-toning voices. The stray notes settled into one extraordinary chord, two hundred voices echoing from the ceiling and walls, swelling and fading, swelling and fading. Together the voices rose one last time, then faded to pure silence.

I held my breath, not moving a muscle. Gradually, people knelt. I dropped to my knees and touched the floor, still reverberating from the chant. Next to me, a woman lowered her face and kissed the ground.

Eventually, people settled back into their seats. From near the North altar, several graces stepped forward bearing overflowing baskets of bread and fruit. Antonio pronounced a blessing on the harvest, and the food was distributed among the celebrants, each person passing some to the next with the words, "May you never hunger... May you never thirst..."

I joined those around the perimeter of the circle, figuring it was a good chance to search for Angie. I made a circuit of the room, checking around each altar, expecting every moment to spy her. But she was nowhere to be found.

Had she really left? Surely I was overlooking her. Or maybe she had gone out for some fresh air after the singing and dancing.

Or maybe — maybe she had gone outside to think something over. Maybe she was having a change of heart. Find her, I flashed. Find out. I made my way to the door and out into the lobby. The lights were jarring, the cool air bracing. A dozen people stood or sat around the lobby, refugees from the ritual. But no sign of Angie. Maybe in the women's room?

Just then I spotted Sara coming out of the restroom. I walked up to her and asked, "Have you seen Angie?"

She seemed startled, as if still in a trance. "Yeah," she said. "She went outside." As I started toward the door, Sara called after me. "That was a while ago. I thought she was leaving."

Leaving? I went out front. Nothing. Was she really gone? Maybe she got sick, and couldn't find me to say she was going.

Or maybe... maybe the ritual was too much a reminder of the past that she was leaving behind. Or maybe she could sense how much I wanted to ask her to stay. And she didn't want to deal with it...

I stood staring at the sidewalk. The streetlights cast an anemic glare on the pavement. Why go back inside? If Angie had left, why shouldn't I? I wouldn't even be here if not for her. Was it really my ritual?

But something felt unresolved. Angie's leaving wasn't adding up. Besides, I'd gone on a journey to the Isle of the Ancestors — was it smart to skip the ride home? I wasn't quite done with the Spiral Dance. Or maybe it wasn't quite done with me. Slowly, I gave in. I slipped back through the doors into the dark ritual space. My eyes had trouble adjusting, and I took a seat on the floor near the North altar just as our boat came aground in San Francisco. I patted the floor. San Francisco. We're home.

Soon we were bidding "hail and farewell" to the ancestors. "Hail and farewell," I said along with the rest.

The men and women who had invoked God, Goddess, and the Directions came to the center. In reverse order of the invocations, singers and dancers thanked and devoked first the Earth in the North, then water in the West.

Karina's closing words for the South drew me fully back into the spirit of the ritual. "We release you, fire. But help us remember that you burn in us always — in our passion for one another, in our passion for justice, and in our passion for all living beings. Go if you must, stay if you will. Hail and farewell."

Go if you must, I thought. Stay if you will. Maybe that was the secret. What if I could say that to Angie? "Stay if you will." No pressure, just an invitation. Of course, first I had to find her. Was she somewhere in the room? I looked around the circle, but with the shadows, there was no telling. "Go if you must." Well, if she had left, there wasn't much I could do besides accept it.

Accept it. It seemed like the story of my life. I thought about LAG, about all of our efforts to breathe life back into the group. How little we had to show for it. Maybe we'd reached the end of the road. Time to accept the inevitable. Go if you must. Hail and farewell.

I turned my attention back to the ritual as East, the last direction, was devoked. Then, as if on an unspoken cue, voices throughout the room rose in a closing litany: "By the Earth that is Her body, by the air that is Her breath, by the fire of Her bright spirit, and by the waters of Her living womb — the circle is open, but unbroken. May the peace of the Goddess go in our hearts. Merry meet, merry part — and merry meet again!" On the final words, the voices rose to a shout. The drummers cut loose, and dozens of people flowed into the center of the circle in a free-form dance.

Standing back near the North altar, I searched one last time for Angie, half-expecting her magically to appear in the center, dancing and beckoning to me to join her. Wouldn't that be the perfect ending?

But it wasn't to be. Sadly, I turned toward the door. What had I expected, anyway? A miracle? Maybe it was time to stop asking for miracles. Time to think about what could be learned, so I didn't go on repeating the same mistakes for the rest of my life. I needed to do some serious thinking.

The drumming was good, but nothing was holding me. Why not head for BART, ride out to North Berkeley, and take a long walk home? Get a little distance, and maybe everything would come into focus.

Nothing was holding me, but I found it hard to leave. I should say goodbye to Sara or Doc or Antonio. Let them know I liked the ritual. I looked around the still-crowded room — and spied Karina coming toward me, floating like a Goddess over the sea. I fumbled for a sense of time. Wasn't Karina in prison? Was this a hallucination? Instinctively, I opened my arms and embraced her. She answered, in the flesh, and I squeezed her to me, as if my fervor might keep her free. She'll never go on trial. She'll never go to prison. We'll stop the clock by sheer desire.

We breathed together, and I felt the curve of her body meld into mine. Her thick warm hair rustled across my face. Again we breathed, more deeply. But as we exhaled, she let go of me, and I knew in a flash that she was gone. Even before our bodies separated, her spirit slipped away. Another lost soul. Hail and farewell.

Karina stepped back and pointed toward the door. "Angie just went that way," she said. "She was looking for you."

"Angie?" My eyes darted toward the exit. Angie? For real? Without another word, I headed out the door. My eyes searched the lobby. Find her. No more delays. Time to speak my heart. Stay if you will. Her response was irrelevant. All that mattered was speaking my truth. Stay if you will.

The lobby was a blur of faces, none of which registered. Only one person counted now. Stay if you will. Where was she? I stepped around a knot of people, and like a vision she appeared, walking toward me.

"There you are," she said, as if I were the one who had disappeared.

"Where were you?" I asked. I reached out and took her hand, but sensed that she didn't want to be crowded. "I thought you left."

"No, I just got overheated and felt like I couldn't breathe during the trance," she said. "I needed something cold to ground me, so I went out to the corner store for a bottle of water."

We stood facing one another, holding hands. My mind raced. Ask her now. Stay if you will. I took a breath and tried to say the words, but what came out was, "Are you really moving to Portland? I wish you'd think it over one more time. I really wish you'd come back." I paused, groping for words. "I love you, Angie."

She gazed at me for a long moment. Creases formed on her brow, and she seemed to draw her energy inward. Her eyes flickered, as if chaotic thoughts were racing past. Then suddenly she burst like a coiled spring and threw her arms around my neck. "I'm coming back, Jeff."

I held her to me. Her words echoed in my ears without quite taking hold. "Coming back..." Was it true? "Coming back..." I could scarcely make out her next few sentences. Something about knowing where her home was, and knowing what she needed to be doing. "All through the ritual," she said, "I felt this tugging at my heart, like I was being pulled by the Goddess, or by this community, however you want to see it. These are my people. However much some of them exasperate me, they're still my community. During the trance it just got too intense. I had to get outside and catch my breath. But I knew I was coming back."

Still holding her, I looked into her eyes. "What about school?"

She shook her head. "Social work isn't where my heart is. I'll probably still wind up doing that. But not right now. I need to be here. I felt like I'd given up on myself when I left the Bay Area. There's something here I need to carry through to the end. Even if it never comes to anything, I need to pursue it, to be true to myself."

"You're moving back?" I asked, as if saying it aloud would make it more real.

"Yeah," she said. "There's a room open at Stonehenge, a real room with a door. Ariel told me about it tonight, and said it was mine if I wanted it. Once I heard that, I knew I was meant to be here."

I leaned down and kissed her, a soft touch of the lips at first, then opening, moistening, caressing, like we had never kissed before. Angie leaned back and looked at me searchingly. My eyes opened wide. "I know of another room," I said. "With a great view off the balcony."

As if she had anticipated the question, she arched up and gently pressed her lips to my ear. "One step at a time," she whispered. "I'm sure I'll be spending plenty of time there." I nodded, and we kissed again as if sealing a pact. One step at a time.

Gradually I became aware of voices around us. We stood in the middle of the lobby, still holding one another. The departing crowd swirled past. I looked down at Angie. Her eyes sparkled. "Let's dance." She took my hand and led me back into the ritual space.

In the center of the room, the drummers still pulsed. A small crowd clustered around, bobbing and swaying in time. Sweat, candle smoke, and laughter mingled in the air. Angie pulled me into the circle. She let loose my hand and shimmied. I met her eyes, and my hips picked up the beat. No need to press. Just feel the flow. This was the only moment that mattered. Somewhere among the spirits, I felt Benvenuto smile. I was dancing.

About the Author

LUKE HAUSER is a postgraduate student of parajournalism who was arrested numerous times while researching this book. His writing (under various pseudonyms) has appeared in *GroundWork, Reclaiming Quarterly, Street Spirit, The Berkeley Barb, The San Francisco Bay Guardian, The Indiana Statesman, Z Magazine,* and *The Revolutionary Pagan Workers' Vanguard.* He lives in a collective house in the shadow of San Francisco's Mission Dolores, and is part-owner of People's Park in Berkeley.

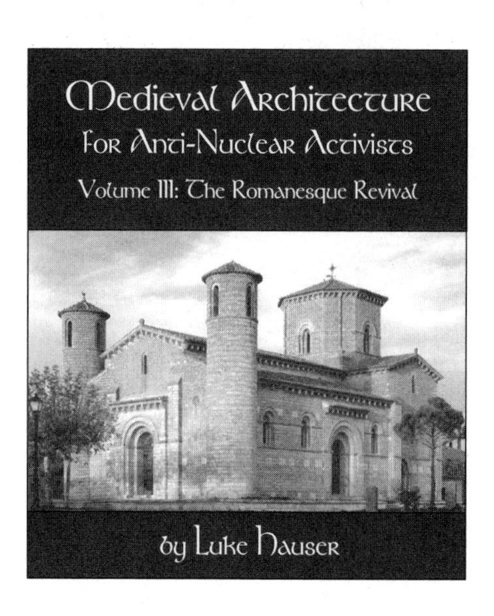

Also by Luke Hauser

Medieval Architecture for Anti-Nuclear Activists (four volumes)

Quasi-Hierarchical Anti-Authoritarianism: An Ontological Analysis

A Child's Garden of Quantum Mechanics

Existential Angst in Five Easy Lessons (second edition)

Improve Your Graffiti Cansmanship! (with inpirational audio tape)

The Direct Action Acrostics Book

Terre Haute Today (tour guide)

Edited by Luke Hauser

The Annotated Lenin-Kafka Correspondence (with a Foreword by U.S. Senator Diane Feinstein)

Olde English Nature Poetry of the Later 1370s

The Complete Pagan Book of Algebraic Geometry

An Illustrated History of the Eight-Track Tape

Poststructural Semiotics and the Quest for Hermeneutic Certitude (junior high textbook)

Appendices

For a guide to the Appendices, turn to the final page of the book

In the mid-1980s, protests of Livermore Lab's weapons programs shifted to the Lab's local test area, Site 300, located east of Livermore in the Altamont Hills. According to the Lab, only non-nuclear "triggers" for nuclear weapons were tested at Site 300. Protesters were skeptical enough to wear radiation suits when they went over the fence in backcountry actions at the sprawling facility (above). Other actions such as the 1985 theater protest at the Site 300 gate (below) used rad suits more for dramatic effect.

Direct Action Handbook

What follows is a much-condensed version of handbooks produced by Abalone Alliance (1981), Livermore Action Group (1982), Vandenberg Action Coalition (1983), and LAG's International Day work group (1983). The 1982 LAG handbook forms the basis for both the material and the graphic design, with sections of text added from the others.

The original handbooks ranged from 48 to 104 pages. The next 35 pages offer a sampling of the material from those handbooks. More will be posted online at www.directaction.org, along with links to present-day handbooks and resources.

LIVERMORE WEAPONS LAB BLOCKADE/DEMONSTRATION HANDBOOK

NONVIOLENT PROTEST & CIVIL DISOBEDIENCE

JUNE 21, 1982

TABLE of CONTENTS

Goals of the Action 1

Livermore Lab

The U.C. Connection 3

Lobbyist for War 4

Why Are We Bombing Nevada? 5

U.S. Militarism 6

The Bomb 7

Nuclear Sites in the USA 8

Process

Nonviolence 9

Consensus 12

Affinity Groups 16

Discrimination Overview 18

Racism 18

Homophobia 19

Feminism 20

Masculine Oppression 23

The Blockade

Scenario 24

Kids 26

Legal 27

Jail 30

Solidarity 32

After It's Over 33

This Handbook was originally conceived as an eight-page supplement to the Diablo Blockade Handbook. But we realized it was important to have the excellent material from the Diablo Handbook on process and the Livermore background material in one place. We experienced both the stress of producing this Handbook in four weeks, and the excitement of working collectively, learning new skills and information, and creating something we think will be useful.

This Handbook is just the youngest descendent in a long line of partial plagiarism of thoughts and graphics which were lifted from the Diablo Handbook, which were lifted from the Pentagon '80 Handbook, which were lifted from the Seabrook Handbook...which were lifted from the mythical, primordial anti-nuclear Handbook. Wherefore and whereas we offer and authorize anyone to use anything from this Handbook.

We see this Handbook as one more step. It is up to all of us to weave more threads into the fabric. The pattern is peace.

GOALS OF THE ACTION

The ultimate goal of the Livermore Action Group is to further the cause of (1) global nuclear disarmament, (2) the demilitarization of American society, and (3) a redirection of economic priorities that provides for a more equitable distribution of wealth and resources at home and abroad.

The Livermore Action Group recognizes that people will participate in this action for a variety of reasons. It is not necessary that you take part for all of the following reasons. This summary is intended to help you clarify your reasons for taking part, by making the necessary connections between the lab, the nuclear arms race, and its threat to peace.

1. To focus public attention on the role of the lab in the arms race and militarism;

2. To stress the importance of conversion of the lab to productive, peaceful use;

3. To disrupt "business as usual" at the Lab, to slow down the development of first-strike and other nuclear weapons;

4. To urge weapons-related employees to reconsider their role in nuclear proliferation;

5. To assert the right and capability of ordinary citizens to express their objections to present foreign policy and to the threat of nuclear war;

6. To make clear to administrators

that they will have to arrest this country's own citizens if they insist on continuing on the path of destruction;

7. To show solidarity with European and world peace and disarmament movements;

8. To call attention to the vested interests which oppose disarmament and pour money into nuclear weapons instead of needed social welfare programs.

STATEMENT of PURPOSE

Livermore Action Group proposes conversion of our nation's two nuclear weapons design laboratories to productive, peaceful use, as a first step towards nuclear disarmament. \LAG affirms that this unilateral initiative would create a

better environment for negotiations between the U.S. and the USSR.

The most formidable obstacle to arms control negotiations is America's thrust to develop a "disarming first-strike" capability. Some of the main proponents of first-strike weaponry are the self-proclaimed "impartial experts" at Livermore and Los Alamos Labs.

At present, the warheads for the highly-accurate, first-strike nuclear weapons such as the Trident, Cruise and the MX missiles are in the final stages of development at Livermore Lab. The lab is also developing three different models of the first-use neutron bomb, which because it destroys living beings while leaving property intact has the potential of greatly increasing the possibility of "limited use" of nuclear weapons.

The weapons labs also conduct underground nuclear weapons tests at Nevada Test Site. Without these tests, the development of new and more destructive nuclear weapons systems would end.

Conversion of the weapons labs would constitute an enormously effective first step toward disarmament without jeopardizing the ability of the United States to defend itself during negotiations toward total nuclear disarmament.

In essence, the Livermore Action Group proposal for a first step toward nuclear disarmament would have the same effect as the Nuclear Weapons Freeze ballot initiative, which calls for a halt to testing, production, and deployment of nuclear weapons. LAG supports the Freeze. However, we are convinced that a more radical approach is necessary. We hope that massive, nonviolent demonstrations and direct action will serve as a catalyst that will encourage people from all walks of life to become active, and that together we will bring pressure on the American government to reverse its nuclear acceleration.

We do not expect to stop work at Livermore Lab for more than a few hours or a few days. However, we expect to focus national attention on Livermore, and to make it clear that we will no longer stand idly by while this administration prepares for global destruction. Stop the bomb where it starts!

Introduction

This section is intended to provide a minimum introduction to our reasons for attempting to convert Livermore Lab to peaceful use. We have put together several articles on aspects of the subject prepared by the LAG Education workgroup. These articles were written by individuals and not consensed to by LAG. We encourage further study of and action against this monster in our midst. If you are interested in more information, please contact the Livermore Action Group Education Collective.

LIVERMORE

The Ivory Tower is a Bomb

The U.C. Connection

The University of California's name and seal are on every nuclear warhead developed by the United States. Officially, U.C. operates the weapons labs under five-year contracts with the Department of Energy. But the University exercises no control or influence over the work on the labs. Rather, it has provided an academic cover — a "cloak of legitimacy — for secret nuclear weapons research.

For its part, the University receives a $5 million yearly management fee from DOE.

continued on next page

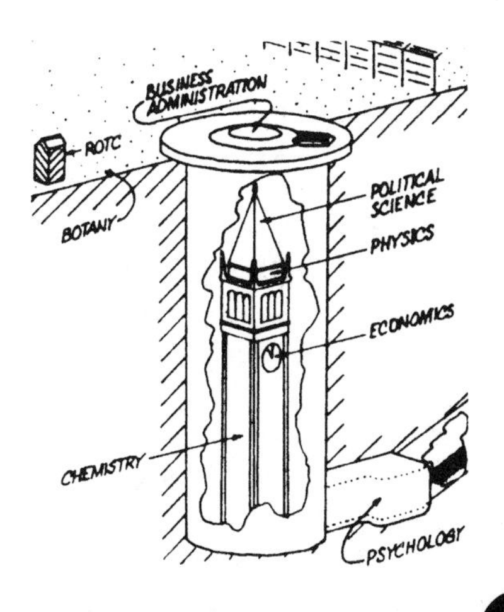

Livermore Lab: lobbyist for WAR

The weapons labs are the most powerful lobbyists in the country against arms control treaties and for new weapons systems. They were instrumental in defeating the negotiations for a Comprehensive Test Ban Treaty in the early 1960s, and again in the late 1970s.

Now, Livermore Lab is lobbying against the California Nuclear Weapons Freeze initiative. Livermore argues that a Freeze now, with the Soviets "ahead," would create an unstable situation, and might actually lead to nuclear war. We need time, the lab says, to develop the new generation of (first-strike) weapons, and then, with these"bargaining chips," we can negotiate real arms reductions. This self-serving argument merely justifies continued weapons work by the labs. In fact, the first-strike weapons under development now represent the most destabilizing development in many years.

Ivory Tower

continued from preceding page

The major benefits to the labs from the University connection are prestige, in that the U.C. name helps in recruitment and retention of scientific personnel, and independence, in that the lab staff enjoys a much greater degree of freedom in its interactions with government officials than would be the case if they were under government or industrial management. It is precisely this independence that has enabled lab officials to exercise powerful influence on weapons policies.

Health and Safety at the Labs

Contrary to official proclamations, Livermore Lab is extremely unsafe, a deadly hazard to all in and around the facilities. The lab is run by people who are aware of the dangers and have withheld critical information from the DOE and from

most of their own employees, and from the public in general.

The Environmental Impact Statement prepared in 1978 by the DOE for Livermore Lab admitted to "routine and unavoidable emissions" of radioactive substances, including plutonium, curium, uranium and tritium. The EIS also reported a history of 17 accidents involving radioactive and toxic substances.

The innumerable health and safety problems at the lab reveal the colossal irresponsibility on the part of management. They risk the lives of employees, the community, and over four million people in the Bay Area with contamination of air, soil, water and vegetation.

No one really knows the outcome of these dangers; will we be faced with higher cancer rates and unknown threats against succeeding generations? The spin-off from the labs' design of first-strike weapons is a first strike against the environment.

Why are we Bombing Nevada?

The nuclear weapons labs and the University of California also need to be held accountable for the ongoing health, safety and environmental risks involved in nuclear weapons testing at Nevada Test Site (NTS). As of June 30, 1979, 537 announced tests had taken place at NTS. President Reagan plans to double the annual number of tests.

Throughout the history of testing in Nevada, the weapons labs and government have knowingly doused thousands of Americans with radioactive fallout from tests. At least 41 of the 441 so-called "safe" underground tests have leaked large amounts of hazardous radiation into the atmosphere, some equivalent to the amount of radiation release din the Hiroshima bomb.

The labs, the Department of Energy, and other government officials have repeatedly ignored and even falsified the health and safety risks for the test site workers and the surrounding communities. This "invisible violence" against out own citizens reflects the willingness of this government to stop at nothing to achieve its ends.

Guns versus Butter

- 25% of the world's research money goes into military research
- The money the world spends on military purposes in 12 hours could probably eradicate malaria from the earth
- 5% of the world's military expenditure could provide school places for 100 million children who do not currently attend school
- The world spends $22 on military purposes for every $1 it spends on development aid to poor countries
- "The money required to provide adequate food, water, education, health and housing for everyone in the world has been estimated at about $18.5 billion per year. It's a huge sum of money... about as much as the world spends on arms every two weeks." — U.N. Center for Disarmament

source: Oxfam America

U.S. Militarism

The War at Home and Abroad

The U.S. is at war. It has been in a state of war or war preparedness uninterruptedly for over four decades. Soon the Reagan administration's yearly military spending will surpass the peak of the Vietnam War.

What is the cause of this massive expansion, which began in the late Carter years? It cannot be explained solely in terms of competition with the Soviet

Union. Primarily, this military build-up is due to the loss of the overwhelming political and economic world dominance of the U.S. government and corporations, which characterized the 1950s through the early 1970s.

This abrupt change in U.S. policy parallels exactly the successful upsurge in third world struggles for self-determination. Since 1975, over a dozen third world nations have seen successful liberation struggles in which elites subservient to U.S. corporate interests were replaced by more popular governments. To maintain their profits, U.S. multinationals have become increasingly dependent on cheap labor and natural resources controlled by repressive governments in South Africa, Taiwan, the Philippines, Central America, South Korea, Malaysia, and other "democratic" allies. U.S. corporations and the local elites they support depend on U.S. power to maintain their privileged positions.

At the same time, the nuclear build-up in Western Europe is an attempt to reassert U.S. political dominance over its allies.

At home, the Reaganites are faced with serious tasks. With an economy already weakened by competition from Japan and Europe (whose economies are not drained by excessive military spending), a way must be found to subsidize military programs without totally destroying the U.S. economic base. This means opening a "second front" in Reagan's war: against workers and the unemployed, against women, Blacks, Hispanics, against the people of America.

A massive transfer of wealth is underway fro poor and working people to the military-industrial complex. Corporate taxes have been drastically reduced, while basic social programs are slashed, if not eliminated. These actions are all designed to redirect funds to corporate profits and to the military build-up needed to sustain them.

We need unified resistance to confront this growing militarism. This is why Livermore Action Group sees the necessity of being part of a broad anti-militarist movement which includes trade unions, civil rights, feminist, and third world groups, churches and community organizations, and anti-intervention movements

The BOMB

What It Would Be Like

What is the purpose of calculating just what the consequences of a nuclear war would be? To ignore the reality of holocaust is to surrender to psychic numbing, which produces disabling cynicism and despair. By having a clear understanding of nuclear annihilation, we are able to stop absurd suggestions of the survivability of nuclear war, including discussions of civil defense. And by knowing the future that nuclear war would bring, we are compelled to act.

The circles of destruction emanating from a nuclear holocaust continue to expand as more is understood. The overkill capacity of nuclear arsenals ensure that much of the land area of the United States and the Soviet Union would be subject to primary effects of the weapons.

IN A NUCLEAR WAR . . .

THESE TARGETS ARE LIKELY TO BE HIT

FALLOUT WOULD ENGULF . . .

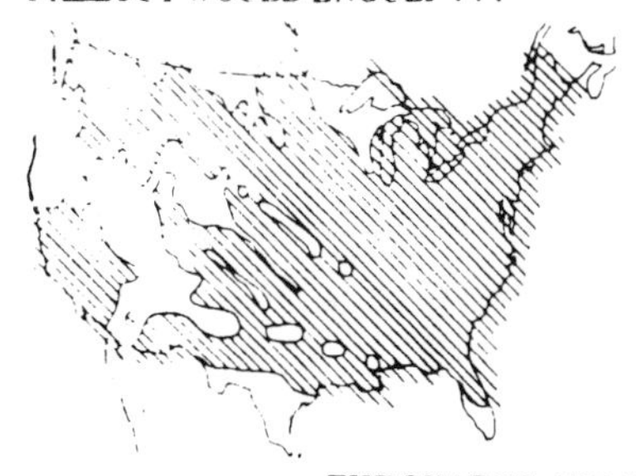

THE SHADED AREAS

After the immediate and local effects, there would be three significant worldwide effects of a nuclear war. First, radioactive material blown into the stratosphere during the explosions would circulate throughout the globe and gradually fall back to earth. This would cause genetic mutations and cancers in organisms on both land and sea, lasting for many generations.

Second, the enormous volume of particulate material blown into the stratosphere would deflect some solar heat from the earth's surface. Cooled by just a few degrees, the climate would change, and global vegetation, including agriculture, would be drastically altered.

Finally, the layer of ozone in the upper atmosphere, which protects life from harmful ultraviolet radiation, would be reduced 30 to 70 percent. It is increasingly evident that only some types of organisms could tolerate this environment; the others would become extinct.

Nuclear Weapons Locations in the United State c. 1980

(most still active, all still toxic)

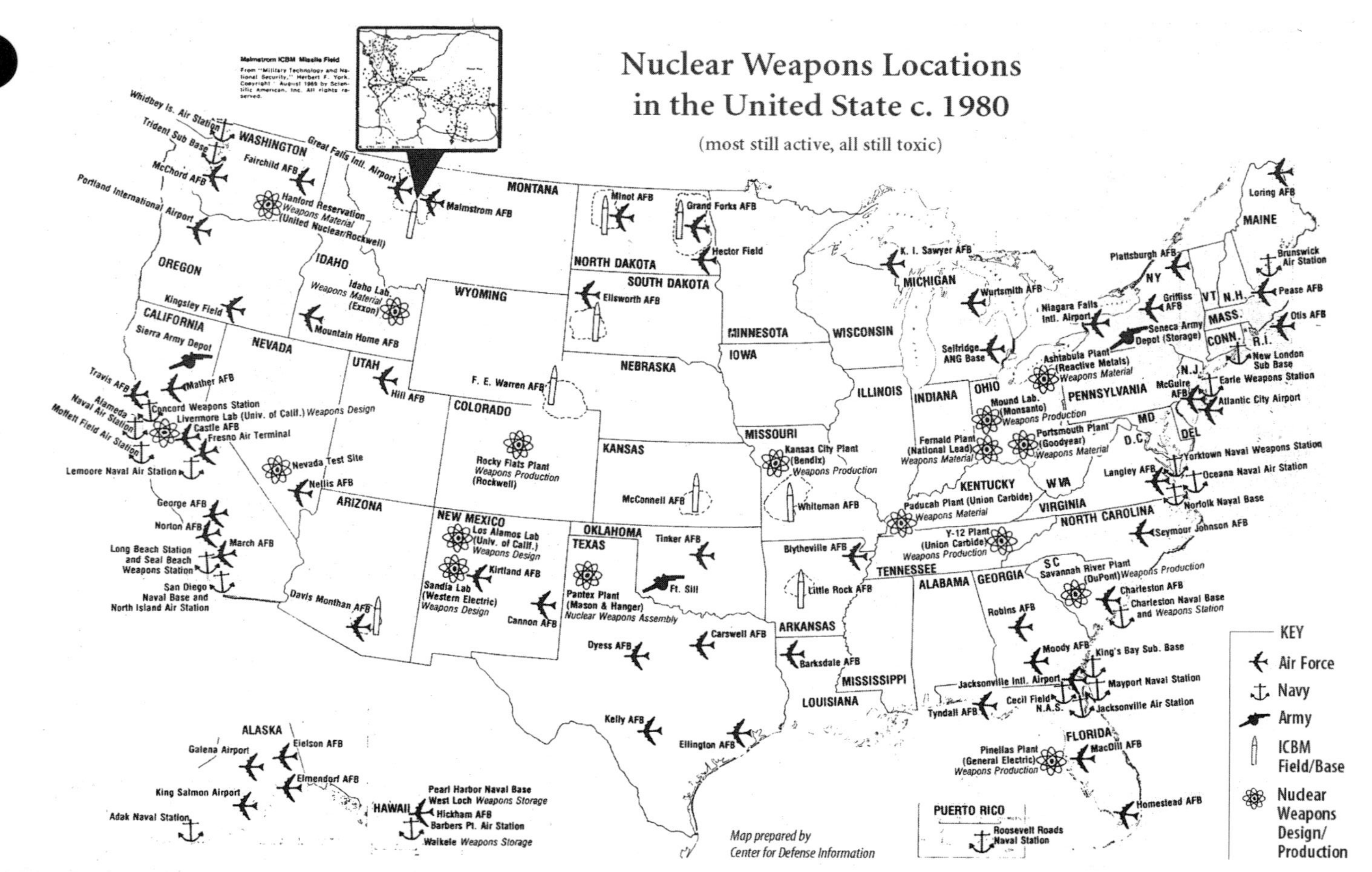

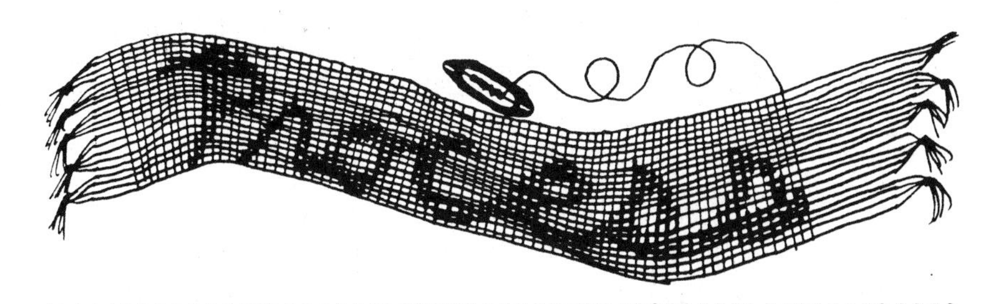

NON-VIOLENCE

Guidelines for Nonviolence

These are basic agreements, rather than philosophical/political requirements. The guidelines are meant to act as a basis of trust among participants who, for the most part, have met only for a particular action. The guidelines are under constant discussion and are seen as our current working understanding, not as statements etched in stone.

1. Our attitude will be one of openness, friendliness, and respect toward all people we encounter.
2. We will use no violence, verbal or physical, toward any person.
3. We will not damage any property.
4. We will not bring or use drugs or alcohol other than for medical purposes.
5. We will not run.
6. We will carry no weapons.

Nonviolence is an alternative to the use of violence to initiate change. Nonviolence minimizes bitterness and isolation in all people affected by it and tries to break the cycle of violence breeding more violence. The use of nonviolence in campaigns has led to many successes, such as ending racial segregation on buses in Montgomery, Alabama, as a result of the 1956 boycott.

A large part of the anti-nuclear movement has decided to incorporate nonviolence into the heart of our strategy. The following working assumptions form a preliminary framework for the understanding of nonviolence:

1. The means must be consistent with the ends.
2. Respect all life.
3. Transform opposition rather than destroy it.
4. Use creativity, humor, and love.
5. Aim for underlying changes.
6. Power lies in social dynamics. We can withhold cooperation from those who abuse power, and remove power from them.
7. Nonviolence is active.

Dynamics of NonViolence

How does one remain nonviolent in the face of riot(ing) police? The first thing is maintaining human contact with the potential assailant—whteher itÆs the police, a counter-demonstrator, or an angry participant from "our" side. Body language is important: especially making eye contact. Listening rather than talking may help prevent conflicts from erupting.

It is crucial that affinity groups discuss and role play, responses to potentially violent situations. For instance, an AG can physically surround someone being assaulted, while continuing to distract or calm the attacker. Active nonviolent responses such as this are, after all, the same idea as the whole blockade, which is intervening against the corporate violence of nuclear power and weapons.

We can show police (among others) another model of human nature, people who are acting for nature and for themselves. This process encourages our opponents' doubts about the rightness of their actions.

Many people comment on the extraordinary tone of nonviolent actions. It comes from the fact that participants are *centered and clear* about what they are doing. Gandhi referred to this as *Satyagraha*. *Satya* is truth, the truth that implies love and human dignity; *agraha* is firmness, the force felt by both actors and opponents when truth and love are acted on. Don't look at this tone as something imposed by leaders in order to have discipline. Rather it emerges freely when, by acting, people take back some control over their lives.

Police Violence

Police are trained to use holds and blows that can break bones or sprain joints. You should be aware of this when you are noncooperating with an officer. You will have to be the one to decide how much to risk, how much to accept.

If you are beaten by police, cover the base of the back of your head at the spine with your hands. Your elbows go over the sides of your head. Lie in a fetal position with your legs drawn up to protect your groin. This is the last stage of dealing with this kind of violence. Communication and sometimes withdrawal should be tried first.

the Politics of NonViolence

The conventional view of political power sees people as dependent on the good will and caprice of the government. Power is seen as something people *have*. Consequently, those without power must kill or destroy their rulers and replace them in their positions in order to wield the selfsame power.

The theory of nonviolence proposes a different analysis: that government depends on people and that political power is variable, even fragile, always dependent on the cooperation of a multitude of groups and individuals. The withdrawal of that cooperation restricts and can even dissolve power. Put another way, power depends on continuing obedience, so that when we refuse to obey our rulers, their power begins to crumble.

In this sense, nonviolence is not passive—nor is it a naive belief in converting the opposition—nor is it a "safe" method of protest, immune from repression. Rather, it is based on a different understanding of where people's power really lies. By acting disobediently, people learn to withhold, rather than surrender, their cooperation. When a group of people recognize this—as the "untouchables" of India did with Gandhi's help—the result is massive noncooperation and obstruction involving the use of social, economic and political power.

The authorities are able to wield power because masses of people passively obey, and because they have the violent means for suppressing dissent—police, National Guard, prison guards. A few disobey and are punished, keeping the many afraid.

Yet there are chinks in this armor. First, the repressive apparatus is made up of human beings whose cooperation is essential. A nonviolent approach undercuts the police rationale for violence—and reveals to neutral parties the extent to which the system relies on violence and force.

When dissent grows and brings force to bear, it astronomically raises the cost of continuing violence against it, until it becomes infeasible and the system breaks down.

CONSENSUS

Introduction

Consensus is a process in which no decision is finalized until everyone in the group feels comfortable with the decision and is able to implement it without resentment. Ideally, the consensus synthesizes the ideas of the entire group into one decision.

The skill of coming to genuine consensus decisions is a real and hard one. It involves a willingness to change and an openness to new ideas. People must be committed not only to expressing their own feelings, but also to helping others with opposite views to express those as well. Because the ideal of consensus is to reach a decision that is not only acceptable to everyone, but is best for everyone, there must be a "bottom line" of shared beliefs about what is best for all concerned. These are the *principles of unity*. These basic agreements will undoubtedly not encompass all the beliefs of each individual in the group, but rather, will help define the working relationship of the members. This may vary from the specific goals of a coalition formed around a single action, to an in-depth, ongoing process of self-definition in a small collective. Whatever their scope, without these basic agreements, and a willingness to work within them, consensus will never succeed. (IntlDay)

Unlike voting, consensus is not an adversary, win/lose method. With consensus, we do not have to choose between two alternatives. Those who hold views different from ours do not become opponents; instead, their views are seen as giving us a fresh and valuable perspective. As we work to meet their concerns, our proposals are strengthened.

Consensus is not the same as a unanimous vote. It does not necessarily mean total agreement. Rather, it means that a proposal has gone through a synthesis process in which everyone has a chance to express feelings and concerns.

Roles in a Consensus Meeting

Facilitator: Helps move the group through the decision-making stages. Takes suggestions for the agenda. Makes sure all necessary roles are filled. Calls on people to speak in turn. By calling on quiet people, soliciting opinions from those who hang back, and limiting those who tend to dominate, a skillful facilitator makes sure every person has a chance to participate fully. Helps the group resolve conflict and make decisions by summarizing, repeating, or rephrasing proposals as necessary. The facilitator should remain neutral on topics being discussed. When an issue arises about which the facilitator feels strongly, he or she should step aside and let someone else facilitate.

Vibeswatcher: Pays attention to the group's process. Stays aware of the feelings people are not expressing. Reminds the group to relax and take breaks as needed. This role is especially important in large meetings.

Other roles: Child care, notetaker, timekeeper.

How Consensus Works

An issue comes up for discussion. For example, an affinity group is trying to decide what its focus will be. After general discussion, someone suggests a *go-round* during which each member has several minutes to speak. One person takes notes and suggestions on a large sheet of butcher paper, so they can be seen by all.

When everyone has spoken, someone attempts to synthesize the ideas into a *proposal*— a suggestion for what the group will do. "I propose we concentrate on the Livermore action." The facilitator then calls for clarifying questions: "Do you mean blockading, or public education, or what?" When the proposal is clearly understood, *additions* may be offered: "I propose we concentrate on Livermore, doing education before the action and support for those who want to be part of the blockade."

The facilitator then asks for *concerns and objections.* A proposal is modified as concerns are expressed. For example, a group member might say, "I'm concerned that a focus on Livermore is too narrow." After discussion, perhaps even another go-round on the subject, the proposal will be modified and modified again. In its final form, it might be something like this: "This group will develop a public education campaign around the impact of U.S. nuclear weapons development on the Third World. The work of Livermore Lab will be a major focus, and we will support those who take part in the blockade." If there are no further objections, the facilitator can call for consensus. If there are still no objections, then you have your decision. If consensus is blocked and no new consensus can be reached, the group stays with whatever the previous decision was on the subject, or does nothing if that is applicable.

Blocking: Any individual in the group may also *block* consensus, but a block should be used very cautiously. *A block*

continued on next page

Consensus

continued from preceding page

is not just a "no" vote, or an expression of disfavor. A block says, "I believe what the group wants to do is wrong. I cannot allow the group to do it—and I am willing to impose this view on other group members because I feel it so deeply." One person may prefer action to education. Another may be afraid to talk to strangers. But they would not block the group's consensus on this proposal unless they believed that the public education program was harmful or unethical. When blocking is used for less serious reasons, it frustrates the consensus process, because it ends discussion and cuts off the possibility of synthesizing new options.

Consensus and Action: The goal of every decision-making process is not just to decide on a solution, but also to carry out that plan of action. It seems that a person's commitment to any decision is in proportion to their sense of participation in that decision. Consensus attempts to involve all members of a group, not just the "leaders".

People sometimes complain that consensus is too time-consuming. Especially when a group is learning to use the process, it may seem cumbersome. But discussion time is compensated by the increased energy and enthusiasm with which people carry out a decision. There is no dissatisfied minority to undermine a decision. Because group members feel part of the decision-making process, they often take on responsibility in new areas.

Spokescouncils: When operating in a large group, each affinity group selects one person to act as their spokesperson. These "spokes" carry affinity groups' opinions and proposals to spokescouncils of all the affinity groups. Spokes try to consolidate, synthesize, and iron out differences between proposals so as to create a proposal agreeable to all. The new proposal is then relayed back to the affinity groups by their spokes, the issues at hand reconsidered by each AG, and a new position (or perhaps the old one) is reached. These new positions are once again brought to the spokescouncil. If consensus can be reached, great. If not, the process may be repeated, or the group may decide to return to the previously consensed upon position. The role of spoke should rotate frequently so that power remains decentralized.

Process Guidelines

One major contribution of the feminist movement to current social change movements is the awareness that effective group process and meaningful personal interactions are crucial factors in developing a successful movement. Nonviolence begins at home, in the ways we treat each other.

Such an awareness stresses that relationships within the group cannot be separated from the accomplishment of political goals. Effective group process, in fact, means valuing co-operation over competition, recognizing the contributions of each individual, and decentralziing power through a non-hierarchical organizational structure.

Process Suggestions

1. *Use go-rounds.* Equalize participation by going around the circle speaking for a specified time.

2. *Value feelings.* Include time in meetings for expressing emotions and for personal interactions.

3. *Meet separately.* Allow time for women to meet with women and for men to meet with men in order to facilitate self-awareness and strengthen each person's particiaption. This applies to other groups as well, such as Blacks and Whites, etc.

4. *Meet in small groups.* Allow time for meeting in small groups during larger meetings so that people who feel uncomfortable speaking in large groups can speak more freely. Small groups will give each person more speaking time as well. A spoke from each small group can report back to the larger group, particularly if proposals have been discussed.

5. *Share skills, rotate responsibilities.*

Affinity Groups

An affinity group is usually composed of 5 to 15 people who have been brought together either at a nonviolence prep, by being in an anti-nuke or other type of group, or just because they're friends. In addition, many affinity groups focus around a specific interest, issue or philosophy, such as opposing sexism or racism in the anti-nuke movement, peace-keeping, being lesbians, Dead Heads or single mothers. An affinity group may exist only for the duration of one action or may continue functioning as an ongoing group.

Affinity groups serve as basic planning and decision-making bodies for an action, including the preparations and aftermath. Each affinity group provides for its own physical needs and makes all the basic decisions about the action, using consensus process. Spokespeople representing each affinity group meet in **spokescouncils** to communicate, co-ordinate and consolidate the different groups' decisions and then bring the co-ordinated information back to their respective groups for their final discussion and approval.

Affinity groups serve as a source of support and solidarity for their members. Feelings of being isolated or alienated from the movement, the crowd, or the world in general can be alleviated through the love and trust which develops when an affinity group works, plays, relates together over a period of time. By generating familiarity and trust, the AG structure reduces the possibility of infiltration by outside provocateurs.

The concept of affinity groups is not a new one; the name goes back to the "grupos de affinidad" of the anarchist

movement in Spain in the early part of this century. But actually affinity groups are the oldest and most ubiquitous form of organization by people seeking to make a better world: what makes more sense than small groups of friends who share an "affinity" working together?

We hope that in organizing for Livermore, many affinity groups will continue on as political/support groups doing anti-nuclear and other things together (for example, anti-war, poetry, gardens, parties, alternative tech, tofu factories, etc). All over the country this is starting to happen.

We feel that affinity groups should meet regularly, or at least several times, before the action to build community in the group, work on their process, plan a blockade strategy, and have a good time together. Group names and even identification such as T-shirts or armbands can help bring a group together. At least one meeting, preferably right after the nonviolence prep, should be devoted to legal and jail preparation, in which everyone's questions, fears, reactions, emotions and attitudes are explored in depth.

Affinity Group Support People

Support people are considered part of the AGs they are doing support for. Among other things they can:

- collect a list of people that members of the AG want to be contacted in case of injury or arrest.
- take care of blockaders' cars, personal belongings, IDs, etc.
- keep in touch with the protesters for as long as possible, keep track of where each member fo the AG is jailed, greet them when they are freed.
- support on the home front: plants, animals, kids, jobs, etc.

Work Groups

Work groups are set up to take care of particular functions for an action. For a mass civil disobedience action, the list of work groups usually includes:

- logistics
- communications
- fundraising
- media
- legal
- outreach & publicity
- nonviolence preps
- jail support
- monitors
- medical

Ongoing communication with affinity groups and other work groups is important. This may be facilitated by representatives of the work groups meeting together as a coordinating council and/or meeting with AG spokes at a spokescouncil.

Work groups must also make budget estimates and work with each other to prioritize distribution of resources.

Discrimination Introduction

In the disarmament movement, it is important not only to struggle against bombs and missiles, but also to struggle against other forms of violence that confront us. Specifically, other violence comes in two forms:

1. Daily physical and/or psychic violence against all people, such as rape or murder, and specifically against oppressed people.
2. Psychic and attitudinal violence within our movement reflected in ways we treat each other and ourselves.

These two forms of violence are strongly interconnected with the creation of weapons of destruction. After all, it is the same system that is responsible: a system based on domination, on the belief that some people have more value than others, and therefore have the right to control others. Because we believe it is the system and all of its forms of violence that we are fighting, we must make a commitment to fight the violence that occurs around us and between us. The Discrimination Section of this handbook specifically addresses these concerns, both within a societal context and within the context of interpersonal relationships.

Racism

Racism, the systematic mistreatment experienced by people of color, is a result of institutionalized inequities in the social structure. Racism stems from a self-perpetuating imbalance in economic, political and social power. The consequences of this imbalance pervade all aspects of the social system and affect all facets of people's lives.

Racism sets groups of people against each other. It distorts our perceptions of the possibilities for change; it makes us abandon our visions of solidarity; it robs us of our dreams of community.

No human being is born with racist attitudes. Racist attitudes are a result of misinformation which has to be imposed upon young people.

Racism continues in part because people feel powerless to do anything about it. But the situation is not hopeless. People can grow and change. Racism can be examined and unlearned.

Before any real change of racist attitudes can happen:

• White people need to realize that it is possible to unlearn racist attitudes, that we do have that power.

• White people need to learn how to get accurate information from and about people of color, to be willing to listen.

• White people must become aware of the ways that our lives have been limited by racism. This will increase the interest of white people in ending racism.

• White people must develop working relationships with all groups working for change, including black, latino and indigenous groups. Don't force your agenda on other groups.

Confronting Homophobia

Many people assume that everyone in the movement is heterosexual, despite the fact that gay people comprise 10 percent of the population and have been a significant force in every major left political movement in the past twenty years.

Historically, gays have been forced to live secretly out of fear of psychological or physical attacks or reprisals. This invisibility hurts us all: it perpetuates stereotypes about gays; it divides us; and it serves to minimize the accomplishments and contributions of gay people.

Unexamined prejudices result from historical condemnation of homosexuality. Gays have been attacked on all fronts: by psychiatry, organized religion, the Right, and the Left (which has viewed gayness as evidence of capitalist decadence). The list is extensive and horrifying, yet repression towards gays is often trivialized and our concerns dismissed as inconsequential.

In the anti-nuclear movement, which encompasses people from a wide variety of political and religious backgrounds, prejudices and stereotypes that lead to negative attitudes toward lesbians and gay men remain unchallenged as long as we remain invisible.

Are lesbians men-haters? This stereotype originated from men feeling threatened by women choosing women as lovers over men, feelings that reflect a cornerstone tenet of a sexist society: women are the property of men and under their control. In recent years, the advent of the lesbian rights movement has allowed for the emergence of a lesbian separatist philosophy, held by a small part of the lesbian population. For many lesbian separatists, the basic premise of this philosophy is the building of a culture, institutions, and relationships with women independent of men, rather than in opposition to men. This is based on the desire not to have to expend energy constantly dealing with sexism and general societal hatred of women.

This concept of separatism is not unique to lesbians and has, in fact, had parallel voices in almost every major liberation movement. Misunderstanding of this philosophy, however, has resulted in the broadening of the man-hating stereotype so that, frequently, it is used to discount women's criticisms of sexism or the desire of women to meet separately from men. It is crucial that this stereotype be confronted and not used as a cover for dismissing strong women.

The treatment of lesbians and gays by the police and jail authorities is another concern. Gays are often verbally abused

continued on page 22

Feminism

It is important to include a discussion of feminism in an anti-nuclear/anti-war handbook for several reasons. We can't stop the arms race simply by opposing nuclear weapons; we must also oppose traditional notions of power. Feminism has evolved from women's experiences: being supportive and nurturant; being victims of violence and oppression; being spiritual and emotional beings. And it offers an alternative concept of power.

Feminist philosophy recognizes the need to not only redistribute power, but to redefine it—power as inner strength, a sense of self not dependent on control or domination of another. Feminist philosophy envisions a society based on support and cooperation, not on fear, intimidation and violence. The recognition that these societal goals and priorities must also exist in *our* process makes feminist analysis an integral part of anti-nuclear protests. We recognize that our means will influence our ends. We are attempting to live our goals instead of just working for them.

Patriarchy

The split which in our society divides women and men is one of the most basic ways in which human beings are devalued. Under patriarchy, which means literally "rule of the fathers," men assume power over women. Women are relegated to limited roles and valued primarily for their sexual and reproductive functions, while men are seen as the central makers of culture, the primary actors in history.

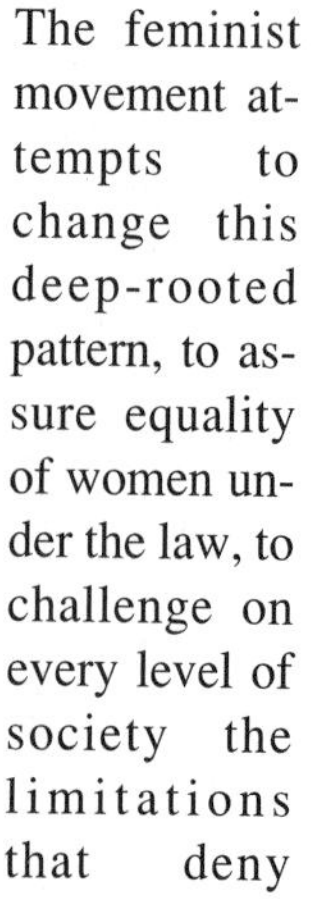
The feminist movement attempts to change this deep-rooted pattern, to assure equality of women under the law, to challenge on every level of society the limitations that deny women—and men—the chance to live our fully-human possibilities.

Patirarchy is reinforced by the language we use,. by the images in our textbooks and on our TV screens, by the fairy tales we hear as children and the popular songs we sing. It is enforced economically: women are clustered in the lowest-paying, lowest status jobs. For every dollar earned by men, women make only sixty cents. Women of color bear the burden of double discrimination.

Patriarchy is also reinforced by violence. Fifty percent of all women are battered at some time in their lives. Fear of rape keeps most women penned in their homes at night and makes hiking trails and lonely beaches places of terror for many women when they are alone. Magazines and movies portray women as objects to be violated. In war, the victors often rape the women of the conquered people.

The feminist movement has actively struggled against patriarchy and for women's self-determination in many areas—economic equality, access to jobs and education, control over our bodies and our sexuality, the right to control our own reproduction.

Feminism and Militarism

Many women see a feminist analysis as crucial to effectively challenge militarism. Patriarchy supports and thrives on war. The split which turns women, or any oppressed group, into *the other* is the same split which allows us to see our enemies as non-human, fair game for any means of destruction or cruelty. Our country's foreign policy often seems directed by teenage boys desperately trying to live up to stereotypes of male toughness. Men are socialized to repress emotions, not to cry, to ignore their needs to nurture and cherish the next generation. Emotions, tender feelings, care for the living and those to come are not seen as appropriate concerns of public policy.

Feminism says that the system which enforces male domination harms both women and men. That system is part of the system which perpetuates racism, classism, heterosexism, and all forms of oppression. In its broadest sense, feminism seeks not only to shake the world, but to remake it.

Feminist Process

We learn sexism at such an early age and in such intimate surroundings—our own families—that the attitudes it fosters are often unconscious. To help each other confront this conditioning, women in the late 60s and early 70s met together in small groups called *consciousness-raising groups.* As stories and experiences were shared, women began to discover that what we thought were personal frustrations or failures often stemmed from our common situation as women. The personal, we found, is political.

The process that developed in these small groups has strongly influenced our process in the peace movement: in fact, we call our process *feminist.* Feminist

continued on next page

Feminism

continued from preceding page

process does not mean that women dominate or exclude men—on the contrary, it challenges all systems of domination, matriarchy as well as patriarchy. The term recognizes the historical importance of the feminist movement in insisting that nonviolence begins at home—in the very ways we treat each other.

When we say that we use feminist process, we mean that the relationships within our groups cannot be separated from the accomplishment of our goals. We mean that we value synthesis and co-operation rather than competition, that we value each individual's contributions to the group and encourage the active participation of everyone involved. We mean that our organizations are non-hierarchical; that power flows from the united will of the group, not from the authority of any individuals. Nevertheless, our groups are not leaderless—each one of us is a leader.

Men's Issues

Although the major changes in women's lives are a result of the work that women have done for ourselves, coalitioning with men to fight sexism is an important ingredient of massive and enduring change. Some men have joined women in this struggle, and from this has emerged a small men's anti-sexist movement that challenges the social order that depends on sexism to control both men and women. Such a movement is helping men become conscious of their own pains and needs, recognize how they dominate others, and give support to each other. As with women struggling to overcome limitations that are conditioned, men can overcome the barriers which prevent them from being full human beings as well.

Homophobia

continued from page 19

by police and as a result feel especially vulnerable to police and jail. It is important that heterosexual and gay blockaders join together to guarantee safety during arrest and/or placement in the general jail population. Our unity can prevent the prison authorities from using homophobia as a "divide and conquer" tool.

Concern for issues beyond nuclear holocaust strengthens our movement by building vital coalitions. Gaining an awareness of lesbians and gay men and other minorities whose experiences have been overlooked will improve our process by encouraging a diversity of people to participate.

by the Non-Nuclear Family AG

Overcoming Masculine Oppression in Mixed Groups

This guide is addressed to men, and to how we can overcome our own oppressive behavior in mixed (male and female) groups. More often than not, men are the ones dominating group activity. Our goals are to rid the society—and our own organizations—of these forms of domination.

The following are some problems for men to become aware of:

- **Hogging the show:** talking too much, too long, too loud.
- **Problem solver:** continually giving the answer or solution before others have had much chance to contribute.
- **Restating:** saying in another way what someone else, especially a woman, has just said.
- **Putdowns and one-upsmanship:** "I *used* to believe that, but now..." or "How can you possibly say that?"
- **Self-listening:** formulating a response after the first few sentences, not listening to anything from that point on, and leaping in at the first pause.
- **Avoiding feelings:** intellectualizing, withdrawing into passivity, or making jokes when it's time to share personal feelings.
- **Seeking attention and support from women while competing with men.**
- **Speaking for others:** "What so and so really meant was..."

The full wealth of knowledge and skills available to the group is severely limited by such behavior. Women and men who feel less assertive than others or who don't feel comfortable participating in a competitive atmosphere are cut off from the interchange of experience and ideas.

As men, we can be responsible to others and ourselves in groups by taking only our fair share of talking time, listening attentively and not interrupting other speakers, giving our ideas in an equal rather than an arrogant manner, minimizing our critical tendencies, and interrupting the oppressive behavior of other men.

If sexism isn't ended within social change groups, there can't be a movement for real social change. Any change of society which does not include the freeing of men and women from oppressive sex role conditioning, from subtle as well as blatant forms of male supremacy, is incomplete.

(adapted from an article by Bill Moyer)

BLOCKADE

scenario

We plan to disrupt business as usual at the labs for as long as possible. Blockaders will attempt to cut off access gates and roads to the lab by engaging in a nonviolent blockade. Blockaders should plan on being arrested.

All blockaders must take nonviolence training and form affinity groups. AGs are encouraged to develop creative nonviolent tactics which prolong the blockade and dramatize our opposition to nuclear weapons. Theatre, props and other nonviolent tactics will maximize the effectiveness of the blockade.

To coordinate affinity group participation for the blockade, there will be regular spokescouncil meetings, consisting of a spoke from each AG. Spokes may express concerns of the AG, exchange information, and discuss proposals for the action. Spokes will then go back to their AGs to discuss proposals in depth, and return to the next council with their AG's concerns and decisions.

The blockade scenario collective is developing the framework for the blockade. This collective will provide for communication, transportation, medics, and other requirements.

AGs will be as autonomous as possible, within the guidelines of the action.

If you are considering blockading June 21st, please contact the LAG office with your name and AG name (if you already have one).

Site Description

Livermore Weapons Lab is located 33 miles southeast of Oakland. The lab is about one mile east of the town of Livermore. It is a large (several square miles) complex of buildings and open fields surrounded by a chain link fence. There are four main vehicle gates, and several pedestrian gates.

Going Limp

An important decision you will have to make is whether or not you will cooperate with police at the time of your arrest. If you decide to "go limp," you should be aware that there is a greater chance of being hurt. Here is some advice from people who have done it before:

• Try to make eye contact and communicate with the person arresting you.

• Try and situate yourself in a way that if you are dragged, you are dragged on your back and heels, instead of on your stomach and knees.

• While linking arms with AG members feels good to you, police have a tendency to view this as defiance, and are more likely to respond with force.

Mace, Dogs and Teargas

We don't expect authorities to use any of these, all of which are dispersal tactics to disrupt the blockade without arrests. However, they are a possibility.

Mace: Mace is an aerosol designed for use against an individual. It causes a burning sensation, particularly to the eyes. Mace victims should wash skin and eyes with a 5% Boric Acid solution, if possible.

Tear Gas: Tear gas is dispensed by helicopter, grenades, cannisters, or pistols. It causes intense tearing and irritation to the eyes. Effects usually disappear a few minutes after an individual is removed from the area. Treatment includes exposure to clean air, washing with plain water, or with mild salt water. Tear gas will affect a whole area, so authorities won't want to expose lab workers. Therefore, blockaders should be sure they are blockading workers.

Dogs: Extreme caution must be used. Remain calm and do not move. Dogs are trained to respond to motion. Make verbal contact with the officer commanding the dog.

The Livermore Community

The Livermore Liaison Collective formed because of our desire to communicate our purpose, concerns and goals to a community supported largely by Livermore Lab salaries. After much discussion with several members of the local community involved in the Nuclear Freeze, we did have supporters from Livermore at our February 1st blockade.

continued on next page

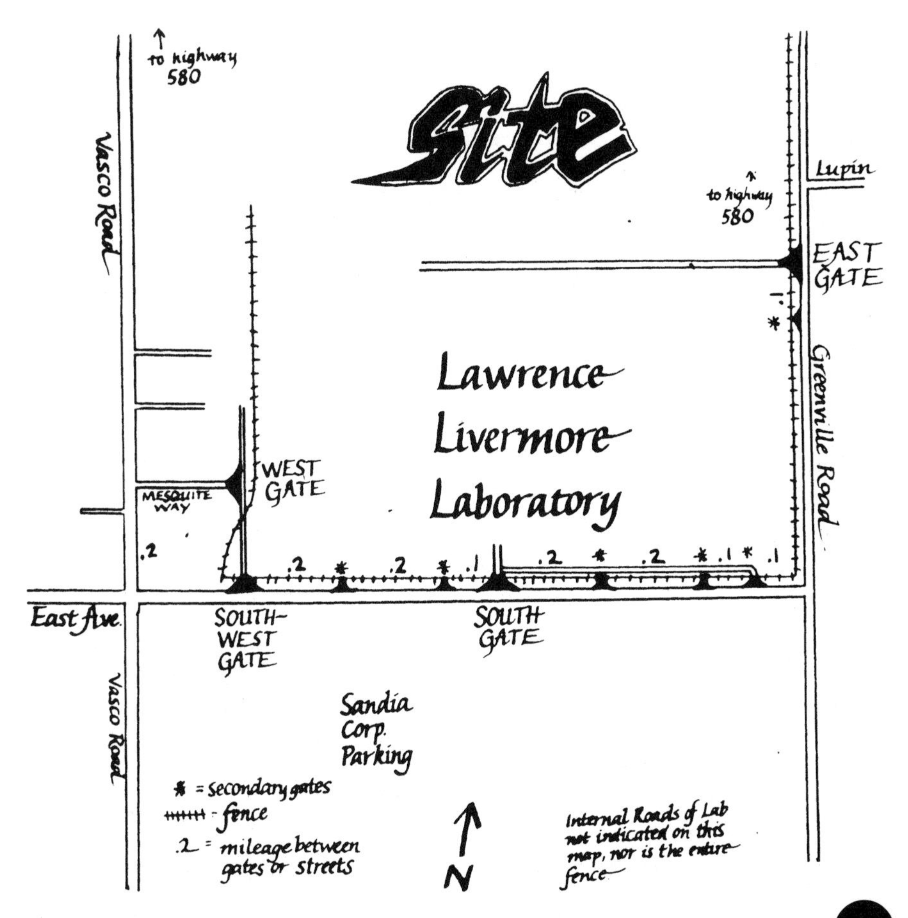

Juveniles: Join Us

We as juveniles have grown up under the threat of nuclear war. We have a right to a nuclear-free future. Through blockading the lab, we can show people in power that what they are doing is not all right with us, and that we will not sit passively and let them ruin our world.

We encourage juveniles to join us in the upcoming blockade. The major difference for juveniles are legalities. People under 18 will need a printed permission slip, signed by parent or guardian. This assures authorities you are not runaways, and authorizes someone to pick you up at juvenile hall. Forms can be obtained from the LAG office.

In past actions, punishment of minors has been light. At the February 1st blockade, the eight juveniles were immediately released to a designated adult.

By Life Squad, an all-kids affinity group.

Blockade Scenario

continued from preceding page

Unfortunately, those in the valley who support our strategy are not numerous. They are working in a community that thrives because of the lab, and therefore feels threatened by our activities.

Constructive dialogue with people in the community and with lab employees is a critical component of nonviolent civil disobedience. We must convey that we don't wish to destroy the lab and rob employees of jobs. Rather, we want the lab to pursue peaceful projects.

We encourage others to join us in opening the barriers and fears that the lab has created against us.

LEGAL

Our approach to the legal system is up to us. We retain as much power as we refuse to relinquish to the government.

The criminal "justice" system functions to alienate and isolate the accused individual, to destroy one's power and purposefulness, and to weave a web of confusion and mystification around any legal proceedings. Jail solidarity, non-

cooperation, and other forms of resistance can be used to reaffirm our position that we are not criminals and that we are taking positive steps toward freeing the world of nuclear terror.

The police may separate us from each other, breaking up affinity groups and possibly isolating individuals. We must develop an ability to deal with the legal system, while trusting in the solidarity of other demonstrators.

Possible Charges

647 — Blocking a public right-of-way. Misdemeanor punishable by up to 6 months in jails and/or $500 fine.

602 K & L — Trespass. Peaceable but wrongful entry on land of another, a misdemeanor punishable by up to 6 months in jail and/or $500 fine.

626.6 — Entry by non-student or non-employee on facility controlled by the U.C. Board of Regents which appears likely to interfere with activities carried on by the facility. First offense, up to 6 months in jail and/or $500 fine. Subsequent offenses carry mandatory jail sentences with no probation.

148—Resisting arrest. Persons who "go limp" may risk this additional charge. Misdemeanor punishable by up to one year in jail and/or $1000 fine.

182—Conspiracy to commit a misdemeanor. Felony punishable by up to five years in jail.

243 — Battery. Any physical contact with an officer. Felony punishable by 2-5 years in jail.

Infractions (traffic tickets) may also be used against some or all blockaders.

In addition, the court may choose to impose harsher sentences on repeat offenders. However, it is unusual for anyone to receive the maximum sentence.

The Legal Process

Police are not required to read you your rights unless you are being questioned. You have the right to remain silent. You are also entitled to confer with a lawyer before you say anything or agree to anything. LAG is organizing a volunteer legal collective for the blockade. Don't be afraid to ask for someone from the legal team if you are confused or need

continued on next page

Legal

continued from preceding page

clarification.

Booking: You will probably go through booking procedure. How much information you give is up to you. Some activists carry no ID and refuse to answer questions. Refusal to comply slows the process down considerably, which may or may not be desirable for the group as a whole.

Citing Out: Authorities may offer to let you go if you sign a citation release form promising that you will appear in court for arraignment. This is called being release O.R. ("Own Recognizance). Failure to appear will result in a bench warrant being issued against you. Because citing out tends to split up group solidarity, the individual decision to cite out should be carefully considered. Further, protesters who cite out may have their arraignments separate from those who remain in jail.

Arraignment: This is an appearance before a judge in which your charges will be read to you, and you will be asked to enter a plea. You will not be alone. Other protesters may be there with you, and lawyers for the action will be present. You are entitled to legal counsel before you plead. If protesters as a group disagree with the way the court wants to arraign you, there are ways of noncooperation (for example, muteness, refusal to enter a plea, to stand, or to speak to the judge). These measures may result in a contempt of court charge. It can be effective, but it is a gamble. You have the right to be arraigned within 48 hours of arrest, not counting weekends or holidays. However, in an "emergency," this right can be ignored.

Pleas: Defendants have the option of pleading not-guilty, guilty, or nolo contendre (no-contest). A not-guilty plea to a misdemeanor or felony leads to a jury trial (juries are not used for infractions).

Never plead guilty. A no-contest plea has the same consequence as a guilty plea as far as sentencing. However, this plea cannot be used as proof of guilt in case of a civil suit against blockaders, while a guilty plea can.

After a guilty or no-contest plea, you will be sentenced, either immediately or at a subsequent hearing. Immediate sentencing helps avoid unequal treatment.

Bail: At arraignment or before, the judge will either set bail or offer to release you on your own

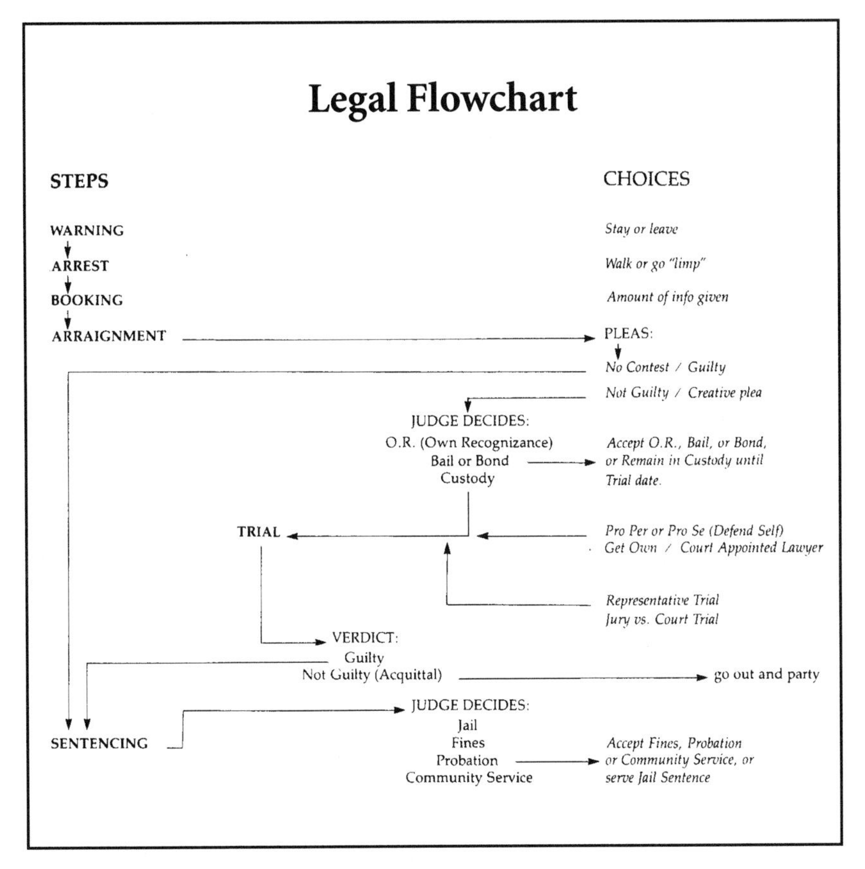

recognizance (O.R.). Bail guarantees your later appearance in court.

If you decline to post required bail, you will be returned to jail to await your next court date. Refusal of bail has been a general commitment of Livermore blockaders. Bail solidarity is a way of ensuring equal treatment to everyone, and ensuring that those who cannot pay are not left in jail.

Trials: The decision to follow through with a not guilty plea is a political one. A trial involves a major commitment of your time, energy and money. It could tie you up for months. For those who wish to plead not guilty, LAG legal workers will offer workshops. Some lawyers may be interested in representing groups of defendants in such cases.

Sentencing: Sentencing is discretionary with the judge, up to the statutory maximum. In lieu if jail or fines, the judge may offer probation, suspended sentence, or community service. LAG blockaders have refused to accept fines, probation or suspended sentences. Opposition to fines arises out of recognition that low-income defendants have no choice but to serve time in jail. Probation and suspended sentences are usually rejected for tactical reasons: they carry a condition that you not be arrested again during the prescribed period, or you risk a much more severe sentence.

Jail is a lonely place. It aims to weaken solidarity, to try to isolate people from each other and reduce one's concentration to dealing with the demands of authority and of one's survival.

You can expect overcrowding, which means frustrating and irritating levels of noise and distraction, little personal space or privacy, and scant regard for cleanliness.

Food will be starchy and dull (don't expect vegetarian menus).

You can expect a complete strip search, possibly including rectal and vaginal examination, which will be the first of many casual assaults on your dignity.

You will be constantly jerked around.

You will finally appreciate the play "Waiting for Godot."

Conflict Among Blockaders

People's motivations for participating in CD will affect their attitudes toward the police and jail guards. Some people blockade as a protest against the multiple structures in society which work together to create a weapons industry. The prison/judicial system is seen as one of these structures. Such people may refuse to cooperate with the authorities at all. Some of these acts serve as personal moral goals; others are initiated as levers to make the legal system mete out equal and fair sentences to all.

For others, blockading stems from fear and outrage over nuclear weapons. Often these people will stress the need to

communicate with the human beings behind the helmets, uniforms and roles. They will talk to police, perhaps befriend the prison guards, and try to use dialogue and persuasion to raise questions about these roles.

The differences between these two approaches will frequently lead to conflicts among blockaders. The stress of the jail situation tends to intensify conflict. Conflicts must be acknowledged and dealt with at the time, or they may become divisive. Conflict is an expression of opposing viewpoints and should not be confused with violence.

Guards

Guards have a great deal of power, and they are aware of this. Because they are human beings, this knowledge tends to have a bad effect on them.They expect the worst out of people. Their principle concern is to preserve order, which demands an atmosphere of unquestioning respect (fear) for authority, supplanting personal responsibility with obedience and submission.

You should not indulge them in their exalted self-image. Expect that they should act with respect and compassion and you may be surprised by the results. But don't forget, in the end, you and they have different jobs to perform. Let them be responsible for keeping order. You are responsible for keeping your conscience. It was your commitment to make decisions for yourself that landed you in jail in the first place, and it remains a good principle to live by, even in jail.

In Jail

• If you want something to happen, make it happen. Don't wait for someone else to think of it.

• Remain aware of how others are being treated, especially those who are "different" or assertive.

• Never point out someone to the guards.

• At all times, know the whereabouts of your AG members.

• Jail fosters dependence. Rely on your own and the group's thinking, and avoid automatically turning to the guards for help, permission, or information.

• Guards often create false crises. Don't be panicked. Take the time you need to meet and reach consensus.

General Population

Some blockaders have been placed in the general jail population and have witnessed the extremely poor conditions under which most inmates live. One primary goal of CD is to make incarceration of blockaders stressful for the government. However, we need to hamper the system as much as possible without negatively affecting the other inmates.

Some ways to minimize our effects on other inmates are:

• Respect that other inmates did not "choose" jail. This may mean avoiding playing around, and recognizing that other inmates don't have the same legal and political support that protesters have.

• Talk with other inmates as much as possible. Communication will increase their support for CD as well as our support for reform of jail conditions.

• Limit our phone calls, and agree to forego personal visits.

SOLIDARITY

The power of jail solidarity lies in two facts. (1) In a mass arrest situation, the authorities need our cooperation to process us. (2) It is expensive for the county to keep us in jail; thus we have great collective bargaining power.

At Livermore in February 1982, blockaders insisted on mass arraignment, equal sentencing for all, and no fines. Judge Lewis said that he wanted to impose a fine, but since blockaders had said they would stay in jail rather than pay a fine, he had no choice but to offer community service as a sentence.

Jail solidarity should not be coercive. If you must get out of jail to keep your job or to take care of your family, you are not breaking solidarity. However, if you cite out you are not assured that your sentence will be the same as for those who exercise collective bargaining.

Solidarity Demands

The following are issues around which solidarity has been exercised in the past:

No bail, no citing out. This keeps us together and in communication, at great expense to the County. As many people as possible should be prepared to stay in jail for as long as necessary to ensure equal and light treatment.

Equal treatment for all. The authorities know the power of our unity and may try to divide us. No one should be singled out for harsher treatment or isolation from the group. Everyone should receive the same sentence for similar actions, and inflated or unfair charges should be dropped.

Mass arraignment. This is the only way we can know for sure that our demands for equal treatment are being met.

We have not maintained jail solidarity with people who have outstanding warrants (pay your traffic tickets before blockading!)

Exercising Solidarity

Around jail conditions: Tactics can include not responding when names are called; all sitting or lying down; milling about; chanting. We can calmly surround a threatened brother or sister, physically protecting them from being taken away. In more extreme cases we can refuse food, or refuse to get dressed.

Regarding sentence demands: The most powerful tactic is to communicate

After It's Over

A large CD demonstration is a very powerful emotional experience. We are likely to be excited, tense, bored and exhausted at the same time.

After the 1981 Diablo demonstration, many of us returned home elated. But we were also very tired and lost. Although we felt very different, our friends, housemates and co-workers seemed to go on as if nothing had changed. We wanted to start work on new actions, but we were mentally and physically exhausted.

Things that may be useful in relieving post-action burnout:

• Plan your response to burnout with your AG before the action. Set a specific date to get together afterward.

• Get your AG together just to talk about the action. The story may need to be told numerous times— like oral history or ancient rituals.

• Make sure everyone gets lots of hugs and emotional support, including non-blockaders who worked hard on support tasks without reaping much of the glory.

• Give everyone (including yourself) the benefit of the doubt. Bickering and irrational behavior may just be temporary.

• After a few weeks or so, plan to work together on a small, easily accomplished task so people will feel useful, but not overwhelmed.

It may take as long to come down off an action as it took to prepare for it!

Solidarity

continued from preceding page

to the judge and DA that if our demands are not met, we will all plead not guilty, ask for individual jury trials, and not waive our right to a speedy trial. We can also refuse to go to arraignment

Be creative: Invent new tactics.

Don't abuse solidarity: Save it for when it really matters.

For solidarity to be effective, it must be addressed before reaching jail. Jail authorities won't wait patiently for us to reach consensus on solidarity before they start employing divide and conquer tactics to weaken our bargaining power.

Some issues that cause controversy include whether to keep solidarity with blockaders who have previous records, are on probation, or have not followed the nonviolence guidelines.

Fact and Fiction

This story is history. Every action is true. Every discussion has its basis in actual dialogs. Every love affair — well, we won't go into that here...

With a single exception (the Bush demo in Chapter Five), every major protest happened on the date ascribed. Some details have been moved to different dates to suit narrative needs. Discussions and interpersonal scenes are fictional, but the actions and topics discussed are true unless otherwise indicated here.

With two exceptions (the RPF and RWP, fictional composites of various Marxist parties, see Glossary), the affinity groups, clusters, and organizations named in the book are authentic. However, attributions of an action to a specific affinity group or cluster are often fictional.

This book is not biography. It is a history of a movement, not the story of specific individuals or affinity groups. Even more so, individuals in the photographs bear no consistent relation to the fictional characters.

The images, except for scenic shots and murals, are from the LAG archives or were loaned specially for this book. Many were not labeled, and some may be matched with the wrong action. No action or words should be linked to any specific individual based on the text, the photographs, or this appendix.

An updated list of changes can be found at www.directaction.org

In General

This history is based on memory, interviews, hundreds of stories in Direct Action newspaper, archival notes and materials, other news accounts, and interviews. Facts are true to the best memory and judgment of the author and others involved. Minor details may be mistaken, but the text can be taken as accurate in most respects, and can be used as the basis of future historical work — with the preceding caveat concerning its not being the biography of individuals or affinity groups.

Some 1980s jargon has been retained. The expressions "Blacks" and "Whites" were usual from the late 1960s through the early 1980s. "Gay" was sometimes used as an umbrella term for gay, lesbian, bisexual, and transgender people.

See Glossary for more on specific groups, actions, etc. See website for more details, links etc.

Direct Action #18, November-December 1984

Prologue / 1984

January 29 Consulate action as described, except all three consulates were co-ed actions, and there was not a separate faith-based action.

February 3 Fictional re-creation, topics true. DA articles true, some from different issues.

March 7 Fictional re-creation. Bank of America stencil true, c. 1984. "Who's illegal" graffiti true. Consulate wrap-up true, "no respect" interchange is from 1986.

April 3 Fictional re-creation, topics true, except A's did not open against Detroit that year.

April 16 Kissinger Demo is factual in all detail, as best as could be done with sometimes-conflicting accounts and memories. The flyer-quote at the top is a re-creation, but the facts in it are true. Not sure whether speech was for Commonwealth Club or some other group.

Chapter I / 1982

May 25 Tougher Targets demo and LAG office true.

June 20 Provo Park meeting true. The film called "Change of Heart," produced by Peter Adair and Associates, played on public TV under the title "Stopping History," but the cluster kept the original name, Change of Heart.

June 21 Action true, but not sure who other clusters at that gate were. Over 1300 arrests on June 21, and about 80 more on June 22, total arrests over 1400. Order of AGs is fictional. "Circle Chant," ©1982 Linda Hirschhorn, from *Roots and Wings,* Oyster Productions, Box 3929, Berkeley, CA 94703.

June 21-22 Jail, court true. For background info on Seabrook and Diablo Canyon, see *Political Protest & Cultural Revolution,* by Barbara Epstein. Deadheads for Peace not in Change of Heart at this point. Serially-torn novel true, probably not Vonnegut, although it should have been. Civil Rights story is a true incident, as is Wavy's story.

July 10 Fictional scene, all details true. Bible incident— narrative based on several conflicting interviews. Freight & Salvage now located in downtown Berkeley. Urban Ecology, see Glossary.

August 17 Fictional scene, topics true. La Peña description is the old mural, re-painted c. 1990. Old mural was by Anna DeLeon, Osha Neumann, Ray Patlan and O Brien Thiele of Commonarts. New mural is very similar. La Peña, 3105 Shattuck, Berkeley CA 94705.

Direct Action #19, February-March 1985

October 9 Livermore funeral march true, except flower sign actually read, "Bombs KiLLL" ("LLL" is a common abbreviation for Lawrence Livermore Lab). The St. Louis Cardinals did well in the playoffs that year, but ultimately lost the 1982 World Series to the Milwaukee Brewers.

October 28 Castro Street as described. Vandenberg and International Day planning probably accurate for this date, although specific meeting-date is invented. Berrigan visit true. Stop-sign action true, the signs were all over Berkeley for a while.

November 9 Patriotic Sing-In true, based on a Direct Action story. Not organized by Commie Dupes. Election results from memory, BCA probably got a majority on all bodies.

November 15 Livermore leafleting true, based on a Direct Action story. Direct Action discussions reflect actual stories. Pinball scene is an idealized re-creation.

Thanksgiving Day Ocean Beach as described. However, the windmill arms probably didn't turn at that time, and don't as of 2003. The Cliff House is being remodeled, and the Camera Oscura is threatened.

December 20 Fictional re-creation of Coordinating Council, which met every Monday night. Topics true, typical for this period. Not certain exactly when we learned of the MX test delay, but probably by this date. International Day Call, see full text in Appendix. Mobilization for Survival true. December 1982 religious actions — a wide variety of faith-based actions took place each December during the early 1980s (and on a smaller scale since). However, the 1982 specifics here are fictional.

January 2 La Peña meeting and Direct Action production true.

January 16 Fictional re-creation.

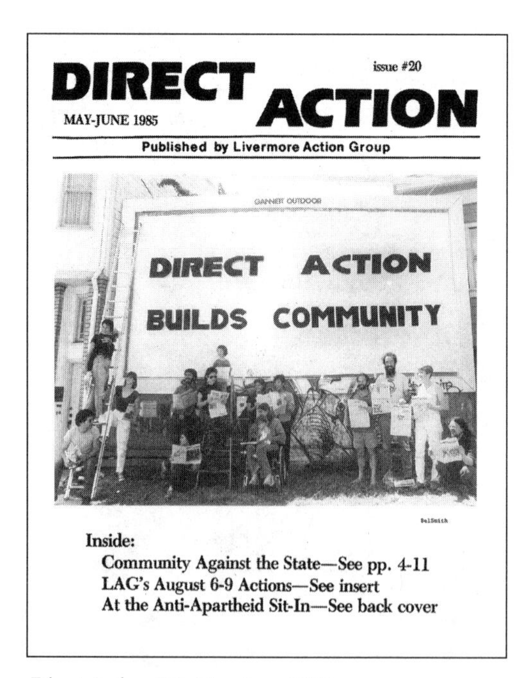

DIRECT ACTION

issue #20

MAY-JUNE 1985

Published by Livermore Action Group

Inside:

Community Against the State—See pp. 4-11
LAG's August 6-9 Actions—See insert
At the Anti-Apartheid Sit-In—See back cover

Direct Action #20, May-June 1985

Chapter II / 1983

January 23-24 Vandenberg action true. Chumash Indian ceremony true.Camp kitchen was coordinated by Turning Tide AG from Bolinas. Poll of affinity groups and clusters true, but details are fictional (although most or all AGs/clusters named were present). The numbers here are invented (except Change of Heart's). Meeting is stylized, but basically true. Action true.

January 28 Fictional scene, topics true.

January 29-30 Concord action true. Description of jail layout from memory. Marines attacking a protester based on hearsay, but probably true.

February 9 Direct Action production description true. Production was done by hand, with electric typewriters, scissors, and gluesticks, on folding tables in people's living rooms. Commie Dupes BART action occurred February 1, 1983.

March 5 Santa Cruz roller coaster true.

March 13 Fictional re-creation, topics true. Love and Rage reference fictional. People's History mural, located at Haste and Telegraph, by Osha Neumann and O Brien Thiele, repainted in the 1990s. People's Park is around the corner form the mural.

March 31 Vandenberg March action true, although exact dates and numbers are fuzzy for this action.

April 12 Fictional re-creation, topics true.

April 30 Fictional re-creation, all pinball references and discussion topics true.

May 22 Fictional re-creation, all details true, except Acorn and Sonomore Atomics references are fictional.

June 8 Vandenberg meeting true, not sure of exact date.

June 19 Vandenberg action true.

June 20 Livermore action true. Truck scene mostly fictional.

June 22-July 1 Livermore action, all incidents and details true unless noted here. Some events may be on incorrect dates, and some sequences are hazily remembered or based on conflicting accounts. More than 1100 arrests on June 20 (early media reports of 800 were incorrect). About 50 more June 22, total about 1200 arrests. Tents, portajohns, chow as described. Dimensions from memory. "Swords to Plowshares" passage from Isaiah 2:4. "We are the Power" chant by Starhawk. Gay Pride parade true, but details are hazy. Baseball radio story true, but specific game fictional. Escape plan true, but not executed. However, one man allegedly did escape from the tents, according to a story remembered years later by someone in his affinity group. Peace Flag true, unsure which day. Many attributions of actions to specific AGs are fictional, although the events and the AG names are both true. Example: "Thousand Cranes by Acorn Cluster." The event happened as described, and Acorn Cluster was present — but attribution of the action to Acorn Cluster is fictional.

Direct Action #21, Summer 1985

Chapter III / 1983

July 4 Jail exit is a reconstruction.

July 8 Fictional scene, topics true. "Strategy Proposal" was actually named the "Campaign Proposal," but otherwise as described.

July 24 Fictional scene, topics true.

July 25-28 Santa Rita events true, not sure of exact dates. Some memories, especially visuals, are hazy. Santa Rita barracks have been torn down, replaced with a Big Brother high-tech jail similar to the one described in the January 1983 Concord action. Lightbulb incident conflates jail incident with a similar set of interactions on Telegraph Avenue in Berkeley. Gabe's story true, from January 1983 Concord action. Kafka is fictional, actual book was Heidegger, which was even drearier. McDonald's is true. "The Minimum Wage" is by the Funky Nixons, to the tune of Hank Williams' "Move It On Over." From the CD, *Still Not Crooks.* Available for $12 postpaid, visit www.groundworknews.org/funkynixons or write GroundWork, PO Box 141414, San Francisco, CA 94114.

August 5 Fictional scene, topics true. BARF 1983, organized by BCA, was rained out. Line-up is fictional, but typical of the period, except Funky Nixons formed in 1990 (see July 25 listing above).

August 22 LAG Congress is a fictional re-creation, topics true.

August 27 Russian River is a fictional re-creation, based on Summer 1985 expedition. Visual memories hazy. For Sonoma outdoors, visit www.sonomacounty.org

September 17 Fictional re-creations, topics true.

September 30 Fictional scene, topics true. Labyrinths at Sibley Park, Oakland.

October 21 Fictional re-creation, topics and details true. Spanish NATO action from c. 1988, when Spain joined NATO. Pinball references, nukecycle true. "Cubeland" c. 1989.

October 24 Euromissiles protest true. Route and specific affinity group actions are fictional re-creations and borrowings from other protests. Direct Action reported 72 arrests. "40 men" is approximate. Embarcadero Plaza described as post-1989 earthquake, without the old bi-level freeway. Nukecycle, Peace Dragon true. Tax resister skit from 1984. Uncle Sam and Betsy Ross from c. 1991. Punks true, but punk AG names might be from a bit later. Gandhi from June 1983 Livermore blockade. "No route map" was typical of later City protests, not sure on this one. "Nukes are a Drag" from c. 1985. Drummers, at least as an organized corps, more typical after 1985. Dancing in the streets true. Die-ins true, tactic borrowed from London "Stop the City" protests of c. 1982-83. Youth Wells Fargo action true, not sure of AG names. BARF, see August 5 above. World Series, no game on Saturday, as Baltimore had defeated Phillies in five games. Iwo Jima action from Spring 1984.

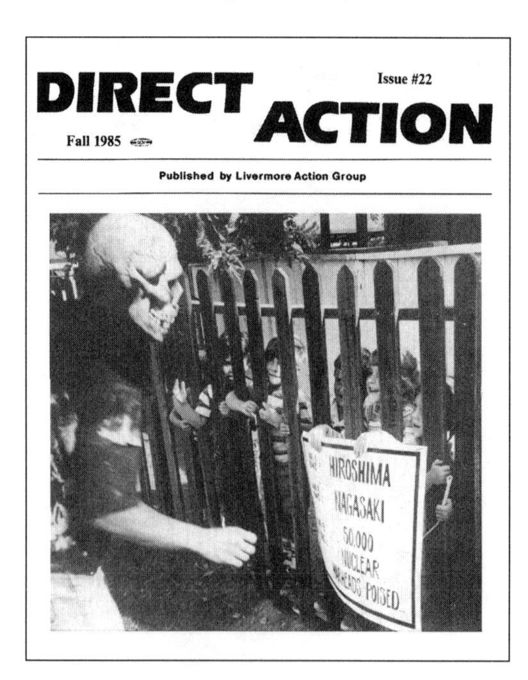

Direct Action #22, Fall 1985

October 25 Grenada invasion and protest true, crowd numbers are estimates. Country Joe, "Screw this!" incident from 1991 Gulf War. Country Joe's classic song, "Feel Like I'm Fixin' To Die Rag," is featured on the on the *Woodstock* album and film.

November 4 Fictional re-creation, topics true. Graffiti action from c. 1987.

November 21 Fictional re-creation, topics true. ERN/Enola Gay true.

Thanksgiving Day Fictional scene, topics true. Mobilization for Survival true.

December 6 Fictional scene, topics true. Garden graffiti from 1998. Beetle Bailey graffiti from Spring 1984, by Apollinaire.

December 11 Fictional re-creation, topics and decisions true. People's Convention true, but RWP is fictional composite of several groups. Actual initiating group for PC was Communist Workers' Party, which dissolved around 1985.

December 22 Fictional scene, topics true.

Chapter IV / 1984

January 7 Fictional re-creation, topics true. Consulate, see Prologue, first scene. Diablo, see glossary. Emergency Response Network was initiated, and many AGs signed up. But Reagan backed off his Central America adventurism, and the ERN was never activated. Later that year, faith-based groups started a national Pledge of Resistance campaign, see Glossary. Balmy Alley true, first painted around this time. Some murals are from later. Romero mural, "Una Ley Inmoral," ©1996 by Juana Alicia, acrylic on wood, nine by twelve feet. Balmy Alley and many other San Francisco murals coordinated by Precita Eyes Mural Arts Center, (415) 285-2311, pem@precitaeyes.org

January 13 Fictional scene, topics true.

January 14 Fictional scene.

January 28 Livermore Peace Lab true. First camp closed in late February. Camp re-opened for two months in Fall 1984, and spawned the Livermore-based Tri-Valley CAREs group (see Glossary).

February 10 Fictional scene, topics true. All sites true. Oregon weapons train action true, around this time (called "White Trains"). Siena Cathedral true.

February 18 Diablo wedding true. Banner action true, different date, not all Deadheads.

February 29 Fictional scene, topics true. Blast Pass, war tax rally, Direct Action layouts, Bit o' Honey all true, dates approximate.

March 4 Fictional scene, topics true. Cal campus true.

Direct Action #23, January-February 1986

March 16 USA Today action true, around this time. Stencil from different action. B of A graffiti, see Prologue, third scene. Burned box around this time. "Disarmament Dividends" was a popular phrase of the time. Logging-road protests true. Nukecycle true. Infiltrator fears true, Alliance for Survival story based on hearsay but likely true.

March 23 Fictional scene, topics true. Ashkenaz is located at San Pablo at Gilman. BARF true, see glossary.

April 2 Fictional re-construction, topics true. Bumper stickers true. Kissinger true, see Prologue, final scene. April Fool's true, broken arm may have been a different demo.

April 13 Fictional scene, topics true.

April 18 Fictional scene, topics true. Windows true. Kissinger, see Prologue, final scene.

April 20 Good Friday is a composite of various Good Friday and Christian actions at Livermore. Nailing the cross true. Summaries of actions true, numbers approximate. Kissinger cop-tire story true. For May 22, see Chapter V.

Chapter V / 1984

May 22 Financial District demo is a composite re-creation of true demo, with details from various protests 1984-1986. Many details based on a Spring 1986 protest. B of A from 1986. Well Fargo from 1986, office at 464 California, stagecoach true (stagecoach still there, please do not climb on it). McDonald's from August 1985 "Happening," based on hearsay. Spiral Dance ending not typical of this period, but possible. More usual from about 1990, and quite common c. 2000. Shopping chant c. 1991.

Direct Action #24, Spring 1986

June 8 Fictional re-creation, topics true. Nicaragua true, but campfire songs are from an activist's trip to a rebel camp in El Salvador about the same time.

June 10 Fictional re-creation, topics true. Action round-up all true, good summary in June 1984 Direct Action. *Nuclear Resister,* www.nonviolence.org/nukeresister, (520) 323-8697.

June 12 Fictional scene, topics true. Bound Together, 1369 Haight Street near Masonic. Mural from mid-1990s, "Remembering American Anarchism," by Susan Greene, quote by San Francisco writer Peter Plate. All demos true, as accurately as possible. Motorcycle burning is a composite of several incidents 1978-1992. "Back to zero" from Fall 1984. "Free speech" quote from Utah Phillips.

June 15 Bush demo from 1988, when Bush the Elder won the presidency. A similar demo against Secretary of Defense Casper Weinberberger happened in Spring 1984, from which some details are taken. Noses from 1988. Barricades typical 1984-1991. Cable cars true. Cops grabbing punks c. 1987. Nukecycle steering true. Union Square has been remodeled.

June 18 Fictional scene, topics true.

June 25 Fictional re-creation, topics true. Graffiti true, around this time. Concord back-country true, around this time.

July 1 Fictional re-creation, topics true. Vacuum true. Jesse Jackson campaign connection true, see Glossary.

July 4 Fictional re-construction. Mime Troupe opens their season on July 4 in Dolores Park every year. Visit www.sfmt.org. Shopping cart calisthenics from a later show. Modern Times is at 888 Valencia near 20th Street, not far from Dolores Park.

July 9 Fictional re-construction, topics true. ERN and Pledge true, see Glossary. Monitors debate true, around this time. Shakespeare speech from *Hamlet* III.i.

July 10 Fictional scene.

July 12 Moral Majority demo re-construction based on interviews and Direct Action story. Mainstream press reports of this action are inconsistent, inaccurate. Kissing Feminists true, probably on this date, story in Direct Action. Reactionary slogan "family values" from slightly later. March to Union Square may be from a different protest. Undercovers true of this period. Limo-hop will happen someday (it is the only incident in the entire book that is taken from the future). Limo-flipoff from mid-1980s, in Berkeley.

July 14 People's Convention is a fictional re-construction, all People's Convention details true. See Glossary for more on People's Convention.

July 15 Fictional scene, topics true.

July 16 People's Convention is a fictional re-creation of the day, all events true, numbers approximate, participating groups typical of the 1980s. Hunter S. Thompson quote from the June 1972 chapter of "Fear & Loathing 1972." People's Convention plenary true. John Deere hat true, or something like it. March true, not sure about dynamics of "take the street." Nukecycle, tractors true. Earth First! probably anachronistic at this date. March fizzle-out true. Confrontation not so definite as shown here. War Chest Tours summary true.

July 17 Fictional reconstruction of the day, all events true.

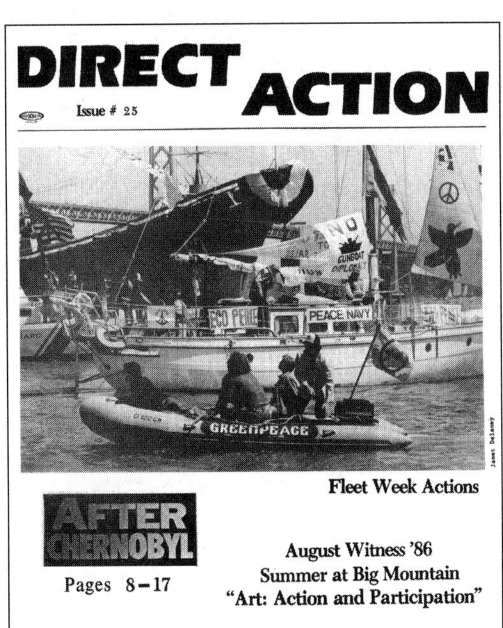

Direct Action #25, Fall 1986

Press release true, computer may be anachronistic. Central America march and theater true. Crosses with names of dead from 1985. At LAG demo, right-wingers actually were carrying an effigy of Jesse Jackson. News cameras true, not sure of stations. "Minimum Wage" and "Screw the Rich" by the Funky Nixons, on their CD, *Still Not Crooks.* Available for $12 postpaid, visit www.groundworknews.org/funkynixon or write GroundWork.

July 18 War Chest Tour true, route is reconstructed. Get Out of Jail Free from c. 1991. "News whores" c. 1988. Some details from other demos 1984-1988.

July 19 All events true, based on interviews, news accounts, with details from other demos of this era. War Chest Tour true. Rock Against Reagan true, specific songs fictional but likely. RAR also performed at the Republican Convention that year. March to Hall of Justice true. Approximate numbers of marchers and arrestees correct, arrests roughly as described. Almost everyone arrested at the Democratic Convention had their charges dropped after the first people put on trial were acquitted by San Francisco juries. Car incident c. 1985. Initiation stories true, colors c. 1998, rappelling c. 1985. Unarrest action from October 1987 protest at Oakland Airport, including MVP. "I'm ready to get arrested" from 1987. Paddywagon from 1997, including "Always Look On the Bright Side of Life," song from Monty Python's film *Life of Brian.*

Chapter VI / 1984

July 26 Fictional scene, topics true. Screens true.

August 2 Fictional scene, topics true. Cal campus true, but brick building is next door to the Philosophy Building.

August 8 Fictional scene, topics true. Bohemian Grove action true. Bohemian Grove Action Network still organizes protests of the annual gathering — for more information visit www.sonomacountyfreepress.com. Contempt story true, but only one person in this case. Five other men received five-day sentences for contempt at a 1984 Livermore court hearing. Thirty-day sentences approximate. Republican Convention actions true, about 130 arrests, according to Direct Action. Karina arrest, see next scene.

August 29 Action is true in detail, based on interviews. Eventual sentence was two years in federal prison.

September 22 BARF true overall. Smash Nancy's China, the piñata, water balloons, volleyball, lots of dancing, Starry Plough selling beer, Mayor Gus Newport speaking, Wavy Gravy as MC, all true. Many other details from LAG and related rallies of this period, especially from BARC in the Park, 1985. Nukecycle true, but happened at a Mime Troupe show, not quite so dramatic. Ron-Off from 1985. Zulu Spear played at Ashkenaz regularly in later 1980s. Anarchist Coffeehouse true, happened almost monthly from late 1984 through about 1989, then sporadically for a couple of more years. PG&E reactor from 1990 Earth Day march. Funky Nixons formed 1990, included several former LAGers, see July 17 listing just above for contact info. Nevada Test Site true, huge protests in later 1980s, with many LAGers in the organizing groups. Nevada Desert Experience still active as of 2003, (702) 646-4814, www.nevadadesertexperience.org (in the 1980s, the group was known as Lenten Desert Experience). Food Not Bombs' participation in BARF is fictional and anachronistic. FNB started in Boston/Cambridge in 1981. The San Francisco chapter started in the later 1980s, and hundreds of people (including many from Abalone, LAG, and VAC) were arrested in the ensuing years of harrassment. The Berkeley/Oakland chapter formed during the Gulf War in early 1991 and was at the center of the defense of People's Park in 1991-92. These and many other FNB groups are active as of this writing, visit www.foodnotbombs.net

September 24 Livermore/Sandia true, 94 total arrests, according to later LAG timeline. Sandia action true. "We're only fighting" from c. 1983.

October 16 Fictional scene. Café Med, Moe Moskowitz, and Julia Vinograd as described. Moe's Books is across the street. Julia's poems are available on Telegraph Avenue. Coming-out story based on 1987 events.

October 27 Spiral Dance generally true. Valencia Street between 16th and 17th as described, description includes spots on both sides of street, but don't worry, there's plenty more. Women's Building, 18th Street near Valencia, as described. Contact www.womensbuilding.org, (415) 431-1180. "Maestrapeace" mural repainted c. 1990 by the Maestrapeace Art Works collective, www.maestrapeace.com. Karina wrap-up true, two-year sentence. Ritual description based on various Reclaiming rituals 1984-2002. The Spiral Dance ritual has taken place in San Francisco nearly every year since 1979 (continuously since the mid-1980s). For more on rituals and magical work, see *The Spiral Dance* by Starhawk. Dancing comes after the God invocation, not the Ancestors (so be ready). "Goddess Song/No End to the Circle" by Starhawk. "Cycles of the Moon" by George Franklin. "Let It Begin" by Starhawk, Lauren Gale, and Amber-Khan-Engel. "Set Sail" by Starhawk and Mara June Quicklightening. All lyrics previously copyrighted and used with permission. Reclaiming, contact www.reclaiming.org, PO Box 14404, San Francisco, CA 94114. Reclaiming publishes a magazine, *Reclaiming Quarterly*, which has featured the works of numerous former LAGers. Same address, or quarterly@reclaiming.org. Siena Cathedral true. For more information and photos of Siena, visit www.terresiena.it

Moon phases — all moon phases in the book are correct.

That's all, folks!

The Direct Action collective pulled off a daring daylight billboard alteration.

Graphics Credits

Many thanks to all of these artists for their generous contribution to our work!

Front Cover Brian Crowley
Back Cover Ted Sahl
8 Unknown*
13 Unknown*
15 Rachel Gertrude Johnson
16 Keith Michael Holmes
17 Ted Sahl
18 George Franklin
19 courtesy Mark McDonald
21 America Narcoleptic
22 America Narcoleptic
23 America Narcoleptic
24 Unknown*
25 Keith Michael Holmes

Prologue

31 belsmith
32 belsmith
35 belsmith
45 Sheila Harrington
46 Virginia Frantz
50 Unknown*
53 Darren Ching
55 America Narcoleptic
56 Keith Michael Holmes
56 Keith Michael Holmes
57 Keith Michael Holmes
58 Keith Michael Holmes
59 Keith Michael Holmes
61 Bette Lee
62 Keith Michael Holmes
64 Keith Michael Holmes
65 Keith Michael Holmes
66 Keith Michael Holmes
67 Keith Michael Holmes
69 Unknown*

Chapter I

71-74 — see those pages
76 Unknown*
77 Unknown*
79 Unknown*
80 Unknown*
81 Unknown*
82 Unknown*
83 Ron Delaney*
84 Unknown*
85 Bay Guardian
86 Bette Lee
87 Bette Lee
88 Ted Sahl
89 Nita Winter
90 Ted Sahl
91 Keith Michael Holmes
106 Heather Hafleigh*
111 Doris Bowles*
117 Karen Kerschen*
120 Lana Fisher*
121 belsmith (graffiti)
121 Eldred (billboards)
126 Darren Ching
129 Steve Stallone
130 Unknown*
131 Ted Sahl
133 Bette Lee
133 Steve Stallone
134 Bette Lee
140 Unknown*
141 Unknown*
143 Unknown*
149 Lana Fisher*
150 Unknown*
151 Unknown*
154 George Franklin
156 George Franklin
157 George Franklin
160 Rafael Jesús González
163 Unknown*
165 Julian Riklon*
168 Unknown*
171 Klatu*
172 Virginia Frantz

Chapter II

175-178 — see those pages
180 Unknown*
181 Unknown*
182 Unknown*
183 Unknown*
184 Bob Thawley
187 Ted Sahl
188 Unknown*
190 Ken Nightingale
191 America Narcoleptic
192 Ted Sahl
193 Bette Lee (2)
193 Bette Lee
193 Ted Sahl
194 Ted Sahl
194 Bette Lee
197 Unknown*
204 Unknown*
207 Unknown*
209 Bette Lee
210 Unknown*
211 Bette Lee
223 Bette Lee
225 Commie Dupes AG
235 Steve Nadel
237 It's About Times
238 Ted Sahl
239 Ted Sahl
241 Bob Van Scoy*
242 George Franklin
249 Unknown*
251 Pat Goudvis*
252 Unknown*
255 Unknown*
259 Janet Delaney
262 Unknown*
264 Darren Ching
265 René Castro
266 Keith Michael Holmes
266 Ted Sahl
266 Keith Michael Holmes
267 Ken Nightingale
267 Janet Delaney
267 Virginia Frantz
268 Keith Michael Holmes
269 Unknown*
270 Unknown*
276 Unknown*
279 Unknown*
281 Jim Doe*
282 Unknown*
284 Unknown*
286 Doris Bowles*
288 Ted Sahl
291 Doris Bowles*
297 Doris Bowles*
298 Doris Bowles*
303 Doris Bowles*
307 Unknown*
308 Jim Doe*
311 Jim Doe*
314 Doris Bowles*
317 Unknown*
324 Doris Bowles*
325 Doris Bowles*
332 Unknown*

Chapter III

335-338 — see those pages
340 belsmith
347 Ken Nightingale
371 George Franklin
372 Unknown*
375 Unknown*
377 Sonoma Tourist Bureau
381 Unknown*
382 Fern Feldman
389 Darren Ching
389 Unknown*
389 Martha Fox*
392 Darren Ching
393 Unknown*
394 Darren Ching
396 Ted Sahl
396 Janet Delaney
397 Unknown*
398 Brian Crowley
398 Brian Crowley
399 Brian Crowley

** All images are from the LAG Archives, or were loaned especially for this book. Most photos and images used with permission. Some credits on archival images were missing, and some known artists (marked with an asterisk) could not be located. If you know the whereabouts of any of these missing artists, please contact info@groundworknews.org or (415) 255-7623 — thanks!*

400 Brian Crowley
401 Rachel Gertrude Johnson
402 Rachel Gertrude Johnson
403 Ted Sahl
404 Keith Michael Holmes
405 Ted Sahl
406 Bob Thawley
407 Rachel Gertrude Johnson
410 Ted Sahl
411 Brian Crowley
413 Keith Michael Holmes
419 Unknown*
420 Bette Lee
424 Bette Lee
425 Unknown*
426 Jack Davis
426 Jack Davis
429 Keith Michael Holmes
429 Bob Thawley
438 Tom Frideg*
441 Keith Michael Holmes
442 Unknown*
449 George Franklin

Chapter IV

451-454 — see those pages
458 George Franklin
459 George Franklin
464 Unknown*
465 Unknown*
468 Ted Sahl
468 Ted Sahl
469 Ted Sahl
470-473 George Franklin
476 Azienda di Turismo, Siena
479 Ted Sahl
480 Unknown*
484 Commie Dupes AG
486 Unknown*
488 George Franklin
491 Francis Arouet*
495 Brian Crowley
495 Brian Crowley
500 George Franklin
505 George Franklin
507 Commie Dupes AG
510 Martha Fox*
519 Unknown*
520 Ted Sahl
520 Ted Sahl
520 Ted Sahl
521 Bette Lee
521 Bette Lee

Chapter V

525-528— see those pages
531 America Narcoleptic
533 Keith Michael Holmes
534 Bob Thawley
534 Bob Thawley
536 Keith Michael Holmes
537 Ted Sahl
538 Keith Michael Holmes
540 Keith Michael Holmes
551 George Franklin
552 M. Collins+
557 Unknown*
561 Unknown*
565 Keith Michael Holmes
566 Unknown*
573 Keith Michael Holmes
574 Unknown*
577 Martha Fox*
583 Darren Ching
593 Unknown*
600 Bob Thawley
602 Bob Thawley
603 Unknown*
608 Keith Michael Holmes
608 Keith Michael Holmes
609 Keith Michael Holmes
609 Keith Michael Holmes
611 Unknown*
612 Unknown*
615 Bob Thawley
616 Unknown*
617 Rachel Gertrude Johnson
618 Bob Thawley
619 Keith Michael Holmes
621 Bob Thawley
622 Ted Sahl
625 Bette Lee
627 Bette Lee
628 Unknown*
631 Keith Michael Holmes
632 Bette Lee
634 Unknown*
634 Bette Lee
637 Unknown*
638 Unknown*

Epilog

646 BGAN
647 BGAN
648 Chris Rossi
649 Chris Rossi
656 Darren Ching (poster)
656 Paul Bloom (graffiti)
657 City Of Berkeley
658 Mark McDonald
660 Rachel Gertrude Johnson
661 Unknown*
662 courtesy Mark McDonald
663 Michael E. Bry/SFMT
663 Michael E. Bry/SFMT
665 Unknown*
666 courtesy Mark McDonald
668 Urban Stonehenge
669 Steve Nadel
672 Darren Ching
674 Ted Sahl
675 Ted Sahl (2)
678 Tori Woodard
679 George Franklin
680 George Franklin
691 Azienda di Turismo, Siena
699 Unknown*
699 Ilka Hartmann

Handbook

Handbook graphics are from the handbooks. Artists unknown unless noted here*

H-1 Darren Ching
H-2 Darren Ching
H-5 Darren Ching
H-10 Osha Neumann (top)
H-11 Osha Neumann
H-13 Peg Averill*
H-15 Peg Averill*
H-16 Peg Averill*
H-18 Peg Averill*
H-19 Peg Averill*
H-20 Bulbul
H-21 Jan Mazur
H-22 Rini Templeton
H-23 Peg Averill*
H-26 Darren Ching (pic)
H-28 Osha Neumann
H-33 Hal Asua*

Appendices

736 Tori Woodard
737 Chris Rossi*
738 belsmith
739 belsmith
739 Bette Lee (2)
739 Ted Sahl
740 Unknown*
741 Allie Light*
742 Big Mountain Support*
743 Janet Delaney
745 belsmith
747 Unknown*
750-751 Various Artists
752 Rafael Jesús González
753 Unknown*
754 Rafael Jesús González
758 Leslie McIntyre*
759 Ted Sahl
760 Unknown*
762 Unknown*
763 Unknown*
764 Darren Ching
765 Unknown*
766 Darren Ching
767 Chris Rossi*
768 Brian Crowley
Back Cover Ted Sahl

German anti-nuclear activists deliver their message to police on a blockade line.

Appendices at www.directaction.org

Even with 768 pages, we couldn't begin to fit everything into this book. So we had to fall back on the internet. Here's a quick guide to the resources you'll find online. If one of these intrigues you and you have absolutely no internet access, send a carrier pigeon to GroundWork, PO Box 14141, San Francisco, CA 94114.

- **Handbook** in printable PDFs — download and print the pages you want
- **Study guide** in printable PDFs — free downloads
- **Direct Action newspaper** — PDF versions of selected pages
- **Photos** — additional photos, color versions of murals, more posters and flyers
- **Stories** — additional actions and narratives posted by readers
- **Discussions and actions** — out-takes, bloopers, alternate scenes, unedited versions
- **Get-involved resources** — books, websites, music, publications, events
- **Bulk discounts** — ordering information and discount schedule

Other Books About LAG

- Barbara Epstein, *Political Protest and Cultural Revolution*
- Starhawk, *Dreaming the Dark, Walking to Mercury, Webs of Power*
- Jim Martin, *1984: The Summer of Hate (from Flatlands Books, see Resources, next page)*
- Susan Moon & Jackie Cabasso, *Risking Peace: Why We Sat in the Road (from Western States Legal Foundation, see Glossary)*

If we missed any books, please let us know for future reprints. Contact info@directaction.org, PO Box 14141, San Francisco, CA 94114.

Bay Area Resources

- ***Bay Guardian*** — free at news boxes, or www.sfbg.com
- ***Street Spirit*** — $1 on East Bay streets
- **San Francisco Mime Troupe** shows — visit www.sfmt.org
- **Radio** — KPFA (94.1 FM), Berkeley Liberation Radio (104.1 FM), KPOO (89.5 FM)
- **The Long Haul** info shop, 3124 Shattuck Ave (near Woolsey), Berkeley, CA 94705
- **Bound Together** anarchist bookstore, 1369 Haight (at Masonic), San Francisco, CA 94117
- **Modern Times** bookstore, 888 Valencia (near 20th), San Francisco, CA 94110
- **Livermore organizing** — see Glossary for Tri-Valley CAREs and Western States Legal

Study and Action Guide

Whether you are an affinity group, a class, a study group, an activist organization, or a circle of friends, this guide moves from reading to discussion to action.

- Chapter-by-chapter guide for developing and applying the issues rasied in the book. Whether you're organizing a revolution or a Solstice ritual (or both), these discussions will shed new light on your work.
- Less talk, more action — local organizing, right where you live, is built into the sessions.
- Ways to share leadership and equalize power within the group.
- Activist, cultural, and legal resources.

Download free printable PDFs from the website. $3 each in print (order one and make copies). Free with five or more books to the same address. Visit www.directaction.org/guide, or contact GroundWork, PO Box 14141, San Francisco, CA 94114.

Resources

Here's a brief guide. A longer list is posted online at www.directaction.org

- **Indy Media**, outstanding user-posted source of grassroots news and photos. Visit www.indymedia.org for links to local sites.
- **Food Not Bombs**, serving free food and building community since 1981. For local groups contact www.foodnotbombs.net, (520) 770-0575.
- **Earth First!** No compromise in defense of Mother Earth, from educational work to tree-sits. Contact www.earthfirst.org, and check out their magazine, *Earth First! Journal*, www.earthfirstjournal.org, PO Box 3023, Tucson, AZ 85702.
- **Precita Eyes Mural Arts Center** is an artists' consortium which coordinates murals and other artwork in San Francisco, particularly in its home neighborhood, the Mission. Contact (415) 285-2311, pem@precitaeyes.org
- **Reclaiming**, an international community of women and men committed to Witchcraft and magical activism. *Reclaiming Quarterly* features reporting on grassroots activism. Contact www.reclaiming.org, PO Box 14404, San Francisco, CA 94114, (415) 339-8150.
- ***The Nuclear Resister*** supports imprisoned anti-nuclear and anti-war activists, and has offered great activist news since 1980. Contact www.nonviolence.org/nukeresister, (520) 323-8697.
- **Art & Revolution** is a collective of artists and activists who revitalize political protest by bridging creative culture with struggles for social justice. A&R brings dance, music, theater, and giant puppets to the streets to bring attention to the critical issues of our times. Contact www.artandrevolution.org
- **Flatlands Books** provides a unique range of nonfiction titles by mail order. Many are unavailable elsewhere, on topics such as suppressed science, the global corporate state, Wilhelm Reich and orgone, mind control, conspiracy, UFOs, lodge brothers, and secret societies. Contact www.flatlandbooks.com, (707) 964-8326 (9-5 Pacific Time).
- **"Free Speech Radio" and "Democracy Now"** shows appear on many community radio stations across North America.

LAG Discography

LAG never reached consensus on its authorized soundtrack, but here are some essential works that will provide a suitable backdrop for reading this book.

Direct Action Production

Various Artists *Soweto Street Sounds*
Ferron *Shadows on a Dime*
Sunny Adé *Juju Music; Live Juju*
Fela Kuti *Live in Amsterdam, Beasts of No Nation*
Grateful Dead *American Beauty, Workingman's Dead*
Bob Marley *Exodus, Uprising*
Sweet Honey in the Rock
Various Artists *Zimbabwe Frontline*

Jeff's Faves

Ferron *Testimony, Not a Still Life*
Bessie Smith
John Lee Hooker *Real Folk Blues*
Talking Heads *Songs About Buildings*

Patti Smith *Horses, Radio Ethiopia*
Woody Guthrie
Muddy Waters *Chess Hits*
Sex Pistols
Elvis *Gold Hits*
Doc Watson

Pinball Classics

The Rolling Stones
The Who
Jimi Hendrix
The Beatles
Bob Dylan
Creedence Clearwater Revival
Grateful Dead *Steal Your Face*
Woodstock *Soundtrack*

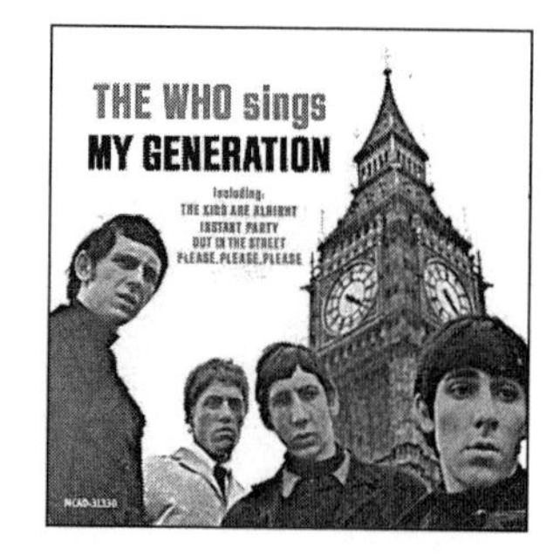

DJ Milhous has threatened to make mixtapes of this music — visit www.directaction.org for info

Raoul's Mix

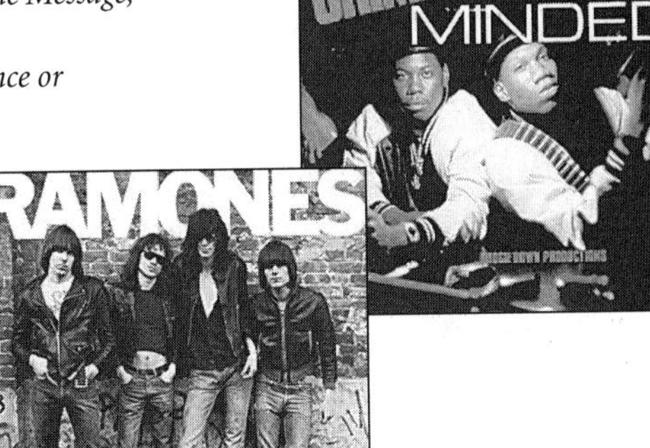

Grandmaster Flash & Melle Mel *The Message, Beat Street*

Dead Kennedys *Give Me Convenience or Give Me Death*

Boogie Down Productions *Criminal Minded*

MDC *Millions of Dead Cops, Multi-Death Corporations*

Run DMC *Run DMC*

The Ramones

Black Uhuru *Brutal Dub*

The Clash *The Clash, London Calling*

Odds & Ends

John Coltrane

Thelonious Monk

Linda Hirschhorn *Roots & Wings*

Dave Lippman *No Sale*

Utah Phillips

Holly Near

John Trudell *Aka Graffiti Man*

Funky Nixons *Still Not Crooks*

Holly's Music

Sukay *Return of the Inca*

Inti Illimani

Reclaiming *Let It Begin Now: Music of the Spiral Dance*

G. S. Sachdev *Full Moon*

Miriam Makeba

Lata Mangeshkar *Golden Voices of Indian Film*

Bedtime

Josquin Des Prez

Guillaume Dufay *Missa Se La Face*

Joseph Haydn *Cello Concertos*

Giovanni Pierluigi da Palestrina *Missa Papae Marcelli, Missa Hodie Christus Natus Es*

J. S. Bach *Cantatas, Cello Suites, Christmas Oratorio*

A CALL FOR

INTERNATIONAL DAY OF NUCLEAR DISARMAMENT

JUNE 20, 1983

PROPOSAL:

A day of coordinated local actions around the world to resist nuclear arms and power, militarism, intervention, and their social and ecological consequences. People will use whatever nonviolent means they think appropriate—civil disobedience, strikes, marches, vigils, demonstrations, individual initiatives, etc.

OBJECTIVES:

To further the causes of 1) global nuclear disarmament, 2) demilitarization and non-intervention, 3) equitable distribution of wealth and resources within and among nations, and 4) a sustainable relationship between the human race and the planet.

To protest, halt, and disrupt the design, production, transport, and deployment of nuclear weapons worldwide for at least one working day.

INTRODUCTION

Stand on the moon and look at the earth. In sunlight and solar wind it hangs, a pearl infinitely precious, whole and entire.

Stand on a mountaintop; stand by the sea. Land, air, water—they move round the great arch of earth to meet themselves again. About the globe the mantle of life clings, no less seamless than what it clothes. There are no breaks or barriers, only a million kinds of continuity.

Yet life threatens life with death. Human beings have distorted the variety of life into oppositions and polarities. Many have forgotten that life cannot be divided, only destroyed. In the pursuit of limited and local gains, we risk the loss of everything.

We are killing each other, and killing our planet. Everything we do affects all of us. We need to work together, consciously, for our common good.

The roots of war are deep, and the A-bomb, the H-bomb and the neutron bomb are its most poisonous flowers. They must be eliminated, for they threaten the very existence of life on earth.

At the same time, if we hope to achieve a lasting peace, nuclear disarmament can only be the beginning, the necessary pre-condition, of a profound process of transformation and rebuilding.

The June 1982 U.N. Special Session on Disarmament demonstrated the unwillingness of the world's nuclear powers to disarm. It is clear that we cannot rely on governments to promote peace without serious pressure from their citizens. We as individuals, working with one another all over the earth, must take upon ourselves the responsiblity of stopping nuclear destruction.

On the days leading up to the Solstice in June 1983, we call for people all over the world to say NO to nuclear weapons and to the increasing world militarism which squanders precious resources needed for basic human necessities.

We call for, in fact, the celebration of an annual world holiday for peace and justice.

THE ISSUES

The threat of nuclear war increases each second. An emergency situation confronts us as the world's nuclear powers move closer to deploying first strike weapons, designed not to deter an attack but to launch one. Two of these weapons, the cruise missiles and the Pershing IIs, are slated for deployment in Europe this year, 1983. Plans to test the MX missile in the Pacific also continue for 1983. These dangerous plans must be resisted with all our will.

Funds for human needs are increasingly siphoned off for war preparation while world unemployment, malnutrition, infant mortality, lack of adequate housing, and other societal ills abound. We must work diligently to change the existing social, political, and economic order, nationally and internationally, wherever it fosters suffering and favors war.

Accelerating militarism increases the likelihood of war, and new "conventional" weapons make war much more violent. Military conscription forces young men, especially poor men, to coerce other people, to kill, and to die. The current military build-up pushes us toward destruction and away from a civilized, peaceable world.

Intervention in the domestic affairs of other countries is bringing death to hundreds of thousands of people each year, and untold misery to others. Wherever intervention exists, it must be opposed, and the right of people to self-determination affirmed.

Discrimination by race, class, sex, age, and religion, is reinforced by a militaristic world. To change that world, we must begin now to live as we would in a more equitable society, and to eliminate these inequities in our daily lives and institutions.

The International Day Call, written by a LAG work group in Fall 1982, spelled out a vision of building a new world, beginning with coordinated direct actions on Summer Solstice 1983. LAG mailed this Call to hundreds of activist groups around the world, with the support of the Mobilization for Survival, the Snake River Alliance, and other networks.

The Call in its final form represented an uneasy compromise between the poetic vision of the Introduction, which spoke for members of the International Day work group, and the list of issues, which was more attuned to Bay Area coalition politics.

THE ISSUES, CONTINUED

Ecological destruction threatens the planet just as surely as does a nuclear holocaust. Immediate steps must be taken to create new ways to live that reward those who work for the enduring health of the land, the air, and the sea, and the health of all who inhabit them. Destructive "development" must be redirected.

Lack of a positive vision of the future hampers us in all we do. Resistance to evil is necessary, but it is not enough. On the International Day let us join one another in imagining and beginning to create a world of peace and justice.

THE DATE—JUNE 20, 1983

Set by the Summer Solstice in the Northern Hemisphere and the Winter Solstice in the Southern Hemisphere, June 20 is a day to affirm life. It is free of ethnic and cultural bias, and emphasizes the integrity of the earth and the universality of the human condition.

We have forgotten our place in nature. Our politics should be rooted in love of the earth. We may gain the vision we desperately need by having our protests and peace festivals coincide with the movements of the earth, the sun, and the moon.

In the emergency brought on by the threatened deployment of the cruise and Pershing II missiles, June 20 gives people time to build international support for European resistance which will culminate in the Autumn of 1983.

1983 is only the start. In 1984, we will continue the dismantling of the machinery of devastation and begin construction of a new world founded on peace. Year by year, we will assemble at or just before the solstice in June, and the balance of our work will tilt gradually from reaction to action, from resistance to creation.

And once peace is achieved—failure is unthinkable; we *will* succeed—the day will be celebrated in rejoicing for as long as there is an earth to roll around a sun and humans here to perceive it. If this vision seems vast, so much the better, for if we destroy ourselves and the world with us, it will be due not to a failure in technology, strategy or tactics, but to a failure in vision.

THE ACTIONS

Planning for actions on or shortly before the International Day of Nuclear Disarmament is taking place at the local level. All decision-making is decentralized, with the only universal commitments being to non-violent actions and to the date.

Participating organizations are encouraged to form coalitions with other groups in their locale to ensure inclusion of the many important issues relating to nuclear disarmament, and to emphasize to the media the coordinated aspect of the International Day.

Many coalitions are already forming which reach out beyond peace groups to include labor, religious, anti-intervention, anti-conscription, human needs, anti-discrimination, and environmental organizations.

Appropriate actions for June 20 are only as limited in scope as our imaginations.

Non-violent blockades, occupations and other civil disobedience at nuclear weapons facilities and military installations, etc., would occur throughout the world.

Legal marches, vigils, and rallies involving theater, speakers, graphic art, music, dance, poetry, prayers, and meditation, etc., would take place everywhere. Peace camps would be initiated.

Non-violent strikes would halt the design, production, transport and deployment of nuclear weapons for at least one working day. Symbolic work stoppages for shorter lengths of time all over the world would proclaim solidarity with these strikesandother non-violent actions.

Conferences, teach-ins, art festivals, religious services, and mass demonstrations during the week and weekend before June 20th would awaken people to the issues involved.

On June 20th itself, people unable to leave their homes or workplaces would telephone friends, public officials, radio and television stations, newspapers, etc., to voice their objection to the nuclear holocaust being prepared for us.

Nuclear Free Zones would be declared in cities, regions, neighborhoods, and buildings.

Businesses and homes would hang anti-nuclear posters and banners on their windows and doors, and create entire window displays devoted to nuclear disarmament.

A prayer in each city and village at sunset on June 20th would completely circle the earth as it spins around the sun.

Like the June 1982 Livermore action, the 1983 action was synchronized with Summer Solstice, connecting the action to the cycles of the Earth. Organizers of International Day aimed to reach beyond specific groups and political cultures and link to a global movement for peace and justice.

The call for actions, rallies, and educational events at weapons facilities was realized the first year. Other aspects, like strikes shutting down weapons plants, were visionary.

THE SPONSOR

Livermore Action Group (LAG) formed following the failure of conventional appeals and lawsuits to convert Lawrence Livermore Laboratory, one of the United States' two nuclear weapons design labs, to peaceful research. LAG members staged six non-violent blockades of the Lab in 1982, the largest resulting in the arrest of more than 1300 people. LAG remains committed to the tactic of non-violent civil disobedience for the purpose of converting or shutting down the Lab.

Livermore Action Group is currently working in coalition with California groups to organize civil disobedience at Vandenberg Air Force Base near Santa Barbara, California, to protest the first test firing of the MX missile. LAG will also undertake another massive blockade of the Lawrence Livermore Laboratory on the International Day of Nuclear Disarmament, June 20, 1983.

This call for action is issued in cooperation with the Mobilization for Survival in the United States.

SPONSOR'S ROLE

Livermore Action Group's role in the International Day of Nuclear Disarmament is that of a clearinghouse for the network of groups organizing actions in their own areas. LAG is offering a handbook, a series of action bulletins, and a common graphic for the International Day.

HANDBOOK

Livermore Action Group will publish a handbook in March 1983 for United States participants in the International Day. The handbook, about 100 pages in length, will include the following sections: a) introduction (nature of the Day); b) process (non-violence, civil disobedience, affinity group structure, consensus); c) planning the action; d) perspectives on the movement; e) information and analysis on nuclear weapons, militarism, intervention, and associated issues; and f) resources (e.g., the location of nuclear facilities). Groups both new and old will find material here to help them in organizing, funding, and carrying out their local actions and in writing their educational literature and publicity. They will also find an extensive presentation of methods and models for working well in groups. The handbook builds upon its predecessors and the experiences and knowledge of more than 50 writers.

HOW TO GET INVOLVED

Organize a non-violent protest in your area on or shortly before June 20, 1983.

Form a coalition with other organizations.

Mail a report of your planned action for inclusion in the action bulletin.

Send in your group's name to be listed as a participant in the International Day.

Distribute this flyer to everyone you know around the world.

Write articles about International Day in your local newspapers.

Return the coupon on this page to:
Livermore Action Group
3126 Shattuck Avenue
Berkeley, California 94705
U.S.A.
Telephone: 415/644-3031

COMMON GRAPHIC

The graphic on this page is offered as a common symbol for the International Day of Nuclear Disarmament. A common graphic would be widely recognized and serve to emphasize the unity of our commitment.

The symbol incorporates three elements: the sun (whose rays are positioned to point to the directions of the compass), the earth super-imposed upon the sun, and the dove (universal symbol of peace) whose wings span the earth.

The symbol could appear on T-shirts, buttons, banners, communiques, and press releases related to the International Day. If you would like to design your own symbol, you might consider incorporating these three elements (the sun, the earth, and the dove) in your design.

ACTION BULLETIN

LAG will also publish a series of action bulletins on a regular basis from March to June 1983. The bulletin will contain news about actions planned on the International Day all over the world. Everyone interested in learning the totality of events on the International Day is encouraged to subscribe to the action bulletin and send articles for it about their planned actions to Livermore Action Group.

Organization ______________________

Contact person ______________________

Address ______________________

____

Telephone ______________________

___ List our group as a participant

___ Send handbook and action bulletins (enclose $7 individual rate or $15 group rate)

___ Send ordering information for International Day posters, T-shirts, more flyers, buttons, bumper stickers, etc.

___ Enclosed is a donation ($5-$5000) to help publicize International Day around the world

(Checks made payable to Capp Street Foundation/Livermore Action Group are tax deductible in the United States.)

Over 300 groups, mainly in the U.S., Europe, Japan, and Australia, answered the Call, with over twenty organizing civil disobedience actions. A sampling is listed on the following pages.

The work group produced a 104-page handbook, which provided material for the handbook in this Appendix (see page 700). Articles also appear in Handbook for Nonviolent Action, published by the War Resisters League. Contact www.warresisters.org, (212) 228-6193.

International Day Participants

a partial list of participants, actions, and events on and around June 20, 1983

San Francisco Bay Area

Berkeley Cycling for Nuclear Disarmament
Berkeley Urban Ecology workshop on cars
Concord CISPES march to Concord Naval Weapons Station
Livermore Livermore Action Group blockade of Livermore Lab
Livermore Hands Around Livermore Lab
Oakland Fellowship of Humanity debate on disarmament
Oakland Pro-Arts driftwood art installation in the mudflats
San Francisco Bay Area Asians for Nuclear Disarmament workshop and film
San Francisco Bay Area Artists for Nuclear Disarmament exhibit
San Francisco International Indian Treaty Council event
San Francisco Buddhist Circle for Peace morning meditation and silent walk
Silicon Valley Mid-Peninsula Peace Center peace camp
Walnut Creek Contra Costans for a Nuclear-Free Future musical festival

California

Chico Chico People for a Nuclear-Free Future demonstration
Claremont Peace and Justice Coalition event
Fort Bragg People for a Nuclear-Free Future event
Fresno Sequoia Alliance civil disobedience action at Lemoore Air Station
Friant Mountain People nuclear free zone campaign
Los Angeles Alliance for Survival peace celebration
Occidental Bohemian Grove Action Network event
Ojai World Peace Movement event
Oxnard/Pt. Mugu Peace Action at Mugu rally and civil disobedience
Palo Alto Community Against Nuclear Extinction (CANE) event
Petaluma HOPE event
Pomona Alliance for Survival peace walk
Riverside Alliance for Survival rally
San Diego Community Energy Action Network civil disobedience at Pt. Loma
San Jose San Jose Peace Center event
San Luis Obispo Vandenberg Action Coalition occupation of Vandenberg AFB
Santa Barbara Nuclear Free California nuclear free zone declaration
Santa Cruz Sisters Rising Affinity Group civil disobedience action at Lockheed
Santa Monica Women's Rand Action rally and tea party at Rand Corporation
Santa Rosa SONOMore Atomics event
Ukiah Coalition for Peace on Earth civil disobedience at recruiting station
Venice Alliance for Survival event
Visalia Sequoia Alliance event
Wilbur Springs Wilbur Hot Springs Group event

continued on next page

International Day Participants

a partial list, continued from preceding page

Northwestern United States

Milwaukie OR People's Test Ban picket at Precision CastParts Corporation
Portland OR People's Test Ban event
Kent WA Puget Sound Women's Peace Camp at Boeing
Kent WA Greenpeace direct action at cruise missile plant
Spokane WA Walk Into the Future to Fairchild AFB
Bangor WA Port Townsend Peace Coalition vigil at Trident Submarine Base
Conrad MT Silence One Silo event
Laramie WY Wyoming Citizens Alliance event
Pocatella ID Peace and Justice Center phone-in to Senator's office
Ketchum ID Groundwater Alliance event
Idaho Falls ID Citizens for Nuclear Weapons Awareness event
Sandpoint, Lewiston, and Blackfoot ID SANE and Ground Zero events
Couer d'Alene ID Pine Cone Alliance event
McCall, Buhl, Boise, Twin Falls, and Nampa ID Snake River Alliance events

Southwestern United States

Tempe/Scottsdale AZ Nuclear Resister vigil at Palo Verde Nuclear Station
Tucson AZ Cruise Conversion Alert rally at Davis Monthan AFB
Big Mountain (AZ) Big Mountain Dineh Nation peace vigil
Las Vegas NV Greenpeace peace procession
Albuquerque NM Disarmament Coalition civil disobedience at Kirtland AFB
Santa Fe NM Project Lighthawk event
Amarillo TX Texas Clergy and Laity Concerned vigil at Pantex weapons plant
El Paso TX El Pasoans for a Nuclear Free Future rally at Fort Bliss
Salt Lake City UT Utahns for a Nuclear Weapons Freeze vigil

Midwestern United States

Cedar Rapids IA Ames Peace Network rally and peace camp
Omaha NE New Covenant Justice and Peace and Omaha Pax Christi events
Emporia KS Emporians for Nuclear Disarmament vigil
Kansas City MO Cowtown Alliance march
West Plains MO Ozarks Area Community Congress leafletting at Southwest Truck Bocy
Chicago IL Disarm Northrup Action Coalition blockade at Northrop Defense Systems
Corydon IN Corydon Peace Group letter-writing campaign
Detroit MI Mobilization for Survival event
Bay City MI Bay Area Peace Coalition leafletting near Wurtsmith AFB
Ann Arbor MI Michigan Alliance for Peace event
Walled Lake MI Michigan Alliance for Peace protest at Williams International
Minneapolis MN Honeywell Project legal demonstration (leading to later direct action)
Madison WI Disarmament Now and Peacemakers direct action at Math Research Center
Milwaukee WI Mobilization for Survival event

Southeastern United States

Washington DC World Federalist Student Division vigil
Baltimore MD Nuclear Free America event
Arlington VA International Disarmament Organization event
Orlando FL People for Disarmament legal protest at Martin Marietta
St. Petersburg FL Immanuel House blockade of General Electric Neutron Devices Plant
New Orleans LA Campaign for Nuclear Disarmament event

Northeastern United States

Groton CT June Coalition civil disobedience at Electric Boat and British Trident
Norwich CT War Resisters League event
Vermont Yankee VT Vermont Yankee Decommissioning Alliance event
Central VT Central Vermont Safe Energy Coalition event
Burlington VT Burlington Peace Coalition civil disobedience at General Electric
Cambridge MA Ailanthus Community civil disobedience at Draper Labs
Westborough MA Worcester Coalition for Disarmament direct action at GTE
New Bedford MA New Bedford Freeze Group protest at Federal Building
Albany NY Knolls Action Project direct action at Knolls Atomic Power Labs
Genesee NY Genesee Valley Citizens for Peace event
New York NY Fourth Wall Repertory Company event
New York NY Mobilization for Survival event
Pittsburgh PA Thomas Merton Center event

Other Countries

Morales, Mexico World Constitution and Parliament Association event
Quandra Island BC Christian Peace Agitators peace boat
Vancouver Island BC Denman Island Peace Group protest at Canadian Forces Base
Victoria BC Greater Victoria Disarmament Coalition vigil at Legislative Building
Tokyo, Japan Japan Citizens' League rally and march with over 100 peace groups
Brisbane, Australia United Nations Association of Australia anti-nuclear march
Sidney, Australia United Nations Association of Australia anti-nuclear march
Adelaide, Australia Campaign Against Nuclear Energy event
Dunedin, New Zealand Peace Action Dunedin rally and letter deluge
Tel-Aviv-Jaffa, Israel International Movement of Conscientious War Resisters event
Leeds, England Headingley Peace Action blockade at Tarmac
Paris, France L'Alliance Internationale pour le Disarmament peace march to Geneva
Vienna, Austria Arbeitsgemeinschaft für Zivildienst street theater
Berlin, Germany Frauen für den Frieden rally
Bielefeld, Germany Christian and nonviolent groups five-day public fast
Bremmerhaven, Germany Nonviolent blockade at Carl-Schurz Kaserne (U.S. Army base)
Trier, Germany Demonstration at Bittburg (U.S. military base)
Krefeld, Germany Friedensinitiative Neuss protest of Vice President Bush's visit
Filderstadt, Germany Banner-hanging and bicycling for disarmament
Dortmund, Germany Gewaltfrie Aktiongruppe Dortmund vigil and demonstration
Ohain, Belgium Brabant-Ecologie event
Milano, Italy Centro per la Nonviolenza program for peace
Copenhagen, Sweden Forsvar-Militaerkntisk Magasin event

Glossary of Groups and Terms

pronunciations in "quotes"

Abalone Alliance Forerunner of LAG, direct action group focused on the nuclear power plant at Diablo Canyon. Organized actions from 1976-1984. *See Diablo Canyon.*

Affinity Group Also AG, small groups for direct action organizing. Everyone participating in actions at Livermore or Vandenberg was expected to be in an affinity group. Some AGs existed for two or three years. Most lasted for one or two actions. Some were intentional groups, such as teachers, anarchists, Catholics, gays, etc. Others were simply a group of people who happened to take their nonviolence prep together. *See Cluster, and also LAG Structure chart, page 766.*

AFSC American Friends Service Committee, "AFSC." Social service wing of the pacifist Society of Friends (Quakers). AFSC played a major role in establishing a series of nonviolence guidelines which many direct actions, including the Livermore and Vandenberg actions, adopted. Also promoted a broader idea of "process," including consensus and feminism.

Anarchist A title loosely used by many organizers of the War Chest Tours, Rock Against Reagan, and the street-protest contingent within LAG. The emphasis was on nonhierarchical, decentralized organizing. Most LAG-affiliated anarchists were committed to nonviolence. Some others who took part in 1984 protests depicted in this book were less so. Bound Together Bookstore on Haight Street was (is) a hub of anarchist organizing in the City, along with a network of collective houses in the Mission and nearby neighborhoods. The collective houses sponsored the Anarchist Coffeehouse, 1984-1989.

Arraignment The first court appearance following arrest. Usually occurs within a couple of working days, or at a later date if you "cited out." At arraignment charges are formally read, and you enter a plea (not-guilty, no-contest, or guilty). Never plead "guilty," or you may face civil liability. Plead "no-contest" only if an attorney you trust assures you of the sentence and it is acceptable. If you have any doubts, plead not-guilty. Blockaders pleading not-guilty are usually released without bail, with a date set for further hearings. If you plead no-contest, you may be immediately sentenced, or a future sentencing date may be set. Arraignment is ordinarily individual, and only solidarity tactics can compel the court to arraign protesters en masse. *See O.R., and Legal Flowchart in Handbook.*

London anti-nuclear "symbolic dyings" like this May 1983 protest...

BARF Berkeley Anti-Reagan Festival, begun in 1982 by Berkeley Citizen's Action. LAG organized BARF III on September 22, 1984. BCA candidates had speaking spots.

BART Bay Area Rapid Transit, light-rail trains that connect the Central Bay Area.

Berkeley Citizen's Action BCA was a progressive electoral slate allied with Congressman Ron

Dellums. Shared an office with LAG, 1982-1985. BCA held the mayor's seat (Gus Newport) and a City Council majority in these years, with a notable record on both local and international affairs. LAGers volunteered with BCA around election time, but otherwise there was little overlap.

Bohemian Grove — *See Fact and Fiction Appendix for September 22, 1984.*

...inspired "die-ins" in San Francisco from October 24, 1983 to the present.

CD Civil disobedience. "Doing CD" was the expression for doing nonviolent direct action. Other expressions included "doing the action" or "getting busted."

Change of Heart Cluster Jeff, Holly, and Angie's cluster, also included Karina, Sara, Doc and Enola Gay, Moonstone and Deadheads for Peace, Alby, Megan, and initially Daniel, Hank, Caroline, and the Commie Dupes. Formed June 1982, dissolved around June 1984. Change of Heart people helped organize the Anarchist Coffeehouse. *See Anarchist.*

CIA Central Intelligence Agency (also known as the Cocaine Import Agency during the Reagan-Bush era). The U.S.'s covert, extra-legal global intervention network, with a long record of election-fixing, assassination, and destabilization around the globe. Especially active in Central America during the early 1980s. Vice President Bush was a former CIA Director. The CIA was officially barred from domestic operations, where quasi-legal groups like the FBI and Cointelpro picked up the slack.

CISPES Committee In Solidarity with the People of El Salvador. U.S.-based organization supporting leftist rebels in El Salvador. The largest of the Bay Area "solidarity" groups, often organized legal protests against visiting government figures. Non-dogmatic leftist orientation, hierarchical structure, more connected to the Bay Area progressive mainstream than LAG, with whom CISPES worked in coalitions. *See El Salvador.*

Cite Out To sign a police citation acknowledging your arrest (but not your guilt) and promising to appear in court on the specified date. The opportunity to cite out is offered at the police's discretion, and is not a legal right. Protesters might accept it to get out of jail faster, or refuse it as a solidarity tactic — particularly if only part of the group is being offered cite-outs. *See O.R., Arraignment, and Legal Flowchart in the Handbook. See also discussions in Chapter II.*

Civil Rights Movement General term for a series of nonviolent direct action protests beginning in the Southern states in the 1950s and gradually spreading across the country. The Civil Rights Movement was probably the most successful and influential nonviolent direct action movement in this country's history. Organized on a mixed model of hierarchical organizations like the NAACP coupled with a decentralized network of churches and community groups, the Civil Rights Movement was a focused, sustained uprising that rewrote laws and social mores. *See discussions in Chapter IV-V.*

Cluster Umbrella group of five to ten AGs. In large actions at Livermore, Vandenberg, and Diablo Canyon, over a hundred affinity groups took part. Most, especially smaller AGs, banded together in clusters. Clusters, not AGs, sent spokes to the jail spokescouncils. A handful of clusters lasted for a couple of years. Most, were ad hoc formations for a specific action. *See Affinity Group, and LAG structure chart, page 766.*

Consensus A complex and much-debated process for bringing a group to a unified decision. Consensus does not mean that everyone agrees with or fully supports the decision. It means that most people support it and none of the others find it morally offensive. LAG, Abalone Alliance, and VAC all used consensus for spokescouncils, affinity group process, and in-jail decision making. To signal consensus (or agreement) in a meeting, hold up both hands and twinkle your fingers. *See Handbook section on Consensus.*

The Pledge of Resistance organized protests at the San Francisco Federal Building in 1984-1985, culminating in a Spring 1985 action with nearly 1000 arrests.

Coordinating Council Weekly meeting of spokes from LAG work groups. Responsible for finances, staff, office, and day-to-day operations. *See Work Group, and LAG structure chart, page 766.*

Cruise Missiles One of the "Euromissiles." Cruise missiles were small, portable missiles launched from air, land, or sea. Computer guidance systems allowed the missile to fly below radar level, posing a huge threat to the Soviet Union's defenses. *See Euromissiles, First Strike.*

Dellums, Ron Congressional representative from Berkeley and parts of Oakland, Ron Dellums was an outspoken opponent of Reaganism in all its forms. One of the two foremost voices of African American politics in the 1980s. Dellums' successor was Barbara Lee, who opposed the war-making efforts of the second Bush administration.

Democrats The more moderate of the mainstream parties. While the Republicans advocated the immediate and total destruction of the environment and the social infrastructure, the Democrats felt it should be done more slowly.

Diablo Canyon Nuclear power plant begun during the last gasp of the atomic-power boom in the early 1970s, situated along an earthquake fault north of Los Angeles. Protests in 1979 and 1981, resulting in over 2000 arrests, ended with the revelation of flaws in the plant's safety plans. But a makeover of blueprints and some timely campaign contributions secured the licensing of the plant, which was crucial in allowing PG&E to pass along the project's massive losses to ratepayers. Abalone Alliance has organized resistance to

Diablo for years, contact (415) 861-0592, www.energy-net.org, abalone@energy-net.org

Direct Action Literally, to take direct action to alter one's environment, whether by creativity, persuasion, or force. As used in the Bay Area for over twenty years, it refers to nonviolent protests in which there is a risk of arrest. The antithesis of direct action is voting, in which we delegate our power. (The name "Direct Action" was also used by at least two small 1980s groups convicted of political bombings, one in Vancouver, BC, and the other in France. A LAG media spoke, asked about one such group, said, "I sympathize with their frustration and anger, but I completely disagree with their response.")

Direct Action Newspaper LAG newspaper published Fall 1982-Fall 1986, 25 issues total. The first two were called the "LAG Rag." By about issue #6, the paper reached 20 tabloid pages (30,000 words). Entire pages of each issue were dedicated to local protests, regional North American events, and European demonstrations and direct actions. Many issues also carried two-page spreads on topics such as the Middle East, the Philippines, the nuclear arms race, Native American news, Central America, and other related matters. *Selected pages of Direct Action may be posted at www.directaction.org*

El Salvador Central American country torn by civil war in which thousands died. Reagan and the CIA supported a right-wing government and its military death squads against a socialist movement called the FMLN. A U.S.-based group called CISPES worked to build opposition to Reagan's policy. *See CISPES.*

Emergency Response Network The ERN was a LAG proposal in Fall 1983 in response to intervention in Central America. The network was never activated. In late 1984 a faith-based group called Pledge of Resistance picked up the idea, leading to a Spring 1985 action at the San Francisco Federal Building in which about 800 people were arrested. Other actions happened around the country at the same time, helping turn the tide against Reagan's policies in the region.

Euromissiles Popular name for the Cruise and Pershing II missiles, part of the U.S.'s First Strike strategy. Deployment of the Cruise and Pershing II missiles in Europe in the winter of 1983-84 prompted the Soviet Union to put their nuclear forces on alert and created the most dangerous standoff between the superpowers since the 1962 Cuban Missile Crisis. *See Cruise, Pershing II, First Strike.*

Feinstein, Diane Mayor of San Francisco c. 1978-1987, California Senator since 1992. A true bi-partisan, Feinstein registered Democrat and voted Republican. Owed her career to millionaire landlord husband, who reaped generous rewards on his political investment.

First Strike The U.S.'s First-Strike strategy called for a sneak attack in which the MX and the submarine-launched Cruise missiles would so devastate the Soviet Union that they would be incapable of mounting a counter-attack. Although never an overt part of U.S. policy, security leaks provided sufficient information for critics to piece together the plan. Critics of First Strike eventually convinced enough policy-makers of the devastation such an attack would wreak on Earth's environment, and the plan was scrapped — after corporations had reaped billions in profits. *See MX, Cruise, Pershing II, Euromissiles.*

Freeze The Nuclear Weapons Freeze campaign was a nonbinding anti-nuclear referendum passed by several dozen cities and states starting about 1979, often winning large majorities. The Freeze was on the California ballot in November 1982. Livermore Lab joined a host of defense corporations in lobbying against it. Faced with that financial onslaught, the Freeze barely passed in California, and the movement faded.

Grenada Caribbean island-state which elected a socialist "New Jewel" government in 1983. In late October 1983, facing a dismal economy and failed policies in the Middle East, Reagan mounted an invasion of Grenada. The elected government was deposed, puppets installed, and Reagan's ratings soared, initiating a pattern that grew familiar during the Bush administrations.

International Day of Nuclear Disarmament A proposal consensed at the August 1982 LAG Congress calling on peace and disarmament groups around the world to do local, decentralized actions around Summer Solstice 1983. LAG planned its second major blockade of Livermore Lab, networked among participating groups, and coordinated media coverage. Over 300 groups, mainly in the U.S., Europe, Japan, and Australia, took part in some way, with about twenty different CD actions. Planners envisioned International Day as an annual event. But dissension within LAG (particularly opposition to the "new-age" tone of the event) sidetracked it and there was never a follow-up. *See International Day Call, page 752, and discussions in Chapters I and II.*

Jesse Jackson African American social activist from Chicago with roots in the Civil Rights Movement. Jackson stepped into the vacuum of 1984 and helped initiate a "Rainbow Coalition" that articulated a vision of peace and justice. He became a credible liberal contender, with about twenty percent of the vote in some primaries. Once Mondale clinched the nomination to face Reagan, Jackson withdrew, but he and the Rainbow Coalition remained a progressive voice in the Democratic Party for years.

Livermore Action Group LAG was a loose organization/network that organized protests at Livermore Nuclear Weapons Lab and elsewhere from 1982-1985. *For ongoing Livermore organizing, see Tri-Valley CAREs and Western States Legal Foundation.*

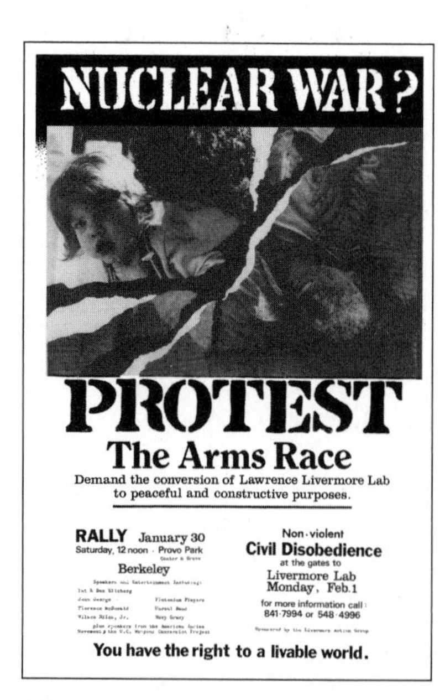

February 1, 1982 poster. 170 people were arrested in this first mass action at the Lab.

Livermore Lab Lawrence Livermore National Laboratory is one of two federally-funded weapons labs (along with Los Alamos). In the 1970s and 80s, LLNL was the designer of the Neutron Bomb and nuclear warheads for the Cruise and Pershing II missiles. Seven thousand research and support personnel used the most sophisticated technology tax dollars could buy to devise new and improved ways to destroy the planet. Livermore Lab, the younger of the two national weapons labs, was founded when Edward Teller and others argued that competition would be beneficial for weapons development.

Los Alamos National Laboratory Livermore Lab's older rival. Los Alamos was the home of the H-bomb. Located in the New Mexico desert, Los Alamos was more insulated from protest than Livermore. However, citizen's groups have tracked Los Alamos's work for years, particularly nuclear waste issues. Contact Los Alamos Study Group, www.lasg.org, (505) 982-7747.

Mobilization for Survival Anti-militarist coalition of several hundred grassroots groups across the U.S., with regional offices in New York City and Milwaukee. The Mobe endorsed International Day in 1983, and many Mobe "locals" participated.

Mondale, Walter Democratic Party nominee/sacrificial lamb to Reagan in 1984. The moderate-liberal Senator from Minnesota was never close to Reagan in the polls after the Summer conventions. Abandoned by corporate election funders, he lost in a landslide.

MX Missile The U.S. military's proposed $70 billion intercontinental ballistic missile whose speed and pinpoint accuracy represented a major escalation of the arms race by the United States. The MX featured multiple nuclear warheads capable of striking Soviet targets with extreme accuracy and force. It was planned as part of a new U.S. first-strike strategy. *See also Vandenberg, First Strike.*

1980-81 study released by the UC Nuclear Weapons Labs Conversion Project, an activist/educational forerunner of LAG.

NATO North Atlantic Treaty Organization, one of two alliances (along with the Moscow-centered Warsaw Pact) that divided Europe during the Cold War era, 1945-1989. NATO was dominated by the U.S. and its nuclear arsenal. The U.S. State Department and the CIA routinely intervened in Western European politics to keep the alliance in line.

Nicaragua Central American country where a 1979 revolution by the openly-socialist Sandinistas toppled a longtime U.S. puppet government. Then-President Carter gave support to the Sandinistas, who worked to rebuild the country. After Reagan came to power, the CIA covertly funneled millions of dollars to right-wing "Contra" rebels trying to destabilize the Sandinistas and restore a pro-corporate government.

Nonviolence LAG, VAC, and Abalone actions were committed to nonviolence. Most actions explicitly used Nonviolence Guidelines., which were printed in the handbooks. Property destruction, which later was more of an issue, was not particularly debated in these years. *See Handbook section on Nonviolence.*

O.R., Own Recognizance To be released from jail with no bail, on a promise to return on a specified date. O.R. release typically follows arraignment, in contrast to "cite out," which can happen from jail or at the arrest site. *See Arraignment, and Legal Flowchart in the Handbook.*

Overthrow Cluster Leftist-oriented cluster, a haven for LAGers like Mort and Craig. Overthrow activists emphasized coalition work, tying LAG's anti-nuclear work to a broad range of social and economic issues. Overthrow also provided a spark for theatrical organizing — the grim reaper, nukecycle, and other props sprung from this cluster.

People's Convention Bay Area Coalition to organize an alternative convention at the time of the 1984 Democratic Convention (other years in other cities). Initiated by the Communist Workers' Party (here "RWP"). LAG took a small part. *See RWP.*

Pershing II One of the "Euromissiles." *See Euromissiles.*

Pledge of Resistance *See Emergency Response Network.*

Plowshares Actions A series of nonviolent direct actions beginning in the late 1960s and continuing to the present, in which activists (often coming from a faith-based perspective) enter a military installation and do symbolic damage to property such as draft files or missile parts. The prophetic image of hammering on a sword to fashion a plowshare (Isaiah 2:4) gives the group its name. Contact Jonah House, (410) 233-6238, disarmnow@erols.com

Process Catch-all term (also "feminist process") for consensus, collectivity, nonhierarchy, etc. AGs were expected to have "good process." *See Handbook on Consensus and Process.*

Reclaiming Anarchist-Pagan group that coalesced during protests at Diablo Canyon, Livermore, and Vandenberg. Today, several dozen local groups around North America and Europe organize rituals and grassroots political actions. Numerous Direct Action writers have written for *Reclaiming Quarterly,* Reclaiming's magazine. Visit www.reclaiming.org, and also www.starhawk.org. *See final scene of Epilog.*

Russia The most powerful of the various states in the USSR. "Russia" was the name by which most Americans knew the entire USSR. From 1945-1989, the word "Russia" called forth the spectre of "Communist Totalitarianism" in all its nuclear terror. *See USSR.*

RPF Revolutionary People's Front. Fictional/archetypal Marxist-Leninist-Maoist party. The RPF has a street-adventurist orientation. There were a couple of dozen alphabet-soup leftist parties in the Bay Area, with 20-100 members each. The RPF and RWP reflect some of the tendencies of these dedicated, dogmatic groups.

RWP Revolutionary Workers Party. Fictional/archetypal Marxist-Leninist party. More coalition-minded than most. Driving force behind the 1984 People's Convention. *See RPF for more on leftist groups.*

San Francisco Mime Troupe *See Fact and Fiction Appendix, September 22, 1984.*

Spokes Spokespeople, i.e., representatives of AGs or clusters to a spokescouncil, which was the main decisionmaking body for actions. *See LAG Structure chart, page 766.*

Tri-Valley CAREs Communities Against a Radioactive Environment, a Livermore Valley-based group which coalesced around the Livermore peace camp in 1984 and has been active ever since in education and organizing around Livermore Lab. Contact www.trivalleycares.org, (925) 443-7148.

UC University of California at Berkeley, also "Berkeley" or "Cal." A beautiful campus marred

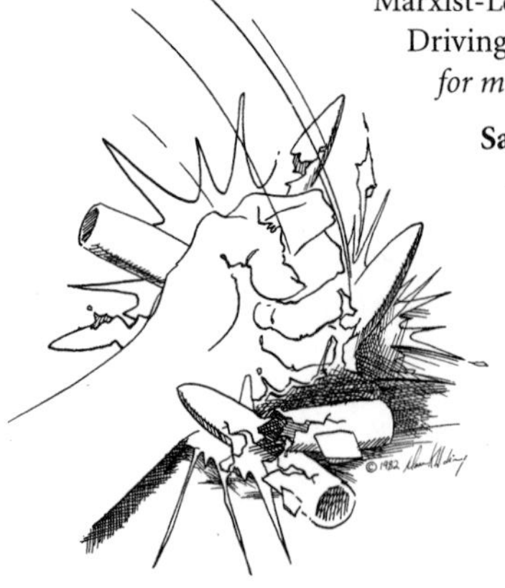

Two graphic facets of LAG. Above, an Overthrow Cluster fist. Top right, an International Day dove.

by a reactionary Board of Regents. At least through 2003, UC managed Livermore and Los Alamos nuclear weapons labs and Nevada Test Site, providing a cloak of academic credibility for the research and testing of weapons of mass destruction.

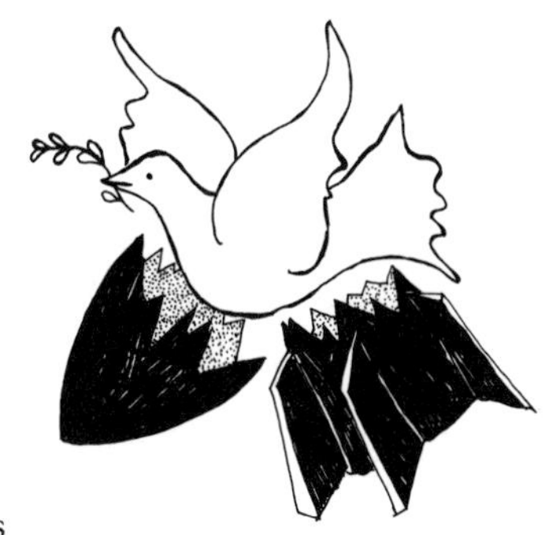

UC Nuclear Weapons Labs Conversion Project Activist/educational forerunner to LAG, focused on research and education about the role of Livermore and Los Alamos Labs in the nuclear weapons complex as well as the University of California's complicity as manager of the weapons labs and the Nevada Nuclear Test Site. The Conversion Project's work gave LAG a factual basis for its critiques, and demonstrated that work through legal channels would not change the policies of these institutions.

Urban Ecology Educational and activist group based in Berkeley working to promote ecological awareness in cities, including urban gardens, planning issues, and transportation. Contact (510) 251-6330, www.urbanecology.org

Urban Stonehenge Anarchist collective household on Potrero Hill in San Francisco, founded c. 1980 and still active in 2003. Core organizing space for the decentralized 1983 Vandenberg actions, the War Chest Tours, and the Anarchist Coffeehouse. *See Anarchist.*

USSR Union of Soviet Socialist Republics, or Soviet Union, commonly called "Russia" in the U.S. The USSR was the second superpower, the only country in the world capable of challenging the U.S. at a nuclear level. The USSR was never remotely the military or economic equal of the U.S., but the Reagan administration manipulated statistics to make it appear that the USSR was "ahead" in the arms race — justifying hundreds of billions of dollars of corporate subsidies for new nuclear weapons. *See Russia.*

Vandenberg Action Coalition VAC was a coalition of peace and anti-nuke groups from around California dedicated to stopping the MX test in 1983. LAG was the largest of the member groups. In practice, LAG tended to pursue its own agenda regarding the MX protests, and VAC became a pole for anarchist/decentralist critics of LAG, leading to a major split among anti-MX organizers. *See Chapter I and II.*

Vandenberg Air Force Base Missile test facility located near Santa Barbara, CA. Tests of the MX missile were planned from Vandenberg in Spring 1983. *See MX.*

War Chest Tours Protests during the 1984 Democratic Convention in San Francisco. Not officially a LAG action, although organizing group included LAGers. Tours targeted military corporations which subsidized both Republicans and Democrats. Several hundred people were arrested. Similar protests were organized at the 1984 Republican Convention in Dallas, and possibly elsewhere in other years. *See Chapters IV and V.*

Western States Legal Foundation Peace and disarmament advocacy group which has kept pressure on Livermore Lab and the national nuclear weapons complex around issues of new weapons programs, toxic waste, and accountability. Contact www.wslfweb.org, (510) 839-5877.

Work Groups Work Groups in LAG were volunteer collectives of five to twenty people organized around specific tasks. Some were stable, others came and went. Around major actions, a hundred or more people would be in work groups, some in several at a time.

Livermore Action Group Structure

LAG developed several elaborate structures on paper. In practice, two kinds of groups met and made decisions concerning LAG: work groups and affinity groups. Each had its own "council," as diagrammed on these pages.

To complicate matters:

- Some people were in both AGs and work groups. Many were in only one or the other.
- The AG Spokescouncils, which met biweekly for several months before an action, formed numerous work groups specific to the given action — encampment, rally, leafletting, medics, scenario, etc. These work groups then sent spokes to Coordinating Council (or if they didn't, that raised more problems).
- Work group members often attended AG spokescouncils. Being some of the most active members of LAG, work group people played key roles in decisions at spokescouncils.

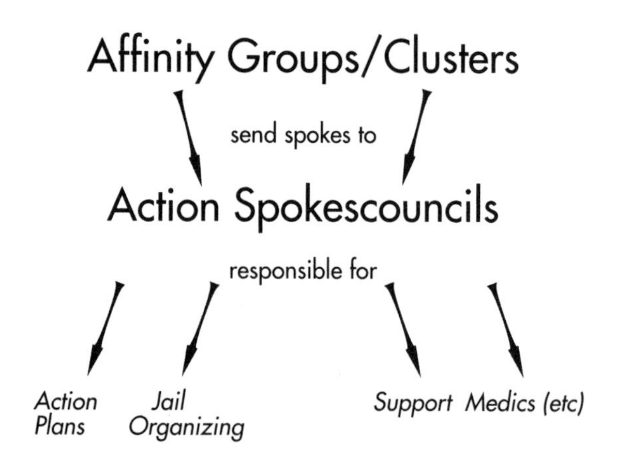

Affinity Groups, Work Groups, & Clusters

See Glossary for information on AGs, work groups, and clusters, which were the basic organizing units of LAG. See also the Affinity Groups, Work Groups, and Consensus section of the handbook.

Livermore Action Group Structure

Ongoing Work Groups

- Newspaper (produced Direct Action from Fall 1982)
- Finances/Fundraising/Canvassing
- Media
- Peace Camp (from Fall 1983)
- Outreach/Coalitions
- Legal
- Office (paid staff + volunteers)
- Nonviolence Preppers (this group also worked with Abalone Alliance, VAC, Pledge of Resistance)

Ad Hoc (specific actions)

- Communications
- Encampment
- Rally
- Scenario/Action Planning
- Leafletting
- Education/Research
- Posters and flyers
- Handbook
- Outside Support
- Medics
- Jail Organizing

Direct Action ran into a financial crisis in mid-1984. The paper bounced back and continued publishing through Fall 1986.

Today, numerous former Direct Action writers contribute to GroundWork and Reclaiming Quarterly magazines and Street Spirit newspaper. See Resources.

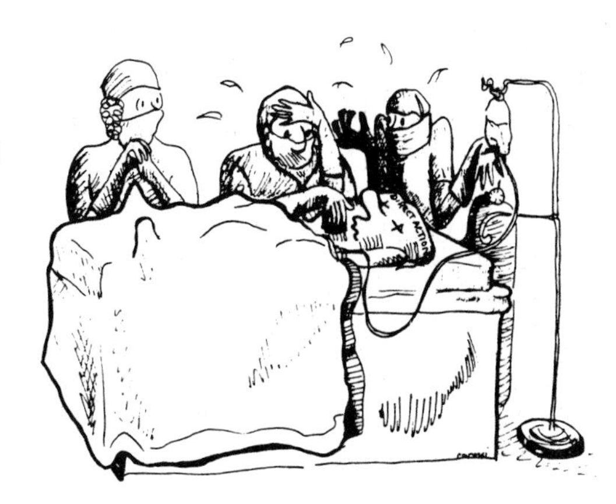

Appendices and Miscellaneous Fun Stuff

In the last seventy pages of the book, you'll find various odds and ends arranged in what our Structural Semiotics Department determined was the most useful order. The LAG structure chart and the glossary are first for quick reference. The International Day pages give a richer sense of that pivotal event. The handbook gives a basic orientation to direct action. Lastly, be sure to consult the LAG Discography to avoid playing inappropriate music as you read a scene.

This Page 768
LAG Structure (affinity groups, work groups, clusters) 766
Glossary of Groups and Terms 758
International Day Participating Groups 755
International Day Call 752
LAG Discography 750
Study Guide 749
Getting Involved/Resources 748
Graphic Credits 746
Fact and Fiction 736
Direct Action Handbook 700
About the Author 698
